THE SAFANARION ORDER BOOKS 1 -3

KEN LOZITO

THE SAFANARION ORDER BOOKS 1 - 3

This is a work of fiction. Names, characters, places, and incidents either are a product of the author's imagination or are used fictitiously.

Published by Acoustical Books, LLC
KenLozito.com

If you would like to be notified when my next book is released, visit **www.KenLozito.com**

ISBN: 978-1-945223-40-2

ROAD TO SHANDARA

SAFANARION ORDER - BOOK 1

1

THE AWAKENING

The university campus was a buzz of bleary-eyed students going to and from class. Some exited the buildings with a slight spring in their step having finished another semester, while others were in such a haggard state that each step was carefully placed as if they walked on a path of eggshells and the slightest misstep would reveal just how unprepared they really were.

Having finished for the day, Aaron left Robertson Hall, home to the college of engineering sciences. Only one final exam separated him from a summer internship before starting graduate school, and he couldn't wait. He headed to the parking lot and quickly located his old-style Jeep CJ7. Aaron had rescued the old CJ from a farm about a hundred miles from his house. His father thought he was crazy, but under the dirt and rust, a beast slept. "Beast" was the Jeep's nickname and was a running joke between him and his father. He'd spent a year restoring it. The black paint shined and the chrome circling the traditional round headlights gleamed. The soft top was down, of course. Unless it was raining, the top to his Jeep always stayed down. There was nothing like driving with the top down and the wind blowing through his hair...freedom.

His mother had sent him a message asking that he cover for one of the horse trainers at his grandfather's stables. He didn't mind helping out and knew that his days working with the horses at the stables were numbered.

The drive out to the stables never took long, and a half hour later he came within sight of the tall hedges that ran the length of the property. He turned onto the long driveway lined with red maples. As he closed in on the main house, Aaron's brows drew forward and he clutched the steering wheel. Bright, flashing red lights from police cars parked outside his grandfather's colonial farmhouse lit up the area. Aaron steered to a stone wall, threw the shifter into park, and climbed out of the Jeep. A knot of police officers and paramedics gathered near the stairway that led to the house. At the top of the stairs, Zeus, his grandfather's wolf half-breed, stood with his head lowered and teeth bared. A deep growl rumbled from Zeus's chest and his ears were pinned back.

Aaron spotted his mother speaking with the police officers. "What's going on? Is Grandpa okay?"

His mother turned to him. "I don't know. We can't get in. Zeus won't let anyone pass."

"Ma'am," a police officer interrupted, "if we can't get the dog out of there, we're going to have to put him down. We can't wait for Animal Control if someone inside needs our help."

"No," Aaron said, stepping up to the stairs. "Let me try."

Aaron heard his mother ask the police officer to give Aaron a chance.

There was no way Aaron was going to let them shoot Zeus. He had been in the family for years. The screen door to the house was propped open. Aaron craned his neck and tried to peer inside, but didn't see anyone. He placed a foot on the first step and stopped. Zeus narrowed his eyes at him and shifted his gaze to the people behind him.

"Easy, boy," he said slowly. "It's me."

Zeus's hackles were raised and his whole body quivered. Aaron took another step forward, and Zeus bared all his teeth, unveiling the peaks of the Rocky Mountains inside his mouth.

Aaron never took his eyes from him, his stare neither challenging nor yielding. "Zeus," he said evenly, trying to get Zeus to calm down with the sound of his voice.

"I need to get in there, boy. Come on," Aaron said.

Zeus's ears perked up, and the wild look in his eyes shifted to the more familiar loving kind that Aaron knew so well. Zeus reluctantly took a step forward.

"It's okay. Show me where he is. Where's Grandpa? Take me to him," Aaron said and walked up the steps as he'd done thousands of times before. Zeus raised his snout, sniffing the air, then turned tail and trotted into the house with Aaron in tow.

Aaron leaped up the last few steps and entered his grandfather's house. He called out, but there was no answer. Everything looked normal and in its place, but something felt wrong. The insides of Aaron's stomach twisted. There was a coldness in the air despite the warm weather outside.

Aaron followed Zeus through the house and down the back hallway leading to the study. He entered the room and found his grandfather lying on the floor.

Oh, no!

His grandfather looked up at him and sighed in relief. Aaron quickly knelt beside him. A trace of blood trailed down the side of his grandfather's mouth. His grandfather, who had always been a vibrant man—even into his eighties—lay helplessly on the floor. He looked wizened and old. Far older than Aaron could recall.

His grandfather gestured for Aaron to lean down. "Come closer," he whispered, placing something in Aaron's hands. "Keep it safe," he gasped.

"What's wrong?" Aaron asked.

His grandfather's face writhed in pain, and he sucked in ragged breaths. "Oh, Aaron. I'm sorry. I'm so sorry..." he said. His body convulsed violently, and his back arched while Aaron held onto him, crying out. Then his body relaxed with a great sigh. Aaron watched in silent horror as his grandfather stopped breathing.

Aaron heard others enter the room. He knelt there clutching his grandfather's lifeless body as the paramedics checked for a pulse. The paramedics labored to revive his grandfather, but nothing worked. He was gone.

Eventually, a gentle but strong hand gripped his shoulder. "It's time to let go, Son," his father beckoned. "Aaron, please," his father said.

Aaron carefully laid his grandfather's head down onto the floor. His father gently ran his fingers over Aaron's grandfather's eyes, closing them. Aaron kept watching his grandfather's chest, hoping that he would see it begin to rise and fall. That this was some sort of mistake. He wanted to believe it more than anything, but he knew the truth.

Aaron stood up and slowly turned, clenching his teeth, trying for all he was worth not to break down and cry. He was eye level with his father, who was also a man of great size, and the sight of his father's eyes brimming with tears made the breath catch in his throat. His mother cried out, and he watched helplessly as she collapsed over his grandfather. His father knelt down next to her and put his arm around her shoulders. Aaron stood there helplessly, watching his parents hold each other.

Aaron opened his hand and looked at the object his grandfather had given him. It was a silver medallion with a white pearl in the center and a carved relief of a dragon holding a rose curling around the front. There was a slight shimmer to it as it caught the light. After studying it for a few moments, he stuffed the medallion in his pocket and walked stiffly from the room.

The rest of the day passed as if it were happening to someone else. Aaron watched helplessly as the white coroner's van took his grandfather's body away. His thoughts raced in every direction, and he tried to get a firm grasp on the emotions welling up inside him. His pulse was racing and his chest felt constricted. He needed to do something—anything—as long as he was moving. He ran over to the stables and saddled Sam, a chestnut stallion, and put as much distance between him and the house as possible. Beyond the stables was a wide-open field bathed in sunshine. The gentle swaying of the grass and distant trees mocked him. Sam snorted anxiously, sensing Aaron's unrest. The trailhead on the far side of the field beckoned him, and he nudged Sam into a gallop.

Aaron glanced over to the side and saw Zeus plowing along next to him. Aaron gave Sam another prod, urging him faster. He wanted to fly, and Zeus flew with him. He veered off the trail and headed into the woods, dodging trees. Faster and faster, cutting each turn tighter until the branches tore at him, scraping through his shirt. He didn't care. He wanted to be reckless and rode as if his life depended on it. Zeus ran with him, darting in and out of sight like a spirit. He didn't know how long he rode, but the edge of the cliffs appeared before him in the waning sunlight, and he stopped. Aaron gazed out at the small valley before him, his heart pounding. Sam snorted and pawed at the ground, feeding off his need to keep moving.

Aaron stepped off his horse and fell to his knees, letting out a silent wail. He felt stripped bare before the world, the mortality that surrounds us every day becoming a reality for him. Grief overtook him, and he let out a piercing scream that echoed through the valley.

Zeus nuzzled his pocket, and he reached inside, taking out the medallion. Why did his grandfather give it to him? *Keep it safe*, he had told him. But safe from what? He traced his fingers along the foreign symbols that surrounded the creamy white pearl in the center. At first, he thought it was silver, but the way the metal felt and shined in the light led him to believe otherwise.

Aaron's grandfather had been his mentor. He had mourned the loss of his wife, Cassandra, who had died before Aaron was born. He had fought wars, but would not speak of them. His past, like his pain, was shrouded in mystery. Reymius was the type of man that when he spoke, you wanted to listen and earn his respect. His calming nature brought out the best in people.

With the sun beginning to settle and his shoulders slumped, Aaron started back to the house. He decided to walk, leading Sam, and Zeus followed. He knew the land well, but he was glad for Zeus's company. The long walk back to the house allowed him to calm down. By the time he arrived at the house, it was dark and deserted. He took care of Sam by way of brushing and giving him some food, and thanked him for the ride. He thought about going into the house, but decided to go to the sparring room instead.

The sparring room was adjacent to the main house, but was only accessible from the outside. He removed his shoes before entering—a habit instilled in him since before he could remember. Hanging along the walls was all manner of weaponry. From staffs to swords of all sizes, Aaron knew how to use them all. His father would say he knew them too well, but Reymius had nurtured Aaron's natural ability with the weapons in the room.

He walked to the center of the room and sank to his knees, facing a marble fountain against the far wall. Water fell gently upon smaller leaf pools, until at last it trickled to a pool at the base. The soft, rhythmic cascade of water soothed him and lulled him into a sense of inner peace. There were two wooden columns on either side of the fountain. His grandfather had carved the columns himself, and the shadows from the soft candlelight caressed the carved relief of roses spiraling up from the base of each column.

He closed his eyes and took slow, deep breaths. He felt a slight vibration through the floorboards. Opening his eyes, he caught a glimpse of something disturbing the water in the fountain. He crossed the room, stared down into the shallow depths, and noticed a small silver ring bobbing among the water plants along the bottom. He reached into the cool water and tugged. Sounds of pins driving into place could be heard under the floor as some unseen mechanism was put into motion. Aaron's breath caught in his throat as a gaping hole opened in the center of the room, revealing stairs that led down into darkness.

Aaron crossed the room and stood atop the narrow staircase, looking down, and a bluish glow emanated from below. He descended the staircase, which opened into a small room where a cylinder hung suspended in midair, surrounded by a blue, pulsing glow. Below the cylinder was a worn stone chest.

Inside his pocket, he felt the medallion grow warm. He drew out the medallion and gasped as the white pearl began pulsing, growing brighter as he brought it closer to the cylinder. Aaron reached out to touch the cylinder, and there was a blue flash of light as the cylinder came to rest upon the chest. A lock clicked from within, and the lid groaned, sending a cloud of dust into the air as it opened. Aaron peered inside. Atop a white cloth bundle was a folded piece of paper with his name written on it. With shaky hands, he reached in and opened the letter.

Dear Aaron,

I fear that as I write this our time together has become short indeed. You have brought joy and light back into a heart that was clouded in darkness and despair. Your grandmother, Cassandra, would have been proud to see you become the man you are today and will rest easier knowing her sacrifice was not in vain. There are things that will happen with my passing that I am powerless to prevent, but I must have faith that you will overcome the obstacles ahead of you. There are things about me that I have never told you, about both my past and where your true home is. One day soon, you will discover that your life is nothing like you thought it would be. You have a power that will arise. I have seen the signs of its coming recently, and so will you when you quiet your mind. The training that I have provided will aid you in reaping the benefits of your coming gifts...and more importantly, will help you stay alive, for there is always a price to be paid for such things. Always remember that fate uses us to its own ends, but it will never take away our right to decide. Choose wisely, and choose quickly. Death comes swiftly to those who tarry in the middle of the road. The things you have found along with this letter are yours. The medallion is your birthright; keep it safe. Both your Faith and your Fate are tied into these items. The Falcon blades are your heritage. Use them well. Worlds will change, but in the deepest, darkest depths, remember who you are. The light of our souls never truly fades, and may the light shine forever upon your path.

Farewell, my grandson.

Reymius Alenzar'seth

Alenzar'seth? That wasn't his grandfather's last name. Frowning, he reached back into the chest to retrieve the cloth bundle. Inside, he found two swords, each resting in a black scabbard; both were the length of his arms. He drew each sword from its scabbard, revealing a strange form of writing along the center of the blades and holes running their length. The swords were surprisingly light in weight and balanced perfectly in his hands. Set in the base of each sword was a crystal. A calling came to Aaron in that moment. A force that had been sleeping within him suddenly rose from the pit of his stomach, filling his chest. He carefully slid the swords back into their scabbards, wrapped them in the white cloth, and picked them up.

The calling had him entranced, guiding him as he exited the sparring room and stepped into the twilight. Zeus walked beside him until the lights of the house faded away and the trees gave way to a moonlit clearing. There were horses grazing nearby. Aaron gazed up at the night sky as the clouds blew past the moon, allowing its light to dance upon the ground. He knelt and set the white bundle in front of him. Unwrapping the swords, he drew them from their scabbards, feeling his grandfather's presence all around him. That same calm and unwavering force that watched Aaron grow from a boy into a man. The swords warmed to his touch as if they, too, were alive.

He closed his eyes and tilted his head, listening. The medallion grew warm in his pocket. The crystals in the hilt of each sword emitted a faint glow. Aaron looked up, believing it was the moon, but the pure white light was coming from within each crystal, pulsating in rhythm with his beating heart. He heard the soft urgings of a thousand voices within.

Wield the blades.

Release the power.

Claim your birthright, Safanarion.

Slowly and with a certain amount of grace, he wielded the Falcons. The pure notes of the bladesong poured forth, ringing out into the night. A force awakened within him, as if the shield that had held it in gave way to an awareness of the world around him. Life's energy surrounded him, pure and simple; its elegant force blazed vibrantly, and he felt his connection to it strengthen. The crystallized light danced upon the ground at his feet. Among the pure notes of the bladesong, Zeus howled. Not a howl of despair, but a howl of triumph. Aaron became infused by his connection to everything around him, losing himself within the music coming through the Falcons. This was his song.

The clearing quickly filled with wild animals. The horses were drawn to this spot and formed a wide circle around him. A nighthawk cried from above. Life's wellspring burst forth inside Aaron, and the crystals in the blades flared brightly. His sorrow momentarily melted away to a brief respite at this gift bequeathed to him by his grandfather.

2

THE THINGS A MOTHER KNOWS

It was the middle of the night when Aaron finally got back to his grandfather's house. His mother sat in one of the rocking chairs on the front porch with a solitary candle for a companion. Her long blonde hair was tied back in a ponytail. She stood up when he came to the bottom of the stairs with Zeus by his side. Relief shined in her red-rimmed eyes as she held her arms open to him.

With each step Aaron took he felt his will not to break down erode. He still saw the memory of her crying in his father's arms.

"Mom, I—" He choked, dropping the white bundle. He hugged his mother and for that brief moment, he was a boy seeking a mother's comforting embrace. "I can't believe he's gone."

"It's okay," she said soothingly. "He would have said it was his time."

"Do they know what happened?" he asked.

"No, they don't know why," she said. "If they did, would it really make a difference?"

Aaron frowned in thought. "No, I guess not."

"Come on, let's go inside and get some sleep," said his mother.

"You're staying here tonight?" Aaron asked.

"It's late, and I just feel like I need to be here tonight, don't you?" she asked.

"Yeah," Aaron agreed.

Zeus whined from behind him and pawed at the cloth bundle that held the swords. Aaron went down the stairs and retrieved the bundle.

"What have you got there?" his mother asked.

Aaron thought about telling her, but decided against it. "Just some stuff I found," he said.

Together they entered the empty house.

A few hours later, Aaron tossed and turned. He couldn't get comfortable despite being exhausted. His mind kept racing. Alenzar'seth, the name his grandfather had signed the letter with—what did it mean?

He gazed out of the window of the guest bedroom. Zeus lay on the floor next to the bed, but Aaron didn't think the wolf half-breed slept any better than he did. Why did his grandfather hand him that medallion? He had clutched it like it was the most important thing he had to give. Then there were the swords. What was he supposed to do with the swords? His thoughts drifted back to the letter.

One day soon, you will discover that your life is nothing like you thought it would be...

The sun was rising when a soft knock came from the door.

"Come in."

His mother opened the door and took a step inside. "Did you sleep okay?" she asked.

"About as good as you did," Aaron answered.

"I see," she said. "Come on down. Your father brought breakfast."

Aaron didn't think he could eat, but he decided it would make his mother feel better if he at least tried. He threw on a pair of jeans and a gray T-shirt and looked at the nightstand where the medallion lay. He considered just leaving it. A ray of sunshine peeked through the window, caressing the edge of the medallion. Aaron sighed, reaching out to grab it, and stuck it in his pocket.

The sweet aroma of cinnamon-raisin bagels wafted from the kitchen table. He sat down and took one as his father came in through the front door. His dad's great size filled the doorway without any effort. Being a carpenter kept him fit and trim.

"Morning," his father said.

"Does Tara know about Grandpa?" Aaron asked, buttering his bagel.

"Yeah, your sister will be out here later," his father answered, then looked at him in a way that made Aaron feel like he was an open book. "Are you all right?"

Aaron heard the echoes of the bladesong in his head, and the medallion warmed in his pocket.

"I guess," he said. "I'm numb really."

Should I tell him about the letter?

"There are no words that I can say that will make this any easier," his father said. "He was a great man, and he loved you. I'll miss him too. I keep expecting him to walk in at any moment. But you know what, it's because we loved him so much that mourning the loss will be hard. By the same token, we can count ourselves fortunate for having him in our lives for the time that we did." He paused and took a sip of his coffee, glancing out the window. "We don't have to talk about this now if you don't want to."

Aaron looked out the same window. The sun was shining with no hint of a cloud in the sky. It was a perfect day outside, and it mocked everything he was feeling. The room felt like it was closing in, suffocating him. He just wanted to run and not stop until he was far away.

"It's fine, Dad. I just need to get some air," he said, rising out of his seat and grabbing his bagel.

He stepped outside, not knowing where he was going, and before he knew it, he was standing inside the sparring room, gazing at the fountain. His breath came in quick gasps. It was dark with all the shades shut. He was taking deep, rhythmic breaths, finding his calm center, when the attack came. A slight shift in the air blared warning bells in his mind, and instinct took over as he tumbled out of the way and came easily to his feet. He ducked again as he heard a staff whistling through the air, missing his head. Aaron spun toward the wall and grabbed his own staff.

Aaron could only make out the shape of his assailant in the dimly lit room. He moved into the center of the room, meeting them head-on. The staff was one of the simplest weapons to use, and in the hands of the right person, among the deadliest. The way his adversary moved with the staff told him that they knew how to use it. His assailant rained attacks down on him. Aaron blocked the attacks and probed with a counter to feel out his attacker. Aaron's size was often deceptive because he was quick as well as big, but all his attacks were blocked. It was like he was practicing with his grandfather. He baited his opponent with an opening. As the staff came down, he shifted to the right and forward, rendering the blow useless, and launched a powerful front kick that sent his attacker across the room. He expected the grunt of a man, but heard the gasp of a woman.

Aaron quickly reached over and turned on the lights, only to see his mother resting on one knee, leaning on her staff. Her hair had been tied back and tucked into a black shirt.

"Reymius has taught you well," she gasped with a pride-filled smile. "I am my father's daughter, Aaron, no need to look so surprised."

"Are you okay?" Aaron asked, kneeling down and helping her to her feet. Aaron had never viewed his mother as anything other than a mother, and it was shocking to think of her as just a person.

"Yeah. You kick pretty hard," she mused, rubbing her side.

"I'm sorry," Aaron said, and left the unasked question hanging in the air for a moment. "But you've never been in here. Not with any of the classes or while he taught me."

His mother nodded. "There was so much I couldn't remember after the accident. What I can remember doesn't make any sense to me. It's like trying to see something through a thick fog," she said, regaining her feet. "One thing I did remember was how to defend myself. I know all of these weapons here, but I don't remember learning how to use them. I know all the forms for gaining flexibility and quieting the mind as you do, but evidently am not so well practiced."

Aaron's hand rested on the pocket of his jeans. He felt the medallion and was trying to decide if he should ask her about it. "When is the funeral going to be?" Aaron asked.

"The day after tomorrow. Tara should be here soon," she said while they walked back outside. Aaron took a last glance at the fountain and the center of the floor where the secret chamber lay hidden.

"Where has she been?"

"She's been away with Alex, looking at places for the wedding reception."

Aaron nodded. His sister had recently become engaged, and he was happy for her. Her fiancé, Alex, was a really good guy. Tara was just a few years older than he and had always looked after him.

"Do you have any exams left?" his mother asked.

"Yeah, one tomorrow. I was thinking of calling the professor to see whether I could have it changed," Aaron answered.

"Well, that's up to you," she said. "Life will go on whether we are ready for it or not."

"Carlowen," his dad called.

"We're out here," his mother called back.

"Jack is here with the paperwork." his father said.

Jack was a family friend who happened to be a lawyer. His mother left him and followed his dad back into the house. Aaron decided to drive to campus and see Dr. Kozak about the final rather than calling. He knew it was an excuse just to do something, but it gave him something to think about besides everything he preferred not to. As he pulled away from the house, he caught a glimpse of Zeus before he disappeared into the trees. Though there was no chill in the air, he shivered.

3

NEW PERCEPTIONS

The drive to campus revived him. He had the top down on his Jeep, and the fresh air did him good. He walked into the humanities building where the sociology department was and went up to the fourth floor. He turned the corner, thinking about what he was going to say, when Professor Kozak came out of his office, heading in his direction. His steel-rimmed glasses caught the fluorescent lighting above, and he appeared to be muttering to himself. His gray hair was in its normal disheveled state.

"Hello, Dr. Kozak. I need a few minutes of your time."

"Sure, Aaron," Dr. Kozak said, looking up at him expectantly, and when Aaron hesitated, he added, "Oh, would you like to step into my office?"

"If that's okay; this is a personal matter," Aaron said.

The office wasn't much bigger than a closet and was jammed with all sorts of books and dusty objects. There was a picture of a mountain whose peak poked above a swath of clouds. The writing beneath it said, "Faith is taking the first step when you don't see the end. The truth is what you find once you get there."

"Do you like the picture?" the professor asked.

"Yeah, I like the caption," Aaron answered.

"Oh really, what do you think it means? I mean, it sounds good, but what does it mean?" the professor asked with a dubious tone.

Aaron paused, considering. "Sometimes in order to get to the truth, you need to take a leap of faith. I supposed it's how one gains wisdom."

The corners of the professor's mouth rose. "Ah yes, you're my philosopher, very good. I am always curious about what people think of that quote. Anyway, what can I do for you?"

Aaron told him about his grandfather's passing and that he wouldn't be able to take the final exam the next day. The professor nodded and conveyed his condolences to him and his family. Aaron liked that about Dr. Kozak: Some professors had an embedded disdain for anyone's lives but their own, but Dr. Kozak was a kindhearted person.

"It's certainly not going to adversely affect your grade if you do not take the final. Not for you, at least. You actually showed up and participated in my class. My goal the entire semester is to get students to think about the world around them, and not be so concerned about grades. The question I had proposed for the final is not far off from the quote you just analyzed for me, which I am happy to say you've hit dead-on. I had hoped you would consider majoring in sociology, but knowing that you are about to graduate, I see I'm too late to recruit you," he said, rising and extending his hand.

Aaron shook the professor's hand and thanked him.

Aaron left the office and took a quick detour to the bathroom. While rinsing his hands, he felt a sick feeling in the pit of his stomach.

Rap!

Rap!

Rap!

The loud noise echoed from outside the bathroom. Aaron yanked the door open. The hallway was empty. The fluorescent lights went out, and all was eerily quiet. Sunlight shined brightly through the entrance at the far end of the hall, but his area was dark. A sudden chill crept down his spine like tiny spiders crawling down his back.

What the hell was that?

The medallion grew cool in his pocket. Aaron stepped out into the hallway and started walking toward the entrance. He felt a presence come rushing toward him, and he spun around, but the hallway was empty. He was all alone.

Aaron quickened his pace down the hallway. He kept looking behind him, but he couldn't see anything. Aaron tried to dismiss the sinking feeling, but was compelled to turn around one last time. He peered into the darkened hallway. There was a loud screech, and something knocked him backward, off his feet. He rolled and was instantly up again, his heart pounding. He scanned about, looking to see who was there. Another blow blindsided him, and he went down. He tasted blood in his mouth while he shook his head, bracing himself. He scrambled back and regained his feet. He leaned back against a glass display case. He scanned out with his other senses, but couldn't detect anybody there with him. In fact, he sensed nothing, as if this place were devoid of life. Then he felt it, the force gathering itself, preparing to strike. Aaron barely got out of the way in time as the blow meant for him shattered a glass display case behind him.

He turned and sprinted down the hallway with the shattering of glass trailing his wake. He reached the end of the hallway, gasping for breath. The lights came back on, revealing a mess of shattered glass as people drawn by the noise filled the hallway. He ducked out of sight, heading down the stairs, but he could have sworn that he'd heard an ominous cackle right before the lights came back on.

As Aaron exited the building, the campus police were rushing in. His chest ached where he had taken the brunt of the blow, and he glanced back at the building. *What the hell was that?*

He took the medallion out of his pocket and ran his fingertips over the carved relief of the dragon holding a rose. On the flip side were two swords, like the ones his grandfather left him. In the center was a white pearl. The medallion was cool now, but he knew that it had reacted to whatever it was back there. Was this what his grandfather's letter warned him about? *One day soon, you will discover that your life is nothing like you thought it would be...*

How could he face something that he couldn't see? But he was able to sense it for a second.

Aaron looked up and saw a hawk flying gracefully, circling to and fro. He followed the hawk's movements, its slight change in its wings to keep riding along the wind. And then he saw it, just a spark at first, but as he focused, he saw the impression of the life force of the hawk shining brilliantly. The hawk, as if sensing him, dived down hard, only to land elegantly on the roll bar of his Jeep. The hawk peered at him, cocking its head to the side, and Aaron calmly looked back. After a moment, the hawk let out a cry and took flight.

Aaron climbed into his Jeep and noticed the thin leather cord he kept hanging from the rearview mirror. He picked it up, looped it through the eyehole on the medallion, and tied it around his neck. He then tucked it inside his shirt. His hands still shook from his encounter with whatever had been in the school. Sirens sounded from more campus police cars speeding toward the humanities building. Aaron put the Jeep in drive and slowly drove away.

Aaron's sister, Tara, waved to him as he parked his Jeep. She stood on the lowest rail on the fence while watching the grazing horses. Her long auburn hair spilled gracefully down her back. His sister turned more than a few heads, but her heart belonged to her fiancé, Alex. She had the ability to get the shyest of people to start talking to her. But today she looked sad. She was grieving just as much as he was, even though Reymius wasn't her true grandfather. His half-sister was four years his senior and remembered precious little of her own mother. Carlowen helped to fill that gap when she married their father, Patrick.

"What's going on?" Aaron asked.

Tara inspected him. "What happened to you?"

Since they were kids, she always knew when he was in trouble just by looking at him. Should he tell her what just happened? *Oh yeah, a freaky ghost attacked me at school today, and I have a medallion that seems to be an early warning device.* That made a lot of sense. Then he remembered the scratches along his face and arms from his wild ride last night.

"Nothing," he lied. "I kinda don't know what to do with myself."

"Yeah, I know the feeling. Don't want to be here like this, but I don't want to go anywhere else either," she said. "Bronwyn came by. She had heard about Grandpa."

"How nice of her," Aaron said.

"I thought so," Tara said, until she noticed him glowering. "Oh come on, Aaron. She's a nice girl. You can't stay mad at her forever."

"Sure," Aaron said. He didn't want to deal with Bronwyn now.

Tara stepped down from the rail and looked up at him in such a way that made him feel small and foolish. "One thing you will have to learn, dear Brother, is that sometimes people make mistakes. No one is perfect. Not even you. Forgiveness may not come easily, but when you care about someone, wouldn't you want a second chance?"

He clenched his teeth without realizing it. "I didn't do anything wrong. She's the one who had the lapse in judgement," Aaron said.

"Be that as it may. You need to make a choice." She paused until he looked her in the eyes. "Did it ever occur to you that the reason this tears you up inside is because you still care for her? Those feelings can't be turned on and off like a light switch."

"Yeah—" he began, but Tara cut him off.

"Look, I'm not condoning what she did, but you should at least talk to her and hear what she has to say. Then maybe you can move on."

Brother and sister faced each other, both unwavering.

"Maybe," was all he would say, and Tara rolled her eyes, muttering about the stubbornness of men while she walked away.

Aaron filled the rest of the day with mindless tasks just to keep busy. His parents were occupied with making arrangements for the funeral. Aaron busied himself with the horses, seeing that they were exercised and fed. When his mind wandered, it kept going back to the same unanswered questions. What was happening to him? Try as he might to go about a normal day, he kept looking over his shoulder.

Often, his thoughts strayed to the swords, so much that he decided to keep them close to where he was working. He opened the white cloth sack to look at them and reached inside to feel them in his hands. They gave him a small measure of reassurance. His grandfather referred to them as Falcons in the letter. He couldn't determine what type of metal they were made from. As an engineering student with a focus in mechanics and materials science, this perplexed him. Certainly not steel, as they were much too light. But they were strong. Each time he held the swords, they felt more at home in his hands, which both comforted and scared him. After all, why would he need swords?

4

DAY TO MOURN

The morning trickled away while Aaron's family prepared for the funeral. The whole idea of a church ceremony for his grandfather annoyed him; after all, his grandfather was not a member of any church that Aaron could remember. They never talked about it. He thought he should have known something like that about his grandfather, and he was beginning to wonder how much he didn't know about the man. An image of the Falcons flashed in his mind, and echoes of the bladesong emanated from within him. He glanced over at them safely tucked away next to his bed. He wasn't ready for them yet, but their calling whispered to him. *I can't exactly walk around with them strapped to my back,* he thought. He wore a dark gray suit and checked his appearance in the mirror before leaving his room. He went down to the kitchen to get something to eat.

"Good morning," his father greeted him.

"Hey," Aaron said. The absurdity of the whole funeral thing still whittled away at him. "Dad, do you think this is right, what we're doing?" he asked.

"What do you mean?"

"Grandpa wasn't even a Christian. I just don't think it's right. Is this funeral what he would have wanted?" Aaron asked.

His father set down his cup of coffee and eyed him for a moment. "Funerals are for the living, Son, as well as the dead," he said softly. "The truth is that your mother and I don't know what he wanted. He never told us. We thought a funeral would be best. Your grandfather touched a lot of lives, and many of them will want to pay their last respects." He took another sip of his coffee before continuing. "I know it's hard, and if you truly feel that this is not right then you do not have to be there. However, I would like for you to come."

Aaron sighed, feeling foolish. "I'll go," he said. How could he do otherwise?

THE FUNERAL WAS OUTSIDE AT THE LOCAL CEMETERY. AARON AND HIS sister exchanged glances more than a few times at the large crowd that gathered. His grandfather had touched more lives than he'd realized, and it filled him with a sense of pride that his grandfather was beloved by so many. Aaron closed his eyes, soaking in the noonday sun. A soft breeze toyed through the air, and the voices of those around him drifted away on the soft eddies of the wind. He breathed in slow, easy breaths. With each exhalation, he sensed the energy of all things around him. He delved deeper within while projecting his own energy out. The energy danced all around and gathered to him. He felt the calling to move the way he did with the Falcons, and then a presence was suddenly there. Aaron's breath caught in his throat as something cold and dark washed over him, and his back stiffened.

Aaron knew it was the same presence that attacked him at the school. He didn't know what to do. The presence felt more potent. Aaron smelled its foulness stealing away the freshness of the air. He opened his eyes to scan the crowd. A hooded figure walked among the people gathered for the funeral. Thunder that no one else seemed to hear boomed in the clear sky. The hooded figure made his way to the other side of the casket, across from Aaron. The figure drew his hands up to remove his hood in a slow, deliberate motion. Aaron's heart thundered as the hood fell away. Soulless black eyes housed in a ghostly white head sneered at him. He had a strong imposing face of high cheekbones and a pronounced chin that dominated his chiseled features. He was completely hairless, and he carried an air of absolute arrogance. The shadows seemed to swirl around him, and Aaron grudgingly met his gaze.

"Ferasdiam has laid her mark upon you, scion of the house Alenzar'seth." His voice was like granite. "A pity," he said and made a show of studying his surroundings with disdain.

Aaron rose to his feet. The crack of a whip sounded, and the being stood directly in front of him. His massive hand reached toward Aaron, and the white pearl in Aaron's medallion flared to life. The being's hand recoiled, and he stepped back with a look of uncertainty flashing across his soulless black eyes.

"Beware, you have this day to mourn. Then you're mine." He screeched the last word with such vehemence that Aaron felt his breath rush past his face.

A hand gently gripped his shoulder, and he looked up to see his mother prodding him to get up. The people at the funeral were beginning to disperse. He got up and scanned the area, all the while hearing the echo of the being's last words, and he shuddered.

Later on he climbed into his Jeep, preferring to drive by himself than ride with his family. He loosened his necktie and tossed it into the center console. He lowered the soft top and tied it off.

"Aaron," a voice called softly from behind him.

The muscles in his shoulders stiffened when he heard Bronwyn call his name. There was a time when her smooth voice sounded like heaven to him, and despite all his efforts to banish her from his heart, her voice still affected him. Why couldn't he just forget her?

He took a deep breath and turned around. "Hello, Bronwyn," he said, and his heart twisted up in knots as she stared back at him with her honey-brown eyes and rich brown hair spilling down her back. She wore a simple black dress, which made her natural beauty appear to be anything but simple.

"I'm so sorry about your grandfather, Aaron. I know how much he meant to you. Are you okay?" she asked.

"My sister said you stopped by yesterday. Thank you, but you didn't have to do that."

"Yes I did," she said. "He meant something to me too, and your family has always been good to me." When Aaron did not say anything, she continued. "I've wanted to see you, but I know—"

All the anguish at her betrayal welled up in him. "Why did you do it?" he blurted out.

Bronwyn took a step closer and put her hand on his arm, her eyes brimming with tears. "I'm sorry, Aaron. I made a mistake. I was wrong and I'm sorry. She paused. "Aaron, please look at me."

Hearing his name from her lips cut his heart in two. Both halves were fighting, one wanting nothing more than to take her in his arms, the other wanting to get as far away from her as possible so the pain would go away.

"How can I ever trust you? I mean, you've taken everything we had and tossed it away the moment you cheated on me. I thought what we had was special and enduring, and you ruined it! You can't get that back!" The bitterness of his words cut him as he saw the pain in her eyes.

"It is special, that's why I'm here. I can only say I'm sorry. I want to be with you. Please, won't you give me another chance?" she asked.

It would be so easy to just take her in his arms and hold her. How he yearned to do that even now in the midst of all the anger and pain, but his anger would not relent. "I don't think you deserve another chance. You stay away from me!" he shouted, earning them some worried looks from the departing funeral procession. "All that we had is dead!" The words left his lips without any thought, his anger taking him to a place where reason and clarity had no sway, and the wisdom of his core began to rebel against grief's foolishness. *She doesn't deserve this.*

"That's not true. I can see it in your eyes," Bronwyn said.

He didn't say anything.

"What we have is not dead," she said.

"I can't be with you," Aaron said.

Those cruel words broke her resolve. Let her be the one to hurt for a while. He climbed back into his Jeep and sped off, leaving her there with tears streaming down her face. His own tears came in bitter defiance to his anger. *You are a fool,* he thought, and struck the steering wheel with his fist over and over again.

He looked into the rearview mirror, and soulless black eyes stared back at him. After a moment, they disappeared, but he heard an echo of mirthless laughter that drained the heat from his blood. The words from his grandfather's letter came to mind. *One day soon, you will discover that your life is nothing like you thought it would be.* Aaron glared at the rearview mirror, and his fist shattered it, and all the while mirthless laughter reverberated in his mind.

5

ANOTHER WORLD

It was midday in the cursed kingdom of Shandara, but one would never know it. Life was all but forsaken, as the lands were covered in decay, and darkness reigned supreme. Whispers of a glorious past lived in the stone remnants found throughout this once lush and proud kingdom in the land known as Safanar. Now wasteland dominated it. The old kingdom of Shandara had been a jewel upon Safanar that was unparalleled, and the palace, a triumph of human and Hythariam kind. Now it was all but a cold corpse. A testament of Colind's recklessness. This was his prison. He was an outcast banished to this forsaken land where he had once been the guardian for all, but now he was just a shadow. It had been more than twenty years since Shandara had fallen. How he longed to feel the warmth of sunlight on his face, drink clean water, and eat food. Oh how he missed the taste of food. Even more, he missed the sunlight on his face, but his prison forbade both.

Colind was a shadow, his soul ripped from his body, which was still imprisoned in the earth, fiendishly preserved as a reminder of a prison he couldn't escape. Sunlight was deadly to him, as it could erase his very essence. The shadows were his home now, as they had been for more than a score of years. Despair claimed him in the beginning, then madness, where he roamed like any other specter, and now a bitter contempt for a prison that had no walls. He was cursed, forever to roam among the place of his failure. This was the price he paid for not being true to the Safanarion Order and not accepting the harsh truth about one of its members. But what parent isn't blind to a child's shortcomings? A feeble argument compared to the destruction it caused, and the silence from all those who had died at the fall of Shandara was his answer.

Here, in the land of shadow, he had little worry about the sun, which was safely tucked away behind a perpetual wall of clouds. Colind still remembered with unwavering clarity those last days. The days when his old friend Reymius had fled Safanar with his only daughter, Carlowen, to stop the evil that was unleashed. He again felt the faint stirrings of a heart that was no longer beat inside him. It had begun the day before, like an itch that needed to be scratched. Beckoning and constant, but gaining in urgency. *Come to Shandara. Return to the palace, Colind. Your role is not yet finished.* The resolute tone was reminiscent of Reymius, but how could that be? If Reymius had, in fact, returned to Safanar, that meant one thing. Reymius was dead. Only he could reach across the planes of death to Colind. A scant flicker of hope that the winds were indeed changing stirred within him.

He closed in on the palace and reluctantly looked up. The legendary ivory walls were scorched and riddled with cracks where they hadn't shattered altogether. Of the twenty towers, a mere six remained standing. He cast his eyes to the ground, unable to stand the sight of Shandara in such a state. He made his way to the sacred grove that lay in the heart of the palace.

Years of existing in the shadows allowed him to instinctively sense when the sunlight was near, and those instincts saved him. Within one pace, the line of darkness gave way to the light, and Colind looked to the sky in awe as shafts of sunlight dotted the once-proud city. His gaze drew downward to the heart of the sacred grove. A pang surged from deep within. The ancient tree of Shandara gleamed under the sun, and the sight of it almost caused him to run perilously into the light.

A glowing figure of a man sitting at the base of the sacred tree slowly looked up and smiled sadly. Colind stopped, unable to go any farther. A barrage of memories swept over him. *Reymius?* The wizened figure nodded in understanding.

"My friend, please tell me that you and Carlowen were spared, that you escaped the fall?" he asked, falling to his knees. The apparition nodded again, and Colind sagged with relief as a great weight lifted from his shoulders. Colind began to speak again, and the luminescent Reymius glided forth, coming before Colind's slumped form. His eyes were full of patient understanding and loving friendship that warmed Colind's lonely heart. For a few fleeting moments, he felt the ground beneath his knees and tasted the sweet air of the sacred grove once again. In one fluid motion, Reymius raised his hand to Colind's forehead, linking them. Images of a young man fanned through Colind's mind.

The heir of Shandara, my grandson.

The Dark One, Tarimus, was already on the hunt, and the trials were about to begin. Colind felt desperation through the link and backed away, knowing what he needed to do. He had to guide Reymius's heir in traversing the crossroads between worlds, facing the perils between life and death.

You are meant to guide, not to interfere. Colind, you are forbidden to interfere. Aaron must choose his own path if there is to be any hope. These are his trials to overcome if the Safanarion Order is to return.

Those cruel words echoed in his mind. Once again, he would be the observer. *Well, we'll see about that.* The specter of Reymius, as if hearing his thoughts, fixed him with a rigid gaze, then faded into the sacred tree and disappeared. Colind glared at the tree for a few moments. He would accept his charge despite his imprisonment. He was *still* a guardian of the land, and he had a debt to the house of Alenzar'seth.

Both he and Reymius had given an oath to protect the land. He would do all that he must in service of the Goddess, despite his loyalty to the house of Alenzar'seth, the keepers of Shandara.

Colind withdrew from the sacred grove and made his way to the gates of the palace. The journey would have been much easier had he simply traveled through the walls, but the part of him that clung to remnants of his humanity refused to give in. He had to travel to the crossroads in order to journey to the home of Reymius's heir. The Goddess saw fit to give him a second chance, and he could not falter. This could be the redemption that he had waited so long for. He now had a chance to set right some of the wrongs that occurred so long ago. To do this, he would need to confront Tarimus once again. Thoughts of Tarimus tore his heart in two, and a single name appeared in his mind with utter contempt: Mactar. *All roads of betrayal lead to your doorstep, and we shall meet again.*

6

THE FOG BEGINS TO LIFT

Aaron looked up at a great marble statue of a dragon that cast its thunderous gaze down at him. Its massive wings were spread wide, and Aaron stood there, taking in the awesome presence before him. The fringes of his vision were blurred to his surroundings, as if he were peering through a window with water streaming down the edges. But the statue was clear and unwavering in his dream. Since he first slept with the medallion around his neck, his nights had been filled with dreams of places he had never seen before. But no matter the dream, sooner or later he would end up in a coliseum with marble columns running down each side, leading to a statue at the end. The statue would sometimes be a tree, intricate in its design and detail as if the stone were once a living entity. He heard the sound of a clock ticking, and the walls of the temple around him were stripped away, revealing a black void. Icy cold ripped the breath from his lungs, and the sinister laughter began.

"The time of mourning is over," a voice thundered from the void. A crushing blow sent Aaron reeling off his feet. The hooded figure that had been at his grandfather's funeral appeared. "I will drink from your soul, Ferasdiam marked. Alenzar'seth's heir," he spat.

Aaron quickly lashed out with his foot. He missed his mark, but was able to get to his feet.

They squared off. This was his dream, and no one had power over him in his own dream. "Who are you?" Aaron demanded.

Lifeless black eyes regarded Aaron. "You're going to have to do better than that."

"Fine!" Aaron said between clenched teeth and charged.

The being disappeared with a cackling laugh, and Aaron cursed himself for a fool. *Remember the hallway at school.* He closed his eyes, claiming the void within, and stretched out his feelings until he found the darkness. Their energies touched for a moment, and the hatred that emanated from this being almost broke Aaron's concentration.

"I found you."

"You know nothing," it hissed back.

Aaron kept a firm hold of his focus and a name appeared in his mind. "You are Tarimus; I know this is your name."

Tarimus howled in such a rage that Aaron's hands went to his ears in a feeble attempt to block out the horrible sound. For a moment, he teetered between wakefulness and sleep.

Aaron opened his eyes and found that he stood upon a dark surface barely visible through the mist that gathered up to his knees as far as the eye could see.

Tarimus floated in the air above him. "Now for your first lesson in power, boy," Tarimus spat, and then he swooped down with lightning speed and struck him.

Aaron felt himself begin to break apart and tried feebly to hold himself together. Then, with a flash of light, he found himself sprawled on the floor of his room. He sprang to his feet, circling around. His breath came to him in labored gasps. He looked at himself in the mirror and saw blood trickling down the side of his lips and two fist marks over his heart where Tarimus had struck him. The medallion lay coolly against his chest.

A hard knock came from his bedroom door. "Aaron, are you okay?" his mother asked as she came in, not waiting for an answer.

He quickly wiped the blood from his face and turned toward her. "Yeah, I'm fine." It was getting to be a habit telling people this.

"I thought I heard something..." She stopped suddenly with her eyes fixed on the medallion. "Where did you get that?"

"Right before Grandpa died, he placed this in my hands and told me to keep it safe."

Carlowen gasped for air, and her eyes grew distant. "Safanar," she whispered.

"What did you say?"

His mother frowned and looked as if she couldn't quite concentrate. "Safanar, our home," she said.

"Our home?"

"We'll talk more in the morning—" She paused, swallowing hard. "I just need some time, okay?" Her eyes darted back to the medallion.

"Do you know what it is?" Aaron asked.

"Yes. It's the crest of our family, but don't show anyone else. I mean no one, Aaron," she said firmly.

Aaron nodded.

Carlowen started to go back to her bedroom, but turned in mid-stride and headed down to the family room. Memories of places long forgotten danced along the edges of her mind, breaking through the walls built long ago. She was standing on a balcony of a palace, watching the sun set over rolling green hills. To her right was a black flag with a gold dragon holding a rose embroidered on it.

"Hey, what's going on?" her husband said, snatching her from her thoughts.

"Everything is fine, Patrick. I thought I heard a noise coming from Aaron's room."

Patrick joined her in the family room. "He's changing more and more every day," he said.

"Yeah, he's growing up," she answered, but in her mind she was still seeing the medallion. The creamy white pearl in the center, surrounded by a dragon clutching a rose protectively. Their family heirloom. The protective walls that had blocked off her memories were slowly crumbling, and she scrambled to make sense of it all. She had seen that medallion before, when it had been worn by her mother. Hazy images of a life long dead invaded her mind. A great white castle lay burning with the acrid smoke stinging her eyes and throat. She blinked back watery eyes. *Shandara, her home.*

Patrick watched the troubled thoughts flow through his wife's eyes. In some ways he knew this woman like he knew himself, but in other ways she was a complete stranger to him. A part of her had always been distant. *Like Reymius,* he thought suddenly. Here but not *truly here.* His death unlocked something in Carlowen, a key to all the memories that were sealed away. It had never bothered him that she couldn't remember her youth. Carlowen loved his daughter and was good to him. Something paramount was happening to both his wife and son, and he felt powerless against it. The only thing he could do was be there for her as he always had been and pray it would be enough. He sat quietly next to her and gently rubbed her back. Her untarnished elegance made the rest of the world fade away. Beneath the beauty was strength and wrought-iron will—the very same strength mirrored in his son.

"It's late," she said. "And you have an early day tomorrow."

Patrick groaned while getting up.

"Go on ahead. I'll be there in a minute," she said.

When she was alone once more, Carlowen knelt straight-backed on the floor. Her breath came in a smooth, even rhythm. The cruel fog in her mind that blocked the memories of her youth was thinning. Glimpses of a stranger's life flashed before her. A world nothing like the one she'd called home for so long. One moment, she was a little girl running through a courtyard with her father growling playfully for the chase. Next, she was in a sparring room much grander than the replica that her father had built at the farm. She squared off against a man dressed in black, whose face she didn't recognize. Next, there was smoke billowing all around her. And screams...

"Take her, Reymius, save yourself," a voice said.

"Cassandra, no!" Reymius pleaded. "There must be another way," he growled.

"There is no other way. You must go. You cannot face the Drake. Go, my love, and live. Protect our future."

Then she was gone, and the world went black. Pain that had been locked away gushed forth, and her world shattered. A lingering feeling touched her thoughts, and she sensed the presence of compassion, whose warm arms surrounded her. She knew this presence, but could not remember his name. His voice echoed in her memories.

"Mom, are you okay?" Aaron asked.

Carlowen opened her eyes to see Aaron above her. Whatever presence had been there, fled. Her son, scanning the room, had felt it too. *Have I been blind all these years?* she wondered. She saw the outline of the medallion beneath his shirt and knew that her son would be leaving her soon. She told him everything was going to be all right.

"Who are the Alenzar'seth?" he asked, his eyes never leaving hers.

"That is the name of our family," she paused, choosing her words. "Tonight, I began to remember all those years lost to me. For so long, I could only remember the time just before you were born, but not now." Her voice trailed off. "It's all right. There's still time." Precious little time, but yes. "We'll talk more in the morning."

As she walked by him he asked, "Who am I, Mother?"

Carlowen turned to look at her son. "No matter what happens, Aaron, you are who you've always been. Nothing will change that." And with that, she turned and left.

Colind watched in silence as Reymius's grandson walked back up the hallway. What a strange world Reymius called home for so long. The safety that once was awarded by this place was gone. It was only a matter of time before their world, Safanar, caught up with them. Colind sensed the impression of Tarimus's rage and utter contempt. The hound had found its prey, or so it would seem, but who would prove the better—the hound or the prey? He stayed at the house that night, dividing his time between Carlowen and her son, watching over them even though neither slept. He was drawn to Aaron and sensed the boy's potential. Power was drawing toward Aaron, but it was a power that he remained ignorant of. How was he supposed to guide Reymius's grandson? Colind couldn't help but think of Aaron as a snowball sailing into the fire as he wondered what Tarimus would do next.

7

DECEPTION

The next day Aaron overslept. His father left him a note asking that he help out with tending to the horses at his grandfather's farm. Aaron had hoped to get some answers from his mother, but his house was empty. He headed over to the horse farm and noted that everything around him seemed clearer than before, as if he possessed a heightened sense of awareness of his surroundings. Even the horses, which he got along with fine before, responded better to him.

At the end of the day, he took Ginger, a honey-brown mare, out for a ride in a small meadow. It was off the beaten path, and he preferred its seclusion. He brought the swords to practice with them, melding the bladesong into the forms that were taught to him by his grandfather. Aaron suspected that his grandfather trained him with the Falcons in mind. These swords felt as if they were made for him. In light of current events, he wondered if his grandfather had always been preparing Aaron for what he was about to face. He just didn't know what he should do now. He needed to talk to someone about all this, someone who would understand, but who? His mother had avoided him this morning. She struggled with her own returning memories, and Aaron preferred to give her some space, but he needed answers. Who knew when Tarimus would strike again? With the Falcons in his hands he felt more secure, but he couldn't bring them with him wherever he went.

Aaron headed back, allowing Ginger to have her stride, and it wasn't until he came within view of the stables that he realized he wasn't alone. Another horse, approaching from one of the other trails, came up next to his.

Bronwyn!

She didn't look surprised to see him. The sun bathed the back of her head, giving her brown hair a reddish glow, and he felt his pulse quicken. The anger and resentment had faded to a dull ache as if he were finally exhausted from it all.

"Hi," Aaron said.

Bronwyn simply looked back at him, her eyes revealing nothing and everything at the same time. He'd acted like such an idiot at the funeral, and now he was the one who felt uncomfortable. *It's your own fault for losing your temper.* He looked back at her, forcing all his angst back. She was waiting for him to say something, and she had every right to.

"I'm sorry for what I said at the funeral," Aaron said.

She regarded him for a moment. "It's okay. I know how much he meant to you," Bronwyn said, easing her horse, Abby, next to Ginger as they continued on.

They rode together in silence, which Aaron appreciated, because for the life of him he couldn't think of anything to say. They guided their horses to the stables and began storing their gear. He watched her brush down Abby, her long slender arms moving in smooth, graceful strokes. The light streamed in through the windows, catching her honey-brown hair in a golden hue. When she noticed him watching her, he looked away, quickly feeling foolish, but he could have sworn he saw her smile. How could his heart yearn to reach out to her and recoil at the same time? *Maybe I just need to get away from this place for a while.* He was stowing his saddle, gathering his resolve to walk over to her, when she came up behind him.

"I'm not sure when a good time will be, but at some point we need to talk," Bronwyn said.

"Okay. It's been tough, you know. There's been a lot going on." He stopped, trying to decide whether he should tell her all the things that were happening.

"It's all right if you don't want to talk about it now," she said. "But I'm here in case you do."

Aaron pressed his lips together. "With his death, I am learning that my family has a history that I never would have believed possible." *Yeah, go ahead, tell her that you're from another world; she won't think you're crazy… Am I crazy?* He wasn't so sure anymore. "It's hard to explain."

"I'm sure you'll find the words when you're ready. Now just doesn't seem to be the right time. Just remember, no matter what your family history is, it doesn't define you," Bronwyn said.

Aaron nodded.

"Can I come by and see you later on this week?" she asked.

"I've been running things here, so this is where I'll be most of the..." He grimaced. "I mean, yes, I would like it if you came by."

She smiled, clearly relieved, and for a moment, a glimmer of hope grew in her eyes. She said goodbye and left.

Aaron waited a few seconds, debating on whether he should go after her. *Screw it,* he thought. He came out of the stables, about to call after her, but Bronwyn was heading toward the sparring room. There was something in the way she moved that didn't seem quite right, leaving an icy feeling sliding down to the pit of his stomach. He watched her open the door and stop in the doorway. Her head cocked to the side. She turned around, and Aaron sucked in a breath. The lifeless stare of depthless black eyes hit him like a blow. She flashed a haunting smile and went inside.

"Tarimus," Aaron gasped, then sprinted to the sparring room. He came to the door and stopped. Blindly charging in would be foolish.

"Bronwyn?" Aaron called as he stepped cautiously through the door into the darkness beyond. Aaron reached over and flipped the light switch, but the lights wouldn't turn on. It was so cold he saw his breath. *It's the middle of June!* He halted just inside the door and was looking back at his Jeep, where his swords were nestled behind the backseat, when he heard a voice call his name tauntingly.

"Aaarrronnn. Come on inside, Aaron."

Aaron stepped inside and saw her standing before the fountain between the twin rose columns. She looked like death's mistress with her skin pale as moonlight and her lifeless black eyes regarding him coldly. She held a long black staff, resting one end on the floor.

"Leave her out of this, Tarimus. I'm the one you want."

Tarimus's sinister laugh escaped Bronwyn's lips, leaving their voices juxtaposed, and it sent shivers down his spine. Her beautiful face twisted into an evil cast. "Or what, Ferasdiam Marked? Will you hurt me?"

Bronwyn leaped forward.

Aaron took a step back in spite of himself. "I won't fight you like this."

Bronwyn brought the staff up. "That's good. All you have to do now is die!"

Bronwyn launched herself toward him quicker than he thought possible, raining down blows as she came. Aaron scrambled out of the way of the whirling staff. Her attacks came so fast he didn't have time to think. All his efforts were to avoid being hit as he maneuvered around the room. He couldn't take the attack to her. He had to find a way to free Bronwyn, but how? *Think, damn it!* Then an idea sprang to mind. He broke down the rhythm of attacks quickly in his mind and began grinning whenever Tarimus missed. The attacks became more out of control, and Aaron kept taunting the demon. Then he deftly caught the staff and locked his grip around it.

"What's the matter, Tarimus? Can't you hit me?" Aaron sneered, smiling wolfishly, then shoved the staff back.

Tarimus howled in rage and attacked in earnest. The dance resumed, taking them the length of the sparring room. The staff whirled in an exquisite medley of attacks that would have killed him had his grandfather not spent hours training him.

The goal here is not to fight, but to keep others from harming you and themselves. A true master can prevent someone from hurting them and keep harm from coming to their opponent as well.

He never appreciated that lesson until now.

Aaron laughed as he avoided the staff. With each miss, Tarimus's rage grew. It wasn't inherently obvious, but something kept nagging at the back of his mind. Tarimus possessing Bronwyn's body to try to kill him didn't make sense. Why her when he could have possessed any number of people throughout the day and struck out when he would have least expected it? They were alone...unless...

Aaron stopped abruptly as a piece of understanding clicked into place. He caught the staff again while looking into those nightmarish black eyes and tossed it aside. "You're not trying to kill me."

Tarimus studied him the way a game master regards a pawn, and his lips curled icily.

"What do you want from me?" Aaron asked.

Tarimus seemed to pause, considering. His gaze drew downward, and he whispered, "You couldn't possibly imagine what I want or what I will take from you."

The remaining warmth fled the room as Bronwyn casually walked over to the wall, grabbed a short sword hanging among the rack of weapons, and turned to face him. She slowly lifted her eyes, smiled, and in one fluid motion, plunged the sword into her stomach.

A strangled cry left Aaron's mouth as he rushed in to catch her. Her nightmarish eyes returned to normal. She looked at him in confusion and pain. The sword clanged on the floor, dropping from her bloodied hands. Aaron laid her gently on the floor, tore off his shirt, and tried to stop the blood. *This can't be happening*!

"Bronwyn, you're going to be okay," Aaron said.

This is all my fault. Please.

She let out a gasp and stopped moving.

"Bronwyn, wake up."

Aaron's fingers went to her neck, feeling for a pulse. He couldn't find a heartbeat. His mouth went dry. He drew deep into his core, and his awareness of the world sharpened. A mighty force built within him and remained clouded in mystery. The medallion warmed against his chest, spreading through his arms and legs. Aaron smoothed Bronwyn's hair from her face.

"No," Aaron cried.

He positioned his hands over her chest and started CPR. He counted down from thirty, tilted her head back, and blew a breath of air into her mouth. Aaron repeated this process a few more times and then stopped to check her pulse again.

Nothing.

Aaron leaned in to blow air into her mouth. Bronwyn's eyes opened, revealing sinister black eyes. Aaron scrambled to his feet, watching in horror as the thing that had once been Bronwyn slowly rose. A shimmering purple glow emanated from her body, flashing in waves of darkness until Aaron couldn't see it. An icy wind blew, becoming a ferocious howl that rattled the windows until they shattered.

The glass fragments were sucked into the black void. Bolts of deep-purple lightning flared brilliantly, coalescing around a dark orb. A beam shot forth from the orb and struck Aaron full in the chest. The force of the blow sent him through the windows and beyond the walls of the sparring room.

Aaron dangled in the air several feet off the ground. Sharp pain rattled his bones and he felt as if his life was being drained from him. He gritted his teeth and tried to close his mind to the pain. The raw energy of the bladesong drew up mightily from within, enclosing him in an azure glow. The pain didn't subside; instead, it rose in ferocity, threatening to break his will, but his connection to the orb of blackness began to waver.

A hand reached inside his shirt, grabbed the medallion, and thrust it directly into the beam of light. The medallion flared to life, blazing, and the pain melted away from him.

Aaron looked up and saw his mother standing over him with the medallion thrust forward like a talisman, then everything went dark.

8

FAMILY CREST

Carlowen Jace watched her son as he slept. Patrick had helped her carry him into one of the spare bedrooms of her father's house. She glanced out the window. Patrick was cleaning up the destruction of the sparring room. Carlowen shivered and she looked at Aaron. *They won't get you, my son.* It was as if two worlds collided in her mind and she was struggling to catch up. Her son was strong, but very young. He possessed his father's strength of character, and she feared he would need every bit of it to survive what was coming. He stirred and slowly woke up.

Carlowen had lit a few candles, allowing their warm glow to soothe her. In her lap, the Falcons rested. It had been a lifetime ago that she'd seen her father wield these blades. She ran her fingers methodically over the engraved blades and pommels.

Aaron pushed himself up, and she noticed the wince of pain he tried to hide.

"Next time, perhaps you should keep these a little closer," she said and gestured toward the Flacons.

"I'll try to remember that," Aaron said.

"Are you okay?" Carlowen asked, placing her hand on his arm.

"No, I'm not okay," Aaron blurted out. "Ever since he died, nothing has been the same. Things keep happening to me. Something…Someone keeps attacking me. Do you know what it is?"

Carlowen studied her son. "I'm not sure," she said.

Recent revelations about her life, like her son, left her grasping for a handle on the moment herself. Her life had been here. She had a son here. For her, Safanar was comprised of snippets of a life she was only now starting to remember. It seemed as if Safanar had finally caught up with them. Such an evil so great in its wrath that it reached across worlds to hunt her son down meant one thing—fate was calling her son to return to Safanar. Why else would the power that had been in their family for generations stir within him? Fate was calling him. There was no one else left to call. She took a breath and looked into her son's expectant eyes. They demanded an answer. Had her father known what would happen? Part of him must have suspected. Why else would he have set Aaron on the path to find the swords?

"We are from another world called Safanar. A year before you were born, we were forced to flee our home. Your grandmother sacrificed herself so that we could get free and you would have a chance to grow into a man. She knew I would bear a son who would one day return. Your grandfather almost never spoke of her, because the pain of her passing was always with him. The price of her death afforded us the protection that we so desperately needed, but is now gone with his passing. He must have suspected that Safanar would eventually catch up to us and that he would not be able to protect us any longer."

Aaron shook his head. "How is it that you know all this now, but not before?"

Carlowen regarded her son calmly and pointed to the medallion resting on his chest. "When I saw our family crest again, it was like a long-forgotten world awakened within me."

Aaron traced his fingers along the foreign symbols that surrounded the white pearl in the center. The carved relief of the dragon cradling a single rose caught the candlelight and danced mysteriously with the shadows.

"Who is Tarimus?" Aaron asked.

Carlowen's breath caught in her throat, but the suppressed memories poured forth. "He is a demon sentinel cursed to roam between the world of the living and the world of the dead. He is what stands between you and Safanar. It is he that hunts you."

"Safanar," Aaron said, standing up. "I'm not going to Safanar." He stood there for a moment, collecting his thoughts. "He seems more like an assassin, but even that isn't right. He wants something; otherwise, why wouldn't he just try to kill me and be done with it? With every encounter he seems more powerful, and I don't know how to face him."

Carlowen regarded her son helplessly. The things that were happening were only a reminder that she was powerless to protect her son. She stood slowly and resolutely walked over to him and held out the Falcons. "He needs you to be strong before he feeds upon you. Only then can he claim the power bestowed upon our family for himself."

"What am I supposed to do with swords?"

"Keep them with you. You've keyed them," she said. "What happens when you wield them?"

"I feel invigorated. Strong. I can sense the life force of all around me, filling me." He paused. "There's music when I wield them, and although I've never heard it before, I know the song is mine. It's part of me."

Aaron recounted everything that happened since her father's death. He left nothing out, and with his telling she felt the blood drain from her face. "I feel so alone," he finished.

"Son, you're not alone. Not ever," a firm voice said from outside the room.

The candles in the room flickered, and the bedroom door opened slowly as Patrick stepped in. They shared a look, and something unspoken passed between them. Then Patrick walked up to Aaron and gripped his shoulder. "No matter what happens, Son, we will stand by you," he said firmly.

Aaron frowned. "Did you find Bronwyn?" he asked.

Carlowen glanced at her husband.

"No, there was no one else," Patrick said.

"I have to go. I think he's taken Bronwyn," Aaron said.

"You don't know that, Aaron," Carlowen said. "He will try to confuse you. Use all that you love against you. He is a monster."

"You're right, but I need to find out. I need to know if she's okay. If he has her..." His words trailed off with a shiver. Then he rushed from the room without a backward glance.

Colind watched Reymius's daughter and her husband from the shadows beyond the candlelight. Carlowen's husband had a genuine quality about him that he knew Reymius approved of. He was a good man. It was the tragedies that befell good men that made him truly sick at heart, and on a night like tonight...he smelled blood in the air. Death was coming this night. It was just a matter of when and where.

Aaron barely lifted his foot off the gas pedal, and neither the screech of tires nor blasts of horns swayed him. All fell upon deaf ears as Aaron made his final turn down Orchid Street. Red lights flashed above two police cars parked in front of Bronwyn's house, and his heart sank to his stomach.

He slowly drove down the road and approached the house. Neighbors gathered on the sidewalks, speaking in hushed tones. He turned and looked up at the giant bay window of Bronwyn's house, and for a moment, Tarimus's cold, dead eyes stared back at him, sending an icy drip to the pit of his stomach as the medallion grew cool against his skin.

"Is she dead?" someone asked.

"They don't know. The ambulance just left. The daughter came home acting strange and started screaming frantically. Then she took off. The police are looking for her."

He was too late. Aaron shuddered as the voices trailed behind him. He gripped the Falcons in his lap, but when he looked back up at the window, Tarimus was gone. He closed his eyes and stretched out with his feelings. The life energy of all those around him became apparent, but of the malevolent force that was Tarimus there was not a trace. He needed to meet Tarimus on his own terms, but he didn't know where or when he would appear next. An idea popped into his head. Perhaps he could meet Tarimus on his own terms after all. With a plan formulating in his mind, he sped off.

9

WHAT COMES NEXT

Aaron knelt before a small fire whose flames danced rhythmically before him. Zeus sat beyond the fire, watching intently and sensing the power that gathered around him. Was this how it was supposed to happen? Tonight, he would bring Tarimus to him the only way he knew how. Dreams. *You always have mastery over your dreams if you remember what they are.* Aaron stared at the fire as he gathered himself, converging all thought to separate his consciousness from the waking world. Fire became his world, and he fanned the flames that became his center. He drew deeper into a trance, the energy seeping from below the earth, filling him with a power that he channeled inwardly. Focusing all his thoughts, he let go of the last string keeping him in the waking world and entered the dream state.

Aaron found himself in a burned-out shell of a church. The proud walls held few remnants of their gleaming past, and the white pillars lining the main thoroughfare were cracked with broken pieces on the floor. The soft glow of moonlight entered through the broken remnants of the stained glass windows. His footsteps echoed in the cavernous hall as he walked the length of the main chamber. Before him appeared a great chalice, where a fire flared to life.

The medallion grew cold against his chest. Aaron blinked his eyes, and Tarimus stood before the great chalice of fire. In this place, Tarimus seemed more real than he had before, something more than a ghost. They were in the place between the waking world and the dream world, and Aaron knew by the triumphant smile on Tarimus's face that this is what he had wanted all along.

"Who pulls your strings, Tarimus?" Aaron asked, closing the gap between them.

Tarimus's gaze narrowed angrily. Clearly, he was used to men cowering in fear before him.

"Does a moth truly know fear while he draws helplessly toward the flame?" Tarimus replied coolly.

"Where is she?" Aaron demanded.

Tarimus slowly drew his sword, and a metallic echo rang throughout. "She's no longer your concern," Tarimus said, baring his teeth. "I've watched you, Shandarian. You spurned her. Do you treat all your women with so little respect? What do you care?" he taunted.

"Leave her out of this. Where is she?" Aaron asked through clenched teeth. "Tell me or..."

"Or what?" Tarimus spat. "You'll kill me? I'm already dead and well beyond the reach of the likes of you and your kin."

Aaron jumped back, barely avoiding Tarimus's sword as it whirled through the air, striking the ground where Aaron stood only a moment before. Aaron focused inward and called to the Falcons. He called up an image of the swords in his mind, building it to the tiniest detail, but the image shattered.

"This is no dream, boy," Tarimus spat before delivering a kick that sent Aaron sailing through the air into a stone column.

Aaron's thoughts scattered, and he scrambled to get out of the way. Tarimus was on him in an instant, delivering another crushing blow, sending him sprawling. A bluish orb of light rushed from afar to settle down between the two combatants, giving Tarimus pause, and drew close to Aaron, hovering before him.

A deep voice called from the orb. "Rise, Shandarian."

Aaron's eyes widened as the orb flashed, and the Falcons clanged into his lap. He grabbed each hilt and brought them up just as Tarimus's sword thundered down. Deflecting the blow to the side, Aaron kicked out, sending Tarimus back in surprise.

"NOOOOOO!" Tarimus howled in rage. "Watcher, you are forbidden to interfere," he screamed out to the void.

When Tarimus turned back, Aaron stood ready to face him. He smirked and then wielded the Falcons. The blades flashed into motion, filling the chamber with their mysterious song. Tarimus, for the first time, looked fearful, then he bellowed his battle cry and unleashed a mighty wave of attacks. Wild cracks of steel echoed throughout the church. The power of the bladesong gathered to Aaron and with it an awareness of something much older that lives within the depths of the soul. Visions danced through his mind of the lives of people he'd never seen before. He heard whispers upon the fringes of his hearing. The awareness became more acute and wild in the harsh majesty that binds nature together. The fierceness and golden beauty of the balance of life came to alignment within him, and he drew upon that balance for strength to do what had to be done.

Tarimus sensed the change and howled in denial. "*Ferasdiam*," he spat, and charged yet again. Aaron stood perfectly still. At the last possible moment, he dove to the side, taking a grand swipe with his swords, but his blades passed through Tarimus without making contact. Aaron reeled in confusion, while Tarimus merely laughed.

"I'm not that easy to kill." Tarimus cocked his head to the side. "Can I be killed? I wonder." Dead-black eyes regarded him coolly. "You fight me as if I am alive. I assure you I'm not. Death has no sway over me, boy."

"What about life? Does that sway you at all?" Aaron asked.

"Life," Tarimus said. "These are the halls of what could be your life. Shall I show you what comes next?"

Aaron lashed out with a series of vicious attacks, driving Tarimus back. He'd had enough of these games, and Tarimus was right in front of him. Aaron dove for Tarimus like a falcon on the hunt. He held nothing back and fought with everything he had. The medallion grew warm against his chest, and the Falcons glowed in his hands. Sparks emanated from the clashing blades. With a great sweep of his blades, a jagged cut appeared along the side of Tarimus's face. The demon held the side of his face in disbelief. Tarimus turned, and with a sweeping gesture, he heaved the great chalice of fire off its pedestal, hurling it toward Aaron.

Aaron dove out of the way and scrambled to his feet, putting the Falcons in motion. The bladesong echoed throughout the church. The Falcons were engulfed by a shimmering blue glow. Tarimus made another sweeping gesture, hurling a great oak bench at him. With blades glowing blue, he sliced through the oak bench, scattering it to either side of him.

"Life is what matters to you, isn't it, boy?" Tarimus asked, circling with the appearance of a lazy stride. But Aaron knew better. "What would you do if you knew those that you loved were in danger and no matter what happens, you will never get there in time to stop it?"

Aaron's heart pounded in his chest. Tarimus's words had the ring of truth to them. "Tell me," he said, trying to keep his voice steady. *What have I missed*? he kept thinking. He had been sure that facing Tarimus in this way would force a resolution. The fires in the abandoned church died out in unison, plunging them into darkness save for the moonlit glow through the broken windows.

"Fate has finally caught up with you, Heir of Shandara." Tarimus's voice seemed to echo from every direction. A cold wind blew. "Tonight, they shall weep in their own blood." Tarimus's voice came ahead of him in almost hushed tones. "I unleash *you*, Shandarian. See what has been hidden from you."

A blinding light burst forth from Tarimus's outstretched hand. The light coalesced into an image of Aaron's home. Fire raged throughout the house. Nine men dressed in black stood before the house, and screams came from the burning home. His father burst forth, charging through a window. The centermost man in black lunged forward, drawing his sword.

"Is this real?" Aaron cried. "What have you done? Is this real?"

Aaron screamed as the light shimmered then winked out, and he was once again kneeling before the burning embers of the fire he'd built. Without a backward glance, he dashed off toward his car, but he couldn't shrug off the arresting fear that he was already too late.

10

ANOTHER WORLD

"Beware of the man who has nothing left to lose. You might push too hard, and he will be unable to fulfill his destiny," Prince Tye warned.

"On the contrary, Tye, it is a man who has nothing left to lose that can accomplish great things," Mactar advised the young prince.

"Think about it," Mactar continued. "The Heir of Shandara is within our grasp. Think of the glory that would bring if it were you who brought him before your father, the High King. This lone act will put you first among your brothers. Think of it, Tye, the last remnant of the house Alenzar'seth, holders of the keys to Shandara." He noted the slight tension building within his young companion with satisfaction. Young, power-hungry fools were the easiest to bend to your will with the right motivation, and this fool had means to fulfill this end. Tye was actually quite capable, but he had been forever shadowed by the deeds of his older brothers.

"Absolute secrecy is paramount, Mactar," Tye insisted. "Only my own men will be used for this. The Elitesmen will not be involved."

"Of course, my Lord." Mactar smiled. The Elitesmen could not know about the Heir of Shandara, not for the moment anyway. The utter bitterness he'd felt upon learning that Reymius escaped with that wretched daughter of his tried even his patience. The house of Alenzar'seth once again had cheated annihilation. It was a bitter pill to swallow, but did help to explain why the barrier between worlds continued to hold. Reymius's heir held the keys to great power, and he would be brought to heel and deliver what was due. He wondered how the Elite Grand Master would receive the Heir of Shandara? The complexities of the Elite Council were for another time, Mactar mused, and returned to the task at hand.

"When can we be underway?" Tye pressed.

"Soon, my Lord. Very soon," Mactar answered. "Make ready, and I will send for you shortly."

Tye took his leave, and Mactar strode to a darkened room whose sole occupant was a large mirror. The engraving that encircled the mirror held a powerful spell to allow someone to communicate through the ethereal planes between realities. It was dangerous and unpredictable, as he had learned through another's folly. Mactar lit the candles on each side and called forth to Tarimus.

"I am here, Master." Tarimus appeared instantly. Although Tarimus had answered to him in this manner for years, a new emotion roiled beneath those cold black eyes. Hope. Tarimus had never succumbed to his prison, but he had been leashed, so to speak. His stance betrayed a readiness for action and a hunger for Mactar's destruction.

"The time has come. Tye will be going through," Mactar said, narrowing his gaze.

"Are you sure?" Tarimus taunted. "He is not like the others. Do not underestimate Reymius's heir. He has grown strong. He is different...mindful."

Again, it was there, albeit the last of that statement was added grudgingly. An unspoken challenge and hope, an uncharacteristically human emotion that seemed foreign on Tarimus's now-demonic face. The pieces were falling into place, but what could have given Tarimus cause to hope?

"I trust you've done your part?" Mactar warned.

"Of course," Tarimus answered, stone faced.

"Then he will fall in line and perish when his usefulness is no longer apparent," Mactar said.

"Prince Tye, you say, is making the journey. Ahhh, the youngest son. How clever of you, Mactar."

"I'm glad you think so. He has the power to extract the keys to Shandara from Reymius's heir."

Tarimus appeared to have been on the verge of saying something further when Tye entered the chamber with eight of his men, all dressed in black, adorned with a silver dragon emblem on their chests. These were hard men. All of them battle tested and highly trained, but they were no Elitesman, with one exception. Darven, who had been cast out of the Elite order and had been Mactar's man ever since. Darven would be his eyes and ears on this journey.

Mactar turned back to face Tarimus, who now wore a sardonic smile. Disgusted with Tarimus's taunting, he gathered his will in crushing force and brought it to bear, encompassing Tarimus's essence. He was a hair's breadth from severing his feeble line forever, and Tarimus looked on, waiting to be released, even hungering for it. But Mactar still needed him, and Tarimus knew it.

Mactar turned to address Tye and his men. "The crossroads of fate have brought us here, and each of you has a chance to achieve glory reminiscent of ages long past. As Tye has no doubt told you, the Heir of Shandara of the house Alenzar'seth has been discovered on another plane. Reymius escaped the destruction of Shandara to a world quite different than ours, but its people are no different than you or I. In order for us to obtain the keys, we must capture Reymius's heir, either in body or the essence of his soul. My Lord Prince, you know of what I speak. Let us begin. May Ferasdiam give her blessing to your journey." He almost stumbled on the last words; after all, Ferasdiam was not his god, but of the fools who stood before him. He harbored no faith in anything but himself. Mysteries were meant to be solved and could not be explained away by folklore. He smiled inwardly to himself and began the night's work.

11

AMID THE ASHES

Aaron couldn't get the image of his burning home out of his head. He slammed his foot down on the accelerator as he frantically weaved around cars, blowing through stop signs and lights.

What would you do if you knew those that you loved were in danger and no matter what happens, you will never get there in time to stop it.

Never get there in time! The words were branded in fire in his mind. His family was in danger. All his thoughts were so fixed on getting home that he never once thought about what he would actually do when he got there. Would he see the horrifying visions that Tarimus had shown him? Could he even stop it? Clinging to a fleeting hope, he pressed on.

The tires of his Jeep CJ7 screeched around the corner of his street, and to his surprise, all was quiet. Eerily normal, the flickering streetlights betrayed nothing. He gunned the accelerator and skidded to a stop in front of his house. The medallion became like ice against his skin. Aaron grabbed the roll bar, pulled himself up, and stood there for a moment, scanning the area. A flicker of movement betrayed itself on one side of the house and another on the other side. Aaron drew the Falcons from their sheaths and jumped down. The front bay windows shattered, and his father tumbled onto the front lawn. His face was bloody, and his left arm hung limp at his side as he struggled to rise.

"Dad," Aaron cried, charging toward him.

His father looked up at his call. "Aaron. Behind you!" his father shouted.

Aaron dove to his left, feeling the hiss of a blade on the air where he had been, and was back on his feet instantly. A man in black came rushing toward him, his sword bearing down. Aaron crossed his raised blades and stopped his opponent's momentum through sheer strength. Aaron growled as he charged forward, pulling the Falcons in opposite directions, and sent a glancing blow into his assailant's face. The man cried out in pain, and Aaron kicked him aside.

He turned and saw another man in black standing behind his father. A gold cape hung loosely around his shoulders, and a sword hung casually in his right hand. Four more men in black with a silver dragon emblem on their chests fanned out to either side with blades drawn.

"Take him!" the leader ordered.

Aaron froze in horror as his father scrambled around and wrapped his arm around the leader's neck. The leader struggled for a few seconds, then reversed his blade and plunged it into his father, who fell with a deep sigh.

Aaron's stomach clenched, watching the blade sink in and his heart turned to ice. He screamed out to his father while charging forward. The first black-clad figure rushed him with his sword out, but Aaron didn't slow. He lashed out with one blade, knocking it aside, then with the second blade, he smoothly sliced through his opponent's sword arm. His guttural scream was cut short as Aaron's Falcons took him through the throat.

Aaron cut through the remaining three men as if they were leaves writhing through the wind. All went down lifeless, bathed in red, and the bladesong burned in his mind.

"Well met, Reymius's heir," Tye said.

Aaron snuck a quick glance at his father lying on the ground and was relieved to see his chest slowly rise and fall. He wondered where his mother was. As if in answer to his unspoken question, sounds of a struggle came from inside his house. Aaron called out to his mother while edging his way forward. The leader brought his sword up and moved with leopard-like grace, poised to spring.

"I am Tye, Prince of Safanar. I am here to collect what your family has kept hidden for far too long," he said, and he lunged with his sword.

Aaron unleashed the bladesong into the night. Each probing attack by Tye was driven back in an ever-flowing motion of song and steel. He brushed aside the gnawing questions and brought the attack to his opponent. Tye was good and adapted well to whatever Aaron threw at him. Neither held the upper hand. Aaron felt the power of the bladesong coalescing in him, and he heard the whisperings of countless voices. Urges from within began guiding his hands, and he struggled to maintain control. Panic set in, and he tried to quiet his mind in a failed attempt to quell all that sought to distract him. Struggling and fighting two battles at once quickly exhausted him, leaving him vulnerable to attack.

Tye pressed his advantage, driving Aaron back. Unable to block them out, Aaron opened himself up to the voices within, beginning to seek them out, merging the urges into his own fighting style. The medallion grew warm against his skin, and the crystals within the hilts of his swords began to glow. Tye faltered and was driven back, his sword knocked from his hands as Aaron swept him off his feet.

"Not so quick, boy. Put down your swords," a voice ordered behind him.

Aaron maneuvered to see where the voice had come from and keep Tye in his field of vision.

Mother!

Carlowen Jace stood with a dagger to her throat and an arm pinned behind her back. She would not allow her son to sacrifice himself for her. It was for a mother to sacrifice for the child, not the other way around. She had to act quickly. Her gift to Safanar would be her beloved son. *He will survive the journey there. That is his destiny. Like a bright shining star, he will drive the shadows from Shandara.*

Carlowen tightened up as Aaron lowered his swords, not seeing the dark figure rise up behind him. She drove her elbow back with stunning force, breaking the locked grip that held her. Zeus, snarling from the shadows, charged, tearing at the man. She turned swiftly, twisting the hand that held the dagger, and kicked out with her foot, driving the man into the bushes. She turned, poised to throw the dagger at her son's attacker, when a door of light sprang into being behind them.

"Down!" she cried, and without a moment's hesitation, Aaron dove to the ground.

Something whirled past him, and Aaron bounced back up, seeing his mother standing there, but it was a few moments before his mind allowed him to register that there was a dagger protruding from her chest.

Aaron glanced behind him and saw Tye, who had a dagger lodged in his own throat and a shocked look in his eyes as he sank to the ground. Without a second glance, Aaron ran toward his mother, catching her as she fell. She had blood trickling from her mouth, and his throat thickened. His mother looked up and smiled faintly, struggling to say something. Aaron leaned in to hear her.

"*Be...strong*," she said at last in a half whisper, then lay still and breathed no more.

Aaron knelt there, holding his mother's lifeless form, silently rocking back and forth. The image of his mother's lifeless glazed eyes burned into his mind. Her blood was on his hands. Aaron gently laid her down and slowly stood. The blackness that entered his heart yearned to do unspeakable things. He wanted blood.

The remaining members of the men in black gathered around Tye. Two of them hoisted Tye's body up, and a savage roar came from the door of light. The men hesitated, and one turned to face Aaron. His face was bloodied. He called out, and the rest of them turned to meet Aaron.

"Out of the way, you fools," a voice ordered from beyond the door of light. Then a fiery blue orb came hurling toward Aaron. He brought up the Falcons, and the crystals in the blades flared in a brilliant white light that shielded him. The fiery orb ricocheted from the shield and tore into his house, leaving a gaping hole. The men in black stumbled through the door of light, which was rapidly becoming smaller. Growling, Aaron pulled the dagger from his mother's chest and hurled it through the closing door to the sounds of screams, and then all was silent.

A small explosion came from within the house, and Aaron saw flames spread hungrily. He carried his mother's body away from the burning house and then returned for his father. He came up to his father, who lay staring at the house through the eyes of a broken man. Aaron felt his strength slip away seeing his father like that, but when his father saw him, the broken man disappeared, replaced with the unwavering force that was his father. He wasn't a broken man, but one who faced a journey that visits the doorsteps of all men who dare to live, and those who would die before their time.

Aaron tore off part of his shirt, rolled it up, and pressed it firmly on the wound in his father's chest. "I have to move you," Aaron said, lifting his father as much as he could, then dragging him away from the burning house.

"Your mother?" he asked.

Aaron shook his head, tears streaming down his face. "She's dead. I failed. I couldn't protect any of you."

"No." His father coughed. "You had no control over this, Son. You weren't meant to stop this."

"But Dad, I..." *Should have done something*, he finished to himself.

"No," his father said firmly. "This isn't your fault. There are no perfect solutions. Not in life, Son."

Aaron had no words for the life that was burning away all around him. Everything he had ever known was being stripped away.

"Aaron," his father called out weakly. "Protect Tara."

His father's grip hardened in his hand for an instant before slipping limply away. Aaron knelt, his shoulders slumped, stuck somewhere between shock and disbelief.

Get up, Aaron told himself.

He slowly rose to his feet and brought his mother to rest beside his father. If he focused on just their faces, he could almost fool himself that they were still breathing, but he couldn't stop seeing their bloody remains.

Aaron watched the firemen try to put the fire out, but their efforts were to no avail. The fire would not go out, leaving them to shake their heads in confusion. The EMTs checked him for injuries, and he spent most of the night recounting the events to a policeman, withholding a few facts that would have begged questions that he couldn't answer. When Tara arrived his resolve nearly crumbled. He numbly held her while she wept.

Against the advice of concerned policemen, firemen, and medics, Aaron and his sister stayed in front of his house all night, watching the fire raze his home. At some point, Zeus came up and sat next to him. Eventually, the firemen surrendered their efforts to put out the flames but remained vigilant in preventing the fire from spreading to the other houses.

Aaron kept going over the night's events in his mind. Despite his father's last words, he couldn't help feeling responsible for his parents' death and the danger that now threatened his sister. The danger she was in so they could get to him. He was the key to something, but what? There was no one else he could seek answers from.

Aaron decided that he owed Tara the truth. They shared the same father, and though Carlowen was not her biological mother, she was the only mother that Tara had ever known. Tara silently watched the flames next to him, and in hushed tones, he told her everything. She was in too much shock to do anything more than listen.

"I have to leave. If I don't..."

"Where will you go?" Tara asked.

"To find the men responsible," Aaron said. He yearned to hold the Falcons again, but his swords were safely concealed for the moment. "I don't care how long it takes or how far I have to go. I will make them pay."

"Aaron, you don't—" Tara began, but stopped as some people walked by. "This didn't happen because of you," Tara said.

"Yes it did. This isn't something the police or anyone else can handle," Aaron said.

"You're not responsible for the whole world. Just don't charge off and do anything stupid," Tara said.

Aaron sat there the remainder of the night, mulling things over in his head. He had to meet Tarimus where there was no escape for either of them. Looking back on the events that brought him here, he knew there was no other way. As dawn approached, the unquenchable fire that claimed his house completely and inexplicably went out in the span of a passing breath. Zeus let out a low growl, and the firemen began muttering to each other.

Smoking embers and a burned-out shell were all that remained of the home he'd grown up in, but Aaron wouldn't let himself turn away. He couldn't. He took in the scene in its entirety, allowing it to burn into his mind lest he forget the price of failure. A small voice from within cried out that it wasn't fair. How could he have known? But he should have known that an attack would come, and others paid the price with their lives. *Maybe if he...* He looked around, wearily avoiding the path of "what ifs" for now, and with heavy footsteps, he got in his Jeep and drove slowly away.

FAINT STIRRINGS OF A HEART LONG BURIED ACHED WITHIN COLIND'S chest at the tragedy before him.

Tarimus, what are you up to? Colind wondered, watching Reymius's grandson drive away. *A remarkable man, not at all the fool that Mactar believes him to be. But what does Tarimus believe?* Soon, he would have to reveal himself to Aaron. Power was drawing itself to Aaron, and he was learning to control the power of the Falcons. The balance of life on Safanar was a delicate thing, and the pendulum was swinging wildly out of control. Always the guardians like himself were there to lend guidance and to maintain balance, but he was the last, and he wasn't sure he could truly call himself a guardian anymore with his own dark betrayal haunting him still. Reymius's last days on Safanar were the darkest of both their lives. So much had gone wrong, and evil was allowed to endure. Colind launched himself into the air, riding along the shadows and easily catching up to Aaron.

He kept pace while watching. Was Aaron strong enough to endure the path that he must walk? Colind didn't know, and his perceptions were clouded whenever he tried to think on it. Mactar would soon learn the extent to which he underestimated Reymius's heir and would double his efforts. Colind resolved to do what he must and hope for the best; at times, it was all one could do.

12

PARTING

Aaron woke up to Tara calling his name. His whole body jerked awake, and he sat up, gasping.

"Are you all right?" Tara asked.

"Yeah, it was a bad dream," Aaron answered.

Barely two days had passed since their parents were murdered, and neither one of them had gotten much sleep. Tara's fiancé, Alex, stayed with them, lending support to his sister where he could, for which Aaron was grateful. Aaron had hardly let Tara out of his sight.

They were staying at his grandfather's house...their house now, since they had nowhere else to go. The funeral for their parents was today, and Tara had made him promise that he would stay long enough to attend, which he grudgingly agreed to. Tara didn't realize the danger she was in. Zeus, on the other hand, had hardly left his side these past two days. So Tara had double the protection. At first he'd expected another attack, but nothing had happened. He hadn't even felt the presence of Tarimus.

The funeral was peaceful and quiet and completely at odds with how Aaron was feeling. It was his second funeral in the past few weeks, and he didn't have any tears left. After burying three family members, all he had was smoldering rage, loitering beneath the surface, wanting to lash out at anything and everything around him. He yearned to have his swords in his hands to kill those men again, only this time he would arrive earlier and save his parents.

The funeral procession left, and Aaron was last to leave. He stood in front of the headstones of his parents' grave. Beloved husband and father etched on one and wife and mother on the other. Aaron knelt down and rested his hands on each tombstone. His throat thickened, but his eyes were dry. He stood up and balled his hands into fists. After taking one last long look he turned around and left.

After the funeral, Tara went with their family friends to Alex's house while Aaron slipped away. He changed into his good hiking clothes, which were extremely durable, and left a note for Tara. He advised her to go away for a while and told her that he loved her. He even left Alex a voicemail advising him to take Tara away somewhere on vacation for a few weeks.

The medallion pulsed with a warmth all its own and had done so since the night his parents were murdered. Aaron knew that it had protected him once and hoped it would again. His swords were strapped on his back. At one time he would have felt foolish with them on, but he didn't feel foolish today, just determined.

Standing before the doorway of the ruins of the sparring room, Aaron gathered his will, and then he stepped through. He struggled to quiet his mind. He needed to focus. He closed his eyes, taking deep, rhythmic breaths, and stretched out, feeling the life energy all around him. He felt the familiar presence of Zeus, sometimes savage, sometimes loving, as is all that is wild by nature. He delved deeper into the secret chamber where he had found the Falcons, the medallion, and the cylinder that glowed in a bluish light. He called it forth, and the floorboards shattered as it hovered in front of him, slowly spinning.

"There is no turning back from this," a voice said from the shadows.

Aaron glanced over at the dark corner, trying to see who spoke. "I know, but they will never stop hunting me if I don't do this, and I will find the men responsible."

"Vengeance is a path that you can follow, to be sure, but it usually leads to a place devoid of spirit," the voice answered.

"Who are you?" Aaron asked.

"My name is Colind. I was a friend of your grandfather Reymius. I am sorry for his loss and the loss of your mother. They were both very dear to me," Colind answered.

Aaron saw the old man more clearly. There was a hard edge to him, and his gray eyes carried a slightly worn and haunted expression. "How do I know you are telling me the truth?"

"You can't," Colind said, his lips curving, but the smile did not reach his eyes. "I understand your caution, I do, but as Reymius has told me on countless occasions, the choices we make are all leaps of faith. You will need to decide whether you can trust me or not. Just hear me out and then decide for yourself."

Aaron watched Colind, considering. "Fair enough," he said. "It sounds like something he would say."

It was Colind's turn to consider Aaron's response, and then he laughed. It was a sound that seemed foreign, ripped from the pages of another life. "You surely are your mother's son. She had a backbone to her too and a no-nonsense attitude when she set her mind to a task." The smile felt foreign to his lips and was gone quickly. "Time grows short, and the need is great, for you are in more danger than you realize."

Aaron watched silently, waiting for him to continue.

Colind looked at the cylinder as it hung in midair, slowly spinning, then fixed Aaron with a hard stare. "To travel the crossroads between worlds is perilous by itself, but for you the danger is tenfold, for Tarimus is waiting. Tarimus dwells in the planes between life and death with a foothold in each world, but is denied the release for which he yearns. I know you have unlocked some of the secrets to the Falcons, but believe me, you've only scratched the surface of what you are truly capable of." Colind sighed in frustration. "Your gravest obstacle is Tarimus, and he has played both sides of this battle masterfully. Through your confrontations with him, you have learned much and gained in strength, but when you face him on the crossroads, he will come at you in full strength. In his arena, he will be the master. As a parasite would possess a host, Tarimus will vie for your soul and gain a vessel with the power to return to Safanar."

"A vessel? You mean me?"

"That's really up to you, Aaron. He will try, and he may succeed if you don't find a way to stop him. He is still so full of hate and jealousy." Colind looked away with a pained expression. "He is lost," Colind whispered, and felt tears well up that could never come, because his anger forbade it—anger at Tarimus, at what he had become, and at himself for his gravest failure. Colind studied Aaron. By the Goddess, the last remnant of the shattered house of Alenzar'seth stood before him, stripped of family and the knowledge that was passed down generations.

"How do you know so much about Tarimus?" Aaron asked.

The question was simple enough, but Colind could tell from Aaron's gaze that he was testing him. He decided to be honest and cut straight to the point.

"Tarimus is my son and my greatest failure in life."

"Your son," Aaron hissed, stepping back from Colind.

"He was not always the monster you have seen," Colind said quickly. "Like all men, he was innocent as you are now. And his decisions and my unwillingness to see the truth cost the lives of many."

"There must be more you can tell me. How can I beat him? I wounded him once; I know there must be a way to do so again," Aaron pressed.

"He was once a man, and despite what he has become, the foundation remains."

"Are you alive or dead?" Aaron asked.

"I am banished. My body locked away in an earthen tomb. And my soul is tied to this realm, a punishment for my failure."

"I don't think so," Aaron said quietly. "You are alive. I can sense it in you."

"Don't tell me my own business, boy," Colind barked. "You don't know the half of it."

"I may not know what happened to you, but you have presence, an energy. All life is energy in one form or another. As you stand before me in one form or another. The fact remains that you are alive, and if you are alive then there is always hope," Aaron finished with an inner smile because he supposed he was speaking for the both of them.

Colind stared at Aaron in disbelief. Here was Reymius's grandson, with no knowledge of his lineage or their world of Safanar, lecturing him! He was banished. Banned from the realms of the dead and of life, yet here he was. A whisper on the winds of his mind pleaded with him to yield to this wisdom. Could Aaron be right?

"Now is not the time for this. We need to focus on you," Colind said.

"Okay. Is there a way that I can get through the crossroads without Tarimus knowing?"

"Not a chance. I'm afraid Tarimus is attuned to you as you are him. Both of you will know when the other is near. And there is no one who can guide you through." Colind stopped abruptly as Zeus let out a low growl and barked, looking at each of them. Colind studied Zeus as if seeing him for the first time. "Was this Reymius's companion?"

Aaron nodded, and Colind laughed. "Oh, Reymius, you sly dog," Colind bellowed.

"What is it?" Aaron asked.

"Tell me, Aaron, has Zeus left your side since your grandfather died?"

"Not for long."

"Zeus will be your guide. Reymius prepared him for this. He bonded Zeus to him, and when he died, that bond passed to you. Wolves live in the world of the living, and their spirits roam other realms. He will be your spirit guide on the crossroads to Safanar."

"You can't be serious," Aaron said.

Colind understood Aaron's hesitation, but there was no time. By now, the news of the prince's death would have surely reached High King Amorak, and Aaron was not ready for that battle.

"Is it so hard to believe? Your grandfather surrounded himself with animals, all of which he loved. When I knew him, he had the uncanny ability to know exactly what they needed. He had this ability with people too, and they were drawn to him. He prepared Zeus to be your guide because he knew that there was a strong possibility that you would journey to Safanar. He suspected the protection bought by your grandmother, the Lady Cassandra, would cease with his death. The fact remains, Aaron, you are being hunted. They came once, and they will come again because you have something they want."

Protect your sister. His father's last words echoed in his mind. The best way to protect her was to leave, but part of him felt like a coward for leaving. He took a long look at his grandfather's house with the wraparound porch where friends and family would gather, often joking into the night. Then he turned to the various paths that led through the wooded estate. Pathways he and Bronwyn would take to pass the afternoon away. When he looked once again at the remains of the training room, he clenched his teeth hard. He would have his vengeance, and he would start with Tarimus.

"I will not hide from Tarimus," Aaron said. "But I will accept whatever help you have to offer."

"The crossroads is a place where time can be chaotic. So be mindful of which path you take. You will be drawn to Safanar, whose doorway will resemble the carved relief of those columns," Colind said, gesturing to the remnants of the mahogany columns sticking above the rubble.

"Let's say I make it through somehow, where will I come out in Safanar, and will you be there?" Aaron asked.

"Should you make it through, you will come in through the ancient ruins west of Duncan's Port." As Colind spoke the last word, the cylinder let out a shrieking sound, and a blinding blue light seared the floor. The light expanded with a rhythmic hum to the size of a doorway. Then Colind spoke again, but his voice sounded like it came from a great distance. "Seek Prince Cyrus. He can help—"

The rest of what Colind was about to say was cut off. Aaron scanned the area, but couldn't find him anywhere, nor could he sense his presence. The next two steps he was about to take would forever change his life. He stood rooted in place, watching the door of light. Whispers welling up from deep inside urged him forward. This place where he'd grown up had been his life and would always be part of him. He would carry his home in his heart and hope it would be enough to endure what was to come. For the briefest of moments, he seriously considered running as far as he could, but his parents deserved better.

Aaron slowly took a long look around at the home he loved, and a lump filled his throat. It was then that he saw Tara standing on the porch with his note in her hand. Her eyes were full of concern and brimming with tears. In a moment of unspoken love between the two siblings, they whispered goodbye.

Be strong, his mother's words echoed.

"*Come, Ferasdiam Marked, embrace your destiny*," a voice whispered from the door of light.

Aaron's eyes widened for an instant, then he took a giant leap through with Zeus in tow.

13

THE JOURNEY

An icy charge washed over Aaron's skin as he leaped through the portal. He landed on hard ground and stumbled a few steps. Zeus burst through the door of light, and the cylinder dropped to the ground. Aaron bent over and retrieved the cylinder. He glanced around and found he was in a well-manicured forest. An old brick path stretched away from him. There was no sun or clouds, just a sky cast in perpetual twilight. Trees lining the path swayed gently, and Aaron noticed a natural progression to them. The same type of tree would appear as if it were in each of the four seasons, marking its cycle of life. He walked past the golden autumn leaves of a maple tree towering over the pathway. Then the same tree appeared again, devoid of leaves, and the air was colder.

"I don't suppose you know the way?" Aaron asked, but Zeus just sniffed along the ground a few times before looking back at him.

Aaron started walking down the pathway. The way ahead appeared to just keep going until the path met a distant horizon. Aaron wondered how far they needed to go before they came to the doorway to Safanar. It was quiet on the path. There were no birds chirping or flies buzzing. It was as if he and Zeus were the only ones alive. Something kept gnawing at the back of his mind. The more he thought about it, the more he knew that if he kept going the way he was, he wasn't going to get anywhere. Doing the same thing and expecting a different result is the definition of insanity (thanks, Einstein).

Zeus came to an abrupt stop as if their thoughts mirrored each other's, arriving at the same conclusion. But which way to go, he wondered. They stopped in front of an oak tree in its autumn season, and Aaron remembered the seemingly endless amount of leaf raking he and his father would confront each year. He smiled at the memory and immediately clenched his teeth at the loss of those better days. Both sides of the path appeared exactly the same, and Aaron didn't have a clue as to which way to go. He brought out a silver dollar he had stashed away in his pocket and held it out.

"I guess we'll let fate decide. Heads we go right. Tails we go left," he said, flipping the coin high into the air.

The spinning coin hit its apex, and the medallion grew cold against his chest. The coin remained suspended in the air until a great thunderclap shattered the silence and the coin came hurtling to the ground. The coin was embedded in the earth with heads facing up. A definitive answer if he ever saw one. He decided to leave the coin where it lay as a payment of sorts and headed off the path in what he hoped was the right direction.

Trekking through the forest, he eventually came upon an overgrown path. It was better than wandering aimlessly in the twilight of this place. He quickened his pace to a trot until he came to a clearing. It looked as if someone had drawn an invisible line and decided that this was where the forest would end. A sea of thick fog stretched out before him with an occasional shadow breaching the top of the swirling canopy. He walked to the edge of the fog and extended his hand and moisture began to collect on it.

Zeus eyed him through the savage eyes of a wolf and took a bold step toward the fog with a growing hunger in his eyes. *All right, my friend, I'll follow you.* Holding on to the dense fur on Zeus's back, he plunged into the fog. He held on as if his life depended on it. The fog thickened so much that he could barely see his hand in front of his face. The air grew cold around them, and Aaron stumbled blindly, holding on and trying his best to find his footing, but Zeus quickened the pace. The ground beneath him leveled off and hardened. He was sure they were going down a road of some sort, and there were buildings just beyond the swirling fog. Aaron closed his eyes and allowed his other senses to take the lead. The medallion grew warm against his chest, and he focused on the dragons around the white pearl at the center.

Zeus came to a stop and nudged his hand with his muzzle. Heat began to build in the pearl, and Aaron fed the heat with all his concentration. When he could no longer stand the heat, he reached into his shirt and pulled the medallion out, holding it over his head, but he didn't let go of the power gathering within. Faint whisperings urged him to give over and release his hold upon the power, but he held on a few moments more, until he could bear it no longer. Light rippled from the white pearl in bursts, burning up the fog around him, and Aaron found himself standing within a towering coliseum, all gray with worn stonework throughout. The ground beneath his feet held old dry dirt, stained with blood and the stink of death. A crisp wind blew, and Aaron looked up to discover the stadium full of onlookers, all eerily silent. Whenever he focused to get a better look at them, they went distinctly blurry, but from within his peripheral vision he knew they were there. There was something grim and silent watching him. Judging, leaving Aaron feeling undeniably exposed. Mutterings and hushed tones swept through the coliseum, breaking the silence, and he clearly heard *Ferasdiam Marked and Safanarion.*

"How quaint," a voice called from behind him.

Aaron spun to see a cloaked figure standing behind him, and Zeus let out a deep, rumbling growl.

"You are a long way from home. How honored I am that you've come to mine," Tarimus hissed.

Silence embraced the coliseum as a hush swept over its attendants. This was what he'd come for, to face Tarimus. It was inevitable, despite what Colind had hoped to achieve. Who was Colind trying to protect—himself or his son?

"I know what you want, and if you think you can take my soul, then go ahead and try," Aaron said.

Dead-black eyes regarded him frostily. "I see," he said.

Aaron expected more of a response than this. He knew to the depths of his soul that there would be no waking up from this nightmare.

"I am going to Safanar," he said.

"You walk a fool's path, boy," Tarimus muttered, and then made a waving motion with his hand. A bell clanged throughout the coliseum, and by the third gong, a columned stone doorway appeared at the far end, behind Tarimus. "There is the door. All you need to do is get past me," Tarimus sneered.

Aaron noticed that Tarimus still had the cut on his cheek put there from his blade. He had cut him, but how could he kill Tarimus? With his mouth going dry, he scanned the crowd of the coliseum. All the onlookers watched silently, like judges on a panel. He dropped his backpack to the ground and drew his Falcons.

Let's do this.

If this was going to be his end, then he would be sport for no man or demon.

Tarimus wickedly bared his teeth and drew his black sword, which drank the light. They each regarded the other, poised, and at the same instant, they both charged. The clash of blades rippled through the air.

Aaron spun and was ready for Tarimus. The demon spawn brought his great dark blade to bear. The fury of each hack from the dark blade rattled his hands and arms, but he numbingly held on. *How can he be so quick with a sword that big?* Scrambling, he managed to deflect or dodge the onslaught of attacks. Not blocking quickly enough earned him a shallow slice burning down his side, and a blurring kick sent him into the air. Aaron stumbled to get up, and Tarimus kicked him down again with a furious howl.

"Ferasdiam Marked or not, you will never survive this!" Tarimus spat. "This is no dream world, boy. Here, you are a master of nothing."

A thundering kick sent Aaron down again. Tarimus rained blow after blow on him, until it felt as if it were happening to someone else. Part of Aaron wondered when he would stop feeling the pain, and the other part of him raged for him to get up. That deep core where the greatest reserves of strength reside began to defy logic, and he struggled to his knees.

"Why do you do it? Why get up?" Tarimus stopped kicking him, breathing heavily. "Why fight a battle you cannot hope to win? Are you so eager to die? Would it be so bad to give yourself over to me?"

Aaron looked up, steeling himself for another blow. He hurt everywhere, but the fire within him hadn't diminished in the slightest. He planted his fist into the ground and rose to one knee.

"Why, why do you persist?" Tarimus asked through clenched teeth.

Aaron regained his feet. "Because I choose to."

Tarimus was right about one thing—this was a fight he could not win, not here in this place, but perhaps he could survive, and that was enough.

Tarimus dwells in the planes between life and death with a foothold in each world, but is denied the release for which he truly yearns. Colind had told him a golden truth, which became apparent to Aaron in this moment of bruised clarity. Tarimus needed to learn to let go. This truth gave him purpose, and with that, his strength returned in warm waves flowing through his body. The medallion grew warm against his chest, and a faint blue glow emanated from his discarded backpack.

"It's not too late for you," Aaron said, still hunched and feigning weakness.

"For what?" Tarimus replied contemptuously.

Aaron paused, giving Tarimus a long look, standing straight up before he answered. "To do the right thing. To let it all go and be at peace," Aaron said mildly.

A flash of disbelief crossed Tarimus's face before he began laughing with a mad glint to his eyes. Aaron expected as much, but sometimes words spoken have an uncanny way of coming back to haunt you.

"Do you seek to save me, boy?" Tarimus sneered.

"No, to remind you." Aaron brought up the Falcons and released the bladesong into a swirling harmony that comprised his soul's heartbeat. The voices and life force of those who had come before eagerly came to the brink, their knowledge readily available, but Aaron held them there. This was his fight. The crystals in his swords glowed, casting off a pure white light, blurring in the speed of Aaron's dance. The sound of the audience coming to their feet in unison echoed throughout the great space.

The Falcons felt weightless and required little effort to wield. Aaron poured all feelings, his memories, his rage, and his love into the dance. The faces of family and friends who had come and gone throughout his life flashed in his mind, but he was ever mindful of Tarimus. Random thoughts and experiences flashed by until he saw a shadow of Bronwyn standing before him, her honey-brown eyes silently begging him not to forget her. Her rich dark hair was unkempt, and her clothing was in tatters, but was she alive? She opened her arms out to him, and his throat tightened with the ache of regret. How could he have been such a fool? The love in his heart mocked him for what he'd tried to deny.

The bladesong unleashed a melody that he had never heard before, but fit him the way no other action ever had. He put his heart and soul on the altar and hoped it was enough to appeal to the little humanity that was left in Tarimus. Communication conveyed without words, but rather through raw emotion. The stone facade that framed Tarimus's cold, lifeless black eyes began to shake.

"What are you doing to me?" Tarimus demanded, becoming disoriented and covering his face with his hands in a feeble attempt at denial. "What sorcery is this!" he cried.

Truth. Life. That which you've forgotten. Aaron spoke the words in his mind, which were then conveyed through the dance. The pure white light stretched out its brilliance to encompass all.

Shaking from the struggle within, Tarimus peeled his hands from his eyes, and with a guttural roar, he charged, his dark sword attempting to swallow the light.

Aaron stood his ground, both blurring blades carrying a motion too fast for his mind to track. Thinking at this point was an obstacle. It was his training and awareness unlocked through wielding the Falcons that saved him. The ability to let go, to trust his feelings and to allow nature to take its course would determine this outcome. At last, a final lesson preached by Reymius was understood. No matter how hard he trained, this lesson could not be learned in a sparring room. He engaged Tarimus because there was no other choice, but in his heart he knew his fate lay with Tarimus upon these crossroads between the realms of Earth and Safanar, for Tarimus was the gatekeeper.

Each swing of the blade was countered, and Tarimus howled in rage, but no matter how hard he pressed, he couldn't break through the bladesong. Tarimus at last broke off his attack. Although Aaron stopped the bladesong, the power that gathered did not dissipate; rather it stayed with him, heightening his perceptions.

"Your father never gave up on you," Aaron said.

"Are you still trying to save me, boy?" Tarimus asked. "Don't speak to me of that fool. I have no father," Tarimus spat.

The word father echoed in his mind. Like thunder rumbling before a gathering storm, Aaron at last came for Tarimus. He unleashed the power of the bladesong with each blow, and Tarimus was thrown back, unable to stand against such a force that went beyond the strength of his arms. Aaron's blades cut him again and again, but no blood spilled forth from Tarimus. Their blades locked at the cross sections, and Aaron sent the dark blade spinning away. Sweeping out his leg, Aaron brought Tarimus to his knees. Aaron's vision was hued in red with the blood rage, but he stopped, poised to strike. He could strike Tarimus down with the power gathered and utterly destroy him, but he hesitated. Something wasn't right. If Tarimus dwelt between the realms of life and death, then what could Aaron possibly do? You can't kill what should already be dead. He was battling a ghost. To destroy a soul was something he knew nothing about, and if he did, could he use that knowledge, even on Tarimus?

Yes! a voice demanded. *Destroy him.*

Tarimus, he realized, was but a vessel for someone else's machinations. A prisoner desperately seeking revenge on his jailer. All Aaron needed to do was win his way past Tarimus.

"Colind spoke to me of Mactar. Is it he who holds you within this prison?" Aaron asked. "If I stop him, will that release you?" he pressed.

Tarimus regarded him with a mix of contempt and surprise, then with a fluid motion, he held his hand up. His sword flew to his hand, seemingly of its own accord. Though the coliseum's occupants were silent, their gazes were deafening. Tarimus sheathed his sword, driving it home, and a sense of finality filled the air. Aaron watched warily as Tarimus brought his hands together, and a purple orb of crackling light gathered with intensity above his head. The medallion grew cold against Aaron's chest. Ferasdiam was spoken in hushed tones throughout the coliseum. The gong of a church bell rang in cadence, banishing the whispers into silence. Zeus howled, eerily reminiscent of the night Aaron first tapped into the power of the bladesong. The howl held a calling, and Aaron wanted to heed that call. The columned stone doorway stood with its opening ajar, a shimmering curtain of silvery light blocking the view to the other side.

"I can settle it for both of us," Aaron said, and took a few precious steps toward his pack, where the cylinder glowed. He needed that cylinder if he was going to get to Safanar.

"What will you do in Safanar?" Tarimus asked.

"I seek those responsible for the murder of my family. They shall all pay. This *I swear*," Aaron said. "I will seek out Mactar."

"Vengeance is the path of death. I am responsible for the deaths." Tarimus turned his back to Aaron slowly shaking his head, the purplish orb hanging between them. Aaron wondered what ghosts haunted this demon who had once been a man, Colind's son. Tarimus abruptly turned toward Aaron. The words he spoke seemed reluctant to come out of his mouth, but his facial expression was oddly lucid.

"Perhaps you will succeed where I have failed." He paused, taking in Aaron's measure. "But perhaps not," he hissed, and a menacing glint overtook his face. His arms rose, and the purplish orb flared brighter. "I will have you, Shandarian!"

Aaron barely had time to flinch before the beam of light shot out of the orb, slamming him in the chest. The beam split between the pearl in his medallion and the crystals in the hilt of his swords, forming a blazing pyramid of deep purplish light. The medallion became the focus point, and blinding pain seared his chest, bringing Aaron to his knees. With all his might, he brought up his swords, cutting off the beam and sending it back to its source.

Tarimus stumbled back in shock, but before he renewed his attack, Aaron scooped up his pack and sprinted toward the door to Safanar. Tarimus howled in rage behind him, but Aaron didn't dare turn back. The door to Safanar was his destination. He ran as if the ground were falling away beneath his feet. Closing in on the door, Aaron brought out the cylinder, its bluish glow gaining in intensity.

Aaron thrust the cylinder out, the shimmering silvery curtain parted, and the stone doors began to close. He risked a glance back to Tarimus, but all he saw was the purple orb barreling toward him, screeching louder as it drew in. With the stone doors closing and with Zeus beside him, Aaron leaped through the door to Safanar.

The coliseum's mysterious occupants returned to their seats, and, as one, stared into the space before them. A dismissal hung in the air, and they were all swept away like sand blown in a strong breeze. Tarimus remained there for a few brief moments. "So be it," he whispered and disappeared.

The earth shook, snatching the attention of its people. As it was foretold, the Lords of Shandara would once again walk the lands of Safanar. Ferasdiam had left her mark upon him, and he would be her champion, but the path would be of his choosing. A cold wind blasted its way down, bringing an ounce of relief from the scorching heat of the deserts of Deitmar to the far off plains of the Waylands. Deep in an ancient forest, well protected from the realms of men, the old one stood. The wind carried a strange scent and swept his graying hair back. His eyes scanned the canopy of trees above. He was coming, finally. It set his mind at ease that Reymius did not fail in his task. The last of the ancient house of Shandara had returned. It was left to him to find Reymius's heir and keep him safe above all things, even from himself. Let the forces of shadow be wary, the Hythariam would once again enter the world of men. His golden eyes flashed briefly while he took his first steps on what would be a long journey.

14

A HERO, A FRIEND

Aaron collapsed to the ground, writhing in pain. Coming through the doorway was like plunging into icy waters, but without getting wet. The cold was so sudden that the air was sucked from his lungs. He squeezed his eyes shut, hoping fervently that the pain would pass. The burning on his chest intensified. He struggled to remove his shirt and looked down at his chest, expecting to see blistering skin, but instead saw a perfect reproduction of the carved relief from the medallion. The dragon with his wings spread, holding a rose, and the white pearl in the center. The pain subsided, fading to a harsh, burning ache. The brand was more like a tattoo than a burn, because it had a silvery shimmer reflecting from the dragon scales. With each breath he took, it appeared as if the dragon were breathing.

Thunder rumbled, and he looked up at the dome-shaped ceiling covered with cobwebs. A shadow passed over an opening in the roof, then sunlight streamed lazily in. There were four statues in the room that were equal distances apart, like the points of a compass. A ray of sunshine set the fountain in the center of the room ablaze, and the water reflected the light in glistening waves that shimmered throughout the room.

Aaron slowly got to his feet, still getting his bearings. He put his shirt back on and bit back a gasp.

He'd made it. This was Safanar. The thought looped in his mind, and he had never felt so alone in all of his life. There would be no going home for him. He walked over to the fountain and eagerly dipped his hands in for a drink. Then, he filled the two metal water bottles from his backpack.

The statue on the far side of the temple caught his eye, seeming to glow of its own luminescence. The statue was of a man wearing robes with the hood drawn back, revealing a proud face. His right hand held the remnants of a staff, whose broken haft would have reached down to the floor. The pedestal beneath the statue was adorned with an intricate design of laurel work that drew the eyes to the center. Aaron traced his fingers across the patterns, and the faint whisperings of the bladesong began to awaken within him, urging him on. The center of the laurel work had a round impression. He glanced down at the medallion and held it up. It was a perfect fit. Aaron pressed it firmly into the impression. There was a faint click, and the white pearl in the center glowed. A stone doorway revealed itself off to the right. Aaron peered through the doorway. Faint glowing orbs grew brighter, lighting the pathway beyond. Aaron retrieved his medallion and whistled to Zeus, then went through the doorway.

The passageway sloped downward, twisting to the left. His footsteps echoed down the passageway until he came to the end. The passageway opened into a large, windowless room. Glowing orbs grew brighter as they sprang to life around the room. In the center was a long dark wooden staff driven into the rock floor, and a black cloak hung from the top. Runes were etched along the length of the staff, and a faint breeze toyed with the draping cloak. The musky air almost made him sneeze. Aaron stretched his hand out to the staff, and as his fingers closed around it, the runes flared to life. He tried to draw his hand back, but he couldn't.

"So, one of the Alenzar'seth has returned," a voice called out. "Do you dare claim my Rune Staff for your own?"

Aaron thought for a moment. The voice sounded familiar but different. "I just got here, and the road ahead is long. Please, I could use a good walking stick," he said.

The silence dragged on and then was replaced with a mirthful chuckle. "As did I when fate came knocking at my door, young one."

A ghostly apparition of an old man appeared before Aaron. The man's broad shoulders hinted at the powerful frame he must have had when he was young, but they now stooped with age. His eyes twinkled, showing no signs of age at all. His bushy white eyebrows moved as his face lifted into a smile. Something in his features seemed oddly familiar yet foreign at the same time.

"Uh...hello," Aaron said. "How do you know who I am, and who are you?"

"I had a name once, but that was long ago," the old man mused tiredly. "I am simply known as the Keeper. This staff can light the path of all, even among the darker places of this world. And there are dark places you will be traveling, to be sure. But know this. As with all things, there is a balance with the taking of this staff. To bring light invites the darkness to come take it from you."

"I'm already hunted. Keep the staff," Aaron said firmly, beginning to step away.

"You don't understand. This staff was meant for you as it was for me during my time. You cannot run from your destiny," the old man insisted.

"I walk my own path," Aaron said. "And I make my own destiny."

The old man smiled in a knowing way. "Fate uses us all, son. Failure to play in her game will cost you more than you know."

Aaron unclenched his teeth. "It has already cost me."

"Take the staff and use it well in your journey. That is all I ask. Ferasdiam has already marked you. Take with you another weapon to fight against the maelstrom arrayed against you. Think of it as a long-lost family heirloom." As the old man said the last, he faded away.

"Wait," Aaron cried. "Who are you? Please, tell me your name."

Silence hung in the air for a moment, but Aaron was sure that the Keeper was still there.

"I once was Daverim Alenzar'seth, your ancestor. I, too, served the Goddess once upon a time, and now I have a beloved whom I've kept waiting for far too long. Farewell and good luck."

His ancestor? What were the odds of that? This wasn't at all what he'd expected. Then again, what should he have expected? His life had been anything but normal since his grandfather died and a good deal more brutal. He carefully removed the black cloak from the staff and put it on. Aaron had never worn a cloak before, and it seemed to fit him well, not restricting his movements at all. His swords were well concealed on his hips, and the cloak would make blending in with the people here easier, or so he hoped. Donning his backpack, Aaron reached out for the rune-carved staff once again. At least his sister was safe. He had accomplished that much in coming here. He gripped the Rune Staff and easily pulled it from the ground. As the staff left the soil, a vision of a glowing, yellow reptilian eye seemed to lock onto him instantly. A mighty roar echoed in his mind as Aaron threw down the staff. He shook his head, gasping, then stared at the staff lying on the ground. Zeus eyed him intently, whining softly. Aaron looked back at Zeus, bewildered.

Well, I can't just leave it here.

He cautiously knelt down and picked it back up. The runes glowed briefly and then faded. He ran his hands appreciatively up and down the staff, which was a good weight and perfectly balanced. Aaron wondered how long the cloak and the rune-carved staff had been there as he retraced his steps back up the passageway. He inserted his medallion into the base of the statue, and the stone doorway shut with finality. After taking another drink of water from the fountain, he walked outside.

Aaron emerged from the temple entrance, which was nestled on top of a small hill that overlooked a meadow. The path leading away from the temple was mostly overgrown. He hoped the path would lead him to a town and from there perhaps he could find where this Prince Cyrus was that Colind told him about. Where was Colind? Did he know that he made it to Safanar? He'd hoped that the specter would show himself, but Aaron was alone.

Aaron left the temple, taking the path away. He was the Heir of Shandara. Did that make him some type of lord or a prince? His faint amusement at the thought quickly faded. He'd come here seeking all those responsible for the murder of his family, but he was starting to wonder if he would ever stop paying for things that his ancestors had done. He found himself in the middle of a war where the threat to his life was as real as the air he breathed. A cold shiver ran through him. Was the world always this harsh, or was it that his illusions of the world had been stripped away?

Being a seasoned hiker, he was able to set a good pace and cover a lot of ground. After a few hours, he found a dirt road. The staff helped. He noticed smoke rising in the distance and decided to set off in its direction, hoping to find a town. There was an oddness in the air that nagged at him for a while, until he finally realized it for what it was. The simplicity of it made him snort to himself. There was an enduring silence beyond the sounds of nature. There were no sounds of cars, trucks, planes, or cellular phones. All the things that made up his modern society were gone, leaving him wondering what technology was here. Even when hiking and camping, you brought portable technology with you and could see others with the same.

He went off the road a bit and sat on a fallen tree, taking his ease and closing his eyes. Simply soaking in where he was. The day was growing warm, and the shine of the sun peeked through the canopy of trees surrounding him. Zeus pawed at the ground anxiously, and then he heard the distant sound of galloping horses upon the road.

So much for technology.

Aaron pulled his hood up and crept toward the road, hugging the ground for a better look. The group of riders broke into view and slowed to a stop. All the riders save two wore brown cloaks and sat in their saddles with ease. The remaining two riders that led the group wore dark-blue cloaks. Aaron heard some of the men ask why they'd stopped, and they were answered with contemptuous silence as a blue rider held up his fist. The blue-cloaked riders scanned the area, and as one rider's gaze swept his way, Aaron felt a slight graze upon his senses. When the second blue-cloaked rider turned in Aaron's direction, a large shadow passed overhead, sweeping over them, blocking out the sun.

"Dragon!" one of the men shouted, and some men drew their swords and readied their bows.

"Hold," a blue rider shouted. "That is no dragon. It's a Ryakul. He's on the hunt, but not for us. Let's move out."

As one, the riders left. Aaron moved on as well, but stayed to the forest, following alongside the road rather than walking upon it. *Dragons? Ryakul? What kind of place is this?*

Before he knew it, the sun was setting. He found an old campsite, built a small fire, and ate some of the food he brought with him, but it wouldn't last more than a day. He cursed himself for not thinking to bring more than a day's worth of food, but at least he had water. Not thinking the food situation through left him wondering what else he hadn't thought through before charging headlong on this journey.

Zeus had come back, licking his chops, and settled down close by. Zeus was in his element out in the forest, but this place was still alien to Aaron, with different sounds than back home. He lay back and gazed up at the alien sky. The stars and their formations were all different, and there were two moons, one reddish in color and the other white like home. It was not his first time sleeping out under the stars, only his first time sleeping under them on another world. His first night on Safanar was filled with a dreamless sleep, as if the previous weeks had finally caught up with him. If he dreamt, he was blissfully unaware. He knew that with Zeus there he would be safe enough, and if not, he would at least be warned.

The next morning, he decided to chance walking upon the road, and before lunch, he reached a small town. The town reminded him of the old Western frontier towns he had seen pictures of in history books. Broad, dusty streets lined with worn, but well-maintained buildings—some more elaborately decorated than others. Some of the buildings were made of a type of stone masonry construction rather than wood.

The townsfolk bustled with activity, and although a few glanced at Zeus because of his great size, no one's gaze lingered for long. From under his hood, Aaron scanned the people and buildings as he walked by. He turned down the main thoroughfare to the town's square. A small crowd had gathered, but most walking by were determined to stare straight ahead, ignoring the activity of those around them. Then he heard screams.

Aaron was about to make a quiet withdrawal, but decided to press closer, gaining a better vantage point. A man plainly dressed in a leather apron was being held by the riders in brown cloaks that he saw yesterday. A gauntleted fist slammed home into the man's middle, and he sagged to the ground, gasping for air. Some onlookers cheered, but most looked on with fear, silently praying for a quick conclusion. A small boy that couldn't have been more than ten years of age burst through the throng of people.

"Please," the boy screamed, "don't hurt him. That's my father." Tears streamed down his worried face, and his eyes searched frantically through the crowd for someone to help. But most people in the crowd wouldn't meet his gaze. Those that did would never help by the look of it.

Aaron's pulse raced. *Why doesn't someone do something?* he thought. Another brown-cloaked rider ran up and launched a vicious kick at the man as he struggled to his feet. Aaron clenched the rune-carved staff in his hand.

"No!" the boy cried, and charged feebly to the man who was about to kick again. The rider spun quickly and lifted the child up by his shirt. The man on the ground screamed, struggling to get up, but two men pushed him down with their boot heels, while a third grabbed him by the hair, pulling his head up.

"This boy needs to learn some respect for the guardsmen of the Elite."

The boy's face paled in fear as the dreaded gauntleted fist drew back. The boy's father screamed.

Aaron pressed his way forward. "I don't think so," he growled, and swung the rune-carved staff into the face of guardsman holding the boy. The guardsman's nose exploded into a river of blood as he fell onto his back, releasing the boy to the ground. The other guardsmen were so stunned that, for a few moments, they stared at their companion writhing upon the ground while the crowd seemed to hold its breath.

The guardsmen recovered quickly and drew their swords, fanning out to face Aaron. These were hard men with the seasoned coldness that accompanies those who have faced death in their lives. The crowd quickly scrambled out of the way, and the boy ran to his father's aid.

Aaron held the staff ready and beckoned with his other hand tauntingly for the men to have at him. The first man lunged, and Aaron quickly sidestepped, allowing the guardsman to overextend, then paid him dearly with several crushing blows. While the other guardsmen were strong and skilled, they were no match for Aaron as he weaved in and out between them, delivering decisive blows until he was the only one standing.

He'd never thought his life would become anything resembling a daily life-and-death struggle, but it was becoming that way. He had enjoyed the sparring room back home because there it was competition, it was fun, and it was for learning. If a mistake were made, you worked to correct it next time. But here, if he made a mistake, it could be the end of him. He didn't know why the guardsmen were beating that man, but he couldn't just sit back and let them hurt a child.

"Well, what do we have here?" a voice hissed behind him.

Aaron spun and saw one of the blue-cloaked riders standing before him with his sword drawn. His sword was single edged with serrations on the opposite side, a vile-looking thing.

"I believe your men were out of line," Aaron replied.

The man regarded him coolly. "No, no that won't do at all," he said, circling to one side, dividing his gaze between the fallen guardsmen and Aaron. "But I cannot tolerate such insolence from one such as you. If I did, where would it end?" the man asked with the surety of one who would squash a bug. The arrogance of it darkened Aaron's anger.

"I didn't kill any of your men. I just taught them a lesson," Aaron said.

"You dare raise your hand against a guardsman dispensing justice, a deed punishable by death?"

"Beating a father and son in a town square is what you call justice? What were their crimes?" Aaron asked. "I suppose if I raise my staff against you, that is also punishable by death?"

The murmuring crowd watched the two of them with a sense of fear and of hope. There was no change in the blue rider's demeanor except for his body springing into action, spinning his terrible blade in an all-out attack. Although Aaron was ready for the attack, he was pressed backward by the sheer ferocity of the charge. Aaron remained vigilant in his defense, but would rather have had his swords in his hands than his staff. The man he faced was highly skilled. He anticipated Aaron's movements well and used that to his advantage. Aaron sought the calmness of his inner core until there was nothing left around him except for the man he was facing. His movements became quicker and more precise. The key to his survival was in the boundaries of his own mind. The medallion grew warm against the tender skin of his chest, and the whispers urged his movements. The rune-carved staff grew warm in his hands, and sparks burst forth as blade met wood. Through his opponent's shock, Aaron swept the man's legs out from under him. The remaining people in the town square gasped and looked at Aaron in awe, but none more so than the blue rider who was lying flat on his back.

"My Lord," said several townsfolk as they sank to their knees.

Aaron's mouth dropped open when he realized they were speaking to him. "Ferasdiam," he heard whispered from more than one person. The blue rider erupted from the ground, screaming in rage and flailing his blade. Aaron was ready; he became one with the urgings and whisperings that came from within and was able to move with a mastery he had never felt before. The flow of blade and staff resumed until Aaron struck decisively, sending the man several feet back in a heap. The blade clattered onto the paving stones, out of reach. The man gained his feet once more, with one hand clutching his chest and the other drawn within.

Aaron sensed the energy gathering within the man in a dark foreshadowing. He brought up his staff as the man shot his hand out, sending a cracking blue beam of energy burning toward him. The staff flared to life as a white light encompassed him. The blue lightning glanced off the staff and disappeared into the ground. There was the distinct sound of the snap of a bowstring, and a shaft protruded from the man's chest.

"You are either the bravest or the luckiest man I've ever seen," said a mirthful voice.

Aaron looked up, seeing a young man smiling down at him from his horse. He wore a dark cloak and a wide-brimmed black hat with a rather large feather sticking out one side, reminding Aaron of a Musketeer.

"Here, I brought this for you," he said, holding out the reins to a second horse behind him. "Not to worry. It was his. While you may be handy with a staff, I think we should make our way out of here before all this attention becomes a bit overwhelming." The young man's mirthful smile vanished as he turned to address the crowd. "Let it be known that the Elite are not as infallible as they would have you believe. There are those who can fight them. Spread the tale of this day, but for now, please empty this square. I can already hear the other guardsmen approach."

Aaron took the reins and mounted the horse. The young man regarded him for a moment, then nodded and extended his hand. "I am Verona Ryder, and it is my esteemed pleasure to make your acquaintance, but we must save further introductions for later, my friend. The road calls." And with that, he gave his horse a good kick and galloped away.

Aaron turned to see the boy helping his father to his feet. The father looked as if he were about to say something, but Aaron nodded, gesturing for him to leave. They waved appreciatively, then became lost within the scattering crowd. Hearing the shouts of the guardsmen, Aaron kicked his horse into a gallop, following Verona Ryder.

"You presume much," the Elitesman said, shifting his blue cloak, his disgusted gaze sweeping over both the disoriented guardsmen still gaining their bearings and his dead companion.

"It is more important that we inform Mactar and the High King." The old wizard had been on tenterhooks since Tye's unfortunate demise, but Darven suspected it was a theatrical performance.

"Darven, the Council of Masters must be informed as well. The taking down of an Elite is troubling, even one as pathetic as this one," he said, gesturing toward the dead man. "Do you truly believe that this man is the Heir of Shandara?"

"Oh yes, it's him. I was there the night that Tye was killed. I've faced him before." Darven paused for a moment. "Seth," Darven called, and one of the guardsmen detached himself from the rest. "Follow them. They are taking the same road as you to meet up with your party."

"My identity might be compromised," Seth replied, but Darven cared little for the pitiful doings of an average guardsman.

Fixing the man with a rocky gaze, he said, "Risk is part of the job."

The iciness of his tone betrayed nothing of the empty feeling he felt in his gut. The Heir of Shandara should be dead. He shouldn't have been able to come through the crossroads, not with the safeguards Mactar had in place. He watched Seth's eyes flash briefly in anger, but he schooled his emotions soon enough. Darven brought out two small crystals, both alike in appearance, and handed one to Seth. These crystals were a marvel; when keyed properly they allowed the bearer to communicate with whoever had the crystal's twin. "I want regular reports, but be wary of that man," he said, gesturing to the road. "His name is Aaron, and he is very dangerous." Before the other could raise any questions, he said, "Mactar has plans for him. That is all." He gave a brief salute, and Seth turned and stalked off.

Darven turned back to the Elitesman. "There are forces at work here beyond you and me. We must inform the right people and complete our mission," he said, making a silent prayer for the legendary Elitesmen singular purpose to not manifest itself today. He knew what the Elitesman wanted, and it wasn't as simple as Aaron's blood. Master Elitesmen were ever seekers of those who could be brought to their order, or the alternative, which was the challenge of the hunt. They were a class above men, and their order was a mystery even to Darven, who had been cast out, but he knew enough to show respect and a small amount of fear to those of the Elite order.

"Very well," the Elitesman said, tearing his eyes away from the road. He closed his eyes, his brow wrinkled in concentration, then brought his hands to his mouth and blew out a single melodious note. A raven appeared and shot forth in a blurring dark streak across the sky. "The Elite council will be informed and will pass the information on to the High King," he said to a very stunned Darven. "Let's go," he commanded. The guardsmen and Darven wasted no time in making for the road, for it was unwise to dally when an Elitesman's patience was being stretched.

15

FERASDIAM MARKED

Zeus kept the pace, easily gliding through the surrounding forest, but he also kept his distance, appearing briefly ahead of them in silent beckoning. How long would Zeus stay with him? He had helped Aaron through the crossroads to Safanar—shouldn't he now seek to be with his own kind? They had been riding a short while when Verona asked if he thought they were being followed.

"Probably," Aaron answered. With his luck, it would be a certainty.

Verona eyed him. "Well, let's hope my luck proves true this day, my friend," he said as if hearing Aaron's thoughts.

"Thanks for your help back there," Aaron said.

"You seemed to have things well in hand, although why you would choose to tangle with an Elitesman is beyond me, but I'm glad you did. You've brought hope to that small town and allowed a father and son to escape the poorness of their timing," Verona said, frowning as he stole a glance behind them.

Aaron wanted to ask the obvious question about what an Elitesman was, but doing so would only confirm his proverbial "not from around these parts" status. Verona appeared to be close to his own age, and his instincts told him that Verona could be a friend. What would it cost Verona to be his friend? Aaron wondered darkly. He would gain nothing by being closed off from others, and he needed help if he was going to find this Prince Cyrus. Where was Colind? He had hoped to meet him when he came through.

"I am Aaron Jace," he said, extending his hand, but in his mind he whispered, *of the house Alenzar'seth.*

"Well met, Aaron," Verona said, shaking his hand firmly. "It seems as if luck is not with us, at least in regards to avoiding pursuit." Verona gestured behind them to the distinct dust plume of the riders who were on their trail. "Well, they won't find this fox such easy quarry. Are you with me, Aaron?"

"I'm the one being hunted; perhaps it would be better for you if we went our separate ways."

"Nonsense," Verona replied, shaking his head. "I've got my fair share of trouble following me. Besides, how can I abandon the first person in a generation to take down an Elite? You intrigue me, Master Jace, and it's not mere happenstance that fate put us in the pot."

Aaron looked doubtful as the dust cloud from the riders loomed ever closer. They needed to get moving.

"Colind sent me to find you. I can explain more later, but we have to go now."

"Colind?!" Aaron said. "Let's go."

They kept a sturdy pace for a time, occasionally walking their horses to conserve their strength. The forest grew thick around them, and the road faded to a barely discernible path in some places, but still they pressed forward. A shadow engulfed the sky above them and then disappeared just as quickly.

"Did you see it?" Verona asked, glancing up at the sky.

"No, but earlier I heard the Elitesman refer to something called a Ryakul flying the skies. The guardsman believed it to be a dragon," Aaron replied.

"I see. No, definitely not a dragon. The Ryakul have indeed grown bold if they venture here," Verona said. "Come, I'll tell you on the way. I'm due to meet with some friends in a couple of days, and we must keep moving." Verona took out his longbow and rested it on his lap.

After walking a short distance, Zeus came up silently and nuzzled Aaron's hand. Verona gasped, catching sight of the wolf, and Aaron quickly assured him that Zeus was a friend.

"There are not many men that a wolf would befriend," Verona remarked. "It's an allegiance that has faded with the passage of time, I'm afraid. And I fear our loss from it is greater than theirs."

"He was my grandfather's and has been with me since he died."

Verona nodded. "There are more knowledgeable people who can tell you a great deal about the Ryakul, but since they are absent, I will shamefully attempt to use my meager knowledge to shed some light on the subject."

Aaron couldn't help but smile a bit at the short speech; the man certainly had energy.

"The Ryakul kill indiscriminately, whether man or beast. Dragons appear to be their mortal enemy, but there are few dragons left, and many Ryakul remain, and no one knows for sure the reason why. They do not belong here. There are stories that the Ryakuls came from another world and were released during the fall of Shandara." Verona paused, going around some branches. "Many things were released during that time, but most were imprisoned by Reymius Alenzar'seth before he died at Shandara."

Aaron nearly tripped at the casual mention of his grandfather.

"You know of Reymius?" Verona asked.

"I know him," Aaron replied, but before Verona noted the distinction, he added, "Tell me about Colind, please."

"Ah yes, Colind," Verona said, his eyes hardening. "Do you believe in ghosts,

Aaron? Because I would doubt the validity of my own perceptions if I didn't see what I saw with my own eyes."

"It's not a matter of belief for me anymore. Recently the unexplained has a knack of finding me," Aaron said dryly.

"It was not three nights gone when Colind appeared to me, but at the time I didn't know it was him. You see, Colind, like Reymius, is a man upon which legends have been made, and he's been gone for a long time. He didn't seem like the man that all the stories claimed he was. He was withered and stooped with haunted eyes, but I swear I saw strength in them still. And anticipation. He told me that a new hope was coming to this land and I should watch for it at Duncan's Port. A stranger would appear and I should offer my aid to him. When I saw you in the town, I knew it had to be you," Verona said, watching Aaron. "He said he didn't have much time, but had a message for you, and these are his words exactly. 'Beware the beast that has slept with your family's leaving, for it will wake, yearning for the hunt upon your arrival.' That was all. I'm hoping that it makes more sense to you than it does to me."

Aaron stood in silence, taking in the message that both Colind and Daverim, his ancestor, had warned him about...that he would be hunted. "I had hoped that Colind would be here."

"He found us once; perhaps he will find us again. What did Colind say to you?" Verona asked.

"A great deal, but not enough, it seems. The last thing he said to me was to seek out Prince Cyrus, but I don't know who or where he is."

Verona's eyes widened at the mention of Prince Cyrus. "Do you have any idea why he wanted you to seek out the prince?"

He wasn't sure how much he should tell Verona, who was all but a stranger to him, but how could he expect Verona to help him if he didn't know at least something? "I am a stranger to this place, but I think it would be safer for both our sakes if we didn't delve too much into this right now. I don't know you, and you don't know me—" Aaron stopped himself. "Look, I appreciate all of your help, but if you want to change your mind and go your own way, I will understand. Just point me in the general direction so I can find this Prince Cyrus, and I will make my own way."

Verona stared at him with a look of honest bewilderment. "What kind of man would I be if I abandoned you out here?" he asked, sweeping his hand out, gesturing to the forest around them. "A man of legend asks for my help, which will probably be one of the most significant events to happen in my life, and you ask me if I want to walk away? A charge has been given to me by Colind of the Safanarion Order to help you on your journey. Fate has called upon me, Aaron. Who am I not to heed her call? I promise. Nay, I pledge," he said with his fist across his heart, "that I will see this through to the end and stand by your side as a friend."

The offer hung in the air between them. "You don't even know me. You don't know what you're getting yourself into. Are you willing to risk your life for the words of a ghost?" Aaron asked.

"In this you are mistaken, my friend. I've seen your quality when you stood up to the injustice at the town of Duncan's Port and spared a father and son a horrible end. The winds of change are upon us, and I know in my heart that they have to do with you. So where you go, I follow. As for the trouble that will come of it, well…" He paused with a small, inviting smile. "Trouble has a way of finding us all."

The look of conviction in Verona's eyes left little doubt in Aaron's mind that he meant every word. Back home, his reaction would be that Verona was crazy, but here in this place, he didn't have the luxury of time nor of beating around the bush. Life and death were present in everyday life, but here, out in this world, it seemed to be brought to the forefront. He had a feeling that Verona would prove to be the best friend he would ever know.

"Thank you," Aaron said, shaking Verona's hand firmly. In that single moment, Aaron felt some of the weight lift from his shoulders due to the comfort that only companionship could give.

A short while later, with the sun ebbing away, they reached a clearing. Verona stopped his horse. The woodland around them seemed to draw in its breath in silent anticipation. Aaron's horse snorted nervously, pawing at the ground. An ear-piercing roar came from across the clearing, rattling the trees in its wake and making them jump. A cavernous roar answered, and a dragon launched itself into the air with four Ryakuls in pursuit, their giant bat-like wings whooshing through the air.

The dragon, in all his majesty and savage beauty, reflected the sun, blazing like a star in the sky, and the Ryakuls pursued, swallowing up the light. The Ryakul were the antithesis of the dragon, sharing powerful arms and talons, but that was where the similarities ended. The hide of a Ryakul was glossy black, and its long neck ended in a gaping saber-tusked maw in direct contrast to a dragon's proud head. The dragon turned in midair, roaring its challenge, which the Ryakuls eagerly answered, rising up for their quarry. Aaron's heart thundered in his chest, but he couldn't tear his eyes away from the dragon. The tattoo on his chest throbbed, and the medallion grew warm against his skin. The battle that ensued had a ferocious brutality like nothing Aaron had ever seen. Two of the Ryakuls were brought down in a twisted heap, but not before extracting their toll on the dragon in the form of large gashes along his golden hide. The dragon fought with agility and blinding speed, flourishing teeth and talon alike. The ground shook with its landing, and the remaining two Ryakuls approached warily.

The dragon's gaze fixed upon Aaron, noticing them for the first time. Aaron took a step forward, enamored by the dragon's gaze and feeling utterly exposed at the same time. The Ryakuls lunged toward the dragon, which broke his eye contact with Aaron. Without a thought, Aaron drew his Falcons and charged. As he swept across the clearing, the wind raced past his swords, and a few notes of the bladesong were released. The Ryakuls stopped instantly and turned, their terrible green eyes fixed upon Aaron, who stopped in his tracks. A small breeze tugged at Aaron's cloak. He was rooted in place, feeling nothing but the burning of the dragon tattoo on his chest and the stirring of power from the medallion. He began to wield the Falcons with a savage need to smite the abomination before him. The melodic tune from the bladesong bewitched the Ryakuls long enough for the dragon to seize the opportunity to strike. A powerful swipe with the end of its armored tail nearly severed a Ryakul in half, but instead of blood, black vapor hissed free.

The remaining Ryakul charged toward Aaron, its black wings spread, but it remained on the ground, propelling itself with giant leaps in reckless abandon. The dragon pounced mightily, driving the thrashing Ryakul into the ground. The two beasts were a tangle of claw and talon, each snapping at the other. Aaron closed the distance between them as the Ryakul's soulless green eyes fixed upon him, even with the dragon tearing the life from it. Aaron roared as he leaped, driving his Falcons through the eyes of the Ryakul, avoiding the saber-sized tusks from its mouth.

The dragon eyed him curiously. The boiling rage within him that demanded the death of the Ryakul had subsided, and calmness returned. Aaron sheathed his swords and held out his empty palms, showing the dragon that he meant no harm. He wasn't sure why he sheathed his swords, but it felt right not to arm himself in the presence of a dragon. Perhaps because they shared a common enemy--the Ryakul could be nothing else to him. Verona was right. They were an abomination. The dragon snorted and turned, favoring one of its legs, and limped off.

"Are you okay?" Verona called behind him.

Aaron couldn't take his eyes off the dragon and tried to resist the urge to follow. The dragon looked back and cocked its head at them, then kept going.

"Let's follow him," Aaron said. Verona nodded, clearly at a loss for words. Aaron spoke soothing words to the horses, rubbing gently at their necks, and they calmed down enough to follow the dragon. They kept their distance at first, but with the passage of time, they grew bolder. The dragon turned to look at them a few more times, and when he was satisfied that they were following, he didn't look back again. As time went on, the dragon's breathing became more labored. All the graceful agility the dragon displayed in his battle with the Ryakuls was fading with each strenuous step. Aaron asked Verona if he had any idea where the dragon was taking them.

"I'm not sure," Verona replied. "What happened to you back there?" he asked, seizing the moment for conversation. "One moment you were next to me, and the next you charged. Where did you get those swords? They're like nothing I've ever seen before."

Aaron took a moment to gather his thoughts. He'd been thinking the same thing for a while. Why did he charge into that clearing? "I'm not sure what came over me. When I saw the dragon making his stand against all those Ryakuls, it was as if I had become the dragon and his fight became my fight," Aaron said, absently rubbing the dragon tattoo beneath his shirt. "These swords were bequeathed to me by my grandfather when he died."

Verona swallowed and glanced at the dragon. "There are stories, legends really, about men of the Safanarion Order whose connection to their souls was so in tune and strong that their connection to every living thing was amplified to a level of unspeakable proportions. They could feel the life force of all those around them. Many believed that they could read minds, but perhaps it was due to their heightened perceptions that they were able to know what was in a man's heart, even if that man himself didn't know. Not sure about that. They were more in tune with all forms of life and were therefore both shunned and rejoiced by man. In some cases, like in recent history, they were hunted by those jealous of their power. Legend says that the Safanarion Order's most gifted members were known to have the mark of the Goddess. Ferasdiam Marked, it was called. If what you are saying is true, then perhaps *you* are such a man," Verona said. After considering for a moment, he spoke again. "Who was your grandfather?" he asked in a tone that belied the seriousness of the question.

At some point during Verona's speech, Aaron had clenched his jaw shut and been about to reply, but the dragon had abruptly stopped, its labored breathing coming in gasps.

There is no time.

Aaron heard the words in his mind and looked to Verona for some confirmation that he too heard them, but there was none.

He cannot hear me. Only you as a bearer of our mark can speak and walk among us in this way. Only the bearer of the staff will have the power to aid us and drive away the spawn of shadow. You must come. There is no time.

The dragon swung its mighty head, his golden eyes peering at them intently.

"He looks hungry," Verona whispered nervously.

"No, he won't harm us," Aaron whispered back. He focused himself as he would if wielding the Falcons, and immediately his perceptions sharpened. The power was there at his call; all he needed to do was reach out.

What can I do to help you? Can I ease your pain somehow?

The dragon narrowed its gaze, turned away, and began taking great strides ahead, and they had to leap to catch up.

Just keep up. There is something you must see.

The pace the dying dragon set left them little chance for talking. All their efforts were to simply keep up. The horses grew increasingly nervous, and they decided to lead them rather than ride. They climbed a steep hill, and the setting sun filled the sky behind them in a brilliant orange blaze. Aaron could no longer see the clearing where they'd first encountered the dragon and was amazed at how far they had traveled. Thighs burning with every effort, they crested the hill and were met with a twilight sky on the other side. They stood at the ring of a vast crater where the trees grew thick, blocking their view of its mysterious interior.

Aaron peered down and noticed the occasional stone tower peeking out over the forest canopy. The towers looked old and worn down, as if slowly being consumed by the forest. The dragon thundered down the crater, making its own path, and Aaron followed. The thick gnarled trees gave way grudgingly to the dragon's hapless passing. There was something down there amid the ruins, hidden in the forest. The air felt vibrant with energy, and a sense of calm settle in all around him. He looked at Verona, who nodded his unspoken confirmation that he felt it too. He hadn't answered Verona's question earlier, but he knew sooner or later the subject of his lineage would come up again. A faint mist toiled on the ground as they made their way deeper into the crater. Verona produced a glowing crystal hanging on the end of a chain. The crystal gave them just enough light to see by. As they continued to follow the dragon, Aaron noticed a faint light glowing in the distance.

"What do you think it is?" Verona asked, breaking the silence.

"I don't know. Let's go see," Aaron said quickly.

He barely saw Zeus trotting ahead, the end of his bushy tail just catching the light. Aaron quickened his pace and they emerged into a clearing. A circle of white columns surrounded a pool of water lined with stone. Something in the water was glowing, sending shimmering waves of light dancing upon the trees and columns alike. The light grew brighter as they approached, revealing the statue of a beautiful woman seemingly standing on the water. The trick of the light made her flowing gown shift among the shadows.

The dragon heaved its body down behind the pool with its tail and head wrapped on either side. The light reflecting off its golden hide showered them in a rainbow of color. The eyes of the statue were startlingly lifelike, capturing an essence of pride and strength, making Aaron want stand taller. Through the shimmering light, her appearance changed from a beloved sister to mother to friend to lover, all in cyclical elegance. The darkness that dwelled in his heart inched back grudgingly, but the molten anger and sadness refused to give way completely. He held onto them as he would to a cliff to keep from falling into the void. He would have his vengeance.

Aaron stepped closer, and the rune-carved staff tingled in his hands, sending eddies of energy coursing through him. The dragon tattoo on his chest ached anew, and he winced. The eyes of the statue drew him in and he stood spellbound.

"*You are in the presence of the Goddess,*" the dragon said, and Verona must have heard him, because he sank to his knees, muttering a prayer.

Aaron tore his eyes away from the statue, and the dragon stared pointedly back at him.

"It's a statue," Aaron said.

It's a symbol, the dragon replied.

The tattoo on his chest flared anew, making Aaron wince at the sharp, burning pain.

Cleanse the mark of Ferasdiam with the sacred waters.

The burning intensified, and Aaron scrambled to get his shirt off. He plunged his hands into the cool water and quickly brought them up to his chest over and over until the burning subsided. The pain was completely gone. The dragon markings on his chest no longer appeared fresh, but looked as if they had always been there. Perhaps they had, and coming to this world made the mark of the dragon come forward. He wondered if his grandfather had known about this. What could they have done, regardless? He turned to snatch up his shirt when he heard Verona gasp, staring wide-eyed at him.

"You are one of the gifted, a member of the Safanarion Order. You are Ferasdiam Marked," Verona said, pointing at Aaron's chest.

Aaron snatched his shirt from the floor. His medallion was safely hidden in the folds of his shirt. He put them both on at the same time, keeping the medallion hidden. The medallion had his family crest, which would surely announce who he was, and he didn't want that known until he knew more about the Alenzar'seth.

"I didn't have this mark until yesterday. I don't know where it came from or what it means," Aaron said.

Gaze into the sacred waters and allow the Goddess to show you her vision, the dragon said.

Aaron slowly stepped up to the water's edge, bracing himself for what he was about to see. Verona and Zeus joined him, and he was comforted by their presence. He steadied himself, taking a deep, focusing breath, and gazed into the calm waters. The light deep within the water flared brighter, beginning to pulse, becoming more intense. Aaron looked up, his eyes transfixed on the statue in silent anticipation. Then, in a space between moments, the eyes of the statue opened, revealing an orchestra of images so vast that he felt as if the world both faded away and collided with him at the same time. A dark and dismal land devoid of life, where a lone beacon of light blazed, drawing him closer. He found himself surrounded by the ruins of a vast castle, whose craftsmanship and sheer majestic qualities were clearly evident, even in its dilapidated state. He focused in on a tower, which had a massive carved relief of a dragon caressing a single precious rose, and his mind reeled in recognition of the Alenzar'seth's family symbol. The images shifted to a lone white tree amid a courtyard, which stood in stark contrast to the shadow lands about. Aaron knew immediately that he had to go there. A series of images swept by too fast for him to register, but he recognized Colind and a lone hand bearing the mark of a leaf on its palm.

The land needs a champion. Time is short, and already the sickness spreads. Ryakuls are just the beginning of what was unleashed at the fall of Shandara.

The words and images were synonymous in his mind, and all begged the question of what he could do about this. He was a stranger to this land. This was not his home. The remains of his home were nothing but a burned-out shell devoid of anything to mark the passing of better days. He came here seeking vengeance and to protect those he loved.

The fate of the land falls upon the house of Alenzar'seth, of which you are the last. Guardianship of the land is a legacy shared with the Safanarion Order, who have all but vanished. Fate has chosen you for this.

"I make my own fate!" Aaron shouted at the dragon. "They brought this battle to me. I didn't ask for this," he said, drawing his swords and throwing them down to the ground. "They murdered my—I want Mactar, and in order for me to get to him, I need Colind. Where can I find him?"

The fury erupted like a deadly viper, turning his molten blood to acid. He had been here before, the place where the fires of his rage took him, where he hated everything, including living. His life meant nothing in the face of vengeance; so dark was his vision that everything turned gray and meaningless around him. He struggled against the tumultuous darkness threatening to reign supreme inside him.

Remember who you are! His father's deep voice filled his ears. A lone voice of reason amid a furious storm. This wasn't who he was, he told himself over and over again, and like a spark to a flame, his sense of self returned, but the echo of dark rage remained imprinted upon the edges.

The dragon stared at him pointedly. *Your quest for vengeance will consume you if you let it.*

"It's all I have," Aaron said.

The dragon regarded him, looking exhausted. *The choice is yours. The wanderer dwells in his prison among the ruins of Shandara. Seek him out there if you will, but be warned he is not as he once was.*

The dragon laid his head down with a great sigh and breathed no more. A golden hue surrounded it, his body becoming transparent and then transforming into countless golden sparkles that ascended into the night sky. Aaron's shoulders slumped and his throat thickened. Dragons were the stuff of legends back home, and a real-life encounter with such a majestic creature was awe-inspiring to say the least. They were creatures of high intelligence and purpose, not simpletons ruled by animalistic passion.

The eyes of the statue closed once more, and the light coming from the waters diminished to a soothing glow. While Aaron stood staring at those waters, Verona had built a good-sized fire. Aaron went over to the fire and sat down across from Verona, who absently stoked the flames.

"I can tell that you have experienced a great loss, and for that I convey my sincerest condolences," Verona began. "What passed between you and the dragon I do not know because he gave me my own message. Every man harbors secrets for his own reasons. Fear not that I will press you for yours. I said it before, and I'll say it again—where you go, I will follow. Our paths are connected."

Aaron nodded, not knowing what to say. "Can you tell me about a place called Shandara and what you know of the man Reymius Alenzar'seth?" It was the first time he'd said the name aloud, and it made his heart pound to say it.

"I've never seen Shandara. I was a small boy when Shandara fell, and most of what I know is just stories. You would do well to ask the lore masters when we reach Rexel or Prince Cyrus himself. He was the one whom Colind said you should seek," Verona said.

"That's right, but the dragon said that Colind dwells in his prison among the ruins of Shandara," Aaron replied.

"Shandara was described as a truly wondrous place, home to the Safanarion Order. The Alenzar'seths were of royal blood and keepers of the great seal, a gift from the Hythariam folk, who are themselves legend, but have withdrawn from the world of men. The Shandara that exists today is a land devoid of life and consumed by shadow."

"Not all of it," Aaron said quickly and a bit defensively, which surprised him. "The dragon showed me a white tree that grows among the ruins of a vast palace. That is where I need to go." He could feel the compulsion within fueled by his need for revenge. He would do what must be done, but at what cost?

Verona eyed him. "We will need help if that is our road. We should do as Colind advised and seek out Cyrus, the prince at Rexel. Now about Reymius Alenzar'seth. He was there at the fall of Shandara. In some ways, he bore responsibility for its collapse, and in other ways, he saved the rest of us by staving off what was unleashed there. Misguided use of power and betrayal is what my uncle tells me. Much of what transpired is a mystery to all but those who were at the heart of it. I wish I knew more, but history was never one of my strengths. What I know of Reymius is the stuff of heroes and stories. Despite his birthright, he was ranked high in the Safanarion Order and was something of a diplomat with the Hythariam folk. Now and again there are whispers from small towns about a trapper seeing some of the Hythariam, but they always disappear, some vanishing right before their eyes," Verona finished, stifling a yawn.

Aaron yawned himself. "That's all right. Tell me more tomorrow. We have enough to go on, I think," Aaron replied, settling back on the ground. He rolled up a blanket for a pillow and gazed up at the brilliantly clear night sky. Though his thoughts were not idle, sleep soon came to him as his second day in the land called Safanar drew to a close. Under the watchful eyes of the statue of the Goddess, the weary travelers slept.

16

THE SUMMONS

The mirror's empty reflection hung in silent defiance that gnawed at him. Mactar mulled the whereabouts of Tarimus, staring fixedly into the mirror, which had been empty since the shaking of the earth that announced the coming of Reymius's heir. The blood of the house Alenzar'seth held the key to Shandara. He called to Tarimus through the mirror, but it mocked him again with its silence.

"Prisons don't last forever, nor do prisoners for that matter. Sooner or later, they break or escape. You have much to answer for," a silky voice purred from the window.

Mactar turned, seeing a veiled face, but no one could mistake those depthless blue eyes framed in creamy skin that had made many a foolish man go willingly to his death. Those icy eyes were transfixed upon him and for a moment gave even him pause. Of all High King Amorak's heirs, it was his daughter, Sarah, that was a step above the rest and would not be swayed as her younger brother had been. All the difference a mother can make. This one was a hunter at heart, and the world was her quarry. Not a pampered princess by any means, she possessed a single-minded determination to rival his own. Stepping away from the window with her leopard-like grace, the golden-haired beauty removed her veil. Arrogance was a fitting word to describe all Amorak's heirs, but unlike the bravado of her brothers, she either had true potential or was a grave threat. He couldn't decide which.

"My father will receive you now," she said, holding a purple travel crystal.

"So you've risen in the ranks to the king's messenger?" Mactar taunted, but he knew that Sarah would never give in to so menial an insult. "So be it. I have something for your esteemed father in the other room."

Sarah eyed him coolly, following him. "What are you playing at?"

"Trust me," Mactar said, gesturing to a dark cylinder suspended in the air above a small pedestal.

Sarah waited patiently, her face impassive, and Mactar applauded her for not rising to the bait. Dangerous indeed.

"Your fool's errand cost Tye his life, and no amount of *gifts* will quell my father's anger."

"Perhaps, my dear," Mactar replied patiently. "We will see. Regardless, there are forces at work here beyond the son of the king. Besides, he has two more sons ready to inherit."

A momentary flash of anger arrayed itself across her eyes, but instead of continuing their verbal sparring match, she activated the purple travel crystal, all the while fixing him with a stony stare.

"Won't you be joining us?" Mactar asked, raising an inquisitive brow.

"As much as I would enjoy watching you squirm before my father, I have other duties to attend to and nothing you need concern yourself with."

"Ah yes, would those duties require you to travel to the east? South of Rexel, perhaps?" Mactar replied in a sunny tone. He had gotten the Elitesman report as well when it came to the Council of Masters. The report of a mysterious stranger who had taken down an Elitesman was intriguing to say the least.

The golden-haired beauty regarded him with a look of utter boredom. "Grovel well, my Lord," she said, and then activated the travel crystal, cutting off his response.

Arrogance indeed was his last thought before the flashing of light.

The princess stood among Mactar's vile furnishings and could no longer mask her utter contempt for the home of the Dark Wizard. His slippery fingers were in everything, but so far she had not fallen prey to one of his schemes. She had heard the report about the mysterious stranger who had taken down an Elite, but it wasn't that which drew her attention. It was a restlessness she had been feeling of late. She sought solace at an abandoned church devoted to the Goddess located along the fringes of her father's kingdom. It was one of the few things she clung to in her mother's memory. She'd been there when the earth shook and a soft voice whispered in her ears, *One of the old blood has returned.* That was all that was said, and it happened so fast that she might have imagined it.

She stood silently regarding the mirror that Mactar had watched so intently. There was no reflection, only an inky black void.

Sarah, a slithering voice taunted slowly. *Beware the man marked by dragons,* it hissed.

She grasped the travel crystal and disappeared in a flash of light, but not before she heard a mirthless cackle coming from the mirror.

17

HIDDEN AMONG THE SHADOWS

Aaron snapped awake, gasping for breath, and the dark dreams that held him abated. The sun was chasing away the morning fog, and the lingering unease slowly retreated just below the surface of his thoughts.

"Are you all right?" Verona asked. "Those must have been some dreams. You were muttering most of the night, but I guess that is to be expected given the circumstances," Verona said, glancing at the statue.

Aaron wondered what he had been muttering, and for a moment he considered just telling Verona everything.

"We should get moving," Verona said.

The two men broke camp. They kept a good pace, rotating between riding and leading their horses, each of the mindset that if the time came when they truly needed to run, they could. But avoiding conflict would be preferable. Aaron kept weighing whether he should tell Verona who he was. Caution and honor were warring within him. His life was in Verona's hands just as surely as Verona's was in his own—hadn't he already proved that?

They decided to rest for a bit.

"Who is Bronwyn, if you don't mind me asking?" Verona asked.

Aaron was taking a sip of water and began coughing. "Bronwyn is a girl I knew," he said.

"You mentioned her last night. She was important to you," Verona said.

"Aren't they all?" Aaron asked. "Yes, she was important to me." His tone hardened. "She and others near me were all in danger, but I was too blind to see it and didn't act fast enough. She is dead now." He stood up, drew his swords, and slowly began to wield them. The bladesong whispered on the breeze, aligning the energy around him.

"These were bequeathed to me by my grandfather...*Reymius*," Aaron said, staring directly into Verona's astonished eyes. "I am the grandson of Reymius and

Cassandra, and son to Patrick and Carlowen Jace. I am of the house Alenzar'seth." He quickly sheathed his blades in a single fluid motion. "I'm sorry I concealed my identity. I didn't think it would be fair for you to travel with me and not understand the risks that come with it."

Aaron watched as Verona gathered his thoughts.

"I knew there was something about you, Aaron, when I first laid eyes on you. You are the Heir of Shandara, and I vow that your identity will stay with me until you give me leave to do otherwise," Verona said with a fist across his heart. "I understand your caution. How could you know whether you could trust me or not? I said it before, and I say it again—I will see this through and stand by your side as a friend even in the face of our death."

The man must be crazy, Aaron thought, but he believed every word Verona said. In this world, there could be no time wasted on foolishness.

"Well, well, if you haven't given us a great chase, my Lord," a voice boomed out from the surrounding trees.

"Surrender now and you will only be a little light on coins," another gruff voice called out.

Verona grinned. "If it's more of a chase you want, just say the word, and we'll be off again, you dogs," Verona shouted. The silence was broken by the hearty laughter from the men concealed by the surrounding forest. "Vaughn, Sarik, and Garret, I know it's you. I would advise you to come forward for I'm afraid my friend here has a rather large wolf for a companion who likes to feed on dogs. Even one as great as you, Vaughn."

Three men extracted themselves from the surrounding trees, all with broad smiles. "Well met, my Lord," said the man in the middle, grinning.

"Well met, Vaughn," Verona said, extending his hand to the bear of a man, who had traces of gray in his hair and beard. "May I introduce you to Aaron Jace, another such as we who has a talent for attracting trouble." Aaron shook each of their hands in turn, and all returned a firm handshake. "Where are Eric and Braden?" Verona inquired.

"Camp is set up a few miles north of here. We were hunting for dinner when we quite literally stumbled onto you," Vaughn said, leading the way. "I had expected to meet up with you much sooner and at the wayward point," he said, raising an eyebrow. "Did you get sidetracked again? What was her name?"

"An old friend came to me with a request that I couldn't refuse," Verona answered with a twinkle in his eyes.

Vaughn frowned. "There has been word of some trouble in one of the smaller towns and some cursed Ryakul activity to the east," Vaughn replied, giving a slight glance overhead.

"We don't have to worry about the Ryakuls for now. Aaron and I witnessed an epic battle between a dragon and four Ryakuls." The word dragon was echoed by the other men while Aaron listened silently. *News travels fast, it seems.*

Vaughn glanced at Aaron. "A knack for finding trouble indeed. Dragons are rarely seen during these times. Though it's troubling that the Ryakuls have ventured this far. I wonder what brought them."

Vaughn happened to be looking at Aaron when he said the last, and it got him thinking. Were the Ryakuls hunting him? Hadn't Daverim Alenzar'seth said beasts of shadow would be drawn to him if he took the cloak and rune-carved staff?

"It could mean that the shadow lands are extending beyond Shandara's borders," said the wiry young man called Sarik. It took almost all of Aaron's concentration to not look at Verona at this point, but he felt the tension in the air between them. Instead, he scanned their surroundings as they made their way up the path.

"Peace, Sarik, you speak of what you do not know," Garret said gently.

"It was just a thought," Sarik replied. "The Ryakuls grow bolder with each passing season," he said, adjusting the quiver of arrows poking over his shoulder. "I'm going to see if I have any more luck finding a decent meal for us without you lot plodding through the forest. I'll see you back at camp," Sarik said, trotting ahead of them.

Vaughn picked up the pace, speaking with Verona as they took the lead. Aaron was just as happy to walk and not be on the saddle of a horse for a while. He watched the two men ahead of him and kept an eye out for Zeus, whom he hadn't seen in a while, although he did hear the sounds of other wolves in the distance. Perhaps Zeus had found a home in this place. As soon as the thought came to mind, he caught a glimpse of the smoky gray wolf through the trees, stopping occasionally to peer at him.

"So there really is a wolf," Garret said.

Aaron nodded.

"How did you end up traveling with Verona?" Garret asked.

"I met up with him in a small town south of here," Aaron replied. "He helped me get out of some trouble."

"Well, that sounds about right. Verona can hardly resist a bit of mischief when the opportunity presents itself," Garret replied in a knowing sort of way. "Is that trouble still following you?"

The question was simple, direct, and straight to the point, which Aaron liked. "Yes," he answered.

Garret nodded as if he had expected nothing less. "Not to worry, Aaron, trouble has a way of finding us all from time to time, and it usually doesn't let up easily once it has arrived."

That's putting it mildly, Aaron thought, and he heard the echo of his father saying that you couldn't always avoid trouble when it came, but you could do your part to prepare for it as best you can.

They traveled swiftly to the camp, where Aaron was introduced to Eric and Braden, who were brothers. Both men were like picturesque warriors taken straight from a Greek sculpture, towering above most men and wearing their swords with the graceful ease of one married to the blade. There was no arrogance in their eyes or mannerisms, which instantly commanded Aaron's respect.

Sarik made it back shortly after them, and luck was with him, Aaron noted, since there was a good-sized deer being prepared for dinner. Aaron had worried that he would be looked upon with suspicion as a newcomer to the group, but all of them trusted Verona, and it was by his leave that they reserved their judgment, which Aaron thought was fair enough. When they all sat down to dinner around the fire, Zeus boldly stepped out of the twilight, his eyes locked upon Sarik, who was portioning out the meal. There was no mistaking the wolf's intent. He expected his share, and it was Garret who directed Sarik to set some aside for the wolf. After Zeus devoured his meal, he moved to Aaron's side and lay by his feet.

"So, Aaron," Braden said casually, "Verona tells us that you took down a member of the Elite order."

The rest hushed to an abrupt silence.

"I stopped some men from hurting a father and his son. I've never heard of this Elite Order before I met Verona," Aaron answered, absently stroking Zeus's fur. Most of them masked their surprised reactions well, but all stole a quick glance at Verona, who gave no reaction at all.

"You must be among the luckiest of men," Braden said, taking out a dagger and sharpening it, his powerful arms making precise thrusts with the stone.

"Luck had nothing to do with it, I can assure you," Verona put in quickly. "There is another Elitesman who has been tracking us, so with all possible speed, our road must take us to Rexel."

The men all spoke at once, but it was Vaughn who silenced them. "The prince advised, no, warned you to not return, family or not. We should consider heeding this warning for the time being," Vaughn said.

"Oh, come on now, Vaughn. It has already been a while; perhaps the old man is in a forgiving mood." Verona smiled mischievously.

"Not long enough, I think. He had the guards chase us out of the city the last time," Vaughn said, smiling, and the others laughed. "Why there? Why to the prince? What business is so important that it requires us to go back there?" Vaughn asked.

"Colind the Guardian is alive," Verona said. "He has been a prisoner all these long years, but it's a prison unlike anything I've ever heard of before."

During the ramble of questions, it was Garret whose deep voice spoke up above the rest. "Where is he?" the older man asked.

Verona took a long look at Aaron, who nodded before he answered, and the others noted it. "In *Shandara*," he answered.

Pandemonium. All agreed that it would be impossible to free Colind from his prison because they could never survive the journey. Absolutely no one in their right mind entered Shandara. Aaron wondered if this would be the reaction of the prince as well. He hoped not. Colind was certain that the prince could help in some way, but he never got to say how or why the prince would help him.

"Don't tell me you honestly mean to trek into Shandara to free him," Vaughn said. "That is a fool's errand if ever I heard one; tell him, Garret."

Aaron cleared his throat and drew the others' attention. "No, it's not Verona's intent to trek into Shandara. It's mine," he said, letting the words hang there for a moment while he met all of their eyes. "I am going to Shandara to free Colind, but I was advised to seek the counsel of Prince Cyrus before I go, by Colind himself. So if it's a fool's errand, then I am fortune's fool, for that is my road."

"And I am going with him," Verona finished.

The silence was deafening; Braden even stopped sharpening his dagger in mid stroke with his mouth open. Garret recovered first. Being the oldest among them, he seemed to be the most levelheaded. Aaron did note the concern in Vaughn's eyes; clearly, he looked on Verona as an uncle would look upon a nephew, and their bond was strong.

"That's quite a declaration, Verona," Garret said evenly. "Why would you agree to go on what many of us would consider a suicide mission? Are you that eager to face your final judgment?"

"Did you not hear him?" Verona said, gesturing toward Aaron. "Colind appeared to him just as he did to me. That's what took me away to Duncan's Port. That's where I met Aaron. Colind's own words were that I should offer my aid to a stranger in the town. One who will stand out from the rest, and I believe that taking down a member of the Elite Order is enough to announce that this is who Colind had in mind. Tell them, Vaughn. You were with me when Colind appeared."

Vaughn stood staring at the fire for a moment. "I saw," he began. "I came at the end, but I did see an apparition vanish before my eyes, and I thought I heard his voice. It could have been Colind."

"It could have been dark magic," Garret said. "We've never attracted the notice of the Dark Light Master, but if this one has attracted the Elite's notice," he said, gesturing toward Aaron, "then it will not be long before it brings Mactar's notice as well, and the High King for that matter."

"Gentlemen, please," Verona said. "I won't ask any of you to go farther than you will. But this is where my path goes, with this man for good or ill. I trust in time, if you will allow, that he will earn all of your trust as you have all earned mine. At least travel with us to see the prince; from there, if you feel that we should part ways, then I shall bear no ill will against any man who does so."

There was a brief moment of silence before Braden sheathed his dagger. "I'm not about to abandon you, my Lord, and I believe you have good reasons for this. My sword, as always, is yours." His brother, Eric, nodded in affirmation.

"As is mine," echoed Sarik.

"To Rexel then," Garret said.

"What say you, Vaughn?" Verona asked.

Vaughn sighed. "I say you're all fools. We shall go to the prince at the very least." Vaughn's eyes strayed toward Aaron, and he noticed the hardness within them show for just a moment.

Aaron let out a small sigh and took his leave. He had his work cut out for him if he was going to earn the trust of Verona's companions and find acceptance within the group. All things in time, he supposed, but he hoped he'd be fortunate enough to have the same loyalty and camaraderie that these men showed to each other.

The next morning, the men woke early and ate a quick breakfast before setting out. Zeus set off on his own, occasionally coming into view. According to Vaughn, traveling by horseback they were about five days away from Rexel, home to Prince Cyrus. This puzzled Aaron, who was wondering what type of technology was available in the world of Safanar. When he was at Duncan's Port, he didn't have the time to take note, but all he had seen so far were people traveling by foot or on horseback. Had the people of this world managed to create anything like a car or plane?

He traced the runes along the black staff. A tool against the shadow, but it would also draw their attention. A wizard and his staff, Aaron mused, only he was no wizard. Perhaps the staff wasn't meant for him at all. He could just be its keeper, but for whom, Aaron wondered. He hoped Colind would know what he was to do with the staff. He needed Colind if he was going to stop those who were hunting him. It was thoughts such as these that were both alien to him and also becoming a daily occurrence. He hoped his sister was safe and had managed to find some peace. His throat thickened at the thought of home and all that he'd lost. He lowered his gaze and set a quick pace.

In the days that followed, their path took them through a gnarled old forest, which eventually gave way to grasslands. They passed a few farms along the way. The farmers were friendly enough once they discovered that they were just passing through, for which Aaron couldn't blame them. Living so remotely would require that they keep their guard up. It wasn't until the shoes of his horse broke that they decided to head to a nearby town.

The mood among the men had lightened considerably, especially when Garret took it upon himself to teach Aaron the bow, which he had never shot in his life. His grandfather had taught Aaron many weapons, but a bow wasn't among them, and unlike his swords, he had no apparent affinity toward the weapon. Good old hard work would have to suffice, which suited Aaron just fine, but it did become a joke among the others that he couldn't fire a bow with any degree of accuracy. Nobody would be standing in front of a tree with an apple on their head as a target for him to shoot at any time soon. They were, however, well aware of his accuracy with throwing knives, much to Eric and Braden's delight since they were fond of having contests after supper. Vaughn had adopted the wait-and-see approach, but he watched Aaron closely, and it was becoming increasingly difficult for Aaron to conceal his identity. He began to question Colind's advice in hiding who he was, and he could tell that Verona was caught in the middle. At least there were moments when the anger and pain left him, but they were few and far between. He wondered what would happen if the darkness in his soul consumed him. Who would he become if that happened?

They arrived at a small town by midmorning, and the local blacksmith informed them that he would take care of their horses before midday. This gave them time to resupply, and Aaron used the time to explore the town. All streets led to the town square, where merchants had set up their wares, but what was most notable was an old fountain in the middle of the square. A worn statue of a woman stood gazing up to the sky, reminding him of the statue that he and Verona encountered in the forest. The hot sun blazed down upon his head, feeling like tiny pinpricks on his scalp and reminding him of his need to acquire a hat.

"Do you like the fountain?" an old woman asked, appearing as if by magic beside him.

"Yes," Aaron replied.

The old woman gazed at him intently. "You have kind eyes, child," she stated.

A small smile stole itself onto Aaron's face at her bluntness. "I'm sorry to see that you bear so much pain. Perhaps being in the presence of the Goddess's fountain will bring comfort to a troubled soul, even if it is only for a moment."

Some children began playing games around the fountain, drawing his attention away. When he looked back, the old woman was gone. He gazed at the fountain, allowing his eyes to drink in its splendor, and for that moment at least, he did feel better. He made his way over to a booth where a dusty, black, wide-brimmed hat lay among the wares. Aaron shook the hat, patting it against his side, then tried it on. It fit perfectly. The woman tending the booth eyed him kindly. He wanted to purchase the hat, but had no idea about the currency used in this world. The paper money he had wouldn't be worth much except for kindling the campfire, but the quarters he fished out of his pocket brought a broad smile to the woman's face, and they disappeared quicker than Aaron's eyes could follow. It was good to get the sun off his head.

"Who *is* he, Verona?" Vaughn asked.

"I've already told you all I am permitted to say, my friend. Any more than that would not be appropriate," Verona replied as he watched Aaron from across the square.

"There is something you're not telling me about this man," Vaughn said, his hand gesturing toward Aaron. "Any man who attracts the trouble of the Elite Order we should be wary of and perhaps keep our distance from."

Verona fixed Vaughn with a stern glare. "Aaron will reveal what he wants you to know when he is ready, and until then, you should respect his wishes. He asks nothing of anyone and offers aid when he can." His gaze softened a bit as he put his hand on Vaughn's shoulder. "Perhaps you should consider this, that it is he who is trying to protect us all by only revealing so much. He has his demons to face as do we all, but by and by, I've pledged my friendship, and my word is my bond. What are we without our honor? Nothing but bloodless barbarians and chaos driven at that."

"Vaughn," called Garret as he and Sarik ran up to them from the adjoining street. "Riders approach bearing the black uniform of the High King's guard. They are accompanied by a member of the Elite Order." As Garret said the last, they heard echoes of many horses approaching.

Verona cursed. "Go find Eric and Braden quick. Sarik, stay out of sight and keep your bow ready," Verona ordered. He turned toward Aaron, who had heard the horses and was staying in the shadows as the procession of riders passed. He watched Aaron's face grow grimmer with each passing rider until he saw undeniable recognition followed by a coldness that Verona felt across the way.

The black riders bearing the silver crest of the High King filled the square, and the lively town square hushed to a few low murmurs. The uniformed soldiers stopped in militaristic precision, lining their mounts and surveying the people in the square.

"People of the town, you have among you a stranger who is wanted for crimes against the High King's guards. We know he came this way and is still here. Turn him out, and we'll be on our way. Harbor him, and I'll order this place burned to the ground. The choice is..."

"Murderer!" Aaron sneered, stepping boldly into the street, his black cloak trailing behind him like a swath of midnight.

Vaughn gasped. "What does he think he's doing?"

Watching, Verona strung his bow.

"No need to hold the town by the throat to get to me. You harbor a murderer among yourselves," Aaron said, drawing his swords and stepping boldly forward. A casual breeze toyed with the fringes of his black cloak. "Are you man enough to stand before *me*, murderer?" Aaron taunted, speaking directly to the scar-faced rider to the left of the leader.

The leader looked to the rider and then back to Aaron. "You dare challenge us! Who—form ranks *now!* To arms, men," their leader barked.

The two figures at his side remained motionless. Other men dismounted and drew their swords as one. Two archers remained in the saddle and drew their bows, arrows locked in with deadly precision.

Aaron's eyes were locked on one of the few men still remaining in a saddle. The man's surprise betrayed him. *That's right, you bastard. I'm coming for you.* He still saw the man's eyes that night as he held his mother by knife point and the bold look of determination upon her face as she made her last courageous move to save his life.

None of this was supposed to happen, damn it. She should be alive! I should be home! Aaron's muscles quaked with anticipation, and a subtle, irrevocable truth entered his mind.

I have no home anymore. The thought fanned the flames of his rage.

"By my word, I will order my men to put you down should you not do as I say. Now lay down your swords. We're not here to kill you," the leader said.

Aaron remembered the heat of the fire that took his home. The musky smell of ashes was stuck in the recesses of his nose. *I have no home anymore!* His predatory gaze swept over the men arrayed against him, and they all wore the same scarred face. They were *all that* bastard who cowardly stayed upon his horse, and they would all weep in blood. Seizing the power of the bladesong, he hurled out notes of rigid fury.

Arrows heaved from their bows, furiously seeking their mark, but Aaron was too quick and swept them aside like toothpicks. With the power of the bladesong in him, everything slowed down, giving him ample time to react. The rule when outnumbered was to keep moving and keep striking in order to survive. Movement was life, but it was not survival he sought, but to kill. He cut through three men before they had a chance to counter. In the midst of the other men's hesitation, Aaron saw arrows take down the two archers on horseback and knew Verona was with him. Aaron plunged headlong into the remaining men, whirling his blades into a vortex of death and dismemberment. Compared to the power growing within him, the unenlightened men were as children and died as easily. The whisperings of countless lives filled him with their knowledge, for the soul was an old vessel that never truly died. With each life he took, the fire in his blood roiled in protest. The five soldiers left alive looked fearfully at their fallen companions and threw down their weapons, running past the remaining three on horseback despite their captain's screams of protest.

Aaron charged. His eyes locked on the man whose face had been upon all those he had killed this day. The one who was among those that butchered his family. But before he could make contact with his mark, he was swept aside by an unseen force and knocked from his feet.

"I will deal with this upstart myself," a venomous voice rasped.

Aaron heard mutters of Elitesman from the crowd of onlookers. As he regained his feet, he told himself that what stood before him was just another man like himself, nothing more and nothing less. When one makes his opponent more than what he is, he has already lost, and Aaron would suffer no fear in his heart. The fire inside him yearned for the blood of the scarred man's face, but he knew that he must be wary of these Elitesmen.

The Elitesman drew a slender, curved black blade that appeared to be a distant cousin of a Japanese samurai sword. Aaron brought his Falcons to bear and lashed out with a thunderous attack. If he didn't fight with all that he was, then he would be dead. He moved smoothly and harmoniously, his Falcons an extension of himself, but each swing of his blades was met by the Elitesman's blade, and so the dance ensued. Banishing thoughts of victory and defeat, survival and death, he focused all his efforts on movement, bringing him to a place beyond thought. And in freeing his mind, he achieved a greater awareness that turned the tide of this deadly contest with the Elitesman.

Aaron gained on his opponent, slowly driving him back in a blur of whirling blades. The Elitesman's swordsmanship, like his composure, unraveled as the pattern of his attack became apparent. The Elitesman betrayed surprise as a long slash appeared, running across his chest. Aaron moved with deadly patience, taking the pose of the waiting dragon with his swords held like giant talons waiting to tear at his prey.

The grim-faced Elitesman took his sword with both hands, angling the point of his blade directly at Aaron. Blood flowed freely from the deep slash down his chest. For all his tricks, he was just a man, and he was beaten, a fact they both knew, and yet he would not yield. The Elitesman embraced death like a waiting lover and charged, rushing toward his fate.

Swords clashed with a wild crack of steel, and the Elitesman's blade shattered into pieces. Instead of delivering the killing blow, Aaron kicked out with his leg, sending the Elitesman hurtling off to the side.

Aaron closed in on the guardsman. The man threw down his weapons, crying out for mercy.

"I beg of you. Mercy!" the man said, falling down to his knees. "Don't kill me," he pleaded, his face crumpling in fear.

Aaron stepped forward, his blood running like ice through his veins as he regarded this murderer before him. "You ask me for mercy. There was no mercy from you with a knife held to my mother's throat." He spat, and with a quick flip of his wrist, a shallow cut appeared on the man's face, mirroring the other scar.

"No! No! Please don't kill me. I'm sorry. I was under orders. Mercy!" The man's eyes were wild with fear as tears streamed down his face.

"You are not worthy of *mercy*," Aaron sneered. "I have come for you as I will to all who have brought this war to my doorstep and stole those I loved," Aaron said with his swords at the ready. His will was like iron, and the vengeance gripping his heart yearned to be unleashed.

"Under whose orders were you so compelled to obey?" Braden asked, coming up beside Aaron, his sword drawn as Eric materialized beside him.

The man's eyes were both fearful and defiant at the same time.

"You have but one chance before you die. Who sent you?" demanded Aaron, who was answered with a silent glare of open hatred. This man felt no remorse. Without hesitation, Aaron plunged both swords through the man's chest, and as the life drained out, he grabbed his shirt, holding the dying man up, growling as he did so. His withering glare never left the dying man's eyes. "The others will join you soon," Aaron said, and roughly cast the body aside.

He turned his attention to the Elitesman, who had regained his feet, if a bit wobbly. Upon seeing his approach, the Elitesman plunged his hands into the depths of his robes and brought out a shimmering purple crystal. An aura of light surrounded him, and he vanished.

Send my regards to your masters, Elitesman, Aaron thought bitterly.

Aaron surveyed the carnage around him. Dead men littered the street, and blood was everywhere. The air stank of it. He had allowed his hunger for vengeance to turn him into a monster. The innocence within him cried out in despair from the dark corners of his mind, but his pain yearned for more. Is this what he had become? Was this the purpose for which he had been trained? His eyes swept all the dead men's faces, and he saw them for what they were instead of what his rage demanded they should be. He felt soiled in such a way that no amount of washing would ever get him clean enough. His skin crawled with death. He looked down at his hands still clutching his bloody swords; the gleaming blades were covered with blood. He flung them to the ground in disgust. Sinking to his knees, he vomited. The rage-induced tunnel vision fled, and the truth of what he had done to these men left him disgusted. It was them or him, a colder part of himself said. No, he would not condone his own actions as a mere act of survival and vowed to himself to face men as men and not as what his anger demanded they be.

He heard the sound of a bowstring straining with an arrow nocked, and he looked up from his knees to see the leader of the soldiers taking aim at him. Braden and Eric blocked his view by standing in front of him.

"You might want to think that move through," called Verona with his own arrow nocked, ready to take flight.

"I'm quite certain we'll get you first," Sarik called from the rooftop of the nearest building.

The leader released his bow and returned the arrow to its quiver. "The king shall hear of this," he shouted, turning his horse and leaving the town at a full gallop.

Aaron slowly got to his feet. The wave of nausea left him, and numbness settled in. He nodded gratefully to Braden and Eric, who had put their lives in harm's way to defend him, a fact he would never forget. The crowd of townsfolk gathered and slowly approached.

"Brave warrior," someone said.

"Took down an Elitesman," said another in a loud whisper.

"Who are you, stranger?" the blacksmith asked.

Aaron glanced at Verona, who regarded him in silence, then gave a small nod. Though Colind had strongly advised that he conceal his identity and at one time he'd conceded the point, he just could not hide who he was anymore. It was not fair to those who traveled with him, nor did it feel right to himself. Never in his whole life had he needed to hide who he truly was, and in these dark times, he refused to give his enemies that power over him. They would hunt him regardless of who knew the truth.

"My name," Aaron began, and the crowd leaned in seemingly of its own accord, "is Aaron Jace. Son of Patrick and Carlowen, grandson of Reymius Alenzar'seth. I am the last of the house of Alenzar'seth of Shandara." His eyes swept the crowd, but lingered for a moment on each of the men he traveled with, who over a short span of time he'd come to count as friends and hoped they would remain so. Verona gave him an approving nod, but the others looked shocked. Sarik, who had raced down from the rooftop, turned to Garret, who pursed his lips and nodded to himself.

"The Lords of Shandara have returned," someone gasped from the crowd. "The keepers of the sacred trust have returned."

Eric and Braden shared a brief look before going down to one knee with a fist over their hearts. "By my life or death, I pledge myself to the house of Alenzar'seth and the Heir of Shandara, as was my father's place before me," they said in unison. "We are descendants of the De'anjard, the Shields of Shandara, and our swords are yours." Their words echoed off a stunned crowd, and without exception the onlookers shouted their approval.

The cheering soon died down, and Aaron looked down at the two men kneeling before him, not knowing what to say.

"Please. Please get up," Aaron said quietly. Men shouldn't kneel before other men.

Eric and Braden rose as one, and while their warrior-like demeanor held a resolve to cope with whatever a harsh life saw fit to throw their way, now their eyes brimmed with a hope and purpose they'd not had before. Aaron found himself face-to-face with Vaughn, who looked fearful and shocked as his eyes darted back and forth from Aaron to Verona.

"I want to believe you," Vaughn began, but then words failed to come. "Prove it," he said simply.

It's a fair request, Aaron thought, and he could expect nothing less from the likes of Vaughn. He untied the laces of his shirt, his eyes never leaving Vaughn's, and the dragon tattoo shimmered, dancing amid the rays of the sun under the medallion bearing his family crest.

"By the Goddess," Garret gasped. "He is Ferasdiam Marked. One who is—"

"Marked by fate," Vaughn finished. "And he bears the mark of the house of Alenzar'seth, the Lords of Shandara," Vaughn said in a shaking voice, fearing the truth before his eyes. "My Lord, I have wronged you. Please forgive me."

"No," Aaron said, "you were protecting that which matters most to you. I would count myself fortunate to have someone such as you looking out for me. Verona kept his silence at my request." Aaron extended his hand, and Vaughn shook it firmly. It was liberating to finally reveal who he was to those he wanted to trust so badly. The darkness within him retreated, and even if it was only for this moment, perhaps it would be enough. The others regarded him silently. "We should go. These people are in danger as long as I am here."

"Yes, he's right. We must make haste," Verona agreed. They gathered their horses, and the townsfolk promised that they would hide the dead soldiers. That it would be their honor to aid the Heir of Shandara.

As they came out of the town, Aaron noticed a cloaked figure standing by the edge of the road. The cloak mostly hid the person's face, but Aaron caught a glimpse of the unmistakably beautiful feminine eyes and slender neckline of a woman. Their eyes locked for a moment, and neither looked away. Aaron frowned. He didn't understand why the others rode past her without seeming to notice at all. Her eyes searched his, and he felt as if his soul was laid bare before her. Aaron began to speak but couldn't, and part of him was grateful that he couldn't break the spell over both of them. She took a step toward him and exhaled a breath, her eyes looking regretfully at him, then there was a brief flash of light, and she was gone.

Aaron exhaled the breath he had been holding, searching all around him. "Did you see that?" Aaron asked quickly.

"See what?" Verona asked, puzzled and looking back at him. Eric and Braden drew their swords and immediately started scanning everywhere at once.

"The cloaked woman who was over there," Aaron answered, gesturing toward the far side of the road.

The men exchanged glances. "There was no one. The road is empty as it was moments before."

Aaron was about to protest, but it seemed pointless. Clearly, they hadn't seen her. He still saw her eyes in his mind, and his heart raced. "Do you know how the Elitesman disappeared with a flash of light?" Aaron asked instead.

"He had a travel crystal. Pieces taken from a whole crystal allow the traveler to always return to the source or any place that they know the pattern to. They are not that common," Verona answered.

"That would be useful to have," Aaron mused. "Is there any way we can get to Rexel faster than horseback?"

"Use of an airship would allow us to reach our destination much quicker, but all the Ryakuls in the area make for dangerous skies. Not for pirates, mind you," Verona answered with a twinkle in his eye. "Fear not, my friend, we will make it to Rexel soon enough."

"I just wonder how the Elitesmen are able to track us so easily. There was that group behind us at one point, but now they appear to be coming at us from every direction. Do they all have that travel crystal?" Aaron asked.

"They are a group shrouded in mystery," Verona said. "That is one of their strengths, but it could also mask weakness. I'm sorry, my friend, but I simply don't know."

They rode on in silence after that, chewing up the road quickly as they made their way ever closer to Rexel, where he hoped to find some aid. When he wasn't thinking about the mysterious woman, he knew his companions' questions were mounting up. The first of which came to him from Sarik as they were making camp.

"How did you do it?" Sarik asked. "How did you best that Elitesman?" The other men, including Verona, stopped what they were doing to hear Aaron's answer.

"Are they not 'just' men?" Aaron asked.

"Yeah, but..." Sarik began. "Men I can face, but an Elitesman knows things, just like you know things. How else would you be able to stand your ground against them?"

Aaron had given these Elitesmen a great deal of thought since his first encounter, when he'd met Verona. They had an arrogance to them that he equated to being slapped in the face. Just the thought of them made him tuck in his chin stubbornly.

"My grandfather, Reymius, trained me for as long as I can remember. He, with my father's help, built a school and taught many people, but he never mentioned anyone called an Elitesman. He would drill into me the importance of quieting the mind and moving without thought," Aaron said, smiling a little in remembrance of better days. "He said that sometimes our brains slow us down, and that in order to tap into the greatest strength within, you must let go of all thought. There is knowledge and power to be gained from the spirit, which is far older than the vessels that house it for a time."

Sarik said nothing for a few moments and then got down on one knee and asked, "Will you train me?"

Sarik's question was self-evident in each of their eyes. A sense of hope to stand against a monster that had haunted their footsteps for longer than Aaron could imagine.

"I've never taught anyone. I'm no teacher," Aaron said quickly.

"You carry the lost art of the Shandarian masters within you. We would honor anything you would teach us," Braden said, also going to one knee, followed by Eric.

"Please get up. You are men, for God's sake," Aaron said gently. After a few moments, they did. "It's not right for men to kneel before other men."

"Perhaps it will allow us to stand with you against the next Elitesman, for sure as the sun will rise in the morning, there will be more of them coming after us," Verona said.

Us? Aaron thought. He searched the eyes of all his companions and within them saw something unique and unyielding. Aaron could see the pattern laid before him. These men would be the first to learn what many might come in search of: Reymius's teachings. Was this the reason his grandfather was forced to flee his home? Was this knowledge the reason why war was brought from Shandara to his home? *Keepers of the sacred trust, that's how the townsfolk referred to me.* What sacred trust? He needed to know why his grandfather had to flee this world in the first place. Aaron looked back at Sarik and the others and nodded; he would teach them.

18

FEAST OF SHANSHERU

The city of Rexel stretched extensively upon either side of a river. Even from a distance, Aaron could tell that the city was well thought out in its layout of roads, allowing for efficient commuting from different parts. However, nothing prepared Aaron for the sheer size of the place. On the western side was a palace whose pale spires reached longingly toward the heavens. There were no walls that surrounded the outer city, and the roads led to a main thoroughfare that went straight to the river. He was to seek out Prince Cyrus, who, according to Colind, would be able to help him, but Colind hadn't had a chance to tell him how. *Where is Colind?* Aaron thought for the hundredth time. He was beginning to wonder whether he was on a fool's errand.

"Verona," Aaron called, "I presume that the prince resides in the palace."

"Your presumption is correct, my friend, but I bet you're wondering whether the guards will grant us an audience with the prince," Verona said.

"Something we are all wondering," Vaughn said dryly, "considering how we left the last time."

"Indeed," Verona replied with half a smile. "Aaron, how would you proceed knowing that our…no that's not right, my reception may not be the warmest?"

"I think I'd take my chances knocking on the front door," Aaron replied.

"Ah, the direct approach. Excellent." Verona grinned. "Perhaps you should go first when we arrive." Verona paused for a moment. "Not to worry, my uncle has been kicking me out of the city since I was sixteen years old, and never once has he actually had me thrown into the dungeon upon my return."

"He also never had the guards chase us from the city like the last time," Braden said, nodding to his brother Eric.

"What happened the last time you were here?" Aaron asked.

"A simple misunderstanding concerning a very attractive young lady. Unfortunately, she was betrothed to a pompous peacock of a princeling from the neighboring kingdom of Selapan," Verona replied, and Vaughn grunted something inaudible under his breath.

"It was just a dance," Verona continued, ignoring Vaughn.

"You made the princeling look so much the fool that he challenged you to a duel," Vaughn finished impatiently.

"And taught the peacock a well-deserved lesson," Verona answered. "He won't be bragging about his mastery of the bow anytime soon, or the sword for that matter."

"You also strained the already fragile relations with Selapan," Vaughn responded. "There are consequences for such actions, Verona."

"I'm sure it's all blown over by now," Verona said. "And besides, I'm sure there are other things that hold my uncle's attention at this very moment, given the time of year," he finished with a raised brow.

The dawn of recognition took hold of Vaughn, who quickly looked at Aaron and then back at Verona. He pressed his lips together, considering, but said nothing, waiting Verona out. Aaron wondered what Verona had up his sleeve.

"Coincidence or fate, my old friend?" Verona asked in a flat tone, and Vaughn nodded in understanding that was clearly beyond Aaron at the moment.

"The Feast of Shansheru, which is an ancient celebration to honor the guardians of the ivory tree," Verona said, clearly enjoying himself as understanding registered itself with each of the men, who all looked at Aaron.

"And who would like to inform our newest friend who the guardians of the ivory tree were?" Verona asked, glancing around at the rest of them, grinning. "For seventy years, the ivory tree was safeguarded in Shandara by the noble ruling house of Alenzar'seth. The ivory tree is a symbol of balance given as a seedling by the Hythariam people to Shandara, who repelled the first Ryakul incursion." Verona stopped, smiling at his friend. "So you see, as you are the only living heir of the house of Alenzar'seth, it would be poor manners indeed should my uncle, the prince, deny an audience with *you*, Aaron."

Vaughn shook his head. "All those years of tutoring, and that's all you can remember of the Ryakul incursion and symbolism of the ivory tree? You would think that the incursion was just a few flying beasts and not hordes of monsters. Not to mention when the Hythariam first came to Safanar," Vaughn said.

"Isn't that the gist of what happened?" Verona countered. "I'm sure you and my uncle can speak on this subject for days on end, but we don't have that kind of time, do we?"

Aaron was keenly interested in what they were saying, but became distracted by the flags lining the main thoroughfare into the city. They were of a dragon with his outstretched wings, cradling a rose in his talons. The center was white and pearl shaped, with the etching of a tree. They matched both the medallion and the tattoo on his chest, which he rubbed absently. Shouts of greetings could be heard as they made their way down the street, and a few soldiers cast a wary glance in their direction but waved them on. Aaron noticed a soldier was sent on ahead, no doubt to inform the prince that Verona had indeed returned.

"I don't see any of the airships you mentioned earlier," Aaron said.

"Look over toward the far side of the palace and on the outskirts of the warehouses along the river," Sarik said, urging his horse next to Aaron's. "That's where you will see them take off and land."

Aaron kept a wary eye where Sarik pointed, and he saw something cylindrical rise into the air gracefully, with lines attached to a ship. Wings extend from the main body, and small propellers drop down. The balloon and ship were of equal size, which left Aaron wondering what was being used to fill the balloon because hot air and helium weren't enough to raise a ship that size.

"Do you know how they work? How they can rise straight up into the air? How they are powered?" Aaron asked.

"The crystals are powered through magnified sun beams, which are stored in the crystals. They are rotated as they reach capacity, and energy is drawn from them as needed. As long as sunlight is available, then there is plenty of power," Sarik answered eagerly. "Garret, can you tell Aaron how the engines work?"

"The energy stored in the crystals can be used for more than just lighting the way," Garret began. "Some can be used to ignite a propellant for short periods of time, which can push the vessel in any direction. There are limitations—mostly with storing and tapping the energy, as it is not entirely without risk. There have been fires and explosions known to happen when certain precautions are not met. Airships are relatively new to the world and come with their own share of problems."

"Perhaps we can persuade the prince for a closer look at one should you desire it," Verona added.

"I would like that. Traveling by airship would be much faster than by horse," Aaron replied.

"Indeed, in that you are correct, and they are much more comfortable," Verona said. "I'm not sure if my uncle will be amiable to parting with one of his precious ships, though."

Aaron noted the slightly bitter tone from Verona, which begged the question of how many times Verona had tried to make use of the prince's airships. They both noticed that Vaughn kept looking down the street and behind them.

"Stop fretting, Vaughn. If my uncle intended to have us arrested, the guards would have been upon us already," Verona said confidently.

"Then you don't need to worry about the squad making a beeline right toward us," Vaughn said.

Verona turned, saw the approaching guard, let out a broad grin, and waved to them as they approached. "Well, no use running. We want to get to the palace, don't we?"

"That is indeed our goal," Aaron said with half a smile.

Verona grinned back at him. "Well met, my friend."

Twenty weathered guards approached calmly, and the leader waved back to Verona. "The prince would like to see you, my Lord." His tone was half casual and half stern, but Aaron noticed a slight smile as if he'd had to collect Verona several times in the past.

"I am, of course, at the prince's service, but I must insist that my companions accompany us, for I have urgent news for his grace," Verona answered.

"Of course," the guard said. "After you, my Lord."

The crowds on the streets parted to allow them quick passage, and Aaron quickly lost track of where they were in the sea of city streets. One thing that stood out to him was how clean the streets were and how well kept the buildings. All the people he met were quite friendly, which was a change from the reserved receptions from the smaller towns. Not that the people from the smaller towns weren't friendly, but there was a general mistrust of strangers and a feeling of vulnerability. The realization made him appreciate his home more and more and demanded respect for how far people had come. How would the prince feel about the Elitesmen victimizing the people of the smaller towns, and would he be able to do anything about it?

The walls surrounding the palace grounds had been visible since they had entered the city, and as they got closer, their tallness became much more apparent. They were met at the gates by the palace guards, who took over as escort. The sight of the palace left Aaron's mouth hanging open at the sheer size and meticulous detail of the architecture down to the smallest window. It was not only a place of power, but of beauty as well, and Aaron couldn't help but feel a little intimidated as they got closer.

A steward came to collect them and escorted them through the palace. They didn't need an armed escort because there were guards everywhere Aaron looked, and they were hardly prisoners. The steward brought them to the great hall, which was a cavernous room filled with floor-to-ceiling windows that gave a beautiful view of the palace grounds. Once again, the sheer wealth of the place continued to impress upon him whom he was meeting.

The prince glanced up as they approached and raised his bushy brow quizzically, then he returned his attention to the group of people already before him. A palace guard, of some rank judging by the adornment of his uniform, moved to stand between them and the prince surveying them. Verona spoke a few hushed words to the steward and the guard, but the guard seemed bothered by the sight of Aaron.

"Knight Lieutenant, I will vouch for him upon my honor," Verona said.

"With all due respect, my Lord, the safety of his grace is my responsibility, and I cannot have a stranger so heavily armed in his presence," the lieutenant replied.

"I'm sorry, is there a problem?" Aaron asked, coming next to Verona.

"Yes sir. I must request that you remove your weapons prior to meeting with his grace," the lieutenant answered.

"Why?" Aaron asked before Verona could interject.

The lieutenant narrowed his gaze pointedly before answering. "You represent a security risk to his grace. I must insist that you disarm yourself at once," he said, and grim-looking guards moved in to surround them.

"I see," Aaron said, nodding in understanding and pursing his lips. "I'm sorry, I cannot comply with your request. You see, as all the heavily armed guards here represent a clear security risk to myself and my companions, I would be remiss in my duty to them and myself if I were to let such a risk go unchecked," Aaron countered calmly, returning the knight lieutenant's gaze.

The guards surrounding them gripped the handles of their swords, ready to draw them upon the knight lieutenant's command.

"Come now, what is the hold up over there?" barked the prince from his throne behind them.

The lieutenant turned and bowed. "Your Grace, this man is refusing to disarm in your presence."

The prince's gaze shifted to them.

"Uncle, I will vouch for the quality of this man upon my honor. I humbly ask that you hear us out in your private chambers for I have a tale to tell that I believe you will find most interesting." Verona stopped as the prince held up his hand.

"Ah, my dear nephew Verona, as poetic as always," the prince said with half a smile that vanished instantly when he looked directly upon Aaron. The prince had a hard look to him with his graying beard, like a person who commanded respect. Much like his grandfather Reymius's presence commanded the respect of those around him. "Who are you, sir, that inspires such poetry from my nephew's lips?"

Aaron felt his mouth go dry as he gazed back into the eyes of the prince. "I am Aaron Jace—"

"Uncle, I must insist that we discuss this matter in private," Verona stated again.

The prince's eyes searched the faces of the men standing with Aaron. "Vaughn, I see you've been looking after my nephew these past few weeks. It's good to see you, sir."

"Likewise, your Grace," Vaughn replied. "But I must agree with Verona upon the urgency of the matters we need to discuss with you."

"I see," the prince said. "Yes, it must be of grave importance for you to have returned so quickly after my guards chased most of you out of the city upon your last visit. Don't think for a second I've forgotten about that little stunt, Verona."

Sarik would not stop looking at the floor, his ears red. Eric and Braden calmly surveyed the room. Vaughn and Garret simply nodded, but before Verona could speak, Aaron stepped forward.

"Colind of the Guardians bid me to seek out your council, sir. Please, if I may have a few moments of your time. I've travelled a long way to get here," Aaron said.

The prince looked at Aaron, considering. "You look quite familiar to me. Have I met your father perchance?" he asked.

"I'm quite certain you've never met my father, but you knew my grandfather, Reymius Alenzar'seth," Aaron said.

The prince's gray eyes hardened as he rose from his seat, taking a few steps to stand before Aaron. "That's a bold claim or a fool's claim," he said quietly.

Aaron calmly met the prince's gaze. "The situation calls for both at times, but I assure you Reymius was my grandfather." He had come this far because Colind's last words were that Prince Cyrus could help him get to Shandara. He must journey to Shandara to free Colind from his prison. He needed Colind's help to avenge his family, or he would continue to be hunted—or worse.

The prince studied Aaron for a few moments. "Okay, Verona, we shall do as you requested and retire to my private chambers." He glanced back at the steward. "Please have some food brought up, as I suspect we will be talking for a long time."

The steward bowed and left the great hall. The rest of them followed the prince through a doorway off to the right and entered a smaller room.

They spoke at length, with Verona and Aaron taking turns recounting the events since they had met. The prince was particularly interested in Aaron's home and where Reymius had been for the past twenty-five years, but Aaron could tell he was doubtful. Even showing the medallion and tattoo did little to sway the mind of the prince.

"Surely you must know something about why Reymius left? How he left and why he stayed away?" Prince Cyrus asked.

"I'm sorry, I don't know why he left. Maybe he couldn't get back. My mother's memories were gone, and only bits and pieces returned after he died. All he left me was..." Aaron paused. He had almost forgotten and cursed himself for not remembering sooner. "Would you recognize Reymius's signature if you saw it?" Aaron asked.

The prince waited a few moments, pacing the room, then turned to Aaron. "I believe so, but I can go further than that. I have documents in my possession that bear his signature," the prince said, smiling, and then asked, "You mentioned your mother—is she here?"

Aaron felt like he was punched in the stomach and slowly shook his head. "She died."

The prince's eyes softened. "I'm very sorry for your loss."

Aaron dug into his pack and took out the letter his grandfather had left for him. The letter was folded and worn because he had constantly reread it hoping to glean more information. He carefully opened the letter and passed it to the prince, who took it gently and looked at it intently. After a few moments, he looked up at Aaron.

"You seem like a genuine person, Aaron. I realize this could not have been easy for you. There is a close likeness in this signature," the prince said, and he held up his hand before Verona could interject. "Enough for me to have my scribes pull the documents I mentioned before from the archives so we can compare. However, this will take some time, and I must insist you remain as a guest and attend the celebration this evening." The prince handed Aaron's letter back to him and requested that Verona stay behind a moment.

Aaron nodded, and an agreement was made to speak more tomorrow. They all left the room except for Verona and Vaughn. The prince took a long swallow from his goblet of wine and regarded Verona.

"Do you realize what you're getting yourself into, Verona?" the prince asked. "His likeness to the house of Alenzar'seth is remarkable to say the least. His stance, the way he speaks, all remind me of Reymius when we were young, but I also see Carlowen in him," the prince said with a pained expression.

"Then why don't you believe that he is who he says he is, Uncle?" Verona asked. "Why won't you acknowledge the truth before your eyes? He is a good man, and he is in need of our aid. He challenges the might of the Elite."

"Because if this is true, it will mean war," the prince said in a hardened tone. "War with the High King and the Council of the Elite. Not to mention Mactar the Dark Light Master and his twisted, evil ways. If what Aaron says is true and he is of the house of Alenzar'seth, then he will be the herald of death for many. War of the likes we've never seen."

"My Lord," Vaughn began, "the Alenzar'seth protected the lands of Safanar from shadow for generations. If they are in need of aid, then we should give it to them. They are owed at least that much, regardless of the circumstances surrounding the fall of Shandara."

"I understand what you are saying, Vaughn, but the repercussions of this will be felt by all. Some would argue that it's the Alenzar'seths' failure that cursed the kingdom of Shandara in the first place. I'm not saying I do, but we all need to tread carefully, for this is a slippery slope to be upon."

Verona stood up. "Uncle, I respect your counsel, but I have given Aaron my word. I will see this through with him to the end, wherever that may take us. Right is right. Who are we if we are not men of honor? No better than the High King, the Council, or the dreaded Dark Light Master," he finished quietly, and then he left the room.

The prince was silent for a few moments, deep in thought. "That boy can certainly find trouble wherever he goes. Verona is an idealist. Who will stand with us should we choose to go down this road?"

"Cyrus," Vaughn said gently. He called the prince by his name in private, for they had been friends for a long time. "I've watched over Verona as you've asked. He is a man trying to live up to his principles, much like Aaron. While Aaron may have had a darker time of it recently, or so I gleaned from my charge, it sounds as though he was perfectly happy until Reymius's passing, which leads me to believe that he was safe. Carlowen was safe, and Cassandra's sacrifice was not in vain. Perhaps when the night is darkest, it's the idealists of the world that can light our way and bring others to our cause. It is something to consider." With those words, Vaughn quietly left the prince to his thoughts and the memories he'd helped dredge up from a distant past.

Aaron shook his head, feeling a little frustrated. On some level, he understood the prince's caution because he had literally shown up on the prince's doorstep with this fantastical story. It had all happened to him, and he was still struggling to believe it sometimes. They were being escorted to a suite of rooms for their use, and Aaron found himself walking quietly next to Garret.

"Patience, Aaron. This is a lot to digest for the prince," Garret said. "Your grandfather and the prince were close friends in their youth, and he mourned the loss of your family for a long time. The events surrounding the collapse of Shandara are shrouded in mystery, leaving the most ancient and bright spots of Safanar in darkness," Garret said, placing a gentle hand on Aaron's shoulder.

"I guess I understand," Aaron answered. "But we may not have the luxury of time. I feel that everywhere I go, I place people in danger. If we linger here too long, then something...anything is going to happen," Aaron said with his teeth clenching. He had to keep moving, and yet he was so tired.

"Again, patience. Rest. I'm sure you know the importance of a clear mind when it comes to making decisions. The baths are this way, and I will see that a fresh set of clothes is made available to you," Garret said.

Aaron thanked Garret and grew excited at the thought of being clean and actually sleeping in a bed.

19

A DANCE

The baths were pure joy, and a surprising amount of dirt was left in the pool-sized marble tub. A pretty young girl brought towels and the clothes Garret had promised. Aaron blushed a little at the offer to wash his back, which he politely refused. He did, however, note her slight pause and lingering stare at the dragon tattoo on his chest. Eric poked his head in the door and asked if there was anything he needed, to which Aaron replied something about privacy. Either Eric or Braden was always outside his door. Neither had left his side since entering the palace. When he asked why they were outside his room, they politely smiled and said this was their place. If the room he was in was considered a "guest" room, Aaron wondered what the rest of the palace looked like. The room was cavernous, with tall ceilings, windows with laurel carvings of simple elegance, and a four-poster, king-sized bed. The soft mattress seemed to swallow him up. He fell asleep the moment his head rested upon the pillow.

Later on he woke to a soft knock at the door and noticed the sun was setting.

"Well rested?" Verona asked. He had taken time to clean up as well.

"Very much so. What did the prince want to speak with you about after we left?"

"You," Verona said and chuckled. "You made quite an impression upon him." Verona took in their lavish surroundings. "They don't give these rooms to just any guest. Regardless, I think he wants to believe but is afraid of what it will mean. The world has been limping along since the fall of Shandara. The Council of the Elite and the High King have remained unchecked for far too long. But," Verona said, holding up his hand before Aaron could say something, "they are but a smaller part of a much bigger problem. The Ryakuls aren't the only beasts of shadow to roam the lands, and it is believed by some that they are coming from somewhere within the land of Shandara."

"I'm no prince or king. I am one man. One man cannot keep nations in balance."

"I apologize if I gave that impression. I didn't mean to imply that this falls upon your shoulders. I simply meant that the time for these tyrants is at an end. People will rally behind you because of who you are, regardless of how you view yourself," Verona said.

Rally behind him? Who did they think he was? A few months ago, he was a kid finishing his last year of college.

"Verona, I'm not sure what to say. I came here because I am being hunted and Colind appears to be the only one with the knowledge to help. He is imprisoned in Shandara, and I need to find a way to free him so I can stop those who are trying to kill me. I know nothing of the politics in this world. The High King, Council of the Elite, and this Mactar meant nothing to me until a few days ago." He tried to keep the bitterness from his voice at the mention of the Elite and Mactar. Circles within circles. How far would this journey pull him in?

Verona smiled reassuringly. "I know this is all foreign to you, but it's important that you realize the impact the return of the Alenzar'seth will have on Safanar. Enough of this talk. There is a celebration to attend, and it will be something to behold, even if no one knows that a person in attendance is of the house they are honoring," Verona said with a wink and ushered Aaron out the door.

The clothes he wore were quite comfortable. Brown pants and a midnight-blue shirt that felt light and flexible upon his skin. They walked the corridors of the palace, and Verona joked with Eric and Braden, whom he nicknamed Aaron's Shadows, and for the briefest of moments Aaron wondered how Zeus was doing. He hadn't seen him since before entering the city, but he had no doubt that he wasn't far from him now.

Glowing orbs lit the corridors that led to the great hall, which was awash with light and color reflecting off chandeliers hanging from the ceiling. Giant doors more than twice the size of a man were open to the gardens, where more orbs hung in the air, lighting the party grounds along with the setting sun. The city was alight with color, as the feast extended beyond the palace walls. He had left his swords and staff in his room, but he still had a few throwing knives placed around his person. It never hurt to be prepared. The great hall was lavishly decorated with fresh flowers hung along the walls and tables. Brightly colored banners were arrayed along the way with some depicting the Alenzar'seth coat of arms. The flag of Shandara, he thought, and rubbed the medallion that rested coolly against his chest.

With a few men in his wake, Sarik joined them from among the sea of people who filled the Great Hall and the pavilion set up outside the gardens. While Verona was greeting the men, Aaron seized the opportunity to leave them behind. Aaron went outside to walk among the people, and some nodded in friendly greeting as he passed by. A group of musicians played a gentle tune near a large fountain of the Goddess that matched the one where they had camped a few nights ago. Glowing orbs from within the fountain left the place awash in shimmering light. He wondered how the orbs gave off light because he didn't see any electrical cords to power them. Now that he thought of it, he didn't see any form of electricity here. There were some accoutrements of a modern civilization, like plumbing and those glowing orbs, yet they still used the sword and spear.

He looked around taking in the faces of the people around him and stopped upon a stunningly beautiful woman. Her blue eyes and full cheekbones were unmistakable, for he had seen them before under a hood in a small town. Their eyes locked, his chest tightened, and blood rushed to his face. She had been like a dream on the edge of his thoughts that would disappear if he dared look too closely. The rest of the world around them faded away as he took a step toward her. Her golden-blonde hair was swept up away from her neck, and her eyes calmly searched his, almost challenging him in a way. She wore a gown of deep-sea blue that clung to her form and was both simple and elegant, putting her worlds beyond any girl he had ever seen in his life. The moments ran like quicksand, and his breath quickened as he stepped closer. She held something small in her hand that she kept casually by her side. Aaron silently prayed it wasn't one of those travel crystals.

"Hello," Aaron said, and she regarded him silently for a moment before her lips curved into a small smile. "I've seen you before."

"I've been watching you," she said. They were alone amid a crowd of people, and Aaron couldn't get any words to come out of his mouth. "You have kind eyes," she said, her fingers toying with whatever was in her hand.

Aaron smiled and held out his hand. "Would you like to dance?"

The question slipped out of his mouth without any forethought. She seemed as surprised by the question as he was and stared at his extended hand. Whatever she had been holding was gone when she gently placed her smooth hand in his. The musicians began a song with a slow tempo, for which Aaron was grateful because he only knew one type of dance. His mother had drilled the waltz into him in preparation for his sister's wedding. He placed his right hand on her hip and guided her into the simple elegance of the waltz. After a few moments, he stopped counting the steps in his head. She picked it up quickly, and couples in the area followed their lead. They smiled at one another in the gentle spin as the rest of the world faded away to gray.

"You are not at all what I expected," she said.

"What is it that you expected?" Aaron asked.

"I don't know," she admitted and let out a small laugh.

"I'm Aaron," he said.

"Sarah. It's nice to meet you, Aaron," she replied with a dazzling smile that made his heart melt.

"Sarah," he said, savoring her name in his mouth. "Why have you been watching me?" He asked the question hoping she wouldn't disappear with that cursed travel crystal.

"I want to know more about you," she said. "You've become a person of great interest, even if the people here don't realize it yet. Your actions at the town are even now circulating among powerful people."

Aaron frowned. "Who are you, Sarah?"

"I could ask the same of you, Aaron," was her retort. There was no harshness in her tone, just a determination to stay on equal footing.

"What would you like to know?" Aaron countered.

If she was surprised by such a direct question, she didn't let on.

"Where do you come from?" Sarah asked.

"I'm sure you've never heard of it," Aaron answered. "Earth," he said. He'd never thought he would answer a question quite that way in his life.

"You're right. I haven't heard of it."

"Well?" Aaron asked.

"Yes?" Sarah said with her blue eyes twinkling.

"Where are you from?" Aaron asked.

"Oh, I'm sure you've never heard of it either," Sarah said, her eyes alight with humor. The song ended, and they stood facing each other, but Aaron wouldn't break the silence. He just looked at her expectantly. "Khamearra," she said at last.

"Never heard of it," he said, smiling. "But I assure you, I'm not that interesting."

What am I doing? Aaron thought. He should walk away right now, but he couldn't, and for the first time in a long time, there was no darkness in his heart. The overwhelming desire to keep running was banished as he gazed into Sarah's beautiful blue eyes. They walked, slowly weaving their way through the gardens.

"On the contrary, Aaron, I think you're the most interesting person here. Do you make it a habit to humble Elitesmen wherever you go?" Sarah asked.

"Someone should," Aaron said.

"I'm sure you realize that they will be hunting you even now," Sarah said. "Even here."

He was pleased to hear the concern in her voice, as it was the first indication that she felt one way or another about him. As far as the Elitesmen were concerned, they could stand in line to hunt him.

"They aren't the first," he replied.

They walked in silence, making their way back to the fountain. His heart was at war with itself. He was cursing himself a fool for indulging in this fantasy, for he knew this was something that could never be, whoever Sarah truly was. Yet there was a part of him that defiantly clung to this moment.

"Perhaps with the right help, you'll be able to outrun them all," Sarah said.

"Are you offering?" he asked. After a slight pause, he said, "Well, I don't plan on making it easy for anyone. Perhaps now you can tell me something about yourself, since you seem to know an awful lot about me."

Sarah sighed and looked back at him. He saw uncertainty in her beautiful eyes, and he wanted nothing more than to hold her in his arms and feel the press of her lips upon his. Unless he was an utter fool, he saw a similar desire in her eyes. What was she hiding?

"Maybe another time then," Aaron said after a few moments, hiding his disappointment, but she wasn't fooled.

"I'm sorry," she said at last, pushing a rebellious strand of hair away from her face and taking a step closer to him. "It appears we both have secrets that bind us."

"A harsh prison should we choose to stay within its walls. Do these secrets hold power over us, or we them?"

"All things in time," Sarah said, gazing up into his eyes.

They stood there amid the shimmering golden lights by the fountain. Aaron reached out to Sarah's hand. They stood inches apart from each other, their eyes speaking the words that their mouths refused to say. He leaned in, their lips met, and his heart thundered in his chest. Sometimes a kiss spoke volumes. His thoughts became lost in the alluring embrace of her mouth upon his. Then he heard Verona call his name as he walked around the fountain. Aaron pulled away reluctantly from Sarah, each sharing a small smile with the other. He turned to his friend and was alarmed at seeing sheer shock in Verona's eyes—not directed at him, but at Sarah. Aaron turned back to Sarah as her hand left his arm. She whispered that she was sorry, and then she disappeared before his very eyes.

"It can't be," Verona said in disbelief, with Eric and Braden standing at his shoulders and Sarik bringing up the rear.

"It can't be what?" Aaron asked quickly.

"Unless my eyes have failed me, my friend, you were just kissing the daughter of the High King Amorak of Khamearra. Also, head of the Elitesman Council of Masters. All rulers in our corner of the world are forced to swear fealty and pay homage to his kingdom," Verona said.

Aaron was stunned. "She was the woman I saw as we left the town. She told me her name was Sarah and that her home was in Khamearra," Aaron said. "She wouldn't tell me much." But her kiss told him enough.

Verona nodded. "Did you tell her who you are?" he asked. Aaron shook his head, and Verona sighed, clearly relieved. "Shandara was the kingdom that balanced the power, keeping the High King in check. In essence, you were kissing the daughter of your worst enemy. One of those directly responsible for the fall of Shandara."

Aaron had to steady his breath, allowing his mind to catch up. The daughter of his enemy? Was the High King the one pulling Tarimus's strings?

"She wasn't trying to hurt me," he said.

"That much is obvious," Verona chided, smiling broadly and glancing at Eric and Braden, who laughed in earnest. "I turn my back for a few minutes," he said to them, shaking his head. "Come, Aaron, we should take our ease this night. There is a cask of Rexelian ale that has our name on it," Verona said, patting him on the shoulder.

"She has one of those travel crystals. I think she was feeling me out for information," Aaron said. "Oh, would you stop," he said when they erupted in another bout of laughter. "It felt more like I was being interviewed. Weighed and measured." And with that, the rest of them started laughing so uncontrollably that he had no choice but to join in.

"Well, if that's true, I wish more beautiful princesses would interview me," Braden said, chuckling.

As they walked away, Aaron kept glancing back at the spot where Sarah vanished, hoping that she would return, but she didn't. They found a table and began drinking and telling stories into the night. There were many toasts given in honor of Shandara, to which Verona would give Aaron a nod and a wink. Those who knew who he was would raise their glasses in his direction much to the ignorance of the crowd. There was a single mournful toast of silence for the fall of the house Alenzar'seth, which felt surreal to Aaron. The celebration in its entirety stopped, and silence set in. After a few minutes, the celebration picked back up, but Aaron couldn't help but wonder what his ancestors had done to warrant such respect. Throughout the remainder of the night, Aaron's thoughts returned to Sarah and the way she looked at him with those blue eyes. He found himself remembering the soft curve of her full lips on his and wondered if he would ever see her again. What would he say to her if he did? Daughter of the High King.

THE NEXT MORNING, AARON GATHERED HIS BELONGINGS AND STUFFED them in his pack. He grabbed his cloak, staff, and swords and exited the room to find Sarik waiting outside his door.

"Good morning," Aaron said.

"Morning," Sarik replied. "I'd like to start training today."

There was such enthusiasm in Sarik's eyes, and Aaron hoped he wouldn't disappoint him.

"Good. Me too. Do they have a place that we could use?" Aaron asked. In a place this big, how could they not.

Sarik smiled, clearly excited. "Oh yes. There is an entire courtyard devoted to the martial arts that the guards and guests can use to exercise."

Aaron's stomach let out a loud growl. He was famished. "Breakfast?"

Sarik nodded.

"Lead the way."

Sarik led him through the palace to the kitchens, where they were able to get some food, and then they ate in one of the smaller dining halls. They were soon joined by the rest of the crew.

"Aaron has agreed to start training us today," Sarik said excitedly to the others, who, to Aaron's surprise, looked pleased by this news.

"As I said, I've never trained anyone before, but I'll do my best to pass on the knowledge that my grandfather instilled in me," Aaron said evenly. They all nodded, including Verona, and finished their food.

They soon came to the training grounds, which were easily the size of two football fields. The racks of practice weapons along the walls reminded Aaron of the sparring room back home, only on a much grander scale. There was a section of practice dummies, stumps for uneven footing, walls for climbing, and much more. Prince Cyrus took the conditioning of his soldiers seriously. There were a few groups already there, so Aaron's group walked over to a clear spot for general training and were joined by Vaughn, who looked at Aaron's backpack and said, "Are you going somewhere?"

"Doesn't hurt to be prepared," Aaron said. "Regardless of what is found in the prince's archives, I will be leaving soon."

Vaughn looked the most surprised by this. "I'm sorry. I didn't realize you meant to leave so quickly. I think it's only fair that the prince is aware of your intentions."

"I would appreciate it if you could tell him," Aaron said earnestly. "I mean no disrespect to him, and I am grateful for his hospitality, but I can't afford to loiter anywhere for very long until we find Colind. My presence here puts everyone at risk, and I won't risk the lives of innocent people."

Verona stood between them. "I'm ready when you are, but I urge you to be patient. I suspect we haven't learned all that we could to aid us in our journey."

"Thank you, Verona," Aaron said and then turned to address the rest of the group. "I appreciate all of your help in getting me this far, but I urge you to consider carefully before deciding to come on this journey to Shandara. While I am of the house Alenzar'seth, I am not Reymius," he said, looking at them each in turn. What he saw staring back at him were men resolute of purpose. They really were going to come with him.

"You'd think he was trying to get rid of us," Braden said, glancing at his brother.

"It's okay, Aaron," Garret said. "We're well aware of the dangers, probably more so than you, but we appreciate you giving us the opportunity to leave with our heads held high."

"Now, are we going to stand here talking or train?" Eric asked.

Aaron surrendered; Garret was right. They had more knowledge of what awaited them than he did, but he'd needed to say what he did. He hoped this journey would not end with some or even all of them dead.

"Okay, let's line up," Aaron said, and they warmed up, loosening their muscles as Aaron began with some of the slower forms.

"The most important rule when doing any of these forms is to not think beyond the next move. Push all thoughts away. Breath and body must become one. Even the most basic of moves is worthy of all your attention," Aaron said, pacing up and down the lines. "Each move leads to the next through the natural progression. These forms are used to strengthen your ability to focus your mind. Your mind is the most important weapon and the key for surviving an encounter with an Elitesman." Aaron stopped surveying them as a few passers-by stopped in their tracks at the mention of the Elitesmen.

"That is why you're here, right?" Aaron said. "The Elitesmen are shrouded in mystery, you've told me. Very skilled to be sure, but they are men just the same." They stared back at him, and Aaron could tell they were not convinced.

"Men!" Aaron barked. "Flesh and blood the same as you or I. Men with weaknesses just like you or I. No one"—he paused—"no one is infallible. Any strength can be used against an opponent. Eric and Sarik, come forward." He couldn't have picked men who were more on the opposite sides of the size spectrum. Sarik was all wiry and speed, while Eric was tall, heavily muscled, and strong as an ox.

"A focused mind will measure your opponent in moments and unravel the pattern of their attack so that you can press your own. Or leave. What is more important? The goal you are working toward or victory over the man who stands in your way? Sometimes a way past is all that is required. Sarik is wiry and quick and will use his speed to his advantage at every opportunity, as well he should. Eric is very strong and will swing whatever weapon he holds with mighty force. Each has their place, and it takes a focused mind to survive the encounter." Aaron gestured to Sarik and Eric to return to the line. "As we travel, we will explore the different fighting forms and their applications toward not only self-preservation but the protection of others. Perhaps you may find yourself facing an opponent that you do not wish to harm," Aaron said, and a vision of Bronwyn with the dead-black eyes of Tarimus stared back at him. He swallowed hard. "Believe me, it's not as outlandish as it sounds."

"What happens when we face someone who is more skilled than us?" Sarik asked.

"I'm glad you said when and not if. Return to the basics. Focus and be in the moment; that is the foundation upon which you must build," Aaron said. "There will always be someone who is quicker, stronger, and more experienced out there in the world. Do not let fear or anger overwhelm you. Those are weapons that can cut as deeply as the sharpest sword or knife."

The next few hours were filled with practice and sparring. Aaron was surprised by how much he had to teach. It was like everything that Reymius had ever taught him was there in the back of his mind, eager to be shared. While he couldn't forget where he was given the grandeur of the training yard, he couldn't help but think of the hours spent in the sparring room at his grandfather's house.

The training yard had steadily filled, and as the time passed, they had gathered an audience. Most notable was a boy who couldn't have been more than seventeen years of age, dressed in clothes a bit too fine for the training yard. His companions were two rather large bodyguards that looked to be Eric and Braden's cousins. The boy's expression was of someone who smelled something foul under his nose. When he wasn't watching them and making hushed comments to his companions, he spared a few venomous looks at Verona, which made Aaron wonder what history was there.

Aaron picked up the rune-carved staff. "Let's talk about weapons for a few minutes. Sometimes the simplest of weapons are the most effective. Expensive swords or flashy axes or anything with a lot of finery can be overly complex and come with as many disadvantages as the advantages they offer in combat. A staff is the most common weapon available to anyone and is one all should have a cursory knowledge of."

The boy laughed. "A common weapon for common folk will not stand against a trained swordsman." The boy sneered, drawing everyone's attention and more than a few raised eyebrows.

Aaron smiled patiently at the boy. "A weapon is only limited to the hand that wields it. A farmer with a stick defending his home will most certainly fight harder than any hired soldier."

"A trained swordsman is more than a match for any commoner with a stick," the boy replied.

"I see," Aaron said mildly. "Are you such a trained swordsman? Do you have a name?"

One of the bodyguards stepped boldly forward. "You have the honor of addressing His Exalted Highness, Prince Jopher Zamaridian."

"Would you be willing to put your theory to the test?" Aaron asked, never taking his eyes off the prince.

"You will address his highness by his proper title, Prince Jopher Zamaridian," the guard said harshly, placing his hand on his sword, and Aaron noticed Eric and Braden shift their position.

Aaron kept his gaze upon the boy prince, waiting for an answer. He would be damned if he was going to address this boy by any "proper" title.

After a few moments, the boy held up his hand to the guard. "It's okay. We are guests. I have no issue with putting my theory, as you say, to the test."

"Good, since I am neither a lord nor a prince or a king, I guess I'm as common as they come. Would you care to match your sword against my staff?" Aaron asked and noticed Verona shifting his feet. He would not claim any such title, regardless of his lineage.

The guard was about to protest, but the prince held up his hand, and he reluctantly fell silent.

"A friendly exhibition," Aaron said, and this time he looked at the bodyguard, who fixed him with a hard stare.

"Who will judge this friendly exhibition?" the boy prince asked.

"I will," said a much older voice at the rear of the crowd. Prince Cyrus calmly walked to the front as people made way. "I trust that will be sufficient for you, my Lord," the prince said, addressing the boy with a slight bow.

"Of course, your Grace. I appreciate your taking the time out of your day for this business," the boy said with a respectful bow.

"I think it will be truly enlightening," Prince Cyrus answered, inclining his head. He nodded to Aaron, and he and the boy took up positions facing each other.

While Jopher's sword was indeed flashy, the boy held it as one at home with the blade. When the prince signaled, the boy unleashed a barrage of attacks meant to overwhelm an opponent. Aaron allowed the boy to come at him, giving ground until he sidestepped and gave the princeling a good kick in the backside, which sent him tumbling forward.

Aaron ignored the snickers from the crowd and calmly waited for the boy to gain his bearings. Jopher attacked again, his moves more precise and calculated. Aaron blocked and parried each attack, guiding the boy around in a circle, but he kept coming. The boy was strong, and he was skillful with the sword, at least in that he wasn't mistaken, but his fighting was composed of his arrogance and therefore revealed his weakness. Aaron quickly stepped inside the boy's attack and swept his feet out from under him with his staff. He brought the point of the staff to rest upon the boy's chest.

"Had enough?" Aaron asked calmly.

The boy spat, signaling to his bodyguards. Aaron was waiting for this, but he had hoped the boy had some shred of honor. The two bodyguards charged at the same time, and Aaron moved fluidly against them with a leopard's grace. The whirl of the rune-carved staff humming through the air could be heard as he dealt decisive blows to the bodyguards, sending them sprawling. Aaron spun in time for the boy's attack. Blade met staff only once before Aaron disarmed the boy prince. He swept his feet from under him again with much more force than the first time and planted the end of the staff none too gently upon the boy's chest. Aaron took a quick glance behind him and was relieved to see that Eric and Braden held the bodyguards in place.

"Only a person without integrity dishonors the circle," Aaron said coldly.

The boy feebly struggled to rise, but Aaron held him down.

"You stay there," Aaron said. "Princes and kings can be born, boy, but only men can be made."

Aaron released the boy, who slowly got up rubbing his chest. Eric and Braden released the bodyguards at the same moment. They eyed Aaron as if weighing whether they should seek retribution, but instead came to the boy's aid, guiding him away.

20

COUNCIL OF COMPLACENCY

Sarah needed to think. Aaron's almond-colored eyes flashed in her mind. So enticing. So...sincere. There'd been a few moments where she'd felt like she would tell him anything he wanted to know. And when they'd danced, it was as if they were the only two people in the world. She felt heat rush to her face and chastised herself.

Most of the men in her life had political motives and would only see her as the daughter of High King Amorak. Not all the men in her life had been bad though; some were good friends, but none had made her feel like her heart would race out of her chest. The few brief times she had seen Aaron, he had threatened to suck her into his wake. Even now she wouldn't mind being swept away. She hoped things wouldn't change when he learned who she was. Her thoughts drifted to the small town where he'd revealed he was a descendant of the house of Alenzar'seth, the Lords of Shandara, who were, by her father's account, the sworn enemies of Khamearra.

She wanted to be at his side and found her hand straying to the travel crystal she kept. She snatched it back, knowing that the crystal needed to be recharged. The more sensible part of her warned of the grave danger that would be certain to come by involving herself with Aaron. Would he even accept her once he learned who she was? She had always stood apart from her family, with her three half-brothers always plotting her demise and her mother long dead from an incurable illness. Her father had little time for the daughter he had never wanted in the first place, and when he'd remarried, she was all but forgotten. Sarah brushed those old hurtful thoughts aside. She had felt the change in the air when the ground shook and had almost exhausted her travel crystal tracking him. It was difficult to believe that Aaron was of the house Alenzar'seth. They were an ancient family aligned with the Hythariam people, who themselves were another matter entirely. The voices in the council chambers droned on as they discussed the very person who occupied her thoughts so much of late. She was in a private alcove where she would normally be able to observe without notice, but she sensed someone close by.

"My dear sister, what is the occasion for such a visit?" her half-brother Primus said behind her.

"Primus, how predictable to find you scurrying about," Sarah said. She loathed all of her half-brothers. They were malicious and cruel as boys and only showed signs of growing more evil and power hungry the older they got. Tye was the youngest of the three, with Primus and Rordan being twins.

"Indeed. I myself was on my way to the council when I noticed someone here, and Rordan is already in there. Perhaps I will stay here and spy...excuse me, casually observe from here," Primus sneered.

"Go to hell, Primus. Leave now before you embarrass yourself," Sarah said, brandishing a throwing knife that danced fluidly between her fingers.

"Tisk. Tisk. Such language is unbecoming for *a princess,* even one cast aside and not much more than a brooding mare at that. I'll be sure to send Father your regards," he said, retreating through the doorway.

Sarah took a few moments to calm down, because she really wanted to throw the knife. While she was above such cowardly acts, she knew her brothers were not, and she'd had to keep a watchful eye for as long as she could remember.

Just leave.

She had thought of it before. To just up and leave and never return, but that was before Beck had elected to train her. Beck was an Elitesman, one of the oldest of the order and from a time when it truly was something of which to be proud. Not like it was now. She knew how the Elitesmen were feared, and for good reason—they were among the deadliest warriors of Safanar. Beck would train her at night, away from prying eyes. He trained her in the old ways, from when the order was a sect founded by the Shandarian masters. Now most of the order was power hungry and tyrannical to all those who were not their superiors. Although her father was High King, he was just a member of the Council of Masters, but his word carried much weight. When her mother died, her father changed. She was swept to the side and was all but cast out, except for the occasions where her father was inclined to show her off like some broodmare. She was no man's property, even if that man was the High King. At the age of fourteen, she withdrew to the sidelines and was watched over by Beck at a minor holding outside the capital of Khamearra. That was seven years ago. She once asked Beck why he took care of her, and his only answer was to honor her mother. She never fully understood what that meant, and Beck, being a man of few words, had never explained. She returned her attention to the men in the council when she heard the silky voice of the Dark Light Master himself speaking.

"You have more to add to these proceedings, Mactar," Elite Master Gerric said.

"Indeed, I do. You must acknowledge the evidence points to the return of the Alenzar'seth to Safanar," Mactar said, striding around the room.

"We will be sending a small contingent of Elitesmen to investigate this man and bring him before this council," Gerric answered, his deep voice carrying throughout the chamber.

"A small contingent, you say," Mactar said with raised eyebrows. "Considering what he's done with previous Elitesmen unfortunate enough to cross his path, perhaps the contingent should include a few masters."

"As always, your council is very much appreciated," Gerric began, but Mactar cut him off.

"Underestimate this man at your own peril," Mactar said, his gaze sweeping the chamber.

Gerric clenched his teeth. "This matter is finished. The contingent is already underway, and from our reports there are few places where he could be heading."

Mactar surveyed the council room. The High King was absent, but his son Rordan was in attendance, and the other masters were so blinded by their arrogance that he almost felt sorry for them...almost, but the trap wasn't quite set...yet.

"One more thing if I may. I have another matter to bring forth to this council." When Gerric and the other masters nodded in succession for him to continue, he took a moment and let the silence hang in the air. "The Drake has awoken," he said simply.

Pandemonium.

Mactar waited patiently for Gerric to restore order, but it was long in coming. "It has been reported being seen south of the midland mountains toward Rexel."

Now they will believe, Mactar thought.

"The line of Alenzar'seth is dead. They have been hunted down and dealt with. Reymius is gone," Gerric said, echoing the others. "And..."

"The Drake will not awaken unless the Alenzar'seth has returned to Safanar," Mactar finished. "The keys to Shandara are once again within our grasp, and it appears that the death of Reymius was gravely overrated."

Sarah's breath caught in her chest. The Drake, a demon brought forth when Shandara fell. It had hunted all of the Alenzar'seth down, with one exception it seemed. None of the mighty house could stand against the beast. Reymius had escaped, but where had he gone? Shandara was a place beyond dangerous, and with that thought, she knew that was where Aaron would go. She rose quickly and left the room, leaving the trailing voices of the council behind her. She had to warn Aaron of the danger he was in. Sarah swept down the halls of the palace to gather what supplies she needed, all the while hoping she would get there in time.

21

ESCAPE

"Well, that was an interesting lesson," Verona said, walking with Aaron. "I think you will prove to be a very effective teacher, my friend."

"Thanks. Jopher appeared to know you."

"Indeed. I knew his older brother, whom I had the privilege of teaching one of your lessons to the last time I was in Rexel. Maybe it runs in the family," Verona said, smiling.

"Are all these nobles so arrogant?" Aaron asked, giving voice to his frustration.

"Not all of us," a voice answered behind them.

Aaron turned to see Vaughn and Prince Cyrus. The prince gave Aaron a half smile.

"I meant no offense," Aaron said, inclining his head respectfully. "Where I'm from, we believe all men to be created equal. The rule of law applies to any man, regardless of the assets he calls his own or the armies at his command."

Verona began coughing, and even Vaughn looked slightly alarmed, but quickly got hold of his features. The prince merely smiled, nodding to himself.

"A man's quality is often revealed through his actions and the things he says. In this brief time, I feel confident in saying that the heir of Alenzar'seth is indeed here before my eyes. It is a miracle that you stand before us," Prince Cyrus said. "Whatever aid I may give you on your journey, I will. Your grandfather was a very dear friend of mine, and I'm sad to hear of his passing, but happy to hear that he did find some peace in his life. Please walk with me a while and tell me about Reymius and your mother, Carlowen."

The tension drained from Aaron's shoulders. He told Prince Cyrus about his home, about his grandfather as he knew him, and about his mother and father. Speaking of them was bittersweet, because it reminded him of the home he had lost, but he was grateful for the life he still had.

They eventually made their way to the office of the prince. While the others took their leave, Verona and Vaughn stayed with them. The room was large with windows overlooking the gardens. The prince had lunch brought up, and when they finished eating, he signaled to his steward. The steward walked over carrying a tray with a few documents yellowed with age.

"There is something I would like to show you, Aaron," the prince said, selecting one of the rolls of parchment and unfurling it. "This was written by your grandfather," he said, waving Aaron over. "Please read this here."

Aaron came around the table and examined the parchment. The elegant and precise flow of the script was unmistakably his grandfather's handwriting, which itself was enough to get his attention, but what was written left him speechless. It was a letter to the prince from his grandfather. He turned to the prince, who smiled reassuringly, and Aaron read aloud.

Cyrus, my friend and brother in everything but blood. I urge you to consider what we have spoken about at length. If we are to lead and rule over men, women, and children, then the rule of law must protect them, regardless of home or hearth. The rule of law should be equally applicable, whether commoner or king. I know this is not desirable to those who rule through fear, but at some point we must unite against the tyrants of this land. I have written several volumes on the subject, which are here at the White Rose, that I would like to share with you on your next visit. Cassey believes I may be moving too quickly, but has grown to appreciate that the provinces of Shandara have people at the capital to represent them. This freedom has given birth to such innovation of the likes we haven't seen before. We don't need to rule over the people, but embrace and protect them. Let them be masters of their own destiny.

Your friend,
Reymius

The room was silent.

"Reymius sent me this letter a few weeks before the fall of Shandara. So you see it makes sense that he helped instill in you an appreciation of the law and the freedoms that can come with it. Sadly, I've never seen the volumes that contain the words of which Reymius spoke."

"Was this the reason for the fall of Shandara?" Aaron asked.

The prince shook his head. "There is a power in Shandara that the Alenzar'seth were the custodians of. But it was their innovation that arrayed many against them. They designed the first airships, for example. The concept of people having a say in how they are ruled had spread like wildfire, but has since been suppressed in most kingdoms. What do you intend to do, Aaron?"

The prince didn't exactly dodge the question, but Aaron knew he wasn't being told everything either. "I have no desire for power of any kind. I intend to go to

Shandara to seek out Colind. He is the only person who has the knowledge to help me. Even now, I am being hunted. Just me being here puts you all at risk."

They were interrupted by a commotion outside the door, followed by men shouting. Braden was closest, and with his hand on his knife, he opened the door. Zeus charged through and came to Aaron's side, his fur bristling.

"How did a wolf enter the palace?" the prince asked the steward, who stood panting at the door.

"We don't know, your Grace. One moment the hall was clear, and the next moment it was there," the steward said.

"He is with me," Aaron said. "We must leave. Danger is coming. That's the only reason why Zeus came here from the forests outside the city."

Verona turned to the Prince. "Uncle, please allow us the use of one of your airships. It can't have taken the Elitesmen long to figure out where we were heading."

"But the Elitesmen wouldn't dare travel here." The prince looked up in surprise and then motioned for the guard. "Send out word, and ready the Raven for immediate departure." The guard saluted and quickly left the room. "Gather what supplies you need and meet me at the airfield."

The prince told Verona that he would guide Aaron to the airfield himself.

"Aaron, I wanted to speak to you without the others around," the prince said, and Aaron nodded for him to continue. The prince took a quick glance at Zeus, gathering his thoughts. "I get the feeling that you haven't told us everything," he began. "I'm not saying you've been less than truthful, but I've been a prince for a long time. Long enough to know when someone isn't telling me everything." The prince looked Aaron straight in the eye. "Now, Colind sent you to me because he believed I could provide you with some help, which I fully intend to give, but I also believe that his purpose was twofold. He also wanted me to know that the Alenzar'seth have returned to Safanar. In order for me to really help, I need to know more. Who else besides the Elitesmen Order is hunting you?"

Aaron swallowed, considering how best to answer the prince. "Reymius didn't flee to some distant land on this world. He found a gateway to another world entirely. When he died, the gateway was opened once again, and something evil began to attack me. Tarimus."

"Colind's son!"

"Yes, but he is now enslaved to someone named Mactar," Aaron answered.

For the first time, the prince looked frightened, taking a quick look around them. Then he hardened himself and gripped Aaron's shoulders tightly. "Tread carefully. There is a reason so many fear the Dark Light Master. While you are journeying to Shandara, I will send out word to those who would stand with you, but there is one group that I cannot reach. It must be you who finds them, for they will be powerful allies and will be able to help you against Mactar and the Order of the Elite."

"Who are they?" Aaron asked.

"The Hythariam. They are another race of beings that withdrew from the world of men when Shandara fell. They live upon the edges of the wild, beyond the northern borders of Shandara," the prince said.

"How am I supposed to find them?" Aaron asked.

"I suspect that they will try to find you, and I believe that although they have withdrawn from the world, they are always watching," the prince answered. He quickened his step. Aaron lost track of how many corridors they walked and the different turns they took. At times, he suspected they were underground. When they emerged at the airfield, the sight of the airship made Aaron's mouth drop.

The ship hovered a few feet above the ground, painted black with two silver-and-blue stripes running the length of the ship. Most of the ship was some type of metal with polished wood furnishings. They were joined by Sarik and Garret, who also stood in silent awe of the airship. Verona was already on board with Eric and Braden.

"I never thought I'd get to ride in an airship like that," Sarik exclaimed, rushing forward to get on board with Garret close behind.

A grizzled bear of a man in a silver-and-blue uniform with a golden collar approached the prince respectfully.

"Aaron, I would like for you to meet Captain Nathaniel Morgan. Morgan, I'd like for you to meet Aaron Jace of the house Alenzar'seth."

The captain raised an eyebrow at the mention of Aaron's name, but quickly schooled his features and firmly shook Aaron's hand.

"A fine day for sailing the skies, lad. The Raven is among the finest of airships," Captain Morgan said proudly.

"Captain, if I could have a word," the prince said, and he and the captain walked a few paces away, speaking in hushed tones. A shipman climbing on board offered to take Aaron's pack and staff, which he handed over. His swords were attached to his belt, which he had kept on since the practice yard.

The Raven was immense, and Aaron wondered how many crew there were to fly such a ship. The ship was even more impressive than the airships they had watched take off as they approached Rexel the previous day. They had been here such a brief time. Thinking about last night brought Sarah and the kiss they'd shared at the fountain to his mind. She hadn't been more than a moment away from his thoughts since. He wondered if he would ever see her again.

The captain saluted the prince and nodded to Aaron before walking up the ramp to the airship.

"Aaron, I hope you find what you seek in Shandara, but be warned, while it was once a jewel of the free world, it is now a place of darkness. Safe journey to you," the prince said, reaching out to rest a hand on his shoulder.

Aaron was about to reply when the medallion grew cold against his chest. A second later, he heard Zeus's low growl. Aaron spun, scanning the shipyard.

"Get behind me, your Grace."

No sooner had the prince moved than three identical flashes of light and three figures appeared across the yard.

"You would violate the treaty, Elitesmen!" the prince said.

"We have our orders, your Grace. This one is coming with us," said the center Elitesman, his dark cloak billowing behind him as he pointed directly at Aaron.

"Like hell you are. This is my kingdom, and you have no authority here. To arms, guards!" the prince yelled. Three more flashes of lights erupted with Elitesmen standing some distance behind them. They were surrounded.

Aaron laughed loudly and took a few steps out into the open, drawing everyone's gaze to him. The soft wail of alarm bells could be heard from outside the airfield.

"Is he insane?" Vaughn said aloud to no one in particular.

"No, he's buying time for the guards to arrive. Sarik, get your bow ready and stand over there," Verona said. "No!" he hissed toward Eric and Braden, who stopped in their tracks as they were about to head down. "He's buying time for the prince to escape and needs cover from here. Captain, ready this ship to take off at once. Garret, help him. If we can escape, the Elitesmen will have no reason to stay. Eric, Braden, grab that rope over there and be ready to toss it down." Verona whispered a silent prayer to the Goddess and strung his bow.

"Six of you," Aaron said tauntingly and spared a glance at the prince. Guards began pouring in through the airfield entrances. "Your Grace, please take cover. It's me they want. I will distract them."

He didn't give the prince any time to protest and put more distance between them.

"Well, here I am," he challenged, drawing his swords, further increasing the gap between himself and the prince. As he expected, the Elitesmen remained focused on him.

As one, they Elitesmen drew their weapons. They expected fear, but Aaron refused to give in even though the six that stood around him all had the look of veteran fighters.

"What are you waiting for? I'm right here!" *If it's a fight they want, then let them come.*

The Elitesmen closed in on Aaron, and the first attack came from behind. Aaron quickly dropped to one knee and rolled away, leaping into the next attack. He unleashed the bladesong, and the power coursed through his veins with the whisperings of warriors past echoing in the depths of his mind. He was one with the blades now, and movement in battle was life. Aaron attacked and drove each of the Elitesmen back, becoming the living example of the lesson he had taught his friends earlier. He had no thought beyond the next block, dodge, and attack. His body moved with deadly grace, but he didn't seek the death of these men. Nor they him. They sought to capture him. Then, as suddenly as they had started, the Elitesmen broke off their attack. The leader brought his hands together, and a violet orb formed, crackling with energy. With a powerful push from his arms, the leader sent a beam of energy directly to Aaron, who barely got the Falcons up in time. The force of the blast rattled his bones and had no sign of relenting, but still he held his blades crossed, deflecting the attack. The other

Elitesmen circled around, coming closer, and Aaron knew he was in trouble. He couldn't block the beam and fight the other Elitesmen at the same time. He could chance moving, but he wasn't sure if only one of his blades was sufficient to ward off the attack. There was another flash of light from a travel crystal, and a figure in black emerged and attacked the Elitesmen closing in on him, drawing them away.

The relief he felt was short-lived, as he had to stop the Elitesmen's attack and get out of there. He focused his will on the beam as it hit his swords, and the glow of the crystals in the hilts spread the length of the blades until it covered his arms and surrounded his vision. The power gathered around him, eager to do his bidding, and when he could contain it no longer, he hurled it toward the Elitesmen. A beam as bright as the sun sliced through the Elitesmen's attack, violently knocking him off his feet.

Aaron felt momentarily drained, but looked to the left, seeing that his mysterious protector was overwhelmed by the remaining Elitesmen. With his blades still imbued with energy, he made a broad swipe through the air, sending a rippling wave that sent three of the Elitesmen sprawling and left one engaged with the figure in black. Aaron raced toward them as the figure in black was knocked unconscious, but the Elitesman didn't press the attack. Instead, they turned to face Aaron.

The guards continued to pour into the airfield, circling all of them. Archers filled the ranks between the guards and drew their bows.

"I doubt even an Elitesman will survive a full volley of arrows at this range," the prince warned, joining the guards, and a wall of swords formed around him.

"This doesn't concern you, Prince Cyrus. Call off your guards. There is no need to shed any blood," the last Elitesman on his feet said, with the others beginning to rise.

Aaron heard the humming of the airship's engines grow louder, but he didn't take his eyes from the Elitesmen. He felt a rope hit his shoulder, and he chanced a look above to see Eric and Braden calling to him to grab it. Without any thought, he wrapped his arm around the figure in black and grabbed the rope. The airship quickly lurched into the air with the ground racing away from his feet. Aaron saw flashes of bright light from below, and he knew that the Elitesmen had left. Eric and Braden pulled them onboard.

They gently laid his unconscious protector in black on the deck. Aaron was relieved to see that there were no wounds. He unwrapped the black cloth from around the head and gasped when a swath of golden-blonde hair spilled out onto the deck. His protector in black was Sarah. She opened her eyes, and Aaron sighed with relief.

"You know there are easier ways to get to know me, but I'm grateful that you came when you did," Aaron said, breaking the silence. "Are you all right?" he asked, and he noticed her lips curve into the slightest of smiles before she nodded. Aaron offered to help her up, but she stood up on her own.

"I hope you'll stay longer this time," Aaron said, but before she could reply, Vaughn gasped in surprise and bowed.

"Your Grace," Vaughn said, clearly speaking to Sarah. She nodded with practiced grace and dignity.

"Please," she said, "I would prefer a bit of anonymity for the time being."

Vaughn nodded.

"I'm not going anywhere," Sarah said to Aaron. "But is there somewhere we can speak with a little more privacy?"

Aaron looked to Verona, who answered, "Of course. The captain has some rooms set aside for us to use, and I'm sure it will suit your purposes."

She's here. Aaron kept repeating it in his mind as Verona led them below deck. Why had she returned? How did she know to come to the airfield? Would she disappear again? She said she wouldn't, but... The questions tumbled through his mind, but when she turned to look at him, he decided he didn't care why she was here, he was just happy that she was.

They followed Verona through the ship to a room that was like a lounge, with several chairs and a few desks along the wall. Aaron let Sarah enter the room first and stuck his hand out, blocking Verona and the others from entering.

"I need a few minutes alone here," Aaron said and closed the door in Verona's surprised face. He smiled to himself as he heard them retreat down the hall, grumbling. They were all well intentioned, but there were things he wanted to know from her in private.

"Thank you for coming when you did," he said quietly. "I'm not sure how it would have ended otherwise."

Sarah smiled back at him. "I'm sure you would have thought of something. You really are quite resourceful."

Aaron let out a small laugh. "You took quite a hit, are you sure you're all right?" he asked, taking a step closer to her.

"I'm fine," she replied, pushing a rebellious strand of blonde hair away from her face. "Aaron, I need to tell you..."

Aaron took another step closer and reached out, taking her hand. "Sarah, it's okay."

"No, it's not, there are things that you don't know. You are in grave danger."

Aaron was a bit shocked by how scared she sounded. This had to be something other than the Elitesmen.

"Okay, let's just sit down, and you tell me what you came to tell me," he said, sounding more calm than he felt.

They sat together on a couch by the wall, and warm sunlight streamed through the windows. The day was so calm compared to mere minutes ago, and when she looked at him with those eyes of hers, he felt his heart grow warm in his chest.

"I am the daughter of High King Amorak of Khamearra, where the Elite Council resides. My father was among those who brought destruction to Shandara," she said. "And I know who you are." Her voice cracked. "You're Carlowen's son. Reymius's daughter of the house Alenzar'seth."

Aaron took a few moments before answering her. "Yes, I am, Sarah. Although it seems there were many involved with the fall of Shandara, and I'm afraid there is only one person who knows the whole story," Aaron said, thinking of Colind.

Sarah searched his eyes. "You don't hate me?"

"Hate you! I could never hate you," he said. "I'm not here to avenge Shandara. I'm just trying to stay alive." Aaron smiled at her. "You've risked a great deal to come here, and I can't help but wonder whether you're going to disappear again."

"I'm not going anywhere," she said. "I didn't come here to warn you about my father." She then told him about the Elite Council and how they weren't entirely convinced of who Aaron really was. At least, not before this last attempt to capture him. Then she told him of the Drake. "The Drake was brought forth around the time of the fall of Shandara and the extermination of the Alenzar'seth."

"But what is it exactly?" Aaron asked. He knew there was something he should remember, and it was tugging at the edges of his thoughts.

"It's a beast that is not of this world," she replied. "The last battle invoked a curse that allowed the beast to traverse between worlds. Mactar orchestrated events to allow this to happen, knowing full well what it would do to the kingdom of Shandara and to the Alenzar'seth. Their hearts were the source of their greatest strength and their ultimate weakness. The beast hunted down and murdered them down to the last woman and child. Then it just disappeared."

Aaron's mind raced. He had more questions than he could speak aloud at the moment. "Yeah, but how could me being here awaken this...beast? Where has it been all this time? How would it even know I'm here?" As he said the last, the warning bells in his brain grew louder. There was a knock at the door and in walked one of the crew returning the rune-carved staff.

The staff! "That's it!" he exclaimed, and thanked the crewman.

"I was given this staff shortly after I arrived on Safanar." Given wasn't the right word since his ancestor more or less forced it upon him. He looked back at Sarah and knew she had questions, but she was patient enough to wait him out. "In order for you to understand, I need to tell you...ah, everything," he said, rising.

"Aaron," she said, "how do you know you can trust me?"

Aaron looked at her for a long moment. "Can't I? I know we barely know each other, but when I look into your eyes, I know you would never betray me," he said.

Sarah's breath appeared to catch in her chest. She closed the distance between them, caressed his face with her smooth hands, and pulled him in. Their lips met, and if Aaron could have flown, surely he would have been floating over the rooftops of this world. He felt like there were fireworks exploding brilliantly all around him. They pulled apart from each other, smiling.

"I will never betray you," she said, looking deeply into his eyes.

He wanted to swim for eternity in those bottomless blue eyes, and wondered if he would ever get used to merely standing beside her without his knees getting weak.

They sat together on the couch by the ship's windows. Clouds passed by, and Aaron told Sarah everything. He started at the beginning, when his grandfather died. How his life had changed. He told her about his home and his sister, Tara, who thankfully must be still alive now that he had gone. At least he was able to honor his father's dying wish. He told her of the death of his mother and father, and how they had died to protect him. Aaron turned away from her, his throat thickening with grief. He had gotten so used to carrying it that in these rare quiet moments the weight threatened to crush him.

"You can't protect everyone from everything," Sarah said.

He knew the truth in her words, but he still felt that he should have been able to do more. He should have been able to save his family and Bronwyn. He could have done more, and the cost of not doing so still weighed heavily upon him. Instead of answering Sarah, he told her of meeting Daverim Alenzar'seth and the taking of the rune-carved staff. The beast he saw must have been the Drake waking from wherever it had been sleeping, and now...it was coming for him.

"I need to tell the others about the Drake. Perhaps Vaughn or Garret might know more," Aaron said.

"Aaron," Sarah said, holding on to his hand while they stood up. "Thank you for trusting me."

He took a moment, gripping her hand purposefully. "Thank you for saving me," Aaron replied solemnly and stepped quietly from the room.

After a few minutes, he returned with Verona, who'd been loitering not far from the door anyway. They were later joined by the twins, Eric and Braden, as well as Garret, Vaughn, and young Sarik. As Sarik went to close the door, Zeus nuzzled his way through and settled at Sarah's feet. She was alarmed at first, but when Zeus nudged her hand, she scratched him behind his ears.

"My friends, this is Sarah," Aaron said, making the introductions around the room.

Verona bowed formally to Sarah. "My Lady, it's not that we don't appreciate your timely arrival, but given the circumstances, one could argue that your arrival was a little too timely to be above suspicion," he said without a hint of disrespect.

"You are right to be suspicious," Sarah said, rising and meeting their gazes. "I did not come here expecting that my motives wouldn't be questioned. In fact, I hardly gave any thought to it as I had just learned that a detachment of Elitesmen had been dispatched to capture Aaron. By now, the council will know of its failure and will be better prepared next time they come."

"So why help us?" Vaughn asked.

"I'm here for Aaron," Sarah replied. "I heard a report of a mysterious stranger who took down an Elite, which caused quite a stir. Unlike my father and half-brothers, I still show respect for the Goddess Ferasdiam, like my mother before me. I was meditating at a secret temple that escaped destruction in Khamearra when the Goddess spoke to me."

"What did she say?" Aaron asked, and her gaze softened when she looked back at him.

"She said one of the old blood has returned. I knew I had to search for this mysterious stranger, and I eventually caught up to you in that small town. Prior to that, in another town, I talked to a father and son who spoke very highly of a man who stood up to the injustice of the Elitesmen," Sarah said.

Verona raised an eyebrow and looked at Aaron. "You did see someone outside the town that day. I thought...I don't know what I thought, but I apologize for not believing you, my friend." He turned to Sarah. "How did you appear to Aaron, but remain hidden from the rest of us?"

Sarah smiled at Verona with a hint of a challenge in her eyes. "We all have our secrets."

Verona and a few of the others chuckled. "I had to try. Fair enough, I guess."

"She came to warn us of something called the Drake," Aaron said, and an immediate hush overtook the room.

"The Drake has returned? I had hoped..." Garret spoke first, sharing a glance with Vaughn, but Aaron noticed the shaky note in his voice.

"Mactar believes so, and Aaron confirmed it for me," Sarah answered.

Aaron told them of the events that occurred when he'd first come to Safanar and how he'd come to be in possession of the rune-carved staff. Then he told them of the beast he saw waking when he first put his hands upon the staff. "Daverim Alenzar'seth said the staff would help in the days ahead."

"Perhaps he knew of the Drake and gave you a weapon to fight it with," Vaughn said.

Aaron shook his head. "I'm not too clear on the timeline, but my guess is that the Drake came after Daverim's time."

"He's right," Garret said, "but this was a lost relic of the Safanarion Order. They were the only ones who kept the Elitesmen in check."

"I have something else I need to tell the rest of you. When Verona and I encountered the dragon, it led us to a fountain with a statue of a woman. The dragon said we were in the presence of the Goddess," Aaron said. "It was then that I heard a voice in my head." He stopped, shaking his head slightly, and considered his words. "I'm sorry, but hearing a voice inside my head is not exactly a common occurrence where I come from." He let out a small laugh that the others shared.

"It's not common anywhere, Aaron," Sarah said, and the rest of the room faded to gray while they looked at each other.

Aaron swallowed and continued. "She told me the land is sick and needs a champion. The responsibility for the fate of the land falls upon the house of Alenzar'seth, of which I am the last. Guardianship of the land is a legacy shared with the Safanarion Order, who have all but vanished. Fate has chosen me for this. It's why I was marked. Ferasdiam Marked. Tarimus knew from the onset."

"Tarimus!" Sarah exclaimed. "That's the name Mactar was calling out to." She stopped abruptly, apparently remembering where she was.

"What do you mean exactly?" Vaughn asked.

"Mactar has an ancient mirror in his castle. When my father bade me to summon the Dark Light Master for his role in my half-brother's death, I found Mactar standing before a mirror, calling out to Tarimus, but there was no reply," she answered. "How do you know of Tarimus, Aaron?" she asked.

He knew more about Tarimus than he cared to admit. "He came after my grandfather died. He came for me in my dreams, while I was awake, and used people I care about to get to me." He couldn't keep the bitterness from his words.

"I had to face him upon the crossroads between worlds, but"—he paused again, gathering his thoughts—"I haven't sensed him since coming through the gateway."

"A gateway," Verona said. "Between worlds? You've come from a place a good deal more distant than I originally thought, my friend."

Before Aaron could reply, there was a sharp knock on the door. Sarik opened the door, and a crewman entered.

"The captain wishes a word with you, my Lord," he said, speaking to Aaron. Aaron nodded and began following the crewman out of the room, but stopped and turned to Sarah.

"Don't worry, lad, we'll see that she gets settled in her quarters," Vaughn said, smiling. Aaron let out a small smile and followed the crewman from the room. The others began leaving the room, and Sarah rose from the couch when Verona asked to have a word with her.

"She'll be right there, Vaughn. This won't take but a moment," Verona said. He turned toward Sarah, and she wondered what he was going to say.

"Aaron is a good man," Verona began. "Fate has delivered him a tough hand to play, but a blind man would notice the way you two look at each other. Despite that, I'm still not sure why you're here. Your reasons are your own, and I can respect that, but"—Verona took a moment before continuing—"he's my friend, and he doesn't yet know the ways of this world. It's my job to watch out for him. If you are here for Aaron as you say, then I welcome you with open arms, but I will be ever watchful."

Sarah wasn't lying when she'd said the act of coming was on impulse, but in her heart she knew this was where she was supposed to be. The more time she spent with Aaron, the more she knew she could never go back to her old life.

"You are a good friend, and I have no doubts where your loyalty lies. It's interesting, your comment on Aaron not knowing the ways of this world. I think that could be one of his greatest strengths." What could she possibly tell Verona to put him at ease where Aaron was concerned? "I care for him, Verona. Fate has been pulling on all of our strings it seems."

"Indeed it has," Verona agreed. "Aaron has a way of seeing right to the heart of a matter. Whether he realizes it or not, he is a natural leader. I have but one more question."

"Then ask."

"Your travel crystal?"

"Is depleted," Sarah said, taking out the now-dark crystal.

Verona nodded. "Sarah, I sincerely hope your intentions are true where Aaron is concerned. He could be our greatest hope against"—he stopped, taking a measured look at her—"well, against the darkness springing from Shandara and the tyranny of Khamearra."

Sarah met Verona's gaze evenly. "I understand," she replied, and Verona nodded, leaving her with Vaughn.

22

TRUTHS ACCEPTED

The council chambers of the High King were cold and silent, with the men in attendance not daring to speak. The Elitesmen squad had finished reporting their failed attempt to capture the apparent Heir of Shandara.

"Where is your sister?" High King Amorak asked, but none of the men in attendance was fooled by the calm tone.

"I last saw her outside the main council chambers of the Elite, Father," Primus answered.

The High King regarded his son as a lion observes his prey moments before unleashing his fury. "And you kept this information to yourself," he said coldly.

"I...I didn't think it warranted any attention," Primus stammered.

The High King came before his son. "It's the littlest things that can have the most impact. For example"—the High King made a grandiose gesture to the others present—"it can be a fine line between victory and defeat when there is a breakdown of the perceived importance of an event. Rordan?" the High King called out to his other son.

"Yes, Father," Rordan answered.

"Are the council meetings of the Elite open to the public? Can anyone come and watch them?" the High King asked mildly.

"No, Father, they are not," Rordan answered, pointedly not looking in his twin brother's direction. "But Father," he continued, "Sarah surely is not the one who thwarted the squad's attempt to capture this man."

"Perhaps," the High King answered. "Perhaps not."

"The plan was doomed from the start, your Grace," spoke a hooded figure entering the chambers, who was followed closely by another.

"The only thing learned was that this man can hold his own against six senior

Elitesmen, and quite honestly, I think they got off lightly." Together, the men removed their hoods, revealing themselves to be Mactar and Darven.

The Grand Master of the Elite sneered at Darven, who coolly returned his gaze. Darven was the only living former member of the Elite.

"Your Grace, despite my warnings, the council sent these men to Rexel, alerting not only this man, but also Prince Cyrus that we know that the Heir of Shandara—" Mactar's words were cut off as the High King raised his hand.

"You speak out of turn, Mactar. I have not invited your council," the High King said, holding Mactar at his mercy. The lighting in the room dimmed by an unseen force, and the breath caught in Mactar's throat. He looked toward Darven with panic-stricken eyes.

Darven immediately sank to his knees. "Please, my Lord, release him. Hear what he has to say."

The High King brought his hand up higher, and Mactar's body rose off the floor. "Dark Light Master," he uttered with contempt, letting Mactar's writhing form hang in the air. "Many fear you, but I grow tired of your meddling. I should give you the death you so richly deserve. You have seconds to speak your case, but if you speak in riddles, I will kill you where you stand." The High King's bellow echoed throughout the chamber, and Mactar's body dropped forcefully to the floor.

Mactar gasped for breath. "Thank you, my Lord. As you well know, with the fall of Shandara it was assumed that the line of Alenzar'seth was finally extinguished. The Drake withdrew from the realms of men, and until a few months ago, I believed it as well—that is, until Tarimus appeared, unbidden, in the Mirror of Areschel with news about Reymius Alenzar'seth. Tarimus said a great many things that night, but what was most striking were the words: 'The Lord of Shandara has finally passed from the world of the living through the gateway of an unknown realm and takes his respite in the lands of shadow, awaiting the return.' Tarimus, being a creature between the worlds of the living and dead, could now sense the presence of the Alenzar'seth in this unknown realm. Two of them, in fact." Mactar paused again, watching the High King's expression turn even grimmer.

"Tarimus had enough power to traverse to this realm and was compelled to hunt the heir of Alenzar'seth, but as time went on, he changed, growing madder so that it became almost impossible to control him. I couldn't dissuade him from the hunt. It was almost as if he didn't have a choice. His nature forbade him from not seeking the two. He spoke of a young man who is Reymius's heir, and the second was Princess Carlowen, Reymius's daughter. Tarimus was fixated on the young man, and as he grew in strength, so did Tarimus's power in the place between worlds. This man must have traversed between realms to Safanar, and it was at this moment that the Drake awoke with the shaking of our world, thus proving that this stranger is of the house Alenzar'seth," Mactar said.

"Give us the room," the High King said quietly, and the council chamber quickly emptied, save for his heirs, Mactar and Darven, and Gerric, the Grand Master of the Elite.

"It appears that Tye's strike force wasn't a complete failure after all. And you were there," the High King said to Darven.

"I was, your Grace. I can confirm that Princess Carlowen was in this unknown realm. The last thing I saw before leaving that realm was the knife that left my hands and buried itself into her chest."

The High King nodded and shoved his anger at Mactar to the far corner of his mind. What he was offering was too good to refuse. "How is it that Tarimus did not sense the presence of the Alenzar'seth?"

"All roads lead back to Shandara, your Grace," Mactar said quietly.

"Shandara!" Primus exclaimed. "Are you mad?"

"Take hold of your fear, Brother," Rordan admonished, looking to his father.

"But none can travel to Shandara. The place is cursed. All who go never return. Entire armies have disappeared," Primus responded. Both princes looked to their father. Their eyes demanded an answer, but the High King nodded to Mactar.

"Shandara is the final destination for the heir of Alenzar'seth," Mactar said.

"It is no ordinary hunt of an assassin who lies in wait in the shadows to strike. The Drake can see into the heart of men and will first destroy all those they love, driving the soul mad with despair until it devours their essence," the Elite Grand Master added.

The High King turned his towering form toward Mactar, and a look of understanding passed between them. The heir was key to the true power of Shandara. "I think it's time we set up another force to go to Shandara. I have a present I want delivered to Reymius's heir."

"Father, I will lead the force that will go to Shandara," Rordan said without hesitation, and the High King nodded with approval.

"Both of you will go, but Rordan will lead with Primus as his second. The force will be made up of Elitesmen," the High King said, and then he pointedly looked at Mactar.

"Of course, your Grace, my services are at your disposal," Mactar replied.

23

THE RAVEN

Aaron was led through a series of hallways that ran the length of the immense airship proudly named the Raven. The crewman leading him spoke of the layout and how Aaron would be able to find his way around in no time. Windows along the hallways provided ample lighting during the day, and Aaron noticed dormant orbs along the walls for the night. The interior of the ship was a mix between metal and wood, both polished and ornate. They came to the wheelhouse, and a guard politely opened the door. Captain Morgan was quietly speaking with one of his men when he noticed Aaron and waved him over with a friendly nod of his head.

"My Lord." The captain addressed Aaron formally.

"Please, call me Aaron."

Captain Morgan nodded. "As you wish. Shortly after our auspicious takeoff, one of my crew found an extra passenger hiding among the cargo."

Captain Morgan gestured toward the guards at the door, who immediately brought in a man with a cloth sack pulled over his head. The guards held him firmly. Just then, Verona entered the wheelhouse.

"Well, what do we have here?" Verona asked with half a smile and a wink.

"We're about to find out," Aaron said.

"Indeed, as I was saying," the captain continued, "normally we would set down and send the extra passenger away with the local magistrate, but given the urgency of our trip, we may have to just throw him over the side." The crew laughed hungrily. The man with the cloth sack over his head sagged a little before standing up straight again. "That is, of course, before he said he was with you." The captain raised his hand, and the guard drew off the cloth sack.

It took a few moments for Aaron to realize he was staring at "the Exalted Royal Highness" Prince Jopher.

"My Lord Prince," Aaron said, and Jopher flinched. "I didn't realize you've decided to be with us commoners. What do you think, Verona?"

"It is a peculiar development to say the least," Verona began. "It might be easier to adopt the good captain's policy for unwanted passengers and toss him over the side."

"Please!" Jopher cried, falling to his knees, his disheveled black hair falling into his face. "I have wronged you, sir. My anger got the better of me, and I must atone for my offense. Please let me travel with you to repay my debt."

Of all the things Aaron might have expected to hear, this was not among them. "With me?" Aaron asked, and Jopher nodded vehemently.

Aaron leaned in closer. "What about every other person your royal arrogance has wronged?"

Jopher sagged to his knees, again not meeting Aaron's gaze, and the wheelhouse grew silent.

"It is not me you must atone to, but to people as a whole. Be a better person, Jopher. People were not born to do your bidding, despite what you may have been told. The wrong you've done is to yourself in believing that you are better than everyone else because your father happens to be king in some far-off land."

Jopher took a deep breath. "I will. I promise!"

Aaron regarded the prince and said, "If you were in my shoes, what would you do with someone like yourself?"

Jopher knelt in silence, staring at the floor for a few moments, hardly breathing. "Please," he whispered. "I want to be a better man, and I believe traveling with you will help me achieve that while I aid you in your journey."

"Aaron," Verona whispered, "I know that of which you speak, but the arrogance in him is taught from birth. Consider carefully. He may prove to be an asset."

"More than likely, this journey will bring his death," Aaron replied.

"Perhaps. It's the journey that builds the man, does it not?" Verona asked loudly enough for Jopher to hear.

Aaron narrowed his gaze, studying Jopher, and Captain Morgan cleared his throat.

"I might have a suggestion," the captain said with a wicked gleam in his eye. "We could always use some help in the galley. Perhaps a few days peeling potatoes or scrubbing dishes will go a ways in paying his debt and give you time to consider the boy's offer of aid."

Anger flashed in Jopher's eyes, but he quickly banished it.

Verona laughed out loud. "A fine idea, my good captain."

Aaron nodded, and the guards escorted Jopher from the wheelhouse.

"I hear the same treatment worked on you, my Lord," Captain Morgan said to Verona with a broad knowing smile, and Aaron couldn't help but laugh.

"Oh, my uncle never tires of the tale. We were all young once, weren't we?"

"Some of us were," said the captain. "Now, I have a ship to run, but the prince said you would give me a heading once we were airborne." Before Aaron could reply, the captain interrupted. "The prince filled me in on some crucial details, and the battle with the Elitesmen convinced me of the rest. Perhaps you would join me in the map room as we plot our heading?"

"Of course," Aaron replied, and followed the captain out the door.

The map room was a few doors down from the wheelhouse. The room hosted a desk and a large map as tall as a man that ran the length of the room. The map of Safanar was surprisingly detailed, and it took Aaron a few minutes to find Rexel, which was located almost in the middle.

Verona stepped up to the far side and pointed to a darkened spot on the map. "I believe this is our destination, Captain."

Aaron looked where Verona was pointing and saw Shandara marked in an area of the map that was deliberately darkened, with the words *Land of Shadow* written across the border.

The captain raised an eyebrow and looked surprised, but it passed in an instant. "So it's true then. You are the Heir of Shandara?"

"You make it sound like I'm some sort of king or something. Reymius was my grandfather, and after he died, it was revealed to me that I am of the house of Alenzar'seth," Aaron answered.

Captain Morgan looked sharply at Verona. "He doesn't know?"

"Oh, he knows, my good captain," Verona said with a slight smile. "He just refuses to accept."

"I've told you before, Verona, whatever anyone's plans are, I am no king," Aaron said.

What did his grandfather have in mind for him and the future? Did part of him believe he could run forever? That his mother would never regain her memories? He wished he could talk to his father one last time. Did he know about any of this before marrying his mother?

He turned to the map again, looking at the extremely long distance they would need to travel to reach Shandara. "I didn't realize the road would be this long. How long do you think it will take to reach this border?" Aaron asked.

The captain pursed his lips in thought for a moment. "A few weeks, maybe less, provided we have a good wind and clear skies to sail. As we get closer, we will need to travel only by night to avoid the Ryakuls. They are mostly active during the day, but at least we won't be so visible at night."

Aaron raised an eyebrow, looking from Verona to the captain. "I didn't think of that. Does this ship have a means to defend itself from a Ryakul attack?"

The captain drew himself up. "The Raven has teeth of its own. I'll have my first officer show you around so you and your companions will be able to lend a hand should the need arise."

"Garret told me a little about the crystals used to store energy from the sun. Can this energy be released?" Aaron asked.

"Against the Ryakul, you mean," the captain said, raising an eyebrow in thought. "It might be possible. I would suggest you speak with Hatly. He's the ship's engineer and is the real expert. I've heard some captains play at using the crystals as a weapon and blow themselves up in the process, which is why I've never explored the option. Since Shandara is our destination, though, I think it might be worth the effort and the risk."

"I will speak with Hatly and see if there is a way we can experiment safely," Aaron answered.

"A large crossbow bolt to the chest tends to work the best in my experience, but if you think you can work up something better, then give it a go."

Aaron nodded and left the room with Verona, eager to speak with Hatly. He was extremely curious about the crystals they had here. They had different properties than back home. He was no expert in crystals by any means, but he was fairly certain that they weren't used for storing energy from the sun back home. His hands drifted to his swords with his fingers gliding over the crystals inlaid in the pommel. They seemed to absorb energy, which had been extremely useful on occasion, even saving his life. He also suspected they came into play somehow when he wielded the blades to make the bladesong. Beyond the blades being bequeathed to him by his grandfather, they were as much a mystery to him as everything else in Safanar.

Aaron spent the next few hours speaking with Hatly, who was an easygoing, roll up the sleeves and get the work done sort of man that reminded him of his father. Crystals here in Safanar were a wonder and of a different breed than back home. A combination of different-colored crystals, when powered by yellow crystals, allowed steel to retain its strength but with less weight. However, the base yellow crystal had to be recharged, otherwise the weight of the steel bones of the ship would bring it crashing to the ground. These crystals were found throughout the hull of the ship, embedded in the wooden support beams because if they came in contact with metal, the metal would eventually dissolve into a rusty powder. Hatly assured him that there were many safeguards in place to prevent accidents.

Verona was able to fill in some of the blanks for him regarding the crystals. The richest sources were found in Khamearra and were controlled by the High King. There were stories of a great fire in the sky and how these special crystals were found in small deposits throughout Safanar. Aaron surmised that this planet experienced a large meteor shower that brought the crystals here. When Aaron explained what he had in mind for repelling the Ryakuls, Hatly was interested. The problem with releasing the stored-up energy was focusing its direction. If they broke, they would explode, which was something they all wanted to avoid even with the smallest of crystals. Aaron jokingly mentioned using a slingshot to hurl the crystals into the mouth of the Ryakuls, and Verona's eyes lit up.

"Not a sling, my friend. How about arrows with the shards fastened behind the tips? They won't be able to fly very far or accurately, and I'd wager we would need to wait for our target to get close to conserve our ammo," Verona said.

"That's a good idea, but how will they ignite?" Aaron's question drew a blank stare from Verona, and they both looked to Hatly.

"The crystals we use here on the ship are selected because of their durability. Only fragile crystals run the risk of exploding when they break. But..." Hatly paused, considering, and then reached over to his workbench, uncovering a wooden crate. He withdrew a dark crystal from the bunch and set it down. "This is a spent crystal. All the stored energy has been used up. Perhaps we can break it into the pieces we need and make them a bit more fragile. Then we could allow them to store power in the charging chamber, but we'll need to monitor the time, otherwise they will overload." Hatly went on muttering to himself, seeming to forget that they were still in the room. After a few moments, Verona nodded toward the door, and they quietly left Hatly to his work. In the hall, they met Braden, who was coming to collect them for dinner.

They dined with the captain and his senior officers. The mood was light considering where they were heading. Aaron wondered if Captain Morgan had informed his crew of their destination. The chef had prepared boar, for the tradition on a ship's first day of voyage was to feast in the evening. The food was delicious, with a variety that would surely satisfy even the most finicky of palates. The ale was dark and strong, leaving him feeling more relaxed than he had in a long time. Eric and Braden had resumed their roles as his shadows, never straying far from him. Garret and Vaughn were speaking with the captain, and periodically they would each glance in his direction.

"I see the old men are busy plotting," Verona said, bringing Aaron another pint of ale.

"Thanks, this ale is good," Aaron said. "They don't know what to make of me."

"Possibly," Verona answered. "Perhaps not. Old men talk, and young men drink." Verona smiled and raised his tankard.

"I guess." Aaron snorted, and as he raised his tankard to his lips, Sarah sat down in the seat next to him. He felt his heart quicken in spite of the ale-induced calmness. How did he feel about her? He didn't ignore her, but they both spent a fair amount of time not looking at each other throughout dinner. He felt that everyone must have noticed them not looking at each other. The few times their eyes did meet, Aaron felt heat rise from his chest.

"My Lady, you've found me again," Aaron said with a smile.

"To chance encounters," Sarah answered, raising her glass.

The three of them drank in unison. "What are the odds that the three of us would meet and be here at this particular moment?" Aaron asked.

"It does seem beyond mere coincidence," Verona said wistfully. "Right place, right time." Verona took another swallow of ale, raising an eyebrow.

"I have a question for you," Aaron began. "If I hadn't shown up, what would you be doing right now, you think?"

"That's easy, my friend. I would be looking for trouble. Or is it that trouble would be looking for me and succeeding more than failing," Verona said with a grin.

Aaron laughed with him. "No, seriously. Surely your life is more than looking for trouble."

Verona frowned in thought. "A starlit sky, good ale or wine depending where I am at the moment, and a beautiful lady to share the evening with. That is, of course, until I'm pulled back into the family business."

Sarah laughed, and the sound was music to his ears. Both he and Verona looked at her expectantly.

"I see it's my turn now," she said. "I'll tell you what I'd like to have been doing. Exploring a part of the world people haven't seen before. Where no one knows me. And you, Aaron?" she asked.

The question tumbled through his mind. What would he have been doing if none of this had ever happened? "Back home, I would have been in college, studying mechanical engineering. I like to work with my hands, so things like this airship fascinate me."

"Indeed, I could hardly get a word in edgewise when we spoke to Hatly," Verona said. "The ship's engineer," he said to Sarah.

"Sarik told me that you plan to train with him in the morning," Sarah said.

"He did, did he?" Aaron asked, glancing toward Sarik, who sat at another table with a guilty smile. "Yes." Aaron nodded. "I will be."

"I would like to join him if you wouldn't mind. I'd like to get some exercise," Sarah said with the candlelight caressing her face.

Aaron wondered if she had any idea how beautiful she was when she looked at him like that. Probably not. He would gladly dump Sarik over the side of the ship to spend more time alone with her.

"Of course," he answered, deciding he would thank Sarik instead.

"Good. I'm going to turn in for the night. Until tomorrow then," she said and left the room with more than a few glancing in her direction.

"Do you believe this lot?" Verona mused. "I'd say she only has eyes for you, my friend," Verona continued, and ignored Aaron as he nearly choked on his ale. "I'll admit I'm not entirely sure of her motives for being here, but when her eyes meet yours, well, let's just say there is more than friendship in them. I'd say the same for you, as well."

Aaron felt heat rise in his cheeks and silently cursed himself. "I can't," he muttered.

Verona smiled at him. "I think you already have," he chuckled. "There are times when the heart overrules the mind because it must. I believe this is one of those times. Why don't you go get some sleep? You look dreadful."

Aaron was about to protest, but he was feeling the ale in his veins, and his muscles were like water. He nodded silently and left. Instead of going to his room, he headed out on deck for some fresh air. Sailors nodded in greeting as they went about their tasks, and the cool night air revived Aaron as he stood gazing at the moon. The craters dotting the surface were clearly visible on this night. On the far side of the deck, a door opened, and the princeling, Jopher, appeared wearing a dirty apron and an angry expression. He met Aaron's gaze and took a few steps toward him before a deep voice called him back. Jopher glanced back at Aaron, who calmly looked back at him. Frowning, Jopher returned through the door. *A touch of humility indeed for that one.*

He dismissed thoughts of Jopher while sweeping his gaze across the night sky, taking in the view of the stars. Their clear and vibrant light speckled the sky with foreign patterns, leaving Aaron to wonder whether one of them was Earth. Was he even in the same universe? His passage to Safanar was shrouded in mystery, and these rare moments of stillness left him wondering what connection, if any, there was between Safanar and Earth. Could he ever go back? Would he want to if he could? How did his grandfather and mother go through the gateway between worlds? Could he travel to other places if he wanted? He wondered what his sister was doing and hoped she was safe. They had always been close, and he missed how they used to tease each other. In the midst of all the danger that surrounded him, the bright spot that repelled the darkness within him was Sarah. Despite how he tried to push such thoughts away, they returned in earnest when he least expected them to. Was there a perfect time for love, knowing that death would probably claim him in the near future? The thought tasted bitter in his mouth, but there it was. Unless Colind had an ace up his sleeve, Aaron had no idea what he could do against all that were hunting him. How far could he run? How much could he really fight? The mere thought of it all threatened to overwhelm him at times. Verona and the others looked to him to lead against the High King because of his lineage. When Tye killed his father, he had said he wanted to capture his essence. He had no idea what that meant, but being the last of the Alenzar'seth made him the key to something. All roads led to Shandara, it seemed.

He hoped Colind had the answers he sought to thwart Mactar and the High King. Other than who he was, what could he possibly possess to drive these men to murder an entire family? Who were the Alenzar'seth? If they were like his grandfather, surely nothing they would have done would warrant such action against them. Based upon the letter that Prince Cyrus had shown him, his grandfather had wanted to shift the power from the nobility to the rule of law and allow people to govern themselves. At least, he implied as much. The High King and the Elitesmen were tyrants, holding these people by the throat. It was completely foreign for Aaron to even think of a world in these terms, but was Earth so different? Maybe in some places, but upon the fringes of civilization, the rule of law was fragile at best and most often nonexistent. People deserved better or at least the right to choose for themselves.

24

THE FIRST LESSON

The next morning, Aaron awoke while it was still dark outside. He quietly dressed, gathered his things, and with Zeus in tow, headed immediately for the deck. The sun was beginning to rise, and the brisk morning air drove the remaining sleepiness from him. The deck had a wide expanse of space, which afforded him much room. He put his staff and swords down and warmed up with the fighting forms to increase flexibility, loosening up his muscles. He focused on his breathing and perfection of movement with his body. It wasn't long before Sarik approached silently and copied Aaron's movements without saying a word. Sarik was a quick study and was able to mimic his movements with ease. They worked silently, and a few of the sailors watched from the side. Between forms, Aaron waved an invitation for them to join. A few came over while the others kept watching. He kept to the basic forms, allowing for a good warm-up, and despite the chill of the morning air, beads of sweat formed on him. Before long, they were joined by the others, including Sarah, with whom he shared a brief smile in greeting. Aaron was surprised to see Garret and Vaughn among the group of men that came to train and nodded to each in turn. He noticed Jopher watching among the men who stood to the side. He looked at Aaron with a hopeful expression, which Aaron ignored.

"Good morning. It was customary for my grandfather to begin each training session with a few words, and while we train together, I intend to continue with that tradition. Please, if you will form a circle and take a moment to look at those who stand among you," Aaron said, pausing while they formed a circle.

He took a few moments, considering what he wanted to say. If he was to change things here, he must start with planting the seeds of ideas among these people.

"You all come from different walks of life, from all corners of the world. Each experiences the world in his own unique way and with his own challenges. While we form this circle, we are all equals, and when we break off into smaller groups, the circle stays with us. The circle is how we should embrace the world around us, with neither disdain nor complacence, but with an open mind and compassion. Respect for your fellow man begins with respect for yourselves and thus provides the balance of life. We all breathe the same air and move basically the same way. Breath and movement is life, and this is where we will begin our first lesson..."

Aaron trained with them for the next few hours. Men who worked throughout the night asked if he wouldn't mind having a second training session for those who were duty bound and could not attend. He said that he would and was moved by all the words of praise and appreciation for sharing his knowledge with them.

"Teaching suits you," Sarah said, coming to his side while the others were dispersing. "Now are you up for a bit of a challenge?" she asked with half a smile, holding two pairs of wooden practice swords, and before he could reply, she tossed one at him.

"If you insist. I take it this won't be like our last dance," he said.

"You never know." She smiled back, and then she attacked.

Instincts took over as Aaron barely blocked her attacks. If this was practice, he would hate to face her when she was angry. Sarah broke off her attack, her eyes flashing angrily.

"You will do us both a disservice by not engaging fully. I'm no delicate flower wrapped in silk. Don't hold back, because I won't."

"I apologize, my Lady."

He brought up his swords and decided to dance with Sarah after all. He attacked first, bringing his swords to bear, and Sarah blocked with the grace and agility of a swan skimming across a lake. When Sarah lashed out with her swords, the attacks were quick and powerful, but she never overextended herself. *She's good.* They each probed the other's defenses and thus far were not able to exploit any weakness.

Aaron sensed she was leading him into a trap, as the pattern of her subtle defense taunted him into being more aggressive. Then he felt a tingle upon the edge of his senses, and he found her eyes searching his expectantly. The empty void within gathered essence as if he were wielding the Falcons and invoking the bladesong. His medallion grew warm against his skin as the tingle upon his senses persisted, growing more powerful. Sarah took full advantage of his distraction and swept his feet out from under him. He was flat on his back for an instant before he tucked in and rolled backward, away from the inevitable sword strike that crashed into the spot he occupied a second earlier.

Aaron sprang to his feet, and his wooden blades met Sarah's blinding whirl of attacks. He picked out the pattern and pressed her back with even, purposeful strides. His blades became a moving wall of defense and attack. Sarah was a really good fighter. She gave ground, studying his attack and adapting her own to counter his style. Then the tingle came back as a push on his senses. There could be little doubt that Sarah was doing something to him. He immediately stepped in close, sweeping her outstretched foot toward him just enough to bring her off balance. Their blades locked, and he could feel her breath on his face while she struggled against him.

"What are you doing?" Aaron demanded.

Sarah became still. "You've only scratched the surface of what you're capable of."

Aaron released her, and they stood facing each other, catching their breath. "What do you mean?"

"The lore masters of Shandara were legendary in the feats they performed. It might be safer for you not to discover these skills in the heat of battle," Sarah replied.

"You could have warned me," Aaron said.

"Are you always warned before being tested?"

Aaron's mouth hung open as he was about to reply. Feeling foolish, he closed his mouth quickly. "Point taken," he said. "All right, what do you want to show me?"

"I've felt you take in and harness the energy within yourself," Sarah said.

"When I focus, I can feel the beating hearts of those around me regardless of whether they are human or animal."

"That's because all life is connected. The Elitesmen choose to exploit the bonds of life to bend those to their will. Only the Shandarians, being led by the Alenzar'seth, kept them in check. The bonds of life give you strength, heal your wounds, but there is always a balance. Pull too much, and you will burn yourself out," Sarah said.

"I felt you pushing against my senses. Can anyone do this?" Aaron asked.

"Some—it's been known to manifest only within certain bloodlines." Sarah replied with what she'd learned from Beck, her unorthodox Elitesman teacher.

Aaron frowned, thinking of the whispering voices he heard when he wielded the Falcons and invoked the bladesong.

"I'm not so sure. My grandfather always said that all life is connected and that we can draw knowledge from the soul."

"Let's not get distracted. I said before you've only scratched the surface of what you are capable of, and I meant it. Normally, novices who show promise are given an amulet to help them become more attuned to drawing energy and in some cases store it as well."

"So an amulet would make me a better conductor," Aaron said, rubbing the medallion beneath his shirt. "Something like this," he said, withdrawing the medallion.

Sarah's eyes widened. "I'd say that is a little more than what a novice would be given. And you said you'd never seen this before your grandfather died?"

"No," Aaron said, shaking his head. "It was well hidden."

"Can you tell me what happens when you focus and draw the energy within yourself?" Sarah asked.

Aaron described his heightened sense of awareness and sharpened senses. His connection to living things in his vicinity, as if they were all beating of the same heart. He decided to tell her about the voices he would sometimes hear with the bladesong. "This must sound crazy even for this place," Aaron said.

"No. No," Sarah said, shaking her head and smiling. "It's not crazy at all. It's something wonderful. Something beautiful. You're hearing the voices of past lives. There are those that believe that we live many lifetimes to help us grow."

"If I didn't experience this for myself, I would say that you're a little crazy. The voices aren't speaking directly to me. They're more whisperings and mutterings. Like I'm being urged, but not insistently so. It doesn't invade the void, but complements it. They helped me unravel the pattern of the Elitesman attack."

Sarah reached out and put her hand on his. "To hear so many means you have an old soul. Perhaps ancient, but you will never know who you may have been in another life. Your soul is also made up of pieces from your parents, so each time you are born it's unique."

"That's good I guess, because the implications of that could be scary. It still seems strange though," Aaron said.

"Trust yourself, Aaron. In the end, it's all we really can do. When you draw energy in, you can use it to give you an edge in most endeavors. You can move faster and jump farther than a normal person. You have already done so without realizing it when you faced the Elitesmen in the small town."

"I did? How? I just faced them as I would anyone else," Aaron interrupted, unable to contain himself.

Sarah smiled at him patiently. "Your honesty and integrity serve you well, Aaron. I suspect that when you faced the Elitesmen, you met them as equals. As men. You leveled the playing field, but you were moving just as fast as they were."

Aaron remembered the shocked looks of Verona and the others when he had killed all those men and took down the Elitesmen in the town. He'd been consumed by rage and had thought it was just adrenaline, but perhaps it was something else. "Maybe, but at some point, someone will just be faster or stronger. I wonder what the price is for being able to do such things," Aaron said.

"You could burn yourself out. When you release the energy, your body could release its life essence, leaving the body without a soul. The energy you draw in is meant to be used," Sarah said. "Stand up. It's better if I show you."

"Here?"

"There is no time like the present," she replied earnestly. "Your swords help you channel energy, but you can do it on your own as well."

"Wait a minute. What about the others?" Aaron asked.

"In time, perhaps," Sarah said quietly, answering the rest of his unspoken question.

Aaron glanced over at Verona and Sarik, who were speaking at the far side of the deck. "What do you want me to do?"

"We'll start off with something simple. I want you to clear your mind and begin drawing energy within you," Sarah said.

"Where does this energy come from?" Aaron asked.

"Can you feel the wind blow? There is nothing that you can see that pushes the wind, but there are underlying forces at work that cause the many currents of air to move. It's the same kind of thing. You are tapping into the underlying forces that give life to, well"—she paused, looking around—"everything."

Aaron's brow furrowed as he thought about this. How could something sound so bizarre and make sense at the same time? He cleared his mind, and in his mind's eye he wielded the Falcons, invoking the bladesong. He felt energy draw into him and his senses sharpened.

"Very good, Aaron. I can sense you. Can you sense me?"

Aaron allowed his senses to stretch out from himself, and he saw a faint, golden aura that surrounded Sarah, pulsing with the rhythm of her heartbeat. Then he caught a faint scent. "I smell jasmine," he said suddenly.

Sarah's eyes flashed in surprise. "Jasmine is my favorite flower. It grew near where..." She stopped suddenly and eyed him. "When I was a little girl, it grew near my window. The warm summer night air would fill my room with its sweet scent," Sarah said.

"Elitesmen can sense this?"

"No, their training is twisted. They draw their strength from elsewhere. We will discuss them another time," Sarah replied. "You can use the forces gathering within you to strengthen your body. Specifically, your bones and muscles and all that joins them," she said, looking at the cables that attached the ship to the balloon high above them.

"Then you push," Sarah said, launching herself into the air, jumping over twenty feet and catching hold of the cables that the crew would use to repair the ship.

Verona and the others stopped their conversation and looked up at Sarah in awe. "Well?" she called down to him.

Aaron could feel the energy build within and tried to focus it into his muscles. He squatted down, preparing to jump, and pushed with all his might. He rose about two feet into the air and came back down. His concentration broke, and his hold upon the energy within dissipated. *I'm an idiot.* Aaron glanced at the others and saw a few of them were trying their utmost to keep from grinning.

"I think you need a little more practice," Verona said, smiling as he walked over to Aaron. "Nice to see that you are indeed human like the rest of us."

Aaron shrugged his shoulders and grinned in spite of himself. He looked up at Sarah, and she stared back expectantly. He sighed, getting back on his feet. He then spent the better part of the next hour trying to match Sarah's rather impressive jump. Despite getting up to a whole three feet, he gave in to frustration and stopped.

Sarah assured him that he would be able to jump as high or higher eventually and to give it time. Despite Sarah's assurance, Aaron was frustrated. He put on a brave face, but inside it gnawed away at him. He needed to be prepared for whatever the Elitesmen threw at him—and the Drake. He glanced over at his swords. Perhaps if he were to…

"I want to see him! Get out of my way."

Aaron heard Jopher's shouting amid the crowd of men and a crash of things falling to the ground. Eric and Braden were blocking Jopher's path. Nearby was a deckhand quickly picking up the stacks of tablets that had crashed to the floor. Jopher glanced at the boy, and when he saw Aaron, he took an immediate step in his direction and began to speak. Aaron ignored Jopher as he stepped past him and squatted down to help the deckhand retrieve his tablets. A hush washed over the men on deck. Aaron smiled at the boy reassuringly and handed the remaining tablets to him. The boy thanked Aaron and quickly went on his way.

"Do you know why I won't allow you to be trained, Jopher?" Aaron asked, turning around, and Jopher for once was at a loss for words.

"It's because you don't see people. People are things to you, and until you not only see people, but learn to treat them with common courtesy, then you have no place with me or those around me." Aaron's cold eyes bored into Jopher until he looked away.

"I'm sorry," Jopher muttered, then quickly withdrew back to the kitchens.

The apology was unexpected and surprisingly sincere; perhaps there was hope for Jopher after all. Aaron glanced around and saw Sarah and Verona nodding approvingly.

"If the boy learns the lesson you are trying to teach him, he will be the better for it," Verona said.

"We'll see. It's really up to him," Aaron said.

25

THE HUNTER

Over the weeks that followed they had good travel weather, and Aaron settled into a routine of teaching the men on the ship. After some prompting from Sarik, he even allowed Jopher to join in.

Jopher had put forth a great amount of effort to help those around the ship with any task, and Aaron observed the noble arrogance retreat from his gaze. He didn't think Jopher had ever had any true companions other than servants, and Aaron was glad to see some changes in him take root.

The ship headed steadily east and with each passing day brought him closer to Shandara. What would it look like? Was it really a land of shadow, a place where monsters roamed, a blight upon this world? He stood at the railing with his hand resting casually on his swords and watched the darkening clouds roll steadily in.

"Looks like we might see some weather today," Verona said, coming up next to him. A few sailors shuffled by, securing equipment and making ready for the storm.

"Looks that way."

"Hatly wants to demonstrate the progress he's made with our idea using exploding crystals against the Ryakul," Verona said.

"That's good news. I was in his lab earlier today, and he was extremely close. I've left him some arrows, but we're going to need to think of something better moving forward," Aaron said.

"You're right about that. I doubt an arrow burdened with enough crystal dust to do any sort of damage to a Ryakul will fly more than twenty or so yards," Verona replied, pursing his lips in thought.

Sarah emerged on the far side of the ship, her golden hair cascading down her back with the wind toying playfully at the ends. She smiled at Aaron and walked over.

"You're a lucky man, Verona said. "Normally, I would say she's beyond your reach, but I daresay she has taken a liking to you, my friend."

Aaron laughed and gave Verona a playful shove. "I've got to be crazy, Verona. This can't lead anywhere good for either of us."

"It seems as if your head and your heart are at war with themselves. A monumental struggle fought throughout the ages, to be sure. But, would you like to know a secret truth that many a man pays dearly for and yet still never learns?" Verona asked, his eyes twinkling. Only when Aaron nodded did he continue.

"Love is just love, there is no perfect time."

Aaron chuckled. "That's it? That's your great advice?"

Verona simply shrugged his shoulders, growing silent and using Sarah's arrival as an excuse not to answer. Sarah's blue eyes and smile drove Verona and his sage advice far from his mind. She nodded in greeting to Verona, who said he was going to Hatly's lab.

"Please tell me you're not going to have me try to jump again? I'm still recovering," Aaron said, which brought a small laugh from Sarah.

"No, I promise," she replied, and then her eyes grew serious. "It's up to you now."

"I know," Aaron said. He turned to scan the rapidly approaching clouds, feeling his medallion grow cool against his skin. In the back of his mind, he heard a great swath of giant wings cutting through the air. He glanced at Sarah, who was silently scanning the sky with him. He looked around the deck, and the sailors were going about their normal duties.

"Do you hear that?" Aaron asked.

"Hear what?"

Aaron peered into the sky, but saw nothing except the dark clouds blotting out the sun. He was hearing multiple beating wings now closing in. "Something is coming."

Sarah narrowed her gaze. "I don't hear anything," she said, her hands resting on her sword.

A crash of thunder and lightning tore through the sky, and amid the flash, he saw great winged shapes, dark and sinister, surrounding the ship.

"Ryakuls!" he shouted and was immediately echoed by the sailors of the watch.

There was a flurry of activity as the veteran sailors flew into action. The sailors threw back levers at key points around the ship, and sections of the flooring gave way. Giant crossbows rose from the depths of the ship. The sailors, in teams of four, made ready to fire upon any Ryakuls that breached the clouds, but none came. Ear-piercing roars erupted from above. Eric and Braden were immediately at Aaron's side, their bows at the ready. Captain Morgan arrived on deck, barking orders.

"How many of the beasts have we got?" the captain shouted.

"I see five of them, Captain," Sarik shouted back from the other side of the deck.

A team of sailors near Aaron cursed as they struggled to get a giant crossbow unstuck mid-rise from below the deck. Aaron hopped down the shaft and was immediately joined by Jopher. Without a word, they began searching for what was keeping the gearing stuck. The roars of the Ryakuls pierced their ears as they probed the ship's defenses. Aaron was rocked to the side as something big collided with the ship. Shaking his head, Aaron returned to his feet and began yanking and kicking away the debris from the gearing, until finally the crossbow platform rose to the decks.

A Ryakul slammed onto the deck and roared a challenge. The giant crossbows turned in unison and unleashed a deadly barrage of log-sized arrows, slamming the creature through the chest, forcing it over the side. The turrets were turned back to defend the ship, but no shots were fired as the Ryakuls proved too quick to track in the air. Aaron stumbled as the ship rocked under his feat.

"They're under the ship," a sailor cried.

Aaron ran to the side of the ship and tied a lifeline around his waist, and without a backward glance, he jumped over the side. The wind rushed past his face, and he tensed his muscles, silently praying that the rope would hold. The rope jerked, rattling his bones, sending him toward the armored underbody of the ship, where a Ryakul was clawing away. Aaron raised his heels, using the momentum of his jump, and blindsided the Ryakul, knocking a few talons loose from the ship's bottom.

The Ryakul shook its head and turned viciously toward Aaron with its gaping saber-tusked maw opening for the kill. Aaron drew his sword as he swung back toward the Ryakul, knowing that he was about to die. He roared in his suicidal charge, and Aaron felt the heat of his medallion burn through his shirt, sending a beam of light into the Ryakul's face, blinding it. Aaron barely dodged the rows of deadly teeth and slashed out with his sword, cutting deeply into the beast's long neck. It dropped from the bottom of the ship. Aaron felt a sharp tug on his rope as he was hoisted back up. He heard a swoosh through the air and turned to see another Ryakul closing in, its gaze fixed upon him.

Still hanging by the rope, Aaron kicked away and ran along the side of the ship. He felt heat blast from a great explosion behind him. He turned to see the charred remains of the Ryakul's body falling toward the ground far below them.

A horn blared from within the clouds, and the remaining Ryakuls screeched in reply, breaking off the attack. Aaron looked back up and saw Verona grinning from the side of the ship as Eric and Braden hoisted him up.

"Your idea with the crystals worked," Verona said, holding an arrow whose tip caught the light of the orbs around them.

Aaron thanked Eric and Braden and looked around the deck to find Sarah on the far side. She smiled in relief. Large talons slowly gripped the railing next to her and Aaron's breath caught in his throat. Sarah's perplexed look turned to terror as a great claw gripped her entire body and yanked her over the side.

"There!" Sarik screamed, pointing from above.

The Ryakul flew from under the ship, and Aaron's eyes found Sarah's as the blood pounded in his ears. He reached out, grabbed the crystal-tipped arrow from Verona's hands, and took a few steps back from the railing. He took a moment, gathering the energy from the wind currents into him as Sarah had taught him, and exploded into movement, hurtling toward the side of the ship. He jumped as he never had before. The energy strengthened his muscles beyond the constraints of ordinary men. He mightily pushed with his legs and shot away from the ship like a bullet, gaining on the fleeing Ryakul.

The wind roared past his ears as he reached out and grabbed the beast's leg. He held on with one hand as the beast plunged toward the ground with his added weight. Sarah struggled against the talons, but they held fast. Aaron clenched his teeth around the arrow, not giving a thought that at any moment it might explode, then drew his knife. The ground was rapidly approaching as he slashed deeply across the Ryakul's hamstring, causing black blood to gush forth as the creature howled in pain. The talons around Sarah grudgingly opened, and she fell from the creature's grasp. Aaron followed, turning in midair as he hurled the crystal-tipped arrow into the Ryakul's maw. The explosion pushed Aaron faster, and he caught Sarah in his arms. He summoned the energy from the storm into himself, steeling his muscles and bones to withstand the landing. The impact of his feet slamming the ground sent a wave of dirt into the air. When the air cleared, he placed Sarah on her feet, but she held onto him, gasping for breath.

"How did you—you jumped!"

Aaron shook his head, trying to get the world to stop spinning.

"I guess I needed the right motivation, but please let's not try that again." Lightning streaked across the sky, and the wind howled. The storm had arrived in earnest. They watched the Raven being blown away, unable to fly against such powerful winds. He saw the remaining Ryakuls swarming in the clouds above with one large Ryakul standing out from the rest. Another blast of thunder and lightning revealed a rider upon the Ryakul's back. The gusty winds blew the smaller Ryakuls away, but the large Ryakul struggled to stay in the storm's torment while its rider scanned the ground for them. After a few moments, the rider blew his horn, and the Ryakuls fell into formation, heading away from them.

They took a collective sigh of relief and jogged to the nearby trees to escape the wind and rain.

"Did you see that?" Aaron asked.

"That Ryakul had a rider. I've never heard of that before," Sarah said.

"This wasn't some random Ryakul attack. Someone is controlling them. Could the Elitesmen do this?" Aaron asked.

Sarah shook her head. "The Elitesman cannot control the minds of Ryakuls. Not even Mactar can do that."

Aaron rubbed his medallion, which lay coolly against his chest. It had flared to life when he fought the Ryakul, and he couldn't figure out how it happened. "Could it be the Drake?"

Sarah looked visibly shaken by the question and silently shrugged her shoulders, scanning the sky. "I can't see the ship anymore."

"We'll need a place to ride out this storm. Then I think we should head this way after it passes," Aaron said, pointing to the east. He had studied the map of Safanar in the navigation room on the ship every day since his first day on board, and he knew that heading east would bring him to Shandara. "We can't just sit here and wait for them. Not with that thing looking for us, and besides, when the others don't find us here, they will head east to look."

"You're right. Let's go," Sarah said.

26

AN UNEXPECTED MEETING

After a couple of hours, the storm let up enough that they were able to keep relatively dry if they stuck to the forest. On any other day, Aaron would have enjoyed a hike in the woods, rain or not, but today, without any supplies, he was worried that they would feel the lack of food before long. Sarah, he noticed, didn't share his worries. She knew how to survive in the forest and seemed genuinely amused that he did not.

"Do you not have hunters on your world?" she asked.

"Of course we do, but most people aren't required to hunt. They buy their food at a local market," Aaron said.

"What happens if the local market doesn't have food that day?"

Aaron's thoughts stumbled a bit as he tried to imagine a local supermarket having no food, but he just couldn't imagine it. "It wouldn't happen. I mean, sometimes they might run low because a bad storm was coming, but there are enough markets to sustain people until more food and supplies can be delivered. Sometimes, the food comes in from far away."

"I see," she said and continued to walk.

He had always taken for granted that food was readily available back home. He'd never given more than a passing thought to what he would do should he have to hunt his own food. Why would he? Most people only kept enough food at home to last a few days or a week tops.

"It does seem foolish to me now that I think about it," Aaron said.

"Why would you say that?" Sarah asked. "That is where you came from. If something like food has always been available, then it's easy to see why people wouldn't learn basic hunting skills."

"Basic hunting skills," Aaron repeated. "Not something I would expect a princess to know anything about."

"I assure you my home was not all made of silks and ribbons," Sarah replied frostily.

Aaron looked up in alarm. "I meant no offense. I've never known any princesses before you, but hunting wouldn't seem like something a princess would know anything about. Most girls I've known don't know how to hunt. Then again, most can't handle a sword."

Sarah's gaze softened. "It's okay. Perhaps that's because you've finally met the right girl. The life of a princess for me has been anything but what the stories say. I grew up far from my father's court after my mother died. It was a small manor, and the reason I know anything about how to take care of myself is because of Beck." She stopped, turning to face Aaron. "Beck was an Elitesman. A very old Elitesman before they became the vile sect that you have had the unlucky happenstance to cross paths with. Beck left the order and would train me at night. He understood the danger I was in."

"Danger? From what?" Aaron asked.

"From my brothers and father...the world," she muttered. "I remember my father being kind until my mother died. Then he changed. He became bitter and never had time for me. I don't know why. I was just a little girl. Eventually, he sent me away. Soon after, news came to the manor that he remarried and had more children. Then Beck showed up at the manor one day and asked if I wanted to control my own destiny."

"That's a funny thing to ask a child," Aaron said.

"I was extremely sheltered at the manor, and news from the outside world was slow to arrive, if at all. The manor had a nice library, and I was eager to learn. Beck, in turn, taught me for years. Not just how to defend myself, but how to survive. I once asked him why he came to the manor, and his only reply was to honor my mother since no one else would. I never had many dealings with the Elitesmen, and Beck was more of an outcast. He was already very old when he came, and he died quietly in his sleep a few years ago. I decided to return to Khamearra. I thought that if I could prove myself useful, then my father would look kindly upon me as he once did. I returned to the court at Khamearra, where I was greeted by three younger half-brothers and a father who was all but a stranger to me. The time apart made him more bitter, and the light in his eyes was completely gone. I was tolerated at first, and my father was impressed with how I handled my half-brothers' attempts to have me meet with several unexpected accidents."

Aaron shook his head. "They tried to kill you for simply showing up?"

"They tried but never came close. It amused me for a while to thwart their attempts until my father became bored with the whole mess and ordered them to stop."

"How many brothers do you have?' Aaron asked.

"Three. Primus and Rordan are twins and a year younger than I." She stopped suddenly and looked at Aaron with concern in her eyes. "Tye was my youngest brother."

Hearing the name was like a freight train screaming in his ears. "Tye was your brother," Aaron said quietly.

"Yes," she whispered.

Aaron stomped down the trail in silence with Sarah following. "Did you know what they were planning?"

"No one knew what Tye was up to except Mactar," Sarah replied.

"He murdered my parents," Aaron said through clenched teeth. "Burned my home!"

"I know," she whispered. "I'm sorry, Aaron. Tye got what he deserved."

They walked on in silence, Sarah giving him the time he needed to calm down. What did it change knowing what he knew now? He had no choice now that they were hunting him down. What did this mean for Sarah and him? Regardless of what Sarah had said, they were still her family, and this was going to tear them apart.

"You know where this will lead?" Aaron asked, turning to her suddenly. "It's going to be them or me. Does this change anything for you?"

"How can you be so sure?"

"They're hunting me, Sarah! Mactar, Tarimus, the High King. All of them. It won't stop until either I'm dead or they are. Things are going to become real complicated between us."

"Maybe for some of them. Mactar certainly, but you don't know the whole story. Perhaps there is a way that this doesn't need to end in bloodshed."

"Not end in bloodshed?"

Sarah looked away. "Not everything is black and white, Aaron," she said sharply.

"Not from where I see it," came his terse reply.

"There will be fighting. No one is denying that, but must everything end in death? Must there always be killing?"

"What are you afraid of?" Aaron said, shouting now.

Sarah said nothing at first and took a deep breath. "For you," she said gently, reaching out toward him. "Of what this will do to you. What it already has done to you. I can see the toll it has taken. I've seen good men become twisted in the name of vengeance and survival. I don't want you to lose the good man that you are inside."

Aaron didn't know what to say. She knew there would be fighting but asked why everything had to end in death. Then he remembered the town where he had killed all those guardsmen. In his mind, he'd made them all as evil as the one man among them who had been with Tye that night his parents died. Something dark and sinister was unleashed within him, and perhaps this is what Sarah was warning him about. The dragon had warned him that the path of vengeance led to death. The dragon had not meant death of the body as Aaron had thought, but death of the soul. What choice did he have? The guardsmen from that town would still be dead.

Then it dawned on him.

I'm an idiot.

Had he faced all those men as men and not as what his rage demanded they be, would it have been different? Not to the men who died, but to himself, and that would make all the difference in the world.

"I'm sorry for shouting at you," Aaron said finally. "The dragon Verona and I met warned me against walking the path of vengeance, but the pain of their loss is always with me. When I close my eyes, I see the silver dragon emblem on the black uniform of those men who came to my home. I can still smell the smoke. I can still feel the weight of my mother dying in my arms." It was pure luck that his sister was not at home when the attack came. Fate had been kind enough to grant that much at least. "I don't know if I will ever find peace," Aaron choked. "Would it surprise you to know that prior to a few months ago, I'd never used any weapon to take a life or defend my own? None of this was supposed to happen."

"I'm so sorry this happened to you," Sarah said.

She stood by his side with her hand gently rubbing his shoulder. It felt good, her touch whisking away the dark thoughts. She gave him a smile of understanding. "It hasn't been all bad, has it?"

His lips curved of their own accord. "No, not all bad, and I've met some pretty great people." The burden of the dead still weighed heavily upon his shoulders, but he felt he could bear it better now, and for that he was thankful.

"Present company included?" she asked.

Aaron reached out, taking her hand. "Meeting you was the best thing that ever happened to me, but part of me wishes we had met under different circumstances," he said, imagining what life would have been like if Tarimus had never come.

"Better than not meeting at all," she said, squeezing his hand, and the sparkle in her eyes sent waves of warmth rippling deep within him.

They hiked through the woods, keeping an ever-watchful eye upon the sky, hoping for a glimpse of the ship, but the skies were just a misty gray. The forest grew thicker, and the canopy of immensely tall trees all but blocked out the sky above. Sarah stopped and looked up, scanning the surrounding trees.

"You know we could cover a lot more ground if we used the trees." Sarah winked, then launched in the air, jumping from branch to branch, reaching dizzying heights.

Aaron stared up at her from the ground. He had jumped before in the heat of the moment but wasn't sure he could do it again.

"Are you coming?" Sarah called from above.

Aaron closed his eyes and stretched out with his senses, feeling the energy from the ground beneath him. He called it into himself and felt his medallion grow warm against his chest. He launched into the air and continued to push off the air beneath him. Where Sarah needed three jumps to reach the treetops, he only needed one.

"Let's go," he said.

"Try and keep up, Shandarian," she said, and took off, barely touching one branch before launching to the next.

He launched after her, and slammed into the tree he was aiming for, his shoulder taking the brunt of it. After a few more jumps and with his shoulder only slightly bruised from his collision with several trees, he gained on Sarah. He had to admit that it was fun. He felt as if he were running, taking great strides catching up to Sarah, albeit more clumsily than her graceful leaps. When he caught up to her, she sped ahead of him.

The treetop canopy kept most of the rain at bay, but the damp wind slicked his hair back. He was working, but not breathing all that hard. His body was the conduit tapping energy from wind and the trees. He drew it into himself and released it so fast that it was like a river rolling through him. They soared through the trees like two eagles on the hunt. He focused himself as if he were calling the bladesong with his swords, and the forest ceased blurring by. He could see clearer and with heightened perceptions. He finally passed Sarah and came to halt atop a large branch midway up a tree, which was still over fifty feet from the ground.

"This is amazing," Aaron said.

"Your instincts are really good. The first few times I tried to do this, I crashed," Sarah admitted.

"I nearly did a few times. You make this look so easy. I bounced off a few trees just trying to keep up with you."

Sarah smiled at him. "All things with time, Aaron."

"I wish the others could do this," Aaron said.

"Maybe some of them can. Each person is unique and has varying degrees of ability," Sarah said.

"What do you mean?"

"Your bloodlines are ancient, with ties to the Hythariam folk. You have strength that few achieve, and you learn quickly. This is a good thing to have. The others' abilities will reflect directly upon their personalities and strengths of character. Not everyone is meant to jump so high, nor would they want to. Could you imagine Garret doing such?" Sarah asked.

Aaron thought about it for a second. "Not really, but Verona and certainly Sarik."

"Perhaps," she said. "For some, the effect is subtle. All people draw energy from the world around them. It's just that some are more in tune with it than others."

"Who are the Hythariam?" Aaron asked.

"They are a strange race of men that many believe are from a place across the ocean. They have a darker complexion, almost reddish bronze, with golden eyes, or so the stories say. Many kingdoms sought to align themselves with them because of their knowledge and ingenuity. They were highly skilled craftsman that would make all the grandeur of Rexel seem like the work of children. They allied with Shandara and contributed greatly to building the first airships, but have since withdrawn from our world. They are a secretive race, but occasionally there are sightings among the fringes of settled lands."

"Any idea why they allied with Shandara?" Aaron asked.

"Nothing concrete. More speculation, but I would have thought you would know more about them than I," Sarah answered.

"My grandfather didn't tell me anything about Safanar, much less the Hythariam," Aaron said bitterly. "It's like he deliberately kept me in the dark."

"I'm sure he was trying to protect you. It is possible that he believed that the doors to Safanar were truly closed."

Aaron thought about this for a few minutes, trying to put himself in Reymius's shoes. Reymius couldn't have told him anything—without revealing everything.

"I just wish I could understand more," he said finally.

He wondered what, if anything, his father had known about Safanar. Knowing his father, it wouldn't have mattered to him—he would have taken it all in and dealt with it one thing at a time. They made camp and ate a dinner of nuts, wild berries found nearby, and rabbit courtesy of Sarah's trapping ability. Having no desire to remain wet, they built a small fire to keep warm and dry out their clothes. Each took turns keeping watch, but the night was quiet.

They set off the next morning to a clear sky before the sun had fully risen. There was still no sign of the ship or the Ryakuls, so they continued east, hiking their way through the woods. The trees were much smaller, and traveling as they did yesterday wasn't an option unless one wanted to be impaled. Aaron learned that even though he pulled energy from nearby sources, it was still taxing. He wondered how he could wake up this power in others.

"I wish we could signal the others somehow," Aaron said. "I know they will head east eventually, but I was hoping to see some sign of them by now."

"Your captain is quite experienced. I'm sure he got them through the storm. We need to be patient," Sarah said.

They stopped to rest by a stream later in the day. Although the water was cool and refreshing, Aaron couldn't shake the feeling that whatever had launched the Ryakul attack yesterday was closing in on him. He scanned their surroundings, and all was as it should be—from the crickets to the gentle swaying of the trees. The warnings about the dark things that would hunt him began with Daverim, his ancestor. He had told him to keep the staff close, as it would provide protection, only now the staff was safely aboard the ship and beyond his reach. He'd never taken the time to explore the rune-carved staff. More like never had a chance, but the beast he saw when he first grasped it must have been the Drake. Aaron suppressed the shudder that ran through him. At least he still had his swords, the Falcons, which were no ordinary blades. The Drake hunted the Alenzar'seth to extinction, but how? By all accounts, they were an ancient and powerful family with strong allies. How did the Drake track and kill all of them?

Aaron watched Sarah, who was refilling their only water container. The sun blazed along her blonde hair, giving it a radiance all its own. He had failed to protect Bronwyn from Tarimus, would he be able to protect Sarah from the things arrayed against him? Did she even need his protection? She must have felt his gaze on her, because she turned to him and smiled. He had no choice, because he couldn't deny what was in his heart. He would protect Sarah until his dying breath. What was hard was protecting her from the price she would pay for his love. Though they hadn't spoken the words yet, what was in her eyes was unmistakable.

"I can see smoke rising over there. We should check this out," Sarah said.

"Are you sure? Maybe it would be better if we go around," Aaron said.

Sarah chuckled. "There are good people in the world, I can assure you. We'll be cautious and besides, perhaps those on the Raven will see it too."

Aaron nodded. The campfires were farther away than they looked, and it took the better part of the afternoon to reach the camp. The smell of cooking food made his mouth water as they approached. Aaron counted about thirty wagons constructed as small houses on wheels. All were painted with bright colors that stood in stark contrast to the forest around them. There were children running around playing, and people went along doing their daily chores. Echoes of wood being chopped could be heard on the far side of the camp. They were greeted by a bald older man blessed with a symmetrical head that his lack of hair enhanced. He was followed by a grizzly-looking man with a beard that reached down his chest. He looked as if he could chop down an entire tree with one swing from the axe he carried or wrestle a bear, Aaron couldn't decide which. The older man smiled in greeting while the other looked on calmly.

"Greetings, strangers. I'm Tolvar," the older man said.

"Hello, Tolvar, I'm Aaron," he said, shaking the man's hand. "And this is Sarah."

Tolvar's eyes lit up. "Truly a sight to behold. You surely are the queen of beauty," he said with a slight bow, gently taking Sarah's hand. "This is my son, Armel." Armel nodded to each in turn. "What brings you to our little neck of the woods?"

Aaron and Sarah shared a quick glance. "Chance, I'm afraid," Aaron said, and told Tolvar of the storm and how they became separated from their ship during the Ryakul attack. They were approached by an older woman whose black hair showed streaks of gray.

"Margret," Tolvar called in greeting. "Tonight, we have honored guests. Victims of the recent storm and a dastardly Ryakul attack."

"Good sir," Sarah said, "we seek not to impose upon your generosity. Perhaps there is some way that we may offer aid to your people in exchange for a place by your fire."

"By the Goddess, the sound of her voice is enough to still this old man's heart," Tolvar said, elbowing Aaron's arm. "Or perhaps this young man's, eh?" he said, letting out a hearty laugh.

Aaron's face flushed in embarrassment, and he noticed Sarah's cheeks reddening as well.

"Enough, Tolvar," Margret said. "Of course you are welcome. Courtesy is not dead, now is it? Come along with me, dear, I'm sure the men can find something to occupy their time until supper."

Aaron watched as Sarah allowed herself to be guided away by Margret.

"Women, wives in particular," Tolvar sighed. "I've called that woman wife for more than thirty years, and she still thinks of all men as misbehaving boys. Very well, come with me."

"Aren't you worried that the Ryakuls will see your campfires?" Aaron asked.

"Nonsense, these are no ordinary fires, my boy," Tolvar answered, but didn't say anything more.

They headed in the opposite direction with Armel bringing up the rear. They came upon a smaller wagon that held casks of which one was tapped. Tolvar grabbed three steins and filled them with dark ale. Armel accepted one silently and took a hearty swallow, allowing the foam to gather on his mustache. Aaron took the proffered stein and sipped the dark ale. The rich, bittersweet chocolate liquid rolled through his mouth, leaving hints of malt in its wake. He took a bigger sip, nodding in appreciation to Tolvar.

"That's good," Aaron said.

"Hits the spot, doesn't it?" Tolvar said, and Armel sighed in agreement.

"I have a question about the fires. The ones you say won't draw the Ryakuls," Aaron said.

"Let's just say they burn with a little something extra to keep the beasts at bay," Tolvar answered aloofly. "Why are you so concerned with Ryakuls?"

"Let's just say they have a knack for turning up wherever I happen to be," Aaron answered.

"Ahh, that is unfortunate, and I now understand your concern. You're worried that your presence here will put the camp and my family at risk."

Aaron nodded.

"Well, fear not; we have ways to shield us from unfriendly eyes. You may take your ease here this night without worry."

"Where were you heading when the Ryakuls attacked your ship?" Armel asked.

"Armel," Tolvar admonished, "we mustn't impose upon our guest's privacy."

"It's okay, really. We're heading east," Aaron answered.

Tolvar nodded. "I'm afraid you're heading in the wrong direction if you wish to avoid the Ryakuls."

"I know this, but it's where I need to go," Aaron said, drinking the last of his ale; it was quite good.

Tolvar's eyebrows raised for a moment at Aaron's answer, then he looked at Armel. "Armel, please put that axe away. Perhaps now that we've had some refreshment, you are up for a bit of fun? A game?" Tolvar asked, rising.

"Sounds good."

After refilling their steins, Tolvar led them to a gathering of men who were throwing knives and hand axes. Armel picked up a couple of axes and handed one to Aaron.

"Care for a go?" Armel asked. When Aaron nodded, the big man launched the axe with blurring speed and it buried itself in the center of the target.

Aaron tested the weight of the hand axe and noted that it was pretty well balanced. He held the axe before him, lining it up with his target, and calmly sent the axe into the target, landing alongside Armel's axe, albeit not as deep.

Tolvar laughed with delight. "Not one for brute strength I see."

"Only when the occasion calls for it," Aaron answered, retrieving both axes and handing one back to Armel.

"How about the one over there," Armel said, gesturing toward the farthest target, which was a good sixty paces away. He lined up his shot and sent the axe sailing into the target, where it stuck perfectly center. Armel made it look easy.

Aaron lined up his shot, then brought his arm down, sending the axe just wide of the target. Some of the onlookers laughed, and he looked back at Tolvar and Armel and shrugged his shoulders.

"Try again," Tolvar urged, handing him another axe.

He took a breath and then blocked out the noise of the camp until it was just himself and the target. A slight breeze toyed with the branches overhead, but Aaron was fixed on the target as he brought the axe up. He focused himself, and the bladesong filled his mind, sharpening his perceptions. The familiar tingle spread throughout his limbs as he summoned the energy from the ground below, allowing it to course through his body. He hurled the axe with such force that the tree stump exploded in a shower of splinters. The men around them gasped aloud, but Tolvar nodded to himself and studied Aaron thoughtfully.

"Not bad," Armel said, appearing not to be surprised, and motioned for Aaron to follow.

Aaron was shocked; he hadn't meant to throw the axe like that. He hadn't even known he could do that. They walked to the remains of the target and retrieved their axes. Two men came with a new target and mounted it in place of the old one.

"How about we make this more interesting?" Armel asked. "Do you think you can keep my axe from reaching the target?"

"Are you serious?"

"We know you have strength, but do you have control, I wonder," Armel answered. "It is possible, I assure you. If you like, I will block your next throw even if you throw as you did before."

Aaron looked back at Tolvar, who nodded. He picked up his axe and called the bladesong in his mind. The power answered his call more eagerly than before. He brought up the axe and hurled it with all his might toward the target. A flash of light and a loud clang echoed as the axe buried itself into the ground well short of the target. Laying only a few feet away was Armel's axe. Aaron looked at Armel in surprise, and the man simply smirked back at him and held up another axe tauntingly.

Armel threw his axe five more times, and each time Aaron tried to knock it out of the air like Armel had done to his, only he missed by a wide margin. What was he doing wrong? Armel had made it look so easy. Even when he hurled the axe with all his strength so that the axe blurred from sight, Armel's axe still hit the target first. The big man said nothing but held up another axe, waiting for the next throw with an amused glint in his eyes.

"Might I offer a bit of advice?" Tolvar asked quietly beside Aaron. "Your mind is divided. Focus on one target at a time."

He already was focusing on the target, Aaron thought bitterly, grabbing another axe. He needed to keep Armel's axe from the tree stump, which meant watching Armel's axe and the target...his thoughts scattered as Tolvar's point was driven home. He summoned the bladesong to his mind, and his perceptions sharpened. Taking a deep breath and holding it, he nodded to Armel. When the big man sent his axe sailing to the target, Aaron drew in the energy until he felt he would burst and focused on Armel's axe. Time seemed to slow down, and Aaron saw the pattern of the axe's flight. He unleashed the axe, focusing his energy on its flight, using the air to guide its path. Like a falcon dive bombing his quarry, Aaron's axe forced Armel's into the ground in a cloud of dirt.

"Very good," Tolvar shouted, clapping. The men who watched nodded in approval.

"Well done," Armel said simply.

"Thank you," Aaron said.

"We haven't seen anyone block Armel's axe in a long time, and to be quite honest, his axe needed it," Tolvar said with a smile toward his son. "You know, I haven't seen it done in many years, since before the fall of Shandara, I'd say. Right, Armel?" Tolvar asked, and Armel thought for a moment, then nodded back. "That's right. It was the night we hosted that crowned prince if you can believe that. What was his name?" Tolvar rubbed the back of his neck, and Aaron's heart pounded. "Hmmm...Romus or Ryan? No, that's not right. When you're as old as I am, you lose some of the details," Tolvar said with a furrowed brow.

"Reymius?" Aaron asked quietly.

"Yes!" Tolvar exclaimed, his eyes lighting up excitedly. "It took him many more tries to block Armel's throw," Tolvar said, and Aaron glanced back at Armel, attempting to calculate his age. While the man was older, it didn't add up in his mind.

"Did you know Reymius?" Tolvar asked.

"Yes," Aaron replied, and images of his family played through his mind, from his grandfather's kindly face to his mother's endearing eyes and his father's strong demeanor. A lump grew in his throat. No matter how much time passed, he would never stop missing them.

"Haven't seen his like in a long time. That is"—Tolvar paused, looking at Aaron pointedly—"until today."

Aaron stiffened, and Tolvar put his hand on Aaron's shoulder. "It's all right, son, you are among friends here. Especially a scion of the house Alenzar'seth."

Aaron gaped at him. "How did you know?"

"Trust that some of us see with eyes beyond that of ordinary men. Perhaps in time you will as well." Tolvar smiled sincerely. "It gladdens my heart to know that at least some of you escaped the destruction of Shandara. But it breaks the wanderer's heart not to be able to traverse the lands of Shandara, for they were among the most beautiful in all the world." The sun had dipped low in the sky, and the men started heading back to camp. "Be at ease this night, and know that you are safe here." Tolvar spoke in such a way that Aaron believed him.

The lone roar of a Ryakul drew Aaron's gaze to the sky. It was too far to see, and Tolvar again reassured him that the Ryakul couldn't find them here. Having convinced himself that the mysterious rider of the Ryakul was in fact the Drake, Aaron wondered if the protection of the camp would thwart even the Drake. It was a short walk back to camp, where wood was being piled high for several bonfires. Tolvar took Aaron to a place where they could wash up, and while it wasn't a hot shower, it did feel good to be clean. Aaron kept scanning the crowd for some sign of Sarah, but couldn't find her. They took their ease on one of the many benches that surrounded the bonfires, and Margret walked up and whispered into Tolvar's ear. He smiled and nodded back to his wife.

"Not to worry, Aaron, she'll be along shortly," Margret said, smiling in reassurance.

The sun had set, and the brilliance of the firelight filled the air with a comforting flare. Smells of cooking food made Aaron's stomach grumble as Armel and some others joined them, bringing food that tasted as delicious as it smelled. Sarah's absence kept gnawing away at him, and while he suspected no foul play on the part of his host, the lack of her presence was grating his nerves.

"Aaron, I must take my leave from you at this time, but you should stay here with Armel and the other unmarried men," Tolvar said, and he quickly departed before Aaron could inquire.

Aaron noticed a group of men setting up a variety of drums off to the side, who were soon joined by others carrying different sorts of instruments. A hush swept over the crowd, and he glanced at the other men, but their attention was focused across the way, beyond the bonfires. The drummers beat their drums in unison with their sticks gliding effortlessly through the air. Each beat of the drum was precise and at times so fast that it was chaotic in its harmony.

Colorfully dressed dancers appeared between the bonfires. All the dancers were female, and as they spun, their skirts flared, showing a rainbow of colors and a good portion of their legs. He spotted Sarah spinning and stomping her bare feet in time with the others. Her dark shirt clung to her skin, leaving her bare midriff caressed by firelight. Her long blonde hair rode the air in waves, following the rest of her body as she moved with grace few could hope to achieve. Their eyes locked, and her smile made the heat rise in his chest and melt his heart. He followed her movements, unable to tear his eyes away until she faded from view, going to the far side of the bonfire.

Aaron could feel the rhythm of the music course through him, quickening its pace, and his beating heart rose to keep time. The bonfires flared brilliantly as the dance continued. A familiar presence tickled the edges of his senses. His eyes found Sarah's once again, and she smiled. Aaron extended his senses and was swept away amid the torrent of energy emanating from the crowd as it focused on the dancers. *See with eyes beyond that of ordinary men.* Tolvar's words echoed in his mind. Aaron searched the crowd and found Tolvar and his wife watching him.

A hand gently gripped his shoulder, and Armel nodded toward the dancers. "The choosing is about to begin." Aaron looked at Sarah and back at Armel with raised eyebrows. "Tolvar didn't tell you? You've come to us on a night of the choosing, celebrated with the solstices. Where a woman may choose a man she finds worthy, and if he accepts her laurel crown, he will be with her for as long as they both wish."

Aaron's breath quickened as he turned back to Sarah, swimming in her deep-blue eyes swathed in golden firelight beneath the starlit sky. She smiled at him in that way of hers, and the world around them faded to gray as Aaron finally accepted what his heart had been telling him since they first met. With Sarah, he would always be playing for keeps. He loved her, despite the worlds that separated them and being so far from everything he had ever known. In this place, Safanar, he had found his other half, and in a span between moments, a single wave of truth purged all doubts as he saw the very same reflected in her eyes.

The women resumed their circuit, weaving through the bonfires, and the men fought to keep themselves from giving in to their urges to join in the dance. Aaron wondered if Sarah understood what this dance meant.

Did he?

They had known each other for such a short time, just a few weeks aboard the Raven and a few brief moments in time before that. Was that enough? His father would have told him you only needed a few key moments to realize how you felt about someone.

How do you feel when you look at her, when she's looking back at you?

How do you feel when you watch her, when she's not looking?

And probably the most important, how do you feel when you kiss her? All the rest is whether you want to admit it to yourself.

Aaron recalled the conversation as clear as day. It had been when he had asked his father how he knew that his mother was the one. He smiled a bit in remembrance of gentler days, and then Sarah stood before him, glowing with the firelight caressing her silhouette. She held out her hand to him, and he stared at it for a moment before rising and taking her hand in his. Other men who had been chosen rose and removed their shirts, and Aaron followed suit. The tattoo of the dragon shimmered in the firelight, a living replica of the medallion in his pocket.

The bonfires grew in an unearthly brilliance, releasing bursts into the night sky. Sarah reached up and removed a crown of laurels from the flowers in her hair, and Aaron knelt before her. She gently placed her laurel crown on his head, and he felt an invisible shroud of warmth rest on his shoulders, cascading down his back. Aaron rose to his feet and moved in rhythm with Sarah, and the rest of the world was gone from his mind.

Love is just love, Aaron. There is no perfect time. His father's voice whispered in the back of his mind, and Aaron clutched to this moment. He had never felt happier or more at peace.

The rest of the camp rose to join the chosen, but for Aaron and Sarah the world resided in both their eyes. Aaron felt a hand clamp down on his shoulder.

"Congratulations," Tolvar said, with his wife grinning next to him.

Aaron's reply was cut off as a Ryakul's shriek pierced the night above them, sending a hush over the camp as they looked up in alarm. He could hear the wings beating the air in great swaths as the Ryakul circled the camp. Sarah's hand found his and squeezed in gentle reassurance. A shadowed figure rode the Ryakul, searching, seeming to look upon the crowd but not seeing any of them.

"Are you sure the protection will hold?" Aaron asked.

"It will not breach the protection of this camp," Tolvar replied firmly.

"Are you sure? Whatever that thing is riding the Ryakul, it can sense that something is not right here. Perhaps you should get your people to safety," Aaron said.

The Ryakul stopped circling directly above them. The rider's long howl sawed through the air, causing them to cover their ears in a feeble attempt to block out the piercing sound. Aaron collapsed to the ground, clutching his chest. The dragon tattoo burned and shimmered silver in the darkness. His vision burned red as the pain in his chest threatened to overwhelm him.

"Fight it, Aaron. It calls to you," Tolvar said as he and Sarah crouched by his side.

Aaron braced himself with one hand on the ground and the other clutching his chest. He felt it then deep within the fires of pain, a summons. This was the Drake, and its call stirred something sleeping inside of him. The silvery light of the dragon tattoo pulsed with his heart's rhythm, and Aaron glared up at the sky, feeling the building energy within him as if he had keyed a bladesong of pure molten rage. The voices of his ancestors screamed for vengeance on the Drake, who had robbed them of their lives. He felt his will erode away, wanting to be swept up in the torrent, and at the same time a small voice pleaded caution.

The Drake's call sawed through the air again, and Aaron stood up, firmly answering the call. The dragon tattoo shimmered brightly, sending glowing waves of light into the air. Summoning the energy of this world and the wind into his muscles, he prepared to launch into the air, but Sarah grabbed his arm, forcing him to look into her eyes.

"Stay with me," she pleaded.

Aaron glared back up at the sky, his thoughts scattered by the rage of his ancestors and Sarah's plea.

"It's what he wants. Look at me!" she screamed. "Face this enemy at a time of your choosing and not simply because he calls. Deny him." Her voice pierced him as no other could, and he held onto that rational thought by a string, slowly forcing the power of the bladesong away. He looked into her eyes and just breathed. With each breath he took, he stepped further away from the brink. The voices and urgings had only guided his will until now. They had never risen up to demand action. This new revelation both scared him and reminded him that this power came with a price. A dragon's call answered in the distance, and the Ryakuls gave in to their instinctual hatred and abandoned their search as the Drake struggled for control, flying away from the camp.

Aaron kept breathing, not trusting his voice to speak. He wondered what would have happened had Sarah not been there. He would have rushed to his death. All of those voices...all of that anger, even the echo of it still called out to him. If all of the Alenzar'seth perished against the Drake, how would he be any different?

"Ferasdiam has marked you," Tolvar whispered. "I suspected but..." He stopped in mid-thought. "It's good that fate brought you to us, Aaron. We will spread the word of your coming through the lands. It will reach those who have kept themselves from the world of men for far too long."

"The Hythariam?" Aaron asked.

Tolvar smiled. "Yes, son," he answered quietly.

Aaron could still feel the echoes of voices crying out just beneath the surface of his thoughts and shuddered. He delved deeper, beyond the anger, looking for the root of such hate, and there it was. *Betrayal...Despair...Anguish.* All standing helplessly before a force that one could neither avoid nor fight.

"I was told the Drake hunted down all of the Alenzar'seth and murdered them. Do you know how I can defeat the Drake?" Aaron asked.

Tolvar shook his head regretfully. Aaron frowned, knowing that it was too much to hope for, but he'd had to ask.

"I need to get to Shandara," Aaron said.

"Then it's good that a ship is even now bearing down upon us," Tolvar said, looking up at the night sky.

Aaron looked up and saw the dark outline of the Raven descending toward them.

"We are only shielded from unfriendly eyes," Tolvar said.

Aaron waved up to Verona, who was at the bow of the ship, calling out to the others. A crewman threw down a rope, and Captain Morgan appeared at the side.

"Mr. Jace, my Lady, if you don't mind, I don't know how long the beasties will be gone, but I aim to put as much distance as possible between them and us now that we've found you."

Armel appeared at Aaron's side, handing him two small curved axes. "Two in case you miss with the first one." He winked.

"Go on. We'll spread the word," Tolvar said, and Aaron grabbed the rope and climbed up.

27

REUNION

"I must say it took us a while to find you. Never would I have imagined that you could cover so much ground," Verona said.

"I picked up some new tricks along the way," Aaron replied, sharing a look with Sarah.

"Indeed," Vaughn said. "We saw you leave the ship—" Vaughn paused, looking pointedly at Sarah. "I'm glad that you are safe, my Lady."

"We had to set down to make repairs after the storm finally blew out. We found the remains of the Ryakul. I must say our project using crossbow bolts and arrows laced with crystals is quite effective at keeping the Ryakuls at bay," Verona said.

Aaron recounted the events after he left the ship, leaving Sarik barely able to contain himself with a question as to whether he could fly.

"No, I'm afraid I can't fly," Aaron answered, feeling a bit foolish. "What Sarah has taught me, some of you may be able to do. I barely understand it myself. Sarah is the real expert. But I have something else I need to tell you," Aaron said, waiting for them to settle down. "Some of the Ryakuls are being controlled by the Drake. At least those that attacked the ship were controlled by it. It came for us while we were at the camp."

Vaughn and Verona gasped, while Eric and Braden swallowed hard and Sarik looked questioningly at Garret.

"I need your help. The Drake is responsible for hunting down the Alenzar'seth, and it is coming for me." Aaron shared a brief look with Sarah before continuing.

"I think I speak for everyone here. We will stand with you for the duration of this journey," Verona said.

"I know." He smiled. "I'm not being clear. The Drake's call affects me in ways that you wouldn't feel." The ancestral voices stirred briefly, causing his stomach to clench.

"How does it affect you?" Verona asked.

"It has often been said to me that I am Ferasdiam Marked. One who has been marked by fate with the Goddess's blessing, which is curious because where I come from, there is no Goddess. Apparently, belief is not a prerequisite. When I invoke the bladesong, I feel the blood of my ancestors within me. Calling to me. Their teachings have saved me in the past, but when the Drake called to me, something else happened. I almost lost control to an overwhelming hatred that demands that I kill the Drake."

"No one is doubting your courage, even against the odds of all those arrayed against us," Vaughn said.

"It's more than that. The calling from my ancestors was for the blood of the Drake. I don't know how I'm supposed to fight this thing and survive when they all failed," Aaron said.

"He needs for us to keep an eye on him when the Drake is near to keep him from charging off to his death," Sarah spoke up, sweeping all of them with her steely gaze.

"Sarah," Aaron said quietly, "at some point, I'm going to have to face this thing."

"Like hell you do. And certainly not alone," Verona said.

The air seemed to solidify around them all until Vaughn spoke up.

"Peace, Verona," Vaughn said. "The fall of Shandara was a confusing time, twisted by dark betrayals and many fleeing for their lives from the place that we are destined to travel to. It didn't become apparent to anyone that the Alenzar'seth were being hunted until it was too late. We were preoccupied with taking in refugees and keeping the High King at bay. What are the odds that after the immediate family was killed, the distant cousins faded to obscurity and the beast that hunted them disappeared?"

"Then we head to Shandara as planned, free Colind, and get some answers to light our way. To face the beast now would be to face the darkness without any hope of success," Verona said.

Aaron looked at his friend. "Poetic as always."

Verona grinned and the discussion died down to a few murmurs. Sarah left, saying she would find him later on deck. She knew that's where he would be. Was he really that transparent? Aaron headed to the deck, into the crisp night air, with Verona in tow.

"Did you bring it?" Aaron asked.

"Of course," Verona answered, reaching behind a lockbox on deck and pulling out the rune-carved staff. "Safe and sound."

"Thanks," Aaron said, taking the staff. "Daverim said this would help. When I found it, it was stuck in the ground with his cloak hanging there. I swear, when I first touched it I felt the Drake awaken, but didn't know what it was at the time. It can't be coincidence."

"That's to be sure of. I can't imagine that your long-dead ancestor would insist that you take this staff if he knew that it would draw the attention of the Drake," Verona said.

"You're right. I think he believed that things would be drawn to me no matter what," Aaron said.

His grandfather had said as much in his letter. Surely the Falcons and the rune-carved staff could help him against the Drake. The blades were able to cut Tarimus. Why not the Drake? The only problem was that he would need to face the beast in order to find out, and he suspected that to truly face the Drake wouldn't be as simple as crossing swords with the thing.

"Looks like I missed quite a celebration at that camp. A crown of laurels?" Verona said, snapping him away from his thoughts.

Aaron couldn't help the smile that played across his face. "Yes," he mumbled.

"And Sarah with flowers in her hair. Never thought I'd see the day," Verona said.

"Can I ask you to watch over Sarah? I'm afraid that she will be a target now." How had the Drake known to take her from everyone that was on deck?

"Indeed. As if she needs watching over." Verona chuckled. "The lady more or less threatened that I keep an eye on you. It's strange there was a time such a short while ago when I questioned her motives for even being here. But now I see the way you two look at each other, even when you aren't looking at each other." Verona winked. "Well, it gladdens my heart for you both, but be warned I still suspect that Sarah has secrets that she has not told you yet."

Aaron thought the same thing sometimes, but he had no doubts that she would stand with him. "People have the right to keep some things private. Regardless, I truly believe that if there is something that Sarah needs us to know, then she will tell us at a time of her choosing. Now, speaking of secrets, what about you?" Aaron asked. "Surely there has been a woman who has caught your eye."

"If there was one of such quality as your lady Sarah and she wasn't in love with my dearest of friends, perhaps," Verona finished.

They said nothing for a few moments, both chewing on their thoughts. "Thank you, Verona, for everything."

"No thanks necessary, my friend. The world would be a far lesser place without you in it, of that I'm convinced." Verona gave him a playful shove before walking off.

Aaron stood there, counting himself lucky to have found a friend here in this strange world. He ran his fingers along the staff, tracing the strange runes. Then held it off the ground, feeling its weight. The grain of the dark wood was fine, and the staff itself was balanced. How was he supposed to use this against the Drake? He rested the staff back on the deck and lifted his gaze to the moonlit sky, keeping watch and silently praying that they would go unnoticed.

Sarah watched him cradling his staff from across the deck. The pull of one Aaron Jace was almost too much for her heart to bear. She absently tucked a strand of hair away from her face and with her other hand smoothed out an imaginary wrinkle on her clothing. She must have checked her appearance twenty times before coming out on deck where she knew he would be. Her appearance never concerned her much before, but now things were different. She liked the way Aaron watched her, even more so when he thought she wasn't looking. A smile played over her face, and she sighed. Speaking with Margret and the other women of the camp had helped her come to terms with her feelings for Aaron. She had always kept men in general at arm's distance. Aside from Beck, who was more of a father figure and was the only man she'd allowed into her confidence. Aaron was altogether different. Just being near him made her never want to leave his side. He now held her heart in his hands, and she couldn't even remember giving it away. He was only just starting to accept that he was the last scion of the house Alenzar'seth. He hadn't asked for any of this, and to have it thrust upon his shoulders... She understood all too well how the loss of a loved one could turn your life upside down. Most of her life, she had to contend with what the men in her life would do to her, but with Aaron, she was truly afraid of what would happen if he were to ever leave her behind.

She watched as his hands traced the markings, trying to gain some insight into what the staff could do. Aaron wanted to protect everyone, which was commendable but not always possible. She stepped quietly beside him and rested her hand on his broad shoulder. He looked up at her touch, genuinely surprised, and smiled warmly at her. She felt heat rise from the pit of her stomach, and her heart raced.

"You know, when I first came here I wanted revenge..." He trailed off, looking down at the floor. "And to protect my sister."

"In that order?" she asked.

Aaron seemed startled. "No," he answered quickly. "Maybe. My father's dying wish was for me to protect her, and since I failed up to that point, I wanted to honor his wish. They were after me, so leaving seemed to be the best choice. I don't regret leaving."

Sarah gripped his shoulder firmly. "None of this is your fault. There was nothing you could do to stop what happened. You had no idea what you were dealing with, and you should take comfort in knowing that she is still alive." Aaron stared at the ground stubbornly, and she hoped he saw the truth of her words.

"I hope she is safe. Tara is my half-sister, so they have no reason to take her." His voice shuddered, but the truth passed unspoken between their eyes. They could take his sister to get to him.

"I think you're right but for different reasons," Sarah said gently. "Mactar's hold on Tarimus is fragile at best, and he was only drawn to you when the protection from your grandfather was gone. Your sister, while dear to you, is not Alenzar'seth."

"Thank you," he said. "They wouldn't need to travel so far to get to the people I care about." He turned toward her and reached out, caressing the side of her face. "I love you, Sarah, which both fills me up and scares the hell out of me."

Sarah hushed him to silence with a kiss. "There is no safer place for me than at your side. My heart is yours, my love."

"And mine is yours," he whispered back and kissed her.

They stood together on the deck of the ship, bathed in the pale moonlight, keeping silent watch. Both wayward travelers had found a home in each other, and as their arms intertwined, they basked in the moment for however long it would last.

28

SHANDARA

In the following days, Aaron watched as the land grew more desolate and dark, as if the sun had forsaken this place. He knew they were closing in on Shandara, but he hadn't been prepared for the dreary landscape, as if winter's hold kept the plants dormant, but without the cold. The captain kept the ship along the tree line, hoping to avoid notice, but doubling the watch all the same. Aaron saw shadows moving among the trees and heard the howling of wolves in the distance. Zeus's ears perked up at the sound as he studied the landscape intently beneath them. Aaron caught glimpses of ruined towers along a river below, while abandoned villages and farms dotted the land.

"What drove the people from their homes?" Aaron asked.

"There are dark beasts that roam the land now. They weren't always this far, but they've never ventured farther than Shandara's borders," Verona answered. "Well, to be honest, not many live near the borders of Shandara anymore."

"Dark beasts?"

"Something sickens the land. Like the life is being sucked away."

Aaron pursed his lips and looked at the gray skies around them. "Or it's something underneath that's causing all this. Like a volcano."

"And driving what normally lives underground to the surface? I've never heard of a volcano so widespread as that," Verona said.

"You're probably right about the beasts, but a volcano could darken the skies like this," Aaron said.

"The land has been this way for twenty-five years. It's a bit of a long time for a volcano to produce cloud cover like this."

"It was just a thought," Aaron said.

"Regardless, perhaps when we meet up with Colind, the answers that elude us now will be given," Verona said.

"I hope so."

Sarik walked up and gestured to the far side of the deck where the others were waiting for them. They joined the others, and Verona took his place next to Sarah. Sarik stood between the brothers, Eric and Braden, while Vaughn and Garret stood off to the other side.

"I have an idea that I would like to share with you," Aaron began. "I don't know what we're going to encounter when we finally reach Shandara, but I have no doubt that the Elitesmen are following this vessel. I've asked the captain, and there have been no sightings reported of any other ships in the air, but it's just a feeling I have. Sarah assures me that the travel crystals won't work at the remnants of the city, but they could teleport closer to our destination and beat us there."

"Good enough for me," Braden said, and the others echoed their agreement.

"Through our training sessions, I've been trying to pass along the knowledge I have to help you stand with me against the Elitesmen. I think they're helping, but Sarah has helped me with some new abilities that may not be limited to me. However, they will not manifest the same way for everyone. I'll let Sarah explain," he said, nodding toward Sarah, who joined him.

"The Elitesmen use focused medallions to help quicken the process for an initiate to tap into the energy around us. Until recent years, this was a practice used sparingly because of the danger it poses to an undisciplined mind. However, the irregularities produced by this practice gained weight with the Council of Masters, and now it is encouraged," Sarah said.

"Irregularities?" Verona asked.

"Yes, to open oneself to life's energy is to tap into your soul, and the body is the conduit. Most souls are young, while others are quite old. When you open yourself up, you will be subject to the influence of the experiences of your soul's past, which can be both a blessing and a curse. Only a strong sense of self will shield you from those influences, but within the depths there is knowledge to be gained," Sarah continued.

"Some knowledge is best forgotten. If what you say is true, then you could be opening yourself up to great evil," Vaughn said.

"Only if you were greatly evil in another life," Sarah replied.

"There is a risk that comes with this, Vaughn," Aaron said. "My experience prior to the Drake's challenge was gentle urgings that guided my hand in combat. I was able to gain enough insight to unravel the pattern of attacks that the Elitesmen threw at me. Haven't you ever had a keen insight into a critical situation, and you couldn't pinpoint where the solution came from? Reasoning and experience account for much, but sometimes, when things matter most and the stakes are high enough, you need to go beyond the ordinary."

"Yes, but I suspect Reymius didn't impart any of this knowledge to you. My guess is that he had reason not to," Vaughn said.

"I don't know what he intended, to be truly honest with you. I believe he prepared me as he thought best on the chance that Safanar caught up with him in the end. Sometimes, I wonder if he ever thought he would go back. Opening yourself in this way will allow you to use the currents of energy all around us, but it will reflect on who you are as a person. If you're a physical type of person, then channeling the energy into feats of strength or speed may be possible. If thoughts and strategy are your forte, then greater clarity of thought may be achieved."

Vaughn nodded, conceding the point.

"The danger I was referring to earlier comes from a fractured mind and reckless use of this ability," Sarah continued. "The Elitesmen target certain individuals for advanced training beyond what their martial skills may be. Looking for certain personality traits such as a lack of empathy, being prone to violence, and the use of cunning brutality to accomplish goals."

"That explains my instant dislike for them," Aaron said.

"They can be quite charismatic too," Sarah continued. "Their followers want nothing more than to serve them." Sarah looked as if she were going to say more, but she stopped and shook her head. "We're off topic. Let's continue. The body is a conduit for the connection to the soul, and if it is overloaded, you can burn yourself out, which is why we train. The focus medallions heighten the sensitivity of the user, but we don't have any of those, and honestly, I wouldn't recommend we use them even if we did have them. When Beck trained me, he would have me meditate under various conditions, which allowed me to gradually become more sensitive. Aaron has started you all on a similar path. Practicing the slow fighting forms is a type of meditation for focusing the mind."

"Hold on a minute." Garret spoke up for the first time. "Let's go back to the irregularities you mentioned before with the Elitesmen's use of these medallions. I think it's important to know what we may be facing."

"Please understand that my knowledge is secondhand. I didn't actually train with the Elitesmen. I was trained by Beck, who left the order and was someone who kept himself apart," Sarah replied.

"Fair enough. Anything you can share though would be useful, I think," Garret said.

"Beck spoke of the Council of Masters trying to create a group of specialized Elitesmen who could affect the elements. Like creating fire where there was none. Our perception of fire, for example, is not as acute as someone who constantly obsesses about it," Sarah said.

"Did they succeed?" Garret asked.

"To a certain extent. They learned that the elements had their limitations. The mind-body connection is easier to manipulate than the world around them."

"That's why you had Aaron try that jump before the attack," Sarik said.

"Yes. I had very little doubt that he could achieve it, as he was already using these abilities when facing the Elitesmen, albeit in a more subtle way," Sarah answered.

"When my grandfather died, he left me these swords," Aaron said, drawing the Falcons from their sheaths. "The holes in the blade carry a melody when wielded. The bladesong helped heighten my connection to life's energy all around me. I think I can do something similar with all of you if you're willing to try."

Verona and Sarik gave their assent quickly and were followed by Eric and Braden. Vaughn and Garret, however, exchanged a few glances, and while Vaughn still looked skeptical, Garret then nodded as well.

"Come, Vaughn, let us see if an old dog can indeed learn new tricks, shall we?" Verona prodded with a grin.

Vaughn let out a small laugh. "Perhaps."

"Great," Aaron said. "All right then. Have a seat and close your eyes. Focus on your breathing. Close your mind to all distractions. When you hear the bladesong, try to open yourself up."

When the others sat upon the deck, Aaron was somewhat surprised to see Sarah join them. She regarded him with a slight smile and closed her eyes with the rest. Aaron took a deep breath, focusing himself, and began wielding the Falcons. He felt as if it had been an eternity since he first rode out to that clearing back home in a torrent of sadness and loss while mourning his grandfather. The first time he wielded these swords, the bladesong sending waves of melodic sound through the air had helped him become whole. He and the blades were one, but the connection was deeper than mere metal upon skin. The blades came to life in his hands, and a warmth spread through his core as his perceptions sharpened, seeing the currents of energy surrounding the ship and in the air around them. The more he gathered the energy, the deeper it plunged into his own being. He turned his attention to the others, who resonated a shadowed light of their own as they waited for him to help open the door. He pushed the energy out to each of them, surrounding them with calmness, knocking on the doors of their souls. Sarah's presence filled him up and pulled him in almost to the point where he forgot all else. He had to resist that which he yearned for with all his heart. *Another time...*

He managed to pull himself away and focused on the others. The lifebeat of the others was present, but diminished in vibrancy, and he had to figure out a way to reach them. He swung the Falcons in slow, rhythmic motions, sending eddies of melodic tones into the air. Delicate tendrils of energy reached across the space between them, and he bound the group together. Aaron brought his attention to Sarik and Verona, hoping that youth would allow their minds to be more open than the others'. Sarik's youthful energy burst forth almost instantly, pulsating with vibrant intensity, and Aaron heard Sarik's sharp intake of breath as his awareness of the world around him heightened like never before.

Aaron shifted his attention to Verona, a man of many levels, fiercely loyal to his friends and the ideals of great men. His natural lively manner made one want to engage with him in any gambit conceived at the time. He reached out to Verona, beckoning with the excitement of a great game, and Aaron saw Verona's lifebeat surge forth as his friend broke through. He moved his attention to the brothers, Eric and Braden, and gave more of a warrior's edge to the bladesong. He reached out to Eric and Braden as he had to Verona, but without any response. He pushed out with his blades, sending a thrum of air, which bounced off their chests. He called out to them to rise up and heed the code of the De'anjard. Defend the helpless. Stand the watch. Honor your brothers of the shield. Sacrifice for the greater good. For the briefest of moments, Aaron saw their lifebeats pulse brighter, but they immediately diminished. They were not ready.

Aaron moved on to Garret and Vaughn, both men of some rank, as their word carried weight in Prince Cyrus's court and they were charged to watch over Verona. While Vaughn was clearly loyal to Prince Cyrus, it was Garret that Aaron believed was loyal to Colind. Through the bladesong, he reached out to the older men with an open hand, but there was not a flicker of change in their lifebeat at all. He stopped wielding the Falcons, bringing them to his sides. A lone shaft of sunlight momentarily blazed upon the deck where Aaron stood before being shut out by the perpetual cloud cover. He kept hold of the bladesong in his mind and looked at his companions. Verona and Sarik scanned their surroundings with eyes wide open. Eric and Braden gave him an acknowledging nod, while Garret and Vaughn's attention were on the others. Sarah caught his eye and nodded approvingly. Reaching two out of the six was more than he had hoped for, but Aaron was a bit disappointed that he couldn't reach all of them.

"You mustn't blame yourself," Sarah said, quietly coming to his side. "You can't make blind men see."

"This is amazing!" Sarik exclaimed.

"Is this what you see whenever you wield those swords?" Verona asked.

Aaron swallowed. "Sometimes. I don't need them anymore to focus myself."

"Why is it fading?" Sarik said in disappointment.

"It's not gone. Trust me. You will learn to maintain the connection longer now that you know what it feels like. Try to focus," Aaron said, and turned to scan the sky. "There, focus on the hawk. Take a deep breath. Can you see it?" Sarik's brow furrowed in concentration. "Can you feel its beating heart?"

"I can see it," Verona said in an exhale of breath.

"I can, too," Sarik said.

"But it's not as clear as before," said Verona.

Aaron was about to reply when Eric and Braden stood before him. "We have failed you, my Lord," Braden said.

"No, you haven't. This is only the first time. We will try again. I promise you," Aaron said

"For a moment, I thought I felt something but..." Eric's voice trailed off.

"It will be different for everyone," Aaron said.

Alarm bells shrieked throughout the ship, snapping their attention, and the sailors rushed to their posts.

"My Lord." A shipman approached, gasping for breath. "The captain requests that you join him in the wheelhouse."

"Of course," Aaron answered, and they all fell in behind him.

"Cursed Ryakuls," Captain Morgan grumbled, speaking in low tones with one of his officers. He turned toward Aaron and the others as they entered the wheelhouse. "I hope you have more tricks up that sleeve of yours. Markus!" the captain barked. "Signal below to charge auxiliary engine burst."

"What's happening?" Aaron asked, seeing the crossbow turrets rise from the depths of the ship.

"The watch reports that Ryakuls are following this ship. They are off the stern and on either side, staying just out of crossbow range," Captain Morgan replied.

"They are herding us," Vaughn said.

"Yes, but to where?" Aaron said. "Are they keeping us from Shandara?"

"No, but having them so close and not attacking is enough to set everyone on edge. This is not normal for Ryakul," Captain Morgan said.

Aaron and Sarah exchanged glances. "The Drake. It can control the Ryakuls."

"Yeah, but wouldn't it want to prevent you from reaching Shandara?" Sarik asked.

"If it's herding this ship, then it forces you to get there at a time of its choosing," Sarah said.

Aaron suppressed a shiver as he felt a familiar stirring underneath the surface. He'd held off the blood lust of his ancestors only barely at the camp, and now the Drake was closing in.

"Aaron?" Verona asked.

"This changes nothing. We head to Shandara as planned. We should stay on guard in case the Ryakuls change their mind and attack. How much longer till we get there?" Aaron asked.

"According to the charts, the towers of the White Rose should be visible in the next few hours or so," Captain Morgan replied.

Aaron looked out the windows at the gathering Ryakuls crowding the already darkening skies. At this rate, they weren't going to make it, and he saw that fact reflected in all of his companions' eyes. "Can we outrun them?"

"Only in short bursts. The auxiliary engine burst releases energy stored in the power crystals, which will surge the ship forward, but the Ryakuls will catch up eventually," Captain Morgan answered.

"How many bursts can they handle?" Aaron asked.

"Depends on how quickly the Ryakuls catch up. Sequentially, maybe five before they're blown, and then we're either blown up or stranded. They are an emergency measure at best," the captain answered.

Aaron was silent for a moment, considering. To come this far and die within sight of Shandara would be such a waste.

"Then we fight," he said. "Captain, do the controlled bursts, but don't blow the engines. Perhaps there will be a place within the city walls where we can put down and hold out against the Ryakuls."

"There might be a place if it's still standing." Garret spoke up for the first time. "The Dragon Hall. If we set down within its walls, maybe we could use some of the defenses there."

"The Dragon Hall is big enough for this ship to land in?" Aaron asked, unable to keep the disbelief from his voice.

Vaughn nodded. "You could put the whole of the palace of Rexel within its walls. That is, of course, if it's still standing."

They were interrupted by a shrieking Ryakul that rattled the windows as it passed. "We're out of time. Garret and Vaughn, stay in the wheelhouse. Help the captain find the Dragon Hall," Aaron said.

"Good hunting, Shandarian," the captain said, saluting with his fist across his heart, addressing him in the ancient form for those of the Royal House of Shandara. Aaron nodded back and left the room.

Aaron headed toward the bow of the ship with the rune-carved staff in hand, surveying the number of Ryakuls surrounding the ship. They could really use some help right now. Sailors rushed with practiced efficiency, manning their stations.

"I hope you have a plan, my friend," Verona said, notching one of the special arrows glowing with crystallized dust as Sarik did the same.

"How about not dying?" Aaron said.

The floor beneath their feet shook, and they turned to see the wings extend from the main hull of the ship. Spaced every ten feet were pods swinging into position. The pod caps opened in unison, revealing rows of glowing crystals. Aaron grabbed hold of the side and followed the sailors' examples as they all tied lifelines around their waists. He called Zeus over and tied a lifeline to the wolf, putting crossing loops around his chest so the line wouldn't hurt if it had to be used.

The Ryakuls circled their quarry with ruthless enthusiasm, patiently waiting for the perfect time to strike. Aaron focused himself, drawing upon the energy around them, and his perceptions sharpened. He scanned the sky, looking for some sign of the Drake.

An alarm bell ringing in increments of two from the wheelhouse went off and then the Raven shuddered, groaning under the force of the engines.

"The first burst," Verona shouted over the roaring wind.

The Ryakuls moved in a frenzy to block the advancing ship, swooping dangerously close to the lines securing the balloons and the wings. Aaron grabbed one of the small curved axes given to him by Armel and tracked the approaching group of Ryakuls. He sucked in the energy from the wind, feeling it rapidly spread throughout his limbs while never taking his eyes from the lead Ryakul. The black beast closed in, aiming its talons for the ship's wing. Aaron unleashed the small curved axe, sending it streaking toward his target. The axe shattered the armored tusk below the mouth, causing a small explosion of black blood. The lead Ryakul spun in midair, screaming in pain, and the small group that followed collided, sending a tangled mess toward the surface.

The sailors cheered as the Ryakuls fell behind and the ship broke free of the dark beasts. A call spread among the men on the deck. Alenzar'seth! Alenzar'seth! Alenzar'seth! The call spread throughout the entire ship, and Aaron faced the men while holding the rune-carved staff up in triumph. When the chanting stopped, Aaron saw Jopher making his way through the crowd, holding something in his hand. He knelt before Aaron, holding a broken shard, which he recognized as the remains of the axe he'd just thrown. Aaron thanked Jopher, who bowed and took a few steps back, watching Aaron with wide eyes.

"That was one hell of a shot," Verona said. "Picked up a new trick while you were away?"

"You like that? Unfortunately, I only have one more left," Aaron replied.

"Well, keep it handy."

The engine burst lasted for another twenty minutes, and the Ryakuls became lost in the darkening skies behind them. Verona assured him that the crystals would recharge over time. Aaron stayed at the bow of the ship, gazing over the landscape. In the distance, he saw the faint outline of buildings in the perpetual twilight. His hand traced the rune-carved staff, remembering the dying dragon and his message.

The land needs a champion. Time is short, and already the sickness spreads. Ryakuls are just the beginning of what was unleashed at the fall of Shandara.

The dragon, even Tarimus, had warned him of the path of vengeance. He had been so filled with molten anger that it had consumed him—and now? He looked back at Sarah with her long blonde hair cascading in the wind, glowing with a light all her own. Was she the reason for the change in him? Daughter of the High King. The High King who, along with Mactar, was largely responsible for the destruction of Shandara. Who even at this very moment hunted them. Would this fight tear him and Sarah apart? Cut their hearts until only bitterness and regret remained? He hoped not, but at the same time, he knew he couldn't run from this. Fate was indeed pulling on his strings, and when fate pulled on your strings, there was no choice but to play the game. Walking away was never an option. He knew it when he went through the portal, leaving everything behind to come here.

Sarah tied back her hair and turned toward him with those eyes of hers that stilled his heart. It wasn't fair to think about what he would alter if he could go back and change the course of time, and he shouldn't feel guilty for finding love, but part of him did. As if finding a shred of happiness was an affront to all those who had paid the ultimate price that led him here. They silently gazed at each other, speaking volumes but not saying a word at all.

"Stay close," Aaron said quietly.

"I will," she answered.

Aaron released his breath, nodded to himself, and then waved over Verona and the others. "When Verona and I encountered the dragon, it took us to a fountain with a statue of the Goddess. The dragon showed me images, saying it was the Goddess's message. A glowing white tree standing amid the ruins of a castle is where we will find Colind's prison. There is a tower with a massive carved relief of the Alenzar'seth's family symbol: a dragon caressing a single rose."

"We could use the help of a few dragons," Verona said, looking back at the already gaining Ryakul.

"It's not as if they were numerous to begin with," Sarik said.

"Do you know of the tower?" Verona asked Eric and Braden.

"The towers were part of the main complex of buildings, and if they are still standing, then we should be able to see them," Braden replied.

"Have you ever been there?" Aaron asked.

"We were children, but our parents told us stories. They were among those who escaped the fall, but they believed that the Alenzar'seth would return and that they would be called upon to serve again," Eric replied.

Once again, Aaron was impressed by the level of loyalty and belief the people of Shandara had for the Alenzar'seth. Even though the family had disappeared for over twenty years, the people still persevered, believing that they would one day return.

They decided to spread out and keep an eye on the horizon. Verona divided the explosive arrows between himself and Sarik. Aaron kept tracing his fingers along the rune-carved staff. He had felt stirrings of power emanating from it when he first picked it up and again at the fountain of the Goddess, but nothing since. Not that he'd had much time to spend with it.

He kept thinking about the White Tree and finding the tower. The landscape thus far held the bones of trees and hardly any vegetation, but Aaron could feel energy coiling beneath the surface, wanting to break the bonds that held the trappings of winter firmly in place. A winter without the cold. Colind had said his soul was stripped from his body, which was in an earthen tomb. Was there a way to reunite both body and soul and set him free from this prison?

He focused himself, drawing the energy within as he invoked the bladesong in his mind's eye. The image of the White Tree was brought to the forefront along with his need to find it. The runes on his staff flared brilliantly, sending a beam of light out slightly north of their current easterly heading.

A solitary spot amid a land in twilight was bathed in a lone shaft of sunlight. The Ryakuls' howls were close now, and the rear-mounted crossbows unleashed a volley of special bolts courtesy of Hatly, who was becoming legendary among the Raven's crew. The bolts tore through the sky, streaking into the Ryakuls and exploding.

The beam of light coming from the rune-carved staff stopped, but the runes retained their glow. Aaron felt tendrils of energy along the staff, and the Ryakuls' guttural roars pierced the sky as the shadowy mass of tusk and teeth enveloped the ship. For every Ryakul shot down, another took its place.

A Ryakul emerged from beneath the ship and perched itself on the railing. The Drake's call sawed through the air with such force that all activity on deck ceased. It locked its glowing yellow eyes upon Aaron, and its dark armor drank the light. It clutched a giant, twin-bladed axe that any normal man could barely lift with two hands. Verona and Sarik fired two glowing arrows, which it deflected, sending them flying harmlessly away from the ship. A soldier dropped from above, swinging his sword in a deadly arc, but the Drake swung its axe up, biting into the soldier's armor and sending the already dead man over the side.

Aaron felt the dragon tattoo twinge along the edges and the medallion grow warm against his chest. A single alarm bell rang through the silence. He yelled to Eric and Braden to step back.

"This is not your fight," he said, thundering past with the rune-carved staff clutched in his hand. Aaron stepped down to the main deck, where the Drake waited, poised as doom's herald. The ancestral voices stirred, but Aaron clamped his will down, not giving their bloodlust any footing.

"Here I am," Aaron shouted, and another alarm bell rang in the background. *One more.*

The Ryakul lashed out with its great tusked head at the end of its long neck. Zeus leaped at the same instant, his jaws locking onto the Ryakul's throat, holding on for all he was worth while the Ryakul thrashed about.

The Drake swung down from the Ryakul's back and hammered at the wolf with the haft of his axe. Zeus cried out as the blow sent him across the deck. Aaron brought up the staff, but didn't attack. The Drake studied him as he stood with one hand on the Ryakul as it shook its head, dark blood gushing from its wound.

God, this thing is big.

The Drake was a head taller than Aaron, who was usually among the tallest wherever he went. The third and final alarm bell rang, signaling the imminent engine burst, and the Raven lurched forward.

Aaron flourished the staff, the glowing runes streaking into view, snatching the Drake's attention. At the same moment, two explosive arrows plunged into the Ryakul just as the ship shuddered, gaining speed. The explosive crystal dust blew the Ryakul from the deck, sending the Drake over the side. Aaron rushed to where Zeus struggled to his feet. Zeus took a step and then dropped back down to the deck.

"It's okay. You got him," Aaron said, gently rubbing the wolf half-breed behind his ears. Zeus came to his feet once again and favoring one side, stood ready to go. Aaron gently grazed his hand over Zeus's ribs, and Zeus whimpered. He snatched his hand away and the wolf half-breed lay on the deck.

"He must have broken some of his ribs," Aaron said to Sarah, who came to his side. Seeing Zeus hurt made a lump grow in his throat. He couldn't lose Zeus, who had been his companion since the beginning.

"Aaron, come up here. You must see this," Verona called.

Sarah nodded for Aaron to go, promising to stay with Zeus. He leaped up the steps to the bow of the airship. The Ryakuls were in complete disarray, falling behind as the Raven sped away. The great towers of Shandara reached toward the sky. Some were jagged and cut short, like the spires of a broken crown, but even at this distance, Aaron saw that the capital city of Shandara was immense. The city stretched out, desolate and without a hint of life, and he wondered what the place must have been like when it was bustling with activity. In another life, he would have been born here.

Sarah joined them, taking his hand and silently scanning the city ahead. Zeus stood to his other side, still favoring one of his legs. He felt the energy within the rune-carved staff surge and flash, sending another beam of light toward the center of the city where a space beyond sight was illuminated briefly, until the beam melted away. Someone from the wheelhouse must have seen the beam, because the ship's course changed to head in that direction. There was a great expanse of wide paved roads leading to the city that at one time must have been well kept, but had fallen into disrepair. Aaron looked on, impressed by the amount of traffic the roads must have been able to accommodate.

"For a while there, I didn't think we were going to make it," Sarik said, joining them.

"There are forces at work here beyond any of us," Garret said as he and Vaughn joined them.

"You truly are touched by Ferasdiam," Vaughn said. "I believed wholeheartedly that you were the grandson of Reymius...but..."

Aaron slowly nodded. "Does any of this look familiar to you?" he asked.

"It was ages ago when I was here...as a young man. Don't look so surprised, Verona. I too was young once," Vaughn said. "You would be pleased to know that it was the one place in the world where the legends did not do it justice. The Alenzar'seth believed in the gathering and sharing of knowledge. There were colleges here, where people could learn and more. Gardens were planted throughout the city. To see it like this...so ruined."

"I never thought I would see the towers again," Garret said with slow tears brimming in his misty gray eyes. The rest of the group traded glances while the burned-out shell of a city loomed before them, whispering hints of a gloried past.

29

WHAT SLEEPS MUST AWAKEN

A loud explosion rocked the ship, causing it to list to one side. Orders were given to retract the engine pods for repairs. The crackling of damaged crystals could be heard from within the pods, and the ship lost altitude.

Sailors scurried around the deck, making repairs and gesturing toward the balloon that held the ship aloft. There would be no escaping the Ryakuls a third time, once they caught up again. They needed to land the ship and make repairs within the confines of the city if they were to have a chance.

"Do you think we'll make it to the city?" Aaron asked.

"It's going to be close," Verona answered. The great city loomed before them like a sleeping giant.

"We need to be ready to drop into the city near that tower, but I'm thinking perhaps some should stay behind to help guard the ship—" Aaron began.

"With all due respect, none of us are going to stay behind with the ship," Braden said, his deep voice resonating with his icy glare.

"They have a job to do," Verona said, gesturing toward the sailors, "and so do we, so let's be about it. We're the real targets here."

Aaron surveyed the group, all of whom calmly, but defiantly, returned his gaze with the exception of Sarah, who looked slightly amused. He knew she had no intention of staying behind.

"Nathaniel will have things well in hand. The good captain did serve in the military, which is why the prince selected him for this voyage," Vaughn said. "And most of these sailors have served as members of the guard."

There was a soft clearing of the throat, and Aaron saw Jopher standing behind him. Jopher had his swords and travel pack at his feet, and he wore the common garb of a sailor. His notorious princely arrogance was clearly absent in his sincere gaze. A small group of sailors swung down from the higher observation decks, and a bucket of tools overturned, spilling its contents on deck. Jopher immediately squatted down, helping the sailor retrieve his tools.

Prince Jopher Zamaridian has learned a touch of humility it seems, Aaron thought.

Jopher slowly turned back toward Aaron with his hand across his heart. "Please allow this son of Zsensibar to aid your journey to Shandara," he asked quietly.

"He's earned it," Sarik said quietly, and Aaron could sense the general consensus from the others, who were either indifferent or leaned toward allowing the boy prince to come.

Has being on board the Raven for a month truly changed the boy prince? Aaron wondered. "Okay, you can come. But you follow my lead and take orders when given," Aaron said.

Jopher nodded eagerly and began strapping on his weapons.

The immense city walls rose before them. Their smooth surfaces were made of a light-colored stone. How could any army hope to breach those walls? The others gasped their surprise at the sheer size and thickness, echoing Aaron's thoughts. The walls between what remained of the towers contained massive carved reliefs depicting the Alenzar'seth coat of arms. He studied the damaged sections and noted how the debris dotted the landscape outside of the wall.

"This city fell from within," Aaron said. "Whatever took this city couldn't have come through the walls. So how did they get inside?"

Just beyond the walls, the burned-out bones of the city stretched before him. How many must have died trying to escape what happened here? The mere thought sickened him.

"Could they've used travel crystals to get in?" Aaron asked.

"Only small groups, but there were no travel crystals around during the fall of Shandara," Sarah answered.

The Raven drew steadily closer to the ground, unable to hold its altitude any longer. Aaron scanned the roadways. From the corners of his eyes, the shadows seemed to move, but each time he looked closer he saw nothing out of place. The chill in the air seeped through his clothes, and he shivered. Whatever this place had been, it was now a place of death. A tomb from an earlier time. Though it was the middle of the day, the only light in the area came from the center of the city. Zeus whined, sniffed the air, and then let out a low growl while pacing the deck. The wolf still favored one side, but otherwise looked alert.

Captain Morgan set the Raven down near the Dragon Hall, a large octagonal building in the center of a complex of other buildings. The building was ornately carved to complement the gardens that were part of the complex. Everything appeared functional and beautiful all at the same time. The pride of craftsmanship radiated from it, down to the smallest detail. Shandara made Rexel look like a small country town in comparison. Aaron couldn't shake the feeling that the capital city of Shandara was modern by any measurement back on Earth. What really had him perplexed was how they'd achieved these marvels. The ship landed, heaving its bulk to the ground in a final thud, and a lone howl echoed in the distance.

"I've delivered you to Shandara as promised," Captain Morgan said, coming on deck with an officer behind him.

"As good as your word, thank you," Aaron said. "How long will it take to make repairs?"

The captain surveyed the workings of his crew as they moved about the deck. "How long do you need?" he countered.

"As much time as you can give me," Aaron answered. "If you have any tricks up your sleeve, we'll need those as well. We're not alone here."

Nathaniel nodded. "Good hunting," the captain said, and went off to supervise the repairs.

Aaron and the others descended the gangplank to the surface. Large cracks ran down the walkways, with some extending to the rubbled remains of a building. They moved as quickly as they dared coming out of the complex, leaving the Dragon Hall with its gaping roof behind.

The musky dry air became more apparent the deeper they moved into the city. Deep fissures scarred the roadway, and there were no signs of life among all the scorched remnants. The streets were empty, without a single blade of grass trying to claim what had been made by man. There was a stillness to the air that was only disturbed by each echoing footstep they took. Faint Ryakul howls could be heard far off in the distance. They drew steadily on, not speaking, as if an unspoken agreement had descended upon them to make their way to the towers as quietly as possible.

Seeing the land and the city of Shandara, Aaron wondered if he would have ever been able to make this journey without the help of his friends... *His friends...* Somewhere along the way, they had become more than traveling companions. He looked at Verona, whom Colind had tasked with finding and helping him. He wouldn't be standing here right now if it weren't for Verona. He had hoped that Colind would reach out to him once he was closer to Shandara, but so far he had not.

They turned down another street with a massive tower a short walk away. Aaron gripped the rune-carved staff in his hand and kept scanning the area. So much destruction. Seeing the burned-out buildings that had collapsed on themselves reminded him of his own home. The acrid smoke stinging his nose while he held his sister as she wept on his shoulders. The fires burning away what he'd failed to protect. Watching as the firefighters gave up trying to stop the blazing inferno that consumed his home. The same thing must have happened here in Shandara, but with considerably more destruction. Some of the fissures ran deep into the ground, and Aaron shuddered to think of what escaping from this place must have been like.

How could Grandpa let this happen and then just leave?

He knew that the past haunted his grandfather, but he'd had no idea just how deep those scars really were. To lose your wife and the home you labored to protect in so short a time. Part of him understood his grandfather's need to protect the one remaining person who was wholly dependent upon him. Now that he thought of it, his mother hadn't escaped Shandara entirely unscathed. Something had wiped her memories of this place. Something, or someone, Aaron corrected himself. The stale air of decay invaded his nostrils, and the dark side of anger roiled beneath the surface. So many lives lost for other men's greed, and he was thrust into the middle of their war. Seeing the state of Shandara, how could he not want to fight against all those who were responsible for this? Vengeance in and of itself was not enough anymore. What he wanted was a reckoning, and the two were completely different in his mind. This place was out of balance and spiraling toward destruction that went deeper than the city. He could feel the unrest crawl through his skin. The air felt energized, as if a storm were about to break out at any moment.

Eric stopped in his tracks, motioning for the others to halt. He stepped through the doorway of a building left mostly intact. Braden was peering through the doorway when Eric returned with a broad smile, carrying two metal rods about two feet in length. Eric tossed one to his brother. Each rod had a handled cross section just off-center. Eric grasped the handle, triggering a mechanism that sent small bands across his forearm. The rod extended and then fanned out, forming a golden shield. The shield was adorned with an etched carving of a tree. Braden triggered his shield, which formed in the blink of an eye.

Aaron walked up to Eric and ran his hands along the shield. The seams of the interlocking pieces weren't visible and the smooth solid surface felt cool beneath his fingertips.

"The shield of the De'anjard," Eric said proudly.

Aaron nodded, grasping his shoulder. They collapsed the shields, which returned to their original form just as quickly and silently, leaving Aaron slightly in awe of the craftsmanship used to construct such a thing.

"Aaron," Verona whispered. "It's not that I don't appreciate the calm reprieve from people trying to kill us, but isn't this a little too easy?"

"He's right. I would have thought we'd have seen something by now," Garret said.

The Elitesmen were here, they just hadn't shown themselves yet. A dark shape swooped overhead, and they scattered out of sight. The Ryakuls couldn't have caught up to them that quickly.

"We have to keep moving," Aaron said, and continued toward the tower.

The others followed silently, and both Sarik and Verona had arrows ready to be drawn quickly if needed. The rest had their swords drawn with the exception of Sarah, which didn't fool Aaron in the slightest, as she was among the quickest of them. They rounded the corner of the gateway, passing underneath the tower and heading toward the interior courtyard.

Aaron stopped in his tracks. Beyond the tower, the scarred landscape gave way to a grove of trees, and the smell of fresh pine penetrated the stale air. The runes in the staff pulsed, and he could feel a slight tugging at his core, drawing him into the grove. Aaron focused himself and tried to reach out for Colind, but he couldn't sense him. Zeus whined slightly, perking his ears with all his attention on the grove. A gentle hand touched his shoulder.

"Are you all right?" Sarah whispered.

Aaron nodded and continued forward.

Come on, Colind. Give me a sign.

The gnarled trees of the grove stood tall, lining a straight path, where a white glow radiated. Aaron jogged to its source. The grove gave way to a clearing where a lone white tree stood solitary and majestic, glowing from its own luminance. A border of light surrounded the tree. Zeus pushed ahead, limping past the border, where he seemed to phase out, becoming transparent. A soft rush of air blew back through Aaron as Zeus passed through the border, and the wolf half-breed came to a stop at the tree, wagging his tail. He stood straighter, not favoring his injured side anymore, but something was off. Extreme coldness rolled through Aaron like something had been cut from him. He reached out with his senses toward Zeus, but there was nothing but an expanse of cold.

Sarah caught his arm, reaching toward the barrier, shaking her head. "Death lies beyond that barrier. I can feel it, can't you?"

Aaron called out to Zeus, not bothering to keep quiet. He reached out, but was careful not to touch the barrier. Zeus started to come, but something else grabbed his attention, as if he were being called back.

A hooded figure appeared in a golden cloak, and a hand reached out to gently pat Zeus's head. Aaron's heart stopped in his chest. The stance of the figure was unmistakable, because he had seen it many times while growing up. The figure in the golden cloak was none other than his grandfather, Reymius Alenzar'seth.

He clenched his teeth, feeling the heat rise to his face as he fought blaming his grandfather for leaving him so ill prepared to face the perils that had come with his passing. Then a great weight settled into the pit of his stomach. A deep sadness as the lives lost to bring him here flashed through his mind.

Be...strong... There are no perfect solutions. Not in life, Son. The last words whispered by his parents were always with him. Aaron looked at the shade of his grandfather, no longer with the eyes of youth, but with those of a man in silent understanding. As someone who had walked a few steps along a similar path. Sometimes, we can only do our very best and leave the rest to hope.

Aaron stepped forward, and Sarah grabbed his arm.

"It's okay. This is something I must do. Wait for me," he said. When she nodded, he turned to Verona and the others. "Guard the way. This is something I must do alone."

Verona looked questioningly at Sarah, who nodded. He motioned for the others to fan out around the tree, but they kept their distance from the barrier.

Aaron lifted the rune-carved staff and brought it thundering down just outside the barrier, and the runes pulsed to life. Aaron stepped through the barrier leaving the staff behind. He was instantaneously engulfed in a blazing white light as the world faded away around him.

"Where did he go?" Sarik asked.

"He needs time," Sarah answered. "We must give him time." As she said this, shadows descended upon the grove, spilling beyond the tree line.

"Well done, Sister," a sneering voice called, emerging from the dark. "We couldn't have done it without you."

The shadows retreated, leaving them surrounded by too many Elitesmen to count, but it was her brother Primus who spoke.

"The company you keep nowadays. I must say, Father would not approve. Where is the Alenzar'seth dog? He was here just a moment ago."

Sarah met Verona's cold gaze as she was sure he was weighing whether she had betrayed them or not in his mind. She would not leave. Not when Aaron asked her to wait for him. She wouldn't leave even if he hadn't asked her to stay. Rather than waste time with words, she sent two throwing knives streaking toward Primus and Rordan. The Elitesmen at her brothers' sides easily blocked the knives, but the shock in their eyes was indisputable. If they came for her now, blood would be spilled. The lines had been drawn. She drew her sword with the ease of one married to the blade, its sharp edge gleaming in the light of the Shandarian tree behind her.

Sarah focused her mind, drawing in the energy from this once-proud city. Beck had given her the tools, and the Resistance throughout the land of Khamearra, her purpose. Her brothers drew their weapons, and the Elitesmen surrounding them followed suit. It was time to make a stand.

"Let us not be too hasty." A figure stepped forward, his black cloak billowing behind him. "We care not for any of you. Step aside, and I promise that I will let you walk free of this place," Mactar said, his oily voice dripping with poisonous reassurance. Although Primus and Rordan looked to disagree, they kept their silence.

Eric and Braden brought the shields of the De'anjard to bear and stood poised to attack. Sarah looked at the others and felt a surge of pride as all of them stood rooted in place with fierce resolve in their eyes.

"I believe you have your answer, my Lord," Sarah said.

Mactar looked amused and brought his hands up. A blue orb grew from his hands, crackling with energy. He thrust his hands out, sending the orb blazing toward the twins, and the orb bounced off their shields harmlessly. Gasps of surprise slipped from the mouths of the Elitesmen while Eric and Braden glanced at each other and back at Mactar challengingly. Mactar furrowed his brow, summoned forth an orb of dark energy, and hurled it directly in Sarah's path. An invisible barrier swallowed the blast. Then a voice echoed around them.

"You were a fool to return here, Mactar."

The deep voice of Colind, guardian of the lands, spoke out, echoing around them. Small tendrils of energy seeped out from the rune-carved staff and latched on to each of the defenders. Sarah felt a shield move in place around her and knew they were protected from Mactar's attacks. The Elitesmen drew their weapons in one single motion that spoke volumes of their discipline and training, their black armor making them appear more demon than man.

"Remember what Aaron has taught you. They are men. Face them as such," she shouted.

Verona pulled back a crystal-tipped arrow and sent it streaking toward the ground at Mactar's feet. The explosion sent the Elitesmen into disarray, but Mactar remained untouched, erecting a barrier of his own. Another explosion echoed behind them from where Sarik's crystal-tipped arrow found its mark. Without a backward glance, Sarah charged.

Purpose...

A voice like slabs of granite chafing together spoke.

The land needs a champion... The fate of the world rests upon the last scion of the Alenzar'seth.

The dragon's words echoed in Aaron's mind, weighing down on him. He opened his eyes to a shimmering world of twilight, and the shade of his grandfather stood before him.

"Why didn't you tell me?" Aaron whispered. His grandfather nodded in understanding, but remained silent.

"He can't answer you, Aaron. Not anymore," Colind said, his voice everywhere and nowhere at the same time. "Search your heart for the answers Reymius would have given."

Aaron knew Colind spoke the truth, but he would have liked to hear the answer from his grandfather himself. Reymius was dead, and with Zeus at his side, he knew that Zeus had carried out the last of his master's orders. Zeus was to help guide Aaron to Shandara and with that task complete, could now rest. His only link to the world he knew was severed, leaving him feeling truly cut off from the life he had always known. But he was not alone, and the solace he had found would sustain him.

"I've come to free you, Colind," Aaron said.

"I told you before, boy, I cannot be saved," Colind said coolly.

Aaron heard bitterness in his voice, tinged in a hopeless certainty of one's fate.

"Whatever you may think, you are alive. I can feel it. I can feel your life beat even from this place," Aaron said, and silence answered him. "We need you, Colind. This world needs you. I can't do this without you."

"Your friends need you, Aaron. Even now they are being attacked," Colind countered.

Sarah!

He shifted toward the barrier.

Stay focused, he told himself and stopped.

"Where is your prison?" Aaron asked quickly. He had to leave this place. Time was running out. "I don't know everything that happened at the fall of Shandara, but I know you had a part. Don't you want to help set things right?"

"I have helped!" Colind shouted. "I've given everything. A lifetime of serving the higher cause, and what did it get me? A dead wife and a son who became a monster. A gatekeeper for a pathway between worlds who is also responsible for unspeakable evil."

"Those sound like reasons to fight to me," Aaron replied.

"Those are reasons for vengeance and despair," Colind said bitterly. "Vengeance will only get you so far, and despair is all I have. When Reymius first called me to come aid you, I thought my redemption was at hand, but the more I saw of this world, the more I knew its people have moved beyond the guardians. They need to fight for themselves. Reliance upon a powerful few has left them firmly under the tyrant's boot."

"You're right. They do need to learn to fight for themselves, or all is lost, but there is something you've forgotten. Something that the most stalwart servant of the light can forget. This place has sapped it even from you... Hope," Aaron said.

Silence hung in the air between them, and then Colind replied quietly, "Even for Tarimus?"

Aaron felt bile rise up his throat, and for the briefest of moments he thought of abandoning Colind to his fate. Like Shandara, Colind had spent too much time in the shadows. Who was he to deny a father's hope that his child could be redeemed?

"Tarimus walks his own path, but if he chooses to follow the light, then yes, even for Tarimus."

Colind appeared before him on the cusp of the light barrier, dark smoke billowing around him so thickly that Aaron wondered how he could see. Aaron felt the presence of his grandfather stir behind him.

It's time for you to step back into the light, my friend.

The voice of his grandfather spoke, and a vine of light shot forth from the tree, wrapping itself around Colind's wrists and pulling him in. Colind erupted into screams as his shade made contact with the light, but the vines pulling him forth were relentless, and two more wrapped themselves around his torso. The thrashing shade was pulled forth fully into the light, and bit by bit, the shadow was burned away until only a luminous being remained. Colind's screams ceased, and the shade hung in the air as if he were sleeping. Then, in a flash of light, his shade shot forth beyond the grove to another clearing, into the center of a massive stone prison composed of boulders.

Aaron was pulled back, and the shade of Reymius slowly faded into the tree, beckoning him closer. He stepped forward and put his hand upon the bark. Of all the questions tumbling through his mind, there was one that kept coming to the forefront, demanding to be answered. He had to know why. What was the sacred trust that was imparted upon the Alenzar'seth?

Images spewed forth in his mind of a place where a dark rift hung in a valley. Something pressed against the edges of the rift, desperate to break through. As Aaron drew closer, whatever was struggling ceased its efforts. The rift hung like a dark-stained glass window before him. As he looked through, he saw a gathering horde of creatures in armor, the likes of which he had never seen, swirling like shadows in the dark, poised to come through. The land beyond was barren and dark. Those in front noticed him looking through, sending them into a frenzy with the promise of death and destruction. Whatever was on the other side was definitely not human. A large, heavily muscled creature filled the space just outside the rift, its long neck the size of a tree trunk. It swung its head into view, and wild yellow eyes regarded him with barely contained rage. Aaron jumped back and watched as the creature struggled against the rift, which barely held it at bay. The edges of the rift appeared to fray under the barrage of attacks from the creature beyond it.

Aaron was pulled away from the rift. This was the pledge of the Alenzar'seth. They were guarding the pathway from another world, where an invading army lay in wait, poised to attack. What was keeping this army of darkness from overrunning Safanar? He needed Colind. Was this why he was being hunted? Was this what Mactar had wanted all along?

Aaron pulled his hand from the tree, and the light diminished until it barely surrounded it. The currents of energy he felt were fading fast. He was thrust back into the torrent of the battle surrounding him. The others were cloistered around the tree save for Sarah, who danced between the Elitesmen like twisting death, keeping their attention off the others.

Not so far, Sarah.

The Elitesmen, as if hearing his thoughts, surrounded her. Sarah jumped and was met by multiple black-armored Elitesmen cutting her off. After a few more attempts, she simply stopped and held her sword at the ready, breathing heavily.

Aaron drew his Falcons and called upon the bladesong, summoning the energy from the tree. Immediately, his perceptions sharpened. He took a few steps, leaped up into the air, and landed beside Sarah, who looked at him with both shock and relief.

"I thought I'd even the odds," Aaron said. Not waiting for a response, he engaged the charging Elitesmen.

Aaron became a whirlwind of death, and the Elitesmen fell to his blades. The bladesong coursed through him, and its song assaulted the Elitesmen to the point of distraction. He was able to move as they did, only faster and with much more strength. He tapped the knowledge of his ancestors, who had fought many more battles than he ever could in a lifetime, and their knowledge was his for the taking. He unraveled the pattern of their attacks with increasing ease until they broke off and turned their focus upon his friends. As fast as he was, it would be impossible to protect them all. He shouldn't have expected that the Elitesmen would fight with any semblance of honor. What would he have to sacrifice so that they could survive this? Colind was now buried in his earthen prison, which he must reach. Time was slipping away.

Vaughn and Garret were disarmed first, despite Sarik's valiant attempts to keep the Elitesmen at bay. Sarik was driven back, as was Verona. Eric and Braden fought with their backs to each other with sword and shield, but were quickly surrounded. Jopher managed to get near Sarah, but they too were encircled by a wall of swords.

"Hold!" commanded a man in a violet cloak. "Or they die."

Aaron stopped in his tracks, taking a moment to gather himself. *Think slowly, there must be a way out of this.*

"I'm the one you want," he offered.

"Indeed, the stories are true. You are of the house Alenzar'seth," said the man, whose facial features and blond hair looked oddly familiar. Then he glanced at Sarah, and the family resemblance became apparent.

"You know so much about me," Aaron replied, stepping slowly toward Sarah and Jopher, who were the most heavily guarded.

"I am Prince Rordan. Interesting blades you have. I don't believe I've seen their like before," Rordan said.

Great, another prince. Rordan had confirmed his suspicions that he was Sarah's brother.

"I have, your Grace," Darven said, emerging from the shadows to the prince's side.

Aaron saw the man for the first time. "I know you," he said coldly, remembering the man who had dragged Tye's body through the portal. "You and I aren't finished; before this day is done, I swear I'm going to kill you." As much as he wanted to charge in and claim his vengeance, he also knew that would be the quickest way for his friends to die. They were trying to distract him. It was the only reason the prince came forward. "I would see the face of my enemy."

There was a brief moment of silence before a voice answered. "Your guardian protector is gone. You are all within my power now," Mactar said, appearing as if by magic at Rordan's side. What little light there was in this accursed kingdom of Shandara diminished even more.

For all that he had heard of Mactar prior to this meeting, Aaron had expected more than the wiry man with slicked back oily hair before him. Mactar reminded him of a bad used car salesman, appearing harmless but with an agenda to get the better of you. It was the eyes that didn't fit, appearing dull and dimwitted, but when Aaron peered closer, they became cold and calculating. The man looked directly at him, seemingly aware of everything at once. This was the man who had helped orchestrate the events that drove his grandfather and mother from Safanar? The one who engineered the fall of Shandara? If Aaron had passed him on the street, he wouldn't have given him a backward glance. Many must have underestimated this man to their demise, and the irony was not lost upon Aaron as to how the same applied to him.

"He's not gone," Aaron said with a small, knowing smile.

Mactar frowned, considering. "Well then, time is short for you if the Wanderer has indeed found his way out of shadow, as it were," he said, glancing in the direction of Colind's prison.

He knows.

Aaron continued to take Mactar's measure and added gambler to the list of attributes he was compiling for his enemy. Mactar could be nothing else. He was a puppet master of grand proportions, with the appearance of someone supremely inept.

Beware, a venomous voice whispered along a chilling breeze that danced across his neck, and Mactar's eyes widened in shock as well.

Tarimus!

Aaron tried to sense his presence, but it was gone in an instant. *Why now? Focus. The presence of Tarimus has put Mactar off balance.*

Rordan frowned, looking from Aaron to Mactar. "You speak in riddles, Mactar. Speak plainly if you must speak at all."

A Ryakul screech pierced the sky above them. The Drake was getting closer. He needed to do something. Though his blades were at his side, the bladesong was alive within him. He wondered if Verona or Sarik had more of the crystal-tipped arrows. No time. The energy still churned within him, waiting to be used, and he drew in more.

Mactar sensed this and shouted, "Enough!" He brought up his hands, sending a beam of dark energy barreling toward him. All semblance of ineptness left, revealing the cold-hearted murderer of nations before him.

Aaron barely brought up the Falcons in time to deflect the beam. He could feel the energy churn through Mactar like an inferno. Aaron felt the ground slide under his feet, despite the added strength he was pulling into himself.

Not here! This was Shandara. Home to the Alenzar'seth. Aaron pulled more energy from the tree until he was surrounded with a white glow. A lone shaft of sunlight penetrated the curtain of shadow, illuminating the patch of earth upon which he stood. He heaved the gathered energy out from himself, swallowing Mactar's beam, and spread it out to the Elitesmen. The air crackled and pulsated around them.

Aaron pushed outward, and Mactar, along with most of the Elitesmen, was thrust into the air, blown beyond the grove. The ground rumbled under his feet, and the bark of the tree faded to gray and split. The great tree fell with a colossal crash, and Aaron turned in time to hear Jopher cry out as Primus pulled his sword from Sarah's back.

Sarah fell to the ground as if in slow motion, only to be caught by Jopher, who managed to swing his sword, driving her attacker back while catching her. Something broke inside Aaron, and he released the beast within, giving a guttural roar as he attacked Primus faster than the eye could track. The man's head left his shoulders before surprise could even register on his face.

Aaron circled toward Rordan and the remaining Elitesmen with murder in his eyes. An Elitesmen quickly grabbed the prince and pulled him back into the grove, out of sight.

He turned back to Sarah and dropped his Falcons to the ground. A cry from the depths of his soul ripped through the air, and he fell to his knees, pressing his head onto her chest, listening. *Breathe, damn it. Just breathe.* Then he heard it. The barest hint of a raspy breath. She opened her red-rimmed eyes toward him with a gasp.

"Aaron," Sarah whispered.

"I'm here. I'm with you," Aaron said, grasping her hand in his, ignoring the growing patch of blood beneath her shirt. *Not again. I wasn't fast enough.*

"Remember your power." She sighed and lay still.

No... Not her... He rocked back and forth, and a crack of thunder and lightning split the sky.

"*Why*!" His scream echoed throughout the grove. "Haven't I given enough?!"

The medallion flared coolly on his skin, and the bladesong spread like wildfire within him.

Remember your power.

Sarah's sweet voice whispered from the depths of his mind.

"Aaron," Verona said from behind him.

Aaron sprang to his feet, snatching his swords off the ground, and began to wield the Falcons, pouring his own soul into the bladesong. He would do this.

Give all that he was so that she might breathe again, even if it meant giving everything he had. Instead of drawing energy into himself, he projected it away and into Sarah's still form. The blade's melody rode along the air, harmonizing around them. A golden light radiated from him, stretching toward Sarah's body and lifting it from the ground. Her long blonde hair hung shimmering like a curtain of light beneath her head. Aaron expanded the energy within her as she had taught him to do within himself. Instead of strengthening his bones and muscles, he urged her body to repair itself using the energy from his own soul. Her body healed, slowly at first and then with the rigorous fervor of that which blazed within all life. When her body was whole, she remained frozen in the air before him.

Breathe.

Aaron urged her body to awaken with a burst of energy, and he felt himself become spent. "Please," he whispered before collapsing, and Sarah's body gently sank to the ground.

The path is blocked, Tarimus's venomous whisper returned, and the air stank of his presence.

Release me, Tarimus beckoned. *Release me, and I will ensure her soul returns to its body. Delay, and she will be lost to you forever.*

Release Tarimus? "How could I release you?" Aaron asked aloud to the stunned silence of those around him. "Answer me, Tarimus! How can I release you?" he asked quickly.

"Aaron, you can't," Vaughn shouted, but his protest fell upon deaf ears.

Tarimus appeared before him, his black eyes appearing hauntingly devoid of life at first, but the raised eyebrows and set features denoted the desperation that lay hidden behind the bitterness. Tarimus untied his dark cloak, allowing it to fall into the nothingness that swallowed the area below his thighs. His appearance was slightly out of phase with reality, but for the first time, Aaron saw the scar that ran down the side of his hairless face. The one that Aaron had given him in the dream realm. A golden chain-link belt glowed around his waist, and Tarimus lifted it as if he were lifting a great weight, then let it fall back into place.

He had given so much. Lost so many people he loved. Would it be selfish of him to allow Tarimus back into the world so he could have Sarah? Tarimus was a monster, despite his talk of second chances with Colind. Whatever Tarimus did if he were to release him would be on Aaron's hands. Tarimus was the gatekeeper between the realms, but it had never occurred to him that Tarimus himself could have been trapped, forced to do the bidding of another. Mactar...

"What will you do if I release you?"

"My will will be my own for the first time in many years, but if you must know, I will hunt Mactar. That should suit you," Tarimus replied. "Hurry, time is short, and my hold on her is slipping."

Silence hung in the air as Aaron regarded Tarimus. "What must I do?" he finally asked, lowering his head.

"You must break the chains that bind me as only you can. The paths of the living and the dead are more intertwined here than anywhere on Safanar. Use your blades to cut through these chains. We have but one chance. Do this, and my final act as gatekeeper will be to allow the soul of this one to return to this realm," Tarimus said.

"How do I know you're telling me the truth?" Aaron asked.

Tarimus's lips curved in a mirthless half smile. "Can you afford not to trust me?"

Aaron clenched his teeth. *No, I can't take the chance,* he thought and nodded to Tarimus. He raised his swords and focused the energy within himself, extending it into the Falcons. The crystals within the pommels glowed with a pearly light. Tarimus heaved the golden chain away from his body, piercing the realm of the living. Aaron heard surprised gasps from those around him, and he immediately shut them out of his mind. He focused his will into the edge of his glowing swords, and with a thunderous swing, his blades shattered the golden chains that bound Tarimus.

Aaron staggered as the energy left him, gasping for breath. Tarimus stepped through with a great thud as his boots hit the ground, and he fell to his knees. Aaron straightened himself and watched warily as Tarimus rose to his feet. He didn't say a word. He didn't have to, as Aaron was ready to pounce upon Tarimus at the slightest hint of betrayal, and they both knew it. The others gathered behind him in silence with their weapons at the ready.

Tarimus surveyed the group and said, "You've become much harder since we last met. That is good." Tarimus turned his gaze to Aaron, and with a fist across his heart, he melted away into a dark mist.

Aaron was about to call out, but at the same moment Sarah coughed, sucking in air with harsh gasps. He knelt at her side. All thoughts of Tarimus were purged from his mind as he held her in his arms, watching as the color returned to her face.

"I heard you calling to me," she said shakily. "I tried to come, but the way was blocked. I saw you, but I couldn't reach you no matter how hard I tried. Then I felt myself being pulled...up."

"Don't worry about that. You're safe now. I promise," Aaron said.

Sarah rose to her feet and looked down at her own blood on her shirt. "What happened?"

"Primus stabbed you from behind, and if Jopher hadn't been nearby, it could have been a lot worse," Aaron said.

Sarah looked at Primus's headless body that lay sprawled a few feet away and closed her eyes for a moment.

"And Rordan?" she asked, and Aaron shook his head. "Another time for him then," she said, finding and sheathing her sword forcefully.

They shared a brief look of understanding, and Aaron looked at the others. "We need to move quickly. Colind doesn't have much time."

"What about Zeus?" Verona asked.

Aaron's face crumpled in grief, and he shook his head, tears brimming his eyes. Before anyone could say anything, he went to retrieve the rune-carved staff that stood planted into the ground where he left it. Sarah came to his side and put her hand upon his shoulder. He reached up and grasped her hand, holding it for a second before reaching for the staff. He felt the energy return to him as he carried it. Together, they raced up the path to where Colind's tomb waited. At least he'd managed to save her, but he was still worried about what Tarimus would do now that he was free. He glanced to his side where Sarah was. Worried though he was, he wouldn't change anything.

They only had to run for a few minutes before the path opened to another clearing, where a group of boulders stood stacked upon each other, forming an odd-shaped room.

"We need to spread out and search for a way inside," Aaron said, checking the creases where the boulders met, but all were sealed.

If Colind was awake in there, he would be running out of air anytime now. None of them could find a way inside, and Colind didn't answer their calls. They lined up and tried to move the boulders, but they might as well have tried moving a mountain. The boulders wouldn't budge, even with enhanced strength. The shrieks of the Ryakuls were coming closer.

"There must be a way to move these things," Aaron said in frustration.

"What about the ship?" Verona asked. "I can signal them to come, and perhaps they will have something on board that can help."

"If you send the signal you will give away our position," Vaughn said. "Aaron, can you beat the Elitesmen back as you did before?"

Aaron shook his head. "I used the energy from the tree, and it's gone. The balance of this place is fragile now. I'm afraid I'd only make things worse by drawing too heavily from the energy here." Something skated along the fringe of his thoughts. When Garret was about to speak, he said, "Just give me a minute, please."

He handed the staff to Sarah and knelt facing the boulders. They weren't a natural rock formation. Someone had put them there, and he was willing to wager it was Mactar, but how? Aaron blocked out all the sounds around him so he could listen to the quiet of his mind. The barest hints of crystallized tones echoed from a great distance. He tried to focus on the sound, but it remained elusive. Reaching across the space to a boulder, he felt a distinct vibration emanating from within the rock. He drew his swords, and a few notes from the bladesong reverberated off the boulders, and the vibration increased. He began to wield the blades into a tune that he had never played before. The energy moved through him as before, but it came out through the melody of the bladesong. He focused the energy toward a single boulder. Instead of the notes bouncing away, they were infused into the stone, causing it to vibrate more, and small dust clouds swirled into the air.

"Ferasdiam," Garret gasped.

The boulder lifted a few inches off the ground, groaning as it chafed against its neighbors. Aaron kept the bladesong going and shook his head toward the boulder. Verona gestured for Eric and Braden to follow him, and they all pushed. The boulder moved slowly over the ground. He kept the bladesong focused on the boulder lest it would fall to the ground.

When the boulder moved enough, Sarah slipped inside and emerged with a stooped figure. Garret and Sarik relieved Sarah of Colind's weight and gently laid the old man upon the ground. Aaron released the bladesong, and the boulder dropped down, shaking the ground beneath their feet.

They gathered around Colind, who lay unmoving upon the ground. Aaron leaned his head against his chest and couldn't hear a heartbeat. Aaron brought his fist down twice upon Colind's chest. The old man sucked in air and coughed, and the others sighed in relief. When his breath steadied, he opened his eyes and met Aaron's gaze.

Garret approached from the other side and eased a water skin to Colind's lips, urging him to drink. They watched in silence as Colind slowly drank the water. He looked at his hands, flexing his fingers, then down at his toes, which he wiggled, and then he let out a hearty laugh until he could barely breathe. It was an infectious laugh that soon had most of them joining in.

The clothing he had been buried with had long turned to rags, so Aaron reached into his pack and pulled out his cloak, wrapping it around Colind's shoulders. Colind thanked him and struggled to get to his feet. When Aaron protested, Colind waved him away.

"I've been asleep far too long, my boy," Colind said. He took a few steps and stretched his arms out before him. Colind was tall, approaching his own six-foot-four-inch height.

"I don't suppose any of you brought any food; I haven't eaten in years," Colind said with a twinkle in his eyes. Then he turned to Aaron, reaching out to put a hand on his shoulder. "Thank you for saving this stubborn old fool. I don't know what it must have taken to get you here, but I appreciate all of you coming."

"It was Aaron, my Lord Guardian," Garret said. "He was determined to come here, and the story he told was so compelling that we decided to join him."

"Garret, the last I saw you there was much less gray in your hair," Colind said, seeing him for the first time and reaching out to shake his hand.

"It has been a long while," Garret replied.

"I see you made it to Prince Cyrus's court at Rexel," Colind said, looking back at Aaron.

"Yes," Aaron replied.

"I'm afraid I must apologize to you, Aaron," Colind began. "Reymius forbade me to interfere after our last meeting. He insisted that you find your own way. The way back to your world was closed to me. Unable to be of use, I roamed Shandara and began to doubt that you could ever reach this place. After so many years in my prison, I allowed the darkness and guilt of this place to consume me."

Aaron nodded thoughtfully. "Is he gone then?" he asked quietly.

Colind looked at him for a long moment before answering. "Yes. He held out long enough for you to reach the city and the sacred tree of the Alenzar'seth. And now you know of the trust that has been placed upon your house."

The dark rift flashed before his eyes. "We have to find a way to close it. Whatever is on the other side is trying to get through. Even now it's weakening."

"Close what exactly?" Vaughn asked, but before anyone could answer, a group of Ryakuls streaked into view.

A lone Ryakul perched atop one of the towers still standing, and the Drake unleashed a piercing howl that grated his nerves. The call silenced everything around them. The challenge had been issued, and Aaron knew he had to answer. He took a brief glance at the others, who were all watching the sky, except for Sarah who watched him. Trying to run at this point would be foolish. It was getting harder to deny the ancestral blood. Their yearnings eclipsed his own. Maybe he could buy the others some time.

Aaron sheathed his swords and took the rune-carved staff from Sarah. The dragon tattoo stirred beneath his skin, and the voice of his ancestors' rage roiled to the surface. The Drake was here, searching for him, and perhaps it was time for him to face the beast after all.

"Keep them safe, Verona," Aaron said quietly to his friend.

Keep her safe, he said with his eyes. Aaron squatted down, and the runes flared to life. Drawing energy from the staff, he hurled himself toward a nearby tower to answer the Drake's call.

Sarah began to follow, but Verona grabbed her arm. "We'll be right behind you." Sarah nodded and followed after Aaron as best she could.

Oh, you fool. You stupid...stupid...fool. You're not alone anymore. But it was that same quality that made him do the things that he did that made her love him. She couldn't match his strength or his speed, but please let her be fast enough.

30

THE DRAKE

He landed hard upon the top of the tower, jolting even his enhanced muscles and bones. The medallion grew cool against his chest, and the staff glowed, pulsing in rhythm with his beating heart. The dragon tattoo felt alive on his skin as the power from the staff coursed through him. He turned his gaze to the Drake and felt the rage and bitter despair of the ghosts of Shandara feed into him. Shandara had become the broken heart of the Alenzar'seth, from the rubbled remains of this once great city to the dying land beyond.

But he was here. Against all the odds. Reymius had succeeded because he, Aaron Jace, the last scion of the house Alenzar'seth, stood upon this tower in Shandara. It wasn't fair for a child to inherit the problems of his father, or in this case his grandfather, but what other choice could he make? In life, there were no guarantees of fairness.

There are no perfect solutions, not in life, Son, his father's voice resonated through him.

The forces at work here he could never run from, nor would he even if he could. After the visions from the tree, he knew what he must do. The breach between realms was tied to the Alenzar'seth. Should he perish as the last, the invading horde would be released into the world of Safanar. That is what the Alenzar'seth had fought and died to protect. Through Reymius and his grandmother's sacrifice, this world gained a small reprieve from the coming war. The Drake was a sentinel for the horde and an alien being in the truest sense of the word. The Drake was not of this world or even from Earth. That was all he understood, and if fortune were to smile upon him, he would seek the Hythariam, for they were tied to this, of that he was sure.

Aaron reached for the small curved axe at his belt, running his fingers upon its curve. It was his last one. *In case you miss with the first one.* He smiled at the memory. He wasn't going to miss. No, he intended to make his shot count.

The Drake's call echoed throughout the dead city, dripping its acidic challenge, which sowed the deaths of so many before him. Instead of suppressing the ancestral voices within, he gave in to their urgings and was flooded with their command that he face the Drake. He brought the rune-carved staff up and slammed it down upon the stone floor of the tower, sending a thrum of energy away from him. The figure atop the Ryakul snapped its head toward him, and Aaron roared his own challenge.

Like a hound on the hunt, the Drake launched the Ryakul into the air and the beast roared from its gaping saber-tusked maw. Aaron spun and unleashed the axe, using the energy from the staff and the wind to push the axe through the sky. The axe burned through the Ryakul's head, leaving a gory mess, and the dead beast plummeted toward the ground.

The Drake quickly jumped from the beast to land upon the far side of the tower, across from where Aaron stood. It had to be over seven feet tall with yellow eyes that smoldered like liquid steel from within the horned helmet. The dark armor radiated a slight purplish charge that surged throughout its overlapping layers down to the feet, which ended in black claws. It raised a large armored hand, revealing emerald reptilian skin, and a device rose from its forearm, sending a thin red beam toward him. The beam ran the length of Aaron's body and was gone before he could react.

A scanner? Did it just scan me?

The Drake reached behind and pulled out a long metallic rod. The rod extended, doubling its length, and twin blades emerged from either end. The Drake brandished its bladed staff and charged.

Aaron rushed forward with blinding speed to meet the Drake's attack. The staffs met and sparks burst forth. Aaron spun, halting his momentum as the Drake did the same. Each approached the other more slowly, and Aaron lashed out. The Drake countered, and with each bone-jarring blow, Aaron was driven back. He sidestepped and punched, delivering a decisive blow to the beast's chest. As the Drake was knocked back, it grabbed his arm and pulled itself back up. Then it rained down a blow, sending a shockwave through him and pushing him off balance.

He stepped back and regained his footing, gasping from the blow. It hurt, and he could feel blood trickle down the side of his head. This whole fight was out of balance. Being off balance meant death. The ancestral bloodlust flared inside him, but he clamped down upon their urgings. While they had helped him in the past, he couldn't keep a clear head while under their influence. If he didn't take back control, he was going to die. He was his own master. He banished them to the far corners of his mind, but he couldn't erase their yearning entirely.

As Aaron shook his head to clear it, the Drake charged him again. His feet were swept out from under him, and Aaron rolled to the side as twin blades struck the stone floor where he had been a moment before. Aaron spun, planted the butt of the staff into the Drake's chest, and swung around, striking a powerful blow to its head, knocking it back. He snapped a kick to the knee, sending the Drake down.

The Drake reached out to grab his foot, but Aaron jumped away. Frustrated, the creature ripped its dented helmet off and tossed it over the side. Rows upon rows of teeth took up the inside of its mouth, curving in fiendish delight.

Aaron leaped up to the edge of the tower, balancing upon the very edge and ignoring the dizzying depths below. The creature rose to its feet and leveled its staff, aiming the twin blades at him.

Aw, hell.

Aaron leaped off the edge just before a screeching blast demolished the spot where he had been standing. The wind ripped past him as he plummeted down the tower. He used the wind to slow his descent, but he was still falling too fast, so he shifted the wind to push him to the tower wall. The rubble-strewn ground was closing in. His timing needed to be perfect. He drove his feet into the tower wall, launching himself away and into a large building where the wall had partially caved in. A blur of rafters streaked past his vision until he crashed in a heap on the ground.

Aaron rose shakily to his feet. A gun! The Drake had some type of gun. He hadn't anticipated that. Taking a few seconds to study his surroundings, he realized he was in the remnants of some type of church. Most of the wooden pews had been left standing, and on the far side of the room was a statue of a woman standing resolutely with her head lifted high. The statue was the same as the one the dragon led him to all those weeks ago. The fountain below had long since crumbled to dust. She seemed to regard him coolly, almost challengingly.

Fate has chosen you for this.

The dragon's voice whispered in his mind. Aaron stood up straighter, brought his right fist over his heart, and bowed his head in respect. He didn't know if he believed in the Goddess, but he had been through too much for it to be happenstance. It would have to be enough.

I don't know if you're out there, but I could use a little bit of help on this one.

A loud crash drew his eyes skyward. The Drake had followed him somehow. Aaron jumped up to one of the broken windows on the second floor, where he heard several screeching blasts. He gritted his teeth and dashed forward, onto the roof of a nearby building. A glint of metal caught his eyes, and Aaron headed toward it.

His axe!

He kept glancing back over his shoulder as he retrieved the axe, which was in good shape considering. Now all he had to do was get a shot in before the Drake tried to shoot him again.

Aaron could hear the stomps of the Drake's footsteps throughout the church. It wasn't taking any care to hide its position, or maybe it was trying to lure him into a trap. Aaron reached out with his senses, and the rune-carved staff snatched his attention. There was power there. More than there had ever been before, as if the staff had been infused with energy. He could draw upon the staff's energy instead of disrupting the balance of energy in the city—the city reminded him of a battle-weary ship limping along where one rogue wave could sink it forever.

Out of the corner of his eye, a shadow moved along the roof of the church, and Aaron ducked behind the remnants of a stone pillar. *Sarah...that stubborn...* He'd known she would come. They would always come for each other. Her catlike blue eyes challenged him to protest. Not with the Drake so close. He gestured inside the church, and Sarah nodded, pointed inside, then at him and back at herself. Aaron frowned in thought. She wanted to use him as bait. He tapped the roof loudly with his staff, and the noise from within ceased.

Aaron watched the window on the upper level with unwavering focus, waiting for the Drake to emerge. His breath caught in his throat as the Drake suddenly appeared, crouching on the far side of the roof. Its yellow eyes narrowed when it noticed Sarah for the first time.

"Behind you!" he shouted.

Sarah rolled forward and down to the lower roof, out of the creature's line of sight. The Drake quickly trained its weapon on him and fired. Anticipating the shot, Aaron was already jumping out of the way when the blast scorched the spot where he had been a moment before. He turned in the air and sent his axe streaking into the Drake's chest. Purple sparks burst forth from the creature's armor. Aaron landed lightly on the ground and headed toward where the Drake had fallen.

The alien creature was lying on its back with sparks crackling along its chest armor. *Advanced technology?* There was no time to consider further as the armor began repairing itself as the Drake came to its feet. Aaron gritted his teeth and dashed forward. Green blood oozed down the creature's side. The wound did not slow the creature down as it met his attack. The Drake leaped back and howled to the sky. His call was answered by the Ryakuls closing in on their position.

Aaron pressed the attack, but the Drake hooked his staff and twisted it from his grasp. It tossed his staff to the side and swung its weapon savagely with a satisfied sneer across its face as Aaron scrambled out of the way. The Drake raised its staff with the twin blades, ready to strike, but it was knocked to the side as Sarah struck from behind. The creature quickly spun, caught her blade in his armored hands, and grabbed her by the neck, lifting her from the ground. Molten yellow eyes narrowed as it looked from Sarah to Aaron.

Aaron launched himself from the ground, drawing his Falcons at the same time. The Drake swung Sarah between them, freezing him in his tracks. Sarah struggled helplessly. The Drake drew her closer and breathed a noxious green vapor into her face, and Sarah went limp. Aaron rolled to the side and swung with all his might, severing the arm that held Sarah. The Drake cried out in pain, stumbling backward as Sarah landed roughly upon the ground.

Aaron moved between Sarah and the Drake as it clutched the stump of its arm to its chest. The Ryakuls swooped down and landed all around them, hissing and growling. More were circling overhead. Aaron took a step toward the Drake, which almost sent the Ryakuls into a frenzy, so he stopped.

A bright flash of light illuminated the sky overhead, followed by a thunderous crash. The Raven had arrived. Two smaller crafts hovered next to it by no visible means of propulsion. The crafts were the likes of which Aaron had never seen before on any world. They charged ahead, streaking gold, and fired golden bolts, scattering the swarming Ryakuls.

The Drake watched as the crafts weaved through the Ryakuls. Then it collapsed the staff and leaped atop of the nearest dark beast. Aaron heard Sarah stir behind him, and he chanced turning around. Her face was contorted in pain. Her skin paled to the point where she looked like death's mistress.

"Sarah?"

Her eyes were squeezed shut, and she shook her head violently. Aaron tried to approach her, but when she heard him, she lashed out with her sword. Finally, she stopped writhing and stood smoothly to her feet. Sarah opened her eyes, and Aaron stepped back in horror as molten yellow eyes stared back at him through Sarah's beautiful face.

Aaron tried to step forward, but Sarah growled like a rabid beast, shaking her head in confusion. The Drake let out another howl, and Sarah jumped over Aaron to land next to the Ryakul that the Drake rode upon.

No!

Aaron's heart sank to his feet as he watched the woman he loved leap upon the back of the Ryakul, behind the Drake. Too stunned to even move, he stood there as they launched into the air and flew away from him. The remaining Ryakuls pressed in around him, snapping him back to reality. Aaron sheathed his swords and sprinted to the rune-carved staff, dodging tusk and claw. Screaming Sarah's name, he drew energy from the staff and launched into the air. He landed upon the highest building and launched again, moving past the Raven. A passing glance showed him Verona and the others were already on board.

Aaron focused on the Ryakul carrying Sarah, who briefly glanced back at him with those alien yellow eyes. For the briefest of moments, something vaguely like a human expression played upon her features, but it was gone as quickly as it had come. The air was full of Ryakuls snapping with their great tusked jaws, and he narrowly avoided them in his chase. Then a clawed talon ripped the skin along his back like liquid fire.

Aaron plummeted toward the ground, spinning as he fell. Fiery pain blazed down his back, so much that he couldn't draw upon the staff's energy to do anything. Not even to save himself.

A golden craft swooped under, and strong hands grabbed him, pulling him inside. They laid him down upon a cushioned bench. Aaron opened his eyes and jerked in surprise. He was surrounded by people with golden eyes peering back at him.

"It's all right, Shandarian," one said in a smooth voice.

Aaron blinked, trying to stay conscious, but the pain was too much. "He has her," he gasped, feeling blood pool under his back. He heard insistent muttering in a language that he couldn't understand.

"Who are you?" he asked, drawing their attention.

"You would know us as the Hythariam, and we are most pleased to meet the lost scion of Alenzar'seth. I am called Iranus," an older man said, peeking over the shoulder of the one checking his wounds.

Aaron guessed he was older because he was the only one with white hair, but his chiseled facial features were smooth, hardly showing any signs of age. The golden eyes were unsettling. They were too close to those of the Drake. Dark spots crowded the edges of his vision, and Aaron could feel his consciousness slipping away.

"Please," he whispered, "the Drake has one of my friends...captured."

One of the Hythariam whispered to Iranus, who nodded back. "Be still," Iranus said. "We need to tend to your wounds."

Aaron couldn't help closing his eyes. He reached out with his senses, focusing on Sarah from the bond in his heart. He felt her momentary shock and confusion at his touch and the cold bitter refusal as she shut him out. He flinched inwardly at the icy sting of rejection. *You won't be rid of me that easily, love,* he thought, and then the black abyss pulled him away from his thoughts as he passed out.

Aaron had been brought on board the Raven and carried to his cabin. They had gathered around his bed, but the haggard expression on his friend's face filled Verona with dread.

"Will he make it?" Verona asked, staring at the unconscious form of his friend before him.

"We got to him in time, I think," Iranus answered. "The claws of the Ryakuls are poisonous, which would kill a normal man within minutes...I think we both will agree that he is anything but normal."

"That's not how Aaron would describe himself," Verona said. "What about Sarah?"

"I'm afraid she is under the influence of the Drake now," Colind answered.

"He'll want to go after her."

"I know, Verona. I know." Colind sighed. "It's how the Drake hunted down the Alenzar'seth. He would turn those that they loved into assassins, forcing them either to die by the hands of a loved one or kill them."

"Is there no way we can help her?" Verona asked.

"I don't know," Colind said after a few moments of staring down at Aaron's unconscious body.

"Aaron will find a way. He won't give up on her," Verona insisted.

"That's what I'm afraid of," Colind whispered.

"Why?" Verona demanded, shushing anyone who dared speak besides Colind.

Colind didn't answer right away. He stood there studying Aaron and then looked up at those who had crowded the small room. More stood in the hallway.

"Because we're the reason the Drake hunt the Alenzar'seth in the first place," Iranus said. "The Hythariam are from the same world as the Drake, and its army is poised to invade your world. Should they succeed, this place will burn as ours did. The Hythariam were once many. A proud people. Aaron, with the power of the bladesong, can control the rift between realms, allowing the horde to ravage this world," Iranus said, his golden eyes haunted and cold.

"Aaron wouldn't let that happen," Verona replied.

"Grief has a way dooming the souls of good men," Iranus answered.

"You don't know him," Verona snapped.

Stillness hung in the air, straining the patience of all.

"Come. We've done all we can. We should let him rest," Colind said, ushering people from the room. "Verona, please," Colind said, but Verona shook his head and instead pulled a chair next to Aaron's bed, waiting silently. Eric and Braden closed the door and stood guard outside after the anxious group left the room.

Verona sat in his chair, and Colind sat across from him, lost in his own thoughts. His faith in his friend was unparalleled to anything else, even in Colind's experience. Both waited silently while Aaron recovered from his wounds. Praying for it to be speedy, for the world of Safanar hung in the balance.

ECHOES
OF A
GLORIED PAST

SAFANARION ORDER - BOOK 2

1

HYTHARIAM

Time passed as Aaron slipped in and out of consciousness, occasionally awakening to the muttering of voices, both familiar and not. The steady rise and fall of the airship as it rode the winds was gone, replaced by a soft bed. He forced his eyes open again, ignoring their determination to remain shut. Sunlight and a gentle breeze oozed their way in through the balcony doors on the far side of the room. The harsh burning on his back where the Ryakul clawed him had faded to a dull ache. Stretching his neck, he slowly turned his head, trying to wake up. Stiff limbs quickly yielded to movement as he sat up in bed, rubbing the sleep from his eyes. He was almost naked except for where his wounds had been cleaned and dressed. The skin of his arms and legs was dotted with the remnants of faded bruises. A brown robe hung near a metallic chest across the room. The rune-carved staff rested on the wall near the chest along with his medallion, which sparkled in the sunlight, sending hazy dragon emblems upon the smooth walls. He swung his feet to the floor and bit his lower lip, wincing at the burning pain along his back that flared at his movement. The tiled floor warmed beneath his feet. He took a steadying breath and slowly rose. The more he moved, the less his body seemed to protest.

Aaron crossed the room and pulled the robe on, tying it off at his waist. Its silky fabric felt cool on his skin. His mind still felt muddled, as if he were still waking up. He stepped out onto the balcony into the warm sunlight, allowing it to caress his face. He slowly stretched his arms out to either side, feeling the tender skin protest at first and then give way to the slow movements of his arms. Birds chirped nearby, and a few hawks circled high above him. As he glanced to the side, he saw the outlines of white buildings, which appeared more like pods joined together than the grandeur of the architecture of Shandara. He reached out and ran his fingers along the outer wall, and where his fingers met the surface it turned black. Aaron removed his hand, and the color returned to white. He ran his fingers along the outer doorframe, watching as the surface went from white to dark and back again.

More technology, Aaron thought to himself, and then his thoughts turned to Sarah. She was out there somewhere, under the influence of the Drake. Images of the battle flashed in his mind like lightning. He closed his eyes and tried to draw the energy into himself, but felt as if he were trying to grasp something made of smoke. He couldn't reach out to her. How could the Drake control her so easily? He suppressed a shiver, remembering her baleful yellow eyes looking back at him. With a gasp, he held onto the balcony railing and opened his eyes, filling his vision with the clear skies to keep from seeing her that way, but his last image of Sarah was burned into his mind. He hadn't anticipated the Drake taking a prisoner. Instead, foolishly believing that its only aim was to kill him. His pulse quickened while his hands clutched at the railings.

"You're awake!" Verona said, coming into the room through a metallic door that slid silently into the wall. "They said it would be another day." He poured some water and handed the cup to Aaron.

"Thank you," Aaron said, taking a sip of water. "How long have I been out?"

"Three days. It was touch and go there for a while, my friend. The Ryakul's claws are quite poisonous," said Verona.

"Sarah?" Aaron asked, fearing the answer in his friend's eyes.

"I'm sorry, but we haven't seen her or the Drake since Shandara," Verona said.

Aaron nodded slowly, expecting as much. He sipped the water, tasting the faint hints of cinnamon, and felt his stomach tighten for a moment.

"It's medicine that will help purge the remaining poison from your body."

Aaron remained standing and allowed the queasiness to pass. "Where are we?" he asked.

"We're with the Hythariam, north of Shandara in a place called Hathenwood," answered Verona.

"Is everyone… Did everyone else make it?" Aaron asked.

"Yes." Verona smiled. "Some bumps and bruises and a few shallow cuts, but the Hythariam helped with those as well. The repairs to the Raven will be complete in the next day or so, and the Hythariam are installing some extra things that will help against the Ryakuls," Verona said.

Aaron sighed and felt his shoulders slump in relief. He stretched his neck and rolled his shoulders, still feeling the effects of the medicine. He needed a clear head, and the medicine didn't appear to be helping with that. "I'd like to take a walk."

Verona frowned for a second before giving a small nod. "There is clothing in there," he said, pointing to the chest. "I'll give you a few minutes to change, and then we should get some food in you."

Verona left the room by placing his hand on a pad near the door, and the door slid silently into the adjoining wall. *More technology,* Aaron thought. He walked over to the chest, which didn't have any handles. He placed his palm on top of a pad similar to the one on the door, and a drawer extended from the bottom. The clothes were loose fitting and, like the robe, felt good on his skin. He pulled on black boots that molded themselves to the contours of his feet. He stood up and noted how comfortable they felt while being both sturdy yet almost weightless at the same time. They were a clear improvement over the hiking boots he had brought with him from Earth. He hung the medallion around his neck and grabbed the rune-carved staff. It was a good walking stick, after all.

Aaron exited the room into a quiet hallway where Verona waited. His stomach rumbled noisily, giving Verona the audible clue he needed to lead the way. As they made their way down the hall, a Hythariam appeared, heading in their direction. His golden eyes flashed briefly in surprise, then with a nod to each of them, he turned back the way he had come.

"We've had you on constant watch since arriving the other day," Verona said. "Eric and Braden had only just left your door earlier at my insistence." After Aaron nodded he continued, "I know you want answers, and you'll get them, but I must tell you that it's really good to see you awake, my friend."

"Was it that bad? The poison, I mean," Aaron asked.

"Lethal to most people almost immediately. Even the Hythariam will die if they don't get help in time."

"Colind?" Aaron asked.

"Will be anxious to see you. He's been all but locked in a room with Iranus, Vaughn, and several other Hythariam. I haven't seen much of them since I kept Eric and Braden company."

"Thanks," Aaron said and swallowed a lump down his throat as the image of Sarah's smiling face flashed in his mind. They walked in silence, and the more he moved, the better he felt. Aaron could tell that Verona was holding something back and guessed he didn't want to overburden him. The rune-carved staff proved to be a good walking stick, even on the smooth metallic gray floors. The farther they ventured from his room, the more Hythariam they came across. Most nodded in friendly greeting, but some looked at him with worry in their golden eyes. Those eyes were so similar to the Drake, it was disconcerting.

"Is it much farther?" Aaron asked.

"Not much. We can rest if you need," Verona answered, gesturing toward one of the benches along the wall.

"I'll be fine," Aaron said, waving him on.

The corridors echoed of people walking, and muffled conversations could be heard throughout the place. Wherever they were, there was a bustle of activity. They turned down another corridor, and Aaron smelt food, making his mouth water. He just needed to eat, then he wanted answers.

Verona took him to an open courtyard filled with tables and benches, which was a cross between a garden and an outdoor cafeteria. People took plates of food from several buffet stations strategically placed throughout. Aaron selected food by Verona giving either a nod of approval for some or a vigorous shake of his head for things to avoid. He stuck mostly with vegetables and meat, preferring not to experiment with things he couldn't readily identify.

The Hythariam still glanced in their direction, with some whispering to their companions, and others nodding in friendly greeting. Aaron had never seen so many golden eyes and was surprised to see green ones as well. They were very similar to humans except that their eyes were just a bit bigger and had an almost feline quality to them. They wore clothing of the same quality as he had been given, which Aaron found quite comfortable. Nothing too colorful, and all could have blended easily in a forest if needed. The occasional cyan-colored scarf adorned some of the women, and similarly colored cords were tied around the arms of the men.

They ate in silence, or more like Verona watched as Aaron devoured his meal. The moment the first bite passed his lips, he was filled with an overwhelming need to eat. He was starving. They washed down their meal with water, and Aaron felt his mind clear and more of his strength return.

"You're looking more human now," Verona said.

"Feeling like it, too," Aaron answered.

They were approached by a tall Hythariam with raven hair and green eyes. He had the bearing of a soldier though he was out of uniform. He gave a slight bow to them both and said, "Hello, I am Gavril. Iranus sends his greetings and asks for you to join him and Colind, if you are able."

Aaron shot to his feet, ready to follow Gavril, and Verona rose as well.

"It's not far," Gavril said and led them down a short corridor lined with glass doors. Behind each of the doors appeared to be oval-shaped rooms that hung suspended over tracks heading in different directions. They stepped into one of the rooms, and a panel opened on its far side. Gavril keyed in some of the buttons on the holographic touch screen. "The tram will get us there much faster than on foot," Gavril said, and the door quietly shut behind them.

The tram shot forth, following one of the tracks leading outside. Verona looked delighted, and Aaron reached immediately for something to hold onto before he realized that while they were moving quite fast, he hardly felt as if they were moving at all. Aaron figured the trams must have some type of dampeners to suppress the forces that would put them off balance. Gavril studied their reactions and nodded to himself.

The tram took them outside, and Aaron looked out the window at the complex of buildings from which they left. Some were similar to the style he had seen in Shandara but more modern by comparison. Where Shandara had buildings and gardens complementing each other in their design, the complex of the Hythariam buildings seemed to be more sparse and functional rather than built for appearances. After a few minutes, they approached another set of buildings mostly hidden by the trees, but Aaron saw a few metallic towers strategically placed around a central octagonal dome that peaked over the tree line. The tram entered one of the tunnels near the dome, and Aaron watched the track disappear behind them into darkness. They exited the tram, and Gavril led them away from the platform.

Aaron was growing tired but refused to give in, and he straightened up when he felt himself start to stoop. Gavril pressed his palm to a panel, and the metallic door quietly hissed open. Colind and Vaughn turned immediately and came over to greet Aaron.

"You should not be up and about yet," spoke a silky voice behind him. Aaron turned to see a beautiful raven-haired Hythariam reach inside her pocket and pull out a device. She held the device inches away from his head and slowly scanned down his back.

"Aaron," spoke an older Hythariam, "please forgive my daughter, Roselyn. She is a healer first and person second. Do you remember me? I am Iranus, and I'm most pleased to see you recovering so quickly."

Aaron remembered Iranus, with his long white hair contrasted by his golden eyes. He had been among those on the ship that rescued him when he fell. "I do remember you," he replied.

"Since you're here and not resting in your bed where you should be, give me a moment to examine you," Roselyn ordered and ushered the others away.

The others quickly moved to give the healer room to work, save Verona, who stood rooted in place for once but was clearly at a loss for words. Roselyn raised the device to Aaron's eyes and slowly scanned downward.

"Can you give us a moment please?" she said to Verona, snapping him out of his reverie.

Verona joined the others across the room, giving them some privacy, but he kept glancing back in Roselyn's direction.

Roselyn focused her attention on Aaron and asked him a few questions about the Ryakul wound on his back.

"You're a remarkably fast healer, Aaron," she said sternly. "You don't realize how close to death you were."

"You'd be surprised," Aaron answered quietly. "But thank you."

"Indeed," she said and then leaned in so only he could hear what she was about to say. "You have friends here, Heir of Shandara, but be careful, as all is not what it seems, and the answers given may not be complete in their truthfulness. Some would see the return of the Alenzar'seth as a very grave threat."

Aaron gave a slight nod, and Roselyn moved away.

"He's recovering well. Do not keep him long," she said, looking sternly at Iranus.

"Thank you, my dear. Won't you please join us?" Iranus asked, motioning for them to sit in one of the nearby circles of chairs.

Aaron sat down, and after everyone else was seated, all eyes drew toward him. "First, I'd like to thank you for your help and for giving us a place to stay."

Iranus held up his hand. "No thanks are necessary. It was the least we could do."

Aaron nodded. "Second, where is the Drake, and what did it do to Sarah?"

"We don't know where the Drake is now," Iranus said. "As for what it did to your friend, I need to know exactly what you saw."

"What I saw… " Aaron began, and the image of the Drake holding Sarah up by her neck invaded his thoughts. "It blew some kind of green vapor into her face, forcing her to breathe it in. Then she began to writhe in pain, and after only a few moments her eyes turned yellow like his. When I called to her, she pulled away as if she didn't recognize me. It was like one moment she knew who I was and the next she wanted to kill me. Then the Drake called to her, and she went with it… I could…I could still see…her, but at the same time she was different," Aaron said. "I know, it doesn't make much sense, but that's what I saw."

"It makes perfect sense," Roselyn said and then turned to her father. "The Drake is using a biological delivery agent to spread itself. We suspected, but no one could confirm before now."

"What is it delivering exactly?" Aaron asked.

"A way to control its victims," Iranus said.

There were a few moments of silence until Colind cleared his throat. "Tell him the rest."

Aaron divided his gaze between Colind and Iranus, expectantly.

"I had hoped to give you more time to recover before burdening you with this," Iranus began. "We have observed your world. Where you were raised."

"Earth," said Aaron. For a second, he thought of his sister, Tara, and how he would have liked for her to meet Sarah someday.

"Yes, I've no doubt you are familiar with machines?" Iranus asked and continued when Aaron nodded. "We've developed machines that are smaller than the finest grain of sand. They can live in our bodies and group together to form larger machines to perform any number of tasks."

"We have something similar. We call it nanotech," Aaron said. "It deals with manipulation on a molecular level." His response drew a frown from Verona, but Colind, he noted, didn't look at all out of sorts.

"Excellent, I suspected you would be familiar with the concept," Iranus said. "The Drake used a gas to deliver the Nanites into your friend. It was the Nanites and not the gas that caused her to change."

"But what do the Nanites do exactly?" Aaron asked.

"By themselves not too much, but networked together they can perform complex calculations, including probability, and can adapt to a number of situations. They can form tiny power plants to recharge. Within an organic host, they can convert the movement of the beating heart into energy. When they were first developed, they were coded with a prime directive to keep the body healthy. They worked with the brain and the body, observing the body's reaction to infection. After some analysis, they would help eliminate infections while allowing the body's natural immune system to still function. This was essential so we didn't lose our natural immunity to diseases. We also equipped them with the ability to communicate with other nanotech so knowledge and methods were shared. This went a long way, ultimately eliminating the visible signs of sickness altogether."

"I think I understand. Like a cold, once you start feeling the effects of the cold, you're already sick," Aaron said.

Iranus smiled slightly. "Correct. So, by all outward appearances we 'cured' most diseases entirely, but in truth, the Nanites enabled us to resist them before they were even felt by the body."

"I understand the concept of Nanites, but that doesn't explain what happened to Sarah," Aaron said.

"I'll need to delve a bit into our history to help you understand better," Iranus began. "Particularly how we came from our home world of Hytharia to Safanar. The Nanites' ability to keep the body healthy was only the beginning of their capabilities. We could also use them to manipulate the biological blueprints of a living organism. We learned how to alter the genes for aging, to increase brain function, thus stimulating growth in our ability to calculate, and even increase our bodies' durability and strength."

Iranus paused, allowing for what he said to sink in. The gravity of such a momentous advance in technology was not lost upon Aaron.

"The moral implications of those advances must have been profound," Aaron said after a few moments' thought.

"That's putting it mildly," Roselyn said, speaking up for the first time since she had examined him.

"Aging?" Aaron said. "So, you were able to stop aging entirely? Didn't that lead to overpopulation on your world?"

"Much more than that," Iranus said evenly. "When people live too long, they lose perspective. Organisms such as ourselves were not meant to evade death entirely. So yes, we were able to heal ourselves and delay aging, allowing for the possibility of a fuller life, but some wanted to live forever, believing that since we could, in theory, live forever, that we had a right to do so."

"That doesn't sound so bad," Verona said.

Iranus's lips curved in a knowing sort of way. "It sounds wonderful, does it not? But imagine this, if you will. A whole society that doesn't have to fear death or growing old? You would amass a multitude of knowledge but without wisdom —without the certainty that you were allowed a finite time in this life. People became unmotivated, and their fundamental values changed. Instead of bringing people together into harmony, it drove them apart into chaos. Essentially, we took away the things that made life worth living."

"What did you do?" Aaron asked.

"We decided not to stop aging altogether, but simply slow it down to acceptable levels," Iranus answered.

"How did you decide how long one should live?" Aaron asked.

"We voted on a range and agreed on 200 to 225 years, lifestyle permitting. To prevent constant lobbying in our courts, an agreement was put into place to revisit the age range every 50 years," Iranus said.

"I can't imagine deciding as a society how long one should live," Aaron replied.

Iranus pursed his lips in thought for a moment. "Is it so foreign a concept to you? If you live a healthy lifestyle, you have a better chance to live longer. People, no matter their origin, have this balance, and ours was the next logical step with the resources at our disposal. We were able to manage the genes for aging so that it still took place, but at a much slower rate."

"Still," Aaron said, "even with a majority vote, conflict or even outright war must have been inevitable."

"Yes," Iranus replied solemnly. "There are those who worked in secret to thwart the council's efforts to maintain peace. War, as you said, became inevitable. The precious gift stemming from the Nanites became a weapon. You've glimpsed the remnants of Hytharia through the portal. You've seen firsthand the result upon our world."

"Why Safanar?" Aaron asked. "Couldn't you open a gateway to another world instead?"

"I'm sure they tried, but opening a door doesn't mean you're going to like what is on the other side."

"That's not really an answer, now is it?" Aaron replied.

Iranus smiled. "No, it's not. Safanar was the first successful connection to a habitable world we were able to make. But to understand why we came here, I must explain the situation on Hytharia. Our planet was dying." Iranus began addressing everyone in the room. "In developing our technological prowess, we all but exhausted our natural resources. Something happened to our sun that caused it to age faster than we had originally projected. The lifespan of our star should have ranged in the billions of years, but was eventually reduced to thousands and then hundreds of years. Even then, it should have been enough time for us to find a suitable world to colonize. We utilized every means possible in the search. Sending out probes through space as fast as possible, but these things take time.

"The search for another home became a cycle of destruction for us. Those in power used the impending crisis as a way to justify reckless decisions that eventually put the stability of Hytharia in jeopardy. Super volcanoes killed millions, and a war for the remaining resources necessary for survival reduced our numbers further. Amid all the death and destruction, we found Safanar. Our beacon of hope. A short distance, relatively speaking, but it still took our probe thirty years to find this place. We could never build ships with enough resources to take a significant number of our people here, so we had to find a different solution, but at least we had a target to reach for. This gave us hope and brought the factions of our society back into harmony…for a time.

"The probe continued to send us information and landed on the surface not far from where we are sitting right now. With all the hope that a new home brings, war all but ceased as efforts were focused on viable solutions to get us here.

"The most brilliant scientists of the age were brought together, along with a specialized branch of Hytharia's remaining military factions. They acquired the resources we needed and gave us a place to work."

"Us?" Aaron asked. "You mean you were one of the scientists?"

"Yes," Iranus answered. "Many of us here were part of the original group. It wasn't just scientists, though, but our families as well. We focused on opening a portal between our two worlds. At least that was our end goal. All great things have small beginnings, and we were eventually successful. The calculations involved just to open a portal on the same planet were impressive. Imagine trying to hit a moving target across an enormous expanse of space. What we were able to achieve was startling to say the least, but it did come with its fair share of failure and risk. Now, given the discussion, I won't go into the details of the intricacies of bending space-time. There is simply not enough time for that. So, I will continue." Iranus paused for a moment. "After our first few successful trips to Safanar, we were happy to report that this world was beyond our wildest expectations. We studied the people here and came in contact with one of your ancestors, Aaron. You carry his staff with you here in this very room."

"Daverim," Aaron gasped, his mind flashing back to the abandoned temple he had come to when he first arrived on Safanar. He traced his hands along the rune-carved staff. "But that's…"

"Eighty years ago, yes," Iranus said with a small smile, his eyes growing distant as he remembered his first meeting with Daverim. "Full of life to say the least," Iranus continued. "He was a good man. We allied with the kingdom of Shandara, because the ideals of that kingdom closely matched our own, before the harshness of survival sapped some of our morality from us. In exchange for their help, we agreed to share our technological advances and knowledge. There was actually quite a bit we learned from one another, and we started bringing our people to this world. Shandara was a buffer for us from the rest of Safanar, but it was always our intent to work with all of the kingdoms here.

"When we brought our proposal to our leadership council, a new general was appointed to oversee the whole effort. His name was General Morag Halcylon."

Aaron looked around the room and regarded the cold, expressionless looks of the other Hythariam as confirmation of the sinking feeling he felt.

"We proposed what was in our mandate, which was to find a way to bring survivors from our dying world to Safanar. To live and interact with the people of this world. But others had a different plan," Iranus said bitterly. "They wanted to conquer and rule what they perceived as lesser people. We didn't realize the extent of the ruthlessness of our leadership and the measures taken to provide the resources we needed. They simply took what was needed from others of our home world. Leaving them exposed and in some cases murdering whole cities. I began researching any information I could find about the new general and cursed my ignorant self. General Halcylon was among the most ruthless of our military, who thrived under the guise of survival at the cost of the soul of our people. Most of the council cowered in fear of him, and those that did not were aligned with the means by which he accomplished his goals."

Aaron felt the bile rise to the top of his throat as he tried to imagine what the collapse of a proud civilization like the Hythariam looked like. He realized that like Shandara, nothing in his wildest imaginings would come close to the shadowed horror that lived within the gazes of people who had actually witnessed these events.

"What did you do?" Aaron asked.

"I didn't want to believe it," Iranus began. "We were supposed to be better than this. All of our accomplishments as a people pointed to us being more enlightened than the barbarism being committed. But as great as we were in the good things we did, they were outweighed by the evil done. Evil that was born in the name of desperation under the guise of the good for the many. With my illusions shattered, I alerted others to what was happening and began formulating a plan to get people through the portal to Safanar, people who did not want to bring war to this world."

"Civil war?" Aaron asked.

"Not at first, but yes," Iranus said, his golden eyes becoming steel. "All war is evil, but a war among brothers and sisters is a different kind of evil entirely. We resisted where we could, bringing people through the portal without notice as best we could. At the same time, we didn't want to alert the Shandarians to what was happening for fear that the doors to Safanar would be closed. Daverim, however, suspected that things were deteriorating on Hytharia, and after meeting General Halcylon, he discovered the true intent of the general. He later said that one didn't need to travel so far to know a tyrant when he saw one. After that meeting, Daverim confronted me about the state of Hytharia, and I told him everything. I left nothing out, and he simply listened. Together, we worked on a plan to get as many people as we could off of Hytharia before the portal was to be blocked.

"General Halcylon underestimated the people of Safanar, dismissing them as undeveloped, which couldn't be further from the truth. Where we were strong in science to enhance ourselves, they were strong in their connections to the world and its undercurrents of energy. It's something we've never seen. We used inventions like the Nanites to enhance our bodies, while the Shandarians could do similar things by drawing energy into themselves.

"The plan was to organize a large wave of our people through the portal then block the passage for those who would ravage this world. We had been bringing people through in small groups and were setting up living space with the help of the Shandarians. Daverim came up with a way to block the portal while keeping it open. My job was to see to it that the likes of General Halcylon couldn't open another portal when this one became blocked. We compiled a list of targets so that our work couldn't be followed after we were gone."

"Did it work?" Aaron asked.

"Yes and no," Iranus replied. "There were many sacrifices, and many good people died so that we few survived. We brought as many over as we could, but once those in power finally discovered what we were doing, they moved quickly to thwart us. We had some help on the council from like-minded people. Daverim kept the portal under constant watch along with the Guardians of the Safanarion Order," Iranus said, looking to Colind. "When the fighting appeared on this side as troops came through, Daverim created the barrier."

"How?" Vaughn asked.

"He used the bladesong evoked from the Falcons," Aaron answered. He couldn't help but sympathize with Iranus, who was clearly pained to bring up so many tragic memories, but he needed answers—they all did. The people of Shandara had paid a heavy price in blood to give aid to the Hythariam.

"Yes, that is correct," Iranus said. "Daverim used the bladesong to align the energy from beneath the ground into a barrier that essentially locked the portal open, yet allowed no one through."

"I'm not as well versed on this subject as some," Aaron began, "but my understanding is that what you're describing requires an active connection. How was Daverim able to do this?"

"He was able to connect to the energy deep beneath the ground. That connection is maintained by a living member of the house Alenzar'seth, a secret known only to a few. There is a life energy in this land that is tied to the portal, which forces it to stay open," said Iranus.

"Then how was it maintained when my grandfather and mother left Safanar?" Aaron asked.

"I'm not sure, to be honest," Iranus answered. "Do you know, Colind?"

Colind pursed his lips together in thought, "His soul was able to return to Safanar when he died, so I think it's safe to say that part of him remained connected."

"How does the Drake fit into all this?" Aaron asked.

"The being you know of as the Drake is not of Safanar, but of Hytharia," Iranus said. "We believe that some of Halcylon's people made it through the portal prior to it being locked and were able to send him information."

"How?" Aaron asked.

Iranus looked up to the ceiling. "They couldn't use the portal, but there was nothing stopping them from sending a signal through space. It would take years to reach Hytharia, but it is possible. We didn't find evidence of the Drake until Shandara fell. It appears that those left on Hytharia were able to develop a new weapon to open the portal to this world."

The room was silent for a moment. "You were hoping to wait them out," Aaron said, the pieces fitting into place in his mind. "That was the plan. Block the portal and wait for them to be destroyed with the death of your sun. Except they were able to reach across the stars to get you."

Iranus nodded. "We later figured out that the Drake is a construct of Nanites with a prime directive to open the portal to Hytharia, but these Nanites were different than any we've encountered. Normally, Nanites can be turned off with a kill command, or have their programming rewritten, but not these. They are the perfect sentinels, because they contain all the benefits of normal Nanites, but are able to manipulate the brain on a molecular level, rewriting certain parts, memories for instance, turning love into hate."

Aaron felt his stomach drop out from under him. If what Iranus said was true, Sarah was in more danger than he originally thought. "How long does she have?"

"It's hard to say, but we've seen the process take as little as a few weeks, depending upon how much the subject resists," Iranus answered solemnly. "So, you see, she may already be gone."

"I don't believe that," Aaron said, standing up.

"Wait, what do you mean? How is Sarah already gone?" Verona asked.

"The Drake can rewrite your brain so that you are no longer you anymore," Roselyn answered him.

"She'll fight," Aaron said.

"I'm sorry, Aaron, but it is a fight she cannot win," Iranus answered. "Even if you go to her, which is exactly what the Drake wants, what will you do? We've tried to remove the Nanites, but it always resulted in the death of the person we were trying to save. We've tried augmenting our own to seek and remove them, but the results are the same."

"I won't abandon her," Aaron said.

"I know you won't, Aaron, but you must see reason. What if they're right? What if she's gone?" Vaughn asked gently.

"No!" Aaron slammed his fist onto the table. "I refuse to believe that. I know I can reach her. The Drake doesn't control her fully."

"She left you, Aaron," Colind chimed in. "This is what the Drake does. It turns those that you love against you. It's how it hunted down all of the Alenzar'seth. The ones it wasn't strong enough to stand against, it defeated using cunning and strife to weave a perfect web of destruction, using their greatest strength against themselves."

Aaron's body was rigid, and his muscles rippled with the clenching of his teeth. "I'm not them."

"You think to defy what has been proven over and over by sheer will alone? It's not going to be enough. The Alenzar'seth were once many, but those that survived the fall of Shandara weren't able to stand against the Drake," Iranus said. "I say this not to be cruel, but because I want you to live. Playing the Drake's game is the surest path to meeting your demise. Even for you."

Aaron regarded the Hythariam coolly. "Not playing its game will cost me more than I'm willing to pay. Haven't you been hiding long enough? Convinced it was the best course of action? Tell me, did you stand idly by while the Alenzar'seth were hunted down, slaves to a terrible fate because they refused to yield? Even in the face of death, they fought. They didn't hide in the shadows, nor abandon the ones they loved…neither will I."

Iranus's golden eyes were ablaze with anger. "Do you know how to make war, Aaron?"

"No," Aaron replied, "but I can fight, and it will have to be enough. I will fight for the parts of Sarah that will never submit to the Drake, no matter what technology your people have created. However small, it's worth fighting for."

Colind sighed, "Will you at least consider that Sarah may be beyond your reach and that the person you love is gone?"

Aaron shook his head, feeling the stirrings of the bladesong within him. Sarah's beautiful blue eyes looked back at him when he closed his. I will always come for you. He looked up, his gaze sweeping across the men in the room. Verona stood up and came to his side. Colind returned his gaze evenly, and Iranus's golden eyes narrowed.

"Colind," Aaron said evenly, "I have considered it, and know this. I will never abandon Sarah, not for anything. Not for your war," he said dividing his gaze between Colind and Iranus, "and not for this world."

"She wouldn't want you to sacrifice the world for her," Vaughn said.

"I know, Vaughn, and I won't need to," Aaron said. "That army on the other side of the portal is coming no matter what we do. Whether I live or die, that is one thing that you can count on. The barrier between worlds will fall. If you don't believe me, return to Shandara and study it. Things are wildly out of balance. Now, instead of focusing ourselves on keeping things as they've always been, we should be focused on moving forward."

Aaron felt his energy drain and leaned on his staff, beginning to hunch over. "You can't run from the wind," Aaron muttered to himself.

"What?" Colind asked.

Aaron swallowed, and looked up. "My father used to take us sailing when we were younger, and sometimes we'd be caught out on the water when a storm came. As a child, I was so afraid. All the big waves and wind tossing our boat mercilessly. 'You can't run from wind, son,' he would tell me. 'Trim your sails and face what's ahead.' And he was right. A storm is coming, gentleman, whether you want to believe it or not." Aaron turned and left the room with the dull thumps of the rune-carved staff trailing in his wake.

Roselyn rose and silently followed.

Colind looked at the door and sighed. "He is right. The barrier was always just a temporary measure. We need to prepare."

"He doesn't understand what will be unleashed if the barrier fails. And to abandon all to pursue the Drake..." Iranus said, biting off the last.

Verona cleared his throat. "Without Aaron, none of you would be here. He was lost when I first met him, teetering on the brink of darkness that has claimed many a man's soul. Sarah was the one thing that gave him hope. The one thing that brought the light back in his eyes and gave him some semblance of being whole. So, he cannot do as you would want him to, despite the certainty of the science that supports *your* reasons. They are not his reasons. Your war has cost him almost everything before he was dragged into it. Are you really surprised that he won't follow the path that you've laid at his feet? Should not a strong leader forge his own path, and we, as his friends and comrades, support him as he would for any of us?" Verona asked, his gaze sweeping the room. "You've had more time than he has been alive to do things your own way. Perhaps it's time for a different approach, because to go against Aaron on this would risk...much," Verona said, narrowing his gaze. "If you can't help, fine, but don't tell him that what he intends to do is impossible, because my friend has a knack for doing the impossible." Verona glanced pointedly at Colind, then rose and left the room.

"Aaron, wait," Roselyn called behind him.

"Is this what you warned me about?" he asked, leaning on the staff heavily.

Roselyn's eyes narrowed as she caught up to him. "You need rest. It's only been a few days."

"No, Sarah needs me now," he replied stubbornly, and specks of darkness invaded his vision. Aaron sank to the floor, the last of his strength leaving him. I won't abandon you.

"She has time," Roselyn said gently.

Verona came up silently behind them, but said nothing.

"Don't charge off like the others," Roselyn said. "I believe you are right. There is a way to stop the Drake. We just need to put our heads together, but first you need to recover your strength. You're no good to her like this... "

Aaron felt himself slipping further away, Roselyn's voice growing distant, until he couldn't hear anything at all as the last vestiges of his strength left him.

2

HIGH KING'S WRATH

Mactar expected the others to underestimate the Heir of Shandara, but not himself. The broken window cast a fragmented light as his fingers drummed the now-clutter-free desk in his quarters onboard the airship. He dismissed the mess on the floor, having given his pride a small part of its due. His heart pumped with the excitement of a new challenge. A worthy adversary. Despite this setback, the growing power of the Alenzar'seth put him closer to his goal. In fact, their return drew out the true gatekeepers, the Hythariam. He had witnessed the battle with the Ryakul from afar and had little doubt that the Drake's first battle with Aaron had been enlightening. His lips lifted at the thought of Sarah's betrayal of one Aaron Jace. He was sure he could find a way to turn it to his advantage given some time, but for now he set the thought aside.

Mactar's journey back to Khamearra with Darven, the former Elitesman, and the young Prince Rordan, the High King's remaining heir, was swift and uneventful, even somber. The fact that travel crystals couldn't be used within Shandara's borders still perplexed him. It was as if Shandara was out of phase with the rest of Safanar. Once they were beyond its borders, they were able to use the crystals to shorten their trip. Rordan had been in a fragile state since the battle. Something he had seen had shaken him to his core, and Mactar was going to have to draw it out from him.

The palace of the High King loomed ever closer, and the twin tower of the Elite stood on the far side of the city. The capital city of Khamearra was truly a sight to behold. The busy traffic of airships dotted the sky, and the construction of a bustling city could be heard below. Mactar preferred to have a few moments to himself prior to facing the wrath of High King Amorak once he learned of the death of his son. Primus was such a fool. He allowed petty rivalry to poison his mind. It was never part of his plan to kill Sarah, but he supposed her betrayal by aligning with the Alenzar'seth had pushed Primus over the edge. Rordan, he noted, hadn't spoken of it.

"My lord," Darven spoke quietly. "It is time."

Mactar turned to his loyal companion. "Indeed it is."

Darven's eyes narrowed. "Is there cause for concern? Perhaps we should wait before meeting with the High King?"

Mactar smirked. Darven didn't understand his relationship with High King Amorak. For all Amorak's talk of killing him, there was no escaping the fact that Amorak needed him, which wasn't about to change anytime soon.

"No," Mactar said. "It would be unwise to keep him waiting. Now the fun begins." For all intents and purposes, Darven was his apprentice, but he still had much to learn. The vehemence with which Reymius's heir had singled out Darven was another matter to consider. That was yet another tool at his disposal. A worthy adversary indeed, this Alenzar'seth, Aaron, turned out to be.

They were joined on deck of the High King's airship by the remaining Elitesmen and Rordan. They withdrew their travel crystals and activated them. Teleporting with crystals was much like having the ground pulled abruptly away, only to be plunged into darkness, and then emerge upon the other side.

They landed in the Great Hall of the High King's palace to the immediate hush of all those in attendance. Mactar preferred to make an entrance. The High King, perched on his throne, regarded them coolly as he narrowed his eyes. Amorak rose from his throne and was before his son in an instant, but Rordan wouldn't meet his father's gaze.

"Where is your brother?" the High King asked.

Rordan looked up at his father, his chin trembling. "He is dead," Rordan whispered.

The High King's eyes darted to Mactar.

"It is true. He was killed by the Alenzar'seth," Mactar said.

"Is that what you call it?" Rordan said shakily, his eyes growing distant. "There is no honor in doing battle with someone that can't be beaten. No one can move as fast as he. This Aaron, scion of Alenzar'seth, is a match for any Elitesmen. Primus never stood a chance. If I had faced him, Father, you would have two dead sons instead of just one," Rordan said, hanging his head low in shame.

The High King said nothing, but the air grew colder around him.

"He is Ferasdiam Marked, my lord," Mactar said. "Like you."

The High King nodded and stuck his hand out, gently raising Rordan's head. "This is not your failing, Son. I have sent you out there ill prepared. Something I can remedy."

Rordan's tear-stricken eyes burned with a cold anger. "There is something else. Sarah stands with the Alenzar'seth. She fought by his side."

The High King remained motionless for a few moments, allowing the silence to gather. Mactar felt a torrent of energy gather itself then suddenly the High King lashed out, surprising the Elitesmen. He struck down the Elite Masters who had failed him. Though the High King was unarmed, they were no match. The High King moved with the blurring speed of a shooting star, and the blood of the

Elitesmen gushed forth onto the pristine floors of the Great Hall. Amid the carnage, the High King's body glowed with a luminescence of its own, and the attendees in the Great Hall fled in terror until only Rordan, Mactar, and Darven remained.

"Failure is not to be tolerated!" the High King's voice echoed, his face awash in the blood of his victims. "No heir of Khamearra need fear the Alenzar'seth. It is time for your training to begin, my Son, and together we shall rid the world of the taint of Shandara once and for all!"

Mactar waited a few moments before speaking. Now that the High King's rage had found its victims, he thought it was safe. "There is more, my lord. The Hythariam have come out of hiding. They were at Shandara, while the Drake fought the Alenzar'seth."

High King Amorak smiled wolfishly. "To be expected. I think you'll find we're better prepared for the likes of the Hythariam than we were when Shandara burned. But come, I want you to tell me everything," he growled.

They followed the High King as they stepped over the bodies of the fallen Elitesmen. Amorak, as a council member, could dispense judgment upon the Elitesmen as he pleased without any repercussions. Mactar followed, preparing for what was to come, but as he stepped from the room, something caught his eye. A shadowy reflection of pale skin and black eyes regarding him with pure hatred.

Tarimus?

3

SECLUSION

The rocky ground bit into Sarah's side as the Drake deflected her attack. The days blurred together, split apart by bouts of consciousness. The Drake was always there when she woke, hovering over her like a storm cloud. The cycle was always the same. Upon regaining consciousness, she would attack. The Drake never took any of her weapons and easily thwarted her attacks. It loomed over her, peering at her with yellow eyes filled with a deadly promise. She had felt Aaron reach out to her and wanted to go to him, yet at the same time the very thought of him repulsed her. Her thoughts twisted into a hatred so intense that it yearned for his death. She pictured stabbing him through the heart. The thought filled part of her with a heated joy, while another part of her cried out in denial of such dark thoughts. She would never hurt Aaron.

What was happening to her? Every thought of her love for Aaron became warped into something maddening and sinister, but she still felt him along the fringes of her thoughts. The warmth of his love surrounded her, which part of her embraced while another part pushed away as one would recoil from a poisonous viper.

KILL HIM! a sinister voice bellowed in her mind, followed by images of Aaron suffering by her hand. He would look at her in betrayal with helpless regret, and the euphoria that followed sent her mind spiraling. She denied the images from the confines of her mind. *I would never hurt you, my love.*

The images only intensified with her resistance, and the pain unfurled, spreading from her head to deep inside her muscles. Where warm memories of their time together should have shielded the walls of her heart, instead it only fueled the fires that commanded his death. She cried out at her shattering heart, every waking moment plunging her deeper into a cycle of madness until only bitterness remained. A hate spurned within her from the betrayal that her love for Aaron had caused her. How could he leave her like this?

She heard the cries of a little girl whimpering, and she opened her eyes, frantically searching for the girl. Surrounded by mountain peaks, the frosty air stung her throat, causing her eyes to tear. She was alone except for the Drake, who sat across the way, its yellow eyes watched her mercilessly. Waiting… Expecting …

Sarah drew her sword and charged. She attacked with the ferocity of a cornered animal, abandoning years of training. The Drake wielded about, bringing up its armored forearm to block her attack. She pulled from the energy buried deep in the mountain and hammered at the Drake. The Drake blocked her attack, and as she glimpsed the stump of its arm, Aaron's face flashed in her mind. Her body crumpled to the ground in agonizing pain. The Drake did not attack; instead, it rose steadily to its feet, watching her. She lay helplessly before it, struggling just to breathe. She shook her head to clear it and concentrated on keeping her mind blank. Behind her, she heard the deep rumbling growl of a Ryakul. She sprang to her feet. The beast sat back on its haunches, with its long neck swinging slowly from side to side, licking its chops. The Ryakul blew a tuft of air from its nostrils as Sarah inched closer.

The Drake screeched a warning, snapping Sarah's attention. The Ryakul unfurled its large bat-like wings and in a colossal whoosh, launched itself into the air. The Drake leaped upon its back and took off into the air, leaving her stranded at the top of the mountainside.

Sarah's elation lasted only seconds as the Drake landed farther down the mountain, blocking her only path. If only she had kept a travel crystal. She looked back down at the Drake as it watched her from below. The Drake was toying with her. She could wait up here and die of exposure or head down in the direction of the Drake. Her thoughts drifted to Aaron, wanting to reach out for the ever-present connection she felt. The bout of pain and nausea followed by images of his demise became the only things she saw. There was a part of her that knew the images were a lie, but they felt so real. She began to yearn for the sickening pleasure that followed the images of Aaron dying. The sick pleasure spread through her like a plague, as all the conflicting feelings fractured her mind. She felt the person she was being systematically stripped away. She turned from the Drake's expectant eyes and stepped toward the edge, seeing the dizzying heights below. The barest hints of a promised release urged her forward. She drew in the energy from the depths of the mountain and launched herself away from the edge, hoping the rising peaks below would claim her so the madness would stop. The wind roared past her face and she closed her eyes, welcoming the end of her suicidal leap. Her body jerked to the side as a Ryakul's claws snatched her from the air and away from the death for which she yearned. She pushed against the beast's claws that held her, and when that failed, tried to reach for her knife, but she couldn't grasp it.

The echoes of her screams bounced off the mountains as the Ryakul deposited her in a heap at the Drake's feet. She knelt there powerless and alone, with her shoulders slumped in defeat. Nothing in her life had prepared her for this. She couldn't trust her own thoughts, lest they dwell upon the one thing the Drake was taking away from her. She looked up with bitter defiance as the yellow hue that circled her vision became more prominent.

Her face was wet with tears as she squeezed her eyes shut.

No! she screamed in her mind, momentarily throwing off the shackles she could neither see nor touch but were firmly in place. A shaft of sunlight peeked through the clouds, and its warmth caressed her face for the span of a single breath. Her connection to Aaron pushed to the furthest reaches of her mind, shimmering, calling to her. She drew strength from it. Without hesitation, she reached out to hold onto it with all her might, despite the cost.

Aaron! she called out from within and without, her voice going from a scream of defiance to a cry of pain across the rooftops of the world. For a moment, she heard his gasp of breath across the expanse between them. The plunge into pleasure and pain was swift, and as her mind split apart, she held grudgingly to the thought that she had reached out to him, and that he had heard her.

Aaron awoke crying out Sarah's name. His body was drenched in sweat. He opened his eyes to a room where the walls were blackened as if they'd been burnt except for a solitary spot where Colind and Verona huddled behind a barrier of light.

"Sarah," Aaron gasped doubling over. "I could feel…her pain. So much pain," he said, wincing as he wrapped his arms around himself.

The barrier disappeared, and Colind and Verona rushed to his side. Colind ordered Verona to bring some water.

"Easy now," Colind said.

Verona quickly returned and offered Aaron a cup. He took a sip and looked around the room. "Did I do this?" Aaron asked.

"I'm afraid so, my friend," Verona said. "You were thrashing about, and I was trying to restrain you when Colind barged in and hauled me out of the way. Just in time, I might add."

Colind nodded back to Verona and turned toward Aaron. "What did you see?"

"The last thing I remember was collapsing in the hallway. Then I woke up and heard Sarah calling out to me, and for a second I felt the pain she was in. It was unlike anything I've ever felt. It was her, but at the same time it wasn't."

"It's the work of the Nanites. She is fighting their assimilation," Colind said.

"She's fading. I have to find her. There must be a way to fight them," Aaron said, rising to his feet.

Colind sighed. "Iranus doesn't believe so, and he's not the only one. He wasn't exaggerating when he said they tried everything after the fall of Shandara."

"The Hythariam would have me abandon her, which is something I won't do," Aaron said.

"Everyone will pay the price if you fall now. You're all that stands between the horde and this world," Colind said.

"So Iranus says, but I get the feeling they aren't telling us everything. The only thing I do know is that the Drake has Sarah, and I won't abandon her to that fate."

The door to the room opened, and Roselyn stood in the doorway, looking at the ruined room. "What happened?" she asked.

Aaron was about to answer when he realized that he didn't know what had really happened, and looked at Colind questioningly.

"What I think happened," Colind began, "is you experienced a backlash of energy from your connection to Sarah."

"But how is this possible?" Aaron asked.

"You brought Sarah back from the brink, and used your own lifebeat to feed into her, keeping her alive while her body repaired itself," Colind said. "Extremely risky, as you both could have died or worse—such as being trapped in a world of shadow."

"Some risks are worth taking," Aaron replied.

"Indeed they are," Colind agreed.

"A backlash of energy emanating from a person caused all this?" Roselyn asked, her voice trailing off as she tentatively reached out to the blackened wall. "These walls are resistant to your average fire and heat. Nothing short of a plasma bolt could scorch these walls in such a way, and even then a bolt would only affect a concentrated area. The fact that all of these walls are burnt to such a degree is a testament to the amount of power this 'backlash' unleashed." Roselyn looked at Colind. "Do we need to move him away to a more secure location, away from others?"

Colind shook his head. "No, I don't think so. I'll stay close for the time being and will be able to protect this place and him, should the need arise."

Roselyn nodded. "Very well. I would like to speak with Aaron alone."

"We'll be right outside," Colind said as he and Verona left the room.

Roselyn waited until they left before speaking. "Is your friend always so quiet?"

The question caught Aaron off guard, and it took a few moments to realize she was referring to Verona. *Quiet? Verona?* "Sometimes," he answered.

Roselyn shook her head, dismissing the subject. "I've been speaking with Garret, and he's been telling me about the travel crystals that the Elitesmen use."

Aaron's eyes lit up. "They use them to teleport from one location to another. Do you think they could help with the Nanites?"

"Possibly," she said. "I am thinking that they could cause the Nanites to reset."

Aaron frowned. "What good will that do?"

"It will give us time," Roselyn answered patiently. "Remember, the Nanites are machines. They are doing what they were programmed to do. I'm not familiar with these travel crystals, but I am familiar with the concept of teleportation, and in order for it to work, they must break down our living tissues and reassemble them somewhere else. I believe that this process could reset the Nanites to the state they were in when Sarah first became infected by the Drake."

Aaron perked up at the thought. "Can we get them out?"

"No," she said, "there are too many, but I'm hopeful that we can make them dormant, and then the body will absorb them as it would any foreign agent."

"So we turn them off," Aaron said thoughtfully. "But what about the damage they are doing, can it be reversed?"

Roselyn looked at him with sympathy. "I don't know, to be honest. The measures that we tried in the past were from a distance and had almost no response. This was before we realized that these Nanites were different from what most Hythariam have in their systems. They were designed to be self-sustaining and to help people stay healthy. Not…this."

Aaron swallowed his disappointment. "It's okay. This is a start and is more than what we had before." His back still ached, and he still felt weak. He needed to be outside and breathe in fresh air.

"We have a device that may help with the Nanites," Roselyn said. "It's meant for taking readings from them, but it can also give instructions."

Aaron rose to his feet. "Why are you helping me?" he asked.

Roselyn's golden eyes searched his for a moment. "I've seen enough suffering and heartache at the hands of the Drake. My people have lived in fear of the barrier since it was first sealed. It has taken a toll on us. The decision to withdraw from the kingdoms of this world was not an easy one, nor agreed by all. We came here seeking refuge, and we brought death and destruction in our wake. Some would say we're responsible for all that you've suffered and for the fall of Shandara."

"I don't think that at all," Aaron said.

Roselyn's lips curved into a slight smile. "That is very kind of you to say, but if helping you in some small way atones for some of the wrongs my people have brought here, then it is a worthy cause."

"I appreciate your help," Aaron said. "But the barrier is not going to last. Your people should be helping this world prepare for the horde and General Halcylon."

"We have been, but through subterfuge as opposed to outright alliances. My father was devastated when Shandara fell. He and Reymius were quite close."

"Subterfuge? I hope it's enough. Your father would have me abandon Sarah," Aaron said, unable to keep the bitterness from his voice.

"He is doing what he believes is right. Would you do any less?" Roselyn asked.

"No," Aaron said, "I wouldn't."

He began dressing himself.

"What do you intend to do?" Roselyn asked.

"I'm going after Sarah. There is something I want to try before going after the travel crystals, and I need to be outside to do it."

Roselyn couldn't keep the shock from her voice. "You're leaving? Now? But you're still recovering from the effects of the Ryakul poison."

"Soon, yes. The longer I wait, the less of a chance there is to save Sarah," Aaron replied. "I need to talk to the others. Do you think they will try to stop me?" Aaron asked, thinking of Iranus, who had let fear guide him for too long. *Is brash bullheadedness any less of a folly?*

Roselyn's golden eyes narrowed. "Possibly," she said quietly.

Aaron nodded. "I appreciate your honesty."

He finished dressing in the clothes provided by the Hythariam and strapped on his swords. He still felt a weariness within the depths of his bones, but he didn't have time to wait for a full recovery. Time waited for no one, least of all him, and he wouldn't sit idly by while the woman he loved suffered at the hands of the Drake.

4

INTENTIONS

Aaron left the blackened room to find Verona and Colind waiting outside for him. Verona looked as if he were about to say something when Roselyn came through the doorway. He watched as his friend stared helplessly at the beautiful raven-haired Hythariam. Colind suppressed a slight chuckle and bowed in greeting. Roselyn nodded to each in turn and hurried down the hallway while Verona all but sighed as she left.

"Enjoying the view?" Aaron asked, reducing his normally eloquent friend into a sputter of sounds that could scarcely be called words.

Verona nodded, but said nothing.

"I need to get outside. Someplace discreet would be preferable," Aaron said.

Colind nodded. "I know of a place."

"Verona, would you mind gathering the others, including Captain Morgan?" Aaron asked. For some reason, he couldn't bring himself to address the Captain by his first name, Nathaniel. Verona nodded and set off at a trot down the hallway.

Colind and Aaron continued down the hallway, letting the silence build until Aaron couldn't take it anymore.

"Don't try to talk me out of it. I'm going after Sarah."

"Why would you think that I would try to talk you out of it?" Colind asked.

"I don't know. I just figured you would."

"Aaron, you've brought me back from the world of shadow. I'm not about to stand in your way," Colind said. "I will help you in any way that I can."

Aaron gathered his thoughts for a moment. "But surely, you have an opinion."

"I do indeed have an opinion, and I would surely share it with you if you ask it of me," Colind replied.

"Will I always need to ask?"

"No." Colind chuckled and then grew serious. "Everyone will pay the price if you fall now. You're all that stands between the remnants of the Hytharia military, the horde if you will, and this world."

"So Iranus says, but I get the feeling they aren't telling us everything. The only thing I do know is that the Drake has Sarah, and I won't abandon her. Doesn't it matter that the barrier is already failing?" Aaron asked.

"It matters, but we will need the Hythariam before this is over," Colind answered.

Aaron frowned. "Of all the things Iranus said, he glossed over some important details regarding the Drake. Like how it got here in the first place. It couldn't have broken through the barrier. They couldn't have opened another portal to this world. So that leaves one other possibility," Aaron said as they stepped outside into a small valley. Colind merely looked back, waiting for him to finish. Aaron pointed to the sky, drawing Colind's gaze toward the heavens. "Now do you understand?"

Colind pursed his lips, considering. "You've given this a fair amount of thought, I see, and I agree with you. They must have sent a machine to Safanar across the great expanse of the heavens."

"Which also means that there could be something much worse on the way right now. Waiting is not an option. These people need to prepare themselves," Aaron said.

Colind nodded.

"It's not just us, but the people of this whole world need to be united to face this threat," Aaron said.

Colind took a long look at him. "Vaughn was right about you. For one so young, you have an uncanny ability to see right to the heart of matters."

"There is something else I need to tell you," Aaron said. "Tarimus is alive."

Colind's eyes hardened for a moment. "What do you mean?"

"I mean he is back in Safanar," Aaron said, and he told Colind what had transpired prior to his rescue—about how he had to free Tarimus in order to bring Sarah's soul back to her body.

Colind shook his head. "Well, it appears that all the pieces are on the board. If I know Tarimus, he will go after Mactar. My advice to you would be not to trust him."

Aaron nodded, laying his pack and staff on the ground, then drew his swords.

"What are you going to do?" Colind asked.

"I'm going to reach out to Sarah through the bladesong," Aaron said. "We're connected somehow. I can feel her connection to me, but it's almost like being connected to two different people."

Colind thought about it for a moment then nodded.

Aaron removed his shoes and knelt upon the ground, opening himself up to the energy that surrounded him. He drew it in as easily as one draws a breath. He came to his feet and began to wield the Falcons, releasing the harmony of the bladesong. The melodious tune that was his own rode along the air. The connection to Sarah lay among the furthest recesses of his mind, and Aaron focused his attention there.

He rode along the currents of energy, following the connection to its source. He couldn't tell where she was, but he knew she was there. She was diminished somehow, and it occurred to him that she might be sleeping. But the energy appeared erratic as though two opposing patterns sought to cancel each other out. She had been able to reach out to him before, and he was hoping to do the same. He watched unobtrusively for signs of the Nanites that he knew were in her system, focusing on the patterns of energy and looking for some telltale sign of something artificial. Then he saw it. A pattern that seemed to only react to other patterns of the whole. It took no other actions otherwise. These had to be the Nanites affecting Sarah.

Aaron reached out to block the connection from the Nanites in an attempt to shield Sarah. A spike of energy flashed before him and sent his mind reeling with pain. At that same moment, he heard Sarah's voice cry out in his mind. As if suddenly aware of his presence, she withdrew from him like a scurrying animal avoided a predator. Aaron tried again, only this time both the Nanites and Sarah reacted with vicious certainty, sending shocking pain that jarred his concentration. Aaron tumbled to the ground, and the bladesong left him. He gasped for air. *I can't even reach out to her.*

Colind came to his side. "Can you hear me?"

Aaron nodded as he slowly came back to his senses. "It's like she is there but not completely. I think I made it worse by trying to reach out to her."

"Her time is short, but by all accounts she is very strong. There is still time," Colind said.

Aaron came to his feet as they were joined by the others. Vaughn and Garret, followed by Sarik, Eric, Braden, and Verona. Even Jopher came and nodded shyly to Aaron. It was good to see them all, and after their greetings, Aaron told them about his discussion with Roselyn.

They were joined by Captain Morgan and Roselyn, along with several other Hythariam he didn't know. Then Iranus walked out.

"Are you proposing to journey to the heart of the Elitesmen Order in Khamearra and steal a cache of travel crystals?" Vaughn asked, unable to keep the shock from his tone.

"Not all of us. I think we need to divide our efforts," Aaron said.

"This ought to be good," Garret said. "Never a dull moment, is there?"

Aaron smiled a bit at the comment. The bladesong had invigorated him. "This threat that we're facing affects everyone on this world. This is not my fight or even the Hythariam's fight. This is our fight. We must unite whomever we can. At some point, the barrier is going to fall. It is already weakening." Aaron explained his theory that the military from Hytharia were able to reach Safanar through means other than the portal. Considering that the natives of Safanar had no previous concept of space travel, they were very accepting of the idea.

"The Drake first appeared about twenty-five years ago?" Aaron asked.

"That is our best guess," Iranus said.

"At some point, the faction on Hytharia must have realized that the Nanites didn't work, or at least developed an alternative plan. How long before they could send something else?" Aaron asked.

Iranus exchanged glances with the other Hythariam, all of whom looked shaken by Aaron's question. They spoke quickly in a language that Aaron couldn't understand until Roselyn hissed at them.

"I would say a year at the most," Iranus answered.

"Depending upon when that was, and if they had waited an entire year to prepare something else to reach Safanar to open the portal, when would it arrive? Your best guess," Aaron said. He had them now. Iranus now realized that his tactic was flawed and that all of them were in real danger.

Iranus's eyes grew wide. "About three months from now."

The other Hythariam gasped.

Aaron looked at Colind and the others before addressing Iranus. "Are you able to confirm that? Do you have a telescope or something that can see if there is, in fact, something heading for us right now?"

Now you see, Aaron thought to himself.

The Hythariam conferred among themselves, and one tapped a device above his ear and spoke.

Iranus seemed to nod to himself. "I didn't see it. I didn't see this coming, but hearing it from you, even without the confirmation, I know the truth before my eyes."

"Will you help the people of this world?" Colind asked. "Will you help them stand against the horde that would take their homes from them?"

Iranus glanced at the others, who slowly nodded their approval. "We will stand with you."

"We need to start coordinating with the other nations—" Aaron stopped with a slightly amused expression. "I just realized that I don't know about all the nations of this world, but I think starting with Rexel and— " Aaron motioned to Jopher to step forward, "—will you return to Zsensibar and inform them of the threat to this world?"

Jopher brought his fist over his heart. "It would be my honor." He looked like he was about to say more but remained silent.

"What is it?" Aaron asked.

"It's just that I will need help convincing people of the threat," Jopher said.

Aaron chewed on his lower lip in thought. "He's right. Iranus, it's time for the Hythariam to step back into the spotlight."

"What do you suggest we tell them?" spoke a Hythariam man whom he didn't know.

"I would suggest telling them the truth," said Aaron. "They will find out soon enough if they don't heed the warning."

Colind raised an eyebrow. "Who did you have in mind to travel to Rexel?"

Aaron smiled. "You and Vaughn. Probably Garret," Aaron paused. "And Jopher. Colind, yours will be the voice the Hythariam need to validate their story."

The others protested, but Colind's gaze remained fixed upon Aaron. "I can help with the other 'nations' as you put it, but what will you be doing while we travel?"

An immediate hush swept over the crowd as they waited for his answer.

Aaron glanced at Verona, who nodded back to him. "I'm going to Khamearra to infiltrate the Elitesmen Order."

Verona actually laughed and looked excited. Eric and Braden gave him challenging looks, daring him to leave them behind. Sarik looked concerned for a moment before Verona clamped his hand on his shoulder and whispered something in his ear. Sarik looked back at him and nodded. The others all shouted their protest, save Colind, who called for silence.

"Please explain to the others the rest of your plan," Colind said calmly.

"I'm going to steal a cache of travel crystals," Aaron began. "Then track down the Drake and escape with Sarah, using the crystals. Roselyn has a theory that using the travel crystals will confuse the Nanites in her system, allowing us to make them dormant."

Iranus snapped his golden-eyed gaze toward his daughter. "Theories," he spat.

"Yes, Father, worth a try I think," she replied.

"One doesn't simply trek into the capital city of Khamearra and knock on the doors of the Elitesmen Order," Vaughn said.

"One doesn't walk into Shandara, but we did," Aaron replied.

Vaughn took a deep breath, gathering his patience. "I'm on your side, Aaron. I want you to succeed. I want to help Sarah, but what you propose is…suicide."

"Suicide missions are our specialty," Verona answered. "Hit the enemy where he thinks he is safe. I believe you taught me that, old friend."

Vaughn shook his head. "I don't believe this," he said to Colind and then looked at Aaron. "As powerful as you've become, you are not unstoppable. Everyone has their limits."

"I know I'm not unstoppable," Aaron said softly. "What wouldn't you do to protect the people you love?"

"It's not as simple as that," Vaughn replied.

Of course, not everyone has the strings attached that I do, Aaron thought bitterly. People were looking for him to lead this fight and raise Shandara from the ashes. "I know what's at stake, and I won't debate my leaving with anyone else," Aaron said, sweeping them all with his gaze, thinking of the family he lost to this damned war. I won't lose Sarah, too.

Vaughn nodded. "Okay," he conceded. "How long do you think she has before whatever these Nanites are doing to her have finished?"

Aaron glanced at Roselyn, who shared a brief look with Iranus when another Hythariam dressed in a strange metallic armor whispered something.

"A week," Roselyn said. "Two, at the most."

A week?

He recalled the map of Safanar he had seen in the map room on the Raven. Khamearra was almost across the continent. It had taken them about a month by airship to journey to Shandara. Aaron looked around at his friends and saw the same conclusion reflected in all their eyes. His plan was hopeless. There was no way he could make the journey in time, but it was even worse than that. He intended to return to Shandara with Sarah, this part of the plan he kept to himself. Aaron brought his gaze to Iranus, who immediately knew what he was going to ask.

"I need your help," Aaron began. "You have the means at your disposal to travel faster than what is considered normal here. Khamearra is almost on the other side of the continent."

Iranus appeared thoughtful for a moment. "I know there will be no dissuading you from this."

"I'm going with him," Roselyn interrupted.

Iranus's golden eyes flashed angrily. "No."

"Don't try to stop me, Father," Roselyn replied, and then she softened her gaze. "We owe our aid to the Alenzar'seth, whose shelter of protection we've lived under for these many years."

Aaron watched as Iranus weighed his options, and he could tell that there were none that he liked. Iranus glanced at Colind, who cleared his throat.

"This is what I intend," Aaron began. "For you to provide a way for a small party to accompany me to Khamearra. We will infiltrate the Elitesmen stronghold and use the travel crystals to return here quickly. We will also attempt to make contact with the Resistance in Khamearra."

Colind narrowed his gaze thoughtfully. "What Resistance?"

"Sarah was working with a faction that is looking to overthrow the tyranny of the High King," Aaron said. "A faction loyal to her mother. This faction sent a lone protector, who was loyal to the old order to the Elite. This man trained Sarah. After he died, she returned to her father's court and saw it ruined by the corruption. We may be able to find help there along with the most abundant source of crystals. It makes it a worthy target."

"What if you can't get into the Elitesmen stronghold?" Colind asked.

"Then I will take out as many Elitesmen as I can and take their crystals," Aaron said.

Colind shrugged and glanced at Iranus. "It's not a bad plan."

"Who will be in this 'small' party?" Iranus asked.

Aaron had anticipated the question and shared a brief look at his friends before answering. The fact that he didn't even need to ask touched him. They would follow him anywhere, because they believed he would get them out of any hell that his path took them through.

"Verona, Sarik, Eric, Braden, and Roselyn," Aaron said. He wasn't sure about Roselyn, but he knew the others could hold their own against the Elitesmen. He hadn't been able to reach Eric and Braden with the bladesong as he had been able to with Verona and Sarik, but hopefully there would be time enough.

"I will go as well," spoke a Hythariam in metallic armor that Aaron recognized from the day before. "I am called Gavril Sorindal," he said, bowing his head slightly. "I assure you that I will be an asset. I am formerly of the Hytharia military. My rank would translate to colonel."

Aaron took a long look at Gavril, who had the confident stance of an experienced leader, but he wondered if Gavril would be more of a hindrance than an asset.

Gavril stepped before Aaron and extended his hand. "I was a friend to Reymius and fought by his side at the fall of Shandara." Aaron nodded and shook his hand firmly as Gavril continued. "I would like to bring one other of my crew.

A specialist. He's got experience sneaking into impossible places," Gavril said, sparing a glance at the others.

"Just seven of you?" Iranus asked, barely keeping the shock from his voice.

Aaron grinned. "Seven is considered a lucky number where I come from."

"Well, you are certainly going to need a lot of it," Colind said dryly.

"You as well," Aaron replied. "Any thoughts on how you will convince people of the danger they are in?

"I've had a few thoughts, and Iranus will help with the rest," replied Colind.

Aaron turned to Iranus. "I'd like to leave as soon as possible."

"Indeed," Iranus said. "It would be better to wait until nightfall. We should be able to get you near Khamearra by morning. Could I have a private word with you?"

"Of course," Aaron said, and the others left with the exception of Verona and Colind.

Iranus walked farther into the meadow. "Safanar is a beautiful world, don't you think?"

"I do," Aaron said, and his thoughts returned to Sarah dancing with the other women around the bonfires on the night of the choosing. He had lost the laurel crown she had placed on his head. It was on board the Raven… "Did Tolvar contact you?" he asked, remembering his encounter with the old man before they had reached Shandara. Tolvar had been able to shield them from the Ryakul until the Raven had caught up to them.

Iranus nodded and smiled. "Yes, that is how we knew you were in Shandara."

"I know you don't think much of my chances for saving Sarah," Aaron began, but Iranus held up his hand.

"No, we've both made our points, and you're right. It's time to move on. I wanted to talk to you about my daughter," Iranus said.

"She appears to be able to take care of herself."

"Yes, she can, but it doesn't mean I'm not worried about sending her off," said Iranus. "It is the burden of fathers, I'm afraid."

"I will look after her as best I can," Aaron promised. "I've faced impossible odds at Shandara with Verona, Eric, and Braden, and we would not have survived if we hadn't watched out for one another. In fact, the others will attest that I try too hard to bear the burden myself."

Iranus looked at Aaron evenly. "Desperation has a way of grinding the honor out of most. I don't know you well enough to be a fair judge of your character in that respect, but it is a lesson we learned from our dying world. Desperate people take desperate measures. I just want you to try to be clear-headed about this. None of this is fair, especially for you, but like it or not there is great importance attached to your survival. The people of this world need you."

"Sometimes one can only do the best with the time that one has," Aaron said. "And decide when or where to make a stand."

Iranus's face broke into a smile. "You sound very much like Reymius," he said and then his face turned solemn. "I know what he sacrificed to save your mother and therefore you."

"I didn't know it at the time," Aaron began, "but I saw the emptiness he felt and the scars he had. I don't think he was equipped to deal with the Drake."

"It's worse than that," Iranus said softly. "The form of the Drake you faced was once your grandmother, the Lady Cassandra, Princess of Shandara. It's an unfortunate part of what the Nanites do. Not part of their original programming, I can assure you, but around the fall we came close to creating a true artificial intelligence. That is what I suspect the Drake is, in part. It was sent here to ascertain the barrier and remove it. When it figured out that the barrier was linked to the Alenzar'seth, it conceived this twisted cycle that you are part of now. You have no idea how much it saddens me that one of our most remarkable achievements could be perverted into something so vile and repulsive."

My grandmother? Aaron's mind reeled at the thought. "My grandfather couldn't have known. He wouldn't have left otherwise."

Iranus gripped Aaron's shoulder. "He did," Iranus said gently. "I know because I was there. I helped him escape to the planet you call Earth, but you will never see it in our night sky."

"Why not?" Aaron asked.

"Because Earth is on another dimensional plane than Safanar," Iranus answered. "While we were looking for a way to escape the destruction of Hytharia we figured out a way to open a doorway to another dimension. Same place just in a different universe. In each dimension we were able to open, Hytharia was already destroyed. There was nothing there. When it became apparent that the Drake could not be stopped here on Safanar, I built a new device. A cylinder that over time would charge enough to open the dimensional doorway, and that is how we found Earth."

"Wait a second," Aaron interrupted. "Are you saying that Safanar and Earth are the same planet but in different universes?"

"That is precisely what I'm saying," Iranus answered.

"But nothing looks the same. The geography is all different. The continents are not in the same place. We have only one moon, and the stars don't even match up," Aaron said.

"Different universes. Different rules. Different everything," Iranus said.

"And the Drake is my grandmother?" Aaron asked, still struggling to wrap his head around this.

"It's better to think of it this way," Iranus began. "The Drake's previous form was your grandmother, but your grandmother is dead. She has been completely assimilated by the Nanites. Sarah still has a sliver of hope to avoid the same fate. There were no travel crystals here at the time that Shandara fell. They came from parts of a comet that grazed the atmosphere primarily over Khamearra."

Aaron didn't know what to think and shook his head.

"I thought you should know and have a better understanding what Reymius sacrificed so that your mother could be saved and you could grow up on a world safe from the Drake. It's the only reason I could think of why he never came back."

Me. My mother. Aaron sighed as he saw his grandfather, Reymius, in a new light. "Thank you for telling me. I just don't know what to say."

Iranus nodded. "I know you have the cylinder in your possession. I would suggest showing it to my daughter and telling her its purpose. Perhaps she can figure out a way for it to help in your journey."

Iranus left him to his thoughts, and Colind and Verona quietly approached.

"Did you know about this?" Aaron asked Colind. "About Cassandra, my grandmother?"

Colind looked at the ground with a pained expression. "I knew the Drake had taken her. At the time, we weren't sure how it worked. We thought of the Drake as a separate entity. Reymius suspected it near the end, but at the fall it wasn't just one thing that caused the destruction of Shandara; it was a maelstrom of events happening all at once. Mactar, along with the High King and the Elitesmen, were able to get inside Shandara with Tarimus's help and bring down the walls from within. Mactar trapped me and ... well, you saw the destruction."

After a few moments of silence, Aaron spoke. "Is there anything you can tell me that will help us find what we need in Khamearra?" he couldn't bring himself to think of the Drake as his grandmother. Iranus was right that his grandmother was dead, but part of him wondered if some small part of her was there still. He thought he understood what was at stake for Sarah before, and now...he only had two weeks. Roselyn had implied the longer timeframe was due to her training, which made sense. But he wondered if it was also due in part to the ever-present connection he felt with her. He hadn't sensed it until after he used the bladesong to heal Sarah from her mortal wounds.

Desperate measures. Iranus's warning echoed in his mind.

He had no such ties or responsibilities as his grandfather did. No child of his own to protect. He wouldn't have to make the same sacrifice that Reymius had, but he understood Iranus's fear of events spiraling out of control. Aaron met Colind's concerned gaze and saw understanding mixed with a twinge of fear.

"They need to prepare themselves for war, Colind," Aaron said. "There is no way around this. You must make the leaders of these nations understand this, or they will all suffer the same fate as Shandara."

"I will, Aaron," Colind answered quietly. "Curious word, 'nations.'"

"It is how we refer to other countries or kingdoms," Aaron said, his thoughts drifting back to his life on Earth. He had come to Safanar seeking revenge and to protect his sister, but it had become so much more.

"Verona," Colind said, "listen up. I assume that you will not be leaving Aaron's side for the foreseeable future."

"Your assumption is correct, my lord," Verona answered, joining them.

"Excellent. I will tell you what I know about Khamearra," Colind began.

Across the grand expanse beneath his thoughts, Aaron felt his connection to Sarah splinter. They had precious little time, so he focused on which insights he could glean about Khamearra from Colind.

5

PARTING WAYS

It was late afternoon when the two groups were making ready to depart. Aaron was grateful for everything the Hythariam had done, but was anxious to leave. Colind had shared a great deal about Khamearra with him that should prove useful. They gathered in a field near one of the complexes of dome-shaped buildings.

The Raven loomed overhead, dark and majestic. The crew scurried about their tasks, getting ready to leave as Captain Nathaniel Morgan spoke with a group of Hythariam. Aaron saw where some additional equipment had been installed, which he was told would augment the crystal-powered engines already on the wings. Sarik assured him the new equipment would make the engines safer as well as continuously propel the ship, which gave it a decisive advantage over any other airship native to Safanar.

Captain Morgan possessed the schematics to build and upgrade the remaining ships in the Rexellian Navy. The advantage wouldn't be long lived, as the Hythariam would share the advances with any other kingdom that would ally with them for the coming war. Aaron was appreciative of the fact that the Hythariam not only provided the proverbial fish, but were now willing to teach the people of Safanar how to fish as well. Colind and Garret assured him that the sharing of knowledge would be reciprocated back to the Hythariam, because as the Hythariam were gifted in science, the native people of Safanar were gifted in tapping directly into energy around them. In Aaron's opinion, it would one day equal the advantage of the Nanites and perhaps surpass them, as he could. Aaron had used the power of the bladesong to finish repairing his body and drive the remaining Ryakul poison from his system.

Captain Morgan descended down the gangplank and strode over. "Aaron, glad to see you looking better. No worse for wear, I take it?" When Aaron nodded and shook his hand, he continued. "I wish you were coming with us, but I understand why you can't."

"I'll miss the Raven. She's a great ship, but not as great as her captain," Aaron said.

"That she is," the captain answered, "and that I am," he said, grinning. "Your Grace," he continued, formally addressing Aaron as he would a royal prince or king. "Despite what you say," he said, holding up his hands, halting Aaron's protest, "you are the Heir of Shandara. A king in your own right. There are many who would flock to the banner of the Alenzar'seth should you wish to raise it, and I would count myself fortunate to be among the flock." The crew around them stopped their activities and turned toward them.

Aaron was stuck in mid protest by gratitude. "Thank you," he said finally.

"This world needs the Alenzar'seth! We need Shandara to rise from the ashes!" Captain Morgan's voice barked, snapping the attention of all those gathered. "We need you, Your Grace," he finished, and sank down to one knee, holding his fist over his heart. The crew around them followed their captain, even those upon the ship. Then his friends followed suit. Even Colind and Vaughn went to their knees.

Aaron's heart thundered in his chest as he stood alone among a sea of kneeling men and women. A lone chant carried throughout the field.

Shandara!

The echoes of each syllable permeated through Hathenwood to the rooftops of the world. The Hythariam looked on silently and bowed their heads respectfully toward him. Aaron was overwhelmed by the outpouring of support and committed to himself (and silently to all the people gathered) that he would honor their faith in him. The crew of the Raven had traveled with him, had bled at his side to get him to Shandara. They witnessed the daughter of the High King fall in love with this lost son of the Alenzar'seth. They had grown to love them both as comrades in arms, and until this moment he didn't fully realize that he wasn't alone beyond his closest friends in this quest to save the woman he loved.

Aaron raised his hands, and the men stood up once more and waited expectantly for him to say something. How could he not?

"Thank you. Your support means everything to me. Though our paths take us to different places, we are all joined by this moment in time. Hold onto it, cherish each other, and remember that the crew of the Raven stood with the Alenzar'seth and delivered him safely to Shandara.

"Go forth and spread the word. Tell them of the dangers we face. Call upon their honor to defend their homes, to welcome the Hythariam with open arms, and to harbor no ill will toward them. They have sacrificed as much as the people of Shandara and are worthy of our protection. Tell them we are here, and we will fight this enemy with the strength of this world, for we are mighty! We are Safanarions!" Aaron cried out and he was joined by everyone in the field, including the Hythariam, who perhaps for the first time, to Aaron at least, looked upon Safanar as their home. A home worth defending.

The crowd dispersed. Captain Morgan took his leave, and Aaron noticed that all of them stood a little bit taller, walked with a purpose. He didn't know where the words came from and noted he now considered Safanar almost as much of a home as Earth had been. The idea of a king still sickened him, however. It was too much power for one man, even himself, and would be something he would rectify going forward. But if having a king gave these men the courage they needed to walk the path laid before them, then so be it. To himself, he was a man and not a king. A leader perhaps, but no king.

"You certainly have a way with words, my friend," Verona said, coming toward him.

"Funny," Aaron said, "I always thought of you as having the way with words. Perhaps you're rubbing off on me."

A small golden craft flew silently into view and landed a short distance from them. The wings, if they could be called such, were small and barely extended beyond a few feet in length. From its smooth side, a Hythariam emerged from a door that appeared as if by magic. The Hythariam was followed by Gavril, who waved in greeting and motioned them over.

"Do they have machines like this where you come from?" Verona asked.

"Similar yes, but these look better made and more advanced," Aaron answered. "I wasn't in the military, so I can't really comment on how these compare. They are impressive, and it can get us to Khamearra before Sarah is out of time."

They walked over to the golden craft.

Gavril nodded in greeting to each of them. "I would like to introduce you to Tanneth. He will be joining us, and I'm sure you will find that he is quite resourceful."

Tanneth was of medium build with the same golden eyes that marked most Hythariam. He firmly shook their hands and began checking the outside of the ship.

Aaron ran his hands along the smooth golden surface, which was slightly warm to the touch.

"It's a Flyer-class SPT," Gavril said. "Stealth Personnel Transport. It's fast and silent, with some cloaking abilities. We should be able to make the trip to Khamearra in no time."

Aaron was impressed. "Were these the ones you used at Shandara?"

"Yes," Gavril answered.

"How many of them do you have?" Aaron asked.

"We have ten SPTs in working order," Gavril said. "I know the engineers are working to get some more online."

Roselyn joined them, carrying several packs. Tanneth helped her load them onto the Flyer, and Gavril indicated that they could leave as soon as they were ready.

Aaron noted Verona's almost pained expression when looking in Roselyn's direction. "She's extremely beautiful, but are you going to be able to focus?" Aaron asked.

Verona tore his eyes away and looked toward Aaron, but he could tell that Verona fought to keep his eyes from drifting back. "I don't know what has come over me, my friend. I've been bitten, I'm afraid."

"I can tell, and so can everyone else. You know you could try talking to her."

"I would if the function of my tongue didn't go awry every time she came near me," Verona answered.

Aaron remembered feeling the same thing when Sarah first came into his life and hoped that his friend would get control of himself soon. Roselyn didn't strike him as a type of woman who looked kindly upon a man who behaved with a boyish crush.

Colind approached quietly. "It's almost time," he said.

"Yes and not a moment too soon," Aaron replied.

"I need to ask what your intentions are regarding the barrier," Colind began. "Just so I'm aware."

Aaron calmly returned Colind's gaze. That's what they were all worried about. "I don't know. It's hard to say right now, mainly because we know so little. I'm going to do everything I can to save Sarah though."

Colind nodded slowly in understanding. "Just remember that the people of Khamearra are not the enemy."

"I know," Aaron answered. "But I would think that most people from Khamearra would believe that I am the enemy."

"Some," Colind acknowledged. "There are many factions, but remember they are also a people who live in fear. That is how the High King rules with the Elitesmen working as his right arm. Things were not always as they are now. Remember you may be able to find help in Khamearra." Colind paused, considering his next words. "I wish that I could go with you."

"You are needed elsewhere," said Aaron. "Besides, we'll catch up to you within two weeks," Aaron continued, not voicing what would happen if he failed.

"It seems there is never enough time. May the Goddess's blessings be upon you," Colind said with a slight bow, then pulled Aaron into a quick embrace. "One more thing," Colind began after letting him go. "Remember stealth is the goal. Avoid the High King if you can. He'll be focused on you now, and unlike before, they won't underestimate you."

Aaron understood all too well. "I've killed two of his sons, but it's about time they have something else to think about instead of just hunting me. Where will they stand when the barrier between worlds fails?"

"I suspected that somehow they had been in contact with General Halcylon on Hytharia, but it was never proven," Colind said and went silent as Iranus approached.

"I wanted you to know that we were able to see something heading for this planet," Iranus said. "It's not clear what exactly, but we'll work on it. I can't believe we've been so blind to this threat. We will do everything in our power to help, but, Aaron, I must ask something of you."

"What do you need?" Aaron asked.

"That you return to Shandara," Iranus answered.

"Why? What's there?"

"Up until Shandara fell, we had been working to create a stockpile of weapons to use in the event of the barrier collapsing. We feared they had been lost when the city was all but destroyed. I will send people to search, but I suspect we'll need you in order to find them," Iranus said.

"I'll return to Hathenwood, and together we can search," Aaron said. "I'm just a little surprised that you would need my help with this."

"We're limited by our technology. We, along with your ancestors, decided on this course of action, and it was left to them to hide the weapons as only they knew how," Iranus answered.

Aaron nodded, finally understanding. "They hid it, guarding against an invasion from Hytharia."

"Precisely," Iranus said. "I wish you a quick return, and may fortune smile upon you." Iranus walked away and headed toward his daughter, whom he pulled into a long hug.

"It's time for us to be going, my friend," Verona said quietly by his side.

Aaron nodded and waved goodbye to the others, joining Sarik on the Flyer. Eric and Braden were already on board. He was quickly followed by Roselyn and Verona. *I'm coming, Sarah,* Aaron thought and turned his attention to the display in the front. The display showed a panoramic view of everything around them. Gavril and Tanneth occupied the pilot and co-pilot's seats while the rest of them sat on the benches along the sides. Aaron barely felt the craft lift into the air. Gavril punched in the coordinates that would take them to Khamearra then turned his chair so it faced them.

"The coordinates are set, and we should arrive in about five hours, making the best speed in stealth," Gavril said, then looked at Aaron. "I hope you've got a plan."

"Verona and I put together some ideas, but much of it depends upon what we find when we reach the city," Aaron answered. "We'll need to take a look around."

Gavril nodded. "Reconnaissance. That's a good start."

"Excuse me," Sarik said, drawing their attention. "But how will you blend in?"

Aaron was wondering the same thing.

"The same as you," Roselyn said. "We have something that will make our eyes look the same as yours."

"I have another question, if you wouldn't mind," Sarik asked. "How come you look so…human? The way I understand it is that you are from another world. I guess I'm just wondering how that could be?"

There was a brief moment of silence as the seven of them regarded each other. Gavril and Tanneth looked toward Roselyn, which made sense to Aaron, as she was a scientist.

"It's a good question," Aaron said.

"Yes it is," Roselyn agreed. "The best we can determine is that we are cousins of sorts stemming from the same tree, but have gone down slightly different paths."

"Cousins?" Verona asked, speaking up for the first time since they came onboard.

"Yes," Roselyn said. "We have the same parts, I assure you. We're made up of the same stuff, to be completely blunt about it. We feel pain as you do, emotion as you do. And..." Roselyn glanced at Aaron, "... some of us even have had children with the people of Safanar."

"Why are you looking at me?" Aaron asked.

"Your grandfather, Reymius, chose to marry one of us," Roselyn said. "Your grandmother, Cassandra, was Hythariam. So you see we are not all that different from each other. You and I are truly cousins of sorts."

"How?" Aaron asked.

"Cassandra was Iranus's sister," Roselyn said. "Iranus is my father," she said, addressing the others on the small ship.

Roselyn was right, they were cousins after a fashion through his grandmother. *And now she is the Drake.* Aaron suppressed a shiver; he wasn't sure to what extent anyone else knew of the real tragedy that had befallen his grandparents, but it did explain some of Iranus's bitterness regarding the Drake.

Aaron eyed Roselyn for a moment. "Cousin." He grinned.

A smile lit up her face. "Cousin," Roselyn confirmed.

"Okay back to business," Aaron said. "Do you have a map of the capital city of Khamearra that you can put on screen?"

The Hythariam's reactions to his question were slightly amusing. They were clearly not used to someone other than themselves possessing knowledge about technology. Gavril nodded to Tanneth, who punched in a few keys. An aerial photograph of the city appeared, which confirmed to Aaron that they either had orbiting satellites or had done their own aerial reconnaissance. Verona and Sarik's eyes lit up at the display.

"That is impressive," Verona said.

"Quite," Aaron agreed. "This will help us immensely. How many satellites do you have in orbit?"

Gavril raised an eyebrow. "Thirty-four. We've mapped the surface of this world," Gavril said. "I'm sorry we're just not used to others knowing—"

"About your little toys," Aaron said with a smile, winking at Verona and Sarik. "Get used to it," Aaron said. "They have machines that fly around the world that can take pictures of the land among other things."

"I was among those in favor of sharing knowledge," Gavril replied.

"Look how big the city is," Sarik said.

Aaron looked at the display, frowning. "We should consider splitting up to cover more ground. I only want to spend one day at the most looking around," he said, ignoring the painful spike in his connection to Sarah. He wanted to reach across the expanse to her, but was afraid of the pain he would cause her. Aaron knew in his heart that she was still fighting, and he needed to concentrate on finding the travel crystals.

"It may take more than a day," Verona said gently, and Gavril nodded.

Patience, Aaron counseled to himself. "Fine," he conceded. "But no more than two, or we can throw stealth out the window, and I will start focusing my attention on the Elitesmen."

"I suggest we divide the city into sections and pair off to investigate," Gavril said.

"That sounds good," Aaron answered, and glanced at Eric and Braden's challenging glares. "I won't go anywhere alone."

Some of the areas they would be looking at overlapped, but that was only because he insisted on seeing the Elitesmen stronghold for himself.

"I would like to check these areas myself," Tanneth spoke, gesturing to certain areas of the city, including the Elitesmen stronghold. His quiet tone caught Aaron by surprise as it were the first time he had heard him speak. "Meaning no disrespect to anyone here, but I'll do better on my own."

Gavril nodded his approval.

"Okay," Aaron said. "But be careful."

"I would like to go with you, Master Sorindale," Sarik said, addressing Gavril.

Gavril eyed Sarik for a moment and then nodded.

"I will be joining you two gentlemen, it seems," Roselyn said, looking at Aaron and Verona.

"Welcome," Aaron said and was slightly amused as Verona went a little pale. Sarik and Braden glanced at Verona, noting his silence, and Aaron shook his head slightly. Eric, however, could not keep from chuckling and muttered something about Verona being tongue-tied for once in his life.

The discussion turned to more mundane things, which Aaron only half paid attention to. He was focused on the map of the city before him, committing it to memory, especially the Elitesmen stronghold, where he was convinced a cache of travel crystals was stored. They decided to get what rest they could, with some of them dozing off. Aaron couldn't help but think of this moment as the calm before the storm.

"Are you sure about this?" Iranus asked.

"Aaron must be trusted to walk his own path," Colind answered. "It was Reymius's last command, and you must admit that Aaron has good instincts."

Iranus rubbed his white beard for a moment in thought. "I'm just afraid. You didn't witness the fall of your civilization. Reymius understood and made the ultimate sacrifice."

"Aaron is different," Colind said. "For one thing, he doesn't have a daughter to protect. He has sacrificed, but there will come a time when a line will be drawn and we must choose whether to stand that line with him. Aaron witnessed the cost of Reymius's sacrifices for the greater good, whether he understood the gravity of them or not. He is quite familiar with the results. At some point, the cost of sacrificing for the greater good is too high for those closest to the fight. Aaron is right to expect that the burden be spread to the people of this world. Either we fight and have a chance at surviving, or we stick our heads in the sand and forgo the right to be surprised when annihilation comes for us."

Iranus nodded. "I don't like it, but I understand, and I even agree with you to a certain extent. The Alenzar'seth have given more than we had right to ask of them," Iranus sighed. "I don't know how they could have survived on Hytharia. Our sun has expanded so much so that Hytharia must have become unlivable."

Colind absently grazed his fingertips along his bearded chin, lost in thought. "I had a friend once tell me that we should only worry about things that we have an influence over and acknowledge the things that we do not," Colind said.

Vaughn smiled. "And only take action upon the things that you can directly affect."

"They were very wise and, of course, correct. Who was your friend?" Iranus asked.

"Reymius," Colind said. "I see the same foundation of wisdom in Aaron. Many that he has come in contact with see it as well. It's why people are so apt to follow him."

"Yes, and he hates it as well," Garret said. "He believes whole-heartedly in people thinking for themselves."

"Exactly," Colind said. "And that's why he'll make a good leader. One that we can look to in these troubled times."

"I agree with you, old friend," Iranus said. "We've got a mountains' worth of work to do and very little time to do it in. Good luck in your journey. Our emissaries will have the means to contact us here in Hathenwood. They will show you how to use the comms device as well, so we should be able to keep in contact as needed."

The group split apart into those going on board the Raven and the Hythariam preparing as best they could for a war they had hoped to avoid.

6

DISTRICT CAPTAIN

It was supposed to be an opportunity of a lifetime. Moving to the capital city in his beloved homeland of Khamearra. That was how both he and his wife thought of it six months ago. Nolan's wife still believed at least, but he wasn't so sure anymore. He stood in the bathroom, facing a small oval mirror, methodically rinsing his razor in the sink. *Running water*, he smiled at the thought. When they had first moved into the district captain's residence, they had stood around the sink just to see water come from the faucets. This was the first place he had ever lived in that he didn't have to haul water from a well.

Being among the youngest captain of the guards for his city district, he was committed to looking the part. Not that he was all that young, being just past his thirty-second year. The echoes of his children fumbling through the house, getting ready for school, was soothing to his ears. He should feel fortunate that his children could attend school here. Many others couldn't say the same.

They had gone from living in a charming old house in the country, where his duties required him to travel to the surrounding towns to enforce the High King's Writ, to here. His house wasn't lavish by any means and would be considered a country cottage to those of higher rank, but to him it was a piece of heaven. The house was great. It was the job that made him feel shackled for the first time in his life.

"Nolan," his wife called. "You're going to be late."

Nolan quickly finished shaving and washed the remaining gel off his face. A small grin marked his features as he tied back his shoulder-length black hair into a ponytail. Not as stylish as some other captains, but at least he still had hair enough to cover his head, and for that he was content.

He left the small bathroom and came down the hall to the kitchen, where his family had gathered to break their fast. His wife, Arienh, rounded up his son and daughter and got them to sit at the table. Gathering for family meals was of paramount importance to Arienh, which made him sorry for all the dinners he had missed since taking this job.

Nolan could handle the demands of being a district captain, but it was the undercurrents of the city that worried him…and the Elitesmen. The Elitesmen were above the law and could dispense justice to the point of overruling his authority in his own district. He had learned that the hard way. The Elitesmen perception of justice was significantly different from his own.

He had crossed paths with them but a few times, and they were enough. Since then, he had seen them watching his home. Turning up in places where his wife and children frequented. He especially didn't like the attention they paid his eldest child, Jason, who would reach his twelfth year of age this coming month, the age at which he could undertake an apprenticeship. The children of wellborn nobility and ranking officers tried different apprenticeships before settling into an occupation.

Nolan had once broached the subject of them leaving a few weeks back.

"The Goddess wants us exactly where she intends for us to be. Have faith in that, my love," Arienh had said.

Nolan didn't have the heart to tell her of the Elitesmen watching their comings and goings. Arienh loved the city, and he couldn't take it away from her despite the growing unease he felt whenever he walked through his district. The people were kind, but would rarely make eye contact for fear of causing some type of offense. He had witnessed the abuse some captains imposed upon residents of their districts, but he would stomach none of it in his own. People weren't beaten or tossed into his holding cells without good reason, and in the latter case, only in defense of one's self. He had made that as clear as day to his guards his very first week.

After eating a quiet breakfast with his family, Nolan stepped out of the house to head to the station. He brushed off imaginary dust particles on his otherwise pristine black uniform. The silver dragon emblem showed proudly upon his muscled chest. He walked down the street, nodding in greeting to those passing by. The residents that lived closest to his house had long gotten used to his friendly greetings, which were received warily at first but eventually returned in kind. Across the way, his friend called out to him.

"Good morning, Lieutenant Anson," Nolan greeted.

"Same to you, Captain Nolan," Anson said back, but the mirth was short lived, as his normally sunny features grew serious. "The rumor is that Josef is waiting for you at the station."

Nolan frowned. "Do you know what for?"

Anson raised a brow. "I think you know, sir."

"Enlighten me," Nolan said.

Anson was a good man and one of the earliest at the station to give his support.

"An incident occurred last night near the poor quarter, Josef's Lieutenant… " Anson began.

"Captain Commander Josef," Nolan corrected. Despite both their opinions of the man, he still wore the uniform of the captain commander.

"My apologies, sir," Anson replied. "Lieutenant Renke and his squad followed a group of men returning from their work in the crystal mines. They were beating the group of men, claiming that they had stolen crystals to sell for themselves. Our boys were alerted to the commotion and intervened. They said that when they arrived, the miners had submitted to questioning, but Renke's men were still beating them. We rounded the whole lot up and put them in separate holding cells."

Nolan frowned. "Renke and his guards, too?"

"Yes, sir," Anson answered.

Nolan smiled, slightly glimpsing the crap storm that this was going to cause. Regardless, from the sound of it, his men were in the right, and he would back them up even if Renke's boss outranked him.

"All right, I think I get the gist," Nolan said. "Is there anything else?"

"Yes, Captain Commander Josef was accompanied by an Elitesman," Anson said, unable to keep his voice from shaking. The presence of the Elitesmen were enough to rattle the nerves of the most stalwart of men, and Nolan understood Anson's concern.

"Understood," Nolan said and quickened his pace to the station. So much for a quiet morning.

Ten minutes later, he and Anson rounded the corner to the station headquarters for the district. A three-story, white, stone-faced building big enough to accommodate a hundred guards of the watch stood at a main intersection. He took the steps leading up to the main doors two at a time. When he came through the doors, the clerk behind the desk saluted.

"Captain of the watch is on-site," the clerk cried.

Nolan returned the salute and quickly headed for his office. The mood in the station was more somber than normal, which Nolan attributed more to the presence of the Elitesmen than the Captain Commander. Perhaps it was his own nerves.

Nolan glanced back, and Anson was still on his tail. "Stay close."

Anson nodded and took up the post right outside his office door.

Nolan stepped into his office to find Captain Commander Josef sitting in his chair and the Elitesman standing at the window with his back to him. Josef had the look of someone permanently annoyed with everything and anyone that was unlucky enough to cross his path. Of the districts in the capital city, the captain commander's is the most prestigious because its borders included the palaces of the High King.

Captain Commander Josef looked up at his arrival and scowled.

"My Lord, Captain Commander," Nolan saluted.

The Captain Commander narrowed his piggish eyes. "Nolan, you have some of my men locked up in your holding cells."

"Yes, my lieutenant was bringing me up to speed on my way in this morning, sir," Nolan replied, glancing in the direction of the Elitesman who didn't turn around or make any sound.

"Well," Josef growled.

"Sir?" Nolan asked.

"I want them released," the Captain Commander barked.

"They will be released when I review the case and they've been cleared of any wrong-doing," Nolan replied calmly. "I've only just learned of the incident this morning, and it did only occur last night."

Josef's scowl deepened, and his face became an impressive shade of purple. "Are you refusing an order?"

"No, sir."

"Then why won't you release them now?" Captain Commander Josef asked.

"As I've already said, my lord, I haven't reviewed the case nor checked last night's reports—" Nolan's reply was cut short.

"Don't spout these ridiculous reasons. Those are my men you have locked up, and as your superior officer I'm giving you a direct order to release my men or I'll…" Captain Commander Josef bit off his reply.

"I would caution you against that, my lord," Nolan replied, fighting the urge to clench his fists. "I cannot comply with your order as it would violate our city mandate which is, as you know, to uphold the law of our city. If I were to just release them because of your order, I could be brought up on charges for negligence of duty if any wrong-doing were to be found."

Captain Commander Josef heaved his bulk out of Nolan's chair, glaring menacingly at him. Despite Josef's expanding girth, Nolan knew he had been a brawler in his youth and still enjoyed a good fight. Nolan kept his cool despite Josef's outward display.

Just then, his office door burst open and Lieutenant Anson stepped inside under the guise of delivering reports from the night watch. Anson wore a shocked expression as if he didn't realize anyone was in the room.

"My Lords, I'm sorry for interrupting," Anson stammered, but Nolan knew better. Anson stood, waiting with the files in his hand.

"Thank you, Lieutenant," Nolan said and gestured for him to place the files on his desk.

Anson placed the files on his desk and winked at Nolan before leaving the room.

"Release the commander's men," said the Elitesman, speaking for the first time, slowly turning from the window. "And the miners." His voice didn't hiss, but it still reminded Nolan of a snake.

The Elitesman's icy stare sent shivers down Nolan's spine. He couldn't argue his way out of this, and the Elitesman knew it.

"At once, my lord," Nolan said, bowing his head, knowing that the miners in the holding cell were doomed to a cruel fate.

The Elitesman nodded and turned to address Josef. "Captain Commander, I trust that should satisfy you. Deliver the miners to the Citadel."

The Citadel was the stronghold of the Elitesmen, and there was little chance that they would ever see the light of day again. Nolan felt a pang of regret for the miners settle into the pit of his stomach. *Do something. Help them,* a small voice urged, but there was nothing he could do. The Elitesmen's word was law, and to challenge it often turned out badly for the challenger.

There were rumors spoken in hushed corners about a man who openly challenged the Elitesmen, but he put little stock in them. Who could ever challenge the Elitesmen? Those miners were as good as dead, which is where he would end up if he tried to help them. But he wanted to help. The stink of the Elitesmen autonomy gnawed at him. He was a district captain, and he should be able to protect the citizens in his district and uphold the law.

The Elitesman turned back to Nolan and dismissed the Captain Commander. Josef left the room, still glaring at him. The Elitesman moved closer to him, and Nolan had to fight the urge to grab the sword at his side. He was an expert swordsman. Most captains were, but he had seen some of the things the Elitesmen could do, and he had no desire to test his mettle against any from that order.

"Whenever you're ready, Captain," the Elitesman said.

Nolan nodded. "Lieutenant."

Anson stepped back into the room and saluted.

"Release the captain commander's guards at once. Take a squad and escort the miners to the Citadel," Nolan said.

As Anson saluted, the Elitesman cleared his throat, narrowing his gaze.

"Do we have a problem?" the Elitesmen asked quietly.

"No, sir," Nolan replied.

"I said for the captain commander's men to escort the miners to the Citadel, not your men."

Nolan clamped his jaw shut. He was hoping that his interpretation of the Elitesmen orders would be over-looked. "My apologies, Elitesman," Nolan said.

"You've been here six months, is that right?" the Elitesman asked.

"Yes, my lord," Nolan answered.

"This isn't the first time your 'interpretation' of our orders has almost put you in direct conflict with our will," he hissed.

Nolan swallowed. "My Lord, I was thinking of the well-being of the miners. My only concern was to deliver them safely into the care of your brethren at the Citadel. I meant no offense."

"Perhaps it is my *will* that the miners suffer," the Elitesman spat. "Would you have issues with that?"

The Elitesman knew damned well he would have an issue, and the look in his eyes confirmed it.

"No, my lord," Nolan answered numbly.

"I see," the Elitesman said, striding about the room before turning to face Nolan again. "I would like your men to escort the miners to the Citadel. See to it that they are properly cowed by the time they arrive."

Nolan fought down the nauseous feeling in his sinking stomach as his mind leaped ahead to not only what he was being ordered to do to the miners, but what the cost would be to the men under his command. The spark gave way to the flame of his anger despite his fear of the Elitesmen.

"As you wish, my lord," he said softly.

"I want them driven like livestock through the streets, and I want you to personally oversee their transfer," the Elitesman sneered, his gaze unwavering.

Nolan's hand itched to reach for his sword. He couldn't do this. This was an order he couldn't follow.

"Captain," the Elitesman prodded, "we're very interested in your son. We've watched his progress and have noted his special talents."

Jason! They know!

He had tried to keep Jason's talents secret, but the boy was twelve. No, not my son. Nolan's hand hardened around the hilt of his sword, much to the Elitesman's delight. Nolan stood there for a moment, upon the precipice of openly rebelling against the Elitesman and certain death. The Elitesman, he noted, delighted in his struggle as a spider mercilessly spins his web around his prey.

How could they know about Jason?

"We are keen to get him into the academy of the Elite when he comes of age. That's next month, is it not?" the Elitesman asked.

Nolan nodded, not trusting himself to speak.

"Excellent, I look forward to his training," the Elitesman said in a deceptively sunny tone. "Now I will await you and your men outside. Do not keep me waiting long." The Elitesman finished and left the room.

Nolan stared at the spot where the Elitesman stood until Anson cleared his throat. He released his vice-like grip off the hilt of his sword.

"Lieutenant, gather a squad of men and bring the miners to the front of the station," Nolan said evenly.

"But, Captain, we can't do this," Anson said, his eyes wide with fear.

I have no choice. They are coming for my son.

"We have our orders. Tell the squad to... " His voice faltered. "Bring the whips," Nolan said, turning to face his friend. The look of betrayal nearly broke him as much as the threat to his family had. Almost. There was a line between protecting his friends and comrades and protecting his family. Anson was about to voice another protest. "You have your orders, Lieutenant!" he shouted.

Anson saluted and bowed stiffly. "It shall be done, My Lord Captain."

Nolan felt something break inside him as Anson left the room. Could he really have been so naive to believe that he could have changed things here? The Elitesman had played him as a master swordsman played with a fresh recruit that had never held a blade, and the sting of it burned him inside. The Elitesman was waiting for him outside, and their plan finally dawned on him. For him to drive the miners through his own district like a bunch of animals would prove to all its residents that he was no different than any other district captain that had come before.

7

STRANGERS IN KHAMEARRA

The arrival at Khamearra was uneventful. They had decided to split up and enter the city at different entrances, using the Flyer's stealth mode to drop them off at strategic locations. The sky was beginning to grow brighter as dawn approached and the city began to awaken. The capital city was grand in size, easily four miles wide, and went on a good distance beyond that to the river after. Airships dotted the sky as they went to and fro. The walls of the city were slate gray, a stark contrast to Shandara's pristine white walls. There were houses and other buildings beyond the walls. A grand palace to the western side of the city. *Sarah's home.* Toward the eastern edge was the Elitesmen stronghold from which two dark towers spiraled toward the sky, easily as high as the towers of the palace proper.

Before setting off, Gavril once again emphasized the importance of stealth and that they should focus on reconnaissance only. They had planned to meet at an inn near the center of the city, and Gavril handed out small comms devices about six inches long and thinner than a pencil, but quite durable. They had a range of ten miles and were networked through the Flyer SPT's on-board computer, but they could also communicate back to Hathenwood through the satellite. This gave them some small measure of reassurance that they could at least speak to one another if they needed to, and that help would be on the way if someone were to get into trouble.

Tanneth had all sorts of small devices hidden within his long leather jacket. While not exactly native to Khamearra, its appearance wasn't exactly foreign either. They bid farewell to the others as Aaron, Verona, and Roselyn watched the silent Flyer leave them behind.

Roselyn brought her hands up to her eyes for a moment, and when she took them away, the Hythariam's golden eyes had been replaced with brown eyes matching Aaron's own. She couldn't hide the exotic beauty of her facial features, which were accentuated by her rich dark hair, but that's what hoods were for.

"This should be interesting," Aaron said, beginning to walk down the road to the western gate.

"I agree, my friend. Interesting indeed," Verona said, coming up behind them.

They walked up the road, silently approaching the houses along the outskirts of the walls. The people that were outside took note of their approach with a pointed indifference. The occasional few offered a friendly nod, but most went about their morning tasks, seemingly not to invite attention. They passed through the gates under the wary eyes of the guards in black uniforms with the silver dragon emblems on their chests. Aaron felt a momentary surge of anger at the sight of the uniform. When they were out of earshot of the guards, Roselyn asked him what was wrong.

"I've had a few encounters with men who wore the same uniform as the guards here," Aaron answered, keeping his head low as they passed yet more guards. He had to remind himself that simply because they wore the same uniform these were not the men who burned down his home or murdered his mother and father.

The streets became more crowded the farther they ventured into the city. Whenever there was a group of guards or a passing nobleman, a path instantly opened through the throng of people. The city fully awakened from its slumber and took on a life all its own. It was markedly different from the quietness of Hathenwood or sailing the skies on an airship. Try as he might, Aaron couldn't help but feel out of place among these people. He tried his best not to think of them as the enemy, which became easier the more he observed the silent interplay between the citizens and the guardsman. Not all the guardsmen gave the open appraisal of what could they take from you as they walked by.

Aaron turned his head to the side at the sounds of a struggle to see a man being dragged through an alleyway by a group of guards. The guards occasionally threw the poor sod to the ground, giving him a few kicks for good measure before hoisting him to his feet again.

Verona seized Aaron's arm and shook his head slightly.

"I know what you would do my friend, but we can't make everyone's business our own. Not here."

Aaron nodded reluctantly, unable to decide which bothered him more—seeing such brutality occur in broad daylight or watching the city's denizens go about their way, ignoring the scene. Another group of guards passed, heading toward the alleyway, shouting for the path to be cleared. Aaron quickly got out of the way, but watched as the guards approached the group, carrying the almost-unconscious man. The two groups stopped while the leaders conferred. Aaron noted that the men of each group had their hands upon their swords. After a few terse words that he couldn't hear in their entirety, the new group of guards took custody of the prisoner.

"You see they must take care of their own," Roselyn whispered.

Aaron was glad for the intervention of the guards, but his impression of the city was gravitating toward one of a powder keg, where a single spark would set all aflame.

"How does anyone live like this?" Aaron asked quietly.

"Look who rules these people," Verona said. "They are caught between the tyranny of the High King and that of the Elitesmen."

As if by magic, two figures in dark cloaks moved fluidly through the crowd, making their way like the opposing forces of a magnet. Aaron sensed the gathering energy and knew that these were Elitesmen. He wanted to quell the arrogance right out of them. Sheer will alone kept Aaron from attacking the Elitesmen as they passed. Will and knowing that Sarah's life was in the balance if he failed. He wondered if they sensed him. If only he could sense whether they had a travel crystal with them.

Aaron turned to Verona. "Can you sense them?"

Verona's brow furrowed in concentration and after a few moments. "Yes," he whispered, sounding surprised.

"Good," Aaron said, pleased. Both Verona and Sarik had been practicing the slow forms for meditation while he had been unconscious, and they were slowly increasing their ability to sense the life energy around them. Very soon, they would be able to pull the energy into themselves.

"You can sense them?" Roselyn asked quietly.

"Yes," Aaron answered.

Roselyn frowned and held up a small device in her hand. "I get nothing," she said, putting the device away. "Nothing beyond body heat. I don't think they have any travel crystals on them."

Aaron nodded, knowing that it would have been too good to be true if it were that easy. He turned his attention to the people again and finally understood why Sarah had held them all at arm's length in the beginning. He had assumed she was slow to trust, given the things she had to deal with during her childhood, but now he understood all too well.

Seeing the place she called home put things in a clearer perspective. He knew she aided an underground resistance, but he had no idea how to reach out to them. Aaron felt a cold shiver run the length of his spine and turned to see an Elitesman staring squarely in his direction. *Not yet.* He turned in the opposite direction and headed down a side alleyway away from the droves of people at the market place.

A short while later, they made steady progress toward the Elitesmen stronghold. The massive dark towers stretching their clawed crowns toward the sky loomed ever present in their view. Through strings of conversations and asking seemingly harmless questions, they learned that the city was divided into districts, each run by a captain who then reported to the captain commander.

Despite the oppressive power of the guards, the vibe from each of the districts was vastly different from one to the next. Aaron couldn't determine where the borders of one district ended and another began. The district they were in now was cleaner than any of the others so far, and the people were not quite so downtrodden. Even the guards they passed seemed friendly and stood with pride rather than a challenging stance bent on trouble. He was almost starting to relax when a guard called out to them.

"You three," the guard said.

They all turned to the guard, none of them volunteered to speak first.

"I don't believe I recognize you. Are you lost?" the guard asked.

Verona recovered first. "Yes, my good sir. We have newly arrived to your wonderful city. We are heading toward the central market square. Would it be too much of a bother if you could point us in the right direction?"

The guard stepped closer to them, his eyes lingering on Roselyn, who slowly pulled off the hood of her cloak and returned the guard's gaze in kind.

The guard's eyes flashed admiringly and looked respectfully toward Aaron and Verona. "Yes," the guard said. "Head up this way for three blocks until you come to Main Street East and then turn right. You can't miss it, but it will be eleven blocks whence you turn."

Verona nodded appreciatively, "My thanks to you, good sir. We'll be on our way then."

The three of them walked in the direction that the guard indicated. To do otherwise would arouse suspicion.

"I see you've found your voice," Aaron said quietly to Verona.

"One rises to the occasion," Verona replied with a grin, but the grin faded as his eyes drew toward Roselyn, who walked in front of them. She pulled her hood back up and tucked away her silky black hair. "I don't suppose I could trouble you for a bit of advice?"

"Why not," Aaron grinned, he had been expecting this.

"For the first time, words escape me, my friend," Verona began, still staring longingly at Roselyn's back. "It's stupid to bring this up. Forget I said anything," Verona said quickly and began to walk away.

Aaron grabbed his friend's arm. "It's not stupid. The world doesn't stop simply because of one's problems. I am your friend as you've been to me ever since I arrived here. If I can help, even if it's just to listen, then I will."

Verona smiled. "Thank you, my friend. I know we have bigger things to be concerned about than my boyish crush on our beautiful, fair, and exotic traveling companion."

"Is that all it is then, a boyish crush?" Aaron asked.

Verona was silent for moment, and Roselyn glanced in their direction to be sure they were still following. "No," Verona answered, "it's not."

"Good," Aaron said, "because if it were, I'd thrash you for wasting my time," he said, giving Verona a playful shove.

Verona laughed. "What do I do?"

"You could try talking to her," Aaron quipped.

"What would I say?"

Aaron swallowed a chuckle, because Verona was completely serious and he didn't want to offend. "I suggest being honest and listen. Listening to what a woman has to say is good place to start."

"What if— " Verona stammered, "what if she doesn't feel the same way?"

"There is only one way to find out, but I would suggest picking your moment and taking small steps with a word here and there." Aaron grinned, and Verona shoved him back. That was good. Verona must have it bad if he was asking him these questions. What did he know about women?

Roselyn waved them over. They had come to Main Street East. The sounds of a crowd grew steadily louder, beyond the normal rabble of city life, and they quickened their pace. A large crowd gathered at the intersecting streets, and the closer they got, Aaron could hear the sharp crack of several whips and screams of pain. He pushed his way through the crowd to get a better look. Roughly fifteen men dressed in filthy rags stumbled through the street. Blood stained their backs. He counted twenty guards forming a circle to keep the crowd at bay, while three guards carried long leather whips dripping with blood. They were followed by a grim-faced captain who looked as if he were about to be sick. The grisly group was still a block away from where Aaron stood and approached rapidly. Aaron's hands drifted to his swords as he glanced across the street and saw children interspersed amid the angry crowd.

Aaron noticed the captain glance behind him at the two cloaked figures that followed. *Elitesmen*, he thought, utterly disgusted with the display. Aaron was about to step out into the street when Verona pulled him back.

"Look at them," Verona said. "The guards."

Aaron turned back and studied the guards. They all appeared grim faced and frightened despite the horrendous actions of which they were a part.

"They are afraid," Aaron said. It hadn't occurred to him until this moment that the guards themselves would feel powerless against the Elitesmen. He underestimated the hold that the Elitesmen had upon these people. His first encounter was in a small town remote from any cities; he had assumed the awe of the townsfolk had been exaggerated when he took down the Elitesmen. Now he witnessed a mob of people in a city cowed by merely two Elitesmen. He couldn't absolve the guards entirely in his mind. How could anyone do that to another human being?

"I can't walk away from this," Aaron said to Verona and Roselyn. The latter looking as if she were about to protest, but stopped when Verona gently put his hand upon her shoulder and shook his head slightly.

"I'll be right back," Aaron said, pulling up the hood of his cloak. Then he grabbed a swath of black cloth and tied it so that only his eyes showed and disappeared into the crowd.

"What will he do?" Roselyn asked.

Verona guided her to the outskirts of the crowd so they had a clear view. "I'm not sure. Remind me to tell you about how Aaron and I met at a small town called Duncan's Port. In the meantime, let's watch and help if we can."

Roselyn nodded, and they waited while the poor men under the whips were driven forward.

Crack!

The harsh snap of the whip struck the miner's back, sending droplets of blood flecking into the crowd, with some hitting Nolan's cheek. Anson wouldn't make eye contact with him now. When they had first left the station, Nolan had ordered the men to drive the miners along using the whips to crack the air. More of a theatrical display than anything else. He had hoped that the display would satisfy the Elitesmen, but he had been wrong. Dead wrong, and five of his guards had paid the price with their lives. The side of his head still throbbed from where the Elitesman had thwarted his attack, while another raised his hand, sending a searing blue orb into his chest. His chest still burned from where the orb struck. A warning, the Elitesman had said. The next one would not be aimed at him, but at his wife and daughter. His son, Jason, was too valuable an asset to waste. Jason they would simply take.

Nolan spat the blood from his mouth where he had bit his cheek. The remainder of his squad hardly glanced back at their captain, who had failed to protect five of their number. Though Nolan had only been their captain for six months, he had made it a point to know the men under his command, and he knew that there were some with families whose husbands and fathers would never again come home. His hand lingered upon his sword. How he wanted to lash out and kill the Elitesmen in a torrent of righteous fury, but deep down he knew he would only hasten his own death and doom his own family. He buried his emotions and continued to drive his men forward mercilessly. Let them hate their captain if they could. He would bear the burden of what the Elitesmen had done to all of them in this display of barbarism. Deep within the foundations of his inner core, Nolan knew that he could never absolve himself of the actions taken this bloody day. He turned back to the Elitesman who stared back at him impassively.

Nothing. There is nothing I can do to stop this.

Nolan's hand drifted toward the knife in his belt, toying with rebellious thoughts.

Throw it! a voice in his mind ordered. At the same moment, Anson glanced his way, noting where Nolan's hand had strayed. Nolan looked back at his friend, and Anson nodded back with his own hand tapping his knife.

I'm sorry, Arienh.

It would be a good death. Nolan pulled his knife free and hurled it at the Elitesman, with Anson matching his movements in perfect unison.

The Elitesman's movements blurred, sending both his and Anson's knife harmlessly to the side. The Elitesmen growled and drew their swords, and Nolan did the same. Behind him, he heard the sounds of numerous blades hiss free of their sheaths, and he risked a quick glance to see that all his guards had drawn their swords, grim faced and determined. It appeared he would be testing the Elitesmen's mettle this day.

A dark figure slammed upon the ground between them, startling the advancing Elitesmen. The figure stood tall in silent waiting as a hush swept over the crowd. The Elitesmen lashed out with their blades in a blur, and the dark figure moved equally fast, whirling his staff and blocking their attacks.

Aaron squared off against the two Elitesmen. The bladesong coursed through him, but he did not draw his swords. He held the rune-carved staff steady in his hands and patiently waited for the arrogance of the Elitesmen to win over. They fed upon the fear of those around them. They would contend with someone who could stand against them today.

The Elitesmen attacked as a pair, perfectly coordinated with lethal accuracy, their blades racing to meet him. Aaron shifted through their attacks, drawing upon the energy around them and moving faster than they ever could. In a quick burst, he sent one of the Elitesmen to the ground with a blow from his staff. The other Elitesman, lighter on his feet, danced deftly out of reach, coming to a stop in the middle of the rabble of men the guards had been trying to clear out of the way. Aaron's eyes caught the captain's as they flashed in alarm. He swung his staff in a wide arc, catching the Elitesman that approached from behind. He followed up with a crushing blow to the head, and the Elitesman moved no more.

With a nod to the captain, Aaron drew upon the energy around him and leaped into the air, closing the distance between himself and the remaining Elitesman. The crowd scattered, and the Elitesman snatched a fleeing child attempting to run past him and turned to face Aaron with a wicked gleam in his eyes.

Aaron stopped in his tracks and held his breath. The end of his staff touched the ground next to his feet, and the runes glowed faintly. The Elitesman held his blade to the child's throat. *Why do they always go after the children?* The energy practically crackled down his arms and legs, eager to be released. Aaron saw something move along the crowd's edge, and the Elitesman's sword arm jerked away from the child's throat. Aaron released the energy built up within him and moved so fast that the world stilled around him as he blurred into action. Grabbing the Elitesman by the scruff of his neck, he launched himself into a powerful jump, clearing the buildings around them. Aaron slammed the Elitesman down upon the roof of a small nearby tower. Before Aaron could deliver the final blow, the Elitesman reached inside his pocket and disappeared.

Aaron clenched his teeth, looking toward the dark towers in the distance. Then he slowly leaped down to the street below and headed to where Verona and Roselyn would be waiting.

"Who was that?" Anson asked, coming to Nolan's side.

"I don't know," Nolan said, grateful for the help of the stranger. "Release them and help them get to safety," Nolan said, and the miners disappeared into the crowd.

"What about him?" Anson asked, gesturing toward the dead Elitesman.

"Take the body and burn it," Nolan said. "I want all evidence of it to be destroyed."

Nolan said a silent prayer to the Goddess, rubbing his hand in a small circle upon his brow in a customary show of respect. Anson, who had caught the gesture, stepped up to him and handed him a leather pouch pulled from the

Elitesman's pocket, which Nolan stuffed into his own. The crowd, which had been an angry mob before, began to dissipate.

The guards gathered around after carrying out his orders. Most looked shaken by the events that had taken place. Twenty men looked expectantly at him for orders. Nolan looked at them all with a mixture of sympathy and pride. They had stood with him, ready to defy the injustice of the Elitesmen, knowing full well it would bring them wrath. Some, like himself, had families.

"It was an honor to stand by you on this bloody day, my friends," Nolan said. Friends they were, for from this day forth they could be nothing else. "I fear that the ire of the Elitesmen will be swift. None of us are safe. The Elitesmen will not stop with us. They will visit their retribution where we live. The lives of our families and loved ones are in danger. The city is not safe for us."

"Where can we go?" one of them asked.

Nolan looked back at them helplessly. Where could any of them go now? He couldn't answer the question because he didn't know himself. Anson cleared his throat and gestured to the ground. In the dirt was a sketching of a dragon cradling a rose, with one clawed hand raised before it.

Some of the guards gasped their protests, while others hastily looked around to see if anyone else had seen. Anson quickly brushed away the image.

Nolan looked at Anson, unable to keep the puzzlement from his face.

"The Resistance. We should seek their aide," Anson said. "You're new to the city and don't know how widespread they are."

Judging by the men's reactions, he could tell that more than a few were quite familiar with them.

"We shouldn't talk about this here out in the open. Let's meet in fifteen minutes," Anson said and gave them a location to meet. The guards split into groups of twos and threes and departed.

Nolan looked at his friend. "I need to get my family to safety. Out of the city, if possible."

"I'm not sure if that will be possible. We should be able to get them into hiding," Anson said, leading him down a set of streets farther away from the crowded parts of the district.

They came to an older section of the city where the stonework appeared almost ancient with a lost elegance. Nolan had the distinct feeling that they were being followed, but each time he looked, there was nothing there. Chalking it up to nerves, he kept following his friend. Eventually, they arrived at an old rundown building with a dome-shaped roof that had collapsed in a few places.

They entered the building, which appeared to be as dilapidated inside as the outside except for the pristine fountain with a statue of a woman standing resolute, her gaze sweeping the entranceway. Anson brought his hand to his forehead and made a small circular motion with his thumb and forefinger. It was just the two of them.

"I had hoped to bring you here eventually. You are different from the other captains," Anson said, his gaze lingering upon the fountain. "Better."

Nolan watched his friend. "What are you saying?"

Anson was about to answer him when the other guards arrived. After all twenty arrived, Anson called for quiet.

"My friends," Anson began, "at this point, if you're here, you've accepted that things have gotten so bad that we cannot go back to our old lives. You can, of course, go your separate ways, but after this moment when you learn what you're about to learn, there is no going back, and it would be a danger for us all to allow it."

"What do you mean?" Nolan asked.

"I am a descendant of the De'anjard, Keepers of the Watch. Shields of Shandara," Anson said with his fist across his heart. "We are the heart of the Resistance here in Khamearra. Our main objective is to bring down the Elitesmen and the High King wherever and however we can. Captain Nolan had no knowledge of this and has not participated in any of our activities. He's simply a good man. One that they will never let live because of his commitment to the law and to treating people with a sense of decency."

Nolan's mouth fell open. The De'anjard were the remnants of the Shandarian Army. Many took refuge into neighboring kingdoms, but to learn that after all this time they had kept fighting in whatever way they could was astonishing.

"We can hide your families and your loved ones," Anson said.

"At what price?" one of the guardsman barked.

"Service," Anson said. "To our cause would be ideal, but if you find that you cannot allow yourself to do so, then we will still help you leave the city."

Some of the guards murmured among themselves.

"Was that one of your people who helped us today?" Nolan asked.

Anson shook his head. "No, while there are some older Elitesmen who indirectly serve our cause, none were present today. How could they be? I didn't know we would be transferring the miners. I'm not sure why the Elitesmen wanted those miners brought to the Citadel."

"They wanted to make an example out of me," Nolan said. "This was about their asserting control, but perhaps you are correct. There may be more to their methods than what we are being led to believe."

The guards murmured their agreement, but fell silent when Anson spoke again.

"I'm not the leader of the De'anjard, but I do have the authority to speak for them. Time is short. We can help you escape the injustice of the Elitesmen, but I urge you to take up the cause. If not us, then who will stand up and fight for those who cannot fight for themselves? Give voice to those who cannot speak," Anson leveled his gaze at all of them. "Give shelter to those who wish to escape the storm."

Nolan raised his hand to his friend. "You have my sword. Just help me get my family to safety."

Anson shook his hand. Others spoke up, and they agreed to join the Shandarian Resistance in the home city of the High King. For the first time in months, Nolan felt a sense of pride that could only come from hope. He might die in service to this cause, but knowing that his family would be safe and that he could be of service to a good cause was worth dying for.

Anson split them up into groups of four, giving a different set of instructions to each. He gestured to Nolan to come with him to the various groups. Each group was given a passphrase and a specific action to take at a certain location, the purpose of which was to alert others of the Resistance that they were in need of aid. Help would be provided to gather those with loved ones in need, and after the former guardsman of the High King left, it was just Anson and himself in the old temple.

"Yours will be the riskiest of actions," Anson said.

Nolan raised an eyebrow. "Why is that?"

"Because we need for you to stay in your current place, serving as district captain."

"But," Nolan began.

"Your family will be hidden and eventually smuggled out of the city, but your position as district captain is one we can't hope to pass up. We can come up with some type of cover story for their absence."

Nolan's mind raced. He could see Anson's point. "I agree. I'll help you."

Anson smiled, clearly relieved. "I'll be there with you, my friend. We will protect you as best we can. Now, let us go for there is more work to do before this is done."

"What about the man that helped us?" Nolan asked.

"That's one of the things we need to find out," Anson said, with a wink running his hand through his unkempt brown hair.

As they left the temple, Nolan glanced back at the statue of the Goddess and thought of his wife's words to him when he broached the subject of them leaving the city.

The Goddess wants us exactly where she intends for us to be.

With a respectful nod in the statue's direction, Nolan left the building.

8

RETURN TO REXEL

Dawn approached, and the sun peeked through the clouds. The air was crisp being so close to the mountains near Hathenwood, but since Colind had been released from his prison, he never missed an opportunity to witness the sunrise. The first rays of the sun caressed his craggy old face. Having been deprived of the sun's warmth for a score of years, it was these small quiet moments that made him feel as if he was being born again.

He sat on the deck of the Raven with a large bucket to capture the wood shavings from his carving. A good sharp knife and a couple of other tools gave his hands something to do, whittling away the block of wood. Carving wood was something he hadn't been able to do in a very long time, and it still surprised him how much he missed the simple pleasures in life. He ran his fingers along the fine grain, feeling the density of the old block of wood. Much like himself, he mused. He would often whittle wood to think through a problem, and there was no shortage of those.

His eyes drew east to the horizon where Khamearra was many miles from where he sat. Aaron had occupied much of this thoughts, and despite his preconceptions of the boy, he had grown genuinely fond of him. Boy. He smiled. At Colind's age, anyone younger than fifty was considered a boy. Aaron had shown a remarkable sense of wisdom when dealing with the Hythariam. That's not to say he thought much of his chances of succeeding in his quest, but he understood and agreed with his reasons for trying. Not that Aaron needed or required his blessing, but he still found himself yearning to go with the boy and lend a hand.

"You're up early," Garret said.

Colind looked up at Garret and nodded in greeting. A man well into his fifties, so not a boy. His gray hair had been cropped short, and his eyes were so blue they bordered on silver.

"I've been asleep a long time," Colind said. "In my imprisonment I was unable to enjoy the shine of the sun." His tone was friendly enough, but the terror of being pulled from the shadow back into the world of the living was all too real for him. Mactar had trapped his soul, separating it from his body, leaving it slightly out of phase with reality. He brushed thoughts of Mactar aside lest his mind stray into the reckoning that he would visit upon that evil man in a thousand different ways.

"I wonder how they are getting on," Garret said, glancing to the east.

Colind shifted in his chair. "I'm sure they are fine. They've only just arrived in Khamearra and haven't had enough time to stir up trouble. The boy has quite a following, won't you agree? Present company included."

"That he does. To be honest, I found myself wanting to go with them. What are the odds of them succeeding?"

"I wouldn't bet against Aaron if that's what you mean," Colind said. "I'm not sure, to be honest, based upon everything I've seen and knowing how the Drake hunted the Alenzar'seth. But as Verona put it, Aaron has a knack for doing the impossible," Colind said and raised his hands as living proof to validate the claim he just made.

"I see your point," Garret said. "If there is anyone who can pull off something like this, I believe it's him. He would have walked to Shandara to find the answers he sought. That is the measure of his conviction. He will do no less for Sarah and probably a great deal more."

Vaughn joined them. "It's what he wouldn't do to save Sarah that concerns me."

Colind sighed. They had been over this, and still they came to the same subject yet again. "I think we need to accept the fact that Aaron will do what he needs to do. If those actions bring war to this world sooner than we had planned, then so be it. The Alenzar'seth have sacrificed enough. They gave us almost a hundred years to prepare for this. Besides, Aaron makes a compelling argument, wouldn't you agree?"

Vaughn's bearing changed. He wrapped his arms around himself. "Indeed, he does. I feel foolish for not having thought along similar lines myself, and I know I'm not the only one."

Colind shrugged his shoulders. "None of us did. A fresh perspective is worth its weight. He managed to convince Iranus, which is a monumental feat in itself."

Soft chuckles released the tension. They were all frightened by the looming threat from Hytharia and dealt with their fear in different ways.

"I hope he succeeds," Vaughn said. "I hope he is able to save Sarah. They were good for one another."

An unexpected smile appeared on Colind's face, which was then mirrored on the others' faces as well. This was Aaron's gift, getting people to care. "I never realized you were such a romantic, Vaughn. Can an old dog learn new tricks?"

Vaughn laughed. "Not according to Verona."

"Those two in Khamearra," Garret chuckled. "Now if that doesn't spell trouble for the High King, I don't know what will."

"Eric and Braden will look after them," Vaughn said. "And Gavril seems quite sensible, which leads me to the reason why I sought you out in the first place."

Colind sat up. "Which is?"

"The Hythariam ambassador," Vaughn said.

"Tersellis," Colind said. "I've only just met him, but he seems to be a sensible sort."

"He is quite intelligent," Vaughn replied. "He has been spending quite a bit of time speaking with Jopher."

Despite Aaron's lack of enthusiasm with princely types, Colind knew they were key in preparing for this war. Prince Jopher Zamaridian of Zsensibar, no longer the petulant child, showed the makings of becoming a good man in his own right and would be an asset toward aligning the kingdoms. At least Jopher would be able to bolster their position and lend some credibility in convincing his father, the King of Zsensibar, of the impending invasion.

Colind wouldn't be too surprised if Iranus requested that he resume his place as Guardian of the Safanarion Order. They were an order of extraordinary people whose primary focus was protecting the lands of Safanar and her people. At the peak of their influence, they had members from every kingdom spanning their corner of the world. That is until the fall of Shandara. There wasn't time to reach out to see how many of the old members were even still alive. While the Safanarion Order was aligned with no particular kingdom, they were founded in Shandara, and with his own imprisonment, he suspected the others had faded quietly into the background to avoid being hunted by the High King and the Elitesmen. Most had assumed that Colind had died all those years ago, but perhaps there were more members like Garret, who stumbled across Aaron's path and followed him in the off chance that he was somehow still alive.

The Order was founded by Daverim Alenzar'seth shortly after meeting the Hythariam. The ruling family of Shandara was always striving for the betterment of people as a whole, but Daverim's genius was in founding an independent group that wasn't tied to any kingdom. Perhaps he should think of them as nations? A term he had heard Aaron use to describe the kingdoms here.

Colind now believed that Daverim had suspected that the Hythariam left on their dying world would find a way to reach Safanar, but he and Reymius had been too preoccupied in their youth with changing the world that they lost sight of the looming threat hidden among the shadows. Colind had spent much of his time in the dawn of his imprisonment wondering if the Hythariam that were left on their home world had a role in the High King's rise to power. There was nothing he could prove, but the itch to find out was still there, and he meant to scratch it if he could.

Then there was Mactar, the master architect in the fall of one of the most powerful kingdoms in the history of Safanar. He was going to need an entirely different block of wood to whittle if he were going to crack that nut. He shoved thoughts of Mactar aside, another time for that one.

"Are you still with me?" Vaughn asked.

Colind shook off his reverie and nodded for Vaughn to continue.

"Tarimus," Vaughn began, "we don't know where he is or what he is doing at the moment."

"I know," Colind said. "I think we've got enough to contend with for now. I've spoken with Aaron at length about this. For now, I believe Tarimus is focused on seeking retribution from his jailer. Something I wouldn't necessarily want to get in the way of."

"My Lord Guardian," Garret spoke, "we cannot lose sight of Tarimus, not this time."

Colind sucked in a deep breath and released it. "What would you have me do?" he asked. "We have more pressing matters and cannot afford to go traipsing around the continent after Tarimus. I'm not proposing that we forget about him altogether, but just for the moment while we work to unite the nations of this world. Also, do not believe for a second that I have forgotten Tarimus's role in Shandara's destruction. He will be brought to justice, I assure you."

They grew silent as Jopher arrived on the far side of the deck. He laid out a staff and sword before him. They watched in silence as he practiced the slow forms that Aaron had taught them. The same forms that both Vaughn and Garret practiced when time could be spared. As for Colind, he was too old and had too little time to contend with that. He could draw upon the energy around them without the help of the slow forms.

Colind turned his attention back to Vaughn and Garret. "How do you think Cyrus will react when he learns that our good captain has pledged himself to Aaron?"

"I wouldn't be so naive as to say that he would be overjoyed at the idea," Garret said. "But I don't think he will have a problem with it either. In fact, the more I think about it, the more I think he might ultimately embrace the idea. Rexel has ever been aligned with Shandara."

"And he understands what is at stake," Vaughn said. "He has been quietly preparing for war since we left. With Rexel's central location, I'm sure there will be other leaders there that the ambassador will be keen to meet with."

As if they had summoned him, Tersellis joined them on the deck.

"Good morning, gentleman," Tersellis said. Having learned of their plans to help align the kingdoms of this world against the looming threat from Hytharia, Tersellis demanded to be the one to work with the other kingdoms. It was Colind's understanding that Tersellis was historically passionate about engaging the people of Safanar to share knowledge with them, but the motion was voted down. The sharing of knowledge would be a good thing, but Colind couldn't fault Iranus, and the others of the elected council, for voting to wait. Colind shuddered to think what would be done with the Hythariam technological wonders in the hands of the High King and the Elitesmen.

"I'm glad I found you all together," Tersellis said.

"How are the engines coming?" Colind asked.

Tersellis smiled. "Very good. Their engineer, Hatly, is a quick study. I knew that once we showed the Safanarions how the engines worked, they would be able to build their own in short order and, I suspect, improve upon our design. But don't tell the others I said that," he finished with a wink.

"Excellent," Colind said.

Tersellis's face grew somber. "It seems as if the world has been holding its breath building up to this moment. And now we're finally able to go out into the world and hopefully bring these people together. It shames me that the threat from my homeland is the catalyst for such actions."

Tersellis was not a young man, but it was so hard to tell with Hythariam. According to Iranus, Tersellis was well over a hundred years old. Old enough to bear witness to the fall of Hytharia.

"It is what it is," Garret said.

The Raven lurched forward, gaining speed rapidly. The thrust from the engines gave a quiet whine instead of their normal roar, something in the way that they utilized the energy from the crystals to recycle themselves. Colind expanded his senses and saw the gleaming currents along the wings of the airship. The large balloon keeping the ship afloat in the air now had smaller cone-shaped engines on the sides and one on the top.

Tersellis's wide smile infected them all. "At this speed, I would expect we should be able to reach Rexel by the end of the day."

They had long left Hathenwood behind them and skirted the borders of Shandara, which allowed for little chance to encounter the Ryakuls. The landscape sped by as the engines churned the airship onward until Colind noted the tall spires of Rexel's palace in the distance. A trip that had taken Aaron almost a month, they had been able to make in a day, which was truly a marvel. He felt his chest tighten as the sight of Rexel loomed closer. He and Reymius had been close in age and full of reckless abandon in their youth, and Cyrus, too, later on. A single tear paved its way down Colind's cheek then became lost within the stubble of his gray beard.

Rexel was full of activity, but the presence of so many airships caught Colind's attention. They had built the first airship in Shandara before the fall, and it gladdened his heart that not everything they had worked for was lost in the fires. The Raven flew faster than any other airship, even when they slowed their approach as they came closer to the city. The crew of the Raven waved proudly to the crews of the other ships as they approached the airship yard to the east of the palace. The return of one of their own was greeted with great enthusiasm, but the presence of the guards armed to the teeth could not be missed. There was a city of tents outside the city proper, with fields cleared where temporary barracks were erected for the troops training nearby. Vaughn was right—Cyrus was taking the return of the Alenzar'seth seriously. Cyrus was no fool, and for that Colind was grateful.

The guards on duty at the airfield directed the Raven to a secluded spot on the far side. When the Raven finally landed, the ship was surrounded by a sea of dark-blue-uniformed guardsman adorned with silver hawks upon their chests. Colind's eyes took note of the banners along the way and was surprised to see the flag of Shandara raised with Rexel's own silver hawk. Cyrus was not being too subtle about his alliances.

As they got closer to the city, Captain Morgan flew the flag of Shandara with the dragon emblem grasping a single rose in one of its claws.

"What does the rose symbolize?" Jopher asked.

Colind smiled. "Life," he said. "The Alenzar'seth have always been fond of making statements."

Jopher nodded silently.

"My Lord Prince, if you will," Captain Morgan said from the gangplank leading off the ship. By tradition, the senior ranking nobleman was afforded the honor of disembarking first.

Jopher stood to the side and bowed his head to Colind. "My Lord Guardian," he said.

Many of the crew, including the captain, bowed in respect and voiced their approval. Colind bowed back in return. *It appears that more of Aaron's traits have rubbed off on you, young one.* Colind descended the gangplank to the wide open gaze of Prince Cyrus.

"Am I dreaming?" Prince Cyrus asked. "For if I am, I wouldn't want to wake up for anything." The Prince wrapped his arms around Colind in a firm embrace. "It's good to see you again, old friend."

"You, as well," Colind said.

"I see our mutual friend succeeded in reaching Shandara," Cyrus said. "Where is he?"

"We have much to discuss," Colind answered.

They were joined by the others, who all bowed in respect toward the prince. Captain Morgan saluted with all the practiced formality of having been in the military for the length of his life.

"Your Grace, I must humbly ask to be released from your service," Captain Morgan said.

Prince Cyrus narrowed his gaze and then looked up at the colors flying on the ship. "Why, Nathaniel?"

"I've pledged my service to the Alenzar'seth," Nathaniel Morgan said. "He has saved this ship and all of our lives a number of times. I appreciate everything you've done for me and my crew, but in this I must follow my heart, and it tells me to serve Shandara."

Prince Cyrus put his hand upon Nathaniel's shoulder. "In this we are aligned, my friend, and know that you always have a place here in Rexel." Cyrus glanced up at the ship. "The Raven looks different whence she left?"

"Yes, Your Grace," Nathaniel said. "The engines have been upgraded with the help of our new friends, and that's not all. I have the plans so we can perform those upgrades to the rest of the ships in the fleet. You see, I come bearing gifts," he finished, gesturing toward Tersellis and his two Hythariam bodyguards as they came to join them.

Prince Cyrus's eyes widened as he met the Hythariam's golden-eyed gaze and bowed respectfully.

"Peace be upon you, Gate Keepers of the West," Tersellis said. "We have much to discuss, but know this. The Hythariam are proud to ally with the people of Safanar."

"Peace be upon you," Prince Cyrus said, returning the formal greeting.

"Please join me so that we may take our ease and discuss the important matters that must be addressed."

They were escorted by a group of soldiers dressed in plain, dark blue uniforms.

"My friend, why do these soldiers appear different than the Rexellian Corps?" Colind asked.

"That is because they are not Rexellian," Cyrus answered. "Some of them are, but the soldiers you see in blue are made up of different kingdoms who have agreed to take up arms in our cause. And a number are formerly from Shandara or direct descendants of those that are."

Colind frowned. "Our cause?"

They came to a plain room a short way from the airfield, big enough to accommodate all of them. Spreading around the room, some chose to sit in the proffered chairs, while others including the Hythariam remained standing. Only when Prince Cyrus sat did Tersellis take his seat, which Colind nodded at in approval.

"Yes, our cause," Cyrus answered. "War is coming. If we know anything, it's that the heir of Alenzar'seth would be the herald for war returning to these lands."

"I see," Colind said. "You are, of course, correct. War is coming, but our enemy is not only the High King and the Elitesmen. It's time you learned the truth of why Shandara fell and why it's critical that it be reclaimed."

There was a small commotion from the doorway to the room as an older woman entered, dripping of authority, as most bowed in her direction.

"Sebille, please join us," Cyrus said. "My wife," he said to the Hythariam.

The Lady Sebille stopped, her steely gaze swept the room and widened in shock as it came upon Colind. She slowly circled the room until at last she came before Colind, who stood waiting and took her hand.

"My Lady," Colind said and placed a small kiss upon her hand. Though the years had been many since he had last seen her, he was happy to see her grown into the woman she had become.

"Uncle," Sebille whispered into a hushed silence then turned to Cyrus, who smiled. "Uncle," she cried and pulled him in for a hug.

Colind smiled, hugging her in return. "Back from the dead, little flower."

He watched as his niece sat next to Cyrus and took his hand in hers. It gladdened his heart to see them both happy and alive. He had missed so much because of his imprisonment, but he denied the dark thoughts threatening to intrude upon this happy moment.

The Prince's gaze found Vaughn, and he motioned for him to come forward. "I think we need to start with what happened after you left here."

Vaughn stood up and motioned for Garret and Jopher to join him in the center of the room so they could address the crowd. They each recounted the events that brought them to Shandara, inserting their own take where appropriate.

Colind found himself marveling at the profound impact that one man, Aaron Jace, had upon all of these men before him. By all accounts, Jopher had been the equivalent of a petulant child, only to become a man on this voyage thanks to

Aaron's influence. Aaron himself was barely more than a boy, with the attitude of a much younger man when last he saw him on Earth. The trials of fate had not been kind to him, but they had forged him into the leader that Aaron had become. Men from all walks of life were lining up to follow the lost son of Alenzar'seth, and while some surely were endeared to the family name, there were a number of powerful men in this room that were attached to the man behind the ancient and powerful mantle of Alenzar'seth.

The Prince silently listened to their tale and looked at Jopher with a knowing smile. "A touch of humility can be medicine for the soul," Cyrus said.

Jopher's face flushed for a moment. "Indeed it has, Your Grace."

Tersellis quietly came to the center of the room. "I would like to speak for my people at this point."

Prince Cyrus nodded and thanked the others for recounting events. Colind decided to join Tersellis on the floor as he sensed he would be needed.

Tersellis swept his golden eyes around the room. "As you know, we Hythariam withdrew from the world shortly after the fall of Shandara. We aided the Shandarian refugees as best we could, and then our leadership voted to withdraw ourselves from directly interacting with the outside world until such time as it became necessary to return. I would like for you to understand that this was by no means a unanimous vote and one that our people continue to struggle with. However, recent events and the resurgence of our old alliances have forced a change within the Hythariam. I am honored to say that the time of seclusion for my people is over, and we are proud to stand along the side of men once more to whatever end we may meet. "

Colind listened as Tersellis spoke at length of the origins of the Hythariam and how they came to be on Safanar. For the most part, the room remained quiet as all of them listened to his every word. They were joined by the visiting ambassadors from neighboring kingdoms who were already allied with Rexel. Some were learning the depth to which the Alenzar'seth had shielded their world from an invading horde, including Cyrus, who often glanced in his direction. He and Reymius had planned to bring Cyrus into the Safanarion Order with the knowledge of the Hythariam and their true origins. So many plans executed and so many that didn't see the light of day. He did feel as if he had returned from the dead. Waking up to a world at times only vaguely familiar and not at all like the one he had left all those years ago.

"My Lord Guardian," Cyrus said.

Colind looked up. "Yes?"

"I think many of us would like to hear your take on these events."

"They are true," Colind said. "As real as I am who stands before you. You've all been privy to knowledge that was once only known to a select few, myself, and the Hythariam being the last. None of us were prepared for the High King's attack on Shandara or the betrayals leading up to it. Betrayals by Tarimus, my son, who let the snakes into our beloved city and ultimately led to its destruction." Colind stopped as the murmuring of the men grew in pitch. "Enough! We can talk about the past, or we can prepare and take hold of our future. There is an army on the other side of the barrier, waiting to invade your homes. It is my belief that the promise of power taken from the Hythariam is what motivated the High King to attack."

Cyrus frowned. "It is common knowledge that Khamearra and Shandara have always been at odds, but how could they have known, and who could have made such a promise?"

"They were not always at odds," Colind said. "Just recently."

"Agreed," Cyrus said, "but the actions taken by you few, one could contrive as provoking. The balance of power shifted between Shandara and Khamearra. Some would speculate that the Hythariam were the cause, but Shandara was a place of innovation. The first airships were made there."

"I see your point," Colind said. "It was always our intent to share the knowledge of the Hythariam with the resident nations of Safanar."

"Nations?" Cyrus asked.

"It's a term that Aaron taught me," Colind said. "It's another word for kingdom or empire. I prefer it because it implies a people as a whole rather than a few key individuals."

Cyrus nodded knowingly. "I see the young scion of Shandara has had a profound effect on you, my old friend."

Colind chuckled softly. "He is quite passionate, but it was Reymius who first sparked the flame within me. I see you've begun preparations. There are a number of troops gathered outside the city here."

"Yes," Cyrus said, stroking his beard. "After the Elitesmen showed up here, breaking the treaty we had with the High King to get to young Aaron, I knew the time had come. I had advised Aaron to seek out the Hythariam and hoped that his path would cross theirs in his travels. The High King and the Elitesmen grow more bold with each passing year, traveling through any of the kingdoms they choose, dispensing the *High King's* justice. Reports of their appearance occasionally come from the more remote towns, but for them to come here in my city, I knew that war was only a matter of time. I would have expected to see Aaron and Verona with you, but clearly they are not. Where are they?"

Colind swallowed some water. "They are in Khamearra, attempting to infiltrate the Citadel of the Elite."

Pandemonium.

"It is true," Colind's deep voice rang out, silencing the chaos. "It was not my idea but Aaron's, and as Vaughn and Garret can attest, once the boy sets his mind to something, there is no dissuading him from it. Regardless, in this case I agree with him. He is exactly where he needs to be. Many who once called Shandara home will flock to the Alenzar'seth's banner, and as word spreads that number will grow. The High King will not sit idly by and allow this threat to go unchecked. Cyrus was right to see the signs once he believed that the Alenzar'seth had returned to Safanar. It falls to us to help prepare this world for an invasion of unknown proportions."

"You would have us fight a war on two fronts?" asked an ambassador whom Colind didn't know.

Colind fixed the man with a hard stare. "If it comes to it, then yes, because we have no other choice. Surrender is not an option. We only suspect that the

High King is in league with the Hythariam on the other side of the barrier. The very same faction that sought to rule this world."

"How do we know if things haven't changed on Hytharia?" the ambassador pressed.

"They have not," Tersellis said. "Tell me, would an ally send a beast such as the Drake to your lands? Would an ally send the infestation such as the Ryakul?"

The ambassador grew silent, and Colind continued, "Khamearra is not united behind the High King nor are the Elitesmen. There are those who are allied with the old regime. I've been told upon good authority that Amorak's daughter, Sarah, has been involved with the Resistance in Khamearra."

"Good authority?" Cyrus asked.

"The best," Colind said. "From Vaughn and Garret, who heard it directly from Sarah herself."

"Your Grace," Vaughn said, "you've seen her, but I don't think you realized who she was as she was in disguise. Think back to when the Raven left the castle. A lone figure in black lent their aid to Aaron to help us escape and get you to safety."

Colind watched as the memory came to Cyrus's eyes.

"Ferasdiam," Cyrus whispered.

"Is Sarah with them in Khamearra?" Cyrus asked.

"No," Colind said. "The Drake has taken her prisoner." He had no wish to divulge any more information regarding Sarah and the Drake, and he hoped that Cyrus wouldn't press him right now. Something unspoken passed between the old friends.

"Aaron is in Khamearra, searching for the source of the travel crystals that the Elitesmen use," Colind said. "His presence in Khamearra will be in direct conflict with the tyranny of the High King and the Elitesmen. I suspect he will be the spark to the powder keg of revolution brewing there. Hitting the enemy where he believes he is safe is a wise strategy."

Cyrus frowned, looking worried. "If it doesn't get him killed."

"I believe your nephew, Verona, put it like this," Colind began. "Aaron has a knack for doing the impossible. I can tell you from my conversations with Aaron that he expects us to fight for this world. He makes a compelling argument that the invading horde is the real threat here. He also says that the barrier between worlds is failing. The Alenzar'seth have sheltered this world from the looming threat for almost a century, and now they call upon us to take hold of our future for ourselves. To do otherwise could plunge this world to ruin, just as Shandara is now."

The room was ghostly silent as no one dared to break the spell. Each taking a moment to gather their thoughts.

"Aaron will fight, on that I have no doubts," Colind said. "It falls to us to gather the nations of this world to fight with him. Though our fear might not pass completely, courage does not occur in the absence of fear, but in being afraid and still taking that first courageous step forward."

The group chewed on this for a moment, and Tersellis once again spoke. "We will fight and share our knowledge with any nation who will stand with us against this most grievous of threats."

"Should Aaron fall," Colind began, "should the Alenzar'seth vanish from this world, then we still need to carry the fight on."

"Excuse me," Tersellis said, and Colind gave him the floor. "I realize we're asking you to take a lot of things on faith, but there are some things that we can show you to prove that our claims are, in fact, the truth."

Tersellis removed a gray box from his pocket and set it on the ground in the middle of the room. He placed a silver sphere in the middle, which immediately began to glow and rise several inches into the air.

"Are you able to dim the lights in the room please?" Tersellis asked. After Prince Cyrus nodded his approval, the guards drew the curtains down over the windows, and Tersellis glided a hand across the glowing orbs, dimming them throughout the room.

Tersellis clicked the remote in his hand, and a glowing image of Safanar appeared, hovering in the air, causing some of the onlookers to gasp. The continents of a vibrant blue world teaming with life was displayed with perfect clarity, and the movement of the clouds shifted as the planet slowly spun upon its axis.

"This is your world," Tersellis said. "Safanar as it is today. This image is built from one of our machines we have in orbit around your world. I can explain more later, but for the time being, accept that what I'm telling you is the truth. The next thing I will show you is Hytharia. Not as it is today, but from our last recording of it."

Tersellis rubbed his thumb across the remote, and the image changed. Where Safanar's blue planet vibrantly blazed a moment before, there was now an image of a tarnished sandy world, almost completely devoid of atmosphere with merely a few splotches of green. Colind watched as Tersellis slowly swallowed the pain of seeing his home world, and his two Hythariam companions looked on with stony expressions. Tersellis let the image of the dying world hang there for a few moments before he rubbed part of the remote again, and the image changed to that of many shining dots expanding the length of the room.

"These are stars," Tersellis said. "Some are much like your sun here in this world." He walked over to one side of the room and gestured to a glowing blue orb. "This is Safanar, and on the other side is Hytharia. We estimated that the ship that brought the Drake to this world took almost thirty years to make the trip."

The moments dripped away until Prince Cyrus spoke. "What is that blinking light there? It appears to be heading for our world."

"We're not sure, to be honest," Tersellis said. "We only just learned of it two days ago. We are fairly certain that it is from Hytharia. We are still estimating the size and gathering additional reconnaissance."

"When will it get here?' Prince Cyrus asked solemnly.

"Three months," Tersellis answered. He retrieved the gray box, and the guards opened the curtains, allowing the sunshine back into the room, but the men scarcely dared to breathe.

"You heard it right, gentlemen," Colind said. "We have three months to prepare ourselves. It is an estimate, but I have the highest faith in the Hythariam, and while the timeframe could be off, it will not be by much."

"What are you suggesting we do?" Cyrus asked.

This was the question Colind had been working toward. "Prepare as you've been doing. Allow the Hythariam and Nathaniel to upgrade the airships so they can move faster. They even have ideas for weapons, but we won't have time to outfit and train all the soldiers in their use. Word will need to be spread to all the kingdoms. All of them, not just the ones that at this point in time you're on good relations with. This must be a burden shared by all."

"Where will this invading army be coming from?" the ambassador who spoke before asked.

"Shandara," Colind said. "The barrier is near the capital city of Shandara. I'm proposing that in two months time we begin moving troops into the city. There are resources that can be used as well as something else. Throughout the city are hidden caches of weapons that were put in place for this very day. They are no ordinary swords and armor, but weapons designed by the great lore masters of the Safanarion Order, based in part upon knowledge learned from the Hythariam. The caches are hidden beneath the city, which there are parts of largely intact."

"Three months isn't very much time," the ambassador said.

"You are correct, but it's the time that we have," Colind answered.

"What about Khamearra?" the ambassador asked. "The High King could move against our homes while we are in Shandara."

"The High King is not interested in your kingdoms at the moment," Colind said. "Khamearra is ripe for a civil war, but the focus of the High King and the Elitesmen will be in Shandara. However, the growing trouble in his own kingdom will put him off balance to a certain degree. We're not going to solve all the problems in this room at this very moment. We will be in contact with our friends in Khamearra, who, I expect, will cross paths with the Resistance." The ambassador was about to ask another question when Colind cut him off. "I'm sorry, but I did not get the pleasure of your name?"

"William of Lorrick," the ambassador said with a slight blush.

"Nice to meet you, William," Colind answered.

William of Lorrick chuckled. "Lorrick borders Khamearra. Perhaps we can offer some assistance to the party in the city."

Colind pursed his lips in thought, glancing at Tersellis, who nodded back. "An intriguing thought. Thank you. I think we'll take you up on that offer." The man asked good questions and seemed willing to help. He had anticipated more adversity, but the kingdoms that would offer the most resistance, like Zsensibar, were not present.

Most of the men in the room, despite not knowing all the details, gave their oaths. It was a small thing, but great things often came from small beginnings. Colind and Cyrus shared a brief nod of understanding. The group spoke in earnest about what could be done in the short amount of time that they had. Colind was surprised to learn that the camps outside of Rexel were mirrored in other kingdoms as well. News of the return of the Alenzar'seth had traveled throughout the land. Zsensibar had not joined their coalition so far and held Cyrus personally responsible for its missing prince.

"My Lord," Jopher said to Cyrus. "I wish to return to Zsensibar and convince them of the threat we face."

"Of course," Cyrus said and looked toward Captain Morgan, who nodded back. "We should get things in order here first then speed you to Zsensibar without delay."

Jopher gave a respectful bow and listened to the rest of the proceedings in silence.

Colind watched with a sense of awe as the representatives from the neighboring nations worked together. Perhaps the groundwork that the Safanarion Order had laid for such a day had not been in vain. Once again, the spark of hope beat a bit brighter from within his chest. Colind glanced out the window to the west and hoped that the small group in Khamearra was safe.

9

THE RESISTANCE

With the scattering crowd, Verona scanned the area for a safer spot so they could continue to watch the guards. Eying a nearby side street, Verona noted the ladder that led to the roof, a habit instilled into him since his youth, as trouble always had a way of finding him. He gestured toward the ladder, and Roselyn nodded. They climbed up to the rooftop and kept a low profile. Verona watched as the captain conferred with his lieutenant while scanning the area. *The man is smart.* The captain made a small circle upon his brow, paying tribute to the Goddess Ferasdiam, which was all but outlawed in Khamearra. Roselyn appeared to be about to say something, but Verona motioned for silence so he could listen to the captain address his troops. Colind had stated they would find allies in Khamearra, but until now he had doubted the claim. The city lived in fear of the Elitesmen, which included the guardsman that didn't partake in the corruption so evident throughout the city. The captain, while seasoned, looked to be young as far as district captains went. He should know, as he had his run-ins with district captains in most cities he had visited, be it his home in Rexel or some other kingdom. Verona wondered how long the captain had held his post here in the city.

"What sort of captain tells his men they are not safe in their own city?" Roselyn whispered.

Verona didn't make eye contact with her for fear of becoming tongue-tied, as he had been afflicted of late. "A smart one," he answered.

After the guardsmen took the body of the Elitesman away and the miners all but faded into the crowd.

Verona looked at Roselyn, and even with her golden eyes disguised, they still held her fire and beauty. "We should follow the captain," Verona said and glanced behind them.

"What about Aaron?" Roselyn asked.

Verona glanced up the street, looking for his friend, but said nothing.

"Are you always so quiet?" Roselyn asked.

Quiet? Me?

Verona felt his tongue fill his mouth as he struggled to get it under control under Roselyn's disarming gaze. "No, my lady."

Roselyn reached out to him. "Did I do something wrong?"

Verona mustered up his nerve. "Never, my lady," he answered. "I am curious as to how you caused the Elitesman's arm to pull away from the child's throat?"

Roselyn pulled out a small black oval-shaped device that fit into the palm of her hand. "It can pull most metals with varying degrees of strength. I focused the field upon the sword and pulled," she said with a grin that set his heart pounding. Is this how Aaron had felt when he first met Sarah? How could he stand it?

"I'm sure those children appreciated you keeping them from harm's way. That was very brave of you," Roselyn said.

"Only the worst sort use children as leverage," Verona said. "One can expect nothing less from an Elitesman."

They stood upon the roof, watching the guardsmen go their separate ways, but it was the captain and his lieutenant heading down a side street that held his attention. Roselyn gently laid her hand on his arm, and he saw a cloaked figure coming down the street. Try as he might, Aaron often struggled to blend in, but the man stuck out like a sore thumb. One could easily attribute it to his great size, as he was taller than most men, but Verona knew it was his bearing, the proudness of his stance, resembling that of a stalwart defender to the sound of his voice when he spoke. No, there were some things that could not be concealed. Untarnished idealism exuded from his friend and was absorbed by most in his company, causing them to give more than they ever thought they could. Verona was no fool and knew his life had little direction before crossing paths with Aaron. He had spent most of his life stirring up mischief where he went, but he also tried to help those in need.

Verona sought the calmness within, focusing his energy as Aaron had taught, and reached out toward his friend. Aaron immediately looked up to their position and dashed down a side street.

"Did you just communicate with him?" Roselyn asked.

"Yes. It's something that Aaron was able to teach Sarik and myself," Verona answered.

Roselyn's eyes lit up. "But how do you do it exactly? What did he teach you?"

Verona swallowed. If she was going to keep looking at him like that, it would be a wonder if he would ever form a coherent thought again. "He taught us to be able to see the currents of energy all around us. To be able to draw in their power and use the energy within and outside of ourselves. I can't do all of the things that Aaron can, but there are some things that I can do."

"Can you show me?" Roselyn asked.

"I will try, my lady," Verona answered and focused himself. His perceptions immediately sharpened as before. It was getting easier as both Sarah and Aaron promised. He drew in the energy from the air into himself and then reached out to Roselyn. Her lifebeat pulsed in rhythm with her heart, and a golden hue surrounded her form as the rest of the world faded away. He reached out to her, with the yearning in his heart bearing all the beauty that filled his soul when he thought of her. For the briefest of moments, their energies collided and intertwined.

Roselyn's sharp intake of breath broke his concentration, and the energy dissolved around them. Verona's eyes found Roselyn's shocked expression, but the spell was broken when Aaron joined them on the roof.

"Hello," Aaron said.

Curse you, my friend, Verona thought and gave him the perfect excuse not to be looking at Roselyn though he longed to do so. "No worse for wear, I take it?"

"I'm fine," Aaron said. "I think we should head to the Elitesmen stronghold."

Verona frowned. "I think we should follow the captain this way. There have been some interesting developments," Verona said and recounted what they had overheard from the guards below. He watched as Aaron took a second glance at the looming towers behind them and nodded.

"Good call," Aaron agreed. "The stronghold is not going anywhere."

"That's right, and they refer to it as the Citadel of the Elite," Verona said.

They set off, quietly following the captain and his lieutenant from the rooftops, with Aaron leading the way. Before Verona could follow, he caught sight of Roselyn looking in his direction in that disarming way of hers. She still looked puzzled, but the way she watched him left Verona wondering just what he conveyed across their connection, brief as it was.

They tracked the captain as best they could from the rooftops, but keeping out of sight in the middle of the day posed a bit of a challenge. So far, they had been able to evade detection. The buildings became older and in rougher shape than the other parts of the city Aaron had seen thus far, which impeded their ability to follow as closely as he would have liked.

Aaron scanned the buildings ahead and caught a glimpse of a dome-shaped building that reminded him of the temple he had emerged from when he first came to Safanar. Roselyn slipped on a roof tile, sending it sliding to the ground. The captain suddenly stopped and looked in their direction. They hugged the rooftop, hoping that they could remain hidden. After a few moments, Aaron chanced lifting his head.

"We're going to lose them," Verona whispered.

"I think I know where they're going," Aaron answered and led them in a roundabout way toward the dome-shaped roof he had seen.

The roof had collapsed in a few places, which allowed for them to move in closer. The captain and lieutenant were joined by the other guards that Aaron recognized from before. They settled by one of the openings where they listened to the men speak. The lieutenant stepped to the head of the men and addressed them.

"I am a descendant of the De'anjard, Keepers of the Watch, Shields of Shandara," the man said with his fist across his heart.

Aaron locked gazes with Verona, both eyes wide with shock.

"The De'anjard are here?" Aaron whispered.

"Apparently," Verona whispered back. "We should tell Eric and Braden. Perhaps they might know more."

They listened in silence as the lieutenant spoke to the guards, telling them that he was part of the Resistance in Khamearra and how they had been working toward bringing down the Elitesmen and the High King. Aaron was surprised to learn that the captain was ignorant of any of these activities. He couldn't help but glare at the captain. How could the man partake in such actions, even with an Elitesman pointing a sword at his back?

The lieutenant spoke of older Elitesmen who were indirectly involved with the Resistance, and Aaron wondered if they knew they were serving an organization being headed by the former Shandarian Army. He knew the older Elitesmen did not approve of the current regime, or so Beck had told Sarah while he trained her. Thoughts of Sarah made him yearn to touch the ever-present connection with her that he felt in the furthest reaches of his mind. It took all his will not to open himself to the connection. Not for fear of what he would find, but for fear of the pain he would cause the woman he loved. He silently cursed the Hythariam and their technological advances that gave birth to such a vile creation as the Drake. No, it wasn't their fault, he reminded himself. He was dealing with a computer program of sorts, created with a specific task to bring down the barrier between worlds. As complex and advanced as the Hythariam technology was, the core problem the rogue Nanites were sent to solve was the barrier. After having ascertained the problem, the artificial intelligence afforded by the rogue Nanites created the solution that he was now a part of, and one that he hoped to break free of if he could.

Aaron turned his attention back to the guards as they split up into groups and exited, leaving only the captain and lieutenant in the temple. They spoke in hushed tones, but the bladesong burned inside him and sharpened his perceptions so he could hear the men speak as if he were next to them.

Family. The captain had a family. It was not a sword to the back that the captain feared, it was the threat to his family. Aaron felt a mixed sense of loathing and sympathy for the man. Yet, was he any different? Would he not bring down the barrier between worlds if it would save Sarah's life? The question hung there in his mind, tearing his heart in two. He was torn between doing what he thought to be right by giving the people of Safanar a chance to prepare for the coming war and his heart's desire to save the woman he loved. Aaron glared bitterly at the sky as if it somehow had a part in the hand that fortune had dealt him. The barrier was weakening as the land beneath Shandara continued to unravel. Would weeks or a month make a difference in the survival of this world? *Two weeks at the most.* Roselyn's estimation before the Nanites fully assimilated Sarah to the point that anything worth saving would be gone. Aaron turned back to the two men as they exited the building, and his gaze drifted toward the fountain. The statue of the Goddess stood proudly, her gaze staring resolutely forward. *Focus, Aaron,* he thought to himself.

"Are you okay?" Roselyn asked.

Aaron banished his dark thoughts. "I'm fine. Did either of you hear their names?"

Verona nodded. "I believe the captain's name is Nolan, and his lieutenant's name is Anson."

Aaron brought his comms device out from his pocket and clicked the call button for Eric and Braden. After a few moments and hearing a few grumbles from the device, they heard Eric's voice.

"Yes, hello?"

"It's Aaron," he said. "We just learned something that I think would interest you. The De'anjard are leading the heart of the Resistance here in Shandara."

They waited, hearing the comms device shift hands as more cursing came from the other side. Verona chuckled, and Aaron sighed. They will learn.

"Is there some way you can seek them out?" Aaron asked.

"This is Braden. Eric hates these tiny machines. Did I hear you correctly? The De'anjard are here in the city?"

"Yes," Aaron answered.

"Okay, we'll be on the lookout for the signs. If they really are out there, we will find them," Braden said.

"Good luck," Aaron said, and Braden wished them well.

Verona laughed. "New toys."

"Yeah," Aaron chuckled as he put the comms device away. "This could help us out, if the De'anjard are, in fact, in the city."

"Fate or coincidence, my friend?"

"I'll take what I can get," Aaron answered, glancing back at the statue then turning back to Roselyn and Verona. "Let's head toward the Citadel of the Elite. I just want to take a quick look at the place, and then we can rendezvous with the others."

They made their way back toward the main streets, abandoning the rooftops due in part to the buildings being taller and closer to the looming dark towers of the Citadel of the Elite. The streets were once again filled with people going about their daily lives, but an occasional few glanced at the dark towers with trepidation. There were two dominant towers encased in smooth black stone that could be seen skyrocketing over the fifty-foot walls that surrounded the Citadel. The progression of the walls had an octagonal shape. The wall didn't bother him, as Aaron knew he could clear it if he needed to, but Verona and Roselyn had no chance. He would keep his word despite the urge to charge in blindly, plus he didn't even know if the travel crystals were held within the Citadel walls.

The top of the towers ended in a jagged crown. It was one of the highest structures in the city, rivaling the High King's palace. Between each of the spires were glowing yellow orbs, the purpose of which escaped him. Verona grabbed Aaron's arm and gently pulled him toward the side of the street, and the crowd shifted of its own accord. There were four Elitesmen in their black uniforms along with four teenagers marching among them that couldn't have been more than thirteen or fourteen by Aaron's summation.

"Initiates," Verona whispered.

Aaron clamped his jaw shut and turned back to the group. The Elitesmen strode forward, firm in their authority, followed by their four initiates, who had almost the same arrogant gleam in their eyes. They were followed by a smaller group of younger boys and girls dressed in little more than rags. All looked fearfully at the Citadel of the Elite. Aaron turned toward the gates and saw more guards and Elitesmen upon the towers and along the walls.

One of the boys with dark hair bolted from the group. An Elitesman turned and gestured with his hand, sending a blue orb streaking toward the fleeing boy.

SMACK!

The orb struck, sending the boy down ten feet from where they stood. Aaron felt another set of hands on him and saw Roselyn shake her head helplessly. They couldn't interfere no matter how much he wanted to. Two of the initiates ran over and lifted the boy up. One of the initiates admonished the other for being too rough then carried the scared boy back in line with the others.

A bald man in a dirty white apron glanced in their direction, narrowing his gaze. "New recruits," he said.

Aaron nodded back. "Are they always brought against their will?"

A look of surprise flashed across the bald man's face. "Not to worry, they will soon be like all the rest if they are to survive in there. The Elitesmen Order doesn't tolerate innocence to any degree. Some are used for training and others as targets for future Elitesmen."

The bald man headed back into his shop.

Aaron turned toward Verona. "I had no idea they recruited children."

"Neither did I, my friend."

Roselyn pursed her lips in thought. "Makes sense though, doesn't it? Easier to bend to your will." Roselyn's frosty tone wasn't lost on any of them.

Aaron glanced back at the walls and inventoried all the guards and Elitesmen. "There are so many of them." He summoned the energy into himself and sent it out toward the Citadel. The caw of a crow sounded overhead, and Aaron felt as if the ground were swallowed away beneath his feet. Then the feeling was gone. He glanced back toward the gates and watched as the last of the new recruits went beyond his view. How could anyone let this happen? He was beginning to understand Captain Nolan's predicament regarding the Elitesmen's interest in his children.

"I know that look, my friend," Verona said. "We can't save everyone we come across."

Aaron sighed. "We can't turn a blind eye either."

"What are you suggesting?" Verona asked.

Aaron frowned. "I'm not sure. We cannot do nothing."

Verona put his hand on Aaron's shoulder. "Your heart is in the right place, but we can't do anything about it now. I suggest we circle the walls of the Citadel the best we can. Have a look around and then make for the meeting point with the others."

Aaron stared silently at the gateway to the grounds, refusing to look away, but Verona was right. They couldn't do anything about it right now, but he vowed to himself that he wouldn't abandon those children. The wide-eyed look of the dark-haired boy as the Elitesman's orb struck him was firmly in his mind. There must be a way he could free them. He nodded back to Verona, and they trekked around the walls of the Citadel, noting all the gateways into the complex.

Roselyn deftly held a device in her hands that she said would capture images. All things that they could use.

"I wish we could get a look inside," Aaron said.

"We should ask Tanneth or Gavril," Roselyn said. "Perhaps they have something that we could send that would escape notice."

Aaron sent probes of energy into the Citadel, and each time he encountered that feeling of the ground rushing away from his feet as if there were some type of protection in place to guard against his probing. Aaron felt a slight brush upon his senses that was so fast he thought it was a mistake. He turned back, scanning the way they had come with his eyes drawing toward the rooftops, but no one was there. Frowning, he followed the others.

DARVEN CLUTCHED TO THE ROOFTOP. *THE HEIR OF SHANDARA HERE IN Khamearra?* How could he have traveled here so fast? He knew they didn't possess any travel crystals. No one outside of the Elite and High King carried them. He was the exception, being apprenticed to Mactar. He had idly stumbled upon a presence attempting to probe the defenses of the towers, and he doubted that any of the other Master Elitesmen would have detected it. They sat proudly upon their seat of power, believing they were perfectly safe despite suffering one of the most decisive defeats they'd experienced since the fall of Shandara.

Darven raised his head to watch the distant backside of the man who wanted him dead. He had been there that night on that other world when they had foolishly believed at the time that this boy, Aaron Jace, couldn't be any threat. He was wrong, but where others had died, he had lived. It was a cold comfort to know that the knife he threw that night had killed a princess of Shandara, Aaron's mother. He crept along the rooftops, easily blending in, and followed the Heir of Shandara and his two companions unnoticed.

10

CRYSTALS

The waning afternoon passed into the early evening hours as Aaron and the others made their way to the inn. Despite having memorized the main thoroughfares in the city, they had to rely upon Roselyn, who showed them that the comms device also functioned as a GPS.

"Something else you are already familiar with?" Verona asked.

"Yes," Aaron answered. "But like you, I didn't know how these worked until Roselyn showed us."

They had learned a great deal about the Citadel of the Elite, but without a look inside, Aaron knew they were still flying blind. Roselyn for the most part was quiet, but Aaron caught a few glances in Verona's direction when his friend wasn't looking. Something must have happened between them while he was gone, but he couldn't dwell on it because he still had that nagging feeling of being watched.

"Still have that feeling?" Verona asked, echoing his thoughts.

Aaron nodded. "Yes, but it's so slight that I can barely feel it. It has been with me a while though."

Verona nodded, and Roselyn checked the comms device and shook her head. They came to the inn, and Verona spoke as he was the only member most comfortable with the currency used in Khamearra. Something Aaron hadn't had the time to learn, but thought it important to do so. He scanned the modest first floor of the inn, and after Verona passed the innkeeper a silver mark, he showed them to a private alcove located on the second floor.

Sarik and Gavril waved in greeting, with Gavril looking relieved to see Roselyn, then he nodded to Aaron.

"Safe and sound as promised," Aaron said.

"As promised?" Roselyn asked, glancing at Gavril and himself.

"Roselyn, forgive me, but I promised Gavril and your father that we would look out for you," Aaron answered.

The fire seemed to spike through Roselyn's eyes. "As if I'm the one who needs looking out for."

Gavril held up his hand. "If not your father then how about a beloved uncle?"

The fire flared less brightly in her eyes. "Fine."

Aaron recounted their day's events as Verona went quiet again. Shortly after, they were joined by Eric and Braden. One of whom had a large bruise on his left eye.

"Are you okay?" Aaron asked.

"I'm fine," Braden answered.

"We ran into a small spot of trouble looking for our friends," Eric said.

Aaron nodded silently, agreeing that it was probably not a good idea to speak of the De'anjard in so public a place.

"Were you able to find your friends?" Aaron asked.

"Yes, but they weren't exactly welcoming," Braden said.

"I think we scared them," Eric said. "The sect that came to this city has grown into a very secretive bunch. It took us some time to figure out how to find them, but once we did, we saw signs of them all over the city."

"How?" Verona asked.

"Quite clever actually," Braden answered. "They've stripped down the emblems that were associated with the De'anjard and Shandara. Instead of using the whole family crest, they broke it into pieces. A dragon claw here, a rose there, and sometimes a white tree. We managed to stumble upon one group, which was a mix of normal-looking citizens and some of the city guards. They didn't like that we found them, but before we could identify ourselves, they chose to run or attack. Not a full-out attack. Mostly they were buying the others time to get away. We let them go, but not before one threw something at my head."

"A horse-shoe," Eric chuckled, slapping his brother on the arm.

Aaron smiled. "Good work. Do you think you could find them again?"

"Yes," Braden said.

Aaron turned his attention to Gavril. "Have you heard from Tanneth?"

"No," Gavril said, shaking his head. "I'm not concerned. At least not yet. I expect he will check in via the comms device at some point through the night. Young Sarik and I checked the area near the High King's palace. The place is well protected as one might expect. Being the governing seat, the activity seemed normal. I tried to take energy readings where I could, but there are only small readings coming from inside the palace."

"I have some readings as well," Roselyn said. "Some parts of the Citadel of the Elite were extremely active, and then there were some areas that were quiet. Too quiet, as in no readings at all, as if the place simply weren't there. I've never seen anything like it."

"Is there a way we can get a look inside the place?" Aaron asked.

Gavril nodded. "Tanneth brought some equipment that could work. I'll send him a message. Let me do it because if he is in a position that requires stealth, I don't want to give it away." Gavril brought out his comms device but held it beneath the table and after a few moments, nodded. "Tanneth will do as you ask, but he is asking if you will meet him later tonight."

"Me?" Aaron asked.

Gavril smiled knowingly. "I would say he expects that you will be out and about this evening."

Aaron glanced at the others, seeing slightly surprised looks from some and not from others. "I thought I'd take another look around," he admitted.

Gavril nodded. "I thought as much. We couldn't find any sign of travel crystals in the palace. That is not to say there aren't any there, just that we couldn't detect any. I think focusing on the Citadel of the Elite is our best bet. We did hear about some commotion in that part of the city. Care to enlighten me about that?"

Aaron told them about the events involving the guards and their prisoners and his standoff with the Elitesmen. Then moved on to how the Resistance in the city was being led by the De'anjard, cleverly referred to as Eric and Braden's long-lost friends. He finished with the Elitesmen's recruiting practices that they had witnessed.

"I hate them," Braden said. "I knew they were malicious and cruel, but to take children…"

"I'm with you on that one," Aaron said. "I don't understand how people can just go along with this."

"Do you even know how to keep a low profile?" Gavril asked. "You need to keep a cool head even in the face of what you've seen. A smart warrior knows to make a stand on the battle ground of his choosing."

"I couldn't stand by and let those men be beaten," Aaron said.

"And the children?" Gavril asked.

"If I can help them, I will," Aaron said.

Gavril's lips curved slightly. "Okay, perhaps we can help. But please try to remember that we can't fix all the problems with this city in the short amount of time we are to be here. I applaud your idealism, Aaron, I really do, but there are others that are depending upon you. If we are to be an effective team, we need to function as such, and that includes not charging off, leaving the others exposed."

Aaron thought about Gavril's words for a moment and sighed. "I understand. I'll try to keep that in mind, but someone needs to wake these people up. Who will stand up for them if they cannot stand up for themselves?"

Gavril listened patiently. "I know your intentions are good, and my instincts agree with you, but there is a time and a place to make a stand. We're in hostile territory, and our enemy has us outmanned. If we must strike, we must use the element of surprise. How long do you think it will take them to figure out that you are somewhere here in the city? Outside of overwhelming odds, you are the only person in a generation to go toe to toe with these Elitesmen."

Aaron struggled to get his thoughts in order and took a moment to digest what Gavril was telling him. Other people's lives were in his hands now, and he had to take that into consideration. "Perhaps my being here is the best way to put them off balance. Hit your enemy where he believes he is safe. Regardless, Gavril, I will keep what you've said in mind."

They ate dinner and made plans for the next day. Throughout all of it, Aaron kept seeing the dark-haired boy being struck by the Elitesman's orb and falling down in a heap before him. The sting of being powerless to help had affected him more than he thought. Tanneth was right. He would be going back out into the night, and if he could free those children tonight, then he would.

"Gavril, a word if you please?" Verona asked.

Aaron had just left them, much to Eric and Braden's dismay, himself included, but he understood why Aaron needed to go back out there, and it frustrated him that he couldn't keep up with his friend. Not yet, at least. He and Sarik shared a determined look. They had been practicing everything that Aaron taught them and experimented with things that Sarah had only hinted at. They had come a long way since the decks of the Raven, but Verona knew that they were quite a bit away from being as adept at these abilities as Sarah and Aaron. No, he and Sarik had a long night ahead of them. He glanced longingly at Roselyn, who had followed Aaron out, but said she would be back.

"Verona?" Gavril asked.

"I understand that you believe Aaron's actions to be reckless and even foolhardy at times," Verona said.

"I just want him to act with a bit of caution," Gavril answered.

"He carries the weight of his decisions quite heavily, I assure you," Verona said. "He blames himself for failing to protect his family back on Earth. Part of him realizes that there was nothing more he could have done, but he still feels responsible. He lost someone important to him there. A mere flicker compared to the blaze he has with Sarah, but the dead weigh heavily upon him. He understands how precious a gift life is. It is something that I don't think he can suppress because it comprises the very fiber of his being."

Gavril took a sip of his ale, and his eyes appeared haunted for a moment. "I understand, more than you can realize. I, too, was a boy thrust into a harsh world of danger and sacrifice."

Verona nodded and sipped his ale in silence. "Perhaps if more did as Aaron and made a stand against injustice, then a situation like what we have here in Khamearra could be avoided."

"If only life would cooperate in perfect little pieces. Most people just want to survive and be left alone. But I do agree that at some point enough is enough."

Aaron stepped out from the inn through a side entrance. The air was growing cooler in the night, but the skies were clear. His staff rested easily in his hands though he didn't think he would need it. This would be a night for the Falcons.

"Aaron," Roselyn said, "a moment before you go."

Aaron faced the beautiful raven haired Hythariam and inclined his head attentively.

"Must you go alone?" Roselyn asked. "Couldn't one of us come with you? Verona perhaps?"

Aaron smiled at the mention of his friends name on her lips. "I'll be able to move better on my own tonight, and I don't want to put you in anymore danger if I can avoid it. There is something you can help me with though." He reached inside his pack and pulled out the chrome cylinder. It still glowed with a faint bluish light at his touch. "Your father thought I should show this to you. This is how I was able to travel from Earth to Safanar."

Roselyn's eyes lit up. "A Keystone Accelerator."

Aaron smiled. "Do you know how it works?"

"In theory, yes. This one is still charging as it requires a certain amount of energy to open a dimensional doorway. This is my father's design," Roselyn said, holding it up and examining the device.

"He said as much," Aaron replied. "Do you think you can take a look at it? It's been used twice that I know of, one of those times by me, but I'm wondering if it can do more."

"More?" Roselyn asked.

"Just a thought regarding the Nanites and whether the keystone could help," Aaron said.

Roselyn's eyes narrowed. "What are you saying?"

He should have known his intentions wouldn't escape her notice. "Let's keep this between us, but I've been thinking about the Nanites. In the simplest of terms, they are machines with a purpose to fulfill. It just so happens that the purpose they are fulfilling is grotesque, but ultimately they either need to return to Hytharia or the barrier must be destroyed. It's the only thing that makes sense to me, otherwise a dumb machine would have found another way to achieve its primary programming. The Nanites were created specifically with the barrier in mind. It's a scary kind of intelligence if you think about it."

Roselyn swallowed and nodded. "I see what you mean. Focusing the Nanites upon the barrier wouldn't allow for them to create another craft and journey back to Hytharia through space. So you mean to go through the portal to Hytharia? I'm not sure if what you're asking for is possible with a device this small."

Aaron returned her gaze evenly. "Only if there is no other choice. Could I use the keystone to come back to Safanar?" He was taking a chance by telling her even this much. "Will you help me?"

Roselyn divided her gaze between himself and the keystone she held in her hands, considering. Aaron's heart thundered in his chest as he waited for her answer. She slowly lifted her gaze to him and nodded wordlessly.

Aaron sighed in relief. "Thank you," he whispered and put his hand on her shoulder giving it a slight squeeze.

Roselyn put the Keystone Accelerator away. "Be safe. I know many will flock to the name, your linage that is, but there are those of us here with you that truly are your friends."

Aaron nodded and launched himself silently to the rooftop of the building. The sky was dark, and the shadows were many despite the bright lights of the city. He squatted down and scanned toward the direction of the Citadel of the

Elite. The bladesong churned within as he drew in the currents of energy around him, strengthening his muscles beyond the capabilities of bones and sinew. His perceptions sharpened, and although the night descended upon the city, he could see clear as day. He picked his target—the top of a taller building along the path to the Elitesmen's fortress—and launched himself into the air using his augmented muscles and the wind to push him along the great distance. His black cloak dragged behind him, rippling through the wind, and he spread his arms to slow his descent as he landed upon the stone building.

Aaron scanned the area again and launched into the air, once more relishing the freedom. To keep from a bone-jarring landing, he aligned the many particles hidden in the air to slow his descent. He landed with barely a sound and without damaging the rooftop upon which he now stood. Quite the difference from his clumsy trek through the forest with Sarah. He'd give anything to be back in the forest with her. The next jump brought him close to the Citadel of the Elite, and as he approached, he got his first look at the interior of the fortress grounds. To the far right was an open arena clearly visible by the ring of orbs circling the different levels. He pulled out the comms device, noted the rendezvous point to meet up with Tanneth, and headed that way to wait.

The dark towers loomed overhead, and Aaron stared at them, unable to guess as to how tall they really were. The area nearest the Citadel was quiet, even on the inside as far as Aaron could tell. His grip hardened on the staff as his gaze bored into the Elitesmen's fortress trying to rationalize a likely location for the travel crystals. A sharp pang pierced the walls in his mind through his connection with Sarah. She was in pain again, and the knowledge grated along his nerves. His hands clutched his staff, and the runes glowed softly. Not being able to head straight to her and ease her pain tore at his chest. Unable to resist his need to know, he reached across the expanse and followed the sickening pain toward its source. He dared not go any closer for fear of causing Sarah more pain. He couldn't read her thoughts exactly; it was more like feeling the undercurrents of one's intentions and what he saw in Sarah was a tangled mess of a mind at war with itself.

He recalled the time on the Raven when he tried to open the others to the energy around them, where he had become lost in Sarah's golden blaze that caressed every crevice of his skin. His mind purred at the memory for a moment before another bout of pain snapped his attention.

The tangled mess before him now was a mixture of black and gold, and he watched in horror as the multitude of golden strands comprising Sarah's lifebeat slowly turned black. The Nanites were visiting a fate worse than death with their assimilation of the woman he loved. Twisting her very love for him into its most potent weapon.

The knowledge that the woman he loved was fading before his eyes sent his own core into shambles, breaking his concentration. He opened his eyes, and the runes flared brilliantly under his white-knuckled grip. His anger wound up like a coiled viper yearning to be released. Aaron drew in the energy around him, feeding it into the rune-carved staff. He faced the direction where the Drake was sure to be and brought up the staff.

He stood poised, longing to unleash all the energy he hoarded within him and quench his thirst to kill the Drake. In this moment, he didn't care who the Drake had been before. There was something animalistic inside him that demanded he protect the woman he loved and the ever-mounting frustration of not having done so grated away at him. Growling, he turned back to the towers of the Elitesmen and pictured himself launching headlong in their midst, bringing fire and destruction in his wake. The vision fed the beast inside him that craved to make the world bleed for his suffering. And then he saw Sarah's deep blue eyes that seemed to drink up his soul, staring imploringly at him. The firelight caressing her face dissolved his rage to an angry hiss, and Aaron collapsed to his knees, tears streaming down his face.

I'm so sorry, my love. Each moment you are in pain is my failure.

Aaron wept as he had not allowed himself before, until the tears would no longer come. He knelt with shoulders slumped, giving into the darkness that threatened to overwhelm his heart into hopelessness. Time slipped by as he knelt there in the shadow of the Citadel of the Elite. The moons had risen, claiming the night sky above him. Aaron sucked in a breath, planted the knuckles of his fist into the ground, and rose slowly to his feet. He would not allow himself to fail. He chanted it in his mind like a mantra and drew strength from it. He was here, and there was still time. He pushed aside the despair he'd once given into. Now, he would do what must be done.

Aaron felt a presence off to the side and saw Tanneth patiently waiting. The young Hythariam's golden eyes met his in silent understanding. Tanneth had seen the whole thing.

Aaron strode over and sat next to the mysterious Hythariam that Gavril had vouched for. He did say he had a knack for getting into impossible places.

"I hope you have some good news," Aaron said, still shaking off the remnants of his despair.

Tanneth's lips curved into a slight grin. "Take a look," he said, holding a small black sphere about half the size of a baseball. "These are our recon drones. As you can see, they are quite small, and I deployed several of them earlier today. They have active cameras so we can see everything they are seeing. Plus, they record where they've been. We can track their progress through our comms devices. Here, watch," Tanneth said, bringing up his own comms device as a small video feed showed the drone hovering along the Citadel grounds.

Aaron couldn't help but be impressed. "This is great."

"I thought you might appreciate it, but the drone's capabilities go beyond video," Tanneth said, and he flipped through the different modes, some of which Aaron recognized as infrared and others he didn't know at all.

"I've found something," Tanneth continued. "The base of the far tower is broken out into separate chambers, which are mostly being accessed through an underground network of tunnels that lead away from the city."

Aaron frowned. "The mines would be my guess," he said, thinking of the miners that the Elitesmen were so keen to take into custody earlier.

Tanneth nodded in thought. "That actually makes sense for some of these. There is a chamber higher up where I see some strange activity."

"What do you see?"

"Well, it's some type of momentary spike in energy, only it has a pattern that I'm not able to measure. The spikes occur seemingly at random," Tanneth said.

Aaron kept looking between the display on the comms device and the tower of the Elite before them, his brain making the leap. "Random you say. Were you able to get in there and see what's in the chamber?"

"Things have quieted down now," Tanneth said. "I wasn't able to get a drone in there earlier because of all the activity in the area, but perhaps we'll have better luck now."

Aaron frowned for a second. "Were you able to physically get inside?"

Tanneth nodded. "Only for a short while. I was able to get inside through that structure over there."

Aaron's gaze followed where Tanneth pointed. "The arena?"

"Yes," Tanneth said, and then he asked, "Arena?"

"I'm only guessing at the name. We have structures like those where I come from, but they are often referred to as an arena or coliseum," Aaron said.

"Interesting," Tanneth replied. "I have a drone heading back to that chamber right now. Let's see where it is and hopefully what's inside."

They were already in an alcove off to the side of the street. Tanneth hit a button, and a small holographic display appeared above the device with the image of a dark hallway. The drone hovered a few inches above the ground. Aaron winced as he saw people walk down the passageway, believing they would see the drone, but surprisingly they passed right by.

"The drone is cloaked, and in the waning light they are almost impossible to see," Tanneth explained.

Aaron nodded and continued to watch the display. The drone zoomed down the hall and curved around several stone staircases. The inside of the tower was sparsely furnished, and looked to be more of a work area than a place where people actually lived.

The drone approached a wooden door and paused for a second. Waiting. After a few minutes, Aaron realized that the drone couldn't exactly open any doors. He glanced at Tanneth, who shrugged his shoulders. The drone moved along and came to an open landing near the very center of the tower. There were copper tubes along the walls, running in different directions that reminded Aaron of pipes used for plumbing, only these were about six inches in diameter. Tanneth was about to recall the drone after it had circled around looking for an alternative way into the room, when Aaron noticed something along the ceiling.

"Do you see that opening up there along the ceiling? I can't tell if it is a shadow or an actual hole," Aaron said.

Tanneth saw it and directed the drone toward it. As it closed in, they could tell that it wasn't a shadow, but some type of ventilation shaft that ran inside the walls. The opening had a small screen blocking the entrance. Tanneth brought up a smaller secondary display that held symbols that Aaron didn't recognize. Tanneth entered a sequence into the comms device, and then there was a small flash from the display as the drone cut a perfect hole into the metal screen.

The drone squeezed its way through and headed down the dark airshaft. The display was plunged into darkness for a few moments before a soft purplish glow appeared in the distance. The drone sailed along until it came to another screen, but they could still see the room beyond. In the center of the chamber was a large purple crystal jutting from a black boulder sized rock. The rock was pock marked with channels and holes. Aaron assumed it to be a meteorite that had crashed into the planet at some point. The purple crystal looked to be about ten feet tall and had offshoots protruding in different directions.

The drone used its laser to burn a hole through the screen, and it slowly moved inside the chamber. Secured above the purple crystal was a smaller yellow crystal that reminded Aaron of the crystals that powered the Raven. Along the wall there was a large window with metallic shutters, which were all closed, but Aaron suspected they opened to allow sunlight in to power the focusing crystal. The purple crystal flashed in a momentary brilliance as its discharge was sent to the smaller yellow crystal above and then dissipated. Along the floor were containers filled with different-colored crystals. Aaron noted one filled with crystals that were black, and he recalled when Sarah had shown him her blackened, spent travel crystal as a sign that she had no intention of leaving him.

"Jackpot, Tanneth. See the dark ones there?" Aaron pointed to the container with the black crystals. "Those are spent travel crystals, and I'll wager that this one here has fully charged crystals, considering they're all glowing purple. You did it, Tanneth. You've found the source of travel crystals that the Elitesmen use."

Tanneth nodded, muttering that it was nothing, "More luck than anything else. Now comes the hard part."

Aaron frowned, "Getting inside—"

He was cut off as the drone suddenly went dark. Tanneth frowned and tapped a few commands, and the video feed played back the final seconds before the drone went dark. They couldn't see anything, so Tanneth changed the display to a panoramic view of everything around the drone. There was a movement in the shadows, only revealed from the glow of the crystals. Tanneth paused the feed at the drone's final moments. A silver, blurred image showed something destroying the drone.

A blaring shriek sounded off from the towers, and the inside of the Citadel spawned to life before their very eyes. They shared a brief look and fled down the street away from the Citadel.

NOLAN COLLAPSED INTO HIS CHAIR AT HIS DESK, UTTERLY EXHAUSTED, BUT at least his family was safe, even if a little confused. The agents of the De'anjard were able to move quickly and intercept them all to keep them from harm's way. Part of him was a bit uncomfortable with how easy it was to convince his wife and children to follow the agents of the Resistance simply because they donned a guard's uniform. He shuddered at the thought of what would have happened if the Elitesmen had reached his family first. He hadn't been able to see them, but Anson requested that he write his family a note, which he hastily did, informing them that they were in danger and to trust the people they were with. It wasn't elegant, but it got the point across.

"I'm sorry, Nolan, but it's not safe for you to go to them now," Anson said quietly.

Nolan sealed the letter and handed it to his friend. He was placing an awful lot of faith in the man. The very lives of his family were in his hands, but he understood. "I know. I just don't like it."

"They've already been to your house," Anson said.

Nolan sighed, wishing he had a pint of dark ale in front of him instead of water. "What is to stop them from coming here and taking me by force?"

"Isaac, for one," Anson replied. "He is right outside the door. He was part of the faction that left the Order of the Elite when Shandara fell. He survived the culling, and it was not because he was unskilled."

Nolan glanced toward the doorway to his office and saw the shadow of the quiet old man that stood outside it. Isaac wore a dark leather duster concealing a heap of weapons beyond that were carried by ordinary Elitesmen. What made the hairs on the back of his neck stand on end was the fact that people appeared to ignore Isaac's presence, as if his imposing form wasn't standing there in front of them. He found Isaac's presence unsettling to say the least.

"Are you sure about him, Anson?"

"As sure as I can be. I've worked with Isaac before, and if he didn't want to be here to help, he wouldn't. You can trust me on that."

Nolan nodded. "I don't really have a choice now do I, but you already know that. I gave you my word. I'll do what I can."

Isaac gave a soft knock on the door, and they both looked up as a messenger from the captain commander's office came in. The messenger gave Nolan a salute, retrieved a sealed envelope from his satchel, and handed it to him. Nolan took the letter and read it silently.

"Tell his Grace I will mobilize the guards at once," Nolan said to the messenger, who then left the room.

"What is it?" Anson said.

Nolan reread the letter just to confirm. "Something big is happening. They're mobilizing guards from three districts to converge at an inn. We're to surround the inn and capture all those inside. The Elitesmen will be on site, and we are commanded not to move in until they have arrived. We have fifteen minutes to get there."

Anson nodded and followed him out of the office as Nolan gave orders for the night watch to gather in front of the station. The letter didn't explain much, but Nolan had a sinking feeling that this night was about to get a whole lot more complicated.

11

SACRIFICE

Verona sat at the table talking quietly with Sarik and Eric. Braden left them, heading to one of the rooms they had rented toward the back of the Inn. Gavril stayed with them, occasionally surveying the room. He visibly relaxed when Roselyn joined them. She looked a little upset, but shook her head at Gavril's questioning glare. Instead, she turned to Verona, and for a moment his heart thundered in his chest and he felt the heat rise to his face.

"My Lady?" Verona asked.

"Your friend is something else."

Verona snorted. "He tends to have that effect. What has he done this time?"

Roselyn shook her head, and Verona drank in the sight of her black hair cascading down her shoulders.

"Nothing yet, but he's gone off, so I'm sure we're in for an eventful night. You'd never believe he nearly died a short while ago." She turned to Eric. "Would you mind moving to sit right there, please?"

Once Eric heaved his muscular bulk into the chair, Verona noticed that the view of their table was sufficiently obscured to keep most casual onlookers from observing. Gavril sat forward, waiting. Roselyn pulled a shining cylinder from her pocket, and Gavril gasped.

"Is that…?" Gavril asked.

"Yes," Roselyn answered. "Our absent friend had it. It appears this is how he was able to travel to Safanar in the first place."

"What is it?" Verona asked. He was becoming quite proficient at not stumbling over his tongue when Roselyn spoke to him.

"It is called a keystone accelerator," Roselyn said. "It opens a doorway to other dimensions. In this case, from Aaron's Earth to Safanar."

"I thought Iranus couldn't account for its whereabouts," Gavril said.

"It was a prototype," Roselyn said and looked around at the patrons in the common room. "I'm going to my room to take a look at it in private."

She nodded to all of them, her gaze lingering for a moment on Verona who failed to still his beating heart.

"You, too?" Eric asked after she left.

Verona sighed and glanced back at the men around the table. "What did Aaron say about being fortune's fool? That is what I've become."

Gavril was about to say something, but Verona's gaze snapped to the front of the inn the same instant as Sarik's did. He focused himself, drawing in the energy around them, and stretched his senses away. Verona surged to his feet as he felt the presence of many men surrounding the inn. The rest of the men came quickly to their feet.

"What's wrong?" Eric asked, gripping the sword on his belt.

Verona glanced behind him in the direction that Roselyn had gone. "We're surrounded."

The front doors burst open and men in black uniforms all bearing the silver dragon emblem of the High King poured in. Eric flipped the nearest table, scattering the men in front of them. Verona heard Roselyn scream from behind him, and he dashed down the hall as the common room erupted into chaos.

"Shandara!" Eric bellowed, bringing the shield of the De'anjard to bear as he drew his sword.

Verona nearly collided with Roselyn as she fled down the hallway.

"There are too many that way," she gasped.

"Up the stairs," Verona said.

They took the steps two at a time and came to the landing above the common room. Eric was in the center, drawing the attention of all the High King's guards, using his shield to knock them back two at a time. Sarik was pinned down by a group, and Roselyn gasped as Gavril went down. He had to help them. Verona unslung his bow and smoothly fired an arrow taking down one of the guards holding Gavril down. The Hythariam joined Eric in the center of the fray, fighting the guards hand to hand. There was a growing number of wounded guards littering the floor.

"Go!" Gavril shouted up at them.

Verona grabbed Roselyn's wrist and turned to flee. There were three flashes, and immediately before him were three Elitesmen with their weapons drawn. Verona swung his bow and hurled himself into the Elitesman, knocking one of them off the landing. The other two spun out of the way and shot their hands in front of them. Two blazing metal bands appeared and closed around his wrists and feet, collapsing him into a heap. He heard Roselyn fall to his side. Verona growled, struggling to free himself from the bonds, but there was nothing he could do.

Eric was being overwhelmed as Braden came to his side, tackling three guards at once. The Elitesmen danced amid the men, immobilizing them as they went. First Gavril and then Sarik. Eric saw the oncoming Elitesmen and pushed Braden through a window out the side of the inn.

"Live free, my brother," Eric yelled and faced the Elitesmen.

The forward Elitesman thrust his hands forth, hurling an orb. The orb bounced harmlessly off the shield of the De'anjard back toward the Elitesman. Eric roared and charged forward, launching himself into the air while bringing his shield down upon the first Elitesman and swinging his sword toward the next.

The Elitesman caught his wrist with glowing hands, and Eric came to his knees, crying out in pain as he dropped his sword. The Elitesman sneered over him, and the other rained down blows upon his exposed back. Eric heaved to his feet and swung the Elitesman that held onto his wrist into the other one and brought his shield down in a crushing blow to the man's neck, killing him.

Eric roared as he charged forward, plowing through the guards and shoving them aside. A third Elitesman appeared at his back, and Verona cried out as twin daggers plunged into Eric's side. Eric collapsed to his knees, unable to draw breath as the daggers pierced both his lungs.

Verona strained against his bonds as he watched his friend collapse stiffly to the floor, blood pooling at the Elitesman's feet. The Elitesman looked up in his direction. Their eyes locked, and Verona pulled in the energy around him, wanting for the first time to lash out using what Aaron had taught him. The room darkened until he could only see the sneer of the Elitesman and Eric dying at his feet. Verona projected his rage-filled scream into a thrum of force that sent the Elitesman sailing through the wall of the inn. The last thing Verona saw was an armored fist that knocked him unconscious.

Nolan's men had arrived at the Blue Lantern Inn on the heels of Captain Commander Josef's men. The captain commander sneered in his direction and sent him to cover the back of the inn and alleyways, while his men made ready to storm the front.

"Stop any of the people from escaping. We are to capture these patrons, as they are believed to be the cause of dissidence and destruction near the Citadel of the Elite," Josef said, then waved them away.

Nolan deployed his men to the back of the inn, which itself was a three-story wooden building at least a hundred feet across, including a covered porch. The smell of a smoking hearth laced the air. He was pleased to see so many of the guards that they had met with in the temple of the Goddess return to the station and accompany him tonight. They made up more than a third of the men he had brought with him, and it was those men that he kept closest to him, knowing that he could trust them.

"Do you know anything about this?" Nolan asked Anson in hushed tones after deploying the men to cover the alleys leading away from the inn.

Anson shook his head, and Nolan didn't have time to ask any more questions as they heard the captain commander's men break through the doors of the inn. He kept his men outside, as their orders were to lend support if needed. Screams came from inside the inn, and several patrons attempted to escape out the back. His men took them into custody, and he was pleased that they didn't use an excessive amount of force.

From the commotion inside, it sounded like the captain commander's guards were being met with heavy resistance. A dark shadow crashed through a window and into the middle of the alleyway. Nolan's men retrieved the bear of a man that laid unconscious, struggling to carry him even this far.

After a few minutes, the sounds of struggle died down from inside, and an Elitesman appeared in the doorway.

"You there, Captain," the Elitesmen said. "Take your detainees and interrogate them. If anything appears out of place, you are to send them to the Citadel immediately. Is that understood?"

"Yes, my lord," Nolan answered.

They gathered the people they had captured and slung the unconscious form over a horse and headed back to the district headquarters.

Aaron and Tanneth quickly navigated the rooftops heading away from the Citadel when both their comms devices started blinking red. They stopped, and Aaron scanned for signs of pursuit while Tanneth opened his comms device.

"They're in trouble," Tanneth said.

"Where?" Aaron asked.

"They're still at the inn," Tanneth said.

"I can go faster myself," Aaron said.

Tanneth plunged his hands into his pack and pulled out a golden rod a little more than a foot in length. Tanneth clicked a mechanism on the side of the rod, which fanned out at the points to form discs. He placed it down in front of him and stepped onto the discs, bands extended over his feet. Tanneth keyed a sequence on his wristband and hovered off the ground.

"I think I can keep up with you," Tanneth said quietly.

Aaron smiled and nodded, then launched himself into the air, heading back toward the inn. He glanced back a few times to see Tanneth skating across the air, keeping pace with him. Aaron nodded back to him and really turned on the speed, using the air to propel himself forward, and skipped along the rooftops of the sleeping city. They stopped at a building near the inn. The Blue Lantern where they had agreed to stay for the night was crawling with guards in black uniforms. The silver emblem of the dragon caught the light from the orbs that dotted the street below.

"How could they have found them?" Tanneth asked.

Aaron shrugged his shoulders. "I'm not sure." He didn't think they had been followed, but then his stomach sank. He had that nagging feeling along his senses and cursed himself for not paying more attention. "We may have been followed, but I couldn't be positive, and there wasn't enough evidence…"

Tanneth grabbed his arm. "You couldn't have known. We're in enemy territory. We should assess the damage and decide from there."

Aaron nodded and turned back to face the inn. They moved in closer to get a better look. There were many guards mixed in with a few Elitesmen.

I shouldn't have left them.

People were filing out of the inn, and Aaron saw the unconscious forms of Verona and Gavril, followed closely by Sarik and Roselyn, who huddled nearby.

The energy of the bladesong churned inside him as he drew the Falcons from their sheath.

"No," Tanneth said, grabbing his arm. "If you go down there you will kill them all."

The words of Tanneth penetrated the walls of his anger, but his body was poised to spring.

"You're right," Aaron said, tensing his jaw.

A few moments later, they watched three Elitesmen approach their captured friends, and in a flash of light, they were all gone. Aaron could guess where they were taking them and glanced back at Tanneth.

"We'll be heading back to the Citadel sooner than expected."

"Where are Eric and Braden?" Tanneth asked.

A horse-drawn wagon pulled up, and the guards piled up dead bodies carried out from the inn. Two guards struggled with a large body, and Aaron felt a cry freeze in his throat.

Eric, no!

Aaron struggled against Tanneth's grip. Eric was dead. He scanned the crowd, looking for Braden, but couldn't find him. Aaron refused to believe that Braden would abandon his brother. An Elitesman reached into the wagon and took something from Eric's body.

Aaron sheathed his swords and drew his small curved ax.

The shield of the De'anjard extended in the Elitesman's hands, showing the Alenzar'seth coat of arms emblazoned upon it.

Aaron was poised to unleash the ax and kill the Elitesman holding the shield. The very same shield that Eric unearthed in Shandara with an enormous sense of pride. In a flash, the Elitesman was gone.

Aaron secured the ax to his belt.

"I don't see Braden. Let's circle around and see if he is in the back," Tanneth said.

Aaron nodded, and they circled to the back of the inn. Aaron took grim pleasure at the number of dead and injured guards, knowing full well that Eric had fought to the bitter end.

They said nothing more as they came to the back of the inn. Aaron immediately recognized the district captain from earlier and saw his second in command hovering near an unconscious Braden lying across the saddle of a horse. Aaron sighed in relief as he realized that Braden was breathing and took a small amount of comfort knowing that Braden, for the moment, had escaped the Elitesmen.

"I can't let them take Eric's body like some piece of meat," Aaron said.

Tanneth nodded. "I'll take care of it."

The Hythariam slipped silently away and returned a short while later. "We have a few minutes. Then we should be away from here."

Aaron nodded. The captain was leaving with Braden in tow, and they decided to follow. They would free Braden first before going after the others. A loud explosion painted the street in an orange blaze, and a plume of smoke rose into the air. The streets echoed the cries of the guards at the front of the inn. Captain Nolan, Aaron noted, did not look back but kept heading away from the inn. With a grim nod to Tanneth, they followed Braden's unconscious form amid the guards and the rogue district captain.

12

AN ALLIANCE

Nolan snapped his head back at the sound of the explosion and was about to order his men back, but decided against it. The captain commander's men could deal with the cleanup. He motioned to two guards. "Have a look and see if they need aid. If the commander's men are okay, then return to headquarters." The guards saluted and headed off.

"What do you think caused the explosion?" Anson asked.

"Don't know, but I'm glad that none of us were in front of the inn," Nolan answered, glancing at the rooftop. "I think we have a shadow."

Anson nodded, not looking up. "Do you want me to look into it?"

Nolan thought about it for a minute and shook his head. "No, if it's the Elitesmen then there is nothing we can do, but if it's the same man who helped us earlier today, then I don't want to send him off."

Nolan felt the wheels turning in his mind as the pieces slowly slipped into place. He glanced at the prisoners taken from the Blue Lantern Inn and moved closer to Anson. "I don't think he was alone. I think the whole purpose of the night raid was to capture the man's companions. And if he's following us, then it seems that one of his companions is among our captives."

Anson nodded in understanding and took a closer look at their prisoners. After peering at them for a few seconds, Anson turned back to him. "I think you're right, and I would wager that the unconscious man is tied to this. Look at his build. He has the build of a warrior."

Nolan glanced at the unconscious man and nodded. "I won't give him up to the Elitesmen if I can help it. When we get back to the station, I want him secluded away from the others. Be quick and use only men you trust. Treat his wounds, but post some extra guards just the same, because I doubt when he wakes he will realize we mean him no harm."

"Yes, Captain," Anson said and saluted.

Nolan returned the salute and watched as Anson made his rounds among the men and took point near their mysterious prisoner. It took all his will not to look at the rooftops, being both afraid at what he would find and wary of what he couldn't see.

Aaron and Tanneth followed the guards from the rooftops, keeping pace easily. They kept silent with Aaron still stuck between disbelief and acceptance that Eric was dead. He tried to deny the guilt within that selfishly demanded that he should have fought by his friend's side and could have turned the tide by allowing them to escape.

He gave grief's guilt its due then allowed reason to slowly push those thoughts aside, only to have it start again. Sarah had tried to tell him that he couldn't be everywhere at once, nor could he protect everyone around him, but there could be no denying the fact that they'd been caught in a moment of complacency. Now the Elitesmen had captured all but himself, Tanneth, and Braden. He had thought they could move in the city undetected, but then the incident with the miners occurred. This was all his fault. He had brought the attention of the Elitesmen down upon them, and his friends had paid the price. The blaring truth dragged at the pit of his stomach, making him feel hollow and empty inside. Even though they all knew the risks coming here, Aaron couldn't help but feel responsible. This was the burden of being a leader, and there was nothing he could do for Eric but take the fight to the Elitesmen by striking in the very place where they thought they were safe. He would prove them wrong. He vowed to make the Elitesmen fear the shadows.

Tanneth motioned down to the street, and Aaron noticed that the lieutenant had taken up point nearest to Braden. They must have realized that Braden was somehow connected to him. His thoughts were confirmed when the lieutenant brought Braden into the district headquarters through a side entrance by a small number of guards broken off from the main group.

"Do you have any drones left at the Citadel?" Aaron asked.

Tanneth nodded. "I didn't pull them out. I just had them shut down after we tripped the alarms."

"We need to find out exactly where the others are being held if we're going to have any hope of a rescue," Aaron said.

"What are you proposing?" Tanneth asked.

"I want you to have the drones look for the others. We know that there is a way into the Citadel through the arena, but what if there is another way? I will go and get Braden," Aaron said.

"By yourself?" Tanneth asked.

Aaron shook his head. "I think I have a friend on the inside. They are part of the Resistance and could perhaps mobilize the De'anjard remnants in the city. I won't know until I go down there."

Tanneth nodded and then frowned. "Do you intend to just walk in there?"

Aaron's lips lifted into a small grin. "I thought about it. Just walk in there and ask to see the district captain."

"What makes you think they will let you in?"

"I'll think of something. If things go badly then I'll try and get Braden out by force," Aaron said.

"You're right, we need to divide our efforts if we are to have any hope of success," said Tanneth.

"Thank you for agreeing," Aaron said.

"Let me show you how to call up the video feeds from the drones. I will highlight the important finds in a way that will be easy for you to find," Tanneth said and began showing him the sequences to bring up the video feeds. It was actually quite easy. The Hythariam designed their interfaces for simplicity rather than complexity, which Aaron appreciated.

"I think you have it," Tanneth said after Aaron went through the sequence a few times on his own.

"Be safe," Aaron said.

"Safe journey to you as well," Tanneth said, and then he melted into the shadows, heading back toward the Citadel of the Elite.

Aaron studied the district guard headquarters. The bustle of activity had died down as the night drew on. He could try sneaking in through the side entrance, but dismissed the thought because he didn't want to cross swords with people who could be allies. Going through the front door in this case was the best approach. He leaped down to the street and walked purposefully toward the building, saying a silent prayer for the safety of his friends, hoping that fortune had not entirely forsaken them this night.

The district headquarters with its marbled facade and polished columns appeared more impressive from the street than the rooftops. Aaron walked calmly up the wide staircase without any of the guards giving him more than a passing glance.

He pushed open the metallic gray doors, which yielded easily and required very little force once he engaged the handle. The air had the faintest hints of a musky leather aroma mixed with the sweet smell of a smoking pipe. The inside was swept clean and held the inner trappings of a police station with a duty clerk sitting behind the counter, grumbling to himself. Behind the clerk was a room filled with mostly empty desks. A few guards were stationed throughout, with some polishing their armor or sharpening a blade. More than a few glanced in his direction.

Aaron approached the desk slowly, and the clerk looked up at him.

"Can I help you?" the clerk asked.

"I'd like to speak with Captain Nolan please," Aaron said.

The clerk narrowed his gaze and then glanced at the clock hanging on the wall. "A bit late, isn't it?"

Aaron glanced at the clock and then back at the clerk. "I have some information for him."

The clerk did not look impressed and frowned. "You can leave it with me, and I'll pass it along to the captain. He's quite busy at the moment."

Aaron silently cursed the clerk in his mind and kept his eyes from rolling in annoyance. "I understand that he is busy. I can wait for him, if that will suffice. Can you tell him that I know his family isn't safe and I'm here to help him with that?"

The clerk took a long look at him, seeming to judge whether Aaron was a threat. After a few seconds, he sighed. "You can have a seat over there," he said, gesturing to one of the empty wooden chairs on the far side of the room.

Aaron went over and sat down. The clerk waved over one of the guards and whispered something. The guard nodded and headed toward the back. The minutes dripped past, and Aaron wondered whether his message was being delivered or if they were simply gathering more men to try to arrest him.

After about ten minutes, the captain came around the clerk's desk and stopped mid-stride. His uniform held the golden tips of an officer's wings on his collar, and his dirty blond hair was tied back into a ponytail. The captain looked to be a few years older than himself, and his hazel eyes held an edge to them as they noted the rune-carved staff in Aaron's hands with a flicker of familiarity.

They each appraised the other for a few moments before the man smiled in greeting. "Captain Nolan, at your service."

"Aaron Jace. I appreciate you taking the time to see me, Captain. I know you must be busy. Is there someplace where we may speak privately?" Aaron asked.

The captain nodded. "Of course, if you will follow me," he said and led Aaron through the building toward the back.

They came to the captain's office, and as they entered, Aaron saw an older man off to the side. Without thought, Aaron brought his staff up, and the runes flared faintly.

"Elitesman," Aaron spat, but much to his surprise the older man made no move.

Nolan held up his hands. "It's all right. He is with us and not with the faction you've faced."

Aaron drank in the sight of the old Elitesman in his dark leather duster and his shocking blue eyes alight with energy. They both stared at the other ,scarcely daring to breathe.

The Elitesman slowly held up his hands and bowed his head. "I could hardly stand against one such as you, Ferasdiam Marked. You have nothing to fear from me. I do not stand with the Elite Order, not as it is today. Not since they betrayed the Shandarian masters of the Safanarion Order."

Aaron's breath quickened, and he held the energy within him, waiting for the inevitable betrayal that must come from any Elitesman. It was then he thought of Sarah and the Elitesman named Beck who trained her. Beck couldn't be the only one of the old order of the Elite who did not hold with the current regime's ideals.

"There are none here who can stand against you, but you look to be in need of aid regardless," the Elitesman said.

Aaron stood poised with his staff ready, but he couldn't sense any malice in the Elitesman, nor the superior arrogance that was ever-present in the others he had faced. He relaxed his guard, but kept a firm grip upon the bladesong within.

"I do need help," Aaron said. "You have my friend held captive here, and your Elitesmen brethren have taken the rest."

Nolan cleared his throat. "Your companion's wounds are being treated, and I will take you to him momentarily, but there is something I must know. Were you the man who fought the Elitesmen earlier?"

Aaron slowly nodded.

Nolan's eyes widened. "How?" he whispered.

Aaron glanced at the Elitesman before returning his gaze to the captain. "I am the only living scion of the house Alenzar'seth."

"Ferasdiam," the Elitesman whispered.

"Isaac?" Nolan asked.

The Elitesman Isaac ignored the captain. "The rumors are true. You are Reymius Alenzar'seth's heir. Why would you come here to Khamearra?"

Aaron took a long look at the Elitesman and decided to take a chance. "Did you know a man named Beck?"

The Elitesman's eyes widened in shock, and he took an involuntary step forward. "Yes. He and I were part of a smaller group who broke away from the Elitesmen."

Nolan frowned. "How is it that no one has ever heard of this rogue faction before?"

"We stayed out of sight and let the Elitesmen be, and they stopped trying to hunt us down. But now…"

"Not all of you stayed on the sidelines," Aaron said. "Some of you have worked with the De'anjard here in the city, and the daughter of the High King was too good an asset to let slip through your fingers."

"You know Sarah?" Isaac asked. "We've not had word from her for over a month."

Aaron swallowed. "I know her, and she is the reason I'm here in Khamearra."

"She is in Khamearra?" the Elitesman asked.

"That's not what I said," Aaron answered, but was surprised to hear the note of concern in the Elitesman's voice. "She is the reason I'm here."

The silence hung in the air for a few moments before Nolan said quietly, "I will take you to your friend now."

Aaron followed the other two men from the room after silently insisting that the Elitesman go first. He would be damned if he was going to let an Elitesman at his back no matter what their current allegiance happened to be.

The captain led them down to the lower levels of the building through several hallways to an almost deserted part of the station. Nolan, it appeared, wasn't taking any chances. He stopped before opening the door.

"We moved him here because I wasn't sure when the Elitesmen would return. We were to question the patrons of the inn and report anything suspicious. Having been witness to how the Elitesmen treat their prisoners, I was intending to keep him hidden for his protection."

Aaron nodded. "I appreciate your efforts, Captain. We overheard you and your lieutenant speaking earlier today, and I know the Elitesmen were threatening your family."

Nolan clenched his teeth. "They did, but they are relatively safe for the moment," he said, and then he opened the door.

Braden lay on an old bed in the dusty room, still unconscious. A pitcher of water was by the bedside, and a man in a brown shirt was rubbing a damp towel on his forehead. To the side was the lieutenant.

"Sir," the man in the brown shirt said. "He has minor wounds, and the blow he took to the head just happened to be in the right place. I think he will be fine and should wake up soon."

"Thank you," Nolan said and looked at Aaron. "He's our resident surgeon."

Lieutenant Anson saluted the captain upon entering the room, but Aaron ignored the man as he approached the bed where Braden appeared to be sleeping.

"Do you know what happened to him?" Aaron asked, checking him for any signs of wounds.

The lieutenant shook his head. "We found him in the alleyway next to the inn. He was thrown forcefully from the window. He has not regained consciousness, but as our surgeon said, he will be fine."

Aaron nodded and gently shook Braden, who remained unresponsive. He sent a tendril of energy to Braden and saw that his lifebeat was greatly diminished. Aaron focused the energy around them, pulling it through him and fed it into his friend. The body, as always, was an effective conduit. Something seemed to awaken within Braden, as he felt him grasp at the energy being fed. Braden had become more open to the process as of late than when they had tried on the deck of the Raven a few weeks before.

Braden shot upright in the bed, sucking in a loud gasp of breath and shouting his brother's name. Then he sank back down and looked at Aaron in surprise, still gasping for breath.

"You're going to be fine. Just take it easy," Aaron said.

"The Elitesmen attacked us. The others…" Braden said, his voice trailing off questioningly.

"The others were captured," Aaron said.

Braden rubbed the top of his head. "When I find Eric, I'm going to teach him a thing or two. He threw me out a window."

Aaron felt his lips curve into a smile for a split second despite the lump in his throat. "Braden, your brother was killed in the attack."

Braden looked back at him dumbfounded, as if he hadn't heard him right. Aaron met his gaze and watched as Braden struggled to his feet, shaking his head.

"Dead?" he whispered.

Aaron nodded back, and Braden sank to his knees. His body slumped then immediately went rigid as fire sparked in his eyes. Aaron felt the bladesong churn within Braden as never before. Braden's eyes slowly scanned the room before they settled upon Isaac. His eyes widened in rage, and he lunged for the Elitesman. Aaron caught him in midair.

"No!" Aaron said, struggling against Braden's muscular bulk. "He is not with them." He had to repeat it two more times before Braden stopped.

Braden relaxed enough for Aaron to let him go, but kept a wary look on the other men in the room.

"They saved your life, kept you hidden from the other Elitesmen. Otherwise, you would have been captured with the rest," Aaron said, and this seemed to penetrate Braden's fog of grief. He nodded in appreciation to the other men but still kept a wary eye on the Elitesman. "We need to get into the Citadel of the Elite to rescue our friends. Do you know a way inside?" Aaron asked.

The captain and lieutenant shared an incredulous look, while Isaac the Elitesman looked slightly amused.

"They are no doubt in the holding rooms where new prisoners are taken," Isaac said. "But if they know that they are associated with you, then they may take them to a different place inside the fortress. Probably one of the towers to the Grand Master's Hall. As for getting inside…" Isaac's voice trailed off as he glanced back at the captain. "We'll need the help of the Resistance, which will take some time. I wouldn't advise to go charging off tonight."

"But the others," Braden insisted.

The Elitesman's eyes became cold and calculating. "You stand the best chance at a rescue if we do some planning first. If you charge off at this moment, the only thing you will accomplish is getting them killed, and yourselves, too, for that matter. Have no doubts they will kill them all in the blink of an eye if it means keeping you from getting to them. The Elitesmen are no strangers to ruthless tactics, and right now your friends' worth is in their knowledge about you," he said with his gaze settling on Aaron.

The breath caught in his throat, and Aaron unclenched his jaw to speak. "What are you proposing?" Aaron asked, activating the comms device in his pocket in hopes that Tanneth or even Gavril would be able to overhear them.

"There is still time," Nolan said. "They took everyone from the inn, which was easily over a hundred people."

Isaac kept his gaze upon Aaron. "We use the Resistance to create a distraction throughout the city to draw their attention. They know that you will be coming. There can be no doubt about that. What they don't know is when or how. They've underestimated you up until now, but that luxury is gone. They will send their very best and most dangerous recruits after you."

"I've faced your Elitesmen before," Aaron said.

Isaac nodded. "I believe you, but have you by chance seen how they bring in new recruits?"

Aaron's mind flashed to the children he saw earlier being driven to the Citadel. "Children?" he whispered.

"What's this?" Captain Nolan asked.

"Children," Aaron said firmly.

Isaac nodded, his face grimly set. "They will send the Elite Masters to you, but they will also send their crop of specialized recruits. The ones honed for their ability to work with the energy in ways no sane person would ever think to try. This requires a younger mind more easily manipulated. They can boil your blood from the inside until your veins burst. Trick your eyes into seeing things that aren't there. They are lethal killing machines and not children, despite whatever their appearances are. Are you prepared to face that?"

Aaron swallowed the bile that inched up his throat. "I will do what I must. I will never abandon my friends. And the only thing keeping me from charging off to the Citadel of the Elite is the chance that you may offer a better way to get inside while minimizing the risk to my friends. I don't trust any Elitesman, and if I so much as suspect a hint of foul play, there will be no force on this planet that will keep me from seeking retribution. Rest assured that we may not be able to save our friends, but you can be damned sure we will avenge them."

Isaac searched his cold eyes for a few moments. "Yes, I believe you will," he said, then looked at the others. "Tomorrow night, or rather tonight since dawn is approaching, is when they will be initiating the new recruits at the arena. The Elitesmen will gather there with the new crop of recruits to test them to see if they are worthy of the Order."

"What kind of test?" Captain Nolan asked.

Aaron sensed the fear mixed with relief, as the Elitesmen had been targeting his son for such a fate.

"A series of trials that will allow for the assessment of their physical capabilities, but give light to their cunningness and ruthlessness in their bid for survival," Isaac replied.

"And the prize is induction to the Elite Order at the sacrifice of their innocence," Aaron said, unable to keep the sneer from his voice. He wanted to lash out at the Khamearrans in his midst, but their shocked looks gave knowledge to the fact that none of them had known of the practice.

"I can send word to the Resistance," Lieutenant Anson said. "They will rally, but they will need targets."

"No innocent lives are to be caught in the crossfire," Aaron said.

Anson fix him with a stony gaze. "We hold with the ideals of the De'anjard, my lord. Defend the helpless. Stand the watch. Honor your brothers of the shield. Sacrifice for the many."

Braden brought his fist to his chest as the words of the De'anjard were spoken. Aaron nodded, and Isaac cleared his throat.

"The best distraction is for you to appear in the arena at precisely the right moment. If the Elitesmen believe you to be there, then they will let their guard down, further allowing for a small group to infiltrate the Citadel."

Aaron thought about it for a second, granting that the Elitesman had a point. "Who will go inside to free our friends?"

Isaac's craggy face lifted into a small grin. "I would offer myself, but somehow I don't think you would allow that."

"I'll go," Captain Nolan said, drawing everyone's attention. "And since you're here to protect me," he spoke to Isaac, "then it looks like you'll have to come with me."

Isaac nodded.

"I will go with them. They will need to see a face that they can trust," Braden said in a tone that did not invite any arguments.

Aaron glanced at Braden, concerned for a moment that his friend was too hot-headed for this, but who was he to judge? They were all here because of his need to find the travel crystals. Aaron looked back at the old Elitesman. In what world would he have ever thought to trust the lives of his friends to one of them?

But what other choice did he have? The Elitesman's plan made the most sense and was certainly better than shooting from the hip and making it up as he went.

"There is another thing I would like to ask you," Aaron said. "Travel crystals. Do you know where I can find them?"

Isaac's gaze narrowed for a second. "I know they are charged in one of the towers. Why do you ask?"

"I need them," Aaron answered. "I need to know how I can get inside the tower and what guards them."

Captain Nolan cleared his throat again. "I think we'd be more comfortable if we use my office for this. This way. We can use some of the maps to help in the planning."

Aaron looked back at Braden, who nodded. "That sounds like a good idea. Thank you, Captain."

"Please," the captain said. "Call me Nolan, Your Grace."

"Nolan, please call me Aaron."

Nolan nodded and led the others from the room. Once again, Aaron brought up the rear, but allowed the men to get far enough ahead to bring out the comms device.

"Were you able to hear all that?" Aaron whispered.

"Yes," Tanneth answered. "The plan has merit. And I agree that there is nothing we can do tonight. They have that place locked down tight. I'll continue to have the drones recon for us, and you already know how to access the feeds. If I find something worthy of your immediate attention then I will let you know. But there is one more thing."

"What's that?" Aaron asked.

"Be wary of one of those men with you. I'm not sure he is being entirely forthcoming," Tanneth warned.

Aaron nodded. "I know and thanks. Be careful. I trust your reconnaissance more than another man's knowledge at this point. Were you able to reach Gavril or Roselyn?"

"I don't want to draw unwanted attention to them, but I can tell you that Gavril and Roselyn are still alive. If they can reach out to us, they will. I'm betting that Sarik and Verona are alive, as well."

Aaron frowned. "How do you know about Gavril and Roselyn?"

"Through the Nanites in their system."

"Understood." Aaron put the comms device back into his pocket and caught up to the other men. There was work to be done.

13

RUMINATIONS

This was the longest Mactar had taken up residence at the fabled High King's palace in recent memory, and he hated every second of it. The furnishings were beyond compare, but all the pandering from the pathetic creatures that resided in the palace were beyond his contempt, and distracted him from the real work that required his attention. His scowl deepened at passing servants that knew better than to make eye contact with him. It only took a few examples to convey that he neither needed nor wanted anything a servant had to offer. People were meant to be ruled; subservience had been bred into them for thousands of years. The weak were ruled by the strong and the cunning.

The plush and pomp setting of the High King's court served its purpose for the masses, but the true rulers of Khamearra were the Order of the Elite who functioned as the High King's right hand. High King Amorak allowed them the illusion of a council, which he could squash at a moment's notice. Like all tools, the council served a purpose, unlike his current efforts, but some goals required certain sacrifices. The task of overseeing the training of Prince Rordan, the High King's remaining heir, with the exception of the Lady Sarah, didn't qualify as worthy of his time. The thought of Sarah brought a frown to his face before he could quell it. Sarah alone held true potential, and it was a bit of a shock to see her aligned with this Aaron Jace, the sole heir of the House Alenzar'seth.

Sarah's whereabouts were unknown, even to him, but there could be no mistaking where her loyalties lay. It was terribly vexing to be outsmarted by the likes of Reymius Alenzar'seth. The destruction of Shandara should have been enough to satisfy the ambitions of any man, but now that the Alenzar'seth had returned, the victory over Shandara had become hollow and unfinished. The resilience of the Alenzar'seth was worthy of even his respect.

For all the High King's might, he lacked the intelligence and foresight that would put him on equal footing with the Hythariam. The fact that Amorak was also Ferasdiam marked was truly an accident of fate, by his reckoning. Aaron had proven to be a worthy adversary and would be a rallying cry for the kingdoms of this world to unite behind. Not even the power of the Elite Order would be enough to bring them into line. No, Aaron was the real threat. Having no ties or ambition beyond immediate survival gave him the freedom to act in such a way that even he himself had underestimated. Their confrontation at Shandara was illuminating to say the least. His thoughts drew back to the events as they replayed in his mind.

What connection was there between Sarah and Aaron, he wondered.

Then he saw it. As Aaron transitioned from the crossroads back to this reality, he scanned the battlefield and immediately went to Sarah's side where the Elitesmen were the thickest. Only love would drive one to such lengths as to leap willingly into the fire. Mactar's pulse quickened as the pieces fell into place and a malicious smile oozed its way across his face. It seemed that the princess with the heart of ice had found something in her travels. This was something he could use. Aaron Jace was not as untouchable as it would seem. What were the chances that such a woman would find herself entangled between two Ferasdiam marked, ones touched by fate? There was no precedent for it. Two men, Ferasdiam marked, to shape the world of things to come.

The High King had remained unchallenged since the fall of Shandara, and he still hadn't come to grips with the fact that the Goddess had given her blessing to another. It was true that he himself didn't hold faith with any deity, but it didn't require faith to know the signs of a being with true power. Power that should be his. And yet here he was, observing the young prince with his Elitesman Master to teach him. Rordan had improved, there was no denying that. The Prince could hold his own against most Elitesmen, which in and of itself was an accomplishment shared by few, but in his mind, the Prince would never be a match for Aaron Jace. Reymius's heir had proven to be a worthy adversary and a very grave threat. There was nothing to be gained in not acknowledging the facts before him, and while pride had its place, he would not succumb to its double-edged sword. The window whereby he could take the power of the Alenzar'seth for himself had passed. The one success he could use was the resurgence of the Hythariam. Seeing the land of Shandara had confirmed his theory regarding the stability of the barrier all along. It was failing and it was only a matter of time.

The Drake had the ability to command the Ryakul. This was something he had seen first-hand at Shandara and was something he wanted to exploit. Being able to command a legion of Ryakuls would turn the tide in any war. Mactar's gaze swept the surrounding palace from the practice yard in which he now stood. War was coming, of that he had no doubt. Seeing the Hythariam appear in Shandara with their flying machines only served to whet his appetite of what was promised to him.

"Rordan is making progress," High King Amorak said.

Mactar had not heard him approach, but once the High King let his presence be known there was no mistaking it. "Yes, my lord. He improves every day, but as I have said before, our attention would be better served elsewhere."

The High King kept his gaze upon his son. "You mean your attention? Fear not, Mactar. The call has been sent to mobilize the armies. We will be ready for those who are foolish enough to align with Shandara."

Mactar nodded. "We should continue to hunt the Alenzar'seth and seek out the Drake. I've seen reports of soldiers from various kingdoms gathering in the Waylands near Rexel."

Amorak's eyes narrowed. "Cyrus himself is not a threat, and I believe he has very little chance of uniting the kingdoms of the east against us. Regardless, I have something special in mind for them."

"It's not just them," Mactar said. "The Hythariam have resurged. They are the real threat. They will use the Alenzar'seth as a rallying cry to unite the other kingdoms against us." Partially true, but not something he was especially concerned about.

Amorak turned to him with a raised brow. "I thought you were preoccupied by the fact that Colind's tomb now stands empty? The shadows are lengthening around you, and you are jumping at things that aren't worthy of your attention. Tell me, what is really bothering you?"

Mactar was about to answer the High King when he felt the faintest brush along his senses. A cold touch that hissed at a promise of death, followed by the echoes of a mirthless cackle.

Tarimus!

Mactar pushed out around them with his senses, but the presence was gone. There were times when he thought that madness was indeed consuming him, but at this moment he knew Tarimus had been there. The mirror of Areschel, which had given him dominion over Tarimus, remained closed to him. He had to accept the fact that Tarimus had somehow become free from his prison, but Mactar could not surmise how that could be.

"I felt it, too," Amorak said, glancing around them.

"Now we're both jumping at shadows, my lord," Mactar replied dryly.

Amorak frowned. "I have given thought to your idea about seeking out the Drake, and I agree. To be able to control the Ryakul is too good an opportunity to pass up."

"I'm glad you agree," Mactar replied.

"I assume you mean to leave as soon as possible," High King Amorak said.

"Yes, but there is something that has come to my attention regarding your daughter."

"Has she returned?"

Mactar noted the lack of concern in the High King's tone. "No, I'm afraid she has not. You have spoken with Rordan at length about the events that occurred at Shandara. I've meditated on the events myself and have come to a realization that not only has your daughter allied herself with the Alenzar'seth, but she has fallen in love with the man."

The High King turned, sweeping his gaze around the practice yard not saying anything, but the air felt to have dropped a few degrees. Mactar would have sworn he saw the slightest of twitches upon the High King's face. So he does still care, or is it a matter of pride and possession? Mactar wondered.

"I allowed her to expend her energies with the so called 'Resistance' at my pleasure, but this..." The High King bit off his last word and graced Mactar with a smoldering gaze. "This is unforgivable. The defiance of my daughter will not go unanswered."

Mactar grinned inwardly, but maintained his composure. "What do you intend to do, my lord?"

"Do?" the High King said, then smiled mirthlessly. "She dug her own grave, and now she will lie in it. My course of action will not change. The Alenzar'seth will die. By my hand if need be."

"And Lady Sarah?" Mactar asked.

The High King eyed him. "You always did have a soft spot for her blonde looks. Very much like her mother."

"She has always been quite gifted," Mactar said, which was an understatement given that she had kept at bay the machinations of her half-brothers, the Elitesmen, and himself.

"She will live," the High King said, "and learn the price of defiance. If she was foolish enough to actually fall in love with the enemy then so much harsher the lesson."

Mactar nodded and was silent as his eyes drifted toward every shadowed corner, looking for Tarimus but not finding him.

"I'm sending Rordan to the arena at day's end," the High King said.

"Then I will plan to leave soon thereafter to track down the Drake," Mactar said.

"And how do you plan to do that exactly?" the High King asked.

"By tracking the Ryakul as well as a few other tricks I know," Mactar answered, growing more anxious for the day to end. He could leave now, but he was due to meet with Darven. The former Elitesman had become an asset and was yet another way to put the young Heir of Shandara off balance. But Mactar was ever watchful to see that Darven did not become overly ambitious. Darven had been with the late Prince Tye when they had attacked Aaron's home in a realm called Earth. Mactar would use any means to ensure victory and survival, which included sacrificing his apprentice to Aaron should the need arise. The real victory for him would be to bring down the barrier and allow the other Hythariam faction their due, letting the glories of war ensue and feeding real innovation with the whole world as his playground.

The High King strode over to his son, and the activities in the practice yard ceased. Mactar's eyes scanned the faces amid the crowd, and he saw a pale face with lifeless black eyes peering back at him, but when he blinked, it was gone. He quickly strode over to the spot, but saw nothing to indicate anyone was there other than the men who were already there.

You will never see me coming, Dark Master, a voice hissed.

Rather than spin about, Mactar kept moving in the direction he was going. He reached out and cast a net of energy all around them, intent upon finding Tarimus. A slight tremor pulled his attention toward the roof. He activated the travel crystal in his pocket and emerged on the roof, only to see the dark form of Tarimus grinning as he melted away before his eyes.

14

THE PRICE OF CAPTURE

Verona felt a sharp jab of pain on the side of his head. He pushed his eyelids open and groaned as he tried to sit upright. His vision cleared, and the bitter smell of human excrement hung in the air, biting his nose. A gentle hand helped him sit upright.

"Are you all right?" Roselyn whispered.

Verona sighed and shook his head, coming fully awake. They were in a dark holding cell with bars all around.

"I am still breathing, my lady."

A small smile lit up Roselyn's face, and Verona's pulse quickened.

"Have they hurt you?" Verona asked.

Roselyn shook her head. "No. We're all here, but we've been grouped with some others from the inn. You've been out for hours. They've been taking small groups away."

"Eric?" Verona asked, already knowing the answer but dared to hope anyway.

Roselyn's face drew down sympathetically as she wordlessly shook her head. Verona swallowed down the lump in this throat. There would be time for grief later if they were lucky. He sat up, and his motion aroused the attention of Gavril and Sarik in the neighboring cell. They all looked relieved to see him awake. While all of them appeared bumped and bruised, they were none the worse for wear.

"Is Braden here?" Verona asked.

"The last I saw, Eric had thrown him out of the window. He might have escaped," Roselyn said.

That was something at least. Verona was hopeful that Braden had indeed escaped. "What about—" Verona began, but was cut off as Gavril started coughing and gestured around them. After a moment, Verona nodded. They were not alone and probably being listened to at this very moment.

"They haven't told us what they want," Gavril said and then whispered softly as Sarik coughed loudly, "*Tanneth and Aaron are still free. Neither has tried to make contact which tells me they are planning something.*"

Verona nodded and looked up as the doors on the far end of the room burst forth and a hush swept over the people in the cells. Four Elitesmen walked into the room, dressed head to toe in their customary black uniforms devoid of any markings. He sensed the energy gathered within each of them as if they constantly fed upon it. They glided to a halt in front of their cells, and with a slight gesture, the cell doors opened. Ordinary guards followed the Elitesmen and waved the four of them out of their cells. Verona glanced at the others, but did as he was told. Now wasn't the time to put up a fight, but they needed to escape.

One of the guards yanked off Roselyn's hood, and her silky black hair fell down in waves. The guards openly leered and went to grab her, but in the blink of an eye, Verona seized the guardsman's hand and twisted it, then roughly threw the man into the door of the cell where he collapsed to the floor in a heap.

The Elitesmen hissed. Two appeared on either side of Verona and bound his hands tightly behind him. The guardsman rose to his feet and planted a fist into Verona's stomach, and he collapsed to one knee, expelling his breath. He glanced above him and launched into the air, driving the top of his head into the guardsman's face. Blood geysered from the guard's face, and then the man fell stiffly to the floor, his lifeless eyes staring up at the ceiling.

"He's dead!" the guard gasped after checking on his fallen companion. The other guards moved in and drew their clubs, but one Elitesman stopped them with a wave of his hand.

"Enough," the Elitesman hissed. "Bring them forth now."

Some of the guards protested, and the Elitesman grabbed the nearest one by the throat, holding him several inches off the floor. "Do not believe for a second that I value the life of any guard more than these prisoners. You will obey, or we can find other uses for you," the Elitesman said, letting the guard fall to the ground gasping for breath.

Roselyn spared him a small smile that was gone in a flash, and as the growling guards surrounded him, he knew that his actions had been worth it. He would gladly take the beating of a thousand clubs if it spared Roselyn the leers of the prison guards and what followed them.

The guardsmen guided them away from the holding cells, but not without taking a few shots with their clubs. At least they had left the smell behind. Verona focused his mind, continuing to draw the energy into himself, and began feeding it to his aching parts. His body slowly repaired itself, and the aches faded away completely. Aaron had tried to describe the feeling as aligning one's patterns to their correct course, and he now understood what his friend had meant. He was able to draw upon the energy around them with increasing ease, but holding onto and manipulating it was something both he and Sarik continued to struggle with. Aaron had postulated that the reason he was able to achieve so much was that he had spent a lifetime learning to focus his mind without any thought to using life's undercurrents that surrounded all of them. Aaron had faith that in time they would all be able to do the things he could do, but Verona wasn't so sure.

They were brought into an empty room save for a solitary mechanical wooden chair and a table. On top of the table were knives, various steel spikes, chains, and other tools stained with blood. The pit of Verona's stomach sank to his feet.

Torture.

Roselyn! His eyes drew down in shame. He hadn't been able to protect her or get them to safety.

Some hero I turned out to be.

He banished the useless thought from his mind and focused on an escape plan.

The Elitesmen stood to one side of the room where several windows with wooden shutters were tightly closed, allowing only the faintest traces of sunlight in from the outside. Having Aaron and Tanneth show up now would be convenient, but he had no such illusions that it would happen. He wished he knew the time so he had something to measure against how long they would need to hold out until they were rescued, or, better yet, could escape. The others glanced around their surroundings, taking them in. Gavril's face looked set in stone as he regarded the Elitesmen in the room. The air of defiance grew thick around them much to the amusement of the Khamearrians.

The guardsmen gathered to the side, waiting on the Elitesmen, and Verona glanced at Gavril. The Hythariam colonel was completely at ease, and Verona suspected, judging by the impassive look in his eyes, that if Gavril were by himself, he could have escaped anytime he chose. Gavril met his gaze and gave a slight nod toward Roselyn, and Verona thought he understood. For all of Roselyn's tough exterior, she was no soldier. With the exception of Gavril, who survived the last days of civil war on Hytharia, none of them were prepared for what the Elitesmen were about to do to them. The Elitesmen's ruthlessness was known throughout all kingdoms, and despite Aaron's insistence that they were just men, Verona was afraid. He was not afraid for himself, at least not that much. He had faced death before, but Roselyn and Sarik? One so young shouldn't have these weights thrust upon him. Despite surviving the trek into Shandara, Sarik was barely older than eighteen. Verona glanced at Sarik, who stared back at the four Elitesmen with clenched teeth. Though Roselyn appeared to be the same age as himself, Verona knew she was much older, but she was a healer at heart.

The Elitesmen had done nothing but watch the four of them, who were now all bound at the wrists. Verona looked down at his shackles and noted the smooth surface that held neither lock nor clasp. He focused and probed along the smooth shackles, sensing the energy within that kept them locked together.

"One has been trained," an Elitesman hissed.

Verona looked up quickly. The Elitesmen removed their hoods, revealing bald heads adorned with black tattoos. One stepped forward, coming before him. Verona returned the Elitesman's cold gaze and felt him graze his senses, but Verona did not respond. The Elitesman moved on to Roselyn and reached out, putting his hand under her chin to get a better view of her face. Roselyn met the Elitesman's challenging stare, and then he stepped back and closed his eyes. Roselyn shrugged her shoulders at first and then started shaking off something that she couldn't see.

"*Hythariam!*" the Elitesman hissed.

Gavril roared, and in a single motion broke the shackles that held him and launched himself at the Elitesman. The Elitesman stepped back, attempting to use Gavril's momentum against him, but he spun, kicking the Elitesman back toward the others.

Verona stepped forward, but Gavril held up his hand.

"Protect her. Use what Aaron has taught you," Gavril said, then he spun and threw a small object at the advancing guardsmen.

An explosion rocked the room, capturing both the guards and the Elitesmen by surprise. At the same moment, Verona seized the energy around them and felt Sarik do the same. He projected it outward, shielding them as the flames from the explosion rushed forward. Verona held onto his concentration by a thread, trying to keep the small barrier in place that protected Roselyn and himself. Sarik's barrier sprang up at the same time and merged with his, extending it to protect the three of them.

Gavril went to his knees, bringing his cloak up over him, and the flames bounced harmlessly off him. A strong wind swept through and one of the windows burst open, sucking the flames from the room. The Elitesmen stood unharmed with barriers of their own in place, but the guards that had been in the room were nothing more than smoldering corpses.

The closest Elitesman recovered first and drove his hands forward, sending a blue orb crackling with lightning toward Gavril. He brought up his cloak again, and the orb bounced off harmlessly. Gavril closed the distance between them and fought the Elitesman in a blur of fist and foot.

The other three Elitesmen made no move to interfere, but casually surrounded the lone Hythariam soldier.

Gavril and the Elitesman's arms were locked, each straining against the other. Verona saw the energy gather into the Elitesman, coalescing along his arms.

"This one is strong," one Elitesman observed.

"I think we've seen enough," another Elitesman said.

The Elitesman came up behind Gavril and raised his hand to strike. In a quick motion, Gavril pivoted on his foot and sent the Elitesmen colliding into each other.

The remaining two Elitesmen appeared immediately at his side. One laid his hand upon Gavril's head, who then collapsed to the floor, unconscious.

Roselyn cried out but didn't move from the shimmering barrier kept up by Verona and Sarik.

One of the older Elitesmen frowned at the barrier that separated them. He turned to one of the other Elitesmen. "Fetch Master Gerric."

"What should I tell him?" the Elitesman asked.

"Tell him that our prisoners are the companions of the Alenzar'seth," the Elitesman said, never taking his eyes off Verona.

Verona's mind reeled. This had been a test. A way to get them to reveal themselves. He glanced at the charred remains of the guards and back at the Elitesman, whose lips curved into a cold smile. The Elitesman had gotten what he wanted. The fact that there were ten dead guards mattered not to him. They had revealed themselves. He didn't know how long he and Sarik could keep up the barrier, but he had no intentions of letting it down.

"Now," the Elitesman said, "we can begin."

The door opened, and several cloaked servants carried a table with three small stone chests on top. Heat ripples appeared over one of the chests, while a cold mist swirled out from the center chest. The third appeared to be plain.

Two Elitesmen heaved Gavril into the chair, striping off his boots to expose his bare feet. One Elitesman nodded to the other, and two bands of energy bound Gavril's wrists behind him. The other Elitesman put his hand on Gavril's head, and his eyes popped open. Gavril struggled against the bands that held his wrists and feet, but they didn't budge. The Elitesman dragged his hand across Gavril's face, exposing his golden eyes, which stared grimly back.

The third Elitesman retrieved metal tongs from the table and opened the chest with the heat ripples above it. The lid of the stone chest opened, and the Elitesman reached inside and retrieved a glowing red crystal. The other Elitesman pulled a lever on the chair, and Gavril's exposed feet shot forth in front of him.

Gavril's eyes shot to the red crystal then to his exposed feet and he closed his eyes. His body sagged as if he were almost sleeping.

Heat ripples radiated from the red crystal, and Verona saw beads of sweat dot the Elitesman's face. The Elitesman casually brought the tongs with the crystal to the bottom of Gavril's exposed foot, and Verona winced as the flesh smoked and turn black. Gavril did not cry out and appeared completely aloof to what was being done to him.

The Elitesman withdrew the red crystal, and Verona's mouth hung open in shock as the burnt tissue on the bottom of Gavril's feet immediate healed itself. After a few minutes, the skin appeared unmarked as if it had never been burned.

The Elitesman repeatedly put the smoldering crystal to Gavril's feet, yielding the same result. The Elitesmen glanced at each other and then put the crystal back into the stone chest. Still using the tongs, the Elitesman opened the centermost chest, and a cool mist oozed out. Verona saw the Elitesman's breath as the room grew cooler around them.

Gavril was still in his meditative state and completely unresponsive despite the Elitesmen's attempts to garner his attention.

The Elitesman stuck the metal tongs into the chest and withdrew a white crystal that dripped with cold vapor. The metal tongs iced along the tips and crept toward the handles. The Elitesman quickly brought over the white crystal, and just as it was about to touch the Hythariam's foot, Gavril's whole body jerked, knocking the crystal to the floor at the Elitesmen's feet. Ice quickly branched out from the crystal and encased the Elitesman's leg, and after a few seconds his whole body was frozen. It happened so quickly that the Elitesman didn't even cry out. The others looked on in shock.

"What is happening here?" a man asked from the doorway. He was finely dressed with golden robes cascading over his tunic. His hair was blond almost to the point of being white with only hints of yellow.

The Elitesmen in the room saluted the man and bowed their heads, momentarily ignoring their frozen companion.

"Elite Master Gerric," an Elitesman answered.

"Go ahead, Sevan," the Elite Master said.

"We believe these four are in league with the Alenzar'seth," the Elitesman called Sevan said. "Two of their number have been trained in the Shandarian way."

The Elite Master frowned and narrowed his gaze at the three prisoners huddled behind the barrier.

"A barrier?" the Elite Master said, and his mouth almost curved into an exasperated smile. "Impressive."

"We've tried to break through, but have been unsuccessful," Sevan said. "But this one was caught outside the barrier and is a Hythariam."

"You won't be able to get through the barrier. Not directly at least," the Elite Master's eyes narrowed menacingly. "A Hythariam," he said, and walked over to where Gavril waited strapped to the chair. "I've only heard rumors of your kind."

Gavril said nothing, his gaze unyielding to the Elite Grand Master.

"Their healing capabilities are impressive," Sevan said. "He seems to have the ability to both go into a trance-like state yet be aware of his surroundings at the same time."

Gerric nodded and headed for the door. "Proceed as you were. We'll be gathering at the arena. Learn what you can until then," the Elite Master said and left the room.

Sevan whispered something to one of the Elitesmen, who then left. Verona watched as Sevan retrieved the red crystal and held it near their frozen companion, who then thawed as quickly as he had become frozen. Sevan gestured to the remaining Elitesmen who then carried the injured one from the room.

Sevan returned the red crystal to the chest, and a servant entered. The man had on a gray shirt and plain brown pants. The servant's eyes darted around the room and turned as if to run away, but was blocked by another Elitesman.

"Please come in," Sevan said in a sunny tone.

The man entered the room on shaky legs. "Y… Yes, my lord."

Sevan glanced at Verona and smirked, and Verona felt sick.

"Now we can begin," the Elitesman said. "Why are you in Khamearra? Are you here to kill the High King? Cut the proverbial head from the snake? Are you planning to attack the city? Why are you here?"

Verona silently returned the Elitesman's gaze. The Elitesman stepped forward just outside the barrier and divided his gaze among the three of them, his gaze lingering on Roselyn.

"Surely, you must know that a rescue is not possible," Sevan continued. "Why don't you make it easier on yourself and tell me where he is? We know the heir of Alenzar'seth is in the city."

"Don't you mean easier for yourself?" Verona asked.

The Elitesman's head snapped back toward him, and his eyes narrowed, full of hatred for a moment before smiling. "I mean for you. We both know I can't get through your barrier, but I really don't need to," he said, glancing pointedly back at the terrified servant.

The Elitesman drew a small katana from his hip. "Stick out your hand."

The servant looked at the Elitesman and at Verona before slowly holding up his shaky hand. "P-please, my lord don't... "

The Elitesman brandished his blade and looked back at Verona. "Why are you here!"

Verona said nothing and held back the bile creeping up his throat as he looked helplessly back at the terrified servant.

"As you wish," the Elitesman said and immediately swung the katana.

The servant screamed in pain as his left hand was cleanly severed from his arm. Blood spattered to the floor like runny sap, and the poor man collapsed, clutching the stump of his arm to his chest.

"You bastard!" Verona screamed.

He heard Roselyn cry out behind him.

The Elitesman regarded him coolly. "Your silence cost this man his hand. If you remain so, then it will cost him a good deal more until I get the answers I seek."

"You are a fool if you think any of us will tell you anything," Verona said.

The Elitesman seemed unfazed by Verona's defiance. "Have it your way."

Verona was unable to keep the horror from his face as the Elitesman turned to the servant who was now whimpering, crouched upon the floor as he clutched the stump of his arm.

"Get up," hissed the Elitesman.

Despite his pain, the fear of the Elitesmen was too great for the servant to ignore, and he rose shakily to his feet and glanced at the remains of his hand on the floor. Tears streamed down his face as he looked pleadingly to the group behind the barrier.

Verona glanced at the others. Sarik had his eyes closed, his face a mask of concentration. Roselyn returned his gaze with a pained expression, tears brimming in her eyes. For a moment, Verona wanted to tell the Elitesman something—anything—to spare the poor man in front of him further pain, but he couldn't.

"Very well," the Elitesman said and turned back to the servant. "Take your clothes off."

The servant clumsily unbuttoned his shirt with his remaining hand and let it fall to the floor. The Elitesman's baleful gaze ignited when the servant looked at him, and he pushed out with his hand and sent a blast of air that knocked the servant to the floor.

"I said take off your clothes," Sevan hissed.

The servant scrambled to his feet, quickly removed his pants, and stood naked before them.

Satisfied, the Elitesman walked over to the table, his fingers gliding across the instruments of torture as if he were at a market. He then turned back to Verona with a huge smile that split his terrible face. The servant's eyes darted to the door, but two Elitesmen barred the way.

Verona looked back at the Elitesman he wanted to kill and watched as he selected a large spike with jagged edges from the table.

"This will do," the Elitesman said gleefully and stalked, like a leopard, toward the naked man.

The spike glowed for a moment in the Elitesman's hands as he dragged it across the servant's chest. The man flinched from the touch and appeared shocked when nothing happened. Then the Elitesman let the spike linger upon the man's shoulder, and his face crumpled in pain as a growing patch of blackness grew on the skin.

"Stop!" Verona cried over the servant's screams, but the Elitesman refused to stop. The man writhed on the floor while the Elitesman drove the spike deeper into his shoulder and the blackness continued to spread.

Roselyn buried her face into Verona's shoulder, and he brought his arms up around her.

"You want to know why we're here, Elitesman," Verona screamed. "We're here to kill you and all those like you down to the last man. The oppression of the Elite Order will be wiped from the world like a stain. Kill all your servants if you will, but mark me—before this day is done, I will walk over your cold corpse."

The Elitesman looked unimpressed and drove the spike into the servant's thigh next. The echoes of the suffering screams carried Verona out of time until he was a bundle of fury, but he dared not bring down the barrier, because he knew if he did, then the torture being performed upon the poor man before them would be visited tenfold upon themselves.

15

ANCIENT ALLIES

The hours swept by like a waterfall, and despite the lack of sleep, Aaron felt fine. Anson had left them earlier in the morning to organize the Resistance. Having spent a few hours with the man, Aaron trusted that the distractions created throughout the city would not cause any civilian loss of life. They would target key locations in the most corrupt districts so that it would draw the attention of the Elitesmen and guardsmen alike. Mid-afternoon was the agreed-upon timeframe, and Aaron was impressed at the speed at which the De'anjard Resistance mobilized into action. Anson explained that they already had plans in place to mobilize quickly. Putting the plan into action would be the easy part. They would converge upon the arena after Aaron made his appearance.

Captain Nolan was as good as his word. He kept the less trustworthy of his guards out on patrol or paired with guardsmen either already sworn to the Resistance or loyal to Nolan himself. The privacy was much appreciated. The Elitesman, Isaac, however, was another matter. Maybe it was simply the fact that he was an Elitesman that Aaron couldn't get past, but there was something that Aaron just didn't like. Something in the man's eyes or maybe it was the fact that he had to rely on the Elitesman to help free his friends. Aaron hoped that Verona and the others were able to hold out.

"Why don't we take a break?" Aaron suggested. "I could use some fresh air."

Nolan nodded. "There is a training yard in the back of the building that is normally vacant at this time of day."

Aaron thanked him and nodded for Braden to come with him. A few minutes later, they emerged in a yard that was easily an acre of open space, which this far into the city was truly something to be appreciated. There was a ten-foot wall surrounding the training yard, but Nolan was right, there was hardly anyone here. He and Braden moved off to the side.

"How are you doing?" Aaron asked.

The angry glint had hardly left Braden's eyes. "Anxious to get going. I can't stand the thought of the others being held by the Elite."

Aaron nodded. "Try to keep a clear head. I don't want you to sacrifice your life for revenge."

"Sacrifice is one of the tenets of the De'anjard," Braden replied.

"I know," Aaron said. "Verona and the others are counting on us, but don't let Eric's sacrifice be in vain. He saved your life, and we can't pull this off without you. I need someone I trust to go into the tower."

The jaw muscles on Braden's face flexed at his clenching teeth. "The Elitesmen will pay."

"On that we can agree, and now you stand a better chance at facing them," Aaron said. "I've felt you open yourself up to the energy. You've hardly let it go since this morning."

Braden's eyes shifted as he scanned around them, then he nodded.

"Use it," Aaron said. "Be aware of your surroundings. Part of control comes, in part, from surrendering to it. The Elitesmen like to use cunning and brutality. Don't let your pride be something that they can use against you."

"The whisperings... The voices are many," Braden said. "How do you know which one to listen to?"

Aaron paused a second to form his answer. "You know when we practice the slow fighting forms or do practice sparring. The movements come from your mind and from muscle memory. I think of them as urges, and they compliment my movements. You will get to a point where the voices or whisperings fade away entirely. Hold true to your core being. You are the embodiment of the De'anjard, the Shields of Shandara. Let that be your compass." He wished that there was more time to practice, but time was not a luxury they could afford at the moment.

Braden was silent for a few moments, lost in his own thoughts. "Thank you, my lord. I won't let Verona and the others down."

Aaron put his hand on Braden's shoulder, squeezed, and then asked, "What do you think of the plan?"

Braden frowned. "I would rather join you in the arena, but I think splitting apart is our best option. The Elitesmen will flock to you like moths to a flame. Are you prepared for that?"

Before Aaron could answer, the comms device buzzed in his pocket. After a quick look around, he withdrew it so that both he and Braden could listen.

"I've found them," Tanneth's voice came from the device.

"Are they all right?" Aaron asked.

"They are alive, but Aaron," Tanneth said softly, "it's grim. I don't know how much longer they can hold out."

Aaron shared a hard look with Braden. "We leave now then. Is there anything the drones can do until we get there?" Aaron asked.

"I'll see what I can do," Tanneth said. "I've also added my own bit of distraction. I would suggest avoiding the northern walls of the Citadel this evening."

Aaron nodded. "Okay. We're moving out now. The Resistance should be starting its own distractions throughout the city."

Without another word, they raced back into the building, heading to Nolan's office.

"We need to leave now," Aaron said. "We have their location."

The Elitesman Isaac frowned. "Where?"

"I'm about to show you something that I don't have time to explain right now, but trust that the information I have is accurate," Aaron said.

He brought out the comms device and keyed in the sequence that Tanneth had shown him, which pulled up a small display. It was a simple map of the levels of the tower, and the glowing point near the middle was where Verona and the others were being held captive. Nolan blinked and moved his hands along the hologram, and Isaac's eyes widened at the display.

The Elitesman Isaac swallowed. "I'm sorry, Aaron. That is where they take captives for…interrogation. If your friends are there then time is short. We must make haste."

Aaron nodded and chose not to reveal Tanneth to the group now, preferring to keep that information to himself and Braden. With the sun beginning to wane, they gathered at the front of the district headquarters. The common prattle of the people on the street seemed deceptively calm considering what was about to happen.

"This is where we depart," Captain Nolan said. "Safe journey to us all."

Aaron shook hands with the captain and nodded to Braden. If all went well then they were to rendezvous at Ferasdiam's temple in the old quarter of Nolan's district.

The former Elitesman, Isaac, regarded Aaron for a moment. "You will mostly likely be walking into a trap, but you already knew that."

Aaron met his gaze. "I know, but I think it will not be enough."

Isaac smiled in a knowing sort of way, as an older man indulges a much younger man. "I've never seen anyone with your level of attunement to the energies that surround us. Having faced my share of Shandarians and Elitesmen alike, I know this is not the norm, and I would venture to guess that you are Ferasdiam Marked."

Aaron merely nodded, waiting for the Elitesman to continue.

"The specialist Elitesmen can hurt even one such as you. And I will say this only because I believe that you truly mean to help the Lady Sarah. You are only limited by what you can perceive as possible. Even the specialists have a weakness to unravel. I hope you will survive long enough to figure this out."

Aaron returned the Elitesman's gaze. "If you succeed in helping to rescue my friends, then I won't lump all the Elitesmen together. What will be started today won't end with this day's events, and I hope you are prepared for that, and will remember which side you're on."

Aaron and the old Elitesman regarded each other for a moment and then Braden broke the silence by saying it was time to move out.

Aaron walked to the alleyway next to the district headquarters and brought out the comms device. He needed to see what Tanneth had only hinted about before. The drone hovered near a closed window on an outside wall. The drone's camera showed a translucent frame, as it was in stealth mode. He was able to bring up an image through one of the slits of the wooden shutter and almost gasped at the bloody mess of the room. Gavril remain strapped to a chair with glowing bindings that joined his arms and legs. The others were hovered behind some type of barrier. Sarik had his eyes closed, his brow furrowed in concentration. Roselyn was crying into Verona's shoulder. Verona's face was a mask of rage and horror at the bloody mess before him. The shadow of the Elitesmen hovered just beyond the barrier.

Hold on, help is coming.

Aaron turned off the comms device and tightened his grip on his staff, and the runes flared. He summoned the energy into himself and launched to the rooftop of the nearest building. Aaron turned to the tallest building closest to him and leaped onto the flying buttress, easily a hundred feet from where he now stood. He squatted down, taking in the view of the city. A gentle breeze pulled lazily at his black cloak. Far to the south, a billowing column of smoke rose into the air, soon joined by others throughout the city. The Resistance comprised of the fragmented remnants of the De'anjard were doing their job well. He heard the pops of explosions, followed by more columns of smoke, and alarm bells echoed in the distance.

Aaron faced the great black towers of the Citadel of the Elite, yearning to head straight there, but he knew his role in the plan. They expected him at the arena, and he would not disappoint. Aaron pulled up the drone's map in his mind. He knew of the tunnel network that ran between the arena and the Citadel. The High King's palace was not connected. He drew in more of the energy around him and felt the medallion grow warm on his chest. He leaped to the very top of the tower and faced the arena, which was still a good distance away. Aaron glanced back at the dark towers of the Elite, knowing where the crystal charging station was and with it, his best chance at securing the needed travel crystals. He released the breath he had been holding and strengthened his body, then leaped toward the arena. The wind roared passed his ears, and he used the particles in the air to push him farther along than any jump had the right to go. His cloak flapped behind him like a cape, and he landed within a stone's throw of the arena. He took a direct path, not caring at this point if anyone saw him. By now the others would be making their way to one of the service entrances to the Citadel to free his friends.

Aaron leaped again and landed upon the top of the arena wall, much to the ignorance of the people below. The twin suns were beginning to set, and their flared brilliance had long settled into a deep crimson that bathed the city in a reddish hue. He settled down to wait and watched as the arena was filling with occupants.

MACTAR KEPT CLENCHING AND UNCLENCHING HIS FISTS IN A VAIN ATTEMPT to ignore the growing unrest at Tarimus's abrupt appearance. Tarimus had become an unknown quantity, as no one had ever been shifted out of phase between realms for this long. He truly had dwelt between the crossroads of the soul, and it was troubling to know that he was free. He had subverted Tarimus to his will before, and knew that Tarimus would be seeking retribution for his imprisonment. Part of him relished in the challenge of facing Tarimus much like what Aaron Jace was proving to be. Mactar's brow furrowed in concentration as his mind tumbled through the possibilities. Tarimus had been different since his first encounter with Reymius's heir. It was subtle at first, but now as his mind worked backwards with the benefit of hindsight, he saw a pattern that had been hidden before. Aaron had the power to free Tarimus, but what would make him do so? A woman crossed his vision with a swath of golden hair partially hidden in a hood, and the thought struck him like lightning.

Sarah!

What wouldn't someone do for the one they love? Not that he harbored any such attachments. Knowledge and power were what he cared about, that and the thrill of toying with kingdoms while they squabbled and cast their fearful gaze toward the High King. As if the mighty High King Amorak could have accomplished so much without the likes of him. The High King was simply a means to an end for his otherworldly allies. Mactar's thoughts drifted back to Sarah. Primus had tried to kill her and paid the ultimate price. The fool was no match for her. The only way he could have killed her was to come from behind. Not all the pieces fit together because he didn't fully understand how Tarimus came into play, but there was a connection there. He was sure of it even if he didn't know how. Mactar's gaze swept through the arena and momentarily settled upon Rordan's back, who stood a short way off studying the field. The death of his twin brother had shaken the young prince to his core. As if sensing his thoughts, the prince looked at him, and Mactar gestured for him to come over. The sun was setting, and the rite of the initiates was about to begin.

Rordan came silently to Mactar's side and took the seat next to him. It was a mark of the changes in the young man that he kept silent, rather than filling the air with idle chatter. The grounds of the arena were already set with the course that the new initiates of the Elite would have to navigate. The arena held traps for the unwary as well as hidden caches of weapons and other useful items. The arrangement of debris formed a complex maze with enough corners and dead ends to challenge the young recruits. The center held a wide expanse of open ground where the strongest of recruits would gather. There were many levels of recruits to be tested, from those who had been taken from their homes this very week to initiates who had embraced the order but had not been promoted to full Elitesmen. It had been some time since he had attended one of these events. They were often beautiful in their brutality. One could see what a person was truly made of when stripped away of the preconceptions of civilization. People would conform to a natural hierarchy, giving in to their need to be told what to do, and the illusion of freedom was often enough to satisfy most.

Elite Grand Master Gerric appeared at the podium in a flash of light. Quite theatrical, Gerric never missed an opportunity to convey the power of the

Elitesmen. The crowd came to a hush almost instantly, and Gerric raised his hands.

"Bring out the hopefuls," the Elite Grand Master said.

Across the arena, doors opened and a procession entered gathering just inside the entrance. Mactar looked on, keeping the lack of enthusiasm from his face. The new recruits, not more than children in their own right, would be fodder for the more experienced initiates. The practice kept the Elitesmen strong, as the weak would never survive very long in their midst. Only the strong and the cunning would prosper. The only reason he was here was to meet with Darven, who had so far not seen fit to show himself.

"There seems to be more people than usual," commented Rordan.

Mactar glanced at the crowd. The prince had a point. "Perhaps they expect quite a show."

Rordan nodded but said nothing.

"You're rather quiet this evening, my lord," Mactar said.

He watched as Rordan kept his eyes on the arena's occupants. "I'm here, as is required of me."

"Indeed," Mactar said. "Sometimes true insight can be gleaned even if we are in a place we'd rather not be."

"You're speaking in riddles again," came Rordan's terse reply. "Fine, I'll indulge your game. What insights am I about to glean by watching the slaughter of the new recruits?"

While Rordan was more of a leader than his late brother, Primus, he was the more squeamish of the two.

"Patience and maybe we'll both learn something," Mactar replied.

Rordan turned and glanced up, about to reply, and frowned. Mactar looked behind him but didn't see anything out of the ordinary.

"What is it?" Mactar asked.

"I thought I saw something," Rordan said. "I smell a lot of smoke in the air. Do you?"

Mactar sniffed the air and could detect traces of smoke. "A bit, but not enough to concern me. You saw something?"

Rordan's gaze grew distant before replying. "Nothing worth mentioning," he said and turned back to the arena.

Elite Master Gerric brought up his hands again. "Bring out the initiates."

The doors off to the opposite side of the arena opened, and a small group of initiates walked into the arena. The elder recruits melted into the shadows, allowing the new group of initiates to enter.

"Initiates," Gerric said, "welcome to the proving grounds. This is your one chance to demonstrate your worthiness to join the ranks of the Elitesmen. Each of you was invited because of your potential to rise above all others, but that is not a destiny for all, as there is a price that must be paid. Hidden throughout the arena are these white crystals," the Elite Master said, holding a glowing white crystal above them. "Find them, and you survive to the next round. Failure is never tolerated as an Elitesmen."

"I only sense that about half of the initiates have any potential to tap into the energy," Rordan said.

Mactar raised an eyebrow. "They mix the groups. Some may have actual potential and others ... They serve a purpose. Some things can only be awakened through conflict. What would you change? Do not pretend to be so squeamish. I've seen what you've done to people who cross your path."

The young prince narrowed his gaze. "Things change."

Intriguing, Mactar thought. The prince was taking a fresh look at everything he had taken for granted before, but he still sensed something off about the prince just below the surface. He didn't say anything else but glanced around, looking for Darven.

AARON CROUCHED ABOVE, WATCHING AS THE SMALL GROUP OF CHILDREN moved into the arena. He couldn't believe what he was seeing. He had listened to the announcer and heard the undercurrents of what had not been said. Survival was only guaranteed for those able to find the white crystals. He wondered how many of them there were until the cunning brutality of the events about to take place dawned on him as the last rays of the setting sun faded.

"You stand upon a crossroads." The Elitesman's voice echoed throughout the arena, and Aaron could hear him perfectly. "One of the core tenets of the code of the Elite is to sever all ties from your previous life. Tonight, we will help you do that."

The Elitesman gestured, and glowing orbs ignited, revealing a group of older citizens in twelve individual cages. The initiates turned, and some cried out, reaching toward the cages. Aaron's heart thundered in his chest, and his jaw clenched as he realized what the Elitesmen had done.

"I believe you are familiar with the people locked in these cages," the Elitesman said. "Retrieve the white crystals and bring them back to your loved one's cage, and all will be well. Fail to retrieve the crystals in time, and they will die." The Elitesmen paused for a moment. "There are only six crystals in the arena."

Aaron brought the rune-carved staff to his forehead and closed his eyes for a moment. He couldn't risk contacting Braden through the comms device and had to assume they were close enough to sneak into the Citadel by now. He could wait no longer and be a witness to the imminent slaughter of the children and their families. Even the ones who would survive this test would lose part of themselves, and that he couldn't sit idly by and watch.

The runes along the staff pulsed to life as he gathered the energy around him. Aaron looked behind him at the sprawl of the city. The pieces were in place. He saw the smoke of the fires emanating from key locations, and any minute they would gain the notice of the guardsmen.

Aaron stood poised atop of the arena wall and watched as some of its occupants looked in his direction, noticing the glow of the staff. He launched into the air, the glowing runes of his staff streaking across the sky, and then he landed upon the arena grounds.

"It's him," Rordan gasped, echoing Mactar's thoughts.

"He is here," Rordan said, rising from his seat. "The Alenzar'seth is here."

Off to the side, Mactar glimpsed a pale white head and heard the mirthless laughter of Tarimus.

The Alenzar'seth will plunge your world into a flaming pit of Hell, Mactar! Tarimus's voice hissed behind him. Mactar twisted around ready to attack, but again there was nothing.

"What's wrong with you?" Rordan asked. "Shouldn't we— "

"We should be patient. Let the Elitesmen cast themselves against the Heir of Shandara. A smart man attacks at a time of his own choosing."

Aaron dashed toward the cages, looking for a way to unlock them. The top of each cage held a ceiling of spikes that could at any moment drop and kill the prisoners.

"Leave us. Get the children out of here," a man said from inside the nearest cage.

Aaron was joined by the initiates, none of whom looked more than twelve years of age. He circled the closest cage, looking for a way to stop the spiked ceilings from closing. Everything was enclosed except for the bars.

Bursts of lights surrounded the group as the black-clad Elitesmen appeared. The initiates had spread out to each of the cage fronts, trying in vain to pull the doors open.

The people in the cages screamed for the children to run. Aaron spun around to face the enclosing Elitesmen, stunned by the fact that he couldn't save the people in the cages.

Aaron summoned the energy into the staff and swept outwards, sending out a burst of air that blew back the approaching Elitesmen. A lone silver-clad Elitesman leaped to the top of the cages. Aaron hurled himself at him, and the Elitesman launched himself back behind the black-clad Elitesmen.

"People of Khamearra," Aaron's voice boomed across the arena. "I am Aaron Jace, the last surviving member of the house Alenzar'seth. The Lords of Shandara have returned to Safanar. I am not your enemy. I fight the tyranny of the Elitesmen that hold you under their boot!" Aaron planted the rune-carved staff into the ground. A beacon of light surged from the staff, piercing the night sky in a column of pure white.

A deafening clang came from one of the cages. The spiked ceiling had slammed down, killing the prisoners inside. The mechanisms controlling the spikes of the remaining cages shook all at once, and on instinct, Aaron thrust his hands out, summoning the energy around him, wedging the gearing in place. It took all his concentration to prevent the spikes from falling, leaving his back exposed to the Elitesmen behind him.

The gates nearest to them burst open, and grizzly armed men poured through. If he didn't let the spikes go, he would die. The men rushed past him, screaming their battle cry.

"De'anjard! Shields of Shandara!"

Ordinary soldiers were no match for the Elitesmen, but still they poured forth, coming to their aid. The soldiers separated, some stopping at the cages to free the prisoners and the rest forming a line behind Aaron's back. He cringed inwardly as the first of the soldiers died by his side, unable to defend themselves from the blazing orbs being flung by the Elitesmen, but still they came, buying him and the prisoners time with their lives.

As the soldiers freed the last of the prisoners, Aaron turned to the children. "Run for the exit!"

He released his hold, and the spiked ceilings slammed down to empty cages. Aaron howled in rage for the men dying around him and drew his Falcons, releasing a few notes of the bladesong out into the air.

He moved with blurring speed, charging after the surrounding Elitesmen and wielding the Falcons as he went. Aaron thrust himself into the nearest throng, unleashing the bladesong into the night. At one time, the Elitesmen seemed like a mighty foe, but the ones he now faced were nothing more than an annoyance. The bladesong was his window into untapped knowledge that flowed freely from his soul. The black-clad Elitesmen were merely an obstacle that stood between himself and the silver-clad Elitesman. He moved through them with ruthless abandon, taking them out in droves until he was surrounded by their bodies. None quit the field or ran away. Elitesmen would always choose death over surrender. The silver-clad Elitesman smiled coldly at him before vanishing in the light of the travel crystal.

The surviving solders regarded him in awe, as some brought their fists across their hearts in salute.

"*Ferasdiam Marked,*" was whispered throughout the arena.

Aaron returned the salute. "Run. Go back into the city. Do not throw your lives away. You've helped the children escape. The spirit of Shandara lives on in you. "

More flashes of light emerged around him, and a cold wind blew as the ground rumbled beneath his feet. Eight silver-clad Elitesmen appeared with smoldering red eyes glowering beneath their hooded cloaks. They did not charge, but merely waited. Aaron felt the medallion grow cool against his chest. The bladesong blazed within, surging the energy through him, but he felt something reaching to him.

He was snatched by an unseen force that launched him into the air and slammed him into the ground, drawing him closer into their midst. The medallion grew frigidly cold, almost burning his skin.

"This one is protected," one hissed.

Aaron scrambled to his feet and lashed out with his blades, but his attacks were blocked.

As one, the silver-clad Elitesmen pushed out with their hands, and Aaron leaped into the air as separate bolts of energy singed the area he had been a moment before. He swept his blades out before him, solidifying the particles in the air, and sent them racing into the Elitesmen, startling a few. As he brought up his blades to ward off another blast of energy, he felt his legs sweep out from underneath him. Aaron moved through the sweep, rolling out of the way, and came to his feet. Tendrils of energy latched onto his wrists, attempting to hold him in place. He focused the energy within and, augmenting his strength, pulled several Elitesmen off balance. He dashed forward around another Elitesman who went down to his knees, writhing in pain as his body split open in a hiss. Aaron could spare no more than a glance and was away before he could give any thought to an Elitesman killing one of his own.

He summoned the energy, leaped into the air, and was followed by another Elitesman streaking silver with his sword drawn.

These silver-clad Elitesmen were different from the ones he had faced before. More powerful. A column of flame blazed in the sky around him, and Aaron pushed himself along the air, skating safely out of the way. He landed hard upon the ground, and the crystals in the Falcons blazed white. In a battle such as this, movement was life. With the power of the bladesong, Aaron moved at speeds too fast for the eye to track and then stopped between the Elitesmen, bringing his Falcons to bear. As the silver-clad Elitesmen moved in, he was slowly being overrun.

The notes of the bladesong pierced the air, and all around him glowed white as one voice emerged from all the voices of ancient souls. Aaron pulled the currents of energy from the staff, and a shaft of white light shot forth into the medallion, burning through his shirt. The crystal in the medallion blazed then shot forth the Alenzar'seth family symbol into the night sky. In the heart of Khamearra, home to the High King and the Elite Order, the Shandarian coat of arms of a dragon cradling a single rose blazed upon the night sky for all to see.

A mighty roar streaked through the arena, and the ground behind Aaron thundered and shook, almost sending him off balance.

"*We heed your call, Safanarion.*"

A voice like granite slabs chafing together spoke behind him. The light of his staff reflected off the golden hide of a dragon and washed all in the arena in sparkling brilliance.

The silver-clad Elitesmen hurled orbs of energy, and the dragon exhaled a barrier in front of Aaron, absorbing the orbs. The dragon bounded forth into the midst of the Elitesmen, scattering them, although they regrouped almost immediately. The roar of the dragon shook the ground beneath Aaron's feet, and he charged forward with the Falcons dragging in his wake.

Aaron launched into the air, engaging the Elitesmen, and the ring of the blades echoed throughout the arena. He felt a whoosh of air as the dragon swept out with its tail, pulling him out of the way as it exhaled a blast of energy. The arena lit up as if in the noonday sun, and the rest Elitesmen were caught in the blast and disappeared. The dragon turned its massive head and regarded Aaron with eyes that sparkled of starlight.

"We of the Eldarin honor the one who is marked by Ferasdiam. Seek us out as our numbers are few and there are things you must know."

The dragon launched itself into the air, moving at speeds beyond that of any beast.

The Eldarin? Aaron wondered as he retrieved the rune-carved staff. The beacon that bathed the arena in light before was now gone. The remaining people in the arena were still scattering, trying to get away. Aaron turned to the dark towers of the Citadel looming to the west and launched himself into the air, leaving the silent arena behind.

Had the dragon sought him out, heeding his call? He landed upon the towered walls of the Citadel of the Elite, putting much distance between himself and the arena. He hoped the soldiers of the Resistance had escaped, and his heart ached for the men who died trying to protect him. He released his hold upon the bladesong, and his strength left him, almost bringing him to his knees.

Aaron took a few moments to catch his breath and centered himself, drawing in the energy from the rune-carved staff to heal his wounds. He would need to eat to replenish what his body demanded now, but he could still function. The lack of sleep was catching up with him. His battle with the silver-clad Elitesmen had left him unsettled. They must be the specialist class of the Order that Isaac had referred to and the ones Sarah had hinted about on board the Raven. The thought of Sarah sent a momentary pang to the pit of his stomach, and it took all his will not to reach across the ever-present connection he had with her. He banished his pain and focused on what he must do next, closing the distance to the Citadel of the Elite.

16

DENIAL AND ESCAPE

The air stank of blood and excrement, piercing the confines of his nose. The shield that Verona and Sarik had created held against the Elitesmen's attacks, but did not block the air they breathed. They could do nothing for the man the Elitesman Sevan had tortured before them without a hint of mercy. The brutal efficiency with which the Elitesman had taken to the task had shaken him to his core. The Elitesmen saw people as tools to achieve their own ends, and when one tool broke, another would simply take its place, and the cycle would begin again. The fact that he had killed another human being barely registered with the exception of the effect it had upon him and the others.

Verona's hateful gaze lifted and sought out the Elitesman torturer. The bonds of energy were enough to keep Gavril in place, who had long since given up struggling against them. As they each tried to deny the Elitesman Sevan in their own way, he took pleasure in their failings with fiendish delight. The stalemate they were in left them firmly within the Elitesman's power, and Verona wasn't sure how much longer they could hold out. The screams of the tortured man still echoed in his mind.

"I know you want to kill me," Sevan taunted.

Verona looked away, disgusted, refusing to rise to anymore of the Elitesman's taunts. Instead, his eyes found a momentary respite from this very real version of Hell in Roselyn's golden eyes, so much like his own, but with irises like the sun. They mirrored both the pain and bitterness they felt at the Elitesman's brutality, but Verona could tell that her will was eroding, as was his own. He couldn't sit idly by and watch another person be tortured. Something had to give.

The gruesome remains littered the floor at the Elitesman's feet, and Sevan brusquely kicked them aside, making room, seemingly unfazed that they had once been a person.

"Almost time for our next guest." Sevan grinned and motioned to the Elitesmen by the door.

A hunched old woman limped through the doorway, stumbling as if she couldn't see very well. The old woman stepped into the light, and her eyes shone milky white with only hints of the colored irises that should have been there.

The Elitesman Sevan stood stone still in the shadows, his bloodstained hands resting comfortably upon the edges of his shirt over his chest. Sevan's hands shifted slightly while he watched with a dark, menacing gaze as the old woman stumbled over the dead body of the servant. The lighting in the room grew dimmer around them.

Roselyn cried out, and Verona's breath caught in his chest.

"I can't do this again," Verona whispered to Roselyn.

Roselyn turned toward him, her mouth slightly opened, but no words would come forth.

"I'm sorry," Verona whispered.

"It's all right," Roselyn whispered back to him.

Verona steeled himself, coming to grips with what he must do. If he were to meet his end then so be it, but he would be damned if he would be witness to another tortured innocent for an Order that deserved to burn in Hell for all eternity.

Verona looked back at Roselyn and brought his hand to her cheek, brushing away a silky lock of her raven hair. "We've had no time, my lady," he whispered in a voice that echoed the cracks in his broken heart for what would never be.

Roselyn blinked away her tears and brought her hand to Verona's shoulder, gazing into his eyes. In one swift motion, Verona pulled her in and kissed her lips, feeling the press of her body upon his own. For the span of time between moments, he knew true happiness. The elation blazed along every fiber and yearned for more, but it was not to be. He pulled away and met Sarik's knowing gaze.

The hunched old lady stood in the center of the room, calling out, "Is anyone there, my lord? They told me I was needed here." The woman turned about and stumbled. "I apologize, I don't see very well anymore."

The Elitesman Sevan stood behind her with his challenging gaze, daring Verona to act. In the back of the room, the other Elitesmen's attention drew toward the windows for a moment before looking back at them.

Verona focused himself, drawing the energy in while pulling away from the shield they had created, and Sarik did the same.

Sevan stood poised, his hand raised, clutching a large knife whose edge glinted in the dimly lit room. The old woman spun around completely, looking relieved to see the Elitesman.

"Thank you, my lord. Do you need me to help clean up? I would be happy to do that for you, my lord, but please, I could do with some more light," the old woman said and shuffled toward the windows.

The Elitesman's contemptuous gaze swept the three of them. "There is no hope for you. Your friends will never be able to get to you here."

Verona's heightened senses saw as the blade began its descent. At the same moment, he let the shield go and thrust outward, pushing with all his might, sending a shaft of energy that erupted from his outstretched hand. The Elitesman was knocked backwards off his feet.

The window's wooden shutters burst forth with a blinding white light that blazed from a distance into the night sky, startling them all. The room was still for a moment, and Verona stood with his mouth agape, staring at the Alenzar'seth coat of arms emblazoned upon the night sky.

Aaron!

Verona launched himself across the room and grabbed a ragged spike from the table. His eyes never left the Elitesman as he charged, feeling the energy burn inside as the room blurred around him. He planted the spike into the chest of the Elitesman Sevan.

Two flashes of golden light lit up the room, and the two Elitesmen at the door fell in a heap. Verona turned from his crouch over the dying Elitesman to see that Gavril was free and held some kind of device out from his hands. Sarik and Roselyn were at his side.

Verona turned back to the dying Elitesman who glared back with a crazed loathing as blood frothed in his mouth. Verona grabbed the Elitesman by the shirt and twisted the spike in his chest, growling as he did. The Elitesman cried out in pain.

"I can never hurt you enough, Elitesman," Verona hissed.

"You think you're free," the Elitesman said, spitting up blood. "You will never be free of me. I will haunt your dreams long after I'm gone." The Elitesman's words ended in a gurgled sigh, and his face froze with hatred as the life drained out of him.

DESPITE HIMSELF, MACTAR WATCHED AS THE BATTLE IN THE ARENA unfolded before him. The Alenzar'seth's strength was growing in leaps and bounds. He would soon be a match for the High King, if he wasn't already. The patrons that were not scrambling to leave gasped and cried out as a mighty roar thundered over their heads. The arena was bathed in the golden brilliance of the biggest dragon he had ever seen, appearing as if by magic after the beacon of Shandara pierced the night.

An Eldarin dragon?

Mactar's mind struggled with the truth appearing before his eyes. What trickery was this? The dragons were all but gone from Safanar. The beacon of Shandara blazed through the night sky and then melted away, taking him back all those years ago to the very night that Shandara fell. The great city burned with an unquenchable fire that spread hungrily, devouring anything in its path. The night echoed of countless voices crying out, trapped amid the flames. There had been no beacon then, nor answering call. *This must be a trick.*

His gaze fell once again upon Aaron, who retrieved his staff as the dragon scattered the witless Elitesmen into disarray. Clearly, the Elitesmen believed a dragon was in their midst. Could it be? He dismissed the thought as soon as it occurred. No one had the ability to summon dragons. Rordan stood poised with his hand clenched upon the hilt of his sword. Mactar looked back at Reymius's heir, who was now facing the Eldarin, and something unspoken appeared to pass between them before they both went their separate ways.

Rordan turned to him and said, "He can speak with dragons?"

Mactar shook his head. "This is a trick. The Eldarin dragons are all gone. They have faded into myth."

"*Deny the truth at your own folly, Mactar,*" the voice of Tarimus hissed faintly.

Darven appeared by his side. "my lord."

Mactar narrowed his gaze at the appearance of Darven, taking it in before asking any questions. His appearance was unkempt and his cloak in tatters.

"How did you find him in the city?" Mactar asked.

"Who?" Rordan asked and then said, "You knew the Alenzar'seth was in the city?"

Darven nodded. "Quite by accident, I assure you. It took every shred of knowledge I had to elude him and quite a bit of luck, I'm afraid. He's more acutely in tune with the binding forces around us. It is like nothing I've ever seen. I managed to send word to Gerric shortly before nightfall, hence the appearance of so many Elitesmen."

Mactar nodded. "You've done well. We will be leaving soon."

Rordan's mouth hung open. "Leaving? You can't leave."

Mactar's mouth lifted into a mirthless grin. "I'm quite certain I can leave, my lord Prince."

"Aren't you going to go after him?" Rordan asked.

"What for? He's not after me. At least not yet, and I have pressing business elsewhere. Surely, the Elitesmen will be able to handle one lone Shandarian," Mactar said, somewhat aloof, and nodded for Darven to follow.

"I think you're wrong," Rordan said. "I'm going after him. There must be a reason why he's here in Khamearra, and I intend to find out what it is."

Mactar nodded. "That you should, my lord."

Rordan stalked off into the fleeing crowd, and Mactar wondered if he would ever see the young prince alive again. Should Rordan throw himself at Aaron, Mactar knew who would receive the shorter end of that particular stick.

"We're really not going after Aaron?" Darven asked.

"I would like to know why he's here," Mactar said, "but at the same time I'm happy for the Elitesmen and the High King to contend with him for the moment. If Aaron is preoccupied here, then others will be slower to rally to his call, and we need some time to help us prepare." The advantage of controlling the Ryakuls was too much of an opportunity to pass up and would give him something else to leverage against whoever rallied to the fallen Shandara banner.

A HAND GENTLY PRESSED UPON HIS SHOULDER, AND ONLY WHEN VERONA turned around did he realize that he was still gripping the spike in the dead

Elitesman's chest. He unclenched his grip, and Roselyn pulled him to his feet. They searched the bodies of the Elitesmen, taking what weapons they could.

The beacon winked out, drawing their attention to the windows.

"That was Aaron," Sarik said. "Do you think he—"

"No," Verona said quickly.

Gavril walked over to the window. "Look at the city."

They were high up in one of the towers within the Citadel of the Elite. The orange glow of fires could be seen throughout the city. The blaze seemed to be concentrated at key locations and not spreading to the other buildings. A thunderous sound rocked the ground beneath their feet, and the sky lit up near them in a blaze of angry red flames.

"That was close," Verona said.

"That was Tanneth." Gavril smiled grimly and went to the table to retrieve the comms device that the Elitesmen had taken earlier. "They are coming. We should head out. Tanneth has more surprises in store for the Elitesmen," Gavril said while his eyes darted across the small screen.

Verona nodded. "Let's go," he said and motioned for Sarik to guide the old woman, who was muttering to herself.

Together, they emerged into an empty hallway, and Verona grabbed one of the orbs and threw it on the ground, setting the room ablaze. Verona took point. They heard men shouting throughout the tower and moved cautiously down the hall. Verona kept the Elitesman's blade ready, but he itched to be rid of it, not wanting the taint of anything to do with the Elitesman Sevan to touch his skin.

You will never be free of me.

Verona banished the Elitesman's last words from his mind and moved forward. They came to a stairwell and stopped when they heard a commotion below them. The ring of steel upon steel could be heard, and Verona's pace quickened when he heard Braden's De'anjard battle cry.

Verona and the others took the steps two at a time until they came to an open landing where they found Braden swinging a large steel hammer in one hand and the shield of the De'anjard in the other. Braden fought with two other men. One of whom he recognized as the district captain they had spied upon earlier. The other man he didn't recognize at all.

Gavril unleashed more blasts of energy from the device in his hand, felling more Elitesmen and earning him wary glances from Braden and the others.

"Braden!" Verona called.

Braden smiled in greeting, but Verona noted that the smile did not reach his eyes.

"Verona, all of you? Good," Braden said. "We were having a hell of a time reaching you."

"You keep strange company these days," Verona said, nodding to the other two men, but his eyes never left the older man with the long leather duster. His eyes widened as he felt the traces of energy gathering around the older man. An Elitesman was helping them?

"Desperate times," Braden answered his questioning gaze. "Come, I'll fill you in on the way."

"Where is Aaron?" Verona asked, following Braden and his two Khamearrian escorts.

"Where do you think?" Braden snorted. "Where he can cause the most commotion. He is the reason why the towers are so empty."

Verona nodded. "What is the plan?"

Braden nodded toward Captain Nolan.

"We're going to get away from here and hide out with the underground Resistance here in the city," Captain Nolan said. "I'm Nolan, by the way."

"You have my sincerest gratitude for coming to our aid," Verona said and then he introduced himself and the others.

"We need to move," the old Elitesman barked from farther down the staircase.

"That one is called Isaac," Braden said.

"Will Aaron be meeting us?" Verona asked, catching up with Isaac.

Braden's answer was interrupted as a group of shadows appeared on the staircase. A young group of initiates burst into the staircase, looking startled to see them. They couldn't have been beyond their mid-teen years. Some of their eyes narrowed suspiciously while most looked on nervously.

Before any of them could do anything, Isaac stepped forward.

"Initiates," Isaac's voice spoke with authority. "Where are you heading?"

The group of boys traded glances with one another before one stepped forward.

"Speak quickly, boy," Isaac said.

"My Lord of the Elite," the boy said. "The alarms have sounded. We're to evacuate the tower immediately."

Isaac nodded as if what the boy said was obvious. "Well, don't let us keep you. Move along."

The boy looked as if he were about to say something else then shrugged his shoulders, nodded to the others, and left.

As the staircase filled with people, Isaac led them away down one of the less crowded corridors. Verona glanced at Gavril, who studied the comms device and nodded back to him. He glanced out of a passing window and saw the arena in the distance. It had grown dark and quiet, and Verona hoped that his friend had not bitten off more than he could chew. A soft hand slipped into his, and Verona turned to see Roselyn behind him. For once, he was thankful that in this moment he didn't have to say anything. The message in her eyes was obvious, even to him. Somewhere in the midst of this nightmare he had earned the attention of his beautiful Hythariam Princess. He knew the Hythariam didn't have princesses, but Roselyn could be nothing else to him, except possibly the queen of his heart.

They came through a small doorway, and the cool night air washed over them. Perhaps there was hope for them after all.

17

THE TOWER

Aaron quietly circled the towers of the Elite. He had checked the comms device earlier and, judging from the video feeds, knew that his friends were safe. As safe as they could be given that they were escaping from the home of the Elite. The Citadel grounds weren't nearly as populated now as they had been when last he checked. No doubt his own efforts at the arena had proven tempting enough to draw them out. He crept along and headed for the tower where the travel crystals were being charged. He drew in the energy from around him and cast it out to see if he could detect anyone nearby. He tensed up, sensing an approaching presence behind him.

Aaron leaped down from the wall, landing within the confines of the Citadel. People were still pouring out of the tower entrances farthest from him, but where he stood all was dark and quiet. He was torn between moving on and waiting to see who was trying to follow him. He squatted down, deciding that a few moments' caution was a far lesser risk than having someone follow him inside the tower.

The silhouette of a cloaked figure appeared on the Citadel walls and scanned the area. After a few seconds, the figure dropped down to the ground about twenty yards from where Aaron was hiding. The man stopped abruptly and stood up from his crouched position, then he walked purposefully into the moonlight.

"I know you're there," he said.

Aaron stared at the man standing in the moonlight. "No princely titles this time?" Aaron asked, stepping into the light.

They stood twenty feet apart, and even in the shadows Aaron sensed the barrage of emotions roiling through the young prince, the most prevalent one being fear.

Aaron watched as Sarah's brother stood before him, his hands itching to draw the sword at his hip, but clearly unable to decide what to do. For Sarah, he would give Rordan this one chance at reason. "I'm not here for you, Rordan. I'm here for Sarah."

"The last I saw of my sister she was with you," Rordan said.

Aaron leveled his gaze at the young prince. "She is not here with me."

Rordan drew his sword, holding it loosely by his side, and circled around, but Aaron kept his distance. He sensed the energy gathering around Rordan as it would any of the Elitesmen he faced.

"We don't have to do this," Aaron said, keeping his staff ready in case Rordan attacked. "We don't have to be enemies."

"You killed my brother," Rordan said, his voice shaking.

"After he stabbed Sarah in the back with his sword," Aaron countered. "Primus got what he deserved."

Rordan growled as he charged, flailing wildly with his sword. Aaron calmly sidestepped out of the way, but kept his staff ready. The young prince attacked again, but Aaron didn't engage. Rordan was only a few years his junior, but his world had been stripped raw, and Aaron could sympathize with that. To a point, at least.

"Fight me!" Rordan shouted and swung his sword again.

The bladesong hummed within Aaron, but he needed no focus to avoid the pitiful attacks from the prince.

Rordan stumbled and regained his feet. "Why won't you fight me?" he gasped.

"Because she wouldn't want me to," Aaron answered. "That is the only thing that stays my hand."

"Sarah?" Rordan sank to his knees with his shoulders slumped. "She cares nothing for me."

"No, you are wrong," Aaron said. "It is Mactar who cares nothing for you. Tell me, where is he?"

Rordan frowned. "He is not coming. He believes the Elitesmen should be able to handle you."

Aaron took a quick glance around, but there was no one around except for them. "Where is he going?"

Rordan came to his feet, sneering. "Why would I tell you? I can't stand against you, not even with the training of the Elite. But that doesn't mean that I will help you."

Aaron studied Rordan for a moment, debating in his mind what to say. "Then go. You're at a crossroads, and you need to decide what kind of man you wish to become. There is a war coming that will sweep across this land, and if we are to survive then we will need to stand together. You and I don't have to be enemies."

"You intend to raise Shandara from the ashes?" Rordan asked.

Aaron shook his head. "No. There is a threat to this world that none can escape from. The Alenzar'seth have sheltered this world from an invading army. Take a good look around at those in power. Take an honest look at who counsels the High King and then the king himself."

"You mean Mactar," Rordan mumbled.

"Think about what I said." Aaron turned and headed off to the tower. He needed to move on, and he hoped that Rordan would see reason. He rounded the base and jumped into the air, landing on a ledge four stories from the ground. Aaron looked back and saw Rordan standing in the moonlight with his gaze toward the ground. He knew the bonds of family between Sarah and her half-brothers were fragile, but perhaps Rordan would take what he said to heart. Khamearra would be needed to fight the coming war.

Aaron ducked inside the tower to a dark room. He didn't need any heightened senses to tell him that this tower wasn't empty. He came to the door and listened to see if anyone was out in the hall. When he was sure it was empty, he opened the wooden door and stepped through. Even though he had memorized the layout from the probes, there was a difference between what was on screen and actually standing inside the structure. He turned down a corridor and found a group of men heading in his direction. They looked up at him, and in a split second Aaron walked purposefully forward, taking great strides. As he passed them, some bowed their heads at his passing. He didn't take the time to acknowledge for fear that they would call his bluff. Luck had been on his side, as these weren't Elitesmen.

He came to the hollowed interior of the tower where it opened to a great expanse of space. Lighted orbs hung throughout, giving ample light. The place was bigger on the inside than he had imagined, and was made from the dark stone that capped the outside walls.

Aaron was able to continue up several floors without notice, passing people as if he were just another member of the Elitesmen Order. The farther he ventured, the more it grated at his nerves because he knew at any second that they would discover that he was an intruder. It was interesting to see the various faces of the Elitesmen Order. Not all were clouded with the pristine arrogance that had been prevalent with the other members he had encountered. Perhaps there really were factions within the Order of the Elite. Regardless, he had no doubts that the current indifference of the men and women he passed would evaporate if they discovered him. He had to believe that they would stop at nothing to capture him if they knew who he really was. Unless there were more like Isaac, Elitesmen loyal to an older regime.

Aaron was about midway up the tower when he veered off down a corridor and headed toward the room where the crystals were recharged.

"Hold!" a man called out from down the corridor.

Aaron stopped, and his hand reached inside his cloak for one of his throwing knives.

"You there," the man said again, the heavy thud of his boots echoing down the corridor.

Aaron turned slowly, and the Elitesman's eyes narrowed.

"You!" the Elitesman hissed.

Aaron's hand shot forth and sent a throwing knife at blinding speed through the air, which buried itself into the Elitesman's chest. The Elitesman crumpled to the ground, and Aaron fled down the hallway, expecting to hear an alarm at any moment. A few seconds later, a loud explosion from outside the tower shook the entire place down to the floor beneath his feet. Aaron spun and saw a drone hovering in the air along the ceiling. Aaron nodded to the drone and knew Tanneth was keeping watch, but it still bothered him that the interior of the tower held so few guards.

He came to the marked door outside the crystal charging chamber. The door appeared to be made of solid oak with steel bindings. Aaron ran his hands along the door, feeling around the edges. The door had no handles and no visible means of opening it. The door felt solid under his fingertips. He was sure he could get through the door, but was worried about damaging any of the crystals on the other side, not to mention alert whatever was guarding the crystals. Something inside had taken out the drone earlier, and he wasn't going to take any chances. Not when he was so close to getting what he needed to save Sarah.

Aaron reached out with his senses along the door and could almost see the mechanism inside. Only someone like himself or an Elitesman could open this door. He solidified the particles inside the door and forced the gearing to move. The doorway began to swing open. He pushed it the rest of the way with his hands and entered the room.

There was an enormous crystal suspended in midair, pulsating with a glow that lit the area around them in waves. The air felt charged and almost crackled with energy. Aaron felt the edges of the dragon tattoo on his chest prickle, and the runes on the staff glowed dimly. There were crystal deposits throughout the room, pulsing in rhythm with the main crystal. On the far side was a barrel with glowing purple crystals that could only be the travel crystals.

Jackpot!

He stepped inside the room, and the door closed behind him.

Above the giant crystal was a large open shaft that went straight up to the night sky. The shaft was lined with mirrors all the way up. Aaron guessed that the mirrors were used to amplify the light coming from the outside. He moved farther in, cautiously circling the room. There were all types of crystals, some of which he recognized like the yellow ones that stored energy, but most of the others remained a mystery to him. He scanned the room again, which was empty. He stopped before the pile of travel crystals, withdrew his pack, and stuffed them inside.

"So you are here to rob me?" a voice called out.

Aaron spun around, and saw a giant of a man standing to the side of the charging crystal in the center of the room. The pulsating light distorted his features, so Aaron could not get a good look at him. He quickly closed his pack, now stuffed with the precious purple crystals, and stood up.

The man slowly stepped from around the crystals. He wore a black uniform with a silver dragon emblazoned on his chest that appeared more finely made than any guard's uniform. He wore two katanas on his hips. The set of his high cheekbones and shape of his eyes hit Aaron as if he were kicked in the stomach. Unless he was mistaken, the man before him was the High King of Khamearra, the sworn enemy of Shandara, and Sarah's father.

"You have come here for travel crystals?" the High King asked with a slightly amused expression.

Aaron didn't answer, but stood rooted in place. The prickliness along the dragon tattoo on his chest gained in intensity.

The High King regarded him for a moment, rubbing a spot on his arm. "I don't think we've been properly introduced. I am Amorak," the High King said, but his casual tone did not belie the coldness in his eyes.

"You are Reymius's heir I take it," High King Amorak continued.

"Yes," Aaron replied.

"We went through so much trouble to bring you here to my city, and you up and decide to come on your own. How interesting. Yes, quite interesting, indeed," the High King said, circling toward him.

Aaron sensed the waves of energy exude off the High King in a rigid intensity. "Sarah is in danger," Aaron said quickly, scanning for ways to escape.

"Is she now?" the High King replied. "And how did she get that way?"

Aaron frowned, but kept his distance. "The Drake has captured her."

The High King stepped closer, glowering. "How could you let this happen?"

"I didn't let this happen. We were attacked by your Elitesmen, but you already knew that," Aaron snapped.

"In this you are mistaken," the High King said. "You did let this happen. You brought my daughter to Shandara, and the danger she is in is because of her involvement with you. If you had simply returned with my Elitesmen, she would not be in the clutches of the Drake now."

Aaron clenched his jaw shut, but the truth in the High King's words stung him more than he cared to admit. Curse him, but the High King was right. He was the reason that Sarah was in danger. The seeds of doubt that had been loitering beneath his every action began to firmly take root.

You can't protect everyone, my love.

Sarah's voice echoed within him like a golden beacon, sweeping away the twisted hold the High King had upon him.

"You're wrong. Sarah was there by her own choosing. Primus made his choice when he stabbed her in the back, and I made mine when I took his head from his shoulders," Aaron said and then he leaped into the air, skipping up the shaft emerging into the night sky at the top of the tower. The orange glow of the fires that burned throughout the city dotted his view.

"You didn't think it would be that easy," the High King said, startling him and snatched the rune-carved staff, hurling Aaron to the edge of the tower.

Aaron was on his feet instantly and drew his swords. The bladesong blazed inside him.

The High King smiled in delight. "The Blades of the Alenzar'seth. I have not seen their like in such a long time."

The High King tossed the rune-carved staff off to the side and drew his own dark blades. "Tell me, Shandarian, are you ready to face another Ferasdiam Marked?"

"What do you mean?" Aaron asked.

"Did you think you were the only one?" the High King asked. "You and I are the same, and never before have there been two bearing the mark of Ferasdiam in a generation," the High King said, rubbing his arm. At the same time Aaron felt the sting of the dragon tattoo upon his chest.

"You feel it, too," the High King said.

Aaron kept an eye on the High King, trying to think of some way to escape. "Perhaps it's because you didn't fulfill your purpose that another was required. The land sickens and dies, spreading from Shandara because of what you unleashed."

The High King's face twisted into a sneer. "I crushed your pitiful kingdom and watched as the fires consumed the city."

"Only after Tarimus opened the way for you," Aaron said. "You thought you were conquering a nation, but what you really were was a tool, a blunt instrument playing in someone else's game, and you can't even see it. Mactar used you."

This gave the High King pause. "What are you saying?"

"Mactar isn't loyal to you," Aaron replied.

"You tell me nothing that I don't already know," the High King replied.

"It was only by the grace of the Alenzar'seth that this world wasn't overrun by an invading army from another world. An army that almost won its way to this world except for the actions of my grandfather. It was by his actions and sacrifice that you still live."

"You lie!" the High King howled and lunged for Aaron.

He brought up the Falcons, expecting the High King's attack, and as the blades met, the sky lit up as if lightning had struck the tower upon which they fought. The crystals in the Falcons flared brilliantly as Aaron surrendered himself to the bladesong within. Each movement flowed into the next as a river flows from an icy mountaintop. The bladesong echoed off the rooftops of the towers of the Elite as his blades met those of the High King. Aaron sensed his frustration in their deadly dance. The High King was too used to people falling to his blades, and while he fought with the composure of a master, patient and lethal, he did not expect Aaron to be able to stand against him.

Aaron gave over to the movement that is life, and the urgings of past souls lent their wisdom to his blades. The bladesong churned within, and with it came heightened senses, including those connections he had forced himself to keep at arm's length. The connection to Sarah glowed feebly in his mind, getting weaker and not at all vibrant as it once had been. The brief distraction for the barest of moments was all the High King needed, and Aaron paid the price in blood that ran from a wound down his side. They each broke apart, eyeing the other.

"I'm fighting to save your daughter," Aaron pleaded. He needed to get out of here. This fight with the High King would achieve nothing.

The High King laughed. "You say that as if your actions, even on my daughter's behalf, would hold sway with me," the High King said, and then his features darkened as if he were standing in a shadow's embrace. "They do not. She is your weakness and will be your downfall. If she was foolish enough to be caught by the Drake, then you were her downfall as well."

Aaron's stomach clenched as if he had been kicked, and from the pit did the fires of his love for Sarah rise within him. He drew in the energy around him, including that from the rune-carved staff, which flared from the ground behind the High King. Aaron launched into the air, sending a great swath of energy from the arc of his blades, knocking the High King back. Aaron was before the High King in an instant and kicked out with the side of his foot, sending the High King into the air, tumbling away from the tower.

Aaron seized the rune-carved staff and jumped in the opposite direction. As his feet left the tower of the Elite, the fires of an explosion rose from the bottom of the tower. Aaron turned in mid-air and watched as the tower of the Elite collapsed in on itself. Where there were once two dark towers now only one remained.

18

ESCAPE

They emerged from the tower and found the grounds of the Citadel in complete disarray. The old Elitesman Isaac, as good as his word, had delivered them from the tower. The night air was cool and carried the acrid smoke from the fires. Verona's eyes darted around fearing that the Elitesmen would know of their escape, but they were swallowed up with everyone else fleeing the towers.

"Hurry," Gavril said.

Verona nodded. Gavril had whispered to him earlier that Tanneth was watching over their escape. He glanced up at the bright flashes of light from the top of the tower across the grounds. Braden had retracted his Shandarian shield, but kept his hammer out. Verona wondered how Braden had come by the hammer. The Elitesmen were gathering on the far side of the Citadel grounds where most of the order had been restored. Isaac abruptly changed paths, making a line toward the gates nearest to them.

A figure in black appeared before them in a flash of light and was joined by two Elitesmen, their eyes burning red, clad in silver cloaks. Verona recognized the Grand Master of the Elite. His eyes narrowed upon them and flashed in surprise when his gaze fell upon Isaac.

"You!" the Grand Master of the Elite hissed.

"Gerric," Isaac answered.

"You're supposed to be dead," the Grand Master said.

"You've run the order into the ground, Gerric," Isaac said. "I'm here to set things right."

The Grand Master of the Elite snorted in disbelief. "You cannot hope to stand against us."

Isaac laughed. "Maybe not, but I think just knowing that there are former Elitesmen like me that stand against you is enough to rattle even your cages and those of your lap dogs," Isaac said. He plunged his hands into his leather duster then threw something at the ground. There was a small flash then smoke billowed up at the Elitesmen's feet.

Verona grabbed Roselyn's hand and pushed her toward the exit. She was followed by Sarik and Braden. Gavril brought up the rear, firing golden bolts into the smoke. They were joined by Nolan and Isaac. A loud shriek came from behind them, and Isaac drew his sword.

Verona looked back at Isaac then drew his own sword.

"No," Isaac said. "Tell the Shandarian that there are more Elite of the old code who don't hold with these ideals."

"We can fight with you," Verona said.

Isaac looked around at the grounds of the Elite in disgust. There were young initiates running to escape the fires. Some initiates helped their brethren while others used the disarray as an excuse to strike.

"Fight for *them*," Isaac said, gesturing toward the initiates of the Elite, and smoke swallowed him up as he leaped through.

An explosion rocked the ground beneath their feet as the far tower collapsed to the ground.

"Run!" Gavril shouted.

The Citadel gates burst forth as a mass of people fled for their lives. Roselyn's hand found his and gave him a gentle squeeze as they lost themselves in the crowd. They had escaped. Verona glanced back at the Citadel. The smoke and dust that billowed into the air was overshadowed by the screams of those within who hadn't escaped in time.

Captain Nolan guided them through the streets, leading them away from the chaos. Verona had managed to get the attention of the fleeing Initiates who were all too happy to have escaped the Citadel. They were young, barely more than boys and girls, and hadn't been inducted into the Elitesmen Order yet. Nolan sent them onward with some of his guards that they had met up with.

Verona frowned, scanning the faces of the men with them. "Where is Eric?" he asked.

Braden shook his head grimly, which was reply enough.

Verona swallowed the lump in his throat, knowing that Eric had died the night before when they were taken prisoner. He gripped Braden's shoulder firmly and shared the promised look of grim resolution. The destruction around them was a cold recompense for the lives lost, both the nameless innocent and those of friends and brothers. He hated the Elitesmen, but through Isaac's sacrifice he grudgingly admitted to himself that they were not all the same. He hoped that Isaac did find a way to survive his encounter with the Grand Master. Hoping for the survival of any Elitesman still left him with a bitter aftertaste. Too much of what that order had done to the people of this world could not be swept away.

Captain Nolan brought them to an abandoned building where they were met by Anson along with other members of the Resistance. Anson reported a resounding victory with none of their number being captured or killed.

"Has there been any word from Aaron?" Verona asked.

"Not yet, my lord," Lieutenant Anson answered.

Verona nodded. He wanted to be out there looking for his friend, but knew that staying in one place was the wise choice, at least for the moment. "You must prepare for retribution from the High King and the Elitesmen," Verona said.

"We are prepared to fight," Anson said. "The rumor throughout the city is that a dragon appeared at the arena. When your friend crashes a party, he doesn't go halfway."

"I'm still concerned for the Resistance, and if the fight becomes too much, you should head to Rexel," Verona said.

Captain Nolan frowned. "Why Rexel?"

Gavril cleared his throat, joining them. "Please, Verona, allow me to share what we know."

Verona nodded, and Gavril proceeded to tell them of the barrier between worlds in Shandara and the invading army waiting on the other side. Gavril was able to quell most skeptics with a few displays of the Hythariam comms device and a demonstration of something he called a plasma pistol.

"According to Aaron, the barrier between worlds is failing, and it is only a matter of time before the armies of the former Hythariam military pour through," Gavril said. "We had hoped that our home would be destroyed and would take care of the military faction that was bent on conquering the people of Safanar, but they must have found a way to survive."

"Was the beacon of light we had reports on throughout the city from the heir of Alenzar'seth?" someone from the crowd asked.

Verona stepped up. "Yes," he answered.

Captain Nolan and Anson shared a look. "Thank you for telling us these things. I will circulate this information throughout the Resistance here and decide what to do going forward. I can't commit either way. Khamearra has become a home for many of us, and some will be reluctant to leave. What started off as vengeance of the De'anjard has grown into something much more."

Verona nodded in understanding. "Don't take too long, as time is growing short."

Gavril continued to answer questions, and Lieutenant Anson stepped away to check whether Aaron had shown up at any of the designated meeting points they had agreed on earlier.

Somewhere during the discussion, Verona noticed Roselyn sitting off to the side, working intently on a chrome cylinder at a small table. She looked up and smiled at him as he approached. She was still shaken, he could tell, and so was he if truth be told.

"My Lady, you don't waste any time," Verona said.

Roselyn nodded, turning back to the cylinder. "This is something that Aaron asked me to look at."

"What is it?" Verona asked.

"This is what enabled Aaron to travel from Earth to Safanar," Roselyn said.

Verona frowned. Earth was where Aaron had called home until coming to Safanar. His friend had told him of the place, but try as he might, it was difficult to imagine. Looking at the small device in Roselyn's hands, it amazed him that such a thing was possible, even knowing what he knew.

"I'm updating some of its functions," Roselyn said vaguely.

Verona smiled. "Aaron seeks to protect us all, it seems."

Roselyn eyed him with a raised eyebrow. "Do you know what he intends?"

Verona pursed his lips in thought. "Not exactly, but the question really is what wouldn't he do, and I feel the answers lie in that."

Roselyn's eyes narrowed. "Are all men so bullheaded that they must act alone when there are people able to help them?"

Verona shrugged his shoulders. "Sometimes the occasion calls for it," he said and suppressed a smile as she muttered a curse under her breath. "It's okay to take a moment for yourself, my lady."

Roselyn's hands shook as she held the cylinder. "I can't."

Verona sat next to her and put his arm around her shoulders, and she leaned into him, shaking.

"I can't get it out of my head," Roselyn said. "I can't get him out of my head."

Verona gently rubbed her shoulders. He knew exactly what she meant. They were free from the Elitesman Sevan, but the gruesome acts of torture lingered in the back of their minds.

"I know," Verona said. "I… I just…" He couldn't get the words out, and they both took comfort in the other's embrace.

After a few moments, they released each other despite neither of them being able to find the words. Roselyn resumed her work on the chrome cylinder, which she called the keystone accelerator, and Verona stayed by her side. They were soon joined by the others, although Braden sat off to the side, keeping careful watch even though they were with the Resistance. Within an hour, Anson brought word that they had found Aaron. They gathered their things and set off, heading for another hideout to meet up with their friend. Verona just wanted to leave, putting as much distance between himself and the capital city of Khamearra as possible. He fully supported their reasons for being here, but at the same time he wanted it to just be over.

Captain Nolan supplied them with cloaks and uniforms of the guards so they could move throughout the city more easily. That was the plan, anyway. Verona replaced his sword. He was only too happy to be rid of the Elitesman's blade he was carrying. Both he and Sarik carried bows and a full quiver of arrows. He still didn't see Tanneth, but Gavril assured him that the Hythariam was still out there and would help watch over them as they traversed the city.

Aaron rested upon the rooftop of a shop in the district's market square. The remaining tower of the Citadel of the Elite was a good distance behind him. Things were quiet for the moment, and the smell of smoke was thinning. The wound on his side ached, and he bit back a groan as he removed his cloak and shirt. He scooped some water from a metal bucket on the rooftop and washed the sword slice down his side. The wound was deep, and Aaron worked to steady his breathing, allowing his mind to focus. He reached out to the energy in the staff, and the runes flared dully. He drew it in, speeding up what his body would do naturally if he had been stitched up and bedridden for weeks. The pain faded to a dull ache until the angry pink scar faded away on his skin. He had been lucky. One lesson he learned from his encounter with the Ryakul was that the ability to concentrate and focus was essential when working with the energy. If he couldn't focus then he would die just like anyone else. He rolled his shoulders, remembering the hot pain down his back as the Ryakuls tore at his flesh. He shook off the memory and put his shirt back on as he took in his surroundings. He was looking for a small shop with the emblem of a tree with clawed roots carved into the door. The subtle references to Shandara that could be found throughout the city of Khamearra amazed him. The Resistance had used pieces from the Alenzar'seth coat of arms as their markings throughout the city. Nothing so bold as the complete picture, but pieces that were just enough to give those who knew what to look for the information they sought to find the Resistance. It was the arrogance of the Elitesmen that allowed for their enemy to dwell among them. Aaron wondered if the irony would be lost upon them as perhaps arrogance played its part in the destruction of Shandara.

Aaron's mind drifted to a history class he had in college, where the teacher pontificated that a smart enemy would strike where you thought you were safe. Mactar and the High King had used this tactic to bring about the destruction of Shandara and here Aaron was, instrumental in doing the same to the Elitesmen Order. He knew the Elite Order was not destroyed, but tonight's events had certainly put them off balance just as the High King had put him off balance. His jaw clenched at the High King's dismissal of his daughter, but his mind refused to accept that a father could so easily disregard that their child was in danger, even if that father was the High King. There were things that just didn't add up where Sarah and her father were concerned, and regardless of his understanding, Aaron would move forward with his own plans. He shook his head in frustration and glanced up at the night sky. Except for the faint orange glow, the night was dark, as the moons were still rising. His hand absently rubbed the medallion under his shirt, and he recalled the image of the beacon of light shooting into the sky over the arena. The dragon referred to himself as the Eldarin. Aaron pressed his lips together in thought. How would he seek out the Eldarin? He had no idea where they were, but knew they were the natural enemies of the Ryakuls. Aaron shook his head and lifted his backpack stuffed full of purple travel crystals. He needed to rejoin the others then find Sarah. The Eldarin would have to wait. If his faint connection to Sarah were any indication, time was indeed growing short before the woman he loved was gone forever. His grandfather's haunted eyes flashed before him like a silent prophecy of what would happen to him if he failed. Reymius couldn't have known what became of his grandmother, Cassandra, but Aaron *did* know and he would not condemn the woman he loved to the cruel prison of the Nanites.

Aaron snatched the rune-carved staff off the ground and crept along the rooftops, searching for the shop that bore the emblem of a tree with a clawed foot hidden amid its roots. He expanded his search and found the mark upon the door of a shop along one of the side streets away from the main market square. The shop was dark, and Aaron watched silently. The minutes dragged on, but his patience paid off as he saw shadows move from within the shop. Someone was home even if the lights were not on.

He climbed down to the street and came before the door. After softly knocking three times, he waited to the count of five then knocked twice more. There was a soft shuffle inside, but it was the two shadows that silently approached from either side that gave him pause. Aaron turned and was greeted by two men leveling large double crossbows at him.

"I'm sorry to call so late," Aaron said. "But I was told that there are friends of the shield inside."

The older man with gray in his hair regarded him for a few moments, his eyes widening. "Brothers of the shield are indeed welcome, but for the Heir of Shandara I would lay down my life. It is my honor to be in the presence of the Alenzar'seth once again, Your Grace," the man said, lowering his crossbow and brought a fist over his heart as he bowed his head.

Aaron was about to say something, but the door opened, and the older man brought a finger to his lips, and the three of them stepped inside. He followed the members of the Resistance down a flight of narrow stairs to a storage room that housed long dusty racks. They walked to the back of the room and headed down the farthest aisle. They came to a rack that was covered with old beer steins, and the older man reached toward the back and pulled the top of one of the steins. The wall shuddered for a moment then moved silently back, opening enough for them to easily pass through. The hallway beyond was lit with orbs. They quickly came to an open room that held a few tables and sleeping pallets off to the side. The stone walls were plainly painted, but the air smelled relatively fresh considering they were underground.

The older man turned toward him and regarded him for a moment while his two younger companions waited. They looked to be about the same age as Aaron, and the older man looked to be in his fifties, with a few lines creased upon his face, his beard and hair neatly trimmed. The older man shook his head with half a grin.

"Please forgive me, Your Grace," he said. "I had heard rumors, but to see proof with my own eyes..." The older man went down to one knee with a fist over his heart. "By my life or death I serve Shandara and the ruling house of Alenzar'seth." After a fraction of a second, he was joined by his two younger companions, who repeated the oath.

"Please," Aaron said gently, "don't kneel." Aaron stepped forward and offered his hand to the older man. "I'm Aaron Jace."

The older man rose and took the proffered hand. "I am Nicolas, and these are my sons, Liam and Daniel."

Aaron nodded to each in turn and put his hand out, but it was only with their father's nod of encouragement that they shook Aaron's hand.

"How did you recognize me?" Aaron asked.

Nicolas stood taller, his shoulders back with militaristic precision. "I am a son of Shandara and a member of the De'anjard. I would always recognize the family resemblance of my late Prince Reymius or his daughter, Princess Carlowen."

A proud smile came to Aaron's face, and he nodded.

"I have many questions," Nicolas said. "But I know you're not here to answer my questions. What can I do to help you?"

"I would be happy to answer any questions you have, sir." Aaron replied. "My friends are due to meet up with Captain Nolan and Lieutenant Anson this evening. Are you able to send word to them?"

"At once, Your Grace," Nicolas said and nodded toward Liam, who bowed and left the room.

Daniel approached with a tray of food and water. Aaron thanked them for the food and quickly downed the water.

"I think his Grace could do with something a bit stronger," Nicolas said, and Daniel disappeared down the hallway.

"Please, sir, call me Aaron."

After a few moments, Nicolas nodded, though Aaron doubted he would do so. Daniel returned carrying two steins filled with dark beer.

Aaron raised his stein and took a hearty swallow. "I have things to share with you, but you must have questions for me," Aaron said setting down his stein.

Daniel glanced at his father, who nodded. "Most of my immediate questions surround why you are here in Khamearra and what your plans are moving forward."

"Were you at the fall of Shandara?" Aaron asked.

Nicolas stiffly set down his stein, and shadows from a haunted past glided over his face as he nodded solemnly.

Aaron swallowed. "There are some things I need to share with you, but first I must know—are you the leader of the Resistance here in Khamearra?"

"Goodness, no. In true Shandarian tradition, we share leadership. There are three others besides myself, but beyond that there are very few of the original De'anjard left. Our descendants made a life here in this city, but we've never wavered from our purpose."

Aaron nodded and marveled at the dedication of the De'anjard with their shattered remains spread throughout the world, continuing to fight in their own way. You couldn't buy that type of loyalty, not with all the money in the world.

"I don't know how much you know about the fall, so I ask for your patience —" Aaron began, but Nicolas interrupted.

"You never need to ask for that, Your Grace," Nicolas said then his face softened. "Sorry, Aaron. Part of me doesn't believe that you're sitting here before my very eyes. I was part of the detail assigned with protecting Princess Carlowen, your mother. You have her eyes."

A small lump grew in his throat at the mention of his mother, and while he knew she had been a princess, it was still strange for him to hear of her being referred to as one.

"She lived," Aaron said. "She was happy."

"Was?" Nicolas asked and then reached out and put his hand on Aaron's shoulder. "I'm sorry for your loss."

Aaron nodded, fighting off the bitter torrent of memories. There had always been something to prevent him from properly mourning the loss of both his parents, and it was in rare quiet moments such as these that grief reached out and snatched at him unawares.

Aaron raised his stein. "To those we wished were here and all the lives taken before their time." He took a long swallow from his stein, and Nicolas and Daniel followed suit.

"Well met," Nicolas said appreciatively.

Aaron set down his stein and leaned forward. "There is a looming threat to this world beyond the High King or those seeking retribution for the fall of Shandara..." Aaron told them of the Hythariam and the danger posed by the invading army. How Colind along with ambassadors of the Hythariam were spreading the word and working to gain support from the other nations.

"We need the help of Khamearra against the invading army," Aaron said. "I know there is a small faction of the Elitesmen who have aided your efforts here. You will need their help."

Nicolas looked up alarmed. "Won't you be leading us?"

Aaron knew the question was coming and dreaded giving the answer. "I can't," he said. "To be honest, Nicolas, I don't think I could do anything that you are not already doing, but I will say this. I would much rather see all of the Resistance leave this nation and head to Rexel, where you will find support, than stay and fight the High King and the Elitesmen. We've struck a blow, but they are still powerful, and I wouldn't want you to throw your lives away. I know firsthand how hard it is to leave the only home you've ever known and I realize that many will be reluctant to go, but to not meet this threat head-on could doom this world and give a foothold to an enemy that knows no mercy."

Nicolas gave a small nod and sighed. "You are wise for one so young."

Aaron felt his lips curve into a small smile. "Thank you," he said. "Will you be able to move your people from the city safely?"

Nicolas was silent for a few moments, considering. "There is nothing that can be achieved without risk. Many will need to be convinced. We've moved people from the city before and we do have safe havens setup throughout the land. Some of us always meant to return to Shandara, but—"

"It's not safe," Aaron said quickly. "I wouldn't bring families there, but I fear that this war will take us back to Shandara."

Nicolas nodded. "To where this all began."

Aaron sighed, allowing the silence to stretch between them while he gathered his thoughts. "I don't know where this will end," Aaron said. "I've been to Shandara. We were able to free Colind of the Safanarion Order there, but no one could live there. Not now at least. Perhaps in time the land will heal."

"You have given us much to consider and the events of this night will lend weight to those still in doubt that you do in fact exist," Nicolas said. "How much time do we have before this Hythariam army will invade?"

"It could be as early as three months from now," Aaron replied, and Nicolas's eyes widened in shock.

"Very little time indeed. I'm not sure we could move an army to Shandara in that time," Nicolas said. "We have no time to prepare."

Aaron watched as Nicolas steeled himself to the insurmountable task Aaron was asking him to be a part of. "You will not be entirely without aid. The Hythariam here on Safanar will give aid to any who will join our cause. There are airships being built and augmented with engines that will make the trip possible, but you will have to get your people safely away from the city to meet them. I'm not sure where."

"How will we contact the Hythariam? No one has seen or heard from them, other than rumors, for years," Nicolas asked.

Liam entered the room and bowed his head to Aaron. "Your companions are safe and in Captain Nolan's district. I can take you to them when you are ready, my lord."

Aaron thanked Liam and rose to his feet. He pulled out his comms device. "This is called a comms device and will allow you to call the Hythariam. When we leave, I will give you this one and show you how to use it. The Hythariam have inventions that seem mysterious, but they are not magic. In time perhaps, they will be a commonplace to Safanar."

Aaron activated the comms device. "Tanneth did you get that?"

"Yes, I have their location," came Tanneth's reply. "I will meet you there."

The indicator light dimmed as Tanneth closed the connection, but Nicolas's eyes were wide with shock.

"Mysterious indeed," Nicolas said, rising from his seat. "Let's go meet the others."

They rose, and Aaron watched as Daniel went to the far side of the room away from the entrance. After a moment, a portion of the wall slid away and a dark passageway opened before them. For all the Hythariam technological wonders, Aaron couldn't help but be impressed with the well-hidden secret door as it slid silently upon its hinges, opening the way for them.

"I'm afraid I can't do anything about the smell," Nicolas said. "But at least we will be able to travel through the city unseen. According to my son, the guards are sweeping the city, and regular troops are assembling outside the city walls." He finished attaching a glowing orb to his staff and led the way.

Aaron followed them into the sewers under the city. As they traversed the passageways, his thoughts drifted to his friends. He hoped they were all right. He felt the weight of the travel crystals on his back and wondered if they would be enough to thwart the Nanites. She was slipping. He could feel it and the knowledge gnawed away at him.

Roughly an hour later, through countless turns and passageways, they came to a ladder. Daniel ascended first and gave a series of knocks on the door at the top. A single knock was given in reply, and the door was opened, sending a shaft of light into the dimly lit tunnel. Aaron ascended the ladder and emerged to a crowded warehouse. Curtains hung over the windows preventing light from getting out. There were people tending to wounded soldiers and messengers running about. Nicolas returned a salute to one messenger who greeted them and led them to the other side of the warehouse. As they crossed the way, a hush overtook the people like a wave of silence descending upon them. All eyes were on Aaron, who stood taller than most men. Their eyes lingered on the rune-carved staff and then on Aaron himself. The silence was broken by the sweep of hundreds of feet as all in the warehouse sank to one knee.

"By my life or death, I serve Shandara and the ruling house of Alenzar'seth."

The oath of the De'anjard echoed throughout the warehouse, sending shivers down Aaron's spine. He felt the heat rise to his face, but he let his gaze sweep over those around him. Looking all of these people in the eye was the least he could do considering the loyalty they had shown. His gaze was returned with a proud reckoning in the eyes of those around him. They were a hard bunch and some he recognized from the arena. He nodded to them and they returned a nod in kind. Despite his less than enthusiastic acceptance of being of royal birth, he knew he was something more to these people. A symbol. A leader. And to the smaller group approaching him, a friend.

Aaron leaped atop a small table, feeling that he should say something, and beckoned them all to rise.

"Thank you," Aaron said, his voice traveling through the warehouse. "You honor the spirit of Shandara with your service. I can only stand in awe of what you've accomplished here and at your dedication to the ideals of the Alenzar'seth. Such ideals had merit with my grandfather Reymius. Know that if he were here, you would have had his gratitude, respect, and dedication to the same ideals. I can't imagine what you've had to endure until this day. It is I who pledge to you my life and death to forever serve the spirit of Shandara. The very same spirit I see alive among all of you. The road before us is long, and the battle is not yet won, but we will endure. The spirit of Shandara will endure. The sacrifice of all those before us will never be in vain, for we have something here in this very room that cannot be taken from us."

Aaron paused, his hard gaze sweeping the room as the men and women before him seemed to stand taller. "Honor and courage, never without fear, but always willing to take that bold step forward. These are among the core tenets that the tyrants of this world can never crush. The spirit of Shandara was kept alive because of you and it is you that I should bow to, not the other way around." Aaron knelt down upon the table for all to see and spoke the Safanarion oath. "By my life or death, I serve to protect the world of Safanar and will call brother and sister to all who would take up this cause. Be a shield to those in need. Be an ear for those to listen. Be a voice for those who would speak."

As Aaron spoke, an invisible shroud settled down upon his shoulders. His words had come from the depths of his heart, and he meant every last one of them.

There was a moment of deafening silence until the crowded warehouse erupted with roars of approval. The people stood taller and even those wounded lying in bed held eyes that glimmered with hope.

Aaron leaped down and came face to face with Verona. His friend's eyes held a much harder glint to them, but Aaron was so relieved to see him alive that he pulled him into an embrace.

"Well met, my friend," Verona grinned. "Well met."

Aaron felt as if a fist had unclenched around his heart. Seeing them all alive and safe took a great weight off his shoulders. He glanced at Braden, who nodded grimly in return, and Aaron felt the absence of his brother, Eric, more profoundly than before by the empty spot at his side.

"I'm so glad you're all safe," Aaron said.

"None more so than we are, I can assure you," Verona said with a grin, but his eyes retained the haunted expression that could not so easily be dispelled with a bit of mirth.

Aaron shook hands with Captain Nolan and Lieutenant Anson and noticed for the first time that the Elitesman Isaac was not among them.

Verona sensed his question before he could give voice to it. "He sacrificed himself so we could escape, but he wanted me to give you a message. 'Tell the Shandarian that there are more Elite of the old code who don't hold with these ideals.' When we offered to fight at his side, he looked at the initiates and told us to fight for them. I think the Elitesmen have many factions to their order, and there are some who may join our cause."

Aaron nodded. "I think you are right. Is there any chance that Isaac survived?"

"To be honest, I'm not sure," Verona said.

"We will look for him," Nolan said.

Aaron scratched the back of his head. "It was easier to think of them as all evil, but that is not always the case now."

Verona shook his head, but Braden spoke up. "Most of them are still evil," he said coldly, leaving little room for argument.

Aaron nodded. There would be no easy way forward for any of them. He looked at Gavril. "Tanneth said he would be here soon."

Gavril nodded. "I have no doubts that Tanneth has already taken watch on the roof of this building."

Aaron smiled. Tanneth had done more to help get them this far than Aaron could ever thank him enough for. They sat at a table off to the side and were joined by Lieutenant Anson along with Nicolas, to whom Anson deferred to as one of the leaders of the Resistance.

"It's not safe for all the leaders to gather in one spot, but what is said here will be passed along to them," Nicolas said, and his gaze lingered on Gavril and Roselyn. Both had shed their disguises, and the irises of the golden eyes of the Hythariam shone brightly. "I have not seen your people in a lifetime."

Gavril took the lead and bowed to the Resistance general. "Something we hope to rectify. I will send word to my people, and they will send aid to you." Gavril reached inside his sack and pulled out a comms device. "You can use this to reach our people. Once I show you how to use it, this will help coordinate our efforts better," Gavril said and nodded for Nolan and Anson to come over.

Captain Nolan hesitated for a moment, stopping before Aaron. "Your Grace," Captain Nolan said formally with a fist across his heart. "Many will join our cause, but I wanted to pledge myself to you personally after your actions in the arena and the other day. You have shown me a light worthy enough to beat back the shadows of this world. A light worth following. From this moment forward, you can count on me."

Aaron was momentarily at a loss for words. Before he could say anything, Captain Nolan turned away and joined the others with Gavril.

Verona cleared his throat, and Aaron joined them at the table with Roselyn, Sarik, and Braden.

"The beacon of light at the arena was you?" Verona asked.

Aaron swallowed and nodded and echoes of the Eldarin spoke in his mind. *We of the Eldarin, honor the one who is marked by Ferasdiam. Seek us out as our numbers are few and there are things you must know.*

"We saw the beacon from the tower," Verona said. "I think the whole city saw it. There is talk of a dragon descending upon the arena."

"Yes," Aaron said. "He didn't call himself a dragon, but referred to himself as the *Eldarin*. He said that they honor the one who is marked by Ferasdiam."

"The Eldarin?" Verona said. "I've never heard of them, but if they came to your aid then they are okay in my book."

Aaron smiled at the simplicity that Verona had categorized the world. "I have the travel crystals," he said, opening his pack revealing the horde of glimmering purple crystals.

Verona and Sarik reached in and took two of them out, studying them for a moment.

"Do you know how they work?" Sarik asked.

Aaron's mind screeched to a halt and he looked up in alarm. "No," he said. "I was so focused on getting them that I hadn't considered how they actually worked. I was hoping that Isaac would be able to help."

Aaron reached in and pulled out one of the precious purple crystals. He could feel the stored up energy trapped within the prism confines of the crystal. "It can't be that hard," he said.

Verona shrugged his shoulders and Sarik studied the crystal intently.

Roselyn muttered something under her breath. "Typical. First thing is first. What do we know about how these crystals work?"

Aaron called up the memory of his encounter with the Elitesmen at the airfield in Rexel, but he had been too preoccupied with survival and didn't have an inkling as to how the Elitesmen had used the crystal to teleport from place to place. His mind returned to the Feast of Shansheru, the celebration held in Shandara's honor at Rexel, where he had first danced with Sarah. She had held the crystal in her hand.

That's it!

"They require physical contact," Aaron said. "I remember Sarah having it in her hand the night we danced in Rexel."

Verona nodded, remembering, and Roselyn smiled at Aaron, reminding him of his older sister. "How romantic of you. What else did you see? We need more to go on than that."

Aaron thought about it for a few seconds. "They only have so many charges, but I'm not sure how many. I think since they are mainly used by the Elitesmen, or those trained similarly, then it has something to do with tapping into the energy in the crystal."

"We'll need to test this before you go traipsing off after the Drake," Roselyn said.

Aaron nodded. "Agreed. We need to get out of here tonight. We cannot linger."

Roselyn frowned. "Why?"

"I can feel her fading," Aaron said in a voice barely above a whisper.

Verona and Roselyn exchanged glances, but Aaron did not have time to wonder what had transpired between the two.

"I don't want to reach out to her here," Aaron continued. "We need to be away from the city. Can the ship be recalled to a place of our choosing?"

The others glanced at Roselyn who answered. "Just slow down. Take a moment."

"She doesn't have a moment," Aaron said loudly enough to draw confused looks from those around them. He cast his eyes downward. "I'm sorry. I know you're trying to help."

Roselyn nodded in understanding. "We will get to her in time. I haven't wanted to ask, but have you given any thought as to how to find her?"

He had thought about it constantly. "I can find her through the bond. She is somewhere in the mountain range near Shandara, at least she was yesterday. The Drake knows I will come for her. He is counting on it and therefore doesn't need to move around."

The group was silent for a moment, each taking some time for their thoughts.

"How did you get them?" Verona asked. "The crystals, I mean."

"Oh I went into the other tower to the central chamber after the arena. It seemed to be the place where they recharged all types of crystals."

Verona pressed his lips in thought. "And you made it out undetected?"

Aaron frowned. "Not entirely," he answered. "I met the High King, or rather, he found me in the chamber."

Their mouths fell open, except for Roselyn, who looked questioningly at all of them.

Aaron suppressed a shudder. The High King was powerful. "He is Ferasdiam Marked like me."

Sarik made the sign of the Goddess upon his brow, and Verona leaned in. "Ferasdiam Marked?" he asked, clearly trying to come to grips with this news. "I wish Vaughn were here."

Aaron nodded. "I wish Colind were here, too. If they knew, why wouldn't they have said something?"

"They couldn't have known," Verona said.

Roselyn sighed in frustration and said, "Comms device, gentlemen. Try to raise him on it."

Aaron cursed himself inwardly for not remembering. He brought out the comms device and navigated the small display to Colind's signal, but it was dull, as if his device was offline. Aaron held it up for Roselyn to see.

"That shouldn't happen," Roselyn said, checking her own comms device.

"Never mind about that," Verona said. "Tell us what transpired between you and the High King."

Aaron swallowed some water. "I tried to reason with him. I told him of the invading army and how Mactar is not loyal to his cause, but I'm not sure he believed me. He didn't seem to care about Mactar."

Verona's gaze narrowed. "Did you tell him about Sarah?"

The High King's dismissal of his daughter's life made Aaron clench his teeth, but he nodded and said, "He doesn't care. He said that she was my weakness. People carry no weight in his eyes other than the purpose they serve."

"Did you fight the High King?" Sarik asked.

"I was more concerned with getting away than fighting a battle with him. I had gotten what I'd come for."

"Indeed," Braden said, speaking up for the first time. "You could have struck a blow to cripple Khamearra and cut the head off the snake here."

Aaron met Braden's gaze. "The snakes in Khamearra have many heads. To be honest, I'm not sure it was a battle I could win and to die here in a battle not of my choosing wouldn't accomplish anything. I'm sure the High King and I will meet again."

Braden's eyes still held the fires of anger in them, but he nodded once.

"Where was Mactar during all this?" Verona asked.

"That is an excellent question," Aaron answered. "I don't know and I don't think the lack of his presence was by accident. While I don't know for sure, I can sense his handiwork behind the scenes." Aaron told them of his encounter with Rordan and how Rordan wouldn't tell him anything.

"I can only imagine the restraint it took, given your fondness of arrogant young princes," Verona said, but before Aaron could reply, Verona continued. "I know for whom your actions were dictated, but at some point you will be faced with a choice. Sarah understands that as well."

Aaron nodded slowly. "I'm not here seeking to wage old wars, but for her I gave them this one chance," he said, thinking of when Sarah had asked why everything must end in bloodshed. His mind drifted to their time in the forest where they had jumped to dizzying heights through the trees. She moved with the agility and grace of a swan gliding along a lake against the setting sun, while he stumbled and bumped into a few trees trying to keep up with her. He smiled at the memory, missing Sarah's playful nature and the way she challenged him. How his heart raced as he melted into her arms during the night of the choosing in Tolvar's camp, when she had set her laurel crown upon his head amid the firelight.

Aaron forced the memory aside as Gavril joined them and said, "I think if we have finished our business in the city then we should leave tonight. Tomorrow will prove to be more difficult to move about the city, and I doubt you want to wait idly until the evening."

Aaron looked around at all the members of the Resistance in the warehouse. He wanted to leave. He had to leave, but at the same time he felt a twinge of guilt as if he were abandoning these people. Aaron could feel Gavril's eyes on him.

"This is their fight, Aaron," Gavril said. "They have been waging it for many years."

"I know," Aaron said. "I just wish there was more time. That there was more I could do for them."

Gavril nodded. "You have done much more than you realize. You have given them a path, and with our aid, we will help them reach it. In one evening you've managed to put the Elitesmen off balance, and the fires of hope will blaze throughout this city and all the lands of Khamearra. You've shown the world that they are not unstoppable. That there are those who can oppose them. I think that should you return to this city someday, you will find it a much different place than it is today."

But at what cost, Aaron wondered, taking another look around at all the people. According to Nicolas, there were places like this warehouse throughout the city. The people cast glances in his direction, but they all looked determined.

Gavril reached out to him, and Aaron turned back to him.

"Freedom is never given," Gavril said. "It is won. These people know this truth. They have bled for it and will continue to fight for it."

Aaron's gaze never left Gavril's. The old soldier from the Hythariam home world knew firsthand what it was like to lose freedom in the name of tyranny under the guise of necessity. He was no stranger to true oppression, unlike Aaron, who had never had to cope with it, but only learned of it through history books. Gavril was right. This was their fight, and he had contributed a verse to their battle song, but he couldn't sing it for them.

"It's time for us to leave," Aaron said, and the others around him slowly rose, each choosing of their own accord to stand with him. He nodded appreciatively to each in turn, and he knew that the debt he owed his friends was something that, in his eyes, could never be repaid. They would never call it a debt or view their actions as something owed. They simply stood together in unison with him on this path, wherever it would lead them. The burden of leadership fell heavily upon his shoulders, as it would on anyone's, but Aaron was coming to accept it as he never had before.

19

PRINCES & KINGS

Colind stood on the deck of the Raven, watching as Rexel's airship yard grew smaller. They were heading toward a neutral meeting place between Rexel and Zsensibar, escorting Prince Jopher in hopes of winning support from his father the king. The boy had grown much according to Cyrus. Aaron's influence no doubt.

There were six airships with them, bringing their total to seven. All had been upgraded with the help of the Hythariam, and the newly promoted Admiral Nathaniel Morgan of the Free Nations Army. Morgan was using their little trip as an excuse to put the airships through their paces and practice coordinating attacks and maneuvers. Prince Jopher had taken to sailing the skies and had requested to study under the admiral, to which Morgan agreed while joking about needing more help in the kitchens peeling potatoes. Jopher's face grew red with embarrassment, and Morgan had commissioned the young prince as an officer in the army.

The Free Nations Army was composed of troops from Rexel and its neighboring kingdoms, as well as former Shandarians, with more people joining every day. Colind and Reymius had often spoke of uniting the kingdoms while allowing for their independence. The Safanarion Order had made some progress toward this, but the people of Safanar hadn't been ready before the fall of Shandara. Now, almost twenty-five years later with the power of the High King and the Elitesmen running virtually unchecked, their eyes had opened to the fact that their world would have been a much better place had Shandara not perished.

Colind let the echoes of a gloried past go and focused on the now. He wasn't sure how Zsensibar's King, Jopher's father, would react to his son's enlistment into the military. He hoped they could win their support, as the kingdom of Zsensibar held the second-largest army in their part of the world and mines rich in metals and raw materials that they would need. Being located south of the Waylands, the home of Rexel, afforded Zsensibar to be able to avoid most skirmishes with the High King. Cyrus had told him that Zsensibar's army was well trained despite the questionable practices observed in the kingdom. They practiced a harsh class system of government that left most common people little more than indentured servants. While they didn't outright call them slaves, they could be nothing else in Colind's mind. The Hythariam would be reluctant to share their knowledge with them, and Colind knew Aaron would never approve, but they needed Zsensibar's support. He could see how easily their efforts to save Safanar from invasion could be thwarted if the nations of this world didn't unite.

Colind felt the bottom drop away from his stomach as the ship rose higher into the air and dodged to the side. Tersellis, the Hythariam ambassador, referred to the coordinated airship maneuvers as drills. Well, these drills were going to cause his breakfast to spew all over the well polished deck, which wouldn't help his legendary status in the eyes of the crew.

The enhancements to the ship had included smaller maneuvering engines that helped steer the airship with precision. While the airships could never maneuver as precisely as what the Hythariam's had in Hathenwood, they were a marked improvement over what previously existed.

The heavier fore and aft engines propelled the ships forward. With the additional engines, more yellow crystals were put in place to allow the airships to remain in the air despite the heavier load. Tersellis hinted at future airships that didn't require a cell or balloon to keep the ship in the air, but with the timeframe they had, he doubted that any would be ready in time. There were caches of weapons throughout the ruins of Shandara that had not seen the light of day since before the fall, and Colind hoped there were things there that they could still use. Anything that could give them an edge. Iranus was investigating the ruins of Shandara, but he suspected they needed Aaron to actually open the weapons caches.

Colind lifted his eyes to the west where half a world away, Khamearra lay, and within its capital city, the Heir of Shandara. He kept his frustration in check because part of him felt that he should be by Aaron's side, but they all had a part to play and his required him to be here at this moment. Still, he found it increasingly unsettling that Mactar was out there and he yearned to seek him out. They had unfinished business, and he counted it a fair trade to give his life up to take out Mactar. Safanar would be better off without him. Then there was Tarimus, his son. Almost nothing remained of the boy, Tarimus, but he was still his son, Colind admonished to himself. No amount of time or deeds done would ever change that. But unlike before the fall, he saw the evil that had been in Tarimus. His imprisonment left him with little else to do, and Colind had lost count of how many times he cursed his own foolhardiness for denying the truth before his eyes. Tarimus had always been power hungry and ambitious, but his intentions had been aligned with the Safanarion Order, which was the preservation of this world. He could blame Mactar for bringing Tarimus into his web, but deep down he blamed himself. He was Tarimus's father, and whatever failings were part of his son held an undeniable connection to himself. Even now, after all that had happened, Colind still struggled to think of something that he could have done differently that could change what Tarimus had become. In the end, he knew that the path of 'what ifs' would lead to nowhere, but he still couldn't help wanting to know why. The only way he would get any answers was to face his son again. The thought of facing Tarimus burned like acid in his mouth. It was his duty to bring Tarimus to justice for the part he played in the destruction of Shandara. Tarimus's dark betrayal by aligning with the High King and Mactar, causing the death of thousands of Shandarians, was left to him to address. Better himself than Aaron. He owed Aaron that much at least.

"My Lord Guardian," Jopher said behind him.

Colind turned to see Jopher in a blue officer's uniform standing proudly before him. There was not a hint of the youthful arrogance in his eyes, only the confidence and character one has through achievement, which commanded Colind's respect.

"My Lord, Prince," Colind replied.

"Please, no 'My Lord,'" Jopher replied. "I'm just Lieutenant Jopher of the Free Nations Army."

Colind suppressed a smile. "As you wish, Lieutenant."

Jopher nodded. "The admiral wishes for you to join him on the observation deck off the wheel house."

"I am, of course, at the admiral's service," Colind answered and gestured for Jopher to lead the way. "How are you settling in to your new role?"

Jopher walked ahead, addressing Colind as he went. "Honestly, My Lord Guardian, I love it. Never before have I felt part of something. To be a member of a team. Doing my part, knowing that others depend upon me, and that I in turn depend upon them to do their duty."

Colind smiled at the boy's eagerness and wondered how many other princes could benefit from the disciplined training that Jopher was receiving. Aaron had unknowingly started him on this path. Why not include princesses as well? It would not do to discriminate based upon gender, Colind mused, and he made a mental note to make the recommendation to Cyrus and Morgan later on.

"No need to be so formal with me. You can simply use 'My Lord' and do away with all this 'My Lord Guardian' business," Colind said.

Jopher nearly tripped looking back at him and decided a nod was better than trying to speak, but then said, "As you wish, my lord."

The deck of the Raven had its usual goings-on with members of the crew doing their utmost to ensure that this trip went smoothly. They had a reputation to uphold, as they were the first ship to be upgraded, which paled in the comparison to them actually journeying to Shandara and back again. Colind glanced to the other ships in close proximity. The sailors appeared significantly smaller at this distance, but they moved with the same sense of urgency. Perhaps the discipline of these so-called drills do affect the performance of a crew. It had been a lifetime since he'd had to lead men in such a fashion and his skills were a bit rusty, to be honest. He was a man out of time, and in quiet moments, he wondered if he would ever really find his bearings in a world that had clearly moved beyond him. None of the old faces were there. He missed his dear friend Reymius all the more after learning what the Drake had done to them. Knowing that Cassey was still caught in its web. Iranus said that there was nothing left of the Lady Cassandra, his dear friend Reymius's wife, as she had been fully assimilated by the Nanites. Had Reymius known what had befallen his wife, Colind doubted he would have left even with what had happened to his daughter, Carlowen. They just didn't know what would happen at the time. Reymius must have believed that Cassandra had died to protect them.

"My Lord," Jopher said, and Colind looked up. "It is just through here," Jopher finished, and they came to a gray door. Jopher opened the door and waited for Colind to enter.

Admiral Morgan looked up from a table strewn with maps. His gray hair was tied back and he wore his blue officer's uniform, its gold bars upon the shoulders shone brightly. Morgan gave a nod to Colind and looked at Jopher. "Thank you, Lieutenant. Please remain outside until I call you back in," Admiral Morgan said.

Tersellis, Vaughn, and Garret were already in the room, along with senior officers that he didn't know.

"We should make the meeting point in a little under an hour," Morgan said.

Colind's eyes widened in shock. He knew the new ships were fast, but didn't really expect the improvements to yield what would normally have taken at least a day or two by airship, to be condensed into an hour.

"Impressive," Colind said.

Morgan's neatly trimmed gray beard lifted into a half grin. "I thought you'd appreciate that, my lord."

Colind felt a slight shudder beneath his feet and saw the clouds outside the windows begin to move quickly by.

"We've engaged the new engines," Morgan said proudly. "The crystals powering them are fully charged and will remain so on a day like today. With the help of our Hythariam friends, the stored capacity of the crystals will allow us to operate at full power through the whole night and much into the next day, if needs be."

"That's how they should work," Tersellis said. "I expect that we may see better performance, but we won't know that until we test more."

"Understood," Morgan acknowledged. "Colind, are you able to advise us on how best to deal with the King of Zsensibar?"

With Cyrus remaining at Rexel, this left Colind the most senior among them to deal with the king. Before his imprisonment, he had dealt with many princes and kings.

"I'm going to continue to follow suit of the young Lord of Shandara," Colind said. "I'm going to be direct, as I don't have time to be drawn into long negotiations with the King of Zsensibar." Colind finished and again found his gaze drifting toward the window.

Vaughn frowned. "What is it?" he asked.

They all glanced out of the window and then returned their gaze toward Colind.

Colind had sucked in his bottom lip. "I'm not sure. I'm growing more worried about the group in Khamearra. We have not heard back from them in over a day."

Tersellis brought out what the Hythariam called a comms device. "We know they are still alive and are in Khamearra," he said, nodding to the device.

Colind frowned. "I'm glad the dots are where they should be, but I know something is not right in here," he said, pointing to his heart. "When we finish with Zsensibar, I aim to make a detour to Khamearra if I need to."

The room grew silent, and Tersellis put the comms device away.

Morgan spoke first. "We can head to Khamearra now if you believe they are in danger. I'm certain we can calculate the best speed…"

Colind held up his hand. "I don't know if they are in any more danger today than they were yesterday. It's a feeling I have, but I don't want to take away from our efforts here, and what you need to be doing has to be done back at Rexel."

"How will you get to them in time?" Vaughn asked.

Colind smiled. "Trust in that this old man still has a few tricks up his sleeve. And I assure you that I can get there faster than any ship if I must."

The people of Safanar took his claim at face value, but he could tell the Hythariam were doubtful.

"Iranus sent me a message earlier," Tersellis said. "They've been exploring the ruins of Shandara and marking places of interest. There is a lot of ground to cover and the Ryakul frequent the area in coordinated patterns, as if the beasts are on patrol."

"That's because they are under control," Garret said grimly. "The Drake has some measure of control over the Ryakuls. The only thing that seems to break the Drake's control is when there are dragons in the area."

Tersellis's brow furrowed in thought. "Why is that, do you think?"

Garret shrugged his shoulders. "I'm not sure, to be honest, but it sends them into a frenzy. We've seen it first hand, during our last journey on board the Raven."

"So all we need are some dragons to help us with the Ryakul problem," Tersellis said.

Colind shook his head. "The dragons are creatures of great intelligence and have roamed Safanar long before man ever did. They are worthy of our respect."

Tersellis held up his hand. "I meant no offense, but if they are already natural enemies why wouldn't they help us?"

"It would seem that way wouldn't it," Colind said. "The dragons' numbers are few now. I'm not sure they would help us even if they wanted too. Did Iranus say anything else about Shandara?"

Tersellis nodded. "They were able to confirm the state of the barrier, and Aaron was correct. The barrier is deteriorating fast. Something twists the landscape down to the core around that place and it is spreading."

Vaughn frowned. "Spreading? What do you mean?"

Tersellis was about to answer, but Colind cut him off. "What he means is that the barrier is tethered to this world and Hytharia. The shield upon the barrier on our side is tied to the energy that binds this world together. But the drain and the state of Hytharia is shifting things out of balance. Aaron was right. Time has indeed been growing short."

The men in the room looked grimly back at one another.

Admiral Morgan cleared his throat. "We're still here, and we will rise up to meet this threat."

Colind smiled inwardly, applauding the admiral. "What about the object heading here from the heavens?"

Tersellis met all of their gazes. "Three months. Whatever it is will be here in three months."

"Is there no way we can figure out what it is?" Vaughn asked.

Tersellis shook his head. "They are working on it, but there is no doubt that the object is heading directly toward this planet."

"All right, gentlemen. We have three months, and we need to make every minute count," Colind said and then he nodded his head toward the door.

Morgan called for Jopher to enter the room.

The young prince entered the room, and Colind smiled kindly, motioning for him to join them. Jopher couldn't have been more than eighteen years of age. Perhaps a year older than that, but certainly not more. So young... They all were, including Aaron. *This war will be fought primarily by the young.* The thought tasted like copper in his mouth, but he kept the bitterness from his bearing.

"We've called you in here, because we're heading to meet with your father," Colind began. "I'd like for you to give us your perspective on whether he will join our cause." There, he had said it. He was asking for a son to pass judgment on his father, and while he didn't like it, Colind knew that this was something Jopher would have to face.

Jopher took a long swallow and glanced around the room.

Morgan stood up. "It's okay, son. We understand this will be difficult for you," he said soothingly, putting the young prince at ease.

"Thank you, sir," Jopher said. "Please know that this son of Zsensibar will not abandon his post, nor will I sit idly by while our homes are being threatened."

Colind nodded. "I never had any doubts as to where you stood. It's your father and his advisors that I'm wondering about."

Jopher thought about it for a moment. "He will be shocked and most likely won't believe you. That is until you present him with proof. Then..." Jopher paused, thinning his lips. "Then he will press his advantage, because he will know that you need our kingdom's—apologies—*nation's* help to fight the Hythariam and perhaps the High King. It will be difficult to convey the gravity of the threat."

Colind was impressed with Jopher's summation of their situation. "Very accurate, and your honesty is much appreciated."

"I would like to speak with him before you go to negotiations," Jopher said. "I need to try to explain the things that I've seen."

Colind watched as Morgan shared a proud glance with Vaughn and Garret. "That is perfectly reasonable and will happen, I assure you."

Jopher eyes turned cold for a moment. "And if he doesn't listen then I will lead whoever will come from our homeland to aid this fight."

Colind barely kept his mouth from hanging open and shared a glance with the others. Jopher spoke for the first time as a true prince, a ruler, a leader without a trace of the imperious boy playing at being a man.

"I sincerely hope it doesn't come to that," Colind said. "That is not my intention for bringing you here. Fathers and sons should be able to work together. Would you like to know a secret?"

Jopher looked confused for a moment, but nodded.

"Sometimes men or fathers, kings in particular, can be the embodiment of stubbornness," Colind said with the barest hints of a smile. "Even Admirals," he said dryly, sending a glance toward Morgan, which drew a smile upon Jopher's face. "But I think you will find that if you speak with your father as you've spoken here before us, with the same conviction, that he may be persuaded to our cause. But you must be patient."

Jopher beamed at the compliment. "Yes sir," he said. "There is one more thing."

Colind nodded for Jopher to continue.

"There are practices from my home that are hundreds of years old and looked upon with disdain from the other nations," Jopher said. "I know how we are viewed by nations such as Rexel. We are tolerated because of our strength. Being tolerated for fear's sake is not how any nation should stand. Genuine respect should be held in the highest esteem not only between people, but between nations."

"Well said," Morgan nearly shouted, and the men around the room nodded in approval.

Aaron, if only you could see the seeds that you've sown in this young man bearing fruit, Colind mused.

Their brief moment of celebration was interrupted by the sound of alarms blaring throughout the ship. Morgan sprang toward the door and Colind followed.

They entered the wheel house.

"Admiral on the deck," cried the guard at the door.

"Situation?" Morgan asked.

"General alert, sir," replied one of the sailors. "We're coming to the meeting point and have the royal envoy of Zsensibar in our sights."

"Excellent," Morgan replied.

Colind surveyed the panoramic view from the wheel house windows. They were moving so fast that he looked back at Admiral Morgan in concern. "Should we slow down?"

Admiral Morgan grinned. "Let's make them sweat a bit first," he replied. "Hoist the colors," Admiral Morgan ordered.

Colind heard the order repeated, and after a few moments, watched as dark blue flags appeared toward the bow of the airships and on either side of their flanks. He squinted his eyes and felt them widen in shock as he recognized the flag of Shandara. The dragon emblem grasping a single rose in his claws in white upon a dark blue background. There would be no guessing as to the allegiances and ideals that the Free Nations Army was committed to.

"Signal to the other ships to reduce speed to one quarter," Admiral Morgan said.

The order was repeated and confirmed with militaristic discipline. Within one minute, all the airships had slowed down and approached the mutual meeting place with the Zsensibarians. The king brought a token force of a few thousand men, but had only two airships hovering over a field nearby. Colind could already see that the army on the ground was mobilizing in preparation for their meetings. He whispered a silent prayer to the Goddess for patience and wisdom to be visited upon them all this day.

The Raven was the flagship of this squadron and descended toward the ground, while the remaining six airships maintained their altitude. They staggered approach so no one airship would be an easy target for the army on the ground. Morgan, it appeared, was not taking any chances.

"Shall we, My Lord Guardian?" Admiral Morgan asked, gesturing toward the door.

Colind nodded, and they headed out on deck, where they were joined by the Hythariam ambassadors, Vaughn, Garret, and Jopher, along with thirty soldiers. The soldier's armor gleamed in the sunlight and were accented with blue to match the sailor's uniforms.

A large tent had been setup between Zsensibar's army and the airships with a small force of soldiers near the tent. A white flag whisked in the air under a gentle breeze. They descended the gangplank and Colind suppressed his urge to reassure Jopher when he noticed the young prince's hands fidgeting. But he soon regained his composure, with his shoulders back and his head held high.

Tersellis walked next to Colind. "I've left one of my men on board the Raven in case this meeting doesn't go well. He will monitor through the comms device."

"Let's hope we don't need them," Colind replied.

"I second that," Tersellis said, and he looked around. "This is a tense group."

"With good reason," Vaughn said, coming up next to them. "Dealings with Zsensibar have always been a fragile thing."

"Why is that?" Tersellis asked.

"They are a powerful kingdom with rich natural resources," Vaughn replied. "Their geographical location has allowed them to avoid most wars between the kingdoms, because they can fight without worrying about another kingdom coming in behind to pounce. They've allied with the High King in the past, but I'd say within the last ten years or so, that bond has been deteriorating."

Tersellis nodded in understanding, but did not say anything more.

As they neared the tent, they were greeted by a group of Zsensibarian soldiers, and one held up his hand.

"I am Captain Amir, and upon behalf of his exalted Royal Highness, King Melchoir Nasim, I bid you welcome," Captain Amir said, bowing his head respectfully.

Admiral Morgan bowed back. "I am Admiral Nathaniel Morgan of the Free Nations Army and may I introduce to you My Lord Guardian Colind of the Safanarion Order and Tersellis Ambassador of the Hythariam."

Captain Amir bowed respectfully to each in turn, but his eyes widened at Colind's introduction.

Morgan spoke again. "We are also joined by Prince Jopher, who has been commissioned into the Free Nations Army," Morgan said, and Jopher stepped up from the group of soldiers.

Captain Amir's eyes widened, and then he immediately went to his knees. "Your Royal Highness."

Jopher stepped up. "Rise, Captain," he said. After the Captain came back to his feet, he continued, "Please take me to my father."

Captain Amir regarded Jopher for a moment as if he hadn't heard him correctly and Colind wondered if it was because Jopher had used the word 'please.'

"At once, Your Highness," Captain Amir said.

"Now we wait," Colind said, watching as the two headed toward the tent. The soldiers of Zsensibar split between dividing their gaze upon himself, the airships behind them, and the golden-eyed Hythariam—Tersellis and his bodyguard.

The minutes dragged by, and Captain Amir returned to them. Shouts came from within the tent, and a soldier came out running and whispered something to the Zsensibar Captain.

Captain Amir cleared his throat and narrowed his gaze toward Colind. "His Royal Highness, King Melchoir Nasim, requests your presence. Guardian, if you will follow me."

"One moment if you will, Captain," Tersellis said quickly. "I'm afraid that if your king wishes to speak with us, he will need to join us out here and not in the tent."

Captain Amir barely suppressed a sneer, but Tersellis kept on going.

"I am an Ambassador for my people, the Hythariam. Are we not two nations meeting upon this neutral location under a white flag of truce?" Tersellis asked.

Captain Amir considered this for a moment and then nodded. "Yes, Ambassador."

"Well then, if my understanding of two such nations meeting upon a neutral field is correct and we are not in the providence of King Melchoir Nasim, then he must join us out here if he wishes to speak with this envoy," Tersellis finished respectfully.

Colind silently applauded the cunning ambassador and watched as the Captain struggled with the fact that Tersellis's astute knowledge of Safanarion customs between two nations upon the field put his king clearly in the wrong, and had unwittingly insulted another nation.

"Perhaps the king has been misinformed," Colind said. "Doubtless reuniting with his son, the prince, proved to be a compelling distraction. Wouldn't you agree, Captain?"

Captain Amir regained his composure and nodded. "My Lord Ambassador, please accept my humblest apologies. I will inform the king at once that the neighboring kingdom of the Hythariam are in fact here upon this neutral field."

"Thank you, Captain," Tersellis replied earnestly.

The captain inclined his head respectfully and walked stiffly back toward the tent. Colind couldn't fault the captain's attitude as he was following the orders of his King and historically subjects of Zsensibar's crowned king didn't fare too well when questioning his orders.

The weather was considerably warmer here in the south and sun was shining. Colind took a moment to rejoice in the sun's caress upon his face. After being imprisoned for so long in the shadows, he often found himself being taken aback by the simplest of things. Colind focused himself as the tent flaps were pulled back and King Nasim's retinue exited.

The court that the king of Zsensibar brought to the field was significantly smaller than what Colind had remembered since he last dealt with Nasim, who had been a much younger man at the time. King Melchoir Nasim stood tall among his people, aided in part by the traditional elongated crown that spiraled above his head. The jewels inlaid in gold gleamed and reflected the brilliance of the sunlight, giving a slight aura surrounding the head of the king. His long beard curled down to his chest, adorned with gold beads. Nasim wore light mailed armor under his ceremonial robes and a black handled sword at his side in the traditional curve. The king strode from the tent, taking in the scene before him, but his gaze gave nothing away as it focused upon Colind.

Colind bowed his head respectfully to the king of Zsensibar, and their small party followed suit. "Your Highness."

King Nasim's dark eyes studied him for a moment and then bowed his head slightly. "Guardian of the Safanarion Order," he said softly, which was in contrast to his broad shoulders and well-muscled arms. The king was in perfect fighting shape despite being well into his fifties.

"Peace be upon Zsensibar, Your Highness," Colind replied formally. "May I introduce to you Tersellis the Ambassador of the Hythariam Nation."

The king's eyes strayed to the Hythariam, and Tersellis inclined his head enough to show respect, but not enough to imply subservience. The Hythariam were proving to be very good negotiators indeed.

"Peace be upon the Hythariam," the king replied and then added, "and to the Safanarion Order."

"Thank you, Your Highness," Colind replied.

King Nasim returned his dark eyed gaze to Colind. "My son has told me of a fantastical journey into the cursed kingdom of Shandara. To be honest, I almost had him shackled for telling such lies."

Colind felt Admiral Morgan stiffen behind him and hoped that his normally ornery nature when it came to his men was kept firmly in check. The king's eyes scanned their small group and lingered for a moment upon Vaughn and Garret.

"I can see this does not meet with your approval," King Nasim said. "Seeing the legendary guardian of the Safanarion Order has given me pause in my immediate reaction to the situation surrounding my son. Speaking of which, I do not see Prince Cyrus among you. As my son was in his keeping, I would have thought he would be present upon this field and face me himself."

Most of the soldiers with them were originally from the Rexellian Corps and stiffened at the blow to their crowned prince.

"Please, if I may," Tersellis said quickly. "There are things that I wish to speak to you about that will shed light to the absence of our friend the prince, and I humbly ask you to allay any bad feelings until after you've heard what we've had to say."

King Nasim took a few moments, considering what the Hythariam had said, and with his nose in the air, nodded once.

"Prince Jopher will be present at these proceedings," Colind said, and it was not lost upon anyone nearby that he had addressed the king without his honorific title.

The king's eyes bored into Colind's unyielding gray eyes, but Colind's will was like granite and would not yield to the Zsensibarian king.

Tersellis broke the silence again, "Please, Your Highness, your son was with the party that trekked into Shandara and freed Colind. It makes sense to hear his account firsthand, as he will have much to add."

After a few moments, the king turned his thunderous gaze to Captain Amir and nodded toward the tent. Less than a minute later, Jopher strode from the tent at a quick pace and came to a stop between the two factions with his father, the king, upon one side and the Free Nations Army upon the other. He bowed respectfully toward both and coolly met his father's gaze.

"What ideas have you infected my son with that he does not stand with his kingdom?" King Nasim asked.

Jopher looked uncertainly toward his father and then back at Admiral Morgan, who gave him a nod that was not missed by the king. Jopher moved to his father's side.

"I would know your name," King Nasim said.

Morgan stepped forward. "My Lord, I am Admiral Morgan of the Free Nations Army. The airships you see behind me are a small squadron under my command."

King Nasim's eyes narrowed. "Free Nations Army?"

"Yes, Your Highness," Tersellis answered. "Allow us to explain," he said, gesturing toward Colind, Vaughn, and Garret to step forward.

The soldiers at the king's side stiffened at the movement of so many men near their ruler, but Nasim seemed unimpressed.

"Very well," King Nasim said. "Continue."

Tersellis nodded for Vaughn to begin. Vaughn stepped up and told the king about meeting Aaron and how he was the only surviving descendant of the house Alenzar'seth. Vaughn spoke of their travels to Rexel and beyond, and despite Colind knowing the tale of their journey that took them to Shandara, he was always a bit awestruck by its telling. Aaron had defied all the odds and survived his many encounters with the Elitesmen to get to him. As Vaughn spoke, he had Jopher offer his perspective on the events that they had both been a part of and Colind observed the grudging approval take root in the king's eyes when he looked at his son. There were more than a few times when King Nasim raised his brow at his son's bearing as he told his version of their journey. Jopher's account of his time with Aaron was filled with pure truth and he did not seek to diminish the events that involved him. Jopher even spoke of his time serving on board the Raven in the kitchens like a common servant, which led to his acceptance into the camaraderie of the crew of the Raven. Although the king's gaze took on a dangerous glint when it came upon Morgan, the admiral returned the king's gaze in kind and would not be cowed.

Tersellis cleared his throat and spoke of their actions after Shandara, and how they were working with the nations of this world to help stand against the invading horde from their home world of Hytharia and possibly the armies of the High King. At this point, the king almost rolled his eyes, but waited for him to continue. When Tersellis finally finished speaking, the silence carried on for minutes while the king collected his thoughts.

"Father," Jopher said, "I beg of you to please listen to these men and consider what they have said. I do not wear the uniform of the Free Nations Army to spite you or our home. I wear the uniform to help protect my home and stand with those who would protect this world. This is not an action I've taken lightly nor without a fair amount of thought, but I have sworn an oath."

King Nasim narrowed his gaze. "The best place to protect your home is from within our borders." The king held up his hand as Jopher was about to protest. "I have listened, as you have requested, and now I will speak my piece. The reason why Zsensibar thrives is because we have not been drawn into the wars of the north," the king said, nodding toward Colind and the others. "They would draw us into their war and make their struggles our own, but I assure you they are not."

King Nasim turned toward Colind. "You say this heir of Alenzar'seth is mighty enough to stand against the High King and the might of the Elitesmen? What are our assurances that he will not turn his power upon us should our goals not be aligned?"

The king's question drew blank stares from them, as none had ever pictured Aaron as the tyrant.

The king continued. "How do you know he will not turn on you as High King Amorak has done to you all? Better the enemy that you know than the one you would never see coming. I would have thought the lessons of Shandara's fall would have taught you that."

The king's questions stunned them all to silence until Jopher at last spoke. "Do you trust me, Father?" Jopher asked quietly.

The king turned back toward his son. His gaze taking his measure. "This is not a matter of trust, my son, this is a matter of what is best for Zsensibar, your home."

"I am your son," Jopher said. "I stand among your many heirs to your throne, but I say I am your son with pride as a son should before his father. I would ask that you hear me when I say that your worries where Aaron is concerned are unfounded. He is not and never will be like the High King or the Elitesmen. No matter how much power he attains. It is simply a matter of who he is. He walks his own path and asks nothing of anyone else that he wouldn't do for himself. In fact, I would daresay that Aaron would prefer to do most things himself to prevent his companions from coming into harm's way."

Jopher's statement drew knowing smiles from Vaughn, Garret, and Morgan, which was not lost upon the king.

The king turned his disapproving gaze back to the others. "The young are often easily impressionable."

"Normally, I would agree with you in that regard, your Grace," Colind said. "But on rare occasions such as this, the impressions have the right of it."

Tersellis cleared his throat. "Your Highness, if I may," he began and took out the device he had used to convince the other leaders back in Rexel a few days before.

The king held up his hand and his soldiers took a menacing step forward with their hands upon their swords.

"I think not, Ambassador," the king said. "At this point I will not be swayed by any magical displays you've used to persuade the other kingdoms to your cause."

"Father, please," Jopher began, and the king silenced him with a withering glare.

"A son should know his place," King Nasim said.

"A king should know when to listen," Jopher replied tersely.

The air solidified between them, and in one swift motion, the King spun, striking Jopher with a gloved fist sending him to the ground.

The soldiers, some of which had been sailors who had served with Jopher on the Raven, moved forward, but Colind held up his hands to hold them in their place. While the king had his back to them, the Zsensibar soldiers did not, and Colind didn't want this to turn into a blood bath.

Jopher regained his feet, and the king closed the distance between them in a single stride. "A son should know better than to question the will of his father," he said and raised his fist to strike Jopher again.

Colind watched as Jopher fluidly stepped inside the blow and pinned his father's arm behind him, holding it roughly in place. The king's guards clenched their swords, but waited for the king's command to draw them.

"A son maybe," Jopher said eyeing the guards. "But it is the duty of a prince to stand for what is best for his home even when its King is too stubborn to listen. The threat to this world is like nothing you've ever seen before. None of us have. We cannot cling to our methods from the past if we are to have any hope for our future."

Jopher released his father's arm and stepped away, putting a small amount of distance between himself and his father, but stood resolute, waiting upon the wrath of the king in whatever form it would take. The Zsensibar soldiers stood frozen, waiting the king's word. The king's chest rose and fell as the only visible signs of the rage building inside. He glared around him and as he was about to unleash the full armament of his rage, a screech pierced the sky as the clearing around them filled with answering cries of Ryakuls emerging from the surrounding forests.

Colind heard the blaring alarms from the airships behind them following the roars of the Ryakuls. How had the Ryakuls gotten so close without anyone noticing?

"Treachery!" the king screamed.

Two of the Zsensibar soldiers charged forward with crossbows raised. Colind brought his arms up, poised to lash out, but Jopher swept their feet out from under them, calling out an apology as he did so.

"We're under attack," Admiral Morgan barked, then he turned toward the king. "If we can coordinate our efforts, we may survive this."

The king glared back at the Admiral, taking his measure and then gave a single grim nod.

"Get back to the ship," Colind ordered. "I will do what I can from down here."

Admiral Morgan looked as if he were about to protest, but thought better of it and ordered his men back to the ships.

Colind glanced at Garret. "You should head back with the others."

Garret's bushy gray eyebrows raised in amusement despite the Ryakuls closing in. "Like hell I will, My Lord. I stand with the head of the Safanarion Order."

Colind turned to see Jopher standing before his father, surrounded by a wall of spears. At their approach, some turned and leveled their spears in Colind's direction. He'd had enough and swept his arms out in front of him, opening a hole in the lines of men straight to the king.

"Go on, lad," Colind said to Jopher. "They need you up there. I will look after your father."

The king looked about to protest, but was startled by the roar of a Ryakul plummeting down upon their position.

Colind clawed his hands to his side, summoning an orb of crackling energy like liquid lightning, and thrust his hands out, sending it streaking blue into the black tusked maw of the closing Ryakul. He followed up with another orb, which burst through the Ryakul's black leathery wings. The soldiers formed their lines with spears and shields establishing the front ranks. Arrows flew and the Ryakul crashed into the ground, howling as it came.

The Zsensibar soldiers closed in to finish off the dying beast, and Colind turned back to the king, who nodded back grimly. They were allied for the moment, but he knew he must keep a wary eye upon the king.

"Cover their airships," the king ordered his men, gesturing beyond Colind. "They need time to move into position to cover us."

Stubborn and prideful King Melchoir Nasim may be, but once on task, he quickly adapted to a situation while keeping in mind all available resources, regardless if they were his own or not. If they were to survive this attack, they needed to work together. Garret stayed near his side and drew his sword as Colind scanned the sky. There were ten Ryakuls, each the size of a large building, swooping down upon the Zsensibarian army. Their black hides swallowed the light and their saber tusked maws ripped soldiers apart indiscriminately. The tips of the Ryakuls wings were adorned with blades and each swoop down from the sky above was accompanied with a harsh screech that ended with men being cut down where they stood. The Zsensibar troops were quick to adapt to the Ryakul attack pattern and less men lost their lives to those cursed wings. The troops used their long spears to good measure so when a Ryakul did swoop down upon them, they extracted a heavy toll upon the Ryakul's armored hide.

Five of the airships closed in, with the Raven bringing up the rear. Five

Ryakuls launched up into the air, with one being shot down in a hail of explosive tipped arrows from the lead ship. Of the five Ryakuls upon the ground, four remained alive, while the others changed their tactics and resorted to brute strength, butchering the lines of men before them.

The Raven broke off from the formation, gaining speed, and the remaining four Ryakuls in the air pursued relentlessly. The great airship listed to the side to compensate for the sharp turn it was making and the agile Ryakuls easily followed.

Colind watched as the other airships pursued the Ryakuls, and even from the ground he could see the giant crossbows ready to fire from the bow of the ship. The ground shook beneath his feet catching some of soldiers around them by surprise and causing them to stumble. The ground flew away from Colind's feet as he was swept up into the air and then came crashing down to the earth. A Ryakul leaped over the Zsensibar soldiers to get to him. The saber tusked maw growled viciously as it closed in and the breath seized in Colind's chest. Off to the side a lone voice cried out, and the king dug his spear into the side of the Ryakul's head, catching the beast by surprise.

Colind looked up to find King Melchoir Nasim himself reaching down to pull him back onto his feet. The Ryakul shook its head and roared with the heft of the spear sticking out at an odd angle. Colind drew in the energy causing the ground to crack beneath the Ryakul's feet. The great winged beast sank into the earth, falling off balance as it scrambled with its claws to regain its footing.

The soldiers bellowing their war cry converged upon the beast, slaying it as the very earth beneath its feet kept it rooted in place.

"Thank you, My Lord Guardian," the king said, stepping to Colind's side. "I know the Safanarion Order and Zsensibar haven't always seen eye to eye, but today we fight as one."

They both watched as the Free Nations Army airships lured the more nimble Ryakuls into a chase and were shot down by the other airships, but they did not get away completely unscathed. Some of the airships had taken damage, but all remained in the air.

Despite the bravery of the Zsensibar ground troops, they sustained heavy losses. The field was littered with many of the dead, as the Ryakuls were adept killing machines and held little value to their own numbers. The battle was fierce in its intensity, but over almost as quickly as it had begun, with more than one Zsensibar officer glancing in awe at the Free Nations airships.

The king grimly surveyed the carnage around him, as nearly a third of his troops lay dying amid the Ryakul corpses.

"Your airships are impressive, My Lord Guardian," the king said.

"We would not be your enemies, Your Highness," Colind said. "There is a very real threat to this world. None may simply stay to the side and allow it to pass unscathed. The kingdoms that stand alone will be among the first to fall."

The king met Colind's gaze and nodded. "There are forces at work here beyond a random Ryakul attack. Never before have I seen so many attack at once."

"In this we are agreed, and is a taste of things to come," Colind said. How could anyone have known about their meeting here, and who could have moved fast enough to ambush them? They had assumed the Drake was preoccupied with Sarah's assimilation, but perhaps they were wrong not to keep a closer eye upon its whereabouts. Colind shuddered at the thought of what Mactar could do with the power to command the Ryakul.

Curses, Colind thought to himself. *I'm needed elsewhere.*

The Raven heaved into view, dark and majestic, cutting through the billowing smoke. Colind watched as Jopher leaped down from the gangplank followed by the Hythariam. Jopher ordered a group of soldiers to help with the nearby wounded. The king's eyes showed relief that his son was alive and Colind saw the grudging respect that came when a father recognized that his son was becoming a man in his own right.

Jopher ran over to them and stopped when he saw that they were safe. Following the relief in Jopher's eyes was anger glistening in his gaze as the king came before him.

The king raised his hand as Jopher began to speak.

"You've shown great courage, my son. Both on the field of battle and off," the king said. "Worthy of a Prince of Zsensibar and worthy of its future king."

The men around them came to stand still as a hush swept over those nearby.

"Kneel," commanded the king.

Jopher looked uncertain for a moment, but then did as his father commanded. The king drew his sword and placed it upon Jopher's shoulders.

"Do you, Jopher Zamaridian Nasim, accept the mantle of heir to Zsensibar's throne. To henceforth strive for the preservation of her greatness and defend the independent rule of our kingdom and her patrons?"

"I swear," Jopher said.

"Then rise, first among my sons," the king said and turned toward his soldiers. "Men! I give you my heir. His blood is my blood. His will is my will. Acknowledge your future king."

The soldiers across the field sank to their knees and spoke in thunderous unison, "Jopher Zamaridian Nasim, our future king!"

The soldiers repeated their acknowledgment twice more and Tersellis came next to Colind and quietly asked, "What just happened?"

"The Kings of Zsensibar take many wives, and from their offspring, can select any as the future ruler of that kingdom. Our young friend is among the youngest in a long line of would be heirs and has been put first. Once the King makes his selection known, he cannot simply take it away again," said Colind.

Tersellis nodded and inclined his head in Jopher's direction.

Jopher rose up. "You honor me, Father."

King Nasim shook his head. "No, this day it is you who honor me."

"Father, it is my intention to stay with the Free Nations Army," Jopher said.

Colind noticed how Jopher announced his intention without indicating that it was a want, which was a testament to how much he had grown.

The king frowned for a moment. "We can discuss it along with the many things we need to discuss with this envoy."

Colind's focus drifted away from the conversation, setting his attention northward. He felt the faint stirrings amid the currents of energy up there. A presence that echoed as if from a great distance caught his attention that he had never felt before. He felt his gaze narrow, peering beyond the clouds toward Khamearra, allowing his augmented sight to see beyond those of ordinary men. He rode along the currents, leaving his body behind, and the sky turned dark as night fell upon this part of Safanar. There were few among the Safanarion Order blessed with the sight, and he was among the last. His skills had grown rusty from his imprisonment and he struggled to remain focused, but there was a vibrant presence just beyond his senses. The night darkened around him until a great white beacon of light blazed through the night sky.

The power of the Ferasdiam!

Myths and legend told of the power of Ferasdiam Marked and their ability to call upon the Eldarin, which was what the Lords of Dragons called themselves. Colind felt his mouth open many miles from where he was. The beacon flared brilliantly, pulsating in the rhythm of Aaron's lifebeat. It could be no one else as Aaron alone held the power within him. Colind searched the sky to see if any of the Eldarin would answer the call. The dragon lords had long faded to myth with many doubting their existence.

There was a flash of golden light fading to green as the answering call of the Eldarin pierced the night. A dragon lord hovered above the beacon, its light reflecting off its golden hide. After the barest of moments it winked out of sight, moving at speeds too fast even for him to track, and plunged headlong into the city below.

The *Eldarin* answered the call. Colind was so awestruck that his focus unraveled and he felt himself pulled back to his body. He felt himself collapse to the ground, and Garret was at his side holding him up.

"What did you see?" Garret asked, knowing full well what Colind had been up to.

Colind reigned in his racing thoughts and looked back at Garret, blinking away his confusion. "Something wonderful," he whispered.

Colind stood up. They were mostly alone, with soldiers still moving about and the airships hovering behind them.

"The others are speaking in the king's tents," Garret said. "I told them we would be along when you returned."

"Garret, Aaron has summoned the *Eldarin*," Colind said.

"What?" Garret gasped. "I thought they were a myth."

Colind shook his head. "They are not. I saw one and it was magnificent beyond words."

Garret smiled and Colind couldn't help but join in. "I need to leave."

"What do you mean?" Garret asked, the smile leaving his face.

"I need to travel to the north," Colind answered. "Faster than our airships can travel. Something sets itself against us, and I can guess that the Drake has somehow gleaned our plans and sent the Ryakuls to attack."

Garret frowned. "How would it know what we were doing?"

"I cannot begin to guess at what the Drake is capable of, but I know commanding the Ryakuls is among them," Colind answered. "If others knew that it was possible to command them, then they will seek to press their advantage."

Garret's brow furrowed in thought. "By others you mean Mactar."

Colind nodded. "I have to seek him out. If Zsensibar would join our cause, it will be in Tersellis's hands now."

"How will you even find them? You need help. Let's use the Raven to come to Aaron's aid," Garret said.

"Aaron's in trouble?" Jopher asked, coming up behind them. "I'm coming," he insisted.

Colind suppressed a groan. "I can't take you with me."

Garret narrowed his gaze. "How will you find them?"

"I will follow the currents of energy," Colind replied. "This is not something either of you can do."

"Let us take the Raven. She is the fastest ship and besides, once Jopher informs Admiral Morgan of your intentions, he will head that way anyway." Garret nodded to Jopher who turned around and ran back toward the tent.

"Subtle, Garret. Very subtle," Colind said with only a hint of annoyance.

"You and Aaron suffer from the same affliction of late, believing that you need to do these things all by yourselves. We are a team. When we get closer you can always charge off ahead and beat us there, but perhaps if we leverage our assets we may glean some intelligence on the way," Garret finished.

Colind's mouth curved in a half grin. "Didn't Vaughn say something about old dogs learning new tricks?"

"It was Verona, and I'm not as old as you, but you can see the wisdom in my point, otherwise you would have just charged off," Garret replied.

Jopher returned with not only Morgan, but with King Nasim as well as the others. Colind explained that they needed to leave immediately based upon what he saw unfold in Khamearra. Tersellis was silent for a moment until one of his Hythariam bodyguards whispered into his ear, and he nodded.

"We've finally gotten word from Gavril," Tersellis said. "They've succeeded in Khamearra and after they regroup he expects they will be leaving the city."

Colind shared a look with Garret and Vaughn. Aaron would only quit the city after he had gotten what he came for, and that meant he had the travel crystals in his possession.

"Thank you, Tersellis. Did Gavril report anything else?" Colind asked.

Tersellis shook his head, but something in the Hythariam's golden eyes told him there was more he wasn't saying.

Colind turned to the king. "Your Highness, it appears that some of us need to leave sooner than expected. I hope you will consider carefully what you've been told. We would very much like to call you an ally and friend in the dark days ahead."

Tersellis held out a small comms device and offered it to the king. "You can use this to reach us with your answer."

The king took the device and Tersellis proceeded to give instructions on its use. They headed back to the ships, save Jopher, who stood before his father waiting.

Father and son regarded each other for a moment before the king inclined his head. Jopher's eyes lit up and headed back toward the Raven. The king smiled proudly, which was quickly overshadowed by the worry in his furrowed brows. He turned toward his staff and began issuing orders, taking long purposeful strides through the camp.

Admiral Morgan signaled to two of the airships to head back to Rexel and report in while the remaining four airships would head north toward where they suspected the Drake lay in wait.

King Melchoir Nasim did not commit himself to the Free Nations as of yet, but he had allowed Jopher to return with them, and that was a good sign. Colind doubted whether the king could have actually stopped his son, short of taking the lad into custody, which would not be wise. Morgan assured the king that Jopher would be under his command and that he would look after him. Colind knew that Morgan held no love for the Zsensibar king, but had in fact grown fond of its prince and heir apparent. He joined the Hythariam who consulted their devices and helped pinpoint their heading. Colind would use his own skills to make corrections, because in his experience technology could only get you so far, but he hoped it would be enough.

20

DEMON'S TAUNTING

They had left behind the smoky capital city of Khamearra, using their travel crystals as they went. Mactar was able to leave a few key messages for Rordan to find should he survive the night. He really wasn't sure what Rordan would do, but if he was smart and could follow the breadcrumbs he had left behind, then he may yet be of some use to him. Darven had remained silent and quietly followed him. Darven was a good apprentice, never asking endless amounts of questions, and when it came time to follow orders, he did so quickly. The value the former Elitesman brought was in his ability to act without being specifically told what to do, and he had proven on more than one occasion that he was someone dependable.

It was still nighttime, though the further east they traveled the sooner dawn would arrive. They were in the Waylands, using its centralized location to quickly observe the goings-on near Rexel. Prince Cyrus had become the spearhead uniting the forces behind the Heir of Shandara, and Mactar was impressed with the progress they were making in preparing for war. They just happened to be on the wrong side, which accounted for everyone not serving his purpose. He had wanted to stop to take a quick look around before proceeding further east to the Shadow Lands, as they were known today, but for others they knew it as Shandara. The Ryakuls had always concentrated in that area, and Mactar surmised that the Drake was somewhere within Shandara's borders.

"Are you sure the High King didn't require our assistance?" Darven asked.

"I'm certain of it," Mactar said. "Besides, what we're doing is more important."

"And what is that exactly?"

"The Drake can control the Ryakul," Mactar answered. "And we're going to try to figure out how it does that."

Darven gave a dubious frown. "There has got to be more to it than that."

The same qualities that Mactar appreciated in Darven also came at a price, and that price was he being required to reveal more of his plans than he would have preferred. He should have expected nothing less from Darven.

"Something has always puzzled me about the Ryakuls, but I've never had the time, nor inclination, to give them my full attention," Mactar said. "They restricted themselves to the borders of Shandara, but have recently ventured further and further from its borders. If one were able to control them, then they would be a force to contend with on any battlefield. They could turn the tide of wars, even with the elusive Hythariam."

"Mactar, the Hythariam are not so elusive anymore, and they have aligned themselves with the Alenzar'seth. Many have flocked to his banner at Rexel."

"Indeed," Mactar said. "In that you are correct, but—" He stopped himself, unsure whether he should share the knowledge he had kept hidden for so long. Darven, he noted, simply waited patiently. "They are not the only Hythariam out there."

Darven narrowed his gaze. "What do you mean, not the only Hythariam?"

"You know the Hythariam first appeared on our world about eighty years ago?" Mactar asked, and when Darven nodded he continued, "Things were very different then."

"Hold on a minute," Darven interrupted. "Are you saying that you were there when the Hythariam first came to Safanar?"

"Not exactly," Mactar answered. "I was among the first members of the Safanarion Order."

"The Safanarion Order!" Darven gasped.

Mactar watched the barrage of thoughts play through Darven's face. "It is true, I assure you. Although we didn't call ourselves that in the beginning, and the only person to remember is Colind."

"But that would mean you are over a hundred years old," Darven sputtered.

"There are ways to slow down aging," Mactar replied mildly.

"Yeah but—" Darven began.

"Let's not get caught up in my age," Mactar said. "Just trust in the fact that I was there when the Hythariam first came to our world. I was witness to the barrier when it first came to being. The Hythariam possess powerful knowledge of undreamed potential with a vast array of weapons and soldiers. Most believe the Drake to be demon spawn, but nothing could be further from the truth. The Drake is quite literally not of this world."

"What world is it from then?" Darven asked.

Mactar's gaze grew distant. "What world indeed," came his faint reply.

"Do you know why the barrier went up in the first place?" Darven asked.

"Not entirely," he lied. "There was some type of falling out with the Hythariam. I don't know how the Alenzar'seth created the barrier, but that is not why I'm telling you this."

"Fine," Darven said. "Keep going."

"I suspect that the Ryakuls have something to do with the Hythariam," Mactar said. "I always have, but have never had anything to prove the claim.

Regardless, if the Drake can somehow control the Ryakul, then I want to observe how it's done and, if possible, take that control for myself."

Darven nodded. "I see, but what do you plan to do with the Ryakuls if you are able to control them? I doubt the Drake will sit idly by while you take away something that up until now was solely within its dominion."

"The Drake will only attack if it perceives us as standing between its main objective," Mactar said.

"Which is?" Darven asked.

"The annihilation of the Alenzar'seth," Mactar replied, keeping his own bitterness from his voice.

"Just so I'm clear on what we're doing," Darven continued, "we're to sneak into the den of the Ryakuls and observe how the Drake controls them?"

"That about sums it up," Mactar replied and felt a small chill slink across the back of his neck.

Darven's frown deepened as he stared off to the east. "I wonder how the Ryakuls numbers have grown so much of late."

Mactar schooled his features. "An excellent question, and truth be told, they are not of Safanar either."

"How do you know this?" Darven asked, but was answered by Mactar's contemptible silence.

"*He fills your head with half truths,*" a raspy voice whispered.

Darven drew his sword and scanned the area, poised to attack anything that would dare threaten them.

Mactar seized the energy around them, giving in to his reaction to Tarimus's voice.

"I heard it that time," Darven said. "Come out, Tarimus."

They were greeted with a faint raspy laugh that despite himself had sent shivers down Mactar's spine. Tarimus was back in phase with the world and yet remained so aloof.

"*Your master will betray you Elitesman,*" Tarimus taunted.

Mactar cast out around him, quickly finding where Tarimus hid, but he was gone in an instant.

"Show yourself!" Darven shouted. "How does he move around so fast?"

Mactar felt Darven draw the energy into himself and charge off into the trees quicker than any normal person could see. He aligned the energy within him, allowing his solid form to dissipate, stretching so that he appeared like smoke. The essence of Mactar rose to the tree line and followed his Elitesman apprentice.

Darven charged off, seeking the demon spawn Tarimus. The Grand Master of the Elite had awarded him the rank of Adept because he was so gifted in his ability to use the energy around him. The rank, much like the Order, held little in the way of keeping him within the confines of its practices. It was no mere happenstance that he alone was able to break free of the Elitesmen Order and survive in recent memory. He moved quickly, striking out on a path very few could discern, let alone follow. He gained on Tarimus, who moved in and out of phase dotting the path before him. Darven discerned the pattern of his movements and seized the travel crystal, merging his energy with its own and surged ahead predicting where Tarimus would reappear.

He collided with the specter as they both transitioned back into phase.

Darven had his sword out before him, with its single edge catching fleeting glints of the fading moonlight.

Tarimus slowly rose to his feet and pulled back the hood of his cloak, revealing pasty white skin stretched over a completely bald head. Eyes of inky blackness regarded him.

"All right, Elitesman," Tarimus said, drawing his dark blade that hissed free of its sheath. He brought both his hands up, holding the blade ready with his feet planted shoulder width apart. Tarimus brandished his dark blade, slicing the air around him. Then held it ready behind him as he beckoned with his other hand.

Darven, poised on one leg, angled the sword over his head in observance of the ancient sword forms. For the span of seconds, they stood unmoving, embracing the stillness around them, then Darven charged. Their blades met, ringing out in dawn's early light, signaling the beginning of their deadly dance. The two masters moved through the field, each testing the other's strengths, and assessing any weaknesses.

"You are very good," Tarimus said, breaking off the attack. "But you can never stand against the Alenzar'seth."

Darven swung his sword again, and Tarimus easily danced away.

"Elitesman, you don't even know when you are outclassed. Trust in that you will meet your end by the Alenzar'seth's hand. He knows you were there that night."

"Let him come," Darven said, and he remembered throwing the dagger that took the life of Aaron's mother. Killing was nothing new to him and many had come seeking vengeance. None had succeeded.

"I give you this message. The master you serve will betray you as he has done to all the others that stood at his side."

Darven dashed forward, seeking to cut through Tarimus's twisted face, but his sword only sliced through the air as Tarimus melted away before his eyes. He cast out with his senses, but he was alone.

After a few moments, Mactar appeared behind him.

"Darven, Tarimus seeks to drive us apart. He is bent on vengeance. I'm the one he wants."

Darven sheathed his sword. "Then why all the games? Why not just strike out? He had the element of surprise."

Mactar was silent for a moment. "Tarimus was my prisoner for many years. I know what he wants. He desires to see his victims squirm, putting them off balance so by the time he strikes they are so frozen with fear that they cannot fight."

Darven glanced around them. A blanket of mist covered the ground with the approaching dawn.

"What else did he say?" Mactar asked.

Darven looked pointedly at Mactar, tilting his head to the side. "He said you would betray me."

Mactar's lips curved into a sardonic grin. "You see, he seeks to put us off balance."

"I have no illusions when it comes to your intentions," Darven said. "I am here because you find me useful and I follow because of the knowledge you have."

"Then we know where we both stand," Mactar replied. "Come. We head to Shandara," he said, walking away.

Darven caught up to him easily. "About that. Travel crystals will only get us so far. They don't work in the actual city of Shandara."

"You are correct, but we don't need to get to the city," Mactar said. "Not this time at least. The Drake is not in the city, but somewhere in the northern mountain ranges. And the travel crystals do work in Shandara, but they are dangerous to use there. We can't blindly use the crystals to travel there, but we could travel there by sight."

"You mean to travel to a place within our field of vision," Darven said.

"Precisely," Mactar answered and held up his hand. "I know we would drain the crystal, but as I have said, we can skirt around the borders of Shandara and gain the knowledge we seek."

Darven nodded. "Let's go then, but there is one thing that does bother me."

"What's that?" Mactar asked.

"How does Tarimus keep finding you?"

"That is another excellent question," Mactar said. "When I figure it out, I'll be sure to let you know."

Darven lips curved into a half grin and he nodded. They each brought out their travel crystals and headed north.

21

THE ELDARIN'S PLEA

The cloaked Flyer class SPT silently eased away from the city, much to the ignorance of its inhabitants. Captain Nolan had seen them off and vowed to Aaron that he would do his best to keep the peace. Aaron wished him well and meant it. The De'anjard presence in Khamearra had proven to be something quite special and he hoped to return to them in the future. He rolled his shoulders, loosening them, and sagged into the cushioned seat of the Hythariam Flyer that changed its contours to match his body. Aaron sucked in a deep breath and exhaled while stifling a yawn.

"When was the last time you slept?" Roselyn asked.

Aaron raised his head slowly. "Probably the same time that you did."

"You need rest," Roselyn said. "We all do."

She was right. This journey was catching up with them all. He saw the same bone weary exhaustion mirrored throughout the Flyer. He turned back to Roselyn, whose golden eyes never left his, and nodded.

"Probably best to just agree with her," Verona whispered when Roselyn moved just outside of earshot.

"I am tired," Aaron said, feeling his shoulders slump further with the admission. "But we're so close. Each moment we delay…"

"I know, my friend. I know," Verona said, almost dozing. "Wasn't it you who told us on the deck of the Raven to take a moment to center yourself. Well, this is your moment. Recover your strength. Even working with the energy as we do takes a toll upon us and is not a substitute for actual rest. You won't be any good to Sarah when we find her if you can't think straight."

Aaron smiled tiredly and felt his eyes droop a little. "Glad you were paying attention." He looked back at Verona. "You said when, not if. Thanks."

Verona snorted. "I guess I did. My friend, I've never lost faith in you. You will find a way through this, of that I am convinced. And I will stand at your side watching your back as you do."

He nodded at Verona, sat back, and let his eyes close. Aaron settled his head back and released the breath he had been holding, allowing his mind to relax. He slipped into a dull, dreamless sleep.

A low-level alarm pulled him out of his slumber. He pushed his eyelids open and noticed that the others were all sleeping, save for the Hythariam, who were huddled at the front of the Flyer. Aaron wiped the sleep from his eyes and unbuckled himself from the seat. He had no idea how long he slept, but was sure it couldn't have been that long. He heard the Hythariam speaking in hushed tones as he came up and Tanneth silenced the alarm.

"What is it?" Aaron asked.

Gavril glanced back at him. "Proximity alarm. You're not going to believe this, but we have two dragons flying on either side of us."

Aaron looked at the screen. It was slightly opaque signifying they were still in stealth. The medallion grew cool upon his chest. Just as Gavril had said, there were two enormous dragons flying on either side of the Hythariam craft dwarfing it in size. The dragons were larger than the one that he and Verona had met when he had first came to Safanar.

"Can you come out of stealth? They know we're here," Aaron said.

"Are you sure?" Tanneth said, and Gavril nodded to him after glancing at Aaron.

"What's happening?" Verona asked, joining them and then looked down at the screen. His eyes widened at the sight of the dragons and his eyes darted immediately to Aaron.

"What do you think they want?" Gavril asked.

"Me, I think," Aaron said.

"Doesn't everyone," Verona grinned.

Both dragons had golden hides, but each had their own unique blend of colors with one gravitating more toward greens and the other, blues. The dragon with the bluish hues flew in front of them with a powerful flap of its wings. Aaron focused himself and his perceptions sharpened, seeing the shafts of energy gleaming from the two dragons.

"Do you see that?" Tanneth asked, pointing to one of the charts that sprang up on screen. "That's the energy reading from the dragon. I've never seen so much come from any life form before."

"We should follow them," Aaron said.

The dragon changed course, turning slightly, and Tanneth followed easily. Once the dragon was satisfied they were following, it tucked in its wings and streaked ahead of them. Tanneth increased the flyer's velocity to catch up. The dragon spun in the air, dodging past some tall trees, and Tanneth performed the same aerial stunt matching the dragon. The contest continued for a few moments and then a mountain range loomed ahead. The Flyer hugged the earth and the treetops zipped past them. Despite not feeling any of the inertia they should have been feeling while flying at these speeds, Aaron held onto the seat in front of him just the same.

"They're so fast," Sarik said, joining them. "I've never seen a dragon fly like that. He is not even flapping his wings."

Aaron reached out with his senses and felt the same presence he had felt at the arena. "These are the Eldarin."

Gavril eyed him for a moment, his brows raised in silent questioning.

"The one in front of us is the same dragon that came to my aid in the arena," Aaron said. "It knows I'm Ferasdiam Marked."

"Sir," Tanneth said, and Gavril turned to the front. "We're reaching the limits of the Flyer's ability for atmospheric flight. We cannot go much faster, but I believe they could," the blonde Hythariam said gesturing in front of them. "I think they are testing our abilities."

Gavril nodded. "Stay on course, Tanneth." The Hythariam colonel looked back to Aaron. "I'll be honest, we've never encountered these Eldarin before. Not even during the time of Daverim or Reymius."

"They told me their numbers are few and that there are things we need to know. They helped me against the Elitesmen. I think we should see what they want," Aaron said.

Both of the Eldarin flew ahead of their ship, momentarily disappearing over a mountain peak. The Hythariam flier quickly closed the distance and as they crested the peaks, they were all shocked into silence. Nestled amid the mountains was a valley seemingly carved from the mountains themselves. The surface was flat, but as they got closer they could see the smooth stonework and columns circling the great valley. The Eldarin landed near the center, and Tanneth circled over. The ground was adorned with dragon emblems mostly faded with the passage of time. There were several archways large enough for the Eldarin to easily pass throughout the valley.

Aaron didn't see any roads or trails leading to the valley. "You can only reach this place by climbing the mountain or flying in. I don't see how people would be climbing here unless they already knew of the place."

"Taking us in," Tanneth said, navigating the Hythariam Flyer to land before the two Eldarin.

Aaron was first to step out of the craft and was awestruck by the sheer size of the Eldarin. With the rune-carved staff in hand, he briskly walked out in front of the Hythariam ship and was quickly joined by the others. The Eldarin sat back upon their haunches, lifting their heads to a height equivalent of a four-story building. The vibrant intensity of their gaze made Aaron feel stripped bare, as if there was nothing he could hide from them even if he wanted to. A low rumbling sound echoed throughout the valley. Verona, Sarik, and Braden could be heard muttering a prayer to the Goddess. Aaron took a purposeful step forward, but inclined his head respectfully.

"*Thank you for joining us, Ferasdiam Marked. Normally we would only commune with one who is marked by fate, but we will let our voices be heard by those who travel with you,*" the Eldarin said in unison.

Aaron turned to the others, who nodded back to him that they had understood.

"Thank you for helping me before," Aaron said. "To be honest, I didn't know I was calling anyone."

The two dragon lords eyed each other, appearing to communicate without speaking at all. Then they turned their gaze upon him, sweeping him in a torrent of energy.

"*We have heard of you through the passing of one of our children. You were there at the moment of his transcendence,*" the Eldarin said. "You feel the lifebeat and know of the wrongness of the fallen ones."

Aaron swallowed, absorbing the unspoken words, taking in the Eldarin's juxtaposed voices inside his head.

"The fallen ones?" Aaron asked.

One of the Eldarin tilted his head to the side and an image of a Ryakul sprang before them. The black skin stretched over bat-like wings with its saber tusked maw opening like an enormous cave. The armored tail ended in a spike. Aaron felt the blood course through his veins and his chest fill as if his heart would burst. His teeth clamped down and he felt himself become rigid. The Ryakuls were the enemy.

"*You see. You sense the wrongness of the fallen ones.*"

Aaron steeled his emotions while he searched for the meaning of what the Eldarin were trying to convey to him.

"The Ryakuls attack dragons," Aaron said. "They are the enemy. They serve the Drake."

"*No, Ferasdiam Marked,*" the Eldarin said. "*The fallen ones are also our children. Their songs grow dark as they descend into madness.*"

"Your...children," Aaron gasped. His mind reeled, trying to force the pieces together, and at the same time refused to believe. The Ryakuls were once dragons. "How have your children fallen?"

The Eldarin's powerful gaze shifted behind him to settle upon the Hythariam. Gavril, Roselyn, and Tanneth's golden eyes widened in shock.

Gavril stepped forward. "With respect. We have not caused any of your kind to fall."

The Eldarin shifted their gazes to Aaron. "*One of their kind spreads a sickness that changes what was once beautiful and vibrant into something hideous. They are the fallen.*"

Aaron turned to Gavril. "The Drake is of Hytharia. Who is to say that this is not something it could have done?"

Gavril's eyes grew distant as he considered, and then he shrugged his shoulders and shook his head.

"The Ryakuls attack us on sight," Aaron said, turning back to the Eldarin. "The only way for us to stop them is to kill them, but if you know of a way that we could help them instead, then perhaps there is something that we can do to help you."

The Eldarin regarded each other for a few long moments before turning back to them.

"*We know of no way to help the fallen ones. We seek to protect what is left of our children. They would answer the call of the Ferasdiam Marked and engage the fallen ones to their doom.*"

Aaron looked around him as he finally understood. The Eldarin were concerned with the preservation of the dragons. Their children. That he would call them into battle with the Ryakul and… He turned back to the others.

"We've always wondered where the Ryakuls came from and why their numbers had grown," Aaron said. "The Ryakuls are fallen dragons. Roselyn, do you know of any sickness that could cause something like this? I don't think this is the work of the Nanites."

"Why not?" Verona asked. "I'm not disagreeing, but I'm not sure why it couldn't be Nanites."

Some of the others nodded, save for Roselyn, who returned his gaze evenly.

"It doesn't fit with the timeline," Aaron pressed. "The presence of the Ryakuls predate the Drake by over fifty years. Do you remember Vaughn talking about the Ryakul Incursion and how they were driven back in Shandara. My bet is that there were no recorded instances of the Ryakuls prior to the portal being opened between Safanar and Hytharia. Something is changing the dragons, turning them into the Ryakuls. The two are ferocious enemies, but perhaps we've got it wrong." Aaron glanced at the Eldarin and then back at his companions. "The dragons have been fighting and losing a war for their very survival right under our noses."

"It could be anything," Gavril whispered, looking visibly shaken, his eyes darting back and forth. "Near the end we weren't able to follow decontamination protocols. Something could have gotten through. Some type of sickness…"

Aaron shook his head. "I'm not blaming you. But we need to find a way to help the dragons if we can."

"I don't know of anything off the top of my head that could cause this," Roselyn said. "I would need to return to Hathenwood and search through our repositories of knowledge. Maybe—" her voice cut off as she stifled a cry and looked up, addressing the Eldarin. "I will try to find a way to help your species. I swear it."

Aaron turned back to the Eldarin, feeling his throat tighten. "I'm so sorry."

Each of the dragon lords lowered their heads in acknowledgement.

"*We of the Eldarin will always heed the call of the Ferasdiam Marked. You are the champion of the Safanarion Realm. Do not forget your purpose.*"

The dragon lords launched into the air with grace and majesty, seeming to float up beyond the push of their wings. The wind rushed passed Aaron's face, blowing his dark hair back as the Eldarin disappeared in a blinding flash of light.

"We caused this," Roselyn gasped, looking at Gavril, whose eyes were downcast in shame. "Perhaps it should have been our fate to die on Hytharia."

"No," Verona said firmly, before Aaron could say the same. "This is not your fault," Verona said gently coming before Roselyn. "You saw a way to survive, my lady, to live and your people took it. Would any of us have done differently?" he said, lifting her chin slightly so she would look him in the eyes.

"You couldn't have known this would happen," Aaron said.

Gavril looked up and the old soldier's golden eyes drew down in shame. "I fear this is as bad as it seems," he said softly, drawing all their attention. "On

Hytharia there was such a beast that could spread a sickness through its bite. Most victims would die of the poison, but some did not. They changed. Mutated into a hybrid of the original host and the victim. These beasts were hunted to extinction on Hytharia, however the venom was preserved. This was long before I was born, before we knew our planet was in danger. I first came across the venom during my time in the military. There was a secret special corps established for the enhancement of our soldiers. The program had been long shut down, as with the invention of the Nanites the venom was no longer required. We could enhance our soldiers without turning them into beasts."

"Who would have known about the venom? Iranus or any of the other scientists?" Aaron asked.

"Not a chance. They were just scientists and not associated with weapons research," Gavril replied. "This was strictly military and only the most senior of the military would have access to this knowledge."

"You think this was a weapon," Aaron said. "But how?"

Gavril sighed and took a long haunted glance at the sky. "Before the barrier went up there was fighting here on Safanar. General Halcylon did get some troops across before the barrier closed completely. Perhaps one of them brought it across, or was enhanced with the venom."

Aaron frowned, trying to remember what he saw when he looked through the barrier in Shandara that linked Safanar to Hytharia. The land was desolate, but there was something massive on the other side. A heavily muscled creature with wild yellow eyes beating its claws against the barrier. He blinked away the memory and looked at Gavril in horror, who nodded back grimly.

"You were there when the barrier first went up," Aaron said. "Were there dragons at this battle?"

Gavril looked to be swallowing something vile back down his throat and nodded slowly.

"We didn't realize." Gavril said.

"That's right, you didn't," Aaron said. "But now you know, so now we can do something about it. We must find a way to help the dragons."

"You don't understand, Aaron," Gavril said. "There is no cure for this. The change, once infected, is permanent. The only way is to exterminate all of the Ryakul on Safanar."

Roselyn pulled away from Verona. "It is not enough that we doomed our home world, but look at what we've done to yours," she said and ran off away from the others.

Aaron looked at Tanneth, who quietly shrugged his shoulders. "I was born here. Safanar is the only home I've ever known."

Aaron nodded and watched as Verona slowly closed the distance between himself and Roselyn. When he caught up to her, he simply stood to the side not saying anything for a few moments, and then slowly reached for her. Roselyn turned and buried her head in Verona's shoulder.

"She was a little girl when she came through the portal to this world," Gavril said. "I'm not sure what she remembers of Hytharia, but she is a healer at heart. Knowing that something we made could cause this..."

A searing pain burned across Aaron's chest, dropping him to his knees. He could hear Gavril call out to the others, but it all sounded muffled. The skin on his chest felt like it was being torn open, causing him to cry out. Aaron gasped for breath and pulled down his shirt, but his skin was untouched. The pain lanced across the dragon tattoo as if something was pulling his heart out of his chest.

Oh, Sarah...

He focused himself, calling the bladesong in his mind, and his perceptions sharpened. The lifebeat of the others pulsed around him with glistening clarity, but coming from his chest was the translucent line of energy that had been there since he had healed Sarah's mortal wounds at the hands of her brother Primus.

The pain came again and the line blared red for a moment before turning back to normal. He had to find her now before it was too late.

Aaron drew away from his physical body and heard Verona's voice as if from a great distance telling the others to wait. He hadn't followed his connection to Sarah this far for fear of causing her more pain, but he had to risk it. He needed to find her. Time was running out.

The land and the sky streaked by as he followed the connection, heading east from where they were. He crested over a mountain peak to a valley crawling with Ryakul, as if the ground below were in constant motion, stopping him in his tracks. Below him was a dark sea of black-winged spawn of what were once majestic dragons. The Ryakuls were much smaller than the Eldarin, but what they couldn't account for in size, they more than made up for in numbers. All was strangely quiet, as in this form he couldn't hear anything, but he could imagine the snarling Ryakuls as they shifted their positions. The Ryakuls appeared extremely agitated and frequently snapped at anything close by, including others of their kind.

A large figure stood upon a plateau amid the Ryakuls. The Drake stood poised, surveying the area with one of its arms abruptly ending in a stump from where his swords had severed the hand that held Sarah at its mercy. Even from this distance the smoldering yellow eyes appeared as liquid steel and the black armor held a purplish hue in the sunlight. The Drake's pale alien face gazed up to the sky and despite what Iranus had told him, Aaron was having difficulty believing that the creature had once been his grandmother.

Several of the Ryakuls clawed and bit at each other, snatching the Drake's attention. The Drake brought up its arm and a small display appeared. The effect on the Ryakuls was immediate as they fell writhing in pain and bowed their heads submissively. On a lower plateau, a dark figure curled into a ball with a lone Ryakul standing watch. Aaron closed the distance to Sarah and hovered over her. Her pale skin held black splotches where it was exposed to the cold mountain air. Her arms were clutched around her middle and her eyes were shut tight. He dared not go any closer lest he lose all control and reach out.

Having Sarah's exact location, he began to pull back to his body. The world streaked by until he slowly opened his eyes. Verona knelt next to him, offering him some water. Aaron nodded his thanks and stood up.

"I know where she is," he said. "East of here, less than twenty miles away."

"That's great," Verona said. "Let us be off then."

"We need a plan," Aaron said. "The Drake has a nest of Ryakuls all over that mountain. I don't think we should charge in, as much as I would like to."

"He's right," Gavril said.

"How did Sarah look?" Roselyn asked, her eyebrows drawing up in concern.

"Not good. I don't think she has much time left," Aaron said and described the dark splotches on her skin and how she was curled up into a shaking ball.

Roselyn put her hand on Aaron's shoulder. "She fights. The Drake has not won yet. Have hope."

Aaron nodded and sighed in relief, unclenching his fists. Seeing Sarah like that, with the Nanites doing their worst, had all but sucked the hope from him.

"Do you think the Drake can detect the ship?" Aaron asked.

The Hythariam regarded each other silently before Gavril answered. "No. If we're cloaked then we are completely hidden."

"The Drake is controlling the Ryakuls," Aaron said. "But I think that if we agitated them enough it would break whatever control it was using over them. We need to draw some of them away while I go and get Sarah."

The others considered what he had said, save Verona. "My friend, I know the first thing you want to do is to rescue Sarah, but if we don't handle the Drake then I think your rescue attempt may be doomed to failure."

"The Drake is not going to sit idly by once our presence is known," Gavril said.

"I propose that we split our efforts into two teams," Aaron said. "The first team will stay with the ship and engage the Ryakuls, drawing as many as they can away from the mountain, clearing the way for the second team. The second team, with myself, will attempt to rescue Sarah and if the Drake— No, when the Drake makes its move, then we take it out."

"A good plan," Gavril said. "There is just one thing I don't like about it. We don't know how Sarah will react when she sees you again."

Aaron looked up in alarm, but waited to hear what Gavril meant.

"The Nanites have some control over her," said Gavril. "She may not want to be rescued even if part of her does. She may fight you or any of us that tries to help, but most especially you, Aaron. Seeing you is going to be traumatic for her."

Aaron sucked in his bottom lip considering. "I know. We'll need to capture her."

"What about the travel crystals?" Verona asked. "Do you know how to make them work?"

Aaron's jaw clamped shut in frustration and shook his head. He had probed the travel crystals, but didn't know how to key them. He had hoped to speak to the Elitesman Isaac about it, but never had the chance.

"Sarah knows how to use them. I'll need to reach her," Aaron said.

They were all silent. No one wanted to ask the obvious question of what he would do if he couldn't reach Sarah, but the question was self evident in all of their gaze.

"She is still in there, despite whatever her appearance may be," Aaron said. "I have to believe that there is still a part of Sarah that hasn't been tainted by the Nanites. That is what I'm fighting for."

Verona cleared his throat. "I've said it before, but I feel that I can speak for all of us in that we'll be at your side to see that you at least get to try."

"About the two teams," Gavril began. "I will be with you on the ground, which leaves Tanneth and Roselyn to pilot the ship." Gavril glanced at Roselyn who nodded back. "Sarik, would you join them on the Flyer? I have two reasons for asking this. First, should the ship become damaged and need to be abandoned, then Tanneth and Roselyn will stand a much better chance at surviving with your support. Second, you've shown a keen aptitude for the Flyer's systems and I would like Tanneth to begin showing you how to pilot the ship."

Sarik's eyes darted to Aaron, who nodded encouragingly to the young man.

"I will do as you ask," Sarik said.

"Thank you," Gavril replied.

"So that leaves the rest of us to go on the ground with you, Aaron," Verona said.

Aaron took a moment to consider his next words. "Okay, but if you can avoid it, don't engage Sarah."

Verona and Braden looked at him as if he said the most obvious thing in the world.

"Fine," Aaron said. "If you do, I may be too preoccupied with the Drake to save your sorry asses." This drew chuckles from all of them and they replied in kind. He was glad for the momentary reprieve.

"About the Drake," Gavril continued. "I'm hoping to help even things out."

"How?" Aaron asked.

"The Drake used Hythariam technology against you in your last encounter, which put you off balance," Gavril said. "I will help nullify this threat. Are we agreed that the Drake will need to be destroyed?" Gavril leveled his gaze at Aaron.

Verona and Braden looked at Aaron questioningly. They did not know the Drake's true identity.

"I have no illusions about the Drake," Aaron answered and then faced the others. "Before we left Hathenwood, Iranus revealed to me that the Drake was created using my grandmother as the Nanite host. The previous Drake had infected her at the fall of Shandara. To the best of my knowledge, Reymius had no knowledge of this."

"He didn't know," said Gavril. "None of us did until it was too late. We believed that Cassandra had died in Shandara."

"She did," Aaron replied solemnly.

Gavril sighed, giving a single nod. "By the time we realized what was happening, the Drake all but disappeared."

"I think the Drake is more vulnerable now than before," Aaron said.

"How so?" Verona asked.

"We need to think like a machine," said Aaron. "The Drake's current form is proving to be ineffective, hence it is focusing on switching hosts and doing nothing to repair its current body. I saw that it never repaired the severed arm from when it took Sarah. So we're agreed we take out the Drake and move to capture Sarah."

The others nodded and Roselyn stepped away, heading toward the Flyer, saying she would be right back.

"Here is what I'm thinking we should do, and I'm hoping you'll tell me if this is too crazy," Aaron said and laid out the plan he had been formulating in his mind. It didn't take long as his plan wasn't all that complex, but he kept certain pieces to himself.

"Verona, I need to speak to you alone for a moment," Aaron said.

The others headed back toward the ship, giving them some privacy.

"Here we are, my friend. Again," Verona said.

Aaron grinned in spite of himself. "Indeed. There is something I need to tell you that I won't be sharing with the others. I will face the Drake only because I don't think we can get Sarah out without alerting it. I don't know how this is going to go and I've often heard it said that the best laid plans can sometimes go to waste once a battle starts." Aaron looked at the others for a moment. "If I can get to Sarah and get the travel crystals to work, I intend to head back to Shandara."

Verona's eyes widened. "But the crystals... They won't work in Shandara."

"That is correct, but they can get me near the city and near the barrier, as well. I've felt the imbalance there and believe that I could reach Shandara where others would fail." Aaron said. "I will only do this if there is no other choice and I wanted you to know so you can find us."

Verona nodded grimly. "I understand. I wish we had Colind's counsel for what we're about to do."

Aaron returned his friend's gaze, hoping that fate would deem them worthy of a kind hand in this, but either way, this business would be finished today. He just hoped they were all alive by the end.

Mactar and Darven crouched low amid a tree line's edge before the steep incline of a mountain teaming with Ryakuls. They had been there only a short while and saw that the Drake could, in fact, have some measure of control over the ferocious beasts. The control was barely tenable at best with the Drake's attention focused on maintaining the perimeter. They crept as close as they dared, and had a clear view of the plateau upon which the Drake now stood. It kept looking back at the other plateau where two Ryakuls now sat poised. The other Ryakuls appeared more agitated. Mactar couldn't recall ever seeing so many of the beasts in one place. Fighting among the beasts broke out frequently, which were suppressed when the Drake would activate a device upon its wrists.

Mactar utilized his skills to provoke the Ryakuls so he could focus upon the actions the Drake took to control them. He focused himself, seeing the many lines of energy, but what he was looking for was more subtle. A glowing display appeared above the device on the Drake's wrists. It was pulsing brightly and even with his heightened perceptions, he could barely make out the strumming sound in a freakish rhythm.

The affect on the Ryakul was almost instantaneous as their attention became fixated upon the Drake. Mactar winced at the screeching sounds piercing his ears, and several Ryakuls immediately took to the skies.

Mactar glanced back to Darven, who nodded, indicating that he had seen as well. He was about to speak when a loud boom shook the ground beneath their feet. The Ryakuls on the mountains flapped their wings, sending hundreds of whooshes through the air. A golden ship sped through the clouds and disappeared. Darven looked at him questioningly, and while Mactar had not seen a ship like that in over twenty years, he knew who had access to such technology.

"It's the Hythariam," Mactar said softly. "The Heir of Shandara is here."

"He's not the only one," Tarimus hissed from behind.

THE HYTHARIAM FLYER, WHILE A SUPERB SHIP, WAS ONLY ONE SHIP, WHICH limited their options for approach and reconnaissance. Aaron and the others set down on a narrow ledge of a rock face toward the far side of Ryakul Mountain.

Verona coined the phrase "Ryakul Mountain" and was proud of his vocal eloquence in naming the previously anonymous peak. Regardless, the name stuck with all of them.

"This seemed like a better idea while we were on the ship," Verona said, and Braden grunted in agreement.

"You wanted to come." Aaron grinned slightly. "You could try jumping." While both Verona and Braden could tap into the energy around them, and had accomplished some pretty impressive things with it, they could not jump like he and Sarah could. Back on the Raven before they had reached Shandara, Sarah had told them it would take time. However, the shield that Verona and Sarik were able to create was quite intriguing, and he was sure would come in useful in the future.

"You will be fine," Aaron said. "Tanneth used one of these to follow me through Khamearra when we learned of the attack on the inn. If we weren't about to head into a battle, I'd think the gliders were fun and would join you."

Gavril was helping Verona and Braden strap a glider to their feet. There were two rods upon the ground and Gavril was showing them how to activate the glider through the comms device now strapped to their wrists. At either points of the rod, discs large enough for them to step upon unfolded, forming an oval. Verona and Braden stepped onto the discs and metallic bands extended over their feet, securing them in place.

"Now listen carefully," Gavril said, stepping onto his own glider. "You key in the sequence I've just shown you. Not yet, Verona, just listen first." After Verona put his hands down, Gavril continued. "It's really quite simple. The glider will respond to your movements. If you raise both your knees then the glider will rise into the air. Lean to either side and you will go in that direction. The same also applies to backwards and forwards. Here, watch, I will show you."

The glider at Gavril's feet hovered about a foot off the ground. He brought his knees up and the glider pushed his body into the air. Gavril leaned to the side and the glider followed. The more he leaned the greater the speed.

Gavril spun in the air and returned back to them. "Just push down and straighten your legs to stop moving up or whatever direction you are moving. The glider's systems will respond to you. Once you step on and activate them, they record your weight and adapt to your movements, but you must be careful. There are some safeguards to prevent you from falling, but if you persistently lean too far forward and can't get your feet back under you, you will crash."

"Crashing would be most unfortunate," Verona agreed.

"We just need to use these to go up the side of this mountain. I don't expect you to go into battle on them. When we reach the plateau at the top, just hover over the ground and deactivate the glider through your comms device," Gavril said.

"What happens if the comms device gets damaged?" Verona asked.

"Now *that* would be most unfortunate," Gavril said and the old soldier's face lifted into a grin. "The comms devices are quite durable I assure you, and will not break easily. Let's try rising into the air and coming back down quickly before we make our ascent."

Braden muttered something about flying only being for the birds, but keyed in the sequence into the comms device and his glider hovered in the air. He was joined by Verona, who was unable to keep the smile from his face.

"Class is over. We've been made," Aaron said snapping their attention as a lone Ryakul flew around the corner, appearing as startled to see them as they to see it.

"I'll distract it. You get up the mountain," Gavril said and flew off to meet the oncoming Ryakul.

"Let's go," Aaron said, and he jumped into the air, aligning the particles in the air to push him higher than any strength enhanced jump could take him.

Verona and Braden began rising into the air. Slowly at first, but rapidly gaining speed and closing the distance between them. They were both warriors with excellent balance, which they used to their advantage as they glided up the mountainside.

Aaron landed high above them and waited for his friends to catch up. Gavril was dodging the Ryakul with an aero acrobatic display that he wouldn't have thought possible, even on a glider. The Ryakul's head was fixed upon its prey, and it instinctively flew wherever it led.

The Hythariam gliders were more agile in the air, making the Ryakul seem clumsy as it tried to follow. Gavril fired golden plasma bolts into the Ryakul from his pistol.

Knowing that the Ryakuls were once dragons made him slightly sympathetic toward the feral beasts, but it was only because they were the shadowy reflection of their purer self. Aaron turned back to Verona and Braden and gasped as Verona lost his balance. Braden stuck out an arm to steady him, and they both reached where he was unharmed. They continued to climb, reaching another plateau. Aaron turned to see Gavril blind the Ryakul by shooting out its eyes and the dark beast spun away, plummeting toward the ground.

Gavril caught up to them easily just as the roars of hundreds of Ryakuls echoed off the surrounding mountains. Tanneth had uncloaked the Flyer to draw their attention. Verona, becoming more comfortable upon the glider, drew his bow with an arrow ready and continued to follow them. Aaron kept his jumps small and precise so they could stay together at first, but the closer he got to the top, the more the distance grew between them. Knowing that Sarah was so close, he couldn't help it.

They crested the ridge and settled down low to look at the other side. The air was a sea of black flapping wings as the Ryakuls pursued the Hythariam Flyer as it streaked across the sky like a golden bullet. Aaron turned toward the left, focusing in on the Drake.

The Drake was watching the Flyer as it streaked across the sky and immediately spun, heading toward another peak. Aaron scanned ahead and saw two Ryakul keeping a watchful eye around them.

Gotcha. So much for the plan…

Aaron pointed. "Sarah is over there," he said, grasping the small curved ax from his belt.

"Go," Verona said, "We'll be right behind you."

Aaron gathered the energy around him and the runes on the staff flared to life. He fed the energy into his muscles and launched into the air. He pushed forward, gliding with the wind, and heard the screeching howl of the Drake below him. The Ryakuls snapped their heads in his direction. He unleashed the ax as he bounded off another peak.

The ax streaked silver across the sky, demolishing the Ryakul's head, and its great body slammed down upon the ground as Aaron landed in front of the remaining Ryakul. He dodged the snapping jaws of the Ryakul's saber-toothed maw. The Ryakul swiped with its poisonous talons, barely missing him.

Aaron drew the Falcons, and as the blades kissed the air, notes from the bladesong surged forth within him. He spun and dove into a roll, avoiding another swipe of the talons. Aaron brought up the blades, anticipating another strike, but at the last second the Ryakul spun, sweeping out with its armored tail. Aaron launched into the air, cutting through the Ryakul's hide as he went.

The dark beast roared in pain and sought to overwhelm Aaron as it crashed down upon where he landed. Aaron dove to the side and sliced behind the Ryakul's forward leg, bringing it down. He danced to the other side, cutting through the hamstring of the Ryakul's remaining front legs.

Aaron darted out of the way as the beast swayed and crashed down on its side. One of its wings flapped uselessly as it tried to regain its footing. Aaron circled and drove both his blades into the long neck and black blood spewed forth from the dying beast.

He pulled his blades clean and felt something grab his backpack and swing him away. Aaron tumbled and skidded to a halt inches away from the plateau's edge. He glanced at the dizzying heights of the drop off down below and sprung back to his feet. He nearly stumbled at the sight before him.

Sarah stood with her sword held at the ready. Her eyes glowed yellow, and the black blotches almost completely covered her exposed skin. There was no recognition in her baleful gaze, just a surety of the murderous intent in her eyes.

"Sarah!" Aaron called. "It's me."

Sarah cocked her head for a second and shook it violently.

Aaron was about to step forward when he saw the Drake pull itself over the ledge. The Drake's howl sawed through the air, and Aaron felt the ancestral blood within rise in protest. He dashed forward, closing the distance to the Drake, and brought down his blades in a crushing blow toward the Drake's outstretched arm. The dark swirling armor solidified as his blades made contact and the impact jarred his bones.

The Drake was over seven feet tall. Its great body pulled back, and then an armored fist planted firmly into Aaron's face, sending him flat upon his back.

Aaron shook his head to clear it, losing his focus. The Drake punched hard.

The Drake's eyes peered into Aaron, and then turned its attention to the stump of its left arm. The surface of the arm bubbled up, forming an armored twin of its other arm.

Aaron charged forward, but the Drake shot its hand forth and something rippled through the air, knocking him off his feet and pinning him to the ground. There was a cry behind him as Braden leaped off the glider and landed in front of him, driving the Shield of Shandara in front of them both. The crushing force that kept him pinned to the ground stopped. Aaron came to his feet and saw the glint of metal from the corner of his eye. He spun and his blades met Sarah's. He kicked out with his leg, knocking her off to the side, and turned back toward the Drake.

The Drake leveled its staff and fired upon Braden. The bolt of energy bounced off the shield, but the force of the blast sent Braden sailing through the air and over the edge. Aaron cried out, and Gavril zipped past him over the edge, chasing Braden.

Aaron seized the bladesong and the crystals in the Falcons flared anew. He swept out with his blades, sending out an arc of energy and knocking the Drake back. An arrow flew past Aaron, but bounced harmlessly off the Drake's armor.

"Behind you!" Verona cried, and Aaron turned, bringing up his sword.

Sarah swung her sword at him and then advanced, raining down blows as she came. Aaron met each blow and yielded precious footing upon the plateau. He wielded the Falcons into the bladesong, probing out to Sarah, seeking out the golden core that was her true self and not that tangled mess of the Nanites. He locked her blade in his own and came face to face with her, feeling her ragged breath upon his face.

"Fight them, Sarah," Aaron whispered.

From behind him, Aaron heard Verona cry out, and he risked turning to see that his friend had engaged the Drake in an attempt to give him time to reach Sarah.

Verona's arm hung loosely by his side, and the remains of the glider lay broken at his feet. The Drake hovered behind his friend, and Aaron dashed forward, moving with blurring speed. The twin blades on the end of the Drake's staff began to descend and Verona fell back. Aaron roared, thrusting both his glowing swords in front of him and skipping into the air. He twisted in midair to bring the Falcons down into the Drake's chest; his momentum carried them both over the side to the depths below.

Aaron struggled against the Drake's powerful grip as the wind roared passed his ears. The Drake howled in pain as they bounced along the side of the mountain and several Ryakuls pursued them.

Aaron released his hold upon one of his swords and rained down blows upon the Drake's face with his fist. A dark form swooped underneath them, breaking their fall, and jarred his senses as a Ryakul flapped its bat-like wings to steady itself. Aaron brought his feet underneath him, planting them upon the Ryakul's broad back with the Drake in between and pushed away. His swords twisted free of the Drake, and the pain of it forced the Drake to release its hold upon him.

Aaron was surrounded amid a sea of roaring Ryakuls, tangling themselves up as they each tried to snap at him. He dodged one saber-tusked maw and used his feet to bounce off another. His swords dripped with the black blood of the Ryakuls as their poisonous talons tried to tear at him. He leaped to the back of another Ryakul, plunging his swords into its back, and held on tightly as the beast spun. His white-knuckled grip was locked around the hilts of his swords, but as the Ryakul spun, the blades cut deeper into the beast's hide. The Ryakul leveled off and Aaron saw the golden Hythariam Flyer try to reach him, but it was blocked by the sheer number Ryakuls throwing themselves at the craft. Aaron glanced behind him and then launched himself into the air, pulling his swords free as four Ryakuls, with one carrying the Drake, converged upon the already injured one carrying him. The Ryakuls began to tear their brethren apart, but Aaron was safely away.

He landed upon a ragged cliff and watched the Ryakul tear apart one of their own. He had to force the bile back down his throat. Perhaps it was the knowledge of what the Ryakuls truly were that clawed away at the walls of his heart, or the knowledge that death was the only remedy that could be afforded to the dragons afflicted with this disease. The Drake's call rallied the Ryakul. They dropped the lifeless corpse and closed the distance toward him.

The Drake leveled his staff and fired. Aaron leaped into the air, narrowly avoiding the blast, and charged at the Ryakuls. The beasts' putrid breath invaded his nostrils as he sailed by, lashing out with his blades and slicing deeply into one's hide.

Aaron scrambled off the side of the beast to land upon the back of another. The Drake leveled his staff at him, but as it was about to fire, a blue bolt of energy slammed into it from the side. Small bolts of energy spread across the Drake and the smoking staff fell from its hands.

Aaron looked up seeing Gavril rise up from behind the Drake upon his glider. He nodded grimly toward Aaron.

The Drake pulled back on the Ryakul, forcing it to fly higher. Aaron drew in the energy around him and pushed, launching himself into the air and gaining on the fleeing Drake. The armored tail of the Ryakul was in front of him and he latched on, dragging the beast off balance. The Ryakul crashed onto a mountain plateau and Aaron tumbled away from the tangled mess of tooth and claw. He regained his footing, shaking his head. The Ryakul lay dying with some of its limbs moving feebly, until they stopped altogether.

Aaron glanced at the sky around them, hearing the roar of airship engines at full burst. Streaking into view were four airships firing giant crossbow bolts into the Ryakuls that swarmed the sky like insects.

The body of the Ryakul on the ground heaved and the Drake came out from behind. The Drake's armor sent sparks into the air as it moved and was hanging off in a few places. The two holes in its chest from Aaron's swords had not reformed. The Drake tried to key something into a panel on its arm and screeched a yell into the air, but the call that had previously commanded the Ryakul fell upon deaf ears as the beasts scattered.

The Drake tore the useless panel from its arm and tossed it aside. It cocked its head toward Aaron and for the briefest of moments, the smoldering yellow eyes diminished. Then the beast howled in rage and the yellow eyes flared anew as it charged.

Aaron brought up his swords, easily avoiding the blows of the Drake. He lashed out, cutting through the armor in multiple places. The Drake's attacks grew more feeble and Aaron could sense something growing beneath the surface of its very skin. He cast out, probing with the energy toward the Drake. It was dying, and the Nanites required a living host to survive. A small white light flared faintly from the Drake's dark form as it fell to the ground

---

TARIMUS...AGAIN!

Mactar was at a loss as to how Tarimus had tracked them down again and he hadn't been able to get a clear shot at him. He and Darven decided to split up using the travel crystals. The Ryakuls flew in a frenzy, attacking anything that moved, which included snapping at other Ryakuls. One of his gifts was that of an impeccable memory and having observed the Drake's call, Mactar knew that it was something he could duplicate. The call however, was only half of the means used to control the Ryakuls, with the other half tied to the device upon the Drake's arm. Mactar watched as the Drake pursued the Heir of Shandara in his rather impressive acrobatic display, leaping from one Ryakul to the next. Ferasdiam Marked indeed. He could quite possibly challenge the High King, but not yet. The boy still thought of himself as a man and not one touched by fate.

The Drake was fading, and despite himself, Mactar's gaze was locked upon the battle before him. None of the Alenzar'seth before had stood against the Drake. They all perished one way or another. He engaged the travel crystal to a spot not fifty feet from where Aaron stood over the fallen Drake. He cloaked himself in such a way as to avoid notice, and judging by the state of the Heir of Shandara, he would not looking for him. Mactar quietly waited and listened to what unfolded before him.

"WHO...ARE ...YOU?" THE CREATURE THAT HAD BEEN THE DRAKE ASKED him, struggling to get the words out.

"I'm Aaron," he answered. "Carlowen's son."

The deformed figure of the Drake's face crumpled in pain and grief as it whispered his mother's name. Aaron eyes widened as he realized that some part of his grandmother was still in there.

"Reymius?" his grandmother asked.

Aaron shook his head slightly. "He protected us. My mother found happiness and Reymius took comfort in that."

Cassandra's eyes still glowed yellow, and her face was twisted into something beyond human, but Aaron could tell that the Nanites's hold upon her was fading.

"He didn't know. He thought you had died," Aaron said, trying to give what comfort he could.

Dull yellow eyes searched his as her body spasmed in pain, and she glanced up to the plateau where Sarah was. "She is still in there. She still fights for you."

Aaron felt the tears fall freely and unclenched his jaw to speak. "How can I save her?"

His grandmother's eyes closed and she drew a shallow breath.

"Please," Aaron pleaded. "Can you tell me how to save her? She is my heart... my soul...my everything."

Aaron leaned in as his grandmother struggled to speak, silently begging that fate would allow her to give him this one last message.

"*What...wouldn't...you...do?*" The last words spoken by his grandmother ran together in a great sigh that he could hardly make out.

The remnants of the Drake collapsed to the ground and the crackling energy infused into the armor grew silent. He softly laid his grandmother's head onto the ground and watched as her body dissolved before his eyes. The Nanites that had once been so vibrant, doing their utmost to carry out their task, required a living host to survive, and without them, what was now his grandmother's body came apart, fading away to dust. Aaron unclenched his teeth and howled in frustration. His eyes drew up toward the plateau where he had last seen Sarah. He gathered the energy around him and launched into the air, heading toward Sarah with the echoes of his grandmothers last words in his mind.

What wouldn't you do?

22

THE REACHING

Mactar dropped his shroud and bent to pick up the broken panel the Drake—Lady Cassandra—had discarded. Hearing Aaron speak to the beast yielded nuggets of information that he was ignorant of, and even now his mind raced to catch up with their implications. He stuffed the panel into the folds of his cloak, then someone grabbed him from behind.

Mactar's breath caught in his throat as he felt his body thrown like a rag doll to the ground. He came to his knees and erected a barrier between himself and his attacker. He shook his head, still disoriented, when a flash of light appeared. Darven emerged with his blades ready. Mactar reached out with bands of energy, locking them around the dark cloaked figure in front of him, and dropped his own barrier.

There is no escape this time, Tarimus.

Tarimus drew his dark blade and met the Elitesman. Mactar's bands of energy locked Tarimus in this realm, but he was still free to move about.

Mactar summoned an orb of energy poised to strike, but the two blade masters kept moving. He could take them both out, but Darven still had his uses.

The Ryakuls were scattering and the airships were closing in on their position. The sharp clang of steel hitting the ground snatched Mactar's attention, and he saw Darven being held up by the throat in Tarimus's grip.

Mactar's hand shot forth, sending the orb directly into Tarimus's back and causing him to stagger. He shot another one, but it disappeared into Tarimus's outstretched hand.

Tarimus rose to his feet with an evil knowing smile upon his face.

"Come reap what you have sown, Dark Master," Tarimus spat.

Mactar drew deep within himself, summoning so much energy that the air around them seemed about to ignite. He would squash this rodent once and for all. Gritting his teeth, he charged forward shooting a bar of molten energy toward Tarimus, not caring if Darven would get caught in the blast.

The beam of energy stopped abruptly a foot away from Tarimus, flailing off to the side by a shield of immense power, surprising them both. The backlash could be felt where he stood. Mactar turned to see the face of a dead man standing behind him.

"Father!" Tarimus howled.

Mactar smirked at Colind while engaging the travel crystal, leaving the mountaintop behind.

Colind clamped down on his anger for not taking out Mactar when he had the chance. He was here for his son. What was left of him.

Tarimus turned and dragged the Elitesman to his feet, drawing back his blade to strike. The Elitesman fumbled with his travel crystal, which dropped to the ground.

"No!" Colind commanded and clamped bonds of energy upon Tarimus's wrists. "Let him go, Son."

Tarimus strained against his bonds, growling to the point of sounding more beast than man.

"I want a river of blood to flow, starting with him," Tarimus said, his black eyes narrowing menacingly, striking fear into the Elitesman.

"A river of blood has already been unleashed. Don't add to it," Colind pleaded. "The Elitesman is nothing. Let him go."

"I gave you the Alenzar'seth heir," Tarimus spat, still struggling against the bonds.

"You gave me nothing," Colind said. "You used him to free yourself from your prison."

Colind watched as his son strained against the bonds, his limbs shaking. He felt a great weight shift down in his stomach and a lump grow in his throat. The boy his son had been was gone. There was nothing but a monster before him, twisted and evil. Responsible for countless deaths and who showed no signs of stopping.

Colind held the bonds firmly in one hand and slammed down with the other, causing Tarimus to drop the Elitesman. He held no love for the Elitesman and more than likely the man would die in the near future, but what he fought for was a small redemption for his only son. He sent a shroud of energy that washed over his son, binding him. Tarimus's core was twisted from being trapped between realms. There would be no redemption for his son, only a father's regret for his failure.

"You've always catered to them," Tarimus spat. "The Safanarion Order led by the rulers of Shandara were always first in your priorities."

"Your childish tantrums brought about the destruction of one of the greatest kingdoms this world has ever known," Colind said. "You allied yourself with Mactar and the High King. You let the snakes into Shandara and look what it got you. They used you and when you were no longer useful, they found another way for you to serve. They betrayed you."

"You betrayed me, Father. My only joy all these years was knowing that you were imprisoned just like me. The mighty Safanarion Order pushed into hiding and your precious Shandara brought down by me. Your world burned and I wanted you to burn with it."

Colind released the bonds, having the shroud firmly in place prevented Tarimus from going anywhere. The rage and murderous intent washed off his son in waves, almost staggering Colind in his tracks. He couldn't change that which would not change.

"You're going to have to do it," Tarimus howled. "Yourself. If you want to stop me, you're going to have to kill me. I will never stop. You can't stop me!"

Colind raised his hands and his thunderous gaze bored into Tarimus's black demonic eyes. "Your mother and I brought you into this world, and I'm glad that she never had to see what you've become." Colind glanced to the sky, asking silent forgiveness for what he was about to do. Sometimes the evil was just too great and there were too many lines crossed that even the love of a father couldn't overcome.

"Tarimus, you've broken your solemn oaths to the Safanarion Order and knowingly murdered thousands of people, bringing this world to the brink of collapse. As the head of the order, I will carry out the justice that should have been visited upon you all those years ago." Colind pulled his hands apart, tearing Tarimus's essence into pieces, and felt his own broken heart shatter in his chest. Tarimus thrashed and screamed for a moment before dissolving into the tiniest specs with only echoes trailing their wake.

I'm sorry, my son, Colind kept thinking before he collapsed to the ground, cursing the fate that made him judge and executioner of his only beloved son.

Aaron landed upon the edge of the plateau to see Verona doing his best to avoid being killed by Sarah, whose face was a mask of struggle. Braden was there using only his shield to keep Sarah at bay.

Aaron pulled two travel crystals from his pack and lightly tapped them together. The crystals rang their tones through the air, stopping Sarah in mid-swing of her swords.

"Let her come," Aaron shouted, retrieving the rune-carved staff.

Smoldering yellow eyes bored into him, and Sarah's golden hair rippled like a pendant upon the wind.

"Come and take it," Aaron whispered, leading Sarah away from the others. Verona would fill them in on the rest of his plan when they regrouped.

The purple travel crystal held her attention, and while Aaron knew the untarnished part of Sarah was still locked away inside, he hoped he wasn't too late. She turned to look at the others and poised as if she was about to charge off after them. Aaron closed the distance and blocked her path, forcing a crystal into her hand.

"Use it," Aaron said. "I know you are still in there."

Sarah stared at the crystal in her hand, appearing confused, and flung the crystal away, shaking her hand free of it.

Aaron seized the bladesong inside and forced another crystal into Sarah's hand. He reached across their connection, feeling the woman he loved huddled inside the dark recesses of her own mind, not willing to trust anything, including him. Especially him. Aaron pushed every memory he had across the link. From the first time he saw her outside that small town, to when they danced at the Feast of Shansheru in Rexel.

"Fight it, Sarah!"

He could see her golden core flare momentarily, struggling to break through the sea of blackness. Still Aaron pressed with everything he had, pouring every last look, touch, and breath across, sparing nothing. The sword she held came to rest at her side.

"It's now or never," Aaron said. "Use the crystal."

Aaron could feel her golden core grow dimmer, at last succumbing to the might of the Nanites.

He was too late. She couldn't break free. Sarah was fading.

"Just reach out," he pleaded, cursing himself.

The blackness completely tainted everything, smothering her golden core until the light all but ceased. Then the slightest of shimmers waved through, pushing against the darkness. The travel crystal flared in her hands, and Aaron instantly seized it with his own and then felt himself be sucked in. The world pulled away from his feet and he sank into the purple abyss.

They emerged alone somewhere in a forest. Sarah blinked her eyes, and for a moment they returned to her normal shade of blue. She looked at Aaron in surprise for a few precious seconds before doubling over in pain. When she looked back up at him, her eyes had returned to yellow.

Aaron seized the travel crystal and kept a firm grip upon her arm. He sent a slight tendril of energy into the crystal and built a picture in his mind of a place along the borders of Shandara. The affect was immediate and the ground fell way from their feet. They emerged at an abandoned campsite. The remnants of the bonfires were still there.

"Oh, Aaron," Sarah said, clearly recognizing where he had taken them.

It was working. Using the crystals was resetting the Nanites.

No sooner had the thought came into his mind did Sarah collapse, writhing upon the ground. Aaron brought out the comms device and keyed in the sequence to shut down the Nanites.

Nothing happened.

Aaron keyed it in again, but Sarah cried out in pain.

He grabbed Sarah's arm and used the travel crystal again.

The world faded around them as he picked another place. As soon as they emerged, he brought out the comms device and tried again.

Sarah's eyes searched his and they both waited with baited breath. The Nanites eventually reasserted their control, but it took longer. He grabbed Sarah's arm and activated the crystal, setting a frantic pace of traveling from place to place, and using the comms device to try to shut down the Nanites.

He lost count of how many times he used the travel crystals, going to every place he could think of, but aside from slowing the Nanites down, they always returned. The command sequence given to him from Roselyn wouldn't work. Sarah gained a few minutes before the Nanites resumed their task, slaves to the perverted constructs of a malicious military machine. The likes of which he was powerless to fight. Each time the Nanites took control, the pain she was in shredded the walls of his heart.

Aaron clenched his teeth and growled. He had expended all but a few of the travel crystals with nothing to show for it. Despite himself, Sarah saw defeat in his eyes, and no matter how many times he tried, he couldn't free her of the Nanites.

What wouldn't you do?

His grandmother's last words spoke in his mind.

He pictured one last place and the dark forbidden land that had haunted him since he learned of its existence was brought to the forefront. The travel crystal flared anew and Aaron fed in more energy. They emerged into the land of twilight and the barrier separating Safanar from Hytharia shimmered in the air near them. The crystal cracked in his hands and turned to dust.

"Please," Sarah said weakly. "Let me go, Aaron."

"No," Aaron said. "I have one more crystal left."

Sarah winced away from him. "No, I can't take it anymore. You have to let me go," she groaned, gasping in short breaths. "*Please…* "

Aaron looked on helplessly. He had been sure that teleporting with the travel crystals would reset the Nanites, releasing their hold over her, but they were killing her instead. Aaron caught her as she collapsed to the ground, her body jerking in convulsions. He held her steady until they passed, dividing his gaze between the woman he loved with all his heart and the barrier that kept the Hythariam horde at bay.

What wouldn't you do?

He extended his senses to the barrier and saw for the first time the shafts of energy plunging down into the earth. He was tempted to follow them to their source, but Sarah called to him weakly.

"You mustn't," she gasped. "Don't sacrifice this world for me, Aaron." She looked up helplessly at him. Her eyes alternating from beautiful blue to baleful yellow with both breaking his heart. The Nanites were gaining control again.

"Oh, Sarah," his voice croaked, barely above a whisper. "This world means nothing to me without you."

"You have to do it," she said with her hand reaching toward the knife at his belt.

She wanted to die. The fight was leaving her as the Nanites resumed control.

"No!" Aaron cried. "I've got to save you. There has to be a way!"

Sarah looked up at him in a moment of clarity and her eyes retained their stunning shade of blue. "You already have, my love," she whispered.

Aaron held onto her tightly, tears streaming down his face. He could feel the

Nanites working inside her, carrying out the will of the Drake, slaves to their programming. They couldn't be reasoned with and were a foe that he could not defeat.

There has to be a way, his mind raced, trying to find an answer.

Like a beacon he called through the bladesong, a thought sparked into his mind.

It couldn't be? Aaron glanced at the barrier.

He gently held Sarah to his chest. At any moment, the Nanites would take over and Sarah would become the Drake, continuing the cruel cycle that had killed the Alenzar'seth for trying to protect their home.

He called the bladesong in his mind, drawing upon the power that held the barrier in check. The barrier and the portal to Hytharia were bound together and one couldn't exist without the other. He couldn't force the Nanites from her system or she would die, nor could he command them to shut down, but he could give them what they wanted.

Aaron pressed his lips upon Sarah's, kissing her, and opened himself up. He aligned his lifebeat to hers and called to the Nanites, which were already working frantically to carry out their grisly task of assimilation.

Don't give up, Sarah, he thought as he fed his energy into her. As if sensing his thoughts, he felt her resist the Nanites with renewed vigor and opened herself up to him. His energy merged with hers until either source was indistinguishable from the other, but Aaron knew. His connection to Sarah was like a symphony opening up in his head with each instrument playing a chord of his lifebeat. The Nanites paused in their work, seeing a whole new entity open before them, and they rushed to assimilate. As they raced into Aaron, he closed them off from Sarah. To the Nanites, it would appear as if parts of Sarah went dark, like a lost limb, and were no longer accessible. As they left Sarah and came into Aaron, she became stronger, her body beginning to recover.

Aaron felt his own strength draining, as the last of the Nanites entered into his system, and he closed his connection to Sarah off entirely. He pulled his lips away from hers and collapsed to his knees.

"What have you done?" Sarah cried, grabbing him with both her hands. Her eyes shone with that brilliant shade of blue, like liquid lightning, and the shade of her creamy skin returned to its proper color.

She was saved.

"The only thing I could do, my love," Aaron whispered, and doubled over.

Sarah cried out his name.

Aaron shook his head to clear it. The Nanites were like tiny pinpricks invading his field of vision. Then he rose up through sheer force of will and swept her up in his arms.

"*There's no time*," Sarah whispered into his ear, repeating it over and over.

With each gentle breath of her words caressing his ears, he felt his heart shatter to pieces, and reform because she was saved. That was all that mattered to him, as he held her tightly in his arms.

"We've loved a lifetime's worth, and I wouldn't change it for the world," he whispered.

He released her and stood up, his body responded stiffly as the Nanites invaded his brainstem, vying for control. He stumbled closer to the portal that separated the worlds of Safanar from Hytharia, unbuckling his sword belt. He reached into his shirt and removed the medallion, letting both fall to the ground.

"What are you doing!" Verona cried, finally catching up to them. He held a travel crystal in his hand. Colind and Braden were on either side of him.

Aaron was mere inches from the barrier's threshold and turned back to look at Sarah one final time, leaning heavily upon the rune-carved staff.

Tears were streaming down both their faces and their breaths came in gasps. Sarah's getting stronger while his grew weaker.

"What I must do," Aaron said. "Goodbye, my friend."

His vision took on a yellowish hue as the Nanites gained more control over him. Pain, like hot lightning, lanced through his limbs. He lifted the staff and the runes glowed faintly to his touch. He slammed it into the ground, which gave way enough for the staff to stand on its own and bonded it to Shandara as the barrier had been.

Aaron released the bladesong in his mind, revealing to the Nanites that they were in a new host. There was an immediate spike in activity as per the protocols Aaron had surmised they must take. For the briefest of moments he regained full control of himself while the Nanites reset. He gripped the cylinder in his pocket. It was the keystone accelerator that allowed him to come to Safanar.

There is no other way, he told himself and looked at his friend, his brother in everything but blood.

"Take care of them, Verona," Aaron said, and looked back at Sarah as she struggled to her feet.

"Remember me," he said and brought his hands up to the barrier, severing the tethers that kept it in place. With one final look back at the others and a world he had grown to love, he fell back through the portal to the echoes of his friend's denial, and Sarah crying out his name in his wake.

Aaron slammed into the rocky ground that bit into his skin. Sparks rained down on him and he stumbled away. He saw the portal shimmering in the air between two metallic columns, with bolts of electricity running along them. Thick cables connected the columns to large pylons that gave off an azure glow.

The portal flashed and more sparks rocketed from the top of the columns. Aaron dove to the ground, covering his head, as the columns exploded, plunging the area into darkness. The smoggy air burned his lungs and Aaron looked around him as he felt the Nanites crawling inside his skin, gaining their bearings. After a few moments, the yellowish hue retreated from his vision as the Nanites shut down. He struggled to his feet, and his eyes burned, tearing up, and he couldn't stop coughing. The air was hot upon his skin. He wrinkled his nose in a futile attempt to block the stench of the thin air around him.

Aaron fell to his knees, gasping for a breath of air that would not come. Stars like tiny pinpoints of streaking light closed in on his vision. He fumbled through his pocket, grasping the keystone accelerator. The ground shook with the stomp of many footsteps surrounding him. He forced his eyes to open, blinking rapidly. Despite his blearily eyed vision, he saw that he was surrounded by dark figures, each holding some type of rifle leveled at him in their armored hands.

Aaron could hear shouting in a harsh language he didn't understand. He pulled out the keystone accelerator, desperate to open the way back to Safanar. Rough hands pulled him to his feet, knocking the keystone accelerator from his grasp. An armored fist slammed into his stomach, expelling the remaining air from his lungs. Another figure stepped closer, leveling his weapon at Aaron's head. They studied his face and seemed confused by the way his glowing yellow eyes faded to his normal brown color with hints of gold at the edges.

With the Nanites completely shut down, their primary programming complete, Aaron felt his strength return. He was thankful that the Nanites didn't have any self-destruct mechanism built in upon completion of their prime directive. Something the Hythariam military had overlooked, apparently. They had expected the Drake to return. The ground shook violently underneath him, distracting his captors. Aaron seized the moment and twisted free of the men holding him, sending them sprawling. He squatted down, preparing to jump toward the keystone accelerator, when he heard the snap hiss of a rifle being fired. A net of light collapsed around him, pinning his arms to his sides, and Aaron fell to the ground, helpless before the Hythariam.

One of them spoke in that same language that he couldn't understand as another came to him, slamming a clear mask over his face. The leader spoke again, and he understood one word. Halcylon. They were going to take him to the dreaded Hythariam General that Iranus had warned him about. The one who wanted to conquer Safanar, but had been thwarted by Aaron's ancestor, Daverim. Unable to hold his breath any longer, Aaron sucked in some air through the mask and became light-headed. With his consciousness beginning to wane, he felt himself being dragged across the rugged landscape of a planet that was supposed to have been destroyed years ago, but appeared to be in its final death throes before oblivion.

EPILOGUE

"No, Aaron!" Colind screamed.

Verona was helping Sarah to her feet. She clung to him, crying out Aaron's name.

"We have to get to him, Verona," Sarah cried, struggling to step forward, but Verona held her back and looked at Colind.

Colind nodded and waved over the others from the Flyer.

"Please, my lady," Verona said to Sarah. "Wait here," he said, and left her with Roselyn.

"Quickly now," Colind shouted.

They charged forward, and a shrieking sound came from the portal, as if something were pressing against it from the other side, and then it disappeared.

All became silent as they skidded to a halt where the portal had been a moment before. The darkened land around them seemed to breathe a sigh of relief, already growing brighter in the sunlight.

"Can we open a portal back to Hytharia?" Verona asked, breaking the silence.

Gavril shook his head grimly.

"Is there no other way?" Verona pressed. "Colind?"

Colind's mouth was hanging open. "I… I don't know."

"We have to get him back," Sarah said, leaning upon Roselyn for support.

Verona immediately came to her side. "We will, my lady."

"He was right there," Sarah cried. "We have to get him back," she said again, collapsing, only to be caught by Verona. Braden came up and lifted Sarah's unconscious form into his thick arms.

Gavril blinked away his shock. "We don't have the equipment here."

Verona shared a look with Colind and the others.

"We need to return to Hathenwood," Colind said.

Verona's gaze drew toward the rune-carved staff. The vibrant glow of the runes faded to a whisper of what they once were. He leaned down, retrieving Aaron's swords and medallion, but as he came before the staff, he paused for a moment and glanced at Colind.

Colind focused on the staff. "Let's leave it for now. There are bonds of energy tethering it to the ground. It might be Aaron's link."

"To where?" Verona asked.

"To Safanar," Colind said.

"Right then," Verona said. "Sarik, I want you and Tanneth to stay here standing guard until we return." The others gathered around him and with a nod to Colind, the group disappeared.

IRANUS STOOD IN A ROOM WITH HIS EYES LOCKED UPON THE MAIN DISPLAY of the command center. From here, they could oversee Hathenwood, but also receive communications from the various satellites they had in orbit around the planet. He currently had all the satellites not blocked by the planet locked on their deep-space satellite, which tracked the object that Aaron had cleverly surmised existed.

"Confirmed, sir," the tech said. "Repeat, confirmed; the object has changed course."

Iranus grimly studied the main display as it mirrored the tech's console, giving voice to a fear that all the Hythariam at Hathenwood had hoped to escape. They tracked the trajectory of the incoming object, and it was indeed from their home world. The object had just changed course, denoting some type of intelligence guiding the craft.

"Acknowledged," Iranus answered.

He had hoped the boy had been wrong, but it was confirmed. Hytharia was catching up to them all and time was running out.

AMIDST THE RISING SHADOWS

SAFANARION ORDER - BOOK 3

1

SEARCHING

Sarah's first few weeks at Hathenwood, the only Hythariam city on Safanar, had been spent in a bed, asleep. She slept as if she hadn't slept in months. She probably hadn't in retrospect. The first time she woke, a female Hythariam was standing over her, peering at her with those golden irises that marked most of their race. The eyes—so different and so familiar...*The Drake!* Sarah lashed out, screaming and gasping for breath. Verona pinned her arms down, telling her she was safe.

Sarah glared at him and drew in the energy, strengthening her muscles. Her eyes widened as she sensed Verona do the same.

Was this real? The Drake had tormented her thoughts, bending her mind to its will...but then the memories came rushing back. A portal between worlds. Aaron hunching before it as he took down the barrier. Then he was gone. She could no longer feel the effects of the Drake, but she still remembered. The muscles in her legs and back twitched, expecting the lancing pain to blaze through her following her thoughts of Aaron. She clenched her teeth and her lips drew up into a half sneer on her reddening face. The Drake could never be dead enough for the poisoning that spewed forth from its purpose. She let go of the energy and tried to stop the lump forming in her throat.

"My Lady, Aaron could think of nothing else while you were under the Drake's influence. His first and last thoughts were always of you," Verona said softly, and then he let her go.

She turned to the side and curled into a ball. Her face was hidden by the golden curtain of her hair, her eyes brimming at the ache seizing her chest. *Oh, Aaron, why couldn't you have let me go?* The very same reason she will never let go of him. *This world needs you... I need you.* In the silence that surrounded her, she yearned for his touch, desperate to feel his presence. She closed her eyes, imagining the feel of his strong arms wrapped around her, and having the remnants of his scent in her hair. To feel the press of his lips upon hers.

"He's not gone, Verona."

"I know he's not, my Lady."

Sarah sat up in her bed and swung her feet to the floor, which warmed to her touch. She flexed her toes for a moment and then stood up. Her body was fine, if a little bruised. Aaron was quite thorough when he rid her body of the Nanites. She took a few steps toward the window, and Verona opened it. The crisp mountain air seeped through her clothes to her skin. She was high up in a sea of white square-shaped buildings with the occasional dome-shaped ones poking above the trees. The sunlight caressed her face, and the energy was there, just waiting for her to reach out and use it. Each movement she made, and thought she had, no longer contained the taint of the Nanites. She was free, but at what cost? Sarah turned to Verona. His long black hair was tied back, and his handsome smile was genuine, but she could see the pain in his eyes. The absence of Aaron weighed heavily upon them both.

Verona placed a cloth-wrapped bundle upon the bed and slowly unwrapped it, revealing Aaron's swords and medallion. The crystal inlay on the pommel shone dully inside the room.

"I kept them safe, my Lady, but I think he would want you to look after them."

Sarah came before Verona and put her hand upon his shoulder; an unspoken promise went between them. They would get Aaron back.

"Thank you," Sarah said.

"I will wait for you outside, my Lady," Verona said and quietly withdrew from the room.

Sarah reached out and ran her fingers upon the medallion adorned with the Alenzar'seth family symbol of a Dragon cradling a single rose. The sunlight reflected off the crystal in the center of the medallion, casting small rainbows upon the pristine walls of the room. Her fingers traced the Dragon, much like the tattoo upon Aaron's chest. She hung the medallion under her shirt and proceeded to get dressed. The Hythariam clothing and boots were quite comfortable, and had she bothered to notice, the boots fit the contours of her feet perfectly. Her movements were methodical and numb. She reached toward the Falcons. Aaron's swords. Part of his birthright. Sarah removed the Falcons from their sheaths, feeling them for the first time in her hands. The etchings and holes near the base of the blades would have weakened any normal swords made of steel, but these were different. They created the bladesong come to life. Each blade was about the length of her arm and remarkably light. She had seen Aaron do amazing things with these blades, and while she would safeguard them for his return, they were not hers. She preferred the single edge of a slightly curved blade native to her homeland of Khamearra.

Sarah strapped the Falcons to the belt upon her hips and left the room. Outside, she was greeted by Sarik with a quick smile, and by Braden, who with a grim face brought his fist across his heart. Garret and Vaughn came up to her and gave her a brief hug. Verona stood next to a female Hythariam, whose golden eyes she recognized as belonging to the one she lashed out at.

"Please forgive me," Sarah said.

"No forgiveness necessary. My name is Roselyn."

Sarah took Roselyn's proffered hands and gave her a gentle squeeze.

"Your recovery has been remarkable, but I would still like to make sure everything is okay," Roselyn said.

Sarah caught herself clenching her teeth. She'd had enough experience with Hythariam technology to last a lifetime.

Roselyn's eyes widened. "No, no, just a few scans to make sure the Nanites are completely gone."

Sarah glanced at Verona, who nodded encouragingly, and then back at Roselyn. It was quite obvious that they were together.

"You understand my reluctance, and I appreciate that. I would be happy with whatever aid you have to offer, my Lady," Sarah said.

Roselyn looked relieved and absently reached out to Verona.

"We are so happy to see you recovered," Vaughn said. "Please excuse myself and Garret. We're sure we will see you later this morning."

Sarah nodded to each in turn and followed Verona and Roselyn, with Braden and Sarik coming behind.

Braden came up to her side, and she could feel his connection to the energy around them. "Aaron and I always believed that you and Eric would be able to open yourself up to the energy, given some time. Where is Eric?"

"Thank you, my Lady," Braden said and then glanced at the floor for a second. "My brother was killed in Khamearra."

Sarah felt her stomach clench and reached out to him. "Oh, Braden, I'm so sorry."

"He died a warrior's death, and I avenged him," Braden replied.

Sarah nodded, having no wish to poke such a tender wound. How many had died in Aaron's quest to save her? Her chest tightened, and she felt something heavy drag her down in the pit of her stomach. And now they were without their friend...their leader...their king. *You should have let me go, Aaron. This world needs you.*

They walked in silence until coming to a door. Roselyn raised her palm to a pad of silver outside the door, which flashed as if scanning her hand. She motioned for the others to wait outside, including Verona, and gestured for Sarah to step into the room.

There were a few tables along the side. Verona had come to her room the day before and explained what little he could about the Hythariam technology. The panels on the far walls were screens that showed information. Roselyn walked over and placed her hand upon a pad like the one she saw upon entering this room. A circular section of the white floor darkened and rose a foot into the air, along with a railing.

"Sarah, if you could step up onto the platform, I will get the examination started."

Sarah did as Roselyn asked, and the overhead lights dimmed around her.

"Not to worry; a machine is going to descend from the ceiling above you. The lights coming from them will be able to scan through your clothes and put the information on the screen over here," Roselyn said, gesturing to the nearest monitor.

Sarah glanced up at the ceiling and then back to Roselyn. The Hythariam was beautiful with her exotic facial features and the feminine curve of her body. She could see why Verona was attracted to her but could hardly believe that Roselyn had made the journey with the group that went to Khamearra.

"I'm ready," Sarah said and took a deep breath.

A panel opened up on the ceiling above her, and two mechanical arms descended. At the ends, each arm held glowing metallic disks. A blue line appeared at her feet and slowly expanded, running the length of her body. As the glowing line moved up, she tried to feel it as it passed up above her chest, but felt nothing. The second arm moved down to her feet and began to circle around her. The light emanating from this scanner was a thin red line. The arm slowly circled her body, and Sarah felt a little dizzy for a moment. The arm stopped as the glowing line was at her forehead. Sarah opened herself up to the energy upon reflex and stepped backward, bringing her hands up.

"It's okay," Roselyn said and typed a few keys into the panel on the wall. The arms retracted into the ceiling, and the panel closed.

Sarah stepped off the platform as it sank back down to the floor.

Roselyn motioned for her to come over, and a smaller drawing of her body was on the screen.

"Sarah, I'm happy to tell you that there are no traces of the Nanites in your system. If there were, your scan would look a bit like mine," Roselyn said. She tapped a sequence of symbols, and a similar drawing of Roselyn's body appeared next to Sarah's. Roselyn's display showed tiny pulsating lines flowing through every inch of her body.

Sarah's skin crawled at the image.

Roselyn reached out and gently placed her hand on Sarah's. "What's been done to you is a horror I can't even begin to imagine. The fact that you're standing here beside me is a miracle. We've tried and failed to aid those afflicted with the Nanites that turned them into the Drake only a few times before. At best, we hoped to drive them from you and give you enough aid to pick up the pieces that were left, but what Aaron was able to do has pushed beyond the limits of what we might have been able to accomplish on our own."

Sarah stared down at the floor, her blonde hair covering the side of her face. "I wish he hadn't," she whispered.

Roselyn wrapped an arm around her shoulder, and Sarah allowed herself to be pulled in.

"I tried to end it," Sarah continued, "to take my own life, but it wouldn't let me. It twisted my thoughts until I couldn't tell what was real. I had power over nothing. I know you're trying to help. I look at everything in this room...all this technology, and all I want to do is draw my sword and smash this place to pieces." Sarah gasped an involuntary sob, taking comfort in the embrace of a woman she hardly knew. A woman who had risked her own life to help Aaron save her.

"I hate what was done to you, Sarah. This may be hard to see, but all of this technology here was created with the best of intentions."

Sarah nodded, wiping the tears from her eyes. She needed to be strong. She looked back at Roselyn's sympathetic eyes and allowed herself to believe that this stranger...this outsider...could be a friend.

"Thank you, Roselyn," she said. "I just want him back."

"I haven't known Aaron very long, but I believe with all of my heart that he is fighting to get back to you even now," Roselyn said.

The connection she shared with Aaron that had been so prominent had faded to barely a whisper, and she questioned whether it was there anymore at all. Her heart told her that Aaron was alive, and nothing would convince her otherwise. She wouldn't allow herself to believe that Aaron had died upon the plains of a world in its final death throes.

"What else do these screens tell you about me?" Sarah asked.

"That you're in perfect health, and time will take care of the rest."

Sarah glanced at the door. "He's a good man."

"Aaron?"

"No, Verona."

Roselyn blushed, "Yes, he is, and very sure of himself now. Not long ago I thought I had done something wrong because he was so quiet around me."

Sarah laughed, and the sound of it startled her. "Quiet? Verona?"

"That's exactly what Aaron said," Roselyn snickered.

Sarah shook her head and smiled. *Yes, definitely a friend.*

"We should head to the council chambers, where my father and Colind are meeting with the other leaders to coordinate their efforts," Roselyn said.

Sarah nodded, and they both left the room, joining the others outside. They continued through the building and came to a large elevated platform. There were so many Hythariam that Sarah felt out of place. The Hythariam and the others kept glancing toward the far wall as if waiting for something to happen. A few moments later the section of the wall before them shifted quietly to the side, and a large metallic tube came through the impromptu doorway.

"They are called trams, and they will take us to another part of Hathenwood, my Lady," Verona said.

The tram floated above the glowing points on the track and came to a stop near the platform. She could see other Hythariam through the windows, and after they exited the tram, Sarah and her group got on board. The inside of the tram had benches along the walls, but Sarah preferred to stand. The tram began to move, leaving the building, and as it did so, she couldn't feel the movement beneath her feet. If not for the trees and other buildings speeding by, she would have thought they were standing still.

"I'm glad you're feeling better," Sarik said, coming to her side. "Pretty amazing, isn't it."

Sarah smiled at him and nodded, looking at the city that the Hythariam had built. Parts of it reminded her of what Shandara must have been like before it was destroyed. No, destroyed was too strong a word. There was in fact a lot of destruction, but the bones of Shandara were still there. If they could rid the place of Ryakuls, then perhaps people would journey back and rebuild it.

The Hythariam went to great lengths to include the surrounding landscape into the layout of their small city. The walking paths between the buildings included large trees and colorful plants that should not have been in bloom because of the cooler temperatures. The flowering plants of the gardens offered a choreography of color that was pleasing to the eye and gave her a sense of peace. How long would the peace last, Sarah wondered.

The tram came to a stop inside a dome-shaped building, and they got off. They were soon greeted by an older Hythariam with green eyes that contrasted with the sea of golden eyes she had seen thus far. He had the bearing of a seasoned warrior, from the way he stood and surveyed the area, to the way he moved his arms in precise movements.

"Hello, Sarah, we didn't have a chance to meet before. I am called Gavril."

Sarah returned the greeting and knew from her conversations with Verona that Gavril had also helped Aaron in Khamearra. Roselyn whispered something in Gavril's ear, and he nodded back to her. She could never doubt the sincerity of the people around her, but she could feel a pang of guilt twisting inside her chest at Aaron's absence. She still found herself looking for him, and even here in the crowded atrium outside the Hythariam council chambers she yearned to see him. She needed to know that he was okay. Sarah's breath caught in her throat, and she felt as if something had sucked the air out of the room. The voices echoing throughout the atrium pressed in around her, melding together until they sounded like gibberish. The golden eyes of the Hythariam turned to molten yellow with a malicious glint. Sarah spun around, looking for a window. She needed to get back outside. With her breath coming in gasps, she sprinted away. The others called out to her, but their calls trailed in her wake. She burst through the doorway, elbowing her way through a throng of Hythariam. The molten-yellow eyes of the Drake glared at her from the faces of the Hythariam nearby.

No! You won't take me again!

She burst through the doors and ran out into the gardens beyond.

Faster...I must go faster.

She drew in the energy around her and put on the speed, blurring through the gardens. She could hear sounds of pursuit behind her. She needed the high ground. Sarah leaped to the tallest branch of a tree nearby and stopped. Slowing her breathing, she squatted down upon the tree branch and closed her eyes for a moment, taking in the sounds around her. After a few moments, she opened her eyes and scanned the way she had come. The white dome building peeked above the tree line. She ignored the shouts of her name that came from a short distance away. There was no sign of the Drake, but she could feel its eyes on her, watching and waiting for a moment to strike.

No, the Drake is gone. Aaron killed the Drake.

Sarah dropped down and sank to the ground, wrapping her arms around her body. She rocked back and forth at the base of the tree, telling herself over and over that the Drake was gone.

Where is Aaron? she kept asking herself, but the silence was her only answer.

"My Lady," a voice called to her softly.

Sarah looked up to see Verona squatting before her.

"Are you all right, my Lady?" he asked.

Sarah could feel her heart thundering in her chest and her arms clutching her sides. She took a deep breath and suppressed the urge to keep running until she collapsed from sheer exhaustion.

"It's okay, you're safe now, I promise, my Lady," Verona said, and sat down across from her. "Take as much time as you need. We can head back whenever you are ready, or not at all, if that is what you wish."

Sarah nodded and took another deep breath that shook in her throat. "I'm sorry. I kept seeing...*it.* Verona, I can't get those eyes out of my mind. It's as if there are thousands of Drakes pressing in all around me. Even now at this moment, I feel it will come out of nowhere and drag me back into its clutches while I claw helplessly to escape."

Verona watched her for a moment. "The Drake is gone, my Lady. Aaron saw to that before he came for you. The Nanites that made the Drake possible are inside Aaron, who is now on Hytharia."

Sarah leveled her gaze upon Verona, "And that means they will turn Aaron into the Drake. Don't you see? We have to go after him," she said, rising. "I have to find him," she said as started to head back toward the dome-shaped building.

"Sarah," Verona called, halting her in her tracks. "We will do this together, you and I, but we can't do this alone and certainly not without the help of the Hythariam."

"What if they won't help?"

"I believe that if they can help, then they will. And if not, then we'll find another way. I have the utmost faith that if anyone can find their way back to Safanar, it's Aaron, my Lady."

"You don't understand. The Nanites are too strong," Sarah said.

Verona reach out and put his hand gently upon her arm. "You haven't seen what I have seen, my Lady. Please don't lose faith. Aaron will find a way back."

Sarah searched Verona's eyes, but his faith in Aaron was absolute and would not falter. They didn't know what the Nanites could do. Aaron needed help, but like Verona, she believed in Aaron, she just didn't know how he was going to get back. She slowly nodded, and together they headed back to the Hythariam council building.

On their way back, Sarik and Braden joined them. She could sense them all drawing upon the energy, and each gave her a knowing look. They had come so far since the decks of the Raven. As the group approached the building, they saw Roselyn and Gavril standing together.

"Are you all right?" Roselyn asked.

Sarah nodded. "I think so," she said, glancing at the Hythariam around her but failing to suppress a shudder.

Roselyn followed her line of sight. "Is it the eyes?"

"They are just so similar to the Drake."

"You just need some time," Gavril said.

Sarah nodded, forcing her angst aside; she needed to do this.

"Please, if you will follow me," Gavril said and led them inside the building.

Gavril led them through the atrium and continued down a long hallway. The echoes of voices in a heated discussion could be heard coming from the room at the end of the hallway. There were two Hythariam in brown uniforms standing guard.

"They've already been in session for a while," Verona said.

"Doesn't sound like much of a discussion if people are shouting," Roselyn said.

They entered a grand oval chamber that had thirty-foot windows stretching to the ceiling. The center was open with two platforms where a few men and a Hythariam had gathered. The smooth white benches curved with the room and were filled with occupants. Sarah recognized Colind with his long white hair and eyes of silver. His jaw was set, and he appeared to be only staring at the space in front of him.

"We have evidence of armies gathering near Khamearra," said a dark-haired Hythariam. His maroon shirt was set off by the green cord tied above his elbows.

"There is little doubt that the High King has learned of the Free Nations Army gathering near Rexel, with similar forces massing at the smaller kingdoms, but I remind you that is but one of the threats we face," another Hythariam said. His long, silky-white hair moved in a wave as he addressed the room full of people.

"The one speaking is Iranus. He is one of the leaders of the Hythariam," Verona whispered.

As they entered the room, a slow murmur gained in intensity as many turned in their direction. Colind glanced up, and as his eyes found hers, he stood.

"Ladies and gentlemen, as you've no doubt have surmised, we have been joined by Lady Sarah of the House Faergrace. Please, my Lady, would you join me up here?" Colind asked.

The invitation was clearly for her alone, but the others took the liberty of staying at her side as she walked to the head of the chamber. Braden gave a low growl as one of the Hythariam attempted to block their access to the floor after Sarah had passed. She smiled inwardly, appreciating the support.

"Your Grace, I am Iranus, one of three elected leaders of the Hythariam people, and I bid you welcome to Hathenwood," Iranus said with a slight bow.

"Thank you, but as we are not in my father's court or any other on Safanar, then as a show of respect to the Hythariam, I would propose that you address me by my name, and I shall do the same with you," Sarah said.

She glanced around and calmed herself down as so many golden-eyed Hythariam stared back at her. She had no fear of crowds; being a princess she often had to endure the scrutiny of her father's court, even when she was cast aside after her father married another. The mixed expressions around the room were as she had feared. Some blamed her for their current predicament while others appeared to have no judgment at all.

Colind approached and took her hand in his. "I am relieved to see you looking so well, my Lady."

Sarah could see the strain behind Colind's eyes. "I think we can both agree that we hoped it would be under different circumstances, my Lord."

Colind nodded and squeezed her hand gently.

The dark-haired Hythariam cleared his throat. "I am a bit concerned by the presence of one who has been infected with the foreign Nanites. Are we sure she is not still under their influence?"

Roselyn stepped up next to her and addressed the room. "I'm happy to report that there is no trace of the rogue Nanites left in Sarah's system. She is healthy and free from the influence of the Drake."

Iranus nodded. "That should allay any fears for the risk of having Sarah at this meeting. Wouldn't you agree, Zyven?"

"It does indeed," Zyven answered. "Who better to advise us as to the strategy of the High King than his daughter? If you wouldn't mind, we would like to ask you a few questions."

Sarah studied the Hythariam and knew that if she didn't put a stop to this she would be bombarded by endless questions. It's not that she didn't want to help, it's that she had questions of her own, and given the circumstances she had a right to ask first.

"I will be happy to answer your questions, but first you will need to answer some of mine."

Iranus motioned for Zyven to be seated. "Under the circumstances, it's the least that we can do."

"Has there been any attempt to reach Aaron?"

"No, there has not," Iranus said, looking as if he regretted the words he had just spoken.

"Are you able to open the portal back to your home world?" Sarah asked.

Iranus swallowed. "It's not that simple."

"Then help me understand."

"On the other side of the portal is an army that for the past eighty years has been poised to invade this world. If we were to open a portal back to Hytharia to rescue one man, then we would put thousands more at risk," Iranus said.

Sarah glanced around the room, taking its measure. With the exception of their little group, most had the look of approval to what Iranus had just said.

"This is not just one man. Aaron Jace is on the other side. The only surviving member of the House Alenzar'seth. The rulers of Shandara. The people who opened their doors to you and gave you refuge from your dying world and civil war. Are you all saying that one such as Aaron is not worthy of a rescue attempt?" Sarah asked, her gaze narrowing as it swept the room. Despite what had occurred in her life, she had the blood of kings and queens inside her, and this group was in danger of incurring her wrath.

"I don't think you are aware of what is currently happening here. These lands are upon the brink of war. It's not that we don't want to help, but it's a matter of resources of which we are running dangerously thin. Our foes are many. Even Aaron urged us to prepare for the war with the faction of our race left on Hytharia. He knew the dangers and wouldn't want us to spend countless lives and risk everything to bring him back. It pains me to say this, but he may already be dead," Iranus said.

Sarah felt her body go rigid. "He is not dead," she hissed, glaring at Iranus.

Murmuring began to spread throughout the room, like a rising wave of doubt that she would give no quarter to.

"He is not dead!"

Those closest to her nodded in agreement and echoed their assertions of the same.

"If you're able to open the portal to Hytharia, then I will go and take anyone who volunteers to go with me," Sarah said.

Verona, Braden, and Sarik immediately came to her side, only to be closely followed by Gavril.

Iranus raised an eyebrow at Gavril and smiled sadly. "My Lady, I would join you myself to help get Aaron back, but you don't know the destruction that would be waiting for you on the other side. When a portal is opened, it can be traversed both ways. Hordes of nightmarish creatures could come pouring through and kill everyone in Hathenwood in a matter of minutes. Aaron knew the risk and was even given a way to come back if he could," Iranus said and nodded toward Roselyn.

Sarah turned toward Roselyn, who nodded slowly to her, and Sarah dreaded what she was about to hear.

"It's true, Sarah, Aaron had a Keystone Accelerator in his possession that would have been able to open a way back to Safanar," Roselyn said.

"So you see, if Aaron could have come back, he would have," Iranus said.

Sarah's eyes drew downward as her mind raced for a way to help Aaron. She looked at Colind. "Is it possible to create another barrier?"

Colind pursed his lips in thought and then slowly shook his head. "The only living person with the knowledge on creating the barrier is on the other side of the portal."

Verona frowned. "You mean Aaron? How could that be?"

"He would have had to understand how it worked to be successful in removing the barrier and going through the portal," Colind said.

"I'm still not clear on why he went through the portal to Hytharia," Verona said.

Sarah looked up at Verona. "It's because he couldn't shutdown the Nanites. The travel crystals slowed them down, but nothing could break the cycle."

"She's right," Roselyn said. "The Nanites had a core set of instructions that they based all of their actions on. Their prime directive was to return to Hytharia through the portal. Aaron's ancestor, Daverim, created the barrier, and it was linked to the living members of the Alenzar'seth."

Verona turned toward Colind. "But you were head of the Safanarion Order, how can you not know how the barrier was made? Sarik and I can create barriers, perhaps there is something that we could do."

Colind smiled sadly, and his shoulders slumped as if a great weight were dragging him down. For a moment, Sarah could see something about the old man that she didn't expect: defeat.

"A different kind of barrier, I'm afraid," Colind said. "What you were able to do was powered through your own connections and is not something that can be maintained indefinitely. The Alenzar'seth kept that knowledge close to their chests. Reymius and I were as brothers, but there are some things that must stay within families. What Daverim did was extremely dangerous. He tethered the barrier not only to the living members of the House Alenzar'seth, but to the very core of Safanar. Over time, the energy drain eroded the very fabric of our world. Shandara became a wasteland. Ask yourself, even with the destruction visited upon Shandara by the High King and the Elitesmen Order, should not the land have recovered by now? The presence of the Ryakul would not have stunted the growth of the plant life nearest the barrier. Even the weather over Shandara was out of sync with the rest of the world. So you see, the barrier that protected our world from the Hythariam horde was also sickening the land around it. People were unaware because the Ryakul presence kept everyone out. That is until Aaron and all of you journeyed to Shandara," Colind said with his gaze settling upon the small group with Sarah.

"Aaron wouldn't want us to abandon him," Sarah said.

"On the contrary, Sarah, that is exactly what he would have us do," Colind said.

Sarah closed her eyes, feeling a pang in her heart at the truth in Colind's words. Aaron wanted to protect them all, but she would protect him, even from himself if she had to.

"Then I will apologize to him when next I see him, for abandoning Aaron is something I will never do," Sarah said.

"And neither will we," Verona said, with Braden and Sarik nodding.

Iranus quietly cleared his throat and asked for their attention. "I don't want to give false hope where there very well could be none, but there might, and I stress, *might* be a way."

Colind frowned. "What do you mean?"

"The fact of the matter is that we don't have the resources to build a large Keystone Accelerator to open a portal back to Hytharia and keep it running for any length of time to launch a rescue mission. I would like to see Aaron rescued, and if it were within my power to grant this to you, I would. What I was saying before about there possibly being a way is that in the years after the barrier was first put up, we were preparing for an invasion. We fortified Shandara to specifically be able to deal with the threat from my people. We knew the barrier gave us the breathing room we needed to prepare, but were not sure how long it would last. Together with the Shandarians we created weapons and fortified safe havens for people to gather. Daverim insisted, and I agreed, that the weapons caches hidden throughout Shandara could not be detected by any Hythariam technology. This was to prevent the enemy from using our own weapons against us. The other thing we did was prepare a chamber to open a portal back to Hytharia."

Gasps echoed through the room, and Sarah realized that this was not common knowledge, even among the Hythariam.

"We knew there were still good people left on Hytharia that should not be doomed to suffer the planet's fate. We prepared a chamber that held certain safeguards that could suppress the threat of invasion," Iranus said.

"What safeguards did you put in place?" Sarah asked.

"Ultimately, the chamber would be destroyed, along with anyone inside. However, we wanted to open up communications with the Hythariam still on the other side. Daverim believed, as did I, that a people shouldn't have to suffer such a terrible fate because its leadership had morphed into something malicious and cruel. The Keystone Accelerator we used was able to hold the portal open for an hour before we ran out of power. At first, we launched some scouting missions, and then we started bringing more people through. They were sworn to secrecy, but we began to meet resistance on Hytharia. They had developed a way to detect when a portal was opened. We kept trying for a time after that, but something changed on the other side. The people were different and started to resist us. The groups of Hythariam being brought back started to contain infiltrators in disguise. We started sectioning the newly arrived Hythariam until we learned whether they were serving General Halcylon. There were a number of incidents, and many Hythariam and Shandarians paid the price with their lives. More of the Hythariam on the other side began to change. They began to view us as the enemy. After we lost several scouting teams, we stopped using the chamber. The risk was too great. Years went by, and we began to discuss the idea of going back to Hytharia, but the attack from the High King and the fall of Shandara changed all that. We believed the chamber was destroyed, but we were never able to confirm. The Ryakuls and...well, you've seen Shandara, so 'might be a way' is the best that I can offer."

"It's more than what we had before," Sarah said.

"We are also in need of your aid," Iranus said. "Only those with abilities like your own can help us find the stockpiles of weapons hidden at Shandara. Aaron was going to help us when he returned. Will you help us in his stead? It could very well mean, not just our, but everyone's, survival."

Sarah took a breath, her mind continuing to race as she weighed what her actions would cost. War was coming, and her people were being pulled into it. There were good people in Khamearra, just as there had been on Hytharia, and she felt herself being caught in the middle. So much bloodshed with the sultry promise of more for those craving power. She began to wonder if any of them would survive or if they would all eventually succumb to the fires of war.

Sarah glanced at the large screens on the far side of the room that showed a depiction of the night sky. A blinking dot followed by a red pathway across a field of stars. She could almost feel the fear from the others in the room crawl along her skin. Fear of her father and his Elitesmen, but also something deeper. At times it was difficult to determine the age of the Hythariam in the room, but for some of them the haunted looks of helpless resignation to a dark fate was something she had seen before in Khamearra. The group known as the Resistance had the same desperation about them, clinging to a fleeting hope, that if they could survive another day then perhaps things would change for them. What she was about to do was more than loving Aaron and standing at his side. She was picking a side, but in her heart she knew she had a responsibility to those left in Khamearra, and it was something she would not forget.

"I'll help you," Sarah answered.

She wouldn't abandon Aaron, and some chance was better than no chance at all, which is what she faced now.

Iranus nodded and thanked her. He seemed genuinely relieved to have her help. She was invited to sit, and the meeting continued on while Sarah became lost in her thoughts. It had been two weeks since Aaron had cleansed the Nanites from her system. She had remained asleep for most of that time, which was a blessing because when she did wake up it felt as if the Drake was still controlling her thoughts. Verona had been there each time she awoke and reassured her that she was safe. Although she hadn't known it at the time, she did remember seeing Roselyn there as well. Residual effects of the Nanites' failed assimilation attempt is what she had been told was happening to her. The Nanites had begun training her mind to their twisted purpose, but now her mind was free of them. Their influence would fade with the passage of time or so she hoped.

The meeting finished, and they would be leaving for Shandara soon. With the death of the Drake, the Ryakuls had scattered, no longer claiming Shandara as their own. A camp had been setup inside the city, and Sarah and the others would be heading there to begin searching for the weapons caches and the chamber of which Iranus spoke.

Colind watched Sarah as she and the others left the hall. He hadn't been to Shandara since Aaron had freed him from his prison there. His thoughts were being consumed with Mactar and the death of his son. It was a cold world indeed when a father must visit justice upon his only son. He blamed Mactar for seducing his son with dreams of power, making him a pawn to his own designs. On a much deeper level, Colind blamed himself, and his failure burned him to his core. Reymius, his old friend and Aaron's grandfather, might have told him that Tarimus's failings were his alone to bear, but Colind knew better. Perhaps in time he might see it differently, but he couldn't allow himself that luxury now. He blamed himself, and he wanted to hunt Mactar down. That slippery fallen member of the Safanarion Order had lived too long already, and this world would bear the scars of his designs for many years to come. He could pretend to himself that he would pursue Mactar as some form of justice, but what he wanted was vengeance. He wanted it so badly that he found himself imagining trading his life for it with a perverted sense of glee. His oaths to the Safanarion Order and dead friends be damned. He wanted that man dead more than anything else.

"Colind," Iranus said.

He looked up at the old Hythariam. The hall was empty now. Its occupants had long since left.

"Do you believe we can trust Sarah?" asked Iranus.

"I don't really know her. Just what the others have told me. She wants to rescue Aaron, and those especially loyal to him want to help her. For the time being that should hold this alliance together."

"What do you think she will do if the chamber is destroyed? We can't expend time and resources to go after Aaron. I want to, and don't ever believe that I don't. I hate the thought of him stranded on Hytharia if he is still alive," Iranus said.

This had been eating away at both of them since the moment Aaron had been trapped behind the portal. "For better or worse, Aaron is on his own and beyond our aid. I've said it before—he wouldn't want us to focus on rescuing him with the threats aligned against us. He would want us to prepare. It is our charge to protect the people of Safanar. Aaron understood this. Especially toward the end, by Gavril's account. To honor him, we shall continue preparing for war, and look for a way to possibly bring Aaron back from Hytharia."

Iranus nodded, resigned to the fact that there were limits to what they could do. "There is another thing. I've heard whispers of it since people have learned of Sarah's recovery."

"Quite the romantic story isn't it," Colind said with just a hint of bitterness to his voice.

"That's not what I meant. Some are saying we should hold Sarah in our custody as leverage against the High King."

"That would be supremely stupid of them."

"I agree," Iranus said. "But still I suspect this line of thinking will grow."

Colind nodded, accepting the fact of it. "Well, we'll need to teach them the error of this line of thinking. To hold Sarah prisoner as a means of bargaining with the High King would plant a divide among our own alliance in the Free Nations Army, as well as galvanize the High King's army. We would go from a righteous cause of rebelling against a tyrannical nation to that of criminals taking hostages."

"Let's hope the others see it that way. I've asked Cyrus about her."

"And what did my friend, the ruler of Rexel, have to say?"

"She is her father's daughter in that she has a reputation for being cold and a bit ruthless at times," Iranus said.

"Vaughn told me that they were initially quite suspicious of her when she first showed up on the Raven. But having learned a little bit about the girl, there are reasons why she would cultivate a reputation such as that. You of all people know what it takes to survive in a dangerous place."

Iranus nodded. "Indeed I do, and speaking of such places, will you be going with them to Shandara?"

Colind's first instinct was to say no. There were too many ghosts for him in Shandara. He had spent the better part of his imprisonment there, as a cursed shade sentenced to roam the realm of shadow, but now he was free.

"We've been sending in teams to help clear away the rubble. People will return to Shandara," Iranus said.

Colind drew in a shallow breath and sighed. Perhaps returning to Shandara would help put some of those ghosts to rest. From there he would begin his hunt for Mactar.

"Only for a short while," Colind said. "There are things that I must do. It's time to recall the Safanarion Order, if there are any of them still out there."

"Surely some of them have heard of your return and are making their way to Rexel by now."

"Perhaps, but there are some that live upon the fringes, preferring a more solitary existence."

Iranus nodded. "Then I wish you good luck, and you can always reach me through the comms device."

Colind followed the Hythariam out of the room, then brought out the travel crystal and studied it in the palm of his hand. There were a number left among Aaron's things, and Verona had thought that Colind could use one. He put the travel crystal back into his pocket and headed toward the trams, resigning himself to once again go back to Shandara.

2

A NEW POWER

Far to the north of Khamearra there was a small town nestled in the shadows of a dark keep with a solitary tower. The locals knew better than to venture anywhere near the place. The only indication that someone lived there was the occasional town visit from the deaf mute caretaker. A hundred years ago the place was known as Baerstone Keep, where a small plantation lord resided until Mactar appropriated the keep from him, and it had been his ever since. The townsfolk understood their place, and it was not at the keep unless Mactar brought them there. The occasion that he brought someone to the keep was usually the last anyone ever saw them again. It had been two generations since Mactar had to show the townsfolk that if they left him alone, he would do the same to them.

Mactar stood atop the tower to Baerstone Keep and gazed down at the lights of the town twinkling into the night sky. Dawn was a few hours away, but it was the quiet at this time of night that he preferred to be alone with his thoughts. He had repaired the Drake's metallic bracer that it had used to control the Ryakul. The bracer was only half of what he needed, with the specialized call being the other half to the key of controlling the Ryakuls. That was the theory. He had yet to prove it, but he was getting close. So close that he could almost feel it.

Mactar clasped his hands together and drew from memory the strange strumming sound that the Drake used to command the Ryakuls. Other than the mere memory of the sound, he hadn't been able to crack the inner workings of how the Ryakuls were commanded.

Mactar descended the stairs that led directly toward his trophy room. A collection, of sorts, of all his victories. Hanging on the far wall were the remnants of a flag bearing the Alenzar'seth coat of arms. The fires that engulfed Shandara had blackened the flag so that you could barely discern the once-proud standard. It was meaningless now. Reymius (with the help of the Hythariam) had gotten away, and the House Alenzar'seth had been allowed to endure. Aaron, the sole remaining heir to the ancient House Alenzar'seth, had proven to be more powerful than all his forbearers. Mactar closed his eyes, remembering how Aaron had deftly danced through a sky filled with Ryakuls. Ferasdiam marked or not, the feat had been impressive. It had been weeks since those events occurred, and he hadn't heard anything more of the Heir of Shandara. A worthy adversary. He waved his hand, sending tendrils of energy to the burnt flag of Shandara, causing it to unravel into a pile of dust upon the floor. He would strike a crushing blow against those who would oppose him, and a new order would be upon Safanar.

Mactar came before a window where a dark cylinder hovered over a small pedestal. It was by far the least obtrusive of all his trophies, and it only garnered the attention of the keenest observer. Most of those who had come into this room had grown preoccupied with the objects that gleamed. Only Sarah had noticed the cylinder when she had come to summon him to the High King. How much had changed since all those months ago. High King Amorak was correct—he did have a soft spot for his beautiful and dangerous daughter.

He had been among the first to encounter the Hythariam as they came to Safanar. A shaft of moonlight streamed through the window, reflecting off the cylinder. The device itself was broken, and it was something he would never be able to fix. The only proof he had that there were Hythariam still on the other side of the barrier. A different caliber Hythariam than those fools holed up in Hathenwood. He knew it in name only and had no idea as to the actual location of where the Hythariam called home on Safanar.

Mactar turned from the window and approached his workbench, where two bracers sat. He and Darven had returned to the mountain and found the remains of the Drake's body. They were able to salvage the other bracer and use it as a blueprint to repair the one that the Drake cast aside.

Darven quietly stepped up behind him. The former Elitesman could be the very definition of silence when he chose. This was one of the rare moments where he had truly caught Mactar unaware.

"Any luck at Rexel?" asked Mactar.

"Nothing that we don't already know. They are building airships and outfitting them with things that I've never seen before. They train their troops constantly. I can't get onto the palace grounds, and each time I tried to use the travel crystal to get there the alarms are raised," Darven said, shaking his head. "They've found a way to detect when someone enters the palace grounds by travel crystal. I was able to get into other places, like the airfield and where the barracks are. Looks like you finished repairing the bracers."

"Yes, I believe I've gone as far as I can with them. The airships are different, you said?"

"Yeah, there are additional smaller engines on the wings and on either side of the cells above the ships. I didn't see any of them actually fly, but the Rexellians are working night and day on them. One thing I did learn though. They aren't calling themselves Rexellians or even Shandara's De'anjard."

"What are they calling themselves?"

"The Free Nations Army or FNA for short. They seem to be composed primarily of the Rexellian corps and the remnants of Shandara's armies that settled there, but I also saw other kingdoms represented," Darven said, his voice trailing off.

"What is it?" Mactar asked.

"You'd be surprised what you could learn near the barracks and at some of the inns the soldiers drink at."

"I'm sure it's truly enlightening," Mactar said dryly.

"Usually when kingdoms align against a common enemy, the armies are as likely to fight each other as they are to fight their intended foe, but the Free Nations Army is different," Darven said.

"Different how?"

"Well, they rank by experience. A nobleman may be an officer, but if they are inexperienced then they will be a lower ranking officer. Doesn't matter how highborn they are. And I've seen a number of Hythariam there. Threw me off seeing their darker skin with golden eyes. I've seen some near the palace grounds, but never for very long," Darven said.

"Intriguing," Mactar said. The Free Nations Army at the moment was much smaller than the armies of the High King, but what Darven had described could almost be considered radical. "We'll see how they hold up in a real battle. You can't unlearn a thousand years of practice in a few weeks."

Darven nodded. "And they don't have Ryakuls at their command."

"Technically, neither do we. I think we need to capture a Ryakul. I know you've just returned, but are you ready to leave again?"

Darven smirked. "That almost sounded sincere. I know for a fact that you care nothing for my comfort. If you're ready to go now, then so am I."

Mactar grabbed one of the bracers and tossed the other one to Darven, which he caught easily. The Elitesman's reflexes were never off.

Darven glanced at the far wall where the standard of Shandara had hung. "Wasn't there something hanging on that wall?"

Mactar headed toward the staircase that would take them to the top of the tower. "It used to be something, and now it's dust. Let's go. We've got work to do."

3

PERCEPTION

Despite whatever Mactar had said that night in the arena, Rordan knew what he saw. It wasn't trickery, it was real. The Heir of Shandara had called a Dragon—an Eldarin—to the arena. The Dragon lords were supposed to be a myth. Folklore told children of those marked by fate with the ability to speak to Dragons. It couldn't have been a trick.

He stood alone in his chambers, having dismissed his servants, preferring the solitude of his thoughts. With the deaths of his brothers, Tye and Primus, he was under constant protection of a guard who always had a few Elitesmen among their ranks. Rordan could slip away if he chose and had done so many times before. The sun was up, and the birds that frequented the palace grounds chirped away in their morning routine. He closed his eyes and heard Aaron's voice in his head.

"There is a threat to this world that none can escape from. The Alenzar'seth have sheltered this world from an invading army. Take a good look around at those in power. Take an honest look at who counsels the High King and then the king himself."

Rordan had thought long and hard about what Aaron had said when they met. In his mind, the Alenzar'seth was many things, but a liar wasn't among them. He had debated on sharing what was said with his father, but they had been either locked away meeting with the council of the Elite Masters and the War Council, or with the armies themselves. The armies hadn't been mobilized to this degree since he had been a child. Smaller kingdoms were showing signs of rebelling against his father's authority. There was resistance even here in Khamearra, and the city had been under lockdown ever since, the district captains having orders to arrest anyone out after designated hours. Examples of stragglers had been put on display at every market square in the city. But everyday there was some type of fire. Not near any district headquarters or soldiers' barracks for now, but any inn or brothel that was known to be frequented by the king's guards were targets. When he was in the city last, there were even attempts on his own life. One problem was you couldn't tell where an attack was going to come from, but one thing was certain—anyone could be involved. From the harmless old hag wandering aimlessly through the streets to the most ordinary common folk. Now the guards only traveled with a number of men sizable enough to give the opportunists pause. That's when they started attacking the guards in groups and the Elitesmen became involved. They quelled most of the outright attacks. Yesterday, there had been reports of the letter *F* written on the front of shops in all the marketplaces in the city. The shop owners themselves were ignorant as to how the letters came to be painted upon their shop doors or windows, but they worked quickly to have them removed.

The letter F was painted with a curved sword at the cross section, which was in the style of the surname, Faergrace, the ruling house of Khamearra before his father had ascended to High King. Sarah was among the last of the direct line except for some cousins. Cousins didn't count for much, and none resided in the city, especially when someone like his father had taken out all his opposition. The Faergraces were not a threat.

Ideas could be threats, but what was the real threat here in Khamearra? Was this mysterious army that Aaron spoke of the real threat? How had the Alenzar'seth sheltered this world from anything when they had been gone for longer than he had been alive?

Rordan glanced out the window. *No billowing smoke.* Perhaps this day would be free of attack. A knock at the door came as a subtle reminder that he was expected to leave for the next War Council meeting. He tied on his sword belt and fingered the pommel at his hip. He couldn't defeat Aaron in combat, but did that necessarily mean he couldn't kill the man? He and his brothers had always tried to get the better of each other to win their father's favor. So the fact that Aaron had killed them could be viewed as a favor. He had always thought, especially in Tye's case, that he would have to kill at least one of them. They were still family, and the choice of whether they should die or not should have been up to him. Primus was his twin, and, like it or not, he felt his brother's absence more than he cared to admit. Sarah, on the other hand, was altogether different. They only shared the same father. He hadn't even known he had a sister until a few years ago when she returned to their father's court. Aaron wouldn't fight him. He had said it was because Sarah wouldn't want him to, which he found hard to believe. There hadn't been any sisterly affection before, but that may have been the result of how they had treated her. He and Primus had tried many different ways to have their sister meet with a number of unfortunate accidents. From faulty saddles to an insecure bed onboard an airship where the lines had been cut, causing the ship to tilt precariously to one side. Grease on top of the grand staircase at the palace, which had taken the life of a maid who had fallen down the stone staircase and broken her neck. He smiled at the thought, remembering the popping sound her neck had made and the vacant look in the maid's eyes as she stared lifelessly up at them in a twisted heap. After months of Sarah thwarting their attempts, they had tried to attack her in one of the shadowed passageways that most people didn't frequent. They had only wanted to scare her and scar her pretty face. When she had first come to live at the palace, many had remarked on how beautiful and fair the princess had become. Living up to the Faergrace name. Their attempts to teach Sarah a lesson had failed miserably, and he still had the scar that ran along his side to prove it. At least she didn't scar his face.

Rordan left his rooms, and the guards followed him. An Elitesman walked quietly at his side, and if he was the least bit put off by having lowly guard duty there was no indication of it. The Elitesman was older and one that he had not faced during his training sessions. He wore a silver cloak, and when Rordan glanced at him out of the corner of his eyes, he could have sworn the Elitesman's eyes had a reddish glow to them. Rordan quickened his step and made his way to the council chambers. He paused outside the door and glanced back at the quiet Elitesman, but said nothing as he went through.

There was a large table with a map of the lands strewn across. The map was older and clearly showed Shandara's borders on the side of the map that had unfurled off the table's edge. The table was surrounded by six generals of Khamearra's armies, Captain Commander Joseph and Gerric the Elite Grand Master. An angry red scar split Gerric's pale face, running from his hairline down to his jaw. Rordan wondered who gave him the scar, which had not been there until two weeks ago. The very same night he had encountered Aaron. With the destruction of one of their towers, the Elitesmen had been on the alert ever since.

"My Lord Prince," Gerric nodded in greeting.

The door behind him opened up, and his father came through.

"You're all here, excellent," the High King said. "General Khoiron, I expect that you have a report for us."

Rordan looked up to see a man with more crags on his face than the side of a mountain. His weathered hands looked as if they could squeeze blood from a stone.

"I do indeed, your Grace. Mactar's report of the forces gathering at Rexel proved to be accurate. We've also started seeing reports of troops gathering at these locations," General Khoiron said, marking several places on the map. "And these other ones along our borders are gathering troops as well. There is something about it that I don't like. They are already outfitting their soldiers for war prior to the word going out from the capital, which got me thinking. Either they anticipate what is going to happen based upon all the rumors of the return of the Alenzar'seth and people flocking to the Shandara banner, or they're preparing to rebel."

The craggy general finished speaking, and Rordan noticed some of the other generals looking nervously at the High King.

The High King smiled as he looked at the other men in the room, "Khoiron has been my spymaster for many years, and his army of spies has served us well. His blunt nature may put some off, but I trust his keen insight. Mark the kingdoms and manors that have aroused your suspicions. We'll need to make an example out of some of them if they think to move against us, but it wouldn't serve our cause to punish a loyal vassal. Rordan, I'd like to hear your thoughts."

"My thoughts?"

"Yes, you've been to enough of these council sessions to have an opinion, and

I would very much like to hear your thoughts. Do you think we've missed anything?"

Rordan stood up a bit straighter while his mind raced along with his beating heart. This was his chance to impress his father with some keen observation, but his mind was blank. As the seconds dragged on, the others around the table shifted uncomfortably.

"Father, you've sent out the call for the armies to assemble, and they will come because you commanded it, but something is missing."

"Intriguing, and what would that be?" the High King asked.

"I'm not sure what the rush is for. These other armies, in Rexel, for example, are hundreds of miles from here. If we set out tomorrow with soldiers, airships, and cavalry, we couldn't be there for at least forty days. And that is with a hard march and the weather cooperating," Rordan said, glancing at the other men around the table.

The High King nodded. "Mobility is indeed an issue. What else?"

"We know that the other kingdoms are assembling their armies, but do we know why? Has there been any attempt to talk to them?" Rordan asked. He didn't know where the questions had come from, but now that he had asked them, more questions came to mind. "On the night that the citadel tower was destroyed, I followed the Heir of Shandara from the arena to the tower grounds."

While his father's face remained impassive, the coldness in his eyes sucked the warmth out of the room.

"What happened?"

"I caught up to him with the intent of avenging Primus's death. I attacked him...tried to attack him, but he wouldn't fight me. He told me of a threat to this world that no one could escape from and that the Alenzar'seth has been sheltering us all from—an invading army."

"Ah yes, I've heard the same lies from his own lips atop the tower. An invading army from another world is to come to our world and ravage our lands with war. You would be wise to never trust the words of your enemy," the High King said.

Rordan frowned. "What if he is right, and there is a threat? Is this something we can afford to ignore?"

"There is absolutely zero evidence to support his claim."

"But why come to Khamearra at all? It doesn't make any sense for him to come here just to sow dissension with a lie about an invading army," Rordan said.

"I can shed some light on this, my son. I caught the Alenzar'seth heir stealing travel crystals from the main charging room. He said that your sister had been captured by the Drake and he needed the travel crystals to save her. I offered my aid to him, but instead he chose to attack. So, you see, I offered a hand in friendship, and they strike at my generosity."

Rordan regarded his father for a moment, trying to decide whether his father was being completely truthful with him. Aaron did say he was here for Sarah. He had spoken of the invading army with such conviction that as much as Rordan wanted to see the man dead, he didn't believe that he was lying to him.

"The fact of the matter is," his father continued, "Rexel and other kingdoms like it have resisted royal decrees and interfered with Elitesmen sent on the king's business to apprehend the Heir of Shandara. You've asked for reasons, Rordan. How about our enemies have taken Sarah hostage?"

"But she fought at Aaron's side against us in Shandara," Rordan said.

"They are controlling her somehow, but there is wisdom in your words. I will send word to Prince Cyrus at Rexel, inquiring as to the whereabouts of Sarah, and what his intentions are regarding the forces being assembled there. At the same time we will rally our armies and prepare ourselves," the High King said.

"Offer terms with one hand while arming the other is a sound strategy, your Grace," Khoiron said.

"I will also have word sent to those kingdoms that are already leaning toward aligning with Rexel, announcing our intentions," the High King said.

"But...if you already suspect they are moving against us, wouldn't you be giving away our intentions by contacting them?" Rordan asked.

"Therein lies the problem. Given enough time, these suspect kingdoms could fortify their positions, making the cost of taking them by force more than we could live with. You make an excellent point, and we believe that everyone else will be under the same assumptions. And let us not forget that there is still the issue with mobility. How can we move our forces to where they need to be, when we want them to be there? Grand Master Gerric, would you like to enlighten my son and the rest of the council as to how we will overcome this very important issue?" the High King asked.

The Elite Grand Master's eyes gleamed with anticipation. "My prince, I know you are aware of the focusing crystal, but for the benefit of the others in the room, I will shed some light. As many of you know, Elitesmen are able to travel throughout Safanar with the use of the travel crystals. These crystals allow the bearers to travel to a place of their choosing with a few exceptions. We cannot use them to travel to Shandara. They simply don't work there. And the bearers cannot travel to a place where they've never been. The crystals cannot be used by the common folk, only those who have the ability to manipulate the energy can use them."

The Elitesmen were ever searching throughout the lands for new initiates and quickly squashed any attempt to setup a competing order. Try as they might, Rordan mused, the Elitesmen could never be everywhere at once, and he believed that there could be many out there who could use the energy but kept their gifts hidden.

The Elite Grand Master continued, "What many do not know is there are actually two of the large focusing crystals. One that was in the tower, used to recharge the other crystals, and one hidden underneath the citadel."

"Wasn't the one in the tower destroyed when it collapsed?" Rordan asked.

Grand Master Gerric shook his head, "No. There were safeguards in place to help protect it in the event of disaster. In terms of mobility, we can use the focusing crystals to move our forces pretty much anywhere on Safanar."

Rordan glanced at his father and saw the wolfish smile spread upon his face. "You can move an army anywhere?"

Grand Master Gerric nodded. The other generals in the room looked impressed, but not all.

"I'll believe it when I see it," Khoiron said.

"There are limits," the Grand Master said.

"Of course there are."

"We are limited by the amount of energy used by the focusing crystals themselves. To move a large force like one of your armies can be done twice a day. Any more than that would drain the crystals to the point of uselessness."

The spymaster looked unimpressed. "And you've tested this? You know this will work? You've moved an army before?"

Gerric's brow furrowed in annoyance. "The largest group has been a hundred men."

"That's nowhere near the size of an army. The idea has merit, and if its potential proves to actually bear fruit, then you'll make a believer out of me," Khoiron said and looked to the High King. "Your Grace, there could be a lot of issues with this. Even if we could move an army into enemy territory, the men need assurances that you can get them back to safety. I can see how this could leave us over extended and expose our flank."

The High King smiled. "Your counsel has always been keen. That is why I want you and the other generals to work with Grand Master Gerric and the Elitesmen. For now, experiment within our borders, but well away from the city. No need for anyone else to know we can do this until it's too late for them. Then let them quake in their boots as the armies of Khamearra strike from anywhere and at anytime. Great change is upon us, and we've got work to do."

The other men filed out of the room, but when Rordan went to follow, his father asked for him to stay behind.

"You seem troubled, Son."

"I don't believe Sarah has been brainwashed," Rordan said.

The High King shrugged his shoulders. "Does it really matter?"

Rordan thought about it for a second. "It's all about perception."

"Yes, very good Rordan. Perception is key to having the support you need to accomplish your goals. If people see our cause as just, then many more will flock to it."

"Even if it is based upon a lie?"

His father glanced at him, and for a second Rordan wondered if he had pushed too much. One doesn't simply call a man like his father a liar.

"Love can be a form of brainwashing, Son. How many men have ruined their lives because they thought what they were doing was for love? The idealists of the world will never understand. Make no mistake. This war has been years in the making. They are preparing for war. What's important now is where and how the pieces are played."

"But what about Sarah?" Rordan asked.

"Your sister still has her uses, even if she sides with the enemy. One might say especially if she sides with the enemy," the High King said.

Rordan felt his stomach give way to the ruthless undertone of the intent behind his father's eyes. They were all pawns to him in this game, and it wasn't until now that he fully understood. Should Sarah die, no one would be preoccupied with whose side she had been on. The clear message that would pervade throughout the kingdoms was that the High King's daughter had been murdered by his enemies.

"This offer of peaceful resolution is just for show. You've already decided that we are going to war. This is all to rally the other kingdoms to your cause," Rordan said.

"*Our* cause, Son. Your sister is expendable, but you are my legacy."

Rordan swallowed and suppressed a chill as the realities of his world came to him with greater clarity.

"Come. I want you to work with the generals and the Elitesmen. You are to be more active in the rulership of this kingdom, which is about to get a whole lot bigger."

The fear Rordan had felt before was forgotten. He had won a victory. Risen above the ranks of his other siblings. There was a reason why he had survived and they had perished. It wasn't an accident of fate; it was because he was destined for this moment. He followed his father from the room with dreams of glory dancing around his head.

4

OPPRESSOR'S GAMBIT

Pieces of muffled conversation went on around him as he tried to push open his eyes, but there was some type of cloth covering his face. His tongue lolled around probing the inside of his dry mouth, and he forced himself to swallow. The voices around Aaron grew louder as he lifted his hand to remove the cloth. A gentle but firm hand pressed him back down. He felt the hand slowly lift the cover from his face, and Aaron opened his eyes. Staring back at him were the golden irises of a Hythariam. The Hythariam spoke a few words that he couldn't understand. Aaron shook his head, hoping that his captor would understand that he didn't speak the Hythariam language.

Aaron blinked away his blurred vision and saw two more Hythariam in the room. He was in a gray room with a golden holographic display next to the bed. He tried to sit up and realized his hands were restrained to the edges of the bed. The Hythariam noticed and moved his hands, and the holographic display changed. Aaron felt the bed raise him to a more upright position. The Hythariam tried to speak to him again.

"I can't understand you," Aaron said.

The Hythariam closest to him had on a gray uniform with black bars upon the collar. He glanced at the other Hythariam in a black uniform that stood at the foot of his bed. He had on a belt with a silver plasma pistol holstered to his side. Their eyes locked for a moment, and Aaron met the cold, calculating gaze and knew that the Hythariam in the black uniform was the one in charge.

The holographic display morphed into a miniature version of a human body. The Hythariam in the room were taller with longer limbs. While Aaron's own six-foot-four frame was broader of shoulder and more muscled than any Hythariam he had encountered thus far, he knew they were far from weak.

A panel hissed open from the wall, and the gray-uniformed Hythariam went over and retrieved a metallic halo. The Hythariam came toward Aaron and raised it as if to put on his head. His eyes darted around, and he shifted his body as much as he could to avoid the halo. The bed beneath him glowed amber, and his muscles tensed, becoming rigid, locking him into place. The Hythariam closed in on him. He clenched his teeth, struggling to raise his hand, and beads of sweat dotted his forehead. Aaron closed his eyes, reaching out with his senses, probing for a source of energy, but felt the halo clip around his head. The ends snaked around to the base of his neck. Tiny pinpricks through his skin locked it in place.

Aaron opened his eyes and looked down at his hands. Thin metallic rods extended from the restraints on his wrists into his veins. He felt something cold being pumped into his blood. He stopped struggling against his restraints and drew inward, probing. An icy chill slid down to the pit of his clenching stomach. The Nanites were reactivating in his system. He braced himself for the pain about to erupt across his body, but nothing happened. The back of his head began to throb as a faint headache gained in intensity. Aaron took a deep breath, and after a few moments the pain subsided. He opened his eyes and was able to move his head.

The Hythariam in the gray uniform came closer, his golden eyes searching his own before he spoke. "There, that's better. Can you understand me?"

Aaron's eyes widened as he realized that he understood what the Hythariam had said. His voice sounded as if he were speaking through a tunnel. The Hythariam repeated himself, and this time it was clearer.

"What did you do to me?" Aaron asked.

The Hythariam frowned. "I won't be able to understand you yet. Give the Nanites some time. Your brain will know when to engage the translator until you can learn our language."

The Hythariam glanced toward the holo display, which showed several progress bars, and then disappeared. He gave a nod toward the Hythariam in the black uniform, and they both left the room.

Aaron tried moving his legs, but everything below his neck was still locked in place. He couldn't feel the forces that held him, gritting his teeth he tried again.

The door hissed open, and in walked the two Hythariam from before, now joined by a third. The third Hythariam didn't look older than the other two except for the eyes. They held an aged alienness that reminded him of Iranus. Knowing that the Nanites could prevent aging all together, he had no idea how old the Hythariam in the room really were. They could have been alive for hundreds of years. The eyes were old. Cold and calculating. He had the black uniform matching the other Hythariam in the room, but his had golden tips on the collar. The other two Hythariam stood to the side and silently deferred to him.

"I am called Morag Halcylon."

Aaron took a long swallow. "I'm Aaron Jace."

Halcylon studied him for a moment and tilted his head inquisitively. "You've heard of me?"

Aaron's eyes never left Halcylon's as he nodded.

"You've seen my kind before?"

"Yes."

Halcylon's eyes lit up as he looked at his companions. "We are not the last."

Aaron glanced at the other two Hythariam in the room. The one in the gray uniform remained stone faced, while the other one gave a half smirk.

"You must forgive the way my men took you into custody. You were extremely disoriented and would have died had they not taken you. There is barely any atmosphere left upon Hytharia anymore," Halcylon said.

"I'd be a lot more forgiving if I was able to move."

"Ah yes, Ronan, I think we can drop the restraints now. Our guest knows we don't mean him any harm," Halcylon said, and the Hythariam in the gray uniformed tapped a few buttons upon a black device on his wrists.

The amber light beneath the bed immediately went out, and Aaron was able to move again. He raised his arms and legs freely now, but resisted the urge to spring to his feet. Here before him was the very same Hythariam his ancestor, Daverim, had met. That fateful meeting had led to the creation of the barrier, which kept the Hythariam army from invading Safanar. Aaron looked back at Halcylon and noticed an emblem that resembled a Z.

Halcylon followed Aaron's gaze. "We are the Zekara, protectors of Hytharia."

"Where am I?"

"You're sitting in the last bastion of hope for my people. The Hythariam in this facility are all that is left on Hytharia. We haven't seen one of your kind in a very long time. We've tried every means at our disposal to go through the portal to Safanar, but always the barrier held us at bay."

Aaron watched Halcylon, trying to gain some insight into why his ancestor, Daverim, believed that this Hythariam standing before him was the tyrant that Iranus had described. There was a harshness to his golden-eyed gaze, and Aaron felt as if he were being scrutinized just as closely.

"How did you manage to come through the portal to Hytharia?"

Aaron's mind flashed, remembering how he tricked the Nanites and freed Sarah from their influence. He searched within, but could only feel the faint whispers of his connection to Sarah.

"How long have I been unconscious?"

Halcylon regarded him a moment. "A few days. Your body became ill as you acclimated to this world."

Days? The others would have tried to rescue him by now if they could. Iranus wouldn't take the risk, and Aaron couldn't blame him. He was only one man, but he still wasn't sure what to make of General Halcylon. He looked over at Ronan, and a flash of uncertainty zipped across his face. Aaron began to suspect that he was being lied to.

"What did you do to me?"

"We've injected Nanites into your system. The ones that were in your system were quite different from what we have now."

Aaron glared at Halcylon, "So you know what they've done?"

Halcylon seemed to nod to himself. "When the portal became closed to us, we had to take other measures to ensure our survival. Since we could not force our way through the barrier, we had to come up with another way. We sent a ship bearing a new prototype Nanite, designed with a singular purpose of assessing the barrier and opening the way for us to escape this dying world."

Aaron felt the bile rise in his throat. "I've seen firsthand the results of that singular purpose. Do you realize how many lives were destroyed in the process?"

Halcylon fixed him with a withering gaze that could crack stone. "Do you know how many lives have been destroyed by the actions of your people? Our survival hangs by a thread, and now you are tied to Hytharia's fate, as are we."

At last Aaron saw it. The tyrant of which Iranus spoke. The ruthlessness in Halcylon bubbled to the surface. Ruthlessness bred from desperation. Didn't he go through the portal, as an act of desperation to save Sarah? Halcylon would use any means necessary to ensure the survival of his people, but when Aaron looked into Halcylon's eyes, he saw a hardened edge devoid of any compassion.

"How were you able to come through the barrier?"

Aaron slowly rose to his feet. The Hythariam in the black uniform rested his hand upon the pistol at his hip.

"I took down the barrier and came through."

"You purposefully came through to a dying world. Didn't you have any plans on getting back?" Halcylon asked.

"I had a way," Aaron said, glancing around the room. "But I lost it."

Halcylon gestured toward Ronan. Another panel hissed open, and Ronan retrieved his Keystone Accelerator.

"Is this what you lost?" Ronan asked.

"Yes," Aaron answered, his eyes lingering on the device, gauging his chances of taking the Keystone Accelerator and opening a way home. They didn't look good.

"The portal opened from such a small device would last only seconds before it shut down, if it worked at all," Ronan said.

Halcylon shrugged his shoulders. "Seconds was all he needed. What disturbs me is that you were willing to come through the portal and then head right back to Safanar, but I don't know why. What was the point of you coming here?"

Aaron remained silent.

"Gone quiet now, have we?" Halcylon asked, after a few moments. "Weren't you even curious as to what was on the other side of the portal?"

"I've already seen what was on this side," Aaron said. "An army. An invasion force prepared to rain destruction down upon Safanar. You took action to ensure the survival of your people, and mine have taken action to protect their people."

Halcylon took a deep breath and sighed. "I had hoped to keep this civil. You have answers that I need. The very lives of the remaining Hythariam I'm sworn to protect are at stake."

The halo on Aaron's head buzzed to life, and he dropped to his knees.

Halcylon squatted down so he was eye level with him. "I have an abundance of patience. One way or another, I will get the answers I seek."

Aaron struggled to push the halo off his head. His fingers numbly grasped it, and he pushed. The halo scraped away his skin as it came off his head. He slammed it onto the ground, and the halo bounced away. A plasma blast scorched the ground next to him. Aaron looked up into the barrel of the pistol pointed directly at his face. He felt a strange tingling at the back of his head, and the golden holo display sprang back to life.

"Are we online?" Halcylon asked.

"Yes, we should be able to disseminate his thoughts now. It took a bit longer to calibrate to human physiology, but it did require that he be conscious. I would advise caution though. This one is not like the others," Ronan said.

Halcylon tilted his head inquisitively again studying Aaron. "Still, only human."

Halcylon's cold, dead eyes slid away from him. Aaron tried to get to his feet, but found that his limbs wouldn't work right. His head swam, and the blood drained from his face as he felt something pulling along the edges of his mind. He tried to summon the bladesong, but it remained stubbornly out of reach. He needed a clear head in order to summon the energy within. Aaron blinked slowly as he glanced up at the display above him. Images passed as if from a movie. The breath caught in his throat as his mother and father figured prominently on the screen.

Protect your sister. His father's dying words echoed in the recesses of his mind.

"What is this place? This is not Safanar," Halcylon said to Ronan.

The two Hythariam were too preoccupied with the holo display to pay him any mind, but the soldier in the room watched him intently.

Aaron glanced back at the display, which now was a multitude of images from his own life. He saw Sarah's face, her golden hair shimmered along the display for a moment, and his pulse quickened.

What wouldn't you do... The last words spoken by his grandmother, who had fallen victim to the Drake, whispered in his mind. Aaron closed his eyes and breathed slowly, calming himself. True mastery came from a focused mind. He pulled together the pieces of his consciousness unaffected by the Nanites and ignored the rest. A translucent form of the barrier coalesce in his mind.

"Why is there interference?" Halcylon asked.

"I don't know," Ronan said, his hands waving through the interface like the conductor of an artificial symphony.

Aaron fed the barrier in his mind, and he felt the skin along the tattoo of the Dragon upon his chest begin to stir.

"It's him, sir."

Halcylon's eyes flashed toward Aaron and narrowed. Then he nodded back to Ronan.

Ronan brought up a miniaturization of Aaron's head upon the display. His hand flicked through the options beneath and then turned expectantly to Aaron.

The sensation of the Nanites felt strange, like tiny beads of light invading his vision as they attempted to wrest control of his mind. The barrier held, and Aaron pushed outward. The holo display went dark.

"What happened?"

Ronan's eyes lifted in shock. "He's resisting the Nanites somehow."

Aaron struggled to his feet, glaring at Halcylon as he stood. His legs shook with effort. "I'll never submit to you."

Halcylon grabbed Aaron by his hair, pulling him upright. "I don't need your submission, human. What was that other place we saw?"

Aaron met his gaze and remained silent.

"If you love Safanar so much, perhaps we can go to this other place instead."

Just then, the display came back online, and Aaron heard the voices of himself and Verona as he told him about where he came from.

"Earth," Halcylon smiled wolfishly. "Tell me human, where is this Earth?"

Aaron felt his strength ebbing away as he hung at Halcylon's mercy. "Like Safanar, Earth is beyond your reach, Hythariam."

Halcylon grabbed Aaron by his shirt and flung him across the room. "Safanar is not beyond my reach, human!"

Aaron crashed into the wall and lay sprawled upon the floor.

"Sir, what do you intend to do with him?" Ronan asked.

"He'll stand trial for war crimes against the Hythariam. The Zekara will have justice," answered Halcylon.

"Very good, sir."

Aaron sat up against the wall. The Hythariam soldier leveled his pistol at him, but it didn't matter. He doubted he could stand at the moment. Though the Nanites had ceased their assault, he could still feel them crawling inside him. He had to think of a way to turn them off. Aaron looked up at the holo display, and where there were foreign symbols before, now he could read them.

"The tribunal will meet within the next thirty minutes. I want the prisoner brought to central shortly after it starts," Halcylon said.

The Hythariam soldier stood over Aaron and slapped two metallic shackles to his wrists. Halcylon and the soldier exited the room.

Ronan keyed in a sequence into the display, and Aaron could feel the Nanites go dormant. With his strength returning and his head clearing, Aaron rose to his feet.

"We don't have much time," Ronan said.

"For what?" Aaron asked.

"Tell me, are there any Hythariam left alive on Safanar?"

"You think I'm going to tell you anything?"

"I was part of a special force of infiltrators, tasked by Iranus to bring others from Hytharia back to Safanar."

Aaron clenched his mouth shut and glared at the Hythariam.

"We came through a different portal from Shandara," Ronan said.

Aaron let out a mirthless chuckle. "Now I know you're lying. There was only one portal on Safanar. The one with the barrier put in place to keep the likes of you, and your psychotic leaders, from ruining our world as you've already done to yours," Aaron said nodding toward the door.

"You're wrong. We built another place capable opening a secret portal from within Shandara. Mine was part of the last mission to come here. We were part of a covert mission to bring back more of my people, but something must have happened because the portal never opened back up for us to return."

Aaron pressed his lips together in thought. "When was this covert mission?"

"Twenty-five cycles of our dying star," Ronan answered.

Could it be? Could this Hythariam be telling him the truth? Iranus or the others had never said anything about another portal being used.

"Shandara has been destroyed," Aaron said.

Ronan looked away with a pained expression. "Destroyed...but that would have been impossible."

"I assure you, I've seen it for myself."

"We knew the risks in coming here, but what happened to all of the other Hythariam that were living in Shandara?"

Aaron regarded the Hythariam. He couldn't tell him about Hathenwood, despite the sincerity of the Hythariam before him.

"Please, I need to know."

Aaron leaned back against the wall, staying silent, but part of him wanted to tell him something.

"I can help you. I have already helped you. Do you still feel the Nanites?"

He didn't feel them anymore, but that wouldn't stop someone else from turning them back on. "You could give me the Keystone Accelerator."

"It won't do you any good. The charge has been drained from it."

"Can you remove the Nanites from my system?" Aaron asked.

Ronan slowly shook his head, "This is something I cannot do."

"Then what exactly can you do?"

"You need allies here if you wish to survive," Ronan said.

"I want to live, but I won't betray my friends."

"Halcylon will use you. You have no idea what he's capable of. You don't know what he has done to our people. Everything you see--," Ronan said, but was cut off as the door hissed open and soldiers, armored head to toe, came in.

Aaron instinctively glanced at the wall, looking for a clock. Had thirty minutes passed already? The spartan gray walls had nothing even remotely close to a clock on them. Ronan returned the Keystone Accelerator to the panel in the wall and closed down the holo display.

Aaron had no illusions of a fair trial here, but he'd much rather walk than be dragged to wherever the Zekara wanted him to go.

The towering soldiers in their dark armor filed in around him, and each held some kind of rifle. The soldiers were easily seven feet tall, with their faces hidden behind a helmet. The door hissed open, and they left the room to the musky damp smell of a hallway carved from dark stone. The jagged edges of the hall had an unfinished look, and Aaron wondered how long the Zekara had been there. There was track lighting with cables running along the edges of the floor. They came to a large reinforced door where two more soldiers were posted. Small drones zoomed down the hallway, pausing briefly at small panels that opened, allowing them through.

The large door opened, and a small breeze came through. Aaron's eyes widened at the enormous cavern before them. An intricate network of catwalks sprawled throughout the place. Dark stone walls extended beyond his field of vision, becoming shadows, leaving him to wonder whether they were underground or inside a mountain. A Zekara soldier shoved the butt of his rifle into his back, moving Aaron along.

There was a buzz of activity throughout the place, and Aaron could see thousands of Hythariam going about their business. None of them appeared to look anything like the hordes he had seen when he had peered through the portal and got his first glimpse of Hytharia.

They stepped onto a floating platform. Railings rose up in front of them, and Aaron grabbed on. The floating platform whisked them away, flying overhead toward the central part of the vast cavern they were in. Aaron marveled that the Hythariam carved all of this out to escape the destruction upon the surface. He knew they were technologically advanced, but being able to dig all of this out was a monumental feat in and of itself. Over to the right was small field of green that looked to be a hydroponic garden. There were several throughout the cavern that he could see. Aaron wondered how they weren't running out of air with so many Hythariam about.

"Are there more caverns like this?" Aaron asked.

"No talking!" the solder at his back said and slammed his rifle into Aaron's back again.

Aaron winced and sagged on his feet. He turned back and glared at the soldier.

"Turn around, human," the soldier barked. "Better yet, give me a reason. I want you to. Just one reason. BANG!" he said brandishing his gun. "No tribunal...nothing. Problem solved."

Aaron turned back around, and his soldier escorts grumbled under their breath. Ronan's face was a mask of impassiveness. He couldn't trust him. He could feel it in his gut. As the platform began to descend, Aaron's mind raced, searching for a way to survive this. Even if he could get away, where would he go? The dying planet was a death sentence.

The platform landed in the middle of a small stadium. Several drones zoomed in, and large displays flicked on around the stadium. Aaron's head figured prominently on screen. The Hythariam gathered in the stadium grew quiet as the platform finished its descent. A soldier secured his shackles to a small pillar rising out of the ground and joined his other escorts to stand well off to the side. More soldiers filed into the stadium, circling around the edges.

Murmuring swept through the crowd. Aaron looked at the display of himself. His brown hair had grown past his shoulders. His clothing was almost in tatters, and he looked every inch the criminal that he assumed the Hythariam thought he was. Despite being chained to the small pillar that came up to his hip, Aaron stood taller, with his shoulders back, and faced toward the dais where five Hythariam sat. They must be the judges serving in this tribunal.

The Hythariam in the stadium began to cheer as one of their own stepped down from their ranks and walked midway between the tribunal and Aaron. Halcylon's golden collar sparkled atop his pristine black uniform. He held up his hands, and the Hythariam in the stadium went silent in a hush.

Aaron was a bit surprised that someone of Halcylon's position didn't preside over the tribunal himself, but came to the realization that he didn't need to.

"You know me as your leader, a general of the Zekara, and savior of the Hythariam. Normally, I would sit at the head of the tribunal, but not this time.

This time, I want the decision from this tribunal to be yours, and yours alone. We have here before us a human. One from Safanar. One of the gatekeepers that have kept us from our salvation, along with the traitors of our own kind. The hour is late, but as I have always said, the way to Safanar will be open for us through the portal. We will not perish with our beloved Hytharia. You have put your faith in me. Even when others of our kind took their chances among the stars, leaving us to our fate, trusting their cryostasis tubes to keep them safe while they traveled to the nearest inhabitable planet. A journey that would take them the better part of fifty of our cycles with no guarantee of success once they get there. They could only take a fraction of us, and I was one they had wanted to lead them. Yet I stayed here with you. I did not do this because it was the easy choice; I stayed because it was the right choice, but this is not why I've called this tribunal. I've called this tribunal because of this man...this human that came through the portal, proving that the barrier that has been in place is no longer a factor."

Murmurs spread through the crowd like waves, and Halcylon waited for it to die down before he continued.

"It saddens me to say this, but it was not peaceful intent that brought this human to our dying world. I've spoken with the human, and he cares nothing for you or for the struggles we've had to endure since the portal to Safanar became closed to us. The civil wars we've fought while our enemies have sewn discord among our very brothers and sisters. The Hythariam will endure as we always have. Look at the human."

Almost as one, the shift of thousands of heads turned in his direction, and the glare of golden-eyed Hythariam bored into Aaron. A soldier approached him and cut Aaron's shirt from his body, exposing his muscled chest. The Dragon tattoo of the Alenzar'seth, with its hints of gold and silver, glistened on the large screens throughout the stadium.

The Hythariam screamed their rage and denial, shaking their fists into the air. Aaron's heart thundered in his chest, but he wouldn't allow himself to cower, even in the face of this madness. Halcylon was making him the embodiment of all the wrongs endured by the Hythariam, and the crowd believed him. He wasn't sure how the truth of matters would stand in the face of so much fear and desperation. He looked around the stadium at all the Hythariam. There were men and women, but there were also children. Not many, but enough for him to notice. Aaron couldn't have imagined what it must have been like to have your whole world crumble around you.

"The mark on his chest," Halcylon said, approaching Aaron, "is the mark of the Alenzar'seth, the rulers of Shandara. The very same people who turned their backs on us. I've spoken to the human before calling this tribunal. After speaking with him, I learned that there wasn't a morsel of remorse for what they condemned upon our race. But don't take my word for it. You can hear it from his own lips."

The screens flickered to Aaron in the room from earlier that day, *"You took action to ensure the survival of your people, and mine have taken action to protect their people."*

Halcylon glared at him. "Protect your people! What gives your people the right to visit genocide on the Hythariam?"

The crowd erupted in fury, and Aaron's head whipped around expecting them to charge out from their seats and tear him apart. He focused himself and began probing for a source of energy around him.

"Through the use of the Nanites we have gleaned information of another world entirely that is also thriving with life. Information that our guest would have kept to himself. Earth, another world, a place we could share with the humans and not only survive, but thrive. But no, the Alenzar'seth will never allow that. He would have the gates of Earth and Safanar be forever closed to the Hythariam. Condemn us all to death. What are we to do?" Halcylon asked, spreading his arms wide, inviting the crowd to respond. "Should we hear what the human has to say? I bet he will tell us of a tale of suffering and trials enough to endear himself into our own hearts. Do you want to hear from him? Hear him tell us why we have to die?"

The crowd was united in their screams, lusting for his blood, as if that would give them any semblance of justice. Hytharia was a place of death, and madness was its warden.

Halcylon waved for him to speak. "Speak to us, human. This is your chance to sway the tribunal before they render judgment. The Hythariam are not an uncivilized race."

The way Halcylon almost spat the word, human, left little to the imagination of how his race was viewed by the general. Aaron took a moment gathering his thoughts. He glanced at the shackles on his wrists and felt the stirrings of the bladesong within. He cast his gaze upward to the jagged ceiling of the cavern above, and then at the angry faces of the crowd all around him. There were no arguments he could make that would spare his life. The Hythariam needed someone to bear the blame for their suffering. He could fight and most certainly die here at this moment, upon this world, away from the people that mattered most to him. He glanced at Halcylon, who stood waiting for him to speak with a menacing glint in his eyes. There was only one thing he could think to do and that was to honor the most basic teachings. When his grandfather had died, thrusting him headlong into this mess, his father had told him there were no perfect solutions. Never were truer words spoken. When faced with uncertainty and having to take responsibility for offenses arrayed against you, the truth cannot only be your shield, but the beacon that shines even in the hour of your death.

Aaron looked up to speak to the crowd. "Your general is right. I didn't come here for the benefit of the Hythariam. Nor did I come here to wage a war that began ages ago before I was even born. I came here to save the woman I loved. She was pulled into this conflict, saving my life, but in turn it would have cost her more than I was willing to allow. The actions I took to save her brought me here, and are something I will never apologize for, to anyone. It is true there are Hythariam alive and well on Safanar, and they all grieve for those left behind. I've seen the sorrow that haunts their footsteps and the pain behind their eyes. They grieve for you and given the choice would choose peace over war. It wasn't me that put the barrier in place, barring your people from Safanar. But given the choice, I never would have come here. It is true I took the barrier down, but not for you. They were for my own selfish reasons. The Hythariam on the other side of the portal fear the war you will bring them. They fear your leaders and the measures that will be taken if you were to ever make it to Safanar."

"Measures indeed, tell me, Aaron, what wouldn't you do to protect your people?" Halcylon asked.

"My ancestor, Daverim Alenzar'seth, created the barrier to protect his people and his world. I cannot know what was in his mind when he committed the act. I'm already betting my life that he wouldn't have taken such an action if he hadn't believed it was necessary. You found Safanar through an accident of fate; who says you should live at all? What desperate measures have you taken to survive? The Hythariam on Safanar paint a bleak picture of what life was like on Hytharia and the measures the Zekara had taken to achieve its goals."

"Doing what is necessary is never wrong," Halcylon countered.

"Was it necessary to murder your own people? Sacrifice entire cities so that you should live?" Aaron asked.

Halcylon studied him for a moment. "We've had to make tough choices in order to survive."

"That's exactly the point. My people also made a tough choice in the name of survival, and yet here I stand, waiting to be judged by your tribunal. Who will judge the actions you have taken?" Aaron asked.

"Indeed you are here to answer for the genocide that your people have committed against mine. Can you justify that?"

In that moment, Aaron knew it was hopeless. "It's not genocide if the Hythariam are alive on Safanar. You've had almost eighty years, and are you telling me that in all that time the Hythariam didn't come up with a contingency plan? That it was either make it to Safanar or die?"

Halcylon regarded him with an icy glint in his eyes. "Make no mistake, human. We will be going to Safanar, and when we do, the Safanarions will have much to answer for, as will the Hythariam there."

The roar of the crowd shattered the silence, and Aaron could hear the echoes of the other Hythariam throughout the great cavern outside the stadium they were in. The roars outside were deep and bestial, beyond that of any normal Hythariam. Aaron felt the stirrings of the bladesong within, and the muscles in his arms grew rigid, straining against the shackles on his wrists. He looked at Halcylon, understanding once again why Iranus was so fearful of his coming to Safanar. If he were to die here, then perhaps he could make his death count for something. He pulled the energy in hardening his muscles and skin. He kept his gaze upon the ground and took a breath. In the last second before he would jump, he looked at Halcylon.

The Hythariam watched him, waiting for Aaron to reach out toward him. "Do it, human," Halcylon hissed.

The moments ebbed away, and the only reason Aaron didn't move was because it was exactly what Halcylon wanted. Instead, Aaron turned to the tribunal and waited.

The crowd came to a muttered silence as the five members of the tribunal rose from their seats.

"We of the Hythariam find the human guilty of the war crime genocide against the Hythariam race. His sentence is death to be carried out immediately," a member of the tribunal said.

Halcylon stepped up. "I have a better idea that I would like to present to the tribunal and one that would serve the justice we of the Zekara would seek."

"The judgment has been rendered and cannot be changed."

"Yes, it has. What I propose is that we condemn the human to the same fate that he and the other Safanarions have doomed the rest of us to. When the portal is once again opened upon Safanar, the human will watch and remain alive long enough to bear witness that the way back to his home is right in front of him, but forever beyond his reach. He can die with our beloved Hytharia."

The crowd roared their approval. The cheers of righteous fury changed to fear as the ground shook violently beneath Aaron's feet. Pieces of rock detached from the roof of the cavern and slammed into the ground around them. The Hythariam in the stadium were thrown to the ground. The tremor finally passed, and Aaron noted that Halcylon was completely unfazed by what had happened.

Halcylon turned and waited for the tribunal to respond.

The members of the tribunal regained their feet, and a member spoke. "We find that your suggestion is in keeping with the good faith of our judgment and will be carried out upon the human."

Aaron glared at Halcylon, but he wouldn't move. He wouldn't strike out against the general even though he was such a short distance away from him. They had a way to get to Safanar. A glimmer of hope ignited deep inside Aaron that he may yet be able to return to Sarah. It was that hope that would keep him from casting his life away, and the look on Halcylon's eyes confirmed that this is what the general had planned the entire time. Halcylon had used Aaron as the rallying cry for the Hythariam. As he looked around the stadium at the hateful leers of the Hythariam, Aaron almost doubted that he would live long enough to even see the portal open to Safanar.

"Have no fear, human," Halcylon said, so only Aaron could hear. "The last thing you will see is your home through the pale light of the portal. Mark my words, Safanar will be forever beyond your reach."

Halcylon stepped away, and four soldiers took up guard around him. The Hythariam in the stadium came onto the field, hungry to see their human prisoner who they had condemned to death. All the while Aaron kept thinking that Iranus was not mistaken in his judgment of his own people. The slippery slope stemming from desperate measures in the name of survival had sapped the soul of the Hythariam race, leaving a yearning hatred to the purveyors of their own destruction. War and a struggle to survive had become a way of life for the Hythariam, and the only thing keeping them together was the promise of retribution for all the wrongs that had been visited upon them. It was madness, and Aaron was caught firmly in its web.

5

FALLEN CITY STIRS

Colind looked at the rubble-strewn ground that stretched away from him. Shandara had been his home and his prison. Now it appeared that the fallen city was waking from a fitful slumber. The imbalance of energy and constant twilight were gone. The barrier that held the Hythariam at bay no longer drained the land. Sunlight bathed the city in a warm glow, and the city seemed to breathe a great sigh as if it had cast off a terrible burden. The cries of the dead still echoed in Colind's mind, causing him to wince at times. Nothing remained of the people who couldn't escape, and what fire hadn't consumed the passage of time claimed for its own.

The Hythariam had been slowly clearing the streets and restoring the buildings. At least they had shelter, and the underground springs that fed the city still worked.

"I keep expecting to see a Ryakul lurking around every corner," Garret said.

"They've scattered, but there could still be some here," Colind answered.

"Without the Drake to control them, I'm afraid it's only a matter of time before they terrorize the smaller cities and towns that have little or no defenses," Vaughn said.

Garret frowned, taking stock of the area, "What I don't understand is how the Ryakuls even survived here for so long. What did they eat? It's not as if there was a ready food supply anywhere near here."

Colind's stomach sank, and he closed his eyes, wincing, "They ate the most readily available food supply: other Ryakuls."

They glanced at each other, their mouths drawing downward, disgusted at the thought of this new revelation.

"I've seen it," Colind answered. "My body was trapped and my soul doomed to dwell in the twilight of this place. The past, whatever else it is, is gone."

The silence gave them men a brief respite from bitter thoughts. They turned down a street that had been cleared. The rubble had been moved to a place away from the city. Roselyn, Iranus's daughter and a brilliant scientist, had been able to create smaller Keystone Accelerators for them to use to open portals. They were less powerful than the prototype that Aaron had used, but they did work just fine. They were limited to a few uses in a given cycle and currently had to brought back to Hathenwood to be recharged. Iranus had assured them that new versions of the accelerators would be able to recharge on their own.

"Even though the barrier has been down a month there have been reports of animals returning to the surrounding forests," Vaughn said.

Colind nodded, "That's good. I know Cyrus has been getting a lot of requests from people wishing to return here. Resources at Rexel are being spread thin, but it will do them no good to get here and not be able to feed themselves."

"There is a long road ahead if Shandara is to be rebuilt," Garret said.

Colind nodded, "Yes, but if Shandara is going to protect anybody we need to repair the walls."

"They are using the rubble from throughout the city, reshaping it into pieces to fix the damaged sections, but simply put, it's a big wall," Vaughn said.

"We still have some time," Garret said. "Precious little though there is. Have the others had any luck finding the chamber or the weapons caches?"

Colind shook his head, "The place that the chamber is believed to be is in one of the most damaged parts of the city. They are still working their way toward it, but they need to be cautious lest they destroy the very place they are most eager to get to. As far as the weapons caches go, they think they might have found one. Sarah and the others are heading there now."

Vaughn frowned, glancing where Colind had nodded his head.

"What is it?" Colind asked.

"I'm worried about Sarah. Her patience is growing thin with finding the chamber. Each day that passes, her will erodes away that much more," Vaughn said.

"I want Aaron back too," Colind said.

"Do you think he is alive?" Vaughn asked, and Garret glanced back at them.

"Yes," Colind said without hesitation.

"How can you be so sure? Verona and the others say the same thing. It's as if they won't believe for a second that Aaron may, in fact, be dead."

"It's not blind faith, my friend, I can assure you. Think about it," Colind said. "We know the Hythariam are on the other side. Aaron saw them. So they must be monitoring the portal and would know if someone came through. I believe Aaron is being held captive by the Hythariam on the other side."

Garret swallowed, "Being held captive could be worse than death. This is the same race that created the Drake. I can only imagine what they could do to Aaron, especially if they knew who he really was."

"They know who he is," Colind sighed.

"How?" Garret asked.

Vaughn's eyes grew wide. "He bears the mark of the Alenzar'seth upon his chest."

"Yes, and Halcylon would never forget who is responsible for putting the barrier in place. Given the amount of destruction where the chamber used to be, I have little hope that we will be able to mount any rescue attempt for Aaron. He is on his own."

The uneasy silence dragged on.

"I'm beginning to understand Sarah's attitude," Vaughn said quietly.

"If they know who Aaron is then they will recognize his value. Wouldn't they keep him alive then?" Garret asked.

"That's what I'm hoping for," Colind said.

"There has been some good news. Zsensibar's armies are gathering in the south. King Nasim has been in contact with Cyrus this morning," Vaughn said.

"That is good news. At least now we are only slightly outnumbered by the High King's armies instead of overwhelmingly so," Garret answered.

"Have they moved?" Colind asked.

The Hythariam had set up what they called a command center at their camp in Shandara. Vaughn had spent most of his time in there, meeting with the rest of the Free Nations Army leaders and using the tracking devices of the Hythariam to keep an eye upon the High King's army.

"No, they are merely gathering, but it can't be much longer before they move out. It's just a matter of figuring out where they will go first," Vaughn said. "Also, this morning there have been reports of Ryakul sightings. They are sweeping west of here. Some of the new airships...the FNA Air Corps is what they are calling themselves, have been dispatched to hunt them down. There has also been a shortage of airship captains. They are going to need to start promoting some of the newer recruits up through the ranks sooner than expected."

"Would one of those new captains happen to be a Zsensibarian prince?" Garret asked.

Vaughn smiled, "Indeed, he would. Although it took some convincing. Jopher had been adamant about staying on board the Raven to serve under Morgan, saying he needed more experience."

"Normally I would say that was very wise, but we're going to need for everyone to move a bit faster than they would like," Colind said.

"Admiral Morgan agreed with needing more experience, so he assigned some of the more senior officers to serve under the prince and packed him off onto one the newer airships," Vaughn said.

Colind found himself laughing with the rest of them.

"Anything more on helping the nations that have allied with us in defending their own cities?" asked Colind.

"The Hythariam have some type of cannon. We've seen them in action on the airships, but again there is an issue of powering anything to do with Hythariam technology. I don't think they were prepared for the scope of what's involved. They are preparing weapons and generators to power them, but it's slow going," Vaughn said.

"Perhaps finding some of the weapons caches here will help with that," Colind said.

They headed back toward where the digging was commencing for the chamber. He would be leaving them soon. He needed to find more members of the Safanarion Order. They were needed. Colind glanced at Garret and knew he would be hard pressed to leave the other man behind. Perhaps he shouldn't leave him behind then. Knowing the armies were gathering and war with the High King was imminent, Colind wondered what would be left of them to stand against the Hythariam if they survived. The object in the heavens, a space ship, Iranus had called it, was still heading in their direction. Colind couldn't help but feel as if they were missing something. A looming threat that lurked among the shadows just beyond his reach, but would strike out and catch them all off guard. He had to begin his hunt for Mactar, who was even now roaming free virtually unchecked. His time here in Shandara was at an end, he decided. He would be leaving by nightfall.

6

A CALL FOR AID

It was their third day in Shandara, and Sarah glared at the mountain of rubble before her. This was supposed to be an entranceway that led to the chamber where they might be able to open a portal to Hytharia. Sarah would be surprised if there was a place in this cursed city that had suffered more destruction than where she was right now. She all but scowled at the Hythariam working to remove the remnants of the buildings that used to be here. No one was moving fast enough. One quiet Hythariam, Tanneth, had urged her to be patient and had warned her that they could cause further damage if they weren't careful. Sarah glanced over to her left where the quiet Hythariam stood with Braden. The Hythariam made sense. She just didn't like it. They were about to trek out among the ruins again, looking for the weapons caches that were supposedly hidden throughout the city. *They are there,* she corrected in her mind. It was just her frustration getting the best of her. The more time passed, the more her emotions spun wildly inside her. She even found herself getting angry at Aaron for leaving her. The nights were the worst, when tears came when she least expected. *He's not dead. I will get him back,* Sarah told herself over and over again.

Her fingers caressed Aaron's swords. He had been able to use them to lift a house-sized boulder, allowing them to free Colind from his prison. She had tried the same, but though she could wield Aaron's blades, she couldn't evoke the bladesong with them like he had. Gritting her teeth, she turned away and walked in the opposite direction.

Braden and Tanneth came to her side and silently followed. She remembered how dark Shandara had felt upon their first trek into the city, as if they were all about to be swallowed into the ground. Sarah hadn't realized how profound the feeling was until she came back here. The barrier had been sucking the life out the land surrounding Shandara, and if left in place, would have plunged more of Safanar into darkness. They all believed that Aaron wasn't dead. Not that she needed their faith in that, but it did make her feel a little bit better. She said a silent prayer to the Goddess that he would survive to return to her. They thought Aaron had been captured by the Hythariam military and the dominant faction known as the Zekara. Sarah didn't care what they called themselves, but the fact that they had Aaron and she couldn't get to him burned her up inside. She drew in a shaky breath and tried to keep her anger in check.

"My Lady," Braden said. "We're heading up to the northern part of the city. Nearest the palace. Tanneth scouted it a bit last night, and he thinks he has found something, but will need you to confirm."

Sarah nodded. Next to her only Sarik, Verona, and Braden could tap into the energy enough to determine whether the caches were near. The others had all newly come into their powers, but she pushed them on without mercy. They trained together whenever they made time for it and never complained, urging her to drive them harder. They all knew what was at stake, but deep in her heart Sarah knew it would take more than the four of them to balance an engagement with the Elitesmen.

They were all good men, even the Hythariam Tanneth, and she was grateful for their support. None of them bore her any ill will, but she could sense the uncertainty from some of the other Hythariam, particularly Iranus. His word carried much weight, and while he hadn't said anything directly, there were others on their council that viewed her as the daughter of the High King. Perhaps even some believed they could use her to barter against her father. She was no stranger to this game and wouldn't have survived in her father's court this long without having learned how it was played. She wondered how the Resistance in Khamearra had faired since Aaron's visit. So far they had no news and no contact. Verona had given her one of the leftover travel crystals, and she was tempted to return to Khamearra to see how things were in the city. She entertained the thought of offering to do some poking around on behalf of the FNA, but couldn't do it. They were still her people, even if she didn't stand with her father. Maybe Aaron was right in his belief that there could be no end to this conflict without bloodshed. But then again, Aaron had the chance to face her brother Rordan and chose not to fight him. Verona's account had left her momentarily speechless, and she felt a warmth blossom inside her chest at the thought even now. Despite what had happened to him, Aaron was a good man, which he had proven time and time again. But deep down Sarah knew there was only so much a Dragon would take before it would unleash its fury. She almost found it hard to believe that he had reached out to not only her brother, but her father as well. A fool's plea some would say, but he was *her* fool. Aaron believed wholeheartedly that the people of Safanar needed to unite if they were to have any chance at all to stand against the might of the Hythariam military. She shared his belief that the people of Safanar should unite, but it would be difficult, if not impossible, for them to unite against a foe that for all intents and purposes was a myth. The Zekara were not here. Right now the only armies gathering upon the field were native to Safanar. The perfect time for a strong enemy to sneak in and position itself for a devastating strike was now. In Khamearra there were Elitesmen who followed the old code;

perhaps now they would stand with the Resistance and overthrow the current regime.

They walked deeper into the city, and the blackened skin of the buildings had begun to show flecks of white as the years of weathering stripped away the past. The first time they had seen Shandara, the destruction had a deep effect on all of them. It was one thing to learn about something as part of history, it was quite another to actually see where the event happened. To smell the stale air. To see all the lives that had been twisted and snuffed out by the fires that had consumed the city. Devastation brought about by her father and his victory was celebrated in Khamearra to this day. She felt her stomach rise up and settle back down, as if she were on an airship.

"Tanneth, what did you find last night?" Sarah asked.

"A part of the city that has been virtually untouched."

Sarah nodded and quickened her step.

Birds flew amid the buildings, and fresh nests could be seen, but Sarah was at a loss for where the birds collected the bits required for building them. The forests were quite a bit away from where they were now, but the birds were determined to make a home.

They turned a corner, coming to a wide-open street lined with some of the biggest statues she had ever seen. The statues were of men and women appearing in succession, depicting a person standing at first, then progressed with each showing the movements of the slow forms that Aaron had first taught them onboard the Raven. Sarah allowed her eyes to glide over them down the long thoroughfare, fooling her eyes into seeing the motions of the very still statues.

"This place is amazing," Verona said.

Braden bowed his head, brought his fist across his heart, and whispered the Warden's Oath of the De'anjard. The rest of them bowed their heads in respect, including the Hythariam. As they progressed down the wide street, Sarah's eyes took in the stunning details of the statues. The folds of the clothing draped over lean muscles in each depiction of the slow forms were shown to perfection. The faces carved into the statues were generic ideals, and she drank in the sight of them as did the others. The tension drained away from her shoulders, and she found herself standing straighter, becoming infused with the majestic energy exuding from this place. The succession of statues spoke to the potential in each of them, and Sarah was grateful that amid all the destruction throughout Shandara this place had been spared.

Tanneth stopped in front of a statue about halfway down the street and nodded to Sarah.

"You think there could be something here?" she asked.

The others spread out examining the area, but Tanneth and Braden stayed at her side. The pedestal upon which the statue stood was adorned with an intricate design of laurel work, drawing the eyes toward the center. Sarah traced her fingers, following the path of the design, and closed her eyes. Her fingers glided along, and she could feel Aaron's medallion grow slightly warmer where it rested upon her chest. She drew in the energy around them and focused on the base of the statue. She sent tendrils of energy to follow the laurel vines away from the center to their point of origins that had become distinct. She fed the tiniest morsel of energy into each origin point and retrieved the warm medallion from under her shirt. The origin points glowed, and she heard Braden call the others over. Sarah brought the medallion to the center of the pedestal and pressed it firmly into place. There was a faint but audible click, and the white pearl in the medallion's center flashed momentarily. They heard the grating sound of a stone doorway reveal itself around the corner of the pedestal away from the street.

Sarah hung the medallion back around her neck and followed the others. Faint glowing orbs pulsated to life inside, growing brighter and revealing a stone staircase. Just past the entranceway, the air tasted stale and old, leaving Sarah to guess when the last time someone had ever been down there. Having drawn in the energy, her eyes immediately adjusted to the dark. They came to the bottom of the stairs, and more orbs began to glow, stretching out along the walls away from them.

The orbs nearest grew brighter as did the others, revealing a long room that housed racks of weapons. The racks closest to them held bows and swords covered with a layer of dust, but the farther they ventured, the types of weapons began to change. One rack held golden rods with handles that slipped over your forearm and a grip for your hand.

"Shields, like the one Braden carries," Verona said.

"They're good at deflecting the Elitesmen's attack orbs," Braden said, then looked at Tanneth. "Now you and Gavril can test your pistols against one of these shields and stop asking me for mine."

Tanneth smiled, taking one of the rods off the rack. He attached it to his arm and engaged the trigger in the handle. Within a second, a golden oblong shield fanned out.

"I never get tired of seeing that," Verona said.

"Braden, do you think it can do what you've done with your hammer and shield?" Tanneth asked.

Braden's brow furrowed in thought for a minute. "Too risky to try in here. Would cause too much damage, but we can try later."

"I don't see any more war hammers like yours here," Verona said, gesturing toward the black-and-gold-etched hammer that Braden carried.

"What can you do with the shield?" Sarah asked.

"I found this hammer beneath the Citadel of the Elite. I had assumed it was taken from Shandara at the fall. When I strike the shield with it I'm able to use the energy to focus the vibrations and push things away," Braden said.

"Things?" Sarah asked with a raised brow.

A hungry look broke through Braden's facade. "Elitesmen, my Lady."

"Indeed," Verona said, "and he's been reluctant to give a demonstration ever since."

"Do you think you can teach the others to do it?" Sarah asked.

"Perhaps now that we have more shields, but it's not for the weak. It requires a strong hand to guide the waves coming off it. This may sound strange, but I felt the shield's potential when I focused with the energy drawn within. While my hammer seems to be well suited to the task, it might work with something else," Braden said.

"I think the hammer suits you, my friend," Verona said.

"So you focused these waves, and it pushed the Elitesmen out of the way?" Sarik asked.

"Violently."

"Couldn't they just move out of the way? I mean they can move pretty fast," Sarik said.

"Not fast enough," Braden said.

"I think I'm fast enough," Sarik answered.

Braden laughed. "All the young ones think they are fast enough."

"I don't know, Braden," Verona said. "Sarik is pretty fast nowadays. Like you, my friend, he's picked up a few new tricks."

"As entertaining as this is, I think we should keep moving. Look, Tanneth is leaving us behind," Sarah said.

She always liked their camaraderie. The bond between them was strong, and she felt fortunate to be a part of it. At first to them she had been Sarah, daughter of the High King, but now she was one of their own. She glanced at Braden, who tended to look out for her as an older brother or uncle she never had. Their protectiveness for her stemmed from their loyalty to Aaron, but she appreciated it nonetheless. After all, they accepted her into their group through her own loyalty to Aaron.

"The weapons here are all finely made, but if they were preparing for a war with the Hythariam military, wouldn't they have different sorts of weapons and armor here?" Verona asked.

"These aren't ordinary. The alloys used show signs of the combined efforts between our peoples. But wait," Tanneth said, stepping up to a smooth metallic wall.

He stood there for a moment and brought up his wrist, tapping commands into the comms device. Two panels hissed open simultaneously, and a screen flickered to life. Tanneth stepped up to one of the open panels and began moving his hands in a sequence that Sarah couldn't begin to guess at. The screen in front of them changed.

"This is a map of the city," Tanneth said, his voice growing excited. "And these are where the other weapons and supply caches are hidden."

The map was invaded by blue dots throughout the city with the exception of a flashing yellow one. Sarah recognized the street above them on the map, which had a flashing yellow dot. Tanneth keyed in another sequence, and a section of the far wall pulled back revealing a smaller room.

"Gavril told me that the creation of these rooms was a joint effort with the Shandarians. It required a Shandarian to open the way into these vaults, but it required a Hythariam to access the more specialized weapons and devices," Tanneth explained.

"Why couldn't you bring up a map like this at Hathenwood?" Sarah asked.

"These vaults were here before Hathenwood was built, and for more protection the records of these locations could only be accessed from one of the vaults. It's what we call a closed system," Tanneth explained.

Sarah nodded. "What's so special about the weapons down here?"

Tanneth smiled. "They are a blend of the finest Shandarian craftsmanship mixed with Hythariam technology. Some are powered and are able to shoot bolts of energy, others help with defense, and there are more things like the comms devices."

Sarah studied the map. "Is that the palace?"

Tanneth nodded.

"What's there? That dot looks different from all the rest."

"It was where the city's defenses could be managed. We've been trying to reach it, but it's off the main palace, which is largely intact. When the invasion does happen, Shandara will become the last and best hope for us," Tanneth said.

Sarah glanced between Tanneth and the screen. "What about the other cities?"

"We're doing the best we can, and we will help them as much as we can, but we had years to prepare Shandara for invasion. The expectation was that the frontline battles would be fought here," Tanneth said.

They were interrupted as his comms device lit up.

"Yes, Colonel," Tanneth said as Gavril's face appeared on the screen.

"You've done it, Tanneth. Good work," Gavril said.

"Yes, sir. I uploaded the other locations to Hathenwood. This will allow us to narrow our search. Sarah was able to open the door for us."

"This is great news," Gavril said, sounding relieved, then he looked at Sarah, and his gaze softened. "My Lady, I need for you to return to our base. We've had word from the Resistance."

An icy grip spread throughout Sarah's chest. "We're coming."

Without so much as a backward glance, Sarah headed for the exit. Each step she took, she drew in more energy, lengthening her strides. She emerged into the sunlight with the others quickly following. Tanneth and Braden quickly activated their gliders and stepped on. After a quick look at the others, Verona followed suit. None of them could jump like she could. Sarik gave a half smile and dashed off down the street, blurring away from them. Sarah nodded to the others and launched into the air. The wind brushed past her face, and she felt her long braid trailing behind her. She landed and immediately took off again, closing the distance to their camp. Braden and Tanneth followed her using the Hythariam gliders. The dust clouds rising from the city streets were the only indication of where Sarik was. He could move so fast now, possibly faster than she could. She kept seeing the look in Gavril's eyes in the back of her mind. Her people were in trouble. She was torn between her need to rescue Aaron and her duty to those she swore to stand with.

"Oh, Aaron...I'm sorry," she whispered as she made the final jump that landed her in the middle of their base camp, startling a throng of Hythariam and people working nearby. The others weren't far behind, arriving in their own fashion. Verona and Sarik had come a long way since the decks of the Raven. It would only be a matter of time before they could jump as she and Aaron could.

Braden, she suspected, wouldn't be able to jump like that. His abilities with the energy came in a different form than the others. Braden's abilities centered around his use of strength, which suited the De'anjard perfectly.

Gavril was one of the few Hythariam whose golden irises had a greenish tint, and they flashed in surprise as they came into the tent. The old soldier recovered quickly and nodded toward the display.

An older man's face appeared on screen. The bleeding wound upon his head stained his gray hair, but it didn't look bad.

"I am Nicholas, one of the Resistance leaders here in Khamearra. We need help. We're being slaughtered by the High King's guards and the Elitesmen. They are sweeping the city. There is no place left to hide. A number of our people have escaped and are making their way to Lorric. There are armies massing outside the city walls. They are planning something big. Please help us," Nicholas pleaded before the message went blank.

Sarah swallowed the lump in her throat and closed her eyes. "I need to go to them."

"What about Aaron?" Sarik asked.

Sarah cast her eyes downward as Sarik's question echoed in her mind. "Is the chamber intact?"

Gavril shook his head grimly. "We haven't been able to reach it yet. I'm sorry, but it doesn't look good."

Sarah felt her knees turn to water before every muscle in her body went rigid as she turned away from Gavril. Her eyes welled up with tears threatening to spill over. "I can't help Aaron here," she said in a harsh whisper. "But I can help my people. I'm going to Khamearra," she said, retrieving the travel crystal.

"Not alone you're not, my Lady," Verona said quickly.

The others all nodded with the clear intention of coming with her. She felt her lips lift into the slightest smile, and her eyes softened. "Thank you, but I can't take you all with me. They need you here. I need to be able to move quickly, and I can't do that if all of you come with me."

They all protested at once, saying how they couldn't let her go alone. Only that alone is how she had made her way through the world, that is, until she had met Aaron. She could tell they weren't going to let up, and she had too much respect for them to just up and disappear.

"I can only take one of you with me when I use the travel crystal because it's getting weaker," she lied.

Verona stepped toward her first, but she shook her head. "You're needed here. The Hythariam need you to open the other vaults throughout the city, and Sarik can help you."

"What about the medallion?" Verona asked.

Sarah withdrew it from under her shirt and reluctantly passed it to him. "Take it."

"One second please," Tanneth said. He went over to one of the metallic cases stacked upon the floor and rummaged inside for a minute. He withdrew a round plate about an inch thick and set it atop of the case. The plate came to life as he tapped in commands to his comms device.

"Put the medallion on top," he said.

Verona did as he was bidden. After a moment, the medallion rose a few inches into the air and was bathed in a red glow. An exact duplicate of the medallion came up on the screen. Verona retrieved the medallion and handed it back to Sarah.

"We'll be able to make a copy of the medallion, which should allow us to open the vaults throughout the city," Tanneth said.

Sarah frowned. "Are you sure? This medallion has been infused with the energy of Aaron's ancestors. That cannot be copied with that device."

Tanneth nodded. "You are correct, but I think the medallion's use at the vault was more as a key. The energy to open the vault came from you."

Sarah nodded slowly and hung the medallion back around her neck, relieved that she could at least hold onto this small piece of Aaron. *Foolish girl,* she chided herself. She glanced at Braden and was about to speak when he cut her off.

"Do not think you're leaving me behind, my Lady. Since my Lord is not here to protect, I will protect what matters most to him," Braden said and gently placed his hand upon her arm.

Physical contact was all that was needed to accompany someone using the travel crystal.

Verona stood, struggling with the fact that he wasn't going, but like Braden wanted to look after her. He shared a hard look with Braden and said, "Safe journey to both of you."

"I will send word when I can," Sarah said.

"Please do so," Gavril said. "We can be of aid and make the journey to you using the accelerators, but it will take a few hours. If you can coordinate with us we can help them escape."

Sarah nodded and looked at Braden. "Are you ready?"

Braden nodded, hefted his war hammer from his belt, and gave her a gentle squeeze. Sarah drew in the energy and focused it on the crystal, picturing a place in Khamearra, her home. After days of their frustratingly fruitless search for a way to rescue Aaron, she was eager to be of use, but at the same time she feared what she would find when they got there. With a silent prayer for the Goddess to guide her path, she activated the travel crystal.

Verona stood helplessly as Sarah and Braden disappeared. He silently cursed his duty for a moment, but knew that he was exactly where he needed to be.

"Let's go find the other weapons caches," Verona said.

Gavril reached out to him. "We'll start making plans for the evacuation now and have a team of FNA soldiers standing by."

Verona nodded and left the tent with the others.

7

A WANING HOPE

Aaron had been left in the stadium, chained to the stone pillar. Halcylon had invited all the Hythariam to look upon the human. The soldiers posted would prevent anyone from killing him, but his body ached everywhere. The first stones thrown hurt the worst. The Hythariam here looked at him as if he were some type of animal.

Sometime later, the soldiers had chained his legs to the pillar, making it so that he could hardly move. He occasionally slipped into a restless sleep until the pain in his aching arms from which he hung woke him up. What passed for food was brought sparingly, but the tasteless, slimy white goop was the only thing they served. He had to endure. It was the only way to get back to Sarah. The faces of his friends faded in his mind as more time slipped past. His arms and legs failed to obey him, and his mind felt as if there were a great weight pulling down his thoughts.

The ground beneath him shook, rattling the chains that bound him, and snapped him awake from a dreamless sleep. He was strewn upon the ground but couldn't remember how he had ended up there. He slowly turned his head to the sound of footsteps approaching upon the hard rocky surface. He opened his eyes, and the smoky gray fur of a wolf padded up to him.

"Zeus!" Aaron gasped and started coughing. His grandfather's wolf half-breed that had died at Shandara watched him with his large slate eyes.

Am I dying?

He could hear Zeus's panting, but as Aaron raised his head, the wolf vanished.

"Get him up," Halcylon ordered.

Rough hands grabbed Aaron and brought him to his feet.

"Look at the screen, human," Halcylon said.

Aaron raised his head to watch as the large screen in front of them flickered to life. Elitesmen crowded his field of vision, which then melted away to a sky filled with Ryakuls. The scenes were all disjointed, but all of them had been of events in his life.

"Explain this. How are you able to do these things?" Halcylon asked.

Aaron sucked in a slow breath. "All Safanarions can do this. They've been preparing for you for the last eighty years. When you bring your army to Safanar, you will be hopelessly outmatched. If you come peacefully, they may allow you to live."

Halcylon's golden eyes narrowed. "You lie, human. We can see your memories. We know what's waiting for us on Safanar. You spread ideas like wildfire."

One the Zekara soldiers jammed the end of his rifle into Aaron's stomach.

Aaron collapsed to the ground, his limbs failing to work properly. He struggled to his hands and knees.

Halcylon squatted down to Aaron's eye level. "This shall be the pose of all the Safanarions."

The bladesong flickered inside him, coming from deep within. Aaron could hear the deep growl of the Eldarin. His mind cleared, and he looked into Halcylon's baleful gaze. He struck out with his hand, grabbing the Hythariam by the throat and surged to his feet.

"We will never kneel before you," Aaron growled.

Halcylon's eyes widened in shock as he gasped for breath. The soldiers rained down blows upon his back, and Aaron collapsed to the ground. The bladesong went silent inside him, and he writhed on the floor in pain. When the soldiers stopped beating him, he found himself staring at his feet. The breath caught in his throat. His feet looked deformed, sticking out at odd angles. He blinked his eyes, and they returned to normal. Aaron shook his head, trying to clear it.

"Will it be ready, Ronan?" Halcylon asked, his voice sounding gravelly.

Aaron couldn't even raise his head to see the Hythariam.

"Oh yes, sir. The Akasul won't last long. Maybe a month at the most. We've rushed its development," Ronan answered.

"Will the memories stick?" asked Halcylon.

"We're pushing the boundaries of even the Nanites, but yes, it will work."

"Excellent, the best weapon is the one they'll never see coming," Halcylon said.

The Hythariam walked away, their voices fading. Even the soldiers left him. Chained and weakened as he was, he wasn't going anywhere.

Aaron lay upon the ground, staring up at the column above him, his eyes tracing the lines of it. Something appeared out of place. He closed his eyes, trying to draw in the energy around him, but it was getting harder to do. What once had been so easy was being stripped away. Two green eyes opened and stared at him. The rest of the creature's body blended in with the column.

"Someone is always watching, human," the creature hissed at him.

Aaron tried to speak, but he couldn't form any words.

"Don't try to speak, human. You and I have the same goal," the creature said, and for a moment its body quivered. It crept down lower along the column. Its body was small, only about four feet in length, but its claws were able to penetrate the rocky column with ease. The creature's face was dark, but Aaron could see the points of its teeth when it spoke.

"We both wish to kill Halcylon," it whispered.

Aaron struggled to open his mouth, but couldn't.

"Don't consume what they bring you. It is bad," the creature said.

"Name?" Aaron asked in a voice barely above a whisper.

The creature cocked its head to the side, listening. The creature turned its gaze upon him and moved its head as a hunter studying its prey. "I have no name, only what my captors used to call me...Thraw."

Thraw came inches from Aaron's face, sniffing.

"You smell bad. I'm not sure you will be much use," Thraw said.

"...Fight..." Aaron croaked.

The door of the stadium opened, and the soldiers were heading back his way. Aaron glanced up at the column, but the creature was gone.

8

RETURN HOME

Sarah and Braden stood on a hill just outside the city of Khamearra. They wore ordinary brown cloaks, which for the most part concealed their weapons. Sarah scanned the skyline of the city and noticed the missing tower at the Citadel of the Elite. One still remained, but the blow to the Elitesmen and the lack of one of their towers was a constant reminder that their power was not absolute. Airships dotted the skyline over the city, their hulking masses moving lazily. She had gotten used to the FNA airships that were quicker and more agile.

Her gaze drifted over to the palace, which towered above the city, casting long shadows around it.

"Braden, at some point I will need to go to the palace," Sarah said.

Braden nodded. "Okay."

"Alone."

Braden reared up. "My Lady, I cannot protect you if I'm not there with you."

"I've been looking after myself since I was a child. I know the palace and how to get in and out unseen," Sarah said.

"Then you can get us both in unseen, my Lady."

Sarah sighed. "Very well," she said, deciding not to push the issue, at least not yet.

Braden brought out the comms device and read the small screen. "Tanneth says they are putting together a plan to rescue any of the Resistance we can get out of the city."

"Where will they take them?" Sarah asked.

"Shandara," Braden said, frowning as he read the message again. "Rexel is bursting at the seams, and Shandara is the one place they are least likely to be found."

Sarah nodded. "I see. When can they be ready?"

"In about six hours, but I'm not sure if it's enough time for us. We need to find out what's been done to the Resistance and where they are being held," Braden said.

"First things first then. Why don't we have a look around and then try and make contact?" Sarah said.

"We should find Captain Nolan. He runs one of the interior districts. He gave us aid when we were in the city last. They were starting to lock down the place when we left a few weeks ago."

Sarah nodded and tried to ignore the pang of guilt she felt whenever she was reminded of what Aaron had done for her. If only she hadn't allowed the Drake to capture her...

"My Lady, are you not well?" Braden asked.

"I'll be fine. Let's have a look around."

Sarah drew up her cloak, and the cloudy skies began to drizzle. At least they would have a reason to keep their hoods up. She kept her head down, thinking about the last time she had been home. The Elitesmen Council had sent men to capture Aaron in Rexel. It seemed so long ago, and so much had changed since then.

Braden gasped, snatching her attention. Lining the main streets leading into the city were crudely constructed frameworks where men and women hung suspended by glowing shackles. The dead people were being collected and thrown into a large wagon that took them away from the city. The rank smell mixed with that of a cheap perfume almost caused her to gag as the cart passed by them.

Sarah and Braden looked back up at the people still hanging helplessly, secured by the glowing shackles used by Elitesmen.

"Pay them no mind. They're traitors," a gruff voice barked.

Sarah glared at the guard from under her hood.

"You there, you've the look of a warrior. Volunteers for the High King's army report in at the west gate," the guard said, eyeing Braden.

Braden nodded. "Thank you. I'm certainly here to fight, but can you tell me what these people have done to deserve..." Braden said, gesturing up.

If the guard caught on to Braden's double edged comment, he didn't let on. He narrowed his gaze and said, "They were part of some sort of rebellion in the city. Mind you, there is a curfew in effect. If you're out after dark, up you go," the guard grinned.

Braden nodded, and Sarah didn't trust herself to speak, because if she did they would be fighting for their lives.

They entered the city proper and left the smell of rotting corpses behind. She couldn't believe the barbarism she had just seen, no doubt ordered by her father. She had heard someone remark how there were similar setups for suspected Resistance members at all twelve gates into the city. Her hands balled into fists; these were her people. She clutched her sword and glanced at the passing guards. She couldn't understand how Braden, who wasn't known for keeping a cool head, had been able to remain focused throughout the exchange with the guard. One telling look from him was all she needed. He was just as furious as she, but a smart warrior will fight upon a battlefield of his choosing.

There was the appearance of things settling down the farther they ventured into the city, but the people were on edge and hurriedly retreated into their houses.

"Do you recognize that?" Braden asked.

Sarah looked where he pointed, and her eyes widened in shock. Painted upon the side of a building was a curved sword at the cross section of the letter F.

"It's the sigil for the House Faergrace, my mother's family. They were the rulers of Khamearra before she married my father," Sarah said.

Braden frowned. "I've seen it on a few places throughout the city. Why would they be painted on the sides of buildings?"

"I think they are a reminder of a time before the rise of the High King," Sarah said.

"My Lady, this place is poised to collapse into a war. What would they do if they learned of your presence here?"

They continued walking while Sarah mulled over the question. "More people will die, but they are my people. I can't let this go on."

Braden nodded, pressing his lips together. "What do you intend to do?"

A child's face appeared behind the window above a shop and watched them. After a few moments, the child was ushered away by their mother.

"I'm not sure," she said.

They continued on, coming to the district headquarters, and Braden led them inside. The clerk at the front desk looked up as they entered the room, his eyes registering Braden's towering form filling the doorway.

Braden leaned in. "Is Captain Nolan here?"

The clerk frowned and told them to wait over at the benches off to the side. Ten minutes went by, and Sarah was losing her patience. The answers she sought were at the palace and not in some district headquarters.

A black uniformed guard came up and told them to follow him. The guard led them through the building toward the offices in the back. Sarah glanced at Braden. His face was a mask of impassiveness, but his hand strayed to the war hammer on his belt.

The guard brought them just outside a room and knocked on the door. The door opened, and the guard gestured for them to go inside. Sitting behind a desk was an older man, fit and trim, with his blondish hair tied back into a pony tail.

Captain Nolan dismissed the clerk that was in the room and instructed the guard to wait outside. He pressed his finger to his lips as they left and motioned for Braden and Sarah to come closer.

"I hadn't expected to see you so soon, but I'm glad you're here," Captain Nolan said, clasping hands with Braden.

"Neither did I," Braden said.

The captain tried to glance at Sarah's face under her hood. When she removed her hood, the captain's eyes widened and darted to Braden who nodded.

Captain Nolan immediately bowed his head. "Your Grace," he whispered.

"Quietly, Captain," Sarah said.

"We received Nicholas's message, and the Hythariam are preparing a way to get your people out," Braden said.

Captain Nolan sighed deeply. "It's been bad since you were here last. We were able to get some out of the city, but that stopped last week. They've captured and executed two of the leaders of the Resistance, and each day there are less and less of us around."

"What about help from the Elitesmen of the old code?" Sarah asked.

"They help, but their numbers are few. They work mostly in secret," Nolan answered.

"Your family?" Braden asked.

"They are safely away from the city, on an extended holiday with my wife's family in the country," Nolan answered. "I keep waiting for them to check on that story and come barging through that door to take me away when they find that they're not there. My Lady, I'm glad you are safe. Aaron was quite worried about you but wouldn't go into any details. I wish we had his help now."

A sharp pang of guilt seized Sarah's chest. "As do we all. Please believe me when I tell you that if he could be here, he would."

Nolan glanced between them, noting their troubled looks. "Is he okay?"

Sarah felt her bottom lip quiver for a moment before she clamped down on her emotions, focusing herself upon the task at hand. She calmly met the captain's gaze and shook her head, but before he could speak she said, "I need for you to make contact with the other members of the Resistance. We need to pass the word that we're working on a way to get them out of the city as soon as possible. Are you still able to gather in any of the meeting places?"

"Of course, my Lady. I will send word at once. There are still some places that we can meet, but you must understand most will only come if it means leaving the city. I don't have much to offer in way of hospitality, but I do have a place where you can wait."

"I appreciate that, Captain, but I'm not staying. I'm going to the palace," Sarah replied.

Braden pulled a comms device out from his cloak and handed it to Nolan.

"I know you've seen this before, so we'll be in contact," Braden said.

Sarah leveled her eyes at the captain. "Do you intend to leave with the rest of the Resistance?"

Nolan looked back at her for a few moments. "To be honest, I'm not sure, my Lady. The people in my district need protection, what little that I can afford to give, but my family..."

Sarah laid her hand upon his arm. "I understand, Captain."

"Not that way," Nolan said as they went to open the door to leave his office. "There is another way out of the building," he said and rose from his seat.

Nolan opened the only other door in the room that Sarah had assumed was a closet.

"It might be a tight fit for you, Braden, but it will take you out through the back," Nolan said and stepped inside. The side wall opened up to a small passageway.

Braden leaned into the closet and glanced doubtfully at the passageway. The man was huge and his 'muscles had muscles' as Verona would say.

"He'll be fine," Sarah said with a smile. *He did insist on coming.*

Braden groaned and ducked his head, going into the passage first. The passage wasn't all that long, and Sarah could appreciate its uses for a district captain. They emerged outside near the rear of the building, and Sarah drew up her hood. The rain had stopped, but the cadence of dripping water sounded off throughout the area. There wasn't enough rain to wash the filth that was her father's rule out of the city. She was a princess, but without any real power here. True, she had the Resistance, but her father commanded the armies and the Elitesmen. But the Elitesmen were beginning to fracture, and she wondered if that was a weakness she could exploit.

Sarah drew in the energy around them and leaped to the top of the building next to them. She heard Braden grumble from below as he began to climb up. She looked toward the palace, with its many gray towers and walls that separated it from the city proper. Khamearra was old, and each ruling family had added to the palace, contributing to the grandness that it was today. Normally she looked at the walls and towers with a sense of pride, but now they were washed in blood. The people were crying out for the return of the Faergrace. She needed to find a way to protect her people, but with all the looming threats upon the horizon, it seemed more like an impossible task. If not from her father, then it was the threat of the invading army from Hytharia.

Braden crested the top of the building, slightly out of breath, but he didn't complain.

Sarah held out her hand. "I've got an idea," she said, bringing out the travel crystal.

Braden took her hand, and she used the crystal to take them into a private chamber near her rooms in the palace. Sarah led the way, taking the least used pathways through the palace. More than once they had seen Elitesmen walking the grounds. No doubt Aaron's last visit to Khamearra had set the security of the palace to an all-time high. Something tugged along the edge of her senses. They were passing one of the training areas that her brothers had often used. She wasn't sure who was in the room, but they were certainly channeling a lot of the energy. She cracked the door and peeked inside. Rordan was there, shirtless with his body dripping with sweat. Sarah threw open the door the rest of the way and walked inside.

Rordan turned at her entry, his mouth falling open for a moment, and then he chuckled. "You've returned," he said.

Braden closed the door behind them.

Sarah studied her half-brother for a moment. Last she saw him had been at Shandara, when they had tried to capture them. The spoiled innocence of privileged youth was no longer on his face. He looked older and more dangerous.

"Now this won't do for Father's plans at all," Rordan said. "How is the man you've betrayed us for?"

Sarah ignored the question. "How could you let the city come to this state, Rordan? They are killing people in droves. Not even I thought you were this cruel."

Rordan swallowed. "That is not my doing. That was Father's solution to those foolish enough to openly rebel against him. This all started because Aaron was here."

"I know," Sarah said.

"And now he is gone, but you return...*alone*. What a fortuitous turn of events. I'll have Father disband the armies since you're now here safe and sound," Rordan said with a smile that left his face appearing unhinged.

"What do you mean disband the armies because I'm here? Who would believe that?" Sarah asked.

Rordan turned away from her. "Truths created to fill a need, but it's not all you. The actions of the Alenzar'seth here in the city help put this into motion. Have you seen the Citadel?"

"We can't afford to go to war with each other now. There is another threat to this world; you must help me make Father see reason. The killings must stop," Sarah said.

Rordan looked back at her, narrowing his gaze. "He and I spoke, you know. This Aaron Jace. He told me that we didn't have to be enemies. That I could be better than Father." He looked away from her, his eyes growing distant.

Sarah's heart beamed in her chest. Aaron had reached out to his enemies to unite them all toward a common goal. He had done it for her, and it sent her heart both bursting and tearing at the thought.

"He also spoke of a greater threat to this world, as if war with Father was some inconsequential thing," Rordan continued.

"And what will you do?" Sarah asked.

"Do? What could I do? No one can defy Father. At least not for very long. The Alenzar'seth will learn this soon enough," Rordan said.

"How long will you hide in Father's shadow?" she sneered.

"For as long as he is in power, which will be for some time. No kingdom is safe. There are none beyond our reach now," Rordan said.

Sarah studied him for a moment. He looked as if he almost meant the words, but something in his eyes gave her pause.

"You sound as if you believe that, more or less," Sarah said.

"And how long do you intend to skulk about the palace before going to see Father?"

"How long will you go about pretending that you don't live in fear every moment of every day of your life?"

Rordan stepped toward her, his hands clenched, and Sarah had her sword out and at his throat before he could blink an eye. She could have taken his life then and there, but she wouldn't. Rordan simply stood there with her blade resting upon the side of his neck.

"The next time you raise your hands against me, my blade will cut you, brother or not."

Rordan took a step back with his hands slightly raised from his sides. "I'll send Father your regards, Sister."

"No need. I'm heading there now," Sarah said and left the room.

Braden quietly followed. "There is something wrong with him," he said after a few moments.

"I agree, but what do you mean?" Sarah asked.

"Couldn't you sense it? I've been around all manner of men from murderers to those believing themselves to be heroes, but there is definitely something off about your brother."

"Half-brother," Sarah said quickly and cursed her vanity in trying to separate herself from the likes of Rordan.

"Perhaps it's the voices or the whisperings. You know when you tap into the energy and you hear the whispers of the souls from ages past?"

Sarah's brows furrowed in thought. "You do have a point. I just couldn't see it."

"Not surprising, my Lady. Most have a blind spot when they have family in their sights."

"Thank you, Braden."

"For what?"

"For coming with me."

"It's what Aaron would have wanted."

"I know, but still I appreciate it," Sarah said.

Braden's lips lifted in a half smile. "And you're one of us now. We have to look out for one another. Are we really going to see the High King? I'm here to help protect you, but I have no wish to be captured by the Elitesmen."

Sarah looked away, staring at nothing, but her eyes taking in everything. "I have to."

They walked along in silence down the deserted hallway.

"Eric saved my life by throwing me out a window. In a split second, when the Elitesmen had attacked the inn, his first thought was to get me to safety. He rightly assumed that I wouldn't leave his side and would have fought and died there along with him. He took the decision from me, and I can't forgive him for that. Not now at least, and maybe not ever. So I'm not going to stand in your way and keep you from making a last stand against the High King. However, I think you should consider whether your actions honor the sacrifice that brought you here," Braden said.

Honor...Sacrifice...Duty, Sarah whispered in the depths of her mind.

"I have no intentions of throwing my life away or yours for that matter. If I don't do something to help these people then I wouldn't be honoring anyone's sacrifice," Sarah said, looking out of the windows to the grand expanse of Khamearra. "We need to get them out. All of them."

"Who?"

"The Resistance, they need to quit the city if they wish to live," Sarah said.

A door swung open from down the hallway, and an older man with long gray hair that spilled onto his leather duster beckoned to them.

"Elitesman," Braden said, "we thought you were--"

"Dead?" Isaac asked. "Not yet. Come inside."

Sarah had a throwing knife in her hand and quickly sheathed the blade and followed Braden through the door. The dark and dusty room was little more than an attic, filled with mismatched furniture.

"What happened to you?" Braden asked.

The old Elitesman took in the sight of Sarah as if making sure she was real. Sarah met his gaze. This was the Elitesman that had helped rescue Verona and the others when they were captured by the Elitesmen. He was like Beck, the old Elitesman who came to the manor where she grew up and trained her.

Isaac went down to one knee. "Your Grace, I'm glad the Alenzar'seth was successful. He wouldn't say exactly what had happened to you, just that he needed travel crystals."

Sarah's mind snapped into the hazy memories of using the crystals to help reset the Nanites. It was Aaron's last-ditch effort to save her.

"It's time for you and your brethren to come out of the shadows. The Resistance needs you, and so do I," Sarah said.

Isaac returned to his feet. "Beck always spoke highly of you, your Grace. We've been helping the Resistance where we can. Gerric has the Elitesmen everywhere. They are wise to our presence here in the city."

"We need to get the Resistance out of the city, and rescue as many as we can," Sarah said.

Isaac divided his bushy-browed gaze between her and Braden. "Where can they go?"

"Shandara," Sarah answered.

"No one can get to Shandara. The place is in ruins, and if that weren't enough, the Ryakuls would feast upon any who would go there," Isaac said.

"No more. The Ryakuls are gone. The darkness that sickened the land is gone," Sarah said.

"And the Heir of Shandara?"

Sarah unclenched her jaw. "He's...gone."

"He's dead?"

"No," Sarah and Braden said at the same instant.

"Then where is he?" Isaac asked.

"He's trapped in another realm, and we're trying to get him back," Braden said.

"We got word from Nicholas that the Resistance was in trouble, which is why we're here," Sarah said.

Isaac frowned. "I sense that you're not telling me everything, which is fine. Nicholas's message was putting it mildly. The High King and Elitesmen are culling the inhabitants of Khamearra, murdering anyone who has ties or shows any signs of defiance. So much so that the cracks are beginning to show in the foundation of the Order of the Elite."

Sarah's eyes widened at the implication. "Do you think some would break away?"

Isaac nodded slowly. "We were trying to get the younger initiates out, before they could be corrupted any further, but they are as likely to turn you in as want to escape. The older ones… some may, but fear keeps them inline. It's hard to tell who to trust."

"Where are they holding prisoners?" Sarah asked.

"They don't hold prisoners very long. They are either executed or volunteered into the army," Isaac replied.

"Conscripts," Braden said grimly, "usually don't make good soldiers."

Sarah's mind raced, a plan already formulating in her mind. "We can't help the ones in the army, at least not now, but we can help the people in the city. We should focus there."

"I'm open to suggestions, your Grace," Isaac said.

"The Hythariam are in preparations to send aid. We go tonight," Sarah said, looking around. "We need a map."

Braden brought out his comms device. "I have one, my Lady."

Sarah smiled. "I thought you didn't like to use those things?"

"I don't," Braden grunted, "but they are damn useful, and Tanneth has been teaching me and Verona about them. Sarik is already well versed in how they work. What do you wish to see?"

"A layout of the city," Sarah said.

Braden's beefy fingers tapped in the sequence, and after a few grumbles and suppressed curses, a small map lit up the room in a yellowish hue.

Sarah frowned. "This might be useful if Tanneth or Gavril could follow along, which would help coordinate the efforts from their side."

Braden's brow furrowed in thought, and a smile split his square jaw when Tanneth's voice answered the call.

"Okay, Braden and Sarah," Tanneth said, "I've added Gavril and Verona so they can hear us and see the map."

"Braden, I'm impressed you managed not only to call, but put up a map of the city," Verona's voice chimed in.

Braden glared at the comms device. "That shield of yours won't protect you from me, Verona."

"We'll see, my friend. How are things in Khamearra?" Verona asked, his tone taking a more serious note.

"It's bad—public executions and people being rounded up. We need to get them out," Sarah said.

"How many are left?" Gavril asked.

Sarah glanced at Isaac, who answered. "Thousands of them."

The silence dragged on until Sarah spoke up. "Are you still there?"

"Yes, my Lady," Verona answered. "We're trying to come to grips with this. Who is there with you?"

"The old Elitesman, Isaac," Braden said.

"Not as old as all that," Isaac said quickly.

"Where can they go?" Gavril asked.

"The only place available to them. Shandara," Sarah said. "No buts; they are dying, and they have nowhere else to go."

"We can't use the flyers to get out that many. How many could you get out with the travel crystal?" asked Gavril.

"Not nearly enough. The travel crystal can only do maybe ten people at a time if it's fully charged," Sarah replied.

"Okay, let's take this one step at a time. Are you able to get the remaining members to converge upon a few key locations in the city? Preferably some of the gates, which would be the weak points along their perimeter?" Gavril asked.

Sarah glanced at Isaac, who shrugged his shoulders.

"Tanneth, can you add Captain Nolan? He was our contact when we first entered the city and may be better able to advise us as to what the Resistance can or can't do." Sarah said. "But be discrete; we don't know who will be around him, and he's understandably on edge as it is."

After a few moments they heard Nolan's voice whispering into his comms device. They brought him up to speed and posed the question of organizing the Resistance to converge upon key locations in the city.

"Which locations?" Nolan asked.

Sarah glanced at the city map. "I'm thinking the gates along the east and southeast part of the city. They are farthest away from the palace and the Citadel, and it would take the armies camped outside the city the most time to muster any type of support."

"Sir," Tanneth said, "I think it's time we try them out. It's their only shot at getting out of there."

"I know, I just don't like it. They need more field testing," Gavril replied and sighed. "What Tanneth is suggesting is an all-or-nothing plan. If anyone gets left behind, they will be on their own because we will only get this chance once. Then the High King will fortify against such a strategy again."

"Let's hear it then," Sarah said.

"We bring a small force and hold the three gates that you've suggested. We open a portal at the gates that will take the Resistance directly to Shandara," Gavril said.

Sarah frowned. "I sense a 'but' there. What is it?"

"We've been able to create smaller portals that have two uses before they need to be recharged. The thing is we've only tested them with small groups, and the portal was never open for very long. So to move the amount of people you are suggesting, there is a risk that many could be left behind if the portals fail to remain open."

Sarah took in Braden and Isaac's grim expressions. This was too risky. If they failed, they would effectively be handing the remaining members of the Resistance over to the High King.

"A slim chance is better than no chance at all, but I think the decision on whether they will take that chance should be up to the people we're trying to help. How soon could you be ready to come?" asked Sarah.

"About four hours' time," Gavril answered.

"Nolan, is that enough time to spread the word and get the people to the gates?" Sarah asked.

"Four hours? Barely enough time. They will be able to bring only what they can carry. I will spread the word, but there is another thing to consider. The High King, the guards, and the Elitesmen aren't going to sit idly by while thousands of people race toward the city gates," Nolan said.

"You're right. They won't, but I think I can keep the High King's attention for a little while at least," Sarah said. "Gavril, I'm not an army general, but I've listened in on enough of my father's War Councils to know that if you do this, they will treat it as an act of war. That the Free Nations Army struck first."

"We are already at war, my Lady," Verona said. "Armies are assembling throughout the lands. I'd say that the risk is worth it if we can help the remnants of the Resistance get to safety."

"Verona is right," Gavril said. "We made a promise of support to any who would stand with us. They've done more than their share to aid us, and this will be our chance to return the favor. Also, we can add our own bit of distraction that will draw attention away from where we don't want their eyes to see."

They spent the next few minutes outlining the plan. It was rough and quickly thrown together, but they were desperate. If Sarah hadn't seen the flyer-class SPTs for herself, she wouldn't have believed they would make the trip. Tanneth and Sarik would pilot the Hythariam ships and give support from the air. Given that the airships in Khamearra could do little more than provide target practice, she was confident they would be relatively safe. It was the portals that worried her. Too many things could go wrong. There were so many things that could fail to come together, but people were being killed in droves. Sarah believed that the people who made up the heart of the Resistance would jump at the chance to get to safety; she just hoped that they wouldn't be meeting their own demise.

Braden put the comms device away, and Isaac eyed him.

"Are you able to jump great distances?" Isaac asked.

Braden shook his head.

Isaac frowned. "But you can draw in the energy and enhance your strength?"

Braden nodded.

"Well then, you can land at least if you drop in from a high place, like some alcove somewhere. Just something to keep in mind," Isaac said.

"Perhaps," Braden said, his brow furrowed in thought.

Isaac turned to Sarah. "You've been teaching them?"

"I have, but Aaron was the one who was able to show them their connection for the first time," Sarah answered.

Isaac nodded. "Your Grace, I will spread word to those of us that are left of the Old Order of the Elite. Something for you to consider is that there are some, many, that would see the return of the Faergrace rulership as good for Khamearra."

Sarah met the old Elitesman's gaze. "Would they follow a queen?"

"No, not just any queen, but they might follow you," Isaac said, and then he took his leave of them.

After a few moments Braden broke the silence. "I find that Elitesman infuriating, but he might have a point."

Sarah had hoped to bring her father around, but there seemed to be little chance of that happening. Her mind wandered to her mother's family sigil they had found painted throughout the city. Perhaps that was the people's way of reaching out to her. A war of succession was a bloody thing, and that didn't tempt her at all. What drew her in to even consider the thought was to help the people of Khamearra get out from under the power of the Elitesmen and her father.

Sarah and Braden stayed in the attic, laying out some plans and mostly waiting to hear back from Nolan or Nicholas about the status of the Resistance.

They moved unseen through the palace, collecting little bits of information about the readiness of the High King's army, but what troubled Sarah was all the talk of secrecy. Something big was being planned. Something that would change how wars were fought on Safanar, and she needed to find out what that was.

Try as she might, Sarah couldn't get it out of her head that her actions were providing the spark that would take all of Safanar into war. The histories in all the great libraries glossed over these points. The dates and battles were cold and factual, but provided little insight into the worries and fears of the people who fought them. Were they doing the right thing? Beck had often told her that doing what is necessary is never a bad thing. Perhaps Verona was right and they were already at war, and the good people of Safanar were caught in the middle. Would future generations look upon her actions as the catalyst that changed their world, leading it into one of the darkest times of their history? Is that how they would view Aaron?

"My Lady," Braden whispered. "Nolan sent word. Whoever would leave Khamearra will be at the designated gates. They are going to start assembling now in the surrounding buildings and wait for the signal. They will be ready to go at the beginning of the nighttime meal. That is a few hours after Gavril said they could be ready, but I think that will be fine."

Sarah nodded.

"What is it?"

"When I first became involved with the Resistance, we would achieve specific goals. We worked against corrupt district captains or shipments bound for the Citadel. I never knew they were part of the De'anjard, but now it makes sense. Then they banded together in force, to aid Aaron, and now they are fighting for their lives."

Braden nodded in understanding. "They've always been fighting for their lives. A wise man told me that the tyrants of this world will use the blood of innocents to sap the will of any who would oppose them. Fear and brutality are their primary weapons. There is a time to survive and endure, and then there is a time to fight. This is a time to fight, my Lady."

Sarah smiled sadly. "A truly wise leader would have found a way not to fight at all."

Braden shrugged his shoulders. "We didn't make this world."

They rested for a time, both of them silent in their thoughts.

"I think we should be going now," Sarah said.

Braden frowned. "This is my least favorite part of the plan. I can't protect you if you go in alone."

"We've been over this, Braden. They will kill you on sight. I have the travel crystal if I get into trouble, and failing that, you will be there to rescue me," Sarah said.

"This is no joking matter. Verona told me what the Elitesmen did to them when they were captured."

"I know," Sarah said grimly. "They won't harm me, and if it looks like you won't be able to get to me, then get yourself out of the palace the way we discussed earlier."

Braden shook his head. "I'll be able to get to you, my Lady."

"Yes, but just in case."

"I will get to you, my Lady," Braden said, and the determined look in his eyes left little room to argue.

They left the recesses of the palace and headed toward the Great Hall, where her father would be hosting the evening meal. There was no way to know who would be in attendance, but Sarah knew the Elitesmen would be present. She could feel their presence throughout the palace. She left Braden in an alcove with access to a catwalk that the servants would use to polish the chandeliers that hung above the Great Hall. This would give him the best vantage point.

Sarah made her way down to another level, where she used to observe her father's court. It was in this room where she had last seen her brother, Primus, before he stabbed her in the back at Shandara. She remembered slipping into unconsciousness and then Aaron calling out to her from the dark recesses.

Sarah shook off the bittersweet memories and focused on the Great Hall. Her father's hulking presence resided at the head table with Rordan at his side. Rordan didn't touch his food but kept scanning the room. She wondered whether Rordan had told their father of their little meeting, but in the end she decided it didn't matter.

The noise in the Great Hall grew as the evening meal started in earnest. Sarah said a silent prayer to the Goddess Ferasdiam to guide her way and to watch over her people. She closed her eyes and made a small circle with her thumb upon her forehead. Her hand drifted down to Aaron's medallion that lay nestled against her chest beneath her shirt. Gritting her teeth, she left the room.

Sarah came to the servant's staircase where two guards waited, eyeing her approach. She pulled back her hood, revealing her golden braid. The guards gasped in surprise, and Sarah drew herself up with all the dignity of a princess of Khamearra.

"I will see my father now," Sarah said. One of her hands hidden in the folds of her cloak grasped the hilt of a throwing knife, ready to use it if necessary, but the guards nodded and brought their fists across their heart, bowing their heads in unison.

She moved past the guards and then heard the heavy footsteps as one ran off. She emerged midway into the Great Hall to a sea of nobles and decorated officers of the Khamearrian army. Her hard gaze slid past her nose as she took in the scene before her. Here these people ate and drank their fill, while the dead piled up at the gates. Her hand clutched the hilt to her sword while servants and nobleman alike scurried out of her way.

Some guards with the silver Dragon emblem gleaming upon their pristine black uniforms moved to intercept her. One of the guards held up his hand to block her path. Sarah drew in the energy, enhancing her strength. She reached out and bent the outstretched hand back on itself, and the guard cried out in pain.

"Get out of my way," Sarah said, keeping her eyes upon the other guardsmen.

She proceeded past them without a backward glance. If they were fool enough to get in her way again, she would draw her sword. Sarah's gaze was fixed at the head of the Great Hall, drawing her father's eyes to her. She strode forward, and the High King narrowed his gaze.

"My daughter has returned to us!" the High King's voice boomed across the Great Hall, silencing its occupants.

Sarah came before the head table and glanced at Rordan, who coolly met her gaze. To the side she could sense Elitesmen closing in around her.

"I have returned, Father," Sarah said.

"What a joyous event this is to have you here now, but I'm a bit out of sorts. Where have you been?"

"Why are you having so many of our people executed, Father?"

Sarah's question echoed through the Great Hall, and her father's playful gaze withered.

"I didn't realize I was answerable to you, my daughter. Regardless, these citizens are a sickness that has plagued our beautiful city. I'm afraid that there is only one way to root out such a vile infection."

"Entire families! Why not let them leave?"

"The infection runs deep. Examples must be made, that any who align with the Resistance are to be punished by death," the High King answered coldly.

"You go too far," Sarah shouted. "I stand with the Resistance; will you have me executed?"

Gasps erupted throughout the Great Hall.

The High King leaned forward. "And your Alenzar'seth suitor. Do you now stand with him?"

The Elitesmen inched closer to her. "Come at me if you will, Elitesmen; I never grow tired of dispatching any of you."

The High King's pained expression almost seemed genuine, but she knew better.

"I see you've been infected by the Alenzar'seth. He will be brought to justice, like all the other kingdoms that would foolishly clamor to Shandara's banner."

"He will never bow to you," Sarah hissed. "And neither will I."

The room darkened as the High King stretched out his hand toward her. The medallion became as ice against her skin. Sarah shut her eyes, wincing against the sudden cold. For a second she saw a dark figure chained to a column. The vision appeared as if she were looking through a window with water streaming down, giving occasional glimpses of golden clarity.

Aaron! She saw him.

"She is shielded. Take her!" the High King shouted.

Sarah shook off the vision and leaped to the side, circling around one of the Elitesmen who tried to grab her. She sprang to the top of the nearest table, whose occupants scrambled out of the way. Two Elitesmen chased her, and she kicked out, knocking them off the table.

Sarah jumped to the next table over, bringing her closer to her father, and saw guardsmen pouring into the Great Hall. An Elitesman leaped to the table in front of her, landing hard, sending plates of food crashing to the floor. He drew his sword with practiced efficiency of one at home with a blade in his hands.

Sarah took a step back, drawing her own blade, its single curved edge catching the light around them. The Elitesmen charged, and their blades clanged out. She dashed forward, inside his attack, and pulled him off balance. Sarah spun, deflecting another attack and kicked the Elitesman in the back, sending him face-first off the table. She drew in the energy and jumped to the far side of the Great Hall. She glanced at her father and could have sworn a prideful smile tugged at his lips.

The Elitesmen blurred toward her, passing the guardsmen as if they were standing still. She reached inside her cloak and grasped the travel crystal, but an attack orb glanced off her sword and knocked her off the table and onto her back.

The loud war cry of the De'anjard sounded from above as Braden landed atop of the guardsmen, sending them sprawling. Braden unfurled his Shandarian shield and lashed out with his war hammer. Attack orbs from the Elitesmen blazed into the shield and ricocheted away into the fleeing nobles. Braden let out another war cry and slammed his hammer on his shield. He planted his foot behind him, bracing himself, his face a mask of grim concentration.

Sarah felt the pressure of the sonic waves as they barreled off Braden's shield. Braden focused the blast, sending guardsmen and Elitesmen alike flying through the air. The pressure built up in her ears, blurring her vision. Sarah grabbed the travel crystal and at the same time grabbed Braden's outstretched arm. They were pulled into a purple abyss, bringing them safely away from the palace.

Sarah and Braden gasped, catching their breath. She took them to the first place she could think of, which was near one of the designated gates that the Resistance would use to escape.

"What happened to you back there?" Braden asked.

She got up off the ground. "I had a vision of Aaron."

"Where?"

"I don't know. It was so dark. He was chained to a stone column," said Sarah.

"How were you able to see him? Can you do it again?"

"I...I don't know. They tried to capture me, and the medallion became as ice on my chest."

"What medallion?"

"Aaron's," she said, taking it out for Braden to see.

He studied it for a moment, then they both looked up as two golden Hythariam flyers streaked across the sky. Alarm bells began to ring throughout the city. People were filling the streets, and she heard the guards manning the gates behind them call for archers. Sarah grabbed Braden's arm and used the travel crystal to bring them to the streets below.

She marched up to the guard commander of the gate. "These people are leaving the city."

The commander's eyes widened. "Your Grace, I have orders not to allow anyone to leave."

"I'm giving you a command; you and your men are to quit the gate," Sarah said.

The commander's eyes darted to the approaching crowd and back at Sarah.

Sarah leaned in with a whispered threat. "You can't stop a mob. Save your men."

"Archers, ready bows!" the commander cried.

The guardsmen at the top of the gate towers drew their bows and nocked their arrows.

"Your Grace, if they come to the gate, I will order my men to fire," the commander said.

Sarah drew her sword and in a flash had the end of her blade at the commander's throat. "Call them off," she hissed.

"Stand down," Braden bellowed.

The guardsmen at the tower aimed their arrows down at them.

"I don't want to kill you, Commander, but if you give that order, you will be the first to die," Sarah said.

"With all due respect, your Grace, if I don't give the order, the king will see to it that I die anyway," the commander replied.

Sarah lowered her sword. "You shouldn't have to serve under such conditions. I cannot sit by while my father murders the good citizens of Khamearra. Would you join a cause worthy of laying down your life for?"

The commander met Sarah's eyes, and something gave way inside. He held up his hand, and the archers stood down.

"They will have us executed for this," the commander said and glanced up at the people tied to the poles beyond the gate. "Cut them down," he ordered his men.

Some of the guards looked as if they would protest the commander's orders, but decided against it.

"Thank you, Commander," Sarah said.

"Your Grace, if you're taking these people away would you consider taking a few guardsmen along?" the commander asked.

Sarah studied the commander for a moment and nodded.

Hythariam soldiers, riding upon gliders, swooped over the walls wearing dark armor. The leader removed his helmet, revealing Gavril's face.

Gavril glanced up at the guards and looked at Sarah questioningly. "I'm glad things are so calm here. There was some fighting at the other gates."

"We don't have long," Sarah said.

Gavril nodded and gestured to his soldiers who immediately put the equipment they were carrying on the ground. They opened a tripod of legs and rested a large cylinder atop. The cylinder began to glow, and a beam of light spread out from it, forming a large oval that bent the very fabric of the world around it. A great hum pulsated from the portal as it stabilized into a glittering doorway of light.

A Hythariam soldier tossed a small metallic ball into the air, which zoomed through the portal. The Hythariam soldier studied the readout upon his comms device and nodded toward Gavril.

Gavril waved over toward the crowd, urging them through the portal. At first they approached warily.

"It's all right; you will find safety on the other side," Sarah said. "Please, you must hurry."

Flashes of light erupted around them, and two Elitesmen appeared. Sarah dashed forward, lashing out with her sword. The Elitesmen met her attacks, but she pressed on, hoping to distract them. One Elitesman disappeared in a flash of light. Sarah pressed her attack, keeping the Elitesman on the defensive. She felt the energy flow through her, guiding her blade as she unraveled the Elitesman's defenses. In moments, the Elitesman collapsed to the ground after her blade stabbed him in the heart.

The crowd pushed forward as more and more people disappeared through the portal to Shandara. Sarah jumped to the top of the nearest building, catching a glimpse of the Hythariam flyers as they laid waste to the airships on the far side of the city. A figure leaped up next to her, and Sarah turned, seeing Verona.

"Apologies, my Lady, but I couldn't stay away," Verona said and waved to Braden down below.

Braden nodded up to them and continued to wave people through the portal.

"The Elitesmen will be back anytime now," Sarah said.

Verona nodded grimly, his face darkening at the thought. "The others are all through. This is the last portal."

The gate beneath them came crashing down, trapping the fleeing people on the other side. Sarah and Verona leaped to the ground. The trapped people began to panic. Braden muscled his way through, shouting for them to stand clear, and grasped the gate.

"You can't lift it. We need to hook up a team of horses to get it up," Verona said.

Braden ignored them, the corded muscles in his back straining. He roared with colossal effort, and the heavy gate slowly lifted off the ground. Sarah and Verona quickly pushed a nearby wagon under the gate, and Braden eased the gate down.

As the last of the Resistance raced through the portal, the Hythariam soldiers converged around them. Bright flashes of light lit up the street, and Elitesmen had them surrounded. Attack orbs were flung in their direction. The Hythariam soldiers fired their plasma pistols, catching the Elitesmen off guard. Gavril waved them through the portal, and they retreated from the bloody streets of Khamearra.

They emerged into the quiet twilight sky above Shandara with the great white walls before them. The heart of the Resistance that was the De'anjard rejoiced to return to their homeland after being away for so long.

Sarah looked around her at all the people they had gotten to safety, and her heart ached for all those they had left behind. Verona and Braden stood next to her.

"And this is only the beginning," Verona said.

Sarah walked among her people, and many bowed in her direction. Verona was right, this was only the beginning, and it left her wondering what the price of this war would cost them in the end. Would they look back and deem the price worthy of the cost, or would they dread the silence of thousands of dead souls as their only answer?

9

A DEMONSTRATION

"Dek, I tell you they are out there just beyond the tree line. The whole town is in danger," Resel said.

"Ryakuls, you say?" Dek asked.

"That's what I'm trying to tell you. I was a few miles out, checking my traps, and I heard them out there," Resel said, clenching his dirty hands. "You're on the town council, shouldn't you raise the alarm or something? Send out a search party?"

They were less than a mile outside of town when Dek had been told that Resel was screaming like a madman running from the forest. His eyes narrowed at the otherwise normal tree line. The air was crisp, and the skies were clear. Nothing out of the ordinary for their remote northern town.

"You should send word to Rexel and this Free Nations Army they have there. They could come up here and slay the beasts," Resel said, pacing.

Dek frowned. "It's two days hard riding to Rexel. Plus, they would need time to send someone up here. If the beasts are even out there."

"Oh, they're out there. I heard them," Resel said.

"You heard something, I'll grant you that. But did you see them?"

"I didn't stick around. As soon as I heard those deep growls, loud enough to rattle my teeth, I hightailed it out of there."

"It could have been a bear."

"It wasn't a bear, I tell you. The trees all started swaying violently, though there was no wind. Bears don't do that. I tell you there are Ryakul up near the peak, just like the reports warned there would be."

Dek frowned. Ever since news came in from the other towns that Ryakuls had been attacking some outlying farms, he was getting scared trappers like Resel coming to him with an alleged Ryakul encounter every other day. "All right, calm down, Resel. We'll head back into town, get a few of the hunters together, and go out and see what's got you so spooked," Dek said, putting his hand on Resel's shoulder. He didn't need the old trapper starting a panic.

"Gentleman, pardon me, but did you just say there are Ryakuls around here?"

Dek and Resel turned around, and behind them were two men in black cloaks. The one who spoke was the shorter of the two. He had greasy dark hair and eyes that seemingly took in everything around them.

"We mean you no harm," the taller man said.

Even beneath the cloak, Dek could tell he had the bearing of a warrior. How had they gotten so close to them?

"Yes," Resel said. "Just north of here, about five miles away."

The two regarded each other for a moment and started to head north without another word.

"I'm not sure if there are any Ryakuls up there, but it may not be safe for you," Dek called to them.

"Safer for me and my companion than most. Thank you for the information," the shorter one said, and they continued on.

Dek wasn't sure why, but he felt a cold shiver run down his spine. He motioned for Resel to follow, and together they headed back to town. Both men set a brisk pace, eager to be back among people and away from mysterious strangers who appeared out of nowhere and went looking for Ryakuls.

"Maybe luck will be with us here," Darven said.

"It certainly wasn't with us before. Not that I believe in luck," Mactar replied. They had been hunting for Ryakuls, but without the Drake to control them, the beasts had scattered. Remote towns like these were often reporting Ryakuls seen in the area.

"Just in case there are actually Ryakuls here, let's go over it again so we don't have a repeat like the last time," Darven said.

Mactar resisted the urge to glare at the former Elitesman, who seemed to adopt a particular fondness of pointing out their recent failure. They had a chance encounter with a Ryakul a few nights ago, and when Mactar had tried one of the calls that the Drake had used, the Ryakul launched into the air and flew away. At least it hadn't attacked. Dead Ryakuls were no use to him.

"That wasn't my fault. The bracer failed. Regardless, it's fixed now," Mactar said.

"I hope so. It wasn't you who was out there as bait the last time," Darven said dryly.

Mactar chuckled. "You're not losing a step or two in your old age, are you, Darven?"

"Not in the slightest," Darven replied softly.

Darven had always been gifted, even for an Elitesman, but his ambitions ran beyond those of the Elite Order. Without another word, they both drew in the energy and sped ahead. Anyone watching would have seen them disappear, which wasn't accurate at all. They were still there, but moving at speeds beyond the capabilities of normal eyes to track. It was an advantage that the Elitesmen had perfected, and the knowledge had been given to them by Mactar himself.

Miles went by in mere minutes, and they came to a halt. Mactar extended his senses out away from them and could detect two hidden Ryakuls. He pressed the button on his bracer, and it came to life in a soft glow. Mactar strode into the clearing, and after a few moments Darven followed.

Mactar recalled the memory of the call the Drake had used to control the Ryakuls. He crossed the clearing and could hear the loud snorts of the beasts as they lay in wait. Crossing into the tree line the sunlight above all but vanished, sending them into perpetual twilight. Directly in their path was a Ryakul; its bat-like wings were folded in on themselves, and a low growl came from its saber-tusked maw. Foamy white liquid pooled below the beast's mouth, and its eyes bored into him hungrily.

Mactar locked his eyes on the beast, all the while wondering where the other one was. A piercing scream came from above, and Mactar felt a hand roughly pull him back into the clearing. Sounds of snapping tree limbs filled the air as the Ryakul on the ground followed. A dark shadow crossed the ground, and Mactar saw the second Ryakul swooping down at them.

Got you.

Mactar used the energy, sending out the strumming sound in a freakish rhythm, and the effect on the Ryakul was almost instantaneous. The Ryakul on the ground, the one that had been closing in on them, stopped in its tracks and kept shaking his head. He was so surprised that he almost lost his hold upon the energy. The Ryakul reared back, roaring, and lunged forward, snapping its jaws at him.

Mactar held out his hand and blared the Drake's call. The Ryakul stopped less than a foot away. The beast's wretched hot breath washed over him. The Ryakul closed its mouth and regarded Mactar warily. He sensed the life energy around the Ryakul, but its inner emotions were closed off to him.

"You're mine," Mactar said, and though the beast couldn't understand his words, it understood the meaning behind them.

The second Ryakul landed near them, its massive head sitting atop an elongated neck coiled up like a viper about to strike. Using the Drake's call, Mactar brought his will to bear, and the Ryakul's head lowered in submission. The wild eyes of a predator glared back at him in a mask of pure hatred. Mactar reached out and ran his fingers along the pebbled skin of its neck. He could see the shafts of energy imbued around each of the beasts, being both vibrant and dark. Without controlling them, the Ryakuls were almost mindless, moving on instinct alone.

"I can feel them," Darven said. His own bracer glowed, and the Ryakul allowed him to approach. "How do we tell them what to do?"

Mactar moved away and motioned for Darven to follow. He scanned the clearing for a suitable target. A gnarled old tree with a massive trunk caught his eye. In his mind he pictured the Ryakuls shredding the old tree with their massive claws. As soon as the thought formed in his mind, the Ryakuls snapped their heads in the direction of the tree, but they didn't move. They were waiting for something. Mactar sounded the Drake's call, and the Ryakuls bounded off, decimating the old tree. After the tree was destroyed, the Ryakuls turned on each other, taking grand swipes with their talons and spiked tail. Mactar pressed the button on the bracer, which sent out a barely audible sound, but it snatched the Ryakuls' attention instantly.

"That's interesting," Darven said. "They attacked each other. We'll have to keep that in mind or this could get out of control really quick."

"They seem to react to my thoughts, but I can't gain any insight into theirs. It's as if the beasts are giant living shells. Not fully alive, but not fully dead either. But you're right, we need to practice," Mactar said, then he glanced to the south.

"The town?" Darven asked.

"I could think of worse targets, but we only have two Ryakuls at the moment. Come on; I've got an idea."

Dek called for the hunters to gather in the town square so that Resel could relay what he had heard in the forest. The old fool was sincere if nothing else. He was surprised to see how the hunters listened to the old trapper, confirming some whispered fear lying along the edges of their thoughts. Their grim expressions spoke volumes, and some watched the sky warily.

"We'll need to assemble more men and sweep out to the north," a hunter named Carl said.

"How many men?" Dek asked.

"I'd say at least a twenty. Tell them all to bring their bows," Carl answered.

"Are you sure we're not overreacting? What if we don't find anything?"

"Then we'll be safer for it," Carl said.

"Fine," Dek said. The townsfolk had gathered in the square, waiting for them to convene. Dek stepped away from the others and addressed the crowd. "Then it's decided. We need twenty volunteers to head north of the town to investigate whether there are any Ryakuls in the area."

Hands slowly rose, and before long, they had their twenty volunteers. Dek was about to speak when two brief flashes of light shone along the tree line beyond the village. It happened so quickly that he almost questioned whether he saw anything at all. A loud screech made them all jump, and a blurry, dark form swooped out of the sky. The tips of the wings slashed through the people in the square, washing the paving stones in red.

Dek stood frozen as the dark beast spun about with its spiked tail demolishing the buildings, sending splinters of wood into the scattering people. Some people fell in a mad dash to get away. Hunters fired their bows in a futile attempt to slay the Ryakuls, but their arrows bounced harmlessly off their armored hides.

A second Ryakul landed, tearing at both buildings and people alike. In moments, the town was in ruins, and all Dek could do was watch, unable to move. The Ryakuls caught sight of him and bounded forth. The last thing Dek saw was the cavernous black maw ringed with bloody teeth the size of swords rushing toward him.

"There, you see? An effective test," Mactar said, looking down at the ruins of the town. "Now think of what ten Ryakuls could do to a castle, or fifty to an army on the field."

Darven nodded. "They are impressive. There is no doubt about that. Once we assemble the numbers you have mind, what's our next move?"

The Ryakuls had moved to the outskirts of the town, chasing down anyone who couldn't find cover. As the Ryakuls moved farther away, Mactar heard a few survivors that must have huddled in the basements of the buildings. A few mangled bodies littered the streets with some twitching in their final death throes.

"We'll rejoin the High King's army and prove why we're more effective than any army mustered by man. Even those with Elitesmen among their ranks," Mactar answered.

"You mean to challenge Amorak?"

Mactar chuckled. "Goodness, no, then who would I put in his place? Rordan is too young, and I have no wish to rule in his place. Do *you* want to be king?"

"No, like you, I'm interested in the real power behind the throne and not the illusion of sitting on it," Darven said.

"Hence I keep you around. Now we need to find more Ryakuls," Mactar said.

Darven called to the Ryakuls, and they immediately took flight, heading in a northeasterly direction.

Mactar's eyes narrowed. "Where did you send them?"

"To seek out their own kind. We can follow along and bring them under our power," Darven replied.

"Our power?"

Darven bared his teeth in a wolfish smile. "You need me, and we cannot both search for more Ryakuls and attack the enemies of the High King at the same time. So yes, *our* power."

"Very well," Mactar said, allowing Darven his own illusion.

Rordan stood in the Great Hall of the High King's palace. He would be joining his father in the encampment on the outskirts of the city. Since his sister's appearance, measures had been taken to fortify all the city gates. Reports had steadily come in from three of the gates where an open portal was used by thousands of people fleeing through them. The strangest of these reports were those of black-armored men flying through the air with some type of machines on their feet. Normally such reports would have been dismissed outright, but these came from Elitesmen who had witnessed the events with their own eyes. The Elitesmen, while many things, had never been keen to exaggerate, especially about such a large breach in their defenses. Thousands of people fled the city, people who were no doubt aligned with the Resistance. But the symbol for the Faergraces still showed up. His father's mood had settled into that of a cold fury, and the king had added that those who escaped his grasp would only escape for so long before they were punished.

Rordan activated the travel crystal and emerged on the field outside the High King's tent.

"We will find them. I think we can guess where they went," the High King said.

Rordan stepped inside. They were still talking about the attack last week. The attack that suspiciously occurred when Sarah had paid them a visit.

"What concerns me are these portals," General Khoiron said, his craggy face frowning deeply. "Your Grace, if the enemy has the means to use these portals, then I think we need to move up our timetable."

"In this we are agreed, my old friend. Our reports say they used some type of machine to create the portals. We will circulate the description of it and have it be a target in future engagements," the High King said.

Rordan made his way through the crowded tent. "Mactar sends word that he has been successful, but he needs more time to gather more of them to make a difference in battle."

"Excellent news."

"What has he been successful in doing?" Khoiron asked.

"This, I'm afraid, I will not be sharing with the War Council. Not just yet," the High King said. "Elite Grand Master Gerric, the time for testing with the crystal is over. The attack will be at dawn."

"As you wish, your Grace. What are the targets?"

"These four kingdoms, bordering our lands," said the High King, drawing their attention to the map. "They won't know what hit them. There will be four more kingdoms the day after. Each group will take a contingent of Elitesmen. I expect the cities to fall by the end of the day. Inform the men that they will get their share of the plunder from these cities. That should rally them."

Rordan's heart pounded with excitement. War on this scale had never been possible before. He would be going with Khoiron tomorrow and was eager to test his mettle in battle. A small voice lingered in the back of his mind about the threat to them that Sarah had spoken about, but he banished it as soon as it came. Stepping out of the command tent and seeing the thousands of men assembled that were all part of the High King's army made him more than confident. Knowing full well that there were eight more encampments with as many men in them gave the High King the most powerful army Safanar had ever seen. Safanar would be reforged and would someday be his to rule. Despite himself, his mind drifted to the Heir of Shandara.

He will never bow to you, Sarah had said in the Great Hall, and she had meant it. Even knowing what their father was capable of, she sided with the Alenzar'seth. Sometimes in the quiet moments he thought of his own encounter with him. Could they ever be anything other than enemies?

Rordan followed his father and the other members of the War Council. Anyone who stood against them was an enemy. The sooner the kingdoms learned that lesson, the better they would be. Even if this threat that his sister believed to be lurking over them proved true, it could never stand against the might of the Khamearrian army.

10

LEFT BEHIND

"We've lost it, sir," the Hythariam's gaze bored into his screen, and his fingers danced across the controls with practiced precision. "I'm sorry, one moment it was there, and next it was gone."

Gavril shared a glance with Iranus. "Acknowledged," Gavril said. "Flight team, do you have a visual on the target?"

Eight of their flyers were in the upper atmosphere, waiting to intercept the vessel sent from Hytharia. Iranus still gave himself a mental kick for missing the danger brought to their attention by Aaron. He brushed away the mournful feelings for the young man and focused himself on the screen in front of him. The moments dripped by as they waited in the command center at Hathenwood. The Hythariam and the few Safanarions in the room held a collective breath.

"Negative, we don't have a visual. Permission to sweep the area of the ship's last known trajectory," Tanneth said.

Iranus didn't have high hopes that the search would be successful, but they couldn't afford not to search.

"Granted," Gavril said. "It was a long shot at best. Our satellites aren't military grade."

"I want all the satellites tracking the continent. We can rely on our own search algorithms to alert on anything of Hythariam design," Iranus ordered.

The techs at the consoles began tapping away, carrying out his orders.

Vaughn, one of the few native Safanarions in the room, came quietly to his side. "Do you think they will find anything?"

"The ship must be equipped with military-grade technology, which means it can evade our means to track it. Tanneth will lead the search, and we'll have to wait and find out," Iranus answered.

Gavril came over. The old soldier still had his sleek, black armor on that molded itself to the wearer, almost like a second skin, and was very light in weight. The Hythariam who remembered what life had been like during their last dreadful days on Hytharia all had a deeper set to their jaws and a quieter manner than the others. They hardened themselves for the battles yet to come.

THE HYTHARIAM VESSEL HAD TRAVERSED THE VASTNESS OF SPACE, AND THE onboard ship's artificial intelligence engaged the protocols for the last leg of its journey. The dataset it had for the planet was eighty years old, but the intelligence it yielded was acceptable. Its target was located in a remote central-northern area of the land mass below that had little inhabitants. The AI detected passive scanners and engaged stealth protocols to evade detection. The ship's designers had equipped the vessel with state-of-the-art cloaking technology, so that even if one were standing just outside it, they wouldn't be able to see the ship. The precious cargo entrusted to the AI would be delivered, and the prime directive assigned to it more than thirty years before would be fulfilled.

The ship breached the atmosphere over the planet's vast oceans, away from the marks detected by it sensors. The cloaked ship zoomed across the sky in a staggered approach with its mass displacing the clouds in its wake, but nothing else marked its passing. High above the land the ship flew, rapidly approaching its target. The ship came to a halt and hovered in the air, running a threat assessment of the valley it had chosen for its primary target. The criteria set for the AI was met, and it was green for the final stages of its long journey. In seconds, the onboard computers mapped every inch of the valley below. The ship began its descent using its lasers to cut away a landing area with enough room to carry out its tasks. The countdown timer was engaged. The next actions were essential if it were to achieve its prime directive. Two smaller craft detached themselves from the hull and raced ahead, each two hundred feet in length. They slammed into the ground, anchoring themselves in place. Panels opened up, and the batteries of the trans-dimensional Keystone Accelerators ignited to life, charging up as they waited for the final calculations from the ship.

The main spacecraft landed with the ground giving way to the reinforced landing gear. A small army of machines exited to perform their assigned tasks, reading the area for the host that would come through the portal. The subroutine finished, and the AI ran another check against the star maps of Hytharia's last known position. The AI calculated Hytharia's current position, taking into account the singularity that had been steadily feeding away at the system of planets for which it had been apart. While the data was being fed to the Keystone Accelerator pylons, the AI engaged the passive drones and sent them out, and another subroutine was dedicated to track the positions of all the satellites surrounding the planet.

The small panels opened upon the roof of the ship, and cyber defense drones zoomed into the air, rapidly accelerating away.

Data transfer complete...

The AI waited for the timer to reach zero, giving the drones enough time to take their positions.

The pylons ignited with bolts of energy running the length of each shaft before reaching across to join the other pylon. The energy aligned into a matrix that spread between the pylons, and a portal sheared to life, opening a doorway to a dying world.

ALARMS BLARED TO LIFE THROUGHOUT THE COMMAND CENTER DEEP IN the heart of Hathenwood.

"Sit rep," Gavril said, standing at the central pavilion.

"Energy spikes being reported, sir," the tech said frowning at his screen.

Gavril punched in the command to bring it on the main screen for all to see, but it was completely washed out.

"That can't be right. Run a diagnostic," Iranus said, coming to Gavril's side.

The seconds dripped past while the techs clattered away at their work. "The system is clean, sir; the report is accurate. The energy spikes are everywhere according to our sensors."

Gavril felt as if the floor was suddenly pulled away from his feet. "They've blinded us. The Zekara are coming," he said, giving word to Halcylon's military faction.

"Are you sure?" Vaughn asked.

Gavril's grim face didn't move from the main screen. "I'm sure. This is an act of war. They blinded us to their doings by flooding our systems with false energy spikes reporting from all over the continent. They knew we would be looking for them. Halcylon wasn't taking any chances. With the failure of the Drake, that ship was their last effort and must have an AI with a full-complement cyber warfare suite."

The occupants of the room remained still in a stunned silence.

Gavril turned to Iranus. "We have to find the command center in Shandara; that's where this war was meant to be fought."

"I know," Iranus said, "but we need Aaron to bring the defense online there."

"What do you mean?" Vaughn asked, dividing his gaze between the two of them.

"Hathenwood has been our home since the fall of Shandara, but it wasn't meant to be. Shandara was to be our safe haven in the event of invasion. We poured all our resources there. However, access to the system is genetically encoded to only be brought online by a member of the Alenzar'seth," Gavril said.

"Aaron," Vaughn whispered.

"Yes, Aaron," Iranus said. "Since his return we've been searching for it. Daverim wouldn't safeguard his city to anyone other than his line."

"Surely Reymius would have done things differently," Vaughn said.

"Yes, he would have, but the fall happened so fast. The High King caught everyone by surprise. We couldn't put contingencies in place should all of the Alenzar'seth perish. Plus, Shandara was cut off from everyone by the Drake and the Ryakuls there," said Iranus.

"In addition to the weapons caches, we've been trying to dig our way to the command center amid the ruins," Gavril said.

Vaughn frowned. "Wouldn't it have been destroyed with the city along with any of the defenses you had in place?"

Gavril shook his head. "No, the system never came online, and many of the city's defenses were protected underground. We've been clearing the ruins away, but they can only be brought online by the command center in Shandara."

"What if…" Vaughn began and stopped, "…what if Aaron is dead?"

"Then we'll make every effort to bypass our own security measures in place to bring the system online, but first we need to get access to it. It's buried in a part of the city that is almost completely destroyed," Gavril said and frowned at the main screen. "After all these years we still got caught by surprise."

"We couldn't have known," Iranus answered.

"*I* should have known," Gavril said, then he addressed the room. "Stop tracking energy spikes, it's useless. We need to focus our efforts and narrow potential targets for us to investigate. Let's make a grid and check these areas. The ship will likely choose a place remote from any city."

"How do you know that?" Vaughn asked.

"It's what I would do," Gavril answered.

"They wouldn't have come here?"

Gavril shook his head. "The ship could land anywhere. Halcylon will not charge out and blindly attack. He will evaluate and prepare before he makes his move. He will try to remain hidden while he grows in strength."

"You sound as if you know him," Vaughn said.

"I did know him. I served under him in the military. I'm not sure whether he is alive, but these events with the ship are reminiscent of the tactics used by the general. He was nothing if not effective."

"You almost sound as if you admire him."

"He's crazy. Brilliant, but the good man he may have been is gone. I aim to stop him and take him out if I can," Gavril said.

They resumed their work, and Gavril set himself to the task of facing the embodiment of an old nightmare that hadn't plagued his dreams for eighty years and prayed he was up to the task. He was most senior of the Hythariam military that came to Shandara and knew that if he failed, they all would perish.

THE GROUND RUMBLED, AND PIECES OF THE HOLLOWED OUT MOUNTAIN came crashing down. Aaron stirred awake. He didn't know how long he had been unconscious. Across the stadium an entire section had been pulled away, and a gleaming portal lit up the last bastion that housed the Hythariam, while their planet slowly died.

He was a huddled mass upon the ground with a column digging into his back. Only his eyes moved; the rest of his body felt off, as if his parts were in the wrong place. The Hythariam were flocking to the portal, and Aaron's pulse raced, trying to catch a glimpse of Safanar. Flashes of light washed through the hollowed out mountain as the Hythariam poured through. A long line of equipment trekked across the way and disappeared in a flash, journeying to the place he longed to return. Aaron tried to move his arms, but they wouldn't respond. He forced his lungs to expand, taking in as much of the thin air as he could. He focused his mind, looking inward, trying to make sense of the wrongness he felt to his core. Nothing worked. Part of his mind scattered at the thought before focusing upon the portal. He remembered gaining consciousness in a blurred dream, and when he wouldn't eat, the Hythariam forced the food down his throat. The beast called Thraw he hadn't seen again, and Aaron wondered if he had imagined it all. His eyes shut as if great weights forced them. When he opened them again, the long line of Hythariam heading toward the portal was gone.

"Beautiful is it not, human?" Halcylon asked. "No, don't get up. I doubt you could even if you wanted to."

Aaron lifted his head, which took every ounce of will he had. "Home," he whispered.

Halcylon squatted down, his cold eyes peering at him. "You really are a mess, but *this* is your home now, *human*. You've been sentenced to the same fate that your kind would have visited upon my people. Hytharia has scant time left, and you will be the only one to witness her passing. Initially, I thought to just kill you outright, but I find that this is a fitting end for you."

Halcylon rose to his feet and had to balance himself as the ground shook violently. More of the mountain caved in on itself, and the night sky was exposed on the far side of the cavern. The air began to rush away.

"My time here is up. But know that your beloved Safanar will be in good hands." Halcylon began to walk away, but then turned around. "So much for the strength of men."

Halcylon and his soldiers disappeared through the portal, and after a few moments it vanished, plunging everything into darkness.

Aaron's heart sank as he lifted up his hand in a vain attempt to keep the portal open by sheer will alone, but he had nothing left to give. The air was thinning, and the ground shuddered underneath him. Giant fissures tore the ground open, forming deep chasms.

This is it. I'm going to die. The thought was strangely comforting, but for the deep rumbling of the Eldarin from the recesses of his mind. Aaron tried to focus so he could draw the energy into himself, but failed.

As rocky pieces of the mountain continued to fall, something glittered in front of him that wasn't there before. It took a few moments for the glittering object to register in Aaron's failing mind. He glanced up, and standing before him was a dark figure with green eyes. Hints of the creature's pointed teeth lay inside its mouth, but its body remained blended to its surroundings.

"Thraw," Aaron whispered.

"This is the device you need, human; get us out of here," Thraw said.

Aaron looked at Thraw's form for the first time. The creature had the brown complexion of the Hythariam and a shaggy black mane. Each foot ended in a metallic claw protruding from hairless skin. The green eyes were reminiscent of the Hythariam, both in size and shape, and most importantly intelligence.

"You're part Hythariam," Aaron said and felt his body jerk against the column.

Thraw picked up the small Keystone Accelerator at its feet and shoved it in into Aaron's lap. With a swipe of its claws, the chains fell away from Aaron's arms.

"There is no time, human. You must use the device, or we'll both die," Thraw said.

Aaron's hands clumsily snatched at the Keystone Accelerator in his lap. He swiped at the top, and the cylinder flared to life, casting a bluish light around them. Aaron stared dumbly at the portal to Safanar before him. If his mind had been working right, he would have known that the portal would only last seconds.

Thraw grabbed the human by the arm and leaped through the portal as Hytharia gave a final shudder and the ground beneath them gave way to darkness and flame. The portal closed immediately behind them. Thraw's eyes almost squinted shut in the sunlight. The human lay unconscious in a huddled mass of misshapen arms and legs, which left him to wonder if it would be a mercy to simply kill the human to put it out of its misery.

Hunter senses kicked in, and Thraw leaped into the nearby tree line as more of the humans came running. The beast climbed the tree and watched as the humans gathered around. The sunlight here was almost blinding, as he had never seen the outside, but for images that would play for the Hythariam. The fresh air burned the inside of his lungs, but he bore it all in silence. He had heard the others talk of climate acclimation and had assumed he would need time to get used to his new world. Then it would be time to hunt. His gaze returned to the humans as they carried off one of their own and Thraw set off, eager to be away and do the one thing he had been bred to do: hunt and kill. Only the Hythariam were his prey, and Halcylon was his target.

11

REUNION

Along the outskirts of Shandara the sun was hours away from setting. The rune-carved staff rested with part of its heft sticking up from the earth. Grass had returned in patches, transforming the barren area into the potential for green fields. The staff hadn't been moved or touched since it had been stuck it into the ground. Sarah closed her eyes. She could still see Aaron stumbling toward the portal, the Nanites coursing through his system. Her hands clenched at her helplessness as she kneeled there upon the ground, hardly able to move. The Nanites that Aaron tricked into leaving her body had left her weak and disoriented. She opened her eyes, letting the memory fade. The runes along the staff glowed dully. She knew that the staff was connected to Aaron somehow, and after seeing that her people were provided for, she came here to feel closer to him. Braden was with her of course, and he spoke quietly with the De'anjard that guarded the staff. Her eyes glided over the runes being drawn into the pulsating rhythm. A soft breeze pulled at the wisps of hair that had escaped her braid. No one had wanted to touch the staff for fear of cutting Aaron off from Safanar. Barely two months had passed, and she was no closer to Aaron than she was when she first woke. The rune-carved staff was a mystery, and she had to know its secret. Could it help her find Aaron? More importantly, could it bring him home? She brought her hand up to the staff and could feel the hum of energy along its carved surface. Her fingers grazed overtop, and the quickening of energy from the staff seeped into her fingertips. Sarah quieted her mind and focused on Aaron. She could almost smell his earthy presence in a mixture of fire among the fringes of her senses. The runes on the staff flared brightly for a moment before the staff went dark.

Braden and the De'anjard guard came running over. "What happened?"

"I don't know. I barely touched it, and suddenly it went dark," Sarah said.

They stood there for a moment, not saying anything. All of them staring at the staff.

"Does that mean he's..." the guard asked.

The fear in her eyes was mirrored in Braden's for a moment. "No, he's not gone."

The comms device chimed up, and Braden withdrew it from his pocket.

"Braden. Is Sarah with you?" Verona's voice asked through the device.

"I'm right here, Verona."

"Good. We need for you to return to Rexel. There have been reports of the High King's army attacking," Verona said.

"We'll be right there," Sarah said.

Braden closed the comms device. "You didn't tell him about the staff?"

"I will when we get there," Sarah said, bringing out the travel crystal.

Braden nodded and instructed to the guard to stay with the staff. He took Sarah's hand, and she engaged the travel crystal. Within a moment they emerged at the Free Nation's Army encampment outside Rexel. Verona greeted them. He wore the forest green clothing that the Hythariam wore. Roselyn stood at his side with her hand upon his arm. It was clear that the two were in love. She was happy for them both, but at the same time she felt a tinge of jealousy at their happiness. Sarah clamped down on those thoughts immediately. If it weren't for the efforts of Verona and Roselyn, she might not be standing here at all. Roselyn watched her with the keen golden Hythariam eyes that were almost feline but not quite human.

They exchanged greetings, and Verona led them through the camp.

"I'm glad we were able to help members of the Resistance escape the city, my Lady," Verona said.

"We were able to get a lot of them out, but there are still people there who need our help," Sarah said.

"The Khamearrian army has been attacking our allied nations. Reports are still coming in, except we don't know how they are able to attack so many places at once," Verona said.

"They could be using the travel crystals," Braden offered.

"We thought of that, but the reports speak of a large attack force, laying siege to castles and small cities. Seems like a tall order for a travel crystal, even with the Elitesmen," Verona said and then went into the numbers of the attacking forces being reported.

"You're right. It's too many for the travel crystals traditionally used by Elitesmen, but they certainly aren't marching there, otherwise they would have been seen. They must have found a way to augment the travel crystals to move larger attack forces," Sarah said.

"That's what we're afraid of. We've been advising the nations allied with us to stay on alert, but we're having trouble coming to any of their aid. So far they've hit places close to the Khamearrian border, and not everyone that was hit was allied with the FNA."

"My father is sending a message to the other kingdoms. That no one is beyond his reach. They could attack here at any moment," Sarah said, noting the heightened activity around them.

"What's happening?" Roselyn asked.

A crowd was gathering a short distance from them, so they decided to head over. The crowd was gathered around one person, who stood taller than most of the men gathered around him.

Verona frowned, peering into the crowd. Then his mouth fell open, and he turned to Sarah, "My Lady...The Goddess has blessed us this day. Our wayward friend is back."

The breath caught in Sarah's throat, and she began running. Aaron stumbled along, looking as if he had walked a great distance. Some people came to his aid, but he waved them off. His clothes were in tatters, and he was covered from head to toe in bruises and dried blood, but she didn't care. She ran to him and took him in a fierce embrace, and the crowd around them melted away. Sarah gazed into his honey-brown eyes with hints of gold on the edges, expecting to see the man she loved; instead she found a stranger looking back at her through Aaron's eyes. A sudden coldness sucked the breath from her. The crowd around them cheered. Verona and the others came up behind them smiling.

Aaron leaned in to press his lips to hers, and she flinched back instinctively. A gnawing doubt rapidly spread through her core. *This is not my Aaron.* The people closest around looked at her in shock. Her breath quickened in her chest, and she studied Aaron uncertainly. The crowd around them knew what Aaron had sacrificed to save her, and here she was spurning the miracle of his return, but she couldn't help it. This was not Aaron, and the certainty of it crawled along her skin.

Aaron didn't seemed fazed that she had pulled away. He looked around at the others tiredly and fell to the ground, going unconscious. Verona and Braden carried him away. They pointedly didn't look at her, and some others scowled in her direction before moving on.

Sarah stood rooted in place, unable to move or shake off the feeling that something was terribly wrong. A gentle hand touched her arm, and Roselyn's eyes drew up in concern.

"What is it, Sarah?"

Sarah's eyes darted around, and her breath came in short gasps. "It's not him, Roselyn. I know this must sound crazy, but when I looked into his eyes I swear the man we knew wasn't there."

Roselyn narrowed her gaze inquisitively. "Are you sure? Look at him. He's been through quite an ordeal."

Sarah grasped Roselyn's arms. "It's not him. You have to believe me. He saved me in Shandara using his own life force to keep me from dying. Since then we've shared a connection, and now it's gone."

"It's all right," Roselyn said soothingly. "I will examine him, and we'll be able to see if he is, in fact, Aaron Jace."

"Do whatever you like, but I would know my love if I saw him."

Some of the men passing by glanced in their direction, and Roselyn stepped closer to her. "I have a sample of his blood at Hathenwood. I will get another one from him and compare, but you need to calm down. If you start flinging accusations you may find that there are some here who would harm you."

Sarah clenched her teeth, the muscles in her body becoming rigid. "You know something." It wasn't a question, and the look in Roselyn's golden eyes confirmed it.

"Nothing you don't already know. You're the daughter of the High King. There are some who think you are just a spy. Others believe you to be a perfect bargaining piece to negotiate terms with him. And still others say that you manipulated Aaron into sacrificing himself for you."

Sarah had to fight to keep her mouth from gaping open, but deep down she knew what Roselyn said was true. She had been too preoccupied with trying to find a way to rescue Aaron and help the Resistance to pay the naysayers much mind. If she openly voiced her doubts about Aaron, then they would use it against her.

"I've been blind," Sarah said.

"No you've been working to find a way to help Aaron. We all have. People will talk and have opinions regardless. I want to help you. If that man isn't Aaron then he is not here for our own good, and we need to remove that threat, but what if it is Aaron?" Roselyn asked.

"It's not."

"What if something was done to him that changed him to his very core? Like what was done to you?"

Sarah opened her mouth to reply, but nothing came out. Roselyn had a point.

"He's been gone for months. Who knows what's been done to him in that time," Roselyn said.

Sarah glanced at the backs of the receding crowd. "I have to trust my heart."

Roselyn nodded. "There is just one more thing. If what you suspect is true, then where is the real Aaron?"

Sarah shook her head and scanned the people around them as if Aaron would suddenly emerge.

"Let's go," Sarah said.

They headed in the same direction that Verona and Braden had taken Aaron in. Off to the side of the road, a group of men were stacking sacks of grain into a wagon when a crippled-looking man muttering to himself lurched by, knocking into one of them. The men on the ground shouted and kicked the crippled man who flailed his arms clumsily and his shouts grew louder, sounding like gibberish. The workers screamed at him, and each began laughing and taking a shot. The cripple swung his gnarled hands and tried to wheel around, but stumbled and fell. The workers closed in on him hungrily.

"You men, stop that at once!" Sarah shouted at them.

The men turned around and took note of her golden hair, giving her a slight bow before going back to work. Sarah kneeled down. The crippled man kept his deformed hands covering his face. His clothes were caked with mud, and it was matted through his greasy hair. He drew ragged breaths. Sarah reached out and gently pulled his arms down. Dull-brown eyes darted around before coming to focus on her. He pulled back and squeezed his eyes shut. His mouth opened and closed rapidly. He was hideously deformed as if every bone in his body had been broken. He lurched to his feet and took a few steps away.

"Len," a short man called, coming down the road. He had a homely face and was dressed in simple clothes, but he had a gentle manner to him. He called out again, and the crippled man swung around repeating the name.

"Thank you for looking after him, my Lady. He wandered off the moment my back was turned," the man said.

"It was no problem. Those other men were beating him," Sarah said, glaring at the group of men who had finished loading the wagon and were moving away from them. "I'm sorry, but I didn't get your name."

"Apologies, my Lady, my mum exhausted herself with instilling manners into me, but I'm afraid it was all for naught today. My name is Wes, and this is Len," Wes said with a smile and nod to both Sarah and Roselyn.

"Len," Sarah said, but the crippled man was looking away from them. "That's a strange name."

"Hardly a name at all, my Lady. They found him in the woods yesterday and that was the only word he has said since," Wes said.

"It's very kind of you to look after him," Sarah said.

"Well he's quite strong, and I'm short, so I look after him, and he helps me lift stuff when I need it."

"Len," Len said, his eyes growing distant for a moment, but then darted around following things that only he could see.

They bid the men farewell and headed back into the camp. Sarah caressed Aaron's medallion under her shirt, lost in thought, and before long they came to a heavily guarded tent.

Roselyn started to head inside, but Sarah reached out to her. "I can't go in there."

Roselyn considered her words for a moment and nodded. "We'll meet up later then."

Sarah stood alone outside the tent, and her insides squirmed. She found herself wanting to plunge headlong into the tent and give into the fantasy that Aaron was inside waiting for her, but she couldn't. She heard many voices coming from inside, from Verona's boisterous laughter to Braden's grumbling.

Backing away from the tent, she engaged the travel crystal and left. She emerged under a star-filled sky. The trickling water of a fountain of the Goddess Ferasdiam stood amid a remnant castle long since gone to ruin. At first she didn't recognize where she was until a vision of Aaron burned through her mind. This was a place he had taken her when he had tried to rid her of the Nanites. Verona later told her that the fountain was where a Dragon had spoken to them. She gazed at the stone carving of a woman standing resolute above the pool of water that served as the fountain's basin. Sarah collapsed to her knees, her eyes brimming with tears, and wept. All the while cursing herself for doing so. She twisted around and sat with her back against the fountain walls. She withdrew the medallion from her shirt, tracing the carving of a Dragon cradling a single rose with a crystal in the center. She moaned Aaron's name and sank to the ground, passing out of thought and mind, but for the soft trickle of the water and the resolute stare of the stone carving of the Goddess above her.

12

SHADOWS DESCENT

"I'm here, my Lady," Verona said.

Roselyn looked up from what she had been working on and smiled at him.

"My Lady?" Roselyn asked.

"In this case I mean it quite literally," Verona quipped.

Roselyn laughed and kissed him. "Fool."

"Always for you, my Lady," Verona said, feeling her silky raven hair glide across his hands as she stepped back.

"You should have seen the looks I would get when I asked why you were so quiet."

"I see my reputation precedes me," Verona grinned.

The smiled melted away from her face, and the muscles above her cheekbones rolled as she chewed her bottom lip. He was still learning all her quirks, but this was one he knew well. There was something she wanted to talk to him about.

"How is Aaron?"

Verona noted the slight frown on her face when she asked. "He rests. Braden is with him."

"Did he say anything about how he escaped?"

Verona shook his head. "Not since you examined him yesterday. He more or less passed out."

Roselyn nodded and addressed the flashing light on the screen she was working from. She had setup a small lab with some of her Hythariam equipment that he couldn't even begin to guess how they worked. "What are you working on?"

"I'm running some tests on Aaron's blood."

"What are you looking for?" Verona asked.

"Anomalies. I'm comparing this sample from what we had at Hathenwood," Roselyn said.

Verona frowned. "You kept his blood?"

"It's not as ghastly as you make it sound," Roselyn grinned. "But yes, we did. If you recall, he was infected with the Ryakul poison, and we were trying to help him. Our blood, yours and mine, hold detailed information about us."

Verona nodded. "And why are you comparing his blood samples?"

"He's been gone for months on Hytharia. Captured by my people there. These tests might give us some insight into what has been done to him, if anything. I know on the surface he appears normal, but in the time you were with him has he acted any different?" Roselyn asked.

"He was captured. I don't mean to bring this up, but we both know what that was like," Verona said. The images of the Elitesman Sevan torturing people while he and Sarik kept up a shield still came to him in his dreams.

"I realize that, but Sarah believes that the man that came yesterday isn't Aaron," Roselyn said.

Verona blew out a breath. "Do you realize how crazy that sounds? If I hadn't known about the Nanites and that they were capable of changing the very foundations of our minds, I would think she lost her senses."

"And now?"

"I see Aaron before me. What do you see?"

"I'm not sure what to think. So far the blood tests match, but I have more tests to run," said Roselyn.

Verona came to her side and reached out to her. "What do you see, my Lady?"

"I see Aaron, but Sarah is my friend. She and Aaron are connected in ways we're only beginning to comprehend. If she has doubts, then we should listen to her."

Verona was silent for a moment, considering his words carefully. "Could she still be suffering from some remnant of the Nanites? The way I understand it is that they retrain the mind."

"I've considered that, but don't you find it suspicious that Aaron just showed up here out of nowhere?"

"I thought of it more as a blessing, but I see your point. If he has returned does it also mean the rest of the Hythariam have arrived?"

The comms device chimed from both of their wrists, and Roselyn brought hers up.

"It's a message from Gavril. They want to see us at the command tent," Roselyn said and started packing up her things.

"Roselyn, I think we need to give Aaron some time," Verona said.

"Something we're lacking at the moment. There are too many people who seek to use Sarah as some type of pawn with the High King or believe that she is here spying for him," Roselyn said.

They headed toward the command tent.

"Rumors," Verona said. "She's the daughter of the High King; of course there are rumors. I have no doubts where Sarah's loyalties lie."

"Even if she refuses to believe that Aaron has returned?"

Verona felt his teeth clamp down. "You paint a dark picture, my Lady." His thoughts drifted to Aaron's return and the look on Sarah's face as she pulled away from him. How could she have known anything so quickly? And now Roselyn was running blood tests looking for Goddess knew what. They had enough enemies to face without being suspicious of one another.

Outside of Rexel was a city of tents and makeshift shelters. More permanent structures were being built, but not fast enough to accommodate the Free Nations Army. They came to a behemoth-sized tent, and he nodded to the guards posted outside and entered. There were various groups gathered inside the tent. Some groups were being led by Hythariam there to teach others the basics of how their technology worked. Others were gathered with leaders of the various factions that made up the FNA, poring over maps and discussing tactics. Verona had sat in enough of those to know how useful they were. The maps of Safanar since the dawn of the airships were more accurate than anything they had before, and the Hythariam satellites up in the heavens augmented those as well. He had yet to see so many of the things that Roselyn spoke of, but he had come to trust and rely on the Hythariam technological wonders.

A small crowd gathered at the meeting area, and standing along the outskirts was a familiar face although not as young as he was a few months ago. Jopher had turned into a fine officer.

"Got your feet back on solid ground?" Verona asked.

"For the moment. The admiral put me in command of a ship of my own," Jopher said.

"I don't know how you did it, but you've wormed your way into Nathaniel Morgan's good graces," Verona said.

"I'll tell you how he did it," came Admiral Morgan's voice from behind him. "With honest to goodness hard work. You princely types are all the same. You come to me all high and mighty, thinking that what comes out of your ass doesn't stink like the rest of us. A few weeks or months getting your hands dirty tends to change all that."

"I'm sure you expected it to take months in my case," Verona grinned.

"You both did well. I couldn't be prouder if you were my own sons. The truth of the matter is we need ship captains, and that means some of you will need to grow a bit faster," Admiral Morgan said.

"Did you happen to see my request?" asked Jopher.

"Aye, I did, lad," Morgan said, "You want Hatly, the Raven's engineer. I bet you'd take the Raven too if I was of mind to let you, but I'm not. You're going to one of the newer ships."

"Come now, Nathaniel," Verona said. "You get what you want, which is for Jopher to captain a ship for you, and he gets what he needs, which is an exemplary engineer to keep her flying. You taught him well."

"Too well apparently. Yes, I will approve the transfer," Morgan said after a moment.

"Thank you, sir."

Verona grinned at them both, and the admiral took his leave of them.

"Is it true about Aaron being back?" Jopher asked.

Verona nodded. "Causing quite a stir. He more or less passed out shortly after arriving. Braden is with him. I have a question for you, but not as an officer in the Free Nations Army, but for the heir apparent of Zsensibar's throne."

"That's making waves among my many brothers and sisters still in Zsensibar," Jopher said.

"I can imagine, but they will learn. With Khamearra's armies attacking, we need a commitment from your father. Do you know if he's willing to grant that now?" asked Verona.

"You would think that the sheer fact that I am here would be a measure of his commitment, but I understand what has leaders of the War Council concerned. He will be coming here soon enough," Jopher said.

"Hopefully he doesn't intend to bring his whole army. Resources are spread thin enough as it is, or so my uncle keeps saying."

"Troop movement is going to be one of the topics of discussion. He has used the comms device, but he doesn't like them," Jopher said.

"I actually agree with him in that regard. The comms device has some limitation, and some things are best discussed in person," Verona said.

"Are you getting set in your ways, Verona?" Roselyn asked.

Verona gave her a sly grin. "Not at all, my Lady. There are some I'd rather see in person as opposed to a voice through one of your machines. Your voice, while music to my ears, doesn't hold a candle to actually standing at your side, which is music to my soul."

Roselyn giggled and leaned into him. He brought his arm around her shoulder, and for a brief instant their worries were far away from them. At that moment the thing sitting in the middle of the floor lit up around them. He couldn't remember what it was called. Roselyn would know, but he wasn't of a mind to ask her about that. He was more of a mind of stealing away with her so they could be alone, but there was little chance of that happening. A large display of light showed the people in Hathenwood.

Roselyn eyed him. "Do you remember its name?"

It was almost like she could read his thoughts. "A holographic display," he said.

"What about the device on the floor?"

Roselyn was nothing if not determined to teach him about the Hythariam and their infernal devices that he couldn't remember the names of. It was almost like when he was younger with Vaughn and his history lessons.

"I haven't got a clue, my Lady."

Roselyn stared at him with those golden eyes of hers that would have chased away any of the words that came to mind, except that he knew this was important to her. Jopher stood on the other side of Roselyn and mouthed some words. The answer lit up in his mind like a beacon in the sky. "A holo projector."

"Very good," Roselyn said. "Perhaps you should keep Jopher with you to feed you the answers."

Dammit, she caught us, he thought to himself. "My Lady, you scold me. I am deeply sorry. But I could bring up the finer points of archery."

Roselyn leveled her gaze at him coolly. "You could."

Verona often found it interesting that some rules between men and women, including Hythariam, didn't necessarily apply both ways. Perhaps he was being too hard on her. Roselyn did try shooting an arrow from a bow, but it didn't go well. She had been as bad as Aaron was when they first met.

"Thank you, everyone, for joining us on such short notice," Iranus said. "We have a great many things to discuss."

Sarah came to his side so quietly that he didn't know she was there until she placed her hand upon his arm. Her cheeks were red as if she had been out in the wind, and her eyes held the remnant swollenness of someone who had been crying. Verona went to put his hand upon her back and felt the crisscross of sheathed blades there.

She still carries Aaron's blades.

Roselyn came to Sarah's other side, and they turned their attention back to Iranus.

Iranus began speaking again. "We've got reports of the High King's armies attacking neighboring kingdoms near Khamearra. Not all of them have openly allied with the Free Nations Army, but we believe the High King is sending a clear message to anyone who may have been on the fence about joining us. We must find a way to respond to these attacks. We've put protocols in place so warning can be sent as soon as possible, and a ready force will be on standby all day and night from now on."

A quiet murmuring began at that. Verona had known about the ready forces being assigned as the strategy had been discussed previously, and his uncle, the prince, had informed him that they wanted him to lead one of those forces. Verona almost missed the quiet days when they were just trekking to Shandara, and prior to that, finding trouble in whatever city they had been to in the Waylands. Verona had made his own proposal to the War Council for a more proactive fighting force with aims of striking back at the High King. He was still waiting for the final approval of it, but he had already been trolling through the various FNA camps, looking for a specific type of fighting man. Men who weren't afraid to take risks and were able to improvise. Braden had aims of resurrecting the De'anjard and with his Warden's Hammer he made a formidable addition to any group of men that Verona would put together. Now that Aaron was back, Braden would probably be going back to guarding him. The only thing he could do was to convince Aaron to join him, which begged the question as to whether Aaron was fit to rejoin the fight now that he was back. *If he is back*, said a quiet voice in the back of his mind. He glanced at Sarah through the corner of his eye. Her intentions where Aaron was concerned had always been good, and he wasn't sure why she would believe that the man who came back to the camp yesterday was anyone other than Aaron. Part of him believed it was still some remnant effect of the Nanites, but what if she was right and they were all being fooled? The implications could be disastrous for all of them. It made him uncomfortable to even consider the notion.

"Lady Sarah," the holographic image of Iranus addressed her formally, "do you have any opinion about these attacks?"

"I think you are correct. My father is sending a message that he can strike whomever and wherever he wishes at any time. But as you said, with our allies increasing their readiness they will be better prepared to defend against an attack," Sarah said.

"Thank you. I'd like for you to take a look at what I'm about to display and see if you can tell me what these things are," Iranus said.

The holo changed to a view of the Khamearrian army as if they were looking at it from above. *This must be from one of those machines the Hythariam had in the sky*, Verona mused. Roselyn glanced at him, and he mouthed the word 'satellite' with a half smile. The image zoomed in closer to a circle of black-clad warriors that Verona assumed were Elitesmen. They were circled around some type of large glowing object.

Sarah studied the image for a moment. "It looks like the large focusing crystal that was housed in one of the citadel towers of the Elite."

"A focusing crystal?" Iranus asked.

"Yes, it's used to recharge the other crystals like the ones used for traveling. In the tower they amplify the rays of the sun to power it, and it in turn charges the others. They must be using it to help move the army around," Sarah said.

"Can you offer any insight into how they might accomplish this?" Iranus asked.

Sarah frowned in thought for a moment before answering. "I know how the travel crystals work. The user feeds a bit of the gathered energy into it along with a clear image of where they wish to go. But that large focusing crystal by itself can't do it alone."

"If I understand you correctly, the crystal works in pairs with whoever uses them?"

"That is correct, but a travel crystal by itself can only move small groups of people," Sarah said.

"They must have found a way to use the focusing crystal to increase the ability of a normal travel crystal," Roselyn said. "It's quite smart. We studied the few travel crystals we have and we would need to crunch the numbers, but the power requirements are high. As we've learned with our own Keystone Accelerators to open portals, even in the same dimensional space the power requirements are high to keep the doorway open so enough people can move through. That's why we're limited to two uses per each Accelerator that we use. I would think it is safe to assume that while the High King's army can move about the continent, there are limitations as to how often they can use the focusing crystals before they require recharging."

"We know it's important to them by how heavily it's guarded, but what I'm not sure of is how many of these large focusing crystals they have," Gavril said.

"Two that I know of," Sarah said.

"Then they are priority targets," Gavril said.

"They are also the most heavily guarded," Verona added.

"Worth it if we can cripple their forces for a while," Gavril replied.

"Thank you, all," Iranus said. "All of your input has given us much to consider, but we must move on to our next order of business. We've been tracking an object heading to this planet from space. It was believed that the object's origin is from Hytharia. Early yesterday morning the object made it past our defenses and was able to land somewhere on Safanar."

A tidal wave of questions spewed forth from many of them about the invading horde from Hytharia.

"Give me a moment, and I will tell you what we know," Gavril chimed in. "As Iranus has said, the object beat our defenses, which we can attest to the military-grade technology used to create it." Gavril stopped and brought up a map of Safanar on the display. "Based upon the last known position of the ship, the direction it was heading, the craft came in through the atmosphere over the ocean northwest of Khamearra and then disappeared. We haven't been able to find it, and we have no idea where it went after. We've had people up in the flyers, sweeping different areas of where we expected it to go, but so far it's an extremely slow process."

"Do you know what it could be doing?" Verona asked.

"We're not sure exactly," Gavril answered. "This was a last-ditch effort by the Zekara to gain access to Safanar."

"They're here," Aaron's voice said from behind the crowd, and a pathway opened up for him across from where Verona stood.

Verona's eyes darted to his friend, and he felt Sarah stiffen next to him. Remnant bruises covered his skin in a patchwork of yellows and soft purples. Whispers of his name spread throughout the tent, and Verona realized that for many this was the first time they had ever seen him. The native patrons of Safanar bowed their heads in reverence to the only surviving member of the House Alenzar'seth. Aaron's gaze swept the room as he moved in closer.

"Aaron, I think I can speak for everyone here that we're extremely happy to see you returned to us, but I'm afraid it comes as a mixed blessing since your return would signify that the Zekara have made it to Safanar as well," Iranus said.

"Who are the Zekara?" Verona asked.

"They are what the members of the Hythariam military call themselves," Aaron said. "You must be wondering what has happened to me since going through the portal and how I got free."

"You could say we've spoken about it once or twice, my friend," Verona said, and some of the others chuckled around the room. Aaron, however, barely acknowledged the jibe.

"I was taken prisoner by the Zekara shortly after going through the portal," Aaron said.

"Why didn't you use the Keystone Accelerator to open a way back to Safanar?" Roselyn asked.

"After going through the portal, the Nanites in my system shut themselves down. The atmosphere upon Hytharia was so thin that I began choking. I tried to open a portal back to Safanar, but the Zekara soldiers captured me and brought me to their mountain base. Halcylon is alive, and he's here on Safanar," Aaron said.

Sarah took a step toward him, and Aaron turned his gaze upon her but continued addressing the rest. "They held me prisoner. Put me on trial. That was how all this happened," Aaron said gesturing to the bruises upon his face and arms.

"A trial?" Verona asked.

"I could see that," Iranus said, drawing their attention.

"They held me responsible for the barrier put in place blocking the portal from Hytharia to Safanar," Aaron said. "When they found me guilty, the crowd was allowed to extract their toll."

"How did you survive?" Verona asked.

"I'm sure they wanted to kill me, but Halcylon and his soldiers wouldn't let them."

"How did you return?" Sarah asked, her voice sounding hoarse.

"They gave me enough to eat and drink to barely keep me alive. They had me staked out in the open. Then one day a portal opened, easily the size of a building, and the Zekara started filing through it, taking whatever they could. The planet had become unstable and was in its final death throes. The last thing I saw was a dark figure before something knocked me unconscious, and when I woke up I was out in the forest a few miles away from here," Aaron said.

Verona listened to his friend speaking and almost couldn't believe what had been said.

"So we have an anonymous benefactor for your release," Gavril said with a frown. "How did they even hold you prisoner? A small number of us have seen what you can do to Elitesmen and Ryakuls alike."

Aaron's eyes grew distant for a moment, and he shuddered, "They used the Nanites on me."

Roselyn plunged her hand inside her pocket, brought out a device, and stepped in front of Aaron. She ran the device over his chest and along his arms, then around his face.

"I can detect the Nanites in his system, but they are strange like they are dormant," Roselyn said. "I would like to do a more thorough examination."

Aaron held up his hand. "I've had enough prodding by Hythariam technology for a while, so I will respectfully deny your request."

The words were soft spoken, but it didn't take anything away from the coldness in them. Roselyn backed away, coming to Verona's side. He could tell her feelings were hurt, and he resisted the urge to reach out to her.

"You've been through a lot, my friend, but Roselyn was only trying to help," Verona said.

"I appreciate your help, my Lady, but we have more pressing things to concern ourselves with," Aaron said.

Verona didn't say anything back, but clearly the issue was dismissed.

"When I came into the tent you were speaking about the High King attacking other kingdoms?" Aaron asked.

The discussion turned to what had been previously talked about, and Verona took the opportunity to watch his friend. At times he was just as he had remembered him, and at others he appeared to be a complete stranger. Sarah was silent through much of the conversation, but her eyes never left Aaron. She watched him closely, and more than once did Aaron make eye contact with her, but it held none of the fire it had before. Verona didn't know what to make of it. His mind was at odds with what he wanted to believe, which was that his friend had beaten the odds and had returned to them.

The session ended, and people began leaving the command tent.

"My Lady, I believe you have something that belongs to me," Aaron said, looking at Sarah. "My swords."

"I do indeed have them, but you hardly look like you could wield them. I think I'll hold onto them until you are ready," Sarah said.

"You'll find that I am a quick healer," Aaron said with a smile, standing taller.

Sarah reluctantly removed Aaron's swords from her back, "Perhaps you'd like to have a go in the training area?" she asked and handed his swords back to him.

For a moment Verona wondered whether she was going to give them back or not.

"Not right this second. I'd like to tour the camp," Aaron said, and a number of people standing around practically leaped up for the privilege of showing him around. With a nod in their direction, Aaron left them behind.

Sarah turned to Verona, giving him a pointed look and left.

Verona left the tent with Roselyn silently walking next to him. Jopher had followed them out as well.

"He seems different," Jopher said.

"How so? He was a prisoner until recently," Verona said.

Jopher frowned, putting his thoughts in order. "I don't mean his injuries. All the bowing and formalities, he didn't seem to mind it at all. It was almost like he expected it."

Verona's mind raced, going through the meeting in his mind. "Maybe his imprisonment had more an effect on him than we thought," he said, catching Roselyn's sideways glance.

"It's just not something I expected to see from him," Jopher said, and the comms device buzzed on his arm. "I have to go; my father's envoy is arriving from Zsensibar."

Verona wished him well as he turned and walked away, and then he felt Roselyn's eyes on him as the young officer left.

"I don't know what to say, my Lady."

"I know. It's strange. One moment Aaron is just as he was before, and in the next it's like we're dealing with a complete stranger," Roselyn said.

Verona felt a faint twisting in his stomach at the thought that what if, perhaps, Sarah was right. "It seems that Sarah has her doubts, as well."

The people of the camp went around them, going about their business, and Verona stopped walking when he felt Roselyn place her hand upon his arm.

"Can you blame her?" Roselyn asked. "More than anyone else here, she wants to believe that somehow Aaron has made it back to us."

"I can't argue with that, my Lady. I don't know what I would have done if it were you trapped in a place where I couldn't reach you."

"I know," she said and leaned in to kiss him.

Roselyn left him, saying she had to return to Hathenwood and would be back in Rexel tomorrow.

MORNING CAME MUCH SOONER THAN VERONA WOULD HAVE LIKED, AND HE woke to the sight of Braden, who shed his normally stoic demeanor, shaking him awake with a malicious grin.

"I'm awake!"

"About time too," Braden said.

"Are we under attack?"

The sobering question sucked the mirth right out of his friend.

"No, but there are a group of soldiers we're to assess this morning," Braden said.

Verona nodded and roused himself out of bed, "You've managed to drag yourself away from Aaron?"

"He said he would meet us down there later on," Braden said.

He hadn't slept well last night. After having spent most of the day quietly observing Aaron, and coming no closer to deciding whether it was really him or not, he went to sleep. Mostly he lay awake wondering when the world had grown so complicated. He had sworn to be at Aaron's side throughout the measure of this journey, and at times like these, Verona was left grasping where it would finally lead them.

He and Braden headed outside the city to one of the various training areas set aside for the soldiers in the FNA.

"Have you seen Sarah?" Verona asked.

Braden shook his head. Sarah had left them yesterday, and he had not seen her since.

"I did speak to her through the comms device, and she said she would meet us," Braden said.

"What's so special about this group of soldiers?"

"They were handpicked by Colind, who said they might possess the potential for tapping into the energy," Braden said.

"I haven't seen Colind in a while. The last I heard he was trying to find the old members of the Safanarion Order," Verona said.

Braden glanced the other way, saying nothing.

"When did you become the purveyor of information?"

"What?" Braden asked, a little too quickly.

"You know something. Particularly about Colind," Verona said.

"He instructed me not to say anything."

"Well, now I must know," Verona said.

Braden clamped his mouth shut and put a bit more speed in his step.

"Is this what we've been reduced to?" Verona asked, matching his pace. "Keeping secrets from each other, my old friend? Come on, what is Colind up to that he saw fit to tell the one person whom most wouldn't have thought he would confide in?"

Braden eyed him for a moment before answering. "He hunts Mactar."

"I suspected that such a thing would come to pass in time. What did you say to him when he told you all this?" Verona asked.

"What could I say to him?" Braden asked. "Should I have reminded him of his duty to the Safanarion Order? No, there are some that the world could do without, and if a colossus out of legend wants to make it his mission to take out one of our strongest enemies, then more power to him. Mactar deserves to die."

Verona was silent for a moment, knowing that Braden still mourned the loss of his brother, Eric. They all did. There were times when he expected to see Braden's twin brother at his side, and his absence was a constant reminder that any of them could die along the way.

"I can't argue with that, my friend, but one thing that I have learned, especially in Khamearra, is that we can accomplish so much more if we work together than if we go off on our own."

"Sometimes," Braden said.

They were silent the rest of the way, coming to their designated place in the training area, marked with a white eagle. The soldiers were cloistered together listening to Sarah. Her long blonde hair was braided, and more than one soldier's eyes shone with that cautious admiration that often marked good men when they saw someone as beautiful as the High King's daughter. He had often told Aaron that he was a lucky man, and he meant it. Sarah noticed them approaching and waved them over. Braden told him he would be there in a moment. Young Sarik detached himself from the soldiers and joined them at the front. He supposed he shouldn't think of Sarik as young anymore, it was just that he had taken Sarik into his care three years ago when the lad was fifteen. Sarik was the third son of a minor house in the Waylands, and his father had been overjoyed that the nephew of their prince would take his youngest son into his service. Verona never viewed it as taking anyone into his service, but rather as adopting Sarik as the younger brother he'd never had.

"Sarik is going to demonstrate the slow fighting forms, and I want you to pay particular attention to both his form and his breath control," Sarah said.

The twenty men spread out to get a better look. They ranged in age with the youngest looking about sixteen years of age to some being twice that, but they all lined up and paid attention.

Sarik began moving his body slowly. They both had practiced what Aaron had taught them nearly every day since those days aboard the deck of the Raven. Sarik moved with effortless ease, his whole body becoming one.

"Can anyone tell me the importance of breathing?" Sarah asked.

"Because we like living, my Lady," an older soldier snickered and was quickly joined in by others.

A smile cracked Sarah's face as she joined in. "As do we all. You happened to be quite right..."

"Kay, my Lady," answered the soldier.

"Watch as Sarik moves, his body and breath become one. One cannot happen without the other. When breath is controlled you have greater endurance, which is essential to stay alive," Sarah said, making eye contact with each of them as she spoke. "Suits of armor aren't so common anymore, but those warriors who donned them had to build their endurance to wear them. A smarter, less armored warrior could easily tire out his more armored opponent if he didn't know how to control his breathing. You've all heard of the De'anjard?" Sarah asked.

The soldiers nodded, and some glanced at Braden, who joined them.

"The De'anjard were known throughout the realm as being among the strongest of any fighting force on Safanar. Braden can you tell us why?"

"You can't fight well if you don't breathe well," Braden bellowed.

"Forgive me, my Lady, but we were told you were going to test us to see if we could tap into the energy as you do. When are we going to get to that?" Kay asked, and the question was mirrored upon every one of the soldier's faces.

"In order to open oneself to the energy around them, they must be calm and in control. Mastery of self comes through a quiet and focused mind. Practicing the slow fighting forms will help to train you to focus your mind. Only then you may open yourself up to higher forms of practice," Sarah said.

The men spread out with each trying to mimic Sarik's movement. The rest walked among them and corrected their form as they went. More than once Verona saw Braden watching Sarah as if he were weighing something.

"What's wrong, my friend?" Verona quietly asked.

"The rune-carved staff has been stolen," Braden said.

"And you believe Sarah took it?"

"I'm not sure. There weren't many who knew about the staff or where it was."

"Just all those people at the arena in Khamearra knew about the staff," Verona chuckled.

"The guard on duty was knocked out, and he can't remember anything."

Verona glanced at Sarah who was showing one of the younger soldiers the proper form. The soldier almost looked stunned to be speaking with the princess. "Well, if Sarah did take the staff, I'm sure it was for safekeeping." *Or to keep a certain someone from taking it,* Verona thought to himself.

"And the guard?" Braden asked.

"Now that is something we should be concerned with. If whoever took the staff meant us harm then they simply would have killed the guard. Could you imagine an Elitesman leaving a witness alive?"

"I see your point, Verona. I thought things would have been better when Aaron returned, but instead it's got us all being suspicious of one another."

"Or in this case, Sarah. I agree, my friend, things have gotten more complicated. What I'm about to ask you may seem offhand, but have you noticed anything different with Aaron since his return?" asked Verona.

Braden frowned. "Nothing comes to mind. Aaron has always gone his own way."

"Fair enough," Verona said.

They spent the next hour going through the various fighting forms and then paired the men in groups for some sparring. Verona noticed a group of well-armed Zsensibarian guards making their way through the training yard. Among them a tall, broad-shouldered man with a spiraled crown that sat atop his head. Jopher was with them. Verona liked Jopher, but had never met Zsensibar's ruler. As far as Verona knew, it was a rare event that required Zsensibar's king to venture outside his borders.

At some point Aaron arrived. He had two of the De'anjard with him and a small group of noblemen watching. Aaron waved over to him as he walked over.

"Have you come to join us, my friend?" Verona asked.

"I thought I might," Aaron said, smiling and nodding to the others in greeting. His eyes lingered on Sarah for a moment, who gave him a perfunctory nod.

"I'd like three volunteers and the rest of you to form a circle around us," Aaron said.

Two veteran soldiers stepped up, and one of the younger soldiers, Wesley, Verona believed was his name, stumbled forward. The wiry lad fell in line with the other two men.

"When the Elitesmen attack it will rarely be just you against them. There will be many coming at you all at once and without a shred of mercy. Therefore, the Elitesmen shall be granted none," Aaron said as he slowly stepped toward his three volunteers. "You," Aaron said to Wesley. "How do you think you'd do against these other two?"

Wesley glanced at the other two men, weighing his options. "I'm not sure, your Grace."

Aaron nodded. "Fair enough." He brought out a white piece of cloth about a yard in length. "Here tie this to your belt behind you."

Wesley's brows drew up. He slowly reached out for the cloth and did as Aaron had asked. Verona glanced across the circle at Sarah, whose grim-lined gaze was fixed upon the men in the center.

"The rules are to stay in the circle," Aaron said to the three men. "The job for you two is to bring me that bit of cloth tied to young Wesley's backside."

The two soldiers nodded and turned their attention to Wesley, who gulped and faced his opponents.

"Go!" Aaron said.

The two men charged, and Wesley scrambled out of the way quick as a cat. The men kept doing their utmost to grab the white cloth that trailed in Wesley's wake. After a few minutes, Aaron called for a halt.

"Are you okay?" Aaron asked Wesley, who nodded. "Two on one isn't bad, but I would have thought they would have gotten the cloth by now. I want two more volunteers. Who thinks they can bring me the cloth from young Wesley's backside?"

Two more soldiers stepped forward, and the current men in the center made as if to line up, but Aaron stopped them. "You're not dismissed yet. I want that cloth."

Verona watched as Sarah almost took a step forward, but stopped herself. He himself wondered what Aaron hoped to prove with this exercise.

"Ready? Go!"

Wesley tried to dodge between the four men who surrounded him.

"I want that cloth. That cloth represents life and death. It will mean your death if you don't get it. Hold nothing back," Aaron called.

The men stepped up their effort, and Wesley darted through the circle. The young soldier's shirt was torn as the men grabbed for the cloth.

"Don't let them get it, Wesley; if they do it means you're dead," Aaron said.

The chase went on for a few seconds more until the men were clustered around Aaron, who still stood near the center. In a blurring movement, Wesley cried out as his feet were swept out from under him and the strip of white cloth was held loosely in Aaron's hand. Wesley scooted back away from Aaron's menacing gaze.

"Enough!" Sarah said stepping into the circle. "Five to one is too much to ask anyone, unless you'd like to dance with me, my Lord."

Aaron's head came up as he regarded Sarah for a moment, his face smooth and emotionless. "You of all people should know that there is no such thing as fair when facing an Elitesman."

Sarah helped Wesley to his feet and quietly asked after him. He still looked shaky as he went to the side and sat upon the ground.

Sarah turned her venomous gaze upon Aaron. "I know that the only thing you proved by this display is that of your own prowess, but it lacks any of its former integrity," Sarah said.

The two glared at each other for a moment, and the rest of them looked on in silence. Verona glanced around and noticed Jopher frowning, along with the impassive expression of the King of Zsensibar, who looked on silently. He had been so preoccupied with what was happening in the circle that he hadn't realized that the Zsensibarian envoy had made it to their part of the training yard.

Aaron leveled his gaze at her. "If they don't learn it here, then they are just fodder for the Elitesmen."

"The man I knew would never have taught such a lesson," Sarah said.

"Then maybe you need to accept that the man you knew is gone."

Sarah and Aaron faced off. Though they simply stood facing each other, Verona sensed that violence could break out at any moment. Part of him couldn't move, while the rest of himself urged him to say something.

Verona stepped into the circle. "Why don't we take a break? Clearly we have a difference in teaching methods here."

Verona's voice seemed to dispel the silent standoff, and each backed away.

"My Lady," Aaron called.

Sarah faced him.

"Do you know the whereabouts of my staff?" Aaron asked.

"It's precisely where you left it," Sarah answered.

"That's the thing. It's not there anymore," Aaron said.

"Then perhaps you should keep a better eye on your things," Sarah said.

There were muffled gasps from the crowd of noblemen. The two De'anjard guards started to move, but Braden held up his hand for them to stop.

"My Lord," Braden said. "I'm investigating the whereabouts of the staff. Sarah has been here all morning and couldn't have taken it."

Aaron nodded to Braden. "Thank you. I just asked if she knew where it was. I trust that you will keep me apprised of your investigation."

Verona drew in the energy from the earth, and immediately his perceptions sharpened. He heard Zsensibar's king lean in to Jopher and say, "This is the man whom you chose to follow? He's no different than the High King." Jopher began to respond, but Verona focused his attention elsewhere.

Aaron had walked back to the group of people he had with him. Verona extended his senses, trying to read into those of his friend, but he wasn't very good at this sort of thing and couldn't detect anything. He let go of his connection and noticed Sarah watching him. His mind raced. One moment Aaron was the friend he knew, and in the next he was a complete stranger. He couldn't make any sense of it.

They had decided to take a break for a few minutes, and they broke off into groups. Braden went to Sarah, and the two began quietly speaking. Off to the side, Verona noticed that Wesley stood alone. He had stopped gasping for breath and rose to his feet. Some of the other men came to check on him and then left him, heading to the watering table.

"He's different," Jopher said, coming to Verona's side.

Verona almost asked to whom Jopher was referring, but he knew better. "He was a prisoner for months. Enough time to change any of us, including Aaron."

"I know...I'm just not used to seeing him like this," Jopher said.

"But what is it exactly?"

"I'm not sure what you mean."

"Sometimes Aaron is like he has always been. Patient, especially when teaching. Hard, when the situation calls for it. When Sarah was prisoner to the Drake, he was focused, perhaps a bit rash, but definitely focused. And now...I'm not quite sure what to think," Verona admitted.

Jopher didn't say anything right away. "My father is meeting with Prince Cyrus, and I told them I would catch up."

"Go on then, Jopher, and thank you."

"For what?" Jopher asked.

"For having the courage to say out loud what most of us are only thinking about," Verona said.

A smile lit up Jopher's face at the praise. He nodded and walked away.

Verona found that his mouth was dry, and he went to get some of what passed for refreshment upon the training grounds. He had to settle for water. Heading back, he saw Wesley practicing the slow forms. His wiry body still getting used to the movement he had only just learned this morning. A hunched man watched from behind. One shoulder was lower than the other, and his gnarled hands attempted to mimic Wesley's movements. His misshapen feet lurched over the ground, and his mouth moved as if he were muttering to himself. Verona couldn't hear him, but he knew he was saying something. The man's eyes followed Wesley's movements, but when the young soldier faltered, trying to remember the movement, he continued on, and Verona noted that the crippled man knew the slow forms somehow.

Verona headed over, and a short, plainly dressed man with hair cropped close to his scalp came behind the crippled man and spoke to him. The crippled man waved off the smaller man and moved closer to Wesley. Some of the soldiers had returned and mocked the cripple.

"Mock if you will, gentlemen, but I'll wager he knows the slow forms better than any of you," Verona said.

The men immediately quieted down.

"Apologies, my Lord, he doesn't mean any harm; it's just he has a tendency to wander sometimes," the short man said.

"Not a problem, master?"

The short man grinned. "I'm called Wes, my Lord, and this is Len."

Upon hearing his name, Len's eyes darted around, and he kept repeating his own name.

"Wesley, start again. Let's see if he follows along. The rest of you follow along as well," Verona ordered.

The men immediately lined up. One thing Verona could say about the FNA is that discipline and following orders were a part of their core. Wesley stayed on point. He slowly opened his stance, bringing his arms up. As the soldiers followed in unison, Len stopped muttering to himself, and his eyes seemed to focus on the movement. The men moved through the procession of movement, and Verona was amazed that the crippled man could follow along. He wasn't physically capable of all the movements, but Verona's trained eye could tell that the fundamentals were ingrained there.

Verona joined in. His mind transplanted him to the decks of the Raven, where Aaron had given these lessons to them. Eventually the whole crew had joined in and forged a bond between the men that lasted to this day. No matter what their station, be it soldier, captain, or prince, all were equal in the performing the slow forms.

Perfection of movement is paramount. From movement comes life.

Aaron's words echoed in his ears. Verona felt his connection to the energy around them deepen, and he spread it out away from him. He sensed Sarah's vibrant presence among them. He took in greater breath, and his movement deepened, both powerful and in control. Verona's mind cleared, and he spread his senses to the other men, seeking the spark within them. A blazing presence flashed to the side, snapping away his concentration.

Len was flailing about, waving his arms madly and lurching from side to side like a crab. Wes tried to calm him down, but Len pushed him away. Len grabbed a spear from the nearby rack of weapons and held it awkwardly.

Sarah approached slowly with her palms low and facing outward. Len's eyes widened and the spear dropped from his grasp. His eyes darted all around, and he scurried away, howling as he went.

Verona caught Sarik's eye and nodded toward the fleeing cripple with Wes trailing in his wake. "Just make sure they get out the training area without hurting themselves."

Sarik nodded and set off after them.

Sarah came over to Verona. "I wonder what set him off. Did you see him before? He was able to follow along. If I didn't know better I would say he knew the slow forms."

"In this we are agreed, my Lady," Verona said, and Sarah gave him a sideways glance. "Apologies, my Lady, my uncle believes it to be prudent that I be formal with all manner of nobility. Princesses in particular."

A small smile graced Sarah's face, and she called him a fool. She looked past him, her gaze narrowing. Verona saw Aaron across the training yard, heading away from them. At first Verona believed that it was Sarah that had set Len off, but now he wondered if it was Aaron instead.

"Sarah, you're much better at this than I am. I think a couple of these men might be able to tap into the energy, but I can't be sure."

"With months of training you may be right, for some of them," Sarah said.

"We need Aaron to use his swords. The bladesong helped open the way for Sarik and me," Verona said.

"But not all of you. It took Braden a while, and he will attest that being open to the energy comes at a price. It's not meant for the weak minded. Speaking of which, you've never said whether you've had any problems," Sarah asked.

"I guess I don't have an old soul, because the only voices or urges inside of my head are my own," Verona said.

"That's one way of putting it," Sarah said dryly.

It took Verona a moment to realize that she was joking with him. "And here I almost thought there wasn't an ounce of happiness left in the world. Thank you, my Lady, for proving me wrong."

They dismissed the men, and Verona made some mental notes of whom to include on his own team of men he was building. He set off to find Aaron, hoping that the odd behavior was some sort of misunderstanding and not some nefarious purpose.

13

CATCH OUR BREATHS

General Morag Halcylon surveyed their progress. The Zekara were well on their way to setting up their base of operations. The AI had done its job well selecting this location, which was far enough away that they would know if any of the Safanarions were to come within their vicinity. The traitors living among the humans had no doubt detected the ship's presence, but the combat suite had done its job effectively, and he was quite certain they didn't know exactly where they were. The same also applied to the Zekara. They didn't know where the traitor's nest was that played home to Hythariam who saw fit to break with their own race. They had been gathering intelligence since they arrived, and getting their base of operations up and running was top on his list of priorities, along with running reconnaissance on the inhabitants of this world. He didn't get to his position by being impatient. He would study his enemy, learn the way they did things, and then he would strike. He gave a passing thought to the human they had left behind and knew that he must be dead by now. As a leader of his people, Halcylon couldn't fault the actions of the human's ancestor, but the Hythariam were superior to humans in every way. Something the humans of this world would come to know.

Ronan, his chief science adviser, approached him.

"Is the package away?" Halcylon asked.

"Confirmed; the package has been delivered and has been reporting in, but it won't last long. The process was rushed," Ronan said.

"To be expected; how long do we have?"

"A few weeks before it breaks down completely," said Ronan.

"That's fine. Our timetable won't change. Preliminary reports show various groups are already engaging in combat. That is good for us because it will keep them all occupied, giving us time to prepare."

"What about the other Hythariam here? We detect their comms signals all over the continent," Ronan said.

"The traitors, you mean," Halcylon corrected. He had been drilling into them not to think of the Hythariam here as members of their race, but as traitors.

"Yes, of course," Ronan said.

"They are working on breaking the security in place so we can see the messages. So far they've been unsuccessful," Halcylon said.

"These things take time," Ronan said.

"Indeed, they are the real threat. The primitives here have a rudimentary knowledge of how to make war."

"They're not so primitive," Ronan said.

"They have a few tricks. We're still gathering intelligence, but tricks alone won't save them from the Zekara," Halcylon said.

"The SPT flyers are ready," Ronan said.

"Very good. I want to keep a close eye on our package, and we're still adapting the drones to this world. Plus, I'm reluctant to use them too much. Right now I expect the traitors are scrambling, trying to find out where we are," Halcylon said.

"We're still looking for them as well, but they've had eighty cycles to entrench themselves. The task of finding them may prove more difficult than previously expected," Ronan said.

Halcylon eyed his adviser. "Take a moment and look around, Ronan. We're here and are no longer on a dying planet. Time is again on our side. No longer are we up against the clock. We did it. We're here. Breathe the fresh air. Drink the clean water. This is a living planet and now our home."

Ronan took a moment to look around the camp. The Zekara moved with purpose, but all of them kept looking up at the alien sky above them. Their new home. "You did it. It was you who got us here. Even when those others abandoned our people to take to the stars. You stayed to lead us, and because of that, all of the Zekara will lay down their lives to protect you."

Halcylon nodded to Ronan, and they returned to the task of setting up their new home for their race, and once that was done, they would visit vengeance upon those who believed they were their betters and had doomed them all to a dying world. Before long, these humans would learn to fear the Zekara, and after enough of them died, they would fall on their knees to serve them. Halcylon smiled at the plans he had set in motion so long ago that were only now coming to bear the fruit of his efforts.

14

PERFECT ARMY

Mactar surveyed the forty Ryakuls that he and Darven had brought under their control. Once they controlled the first two Ryakuls, finding more proved easier than they had originally thought. Left on their own, the beasts would hunt for Dragons and in some cases would turn on each other. If they had set off to track Dragons all those weeks ago, finding Ryakuls would have been much easier. Dragons were becoming less common throughout the lands and kept mostly upon the fringes of the realms of men.

"They are the perfect army," Darven said.

"How so?" Mactar asked.

"We can give them any order, and they will carry out those orders or die trying. Once on task, the Ryakuls will never waver from it," Darven replied.

"Unless we deactivate the controller. Then the connection is broken."

"That's right, but we don't have to keep the instructions we give them in the forefront of our minds," Darven said.

"Agreed; they can follow instructions, but I'd be reluctant to just send them off to attack a city on their own. Too many variables. The Ryakuls would throw themselves at an obstacle, but they don't weigh threats very well, which is a shortcoming of them being under control."

Darven shrugged. "Still, I'll take them over an army of conscripts any day."

"Good. I think it's time we gave the High King a demonstration. Now that the Elitesmen have proven that they can move a sizable fighting force with the focusing crystal, the Khamearrian army is going to push deeper into the Waylands, "Mactar said.

"You knew that was going to work?" Darven asked.

"Who do you think gave the idea to Elite Grand Master Gerric?" Mactar smirked.

Darven nodded.

"I am going to have you take half the Ryakuls and meet the armies as they attack," Mactar said.

"I hope the commanders of those armies know to expect me then. I'd hate to have to worry about being shot at by a stray arrow or stabbed by an Elitesman's blade."

"Word has been sent, but the Elitesmen may still take a shot at you just for old times' sake."

Darven shrugged his shoulders impassively. Elitesmen attacks didn't faze him. "What will you be doing while I'm off winning the High King's war for him?"

"I'll continue gathering the Ryakuls. We're going to need them."

"It can't be that long before Amorak sets his sights on Rexel and the heart of their armies there," Darven said.

"That's exactly right, and that is precisely where their defenses will be strongest. We will need more than fifty Ryakuls to take Rexel and break the back of this Free Nations Army," Mactar said.

He marked the locations of the planned attacks on the map that Darven carried. There was no way they could use the travel crystals and bring the Ryakuls with them. It simply wouldn't work even with only one Ryakul, and they hadn't figured out why. The Ryakuls were fast and could make the journey quickly. Darven leaped on top of a Ryakul and signaled to the twenty he would take with him. With a final wave, he took to the skies.

Mactar had taken a short trip back to Khamearra to meet with his network of informants there. He had known his idea with the focusing crystal would work, but wasn't sure Gerric could pull it off. Why do these things himself, when he could have others do it for him? The same applied here, which was why he was sending Darven to attack with the army. His sights were set on much bigger bounty than those of the smaller kingdoms that bordered the Waylands. He would be there to burn Rexel to the ground with a horde of Ryakuls at his back.

The battles, hardly more than skirmishes that the High King's army had fought, served as practice for the real war about to begin. Unlike other wars, there would not be endless marching and razing of town after town. Supply lines would become almost irrelevant, that is, of course, if the focusing crystals used to move the armies around weren't destroyed. So far, this Free Nations Army hadn't answered the threat of the High King, but they had shown up at some of the smaller kingdoms. The results were that castles were better prepared for the attacks, but with the Elitesmen serving as part of the army, the defenses they put together were easily overcome.

Word was spreading of Ryakul attacks on the remote towns, and they had started seeing these towns mount rooftop defenses, but Mactar had no interest in attacking the towns. They were merely a learning tool to be able to take more strategic targets. Sitting on top of a Ryakul while it flew was something Darven put forward as a better way to travel—astride the Ryakuls, rather than using the crystals—and he had to admit that Darven was right. Flying a Ryakul allowed them to send out a signal, summoning more to them. Mactar leaped atop the scaly neck of a Ryakul, and its leathery wings fluttered. With a final command, the remaining Ryakuls took to the sky at the same time and wheeled around heading east. Soon he would meet up with the High King.

15

FIRE FOR FIRE

A dark castle loomed on the horizon, and Colind frowned. Night had descended upon them in the northern reaches of Khamearra.

"That has to be it," Garret said. His salt-and-pepper hair hung past his ears, and although he was into his fifties, he was easily as fit as much younger men.

"It's precisely where Sarah said it would be," Colind said.

He had expected to wander for a while before picking up Mactar's trail, but Garret had the good sense to advise him to ask Sarah, and that he did. She didn't know where Mactar was, of course, but she had been to his castle. The place was little more than a keep with but a single tower.

"It looks...kind of small," Garret said.

"Mactar doesn't hold high regard for pampering," Colind replied.

"Do you really think he's there?"

Colind frowned as he studied the castle. He reached out with his senses, and the castle itself was deserted. "I wish he was there, but the place is empty. I still want to take a look around."

When they had left Shandara weeks before, they had set out to find former members of the Safanarion Order. The task had gone frustratingly slow, because the ones that survived had become adept at hiding themselves. He had been forced to leave messages around that only members of the order would be able to decipher. If any of them got the message, they would know they should make their way to Rexel. He suspected some were already heading to Shandara, and he just needed to be patient.

The town that lived in the shadow of Mactar's castle was quiet, and Colind wondered if they knew whose shadow they lived under. *Probably,* Colind thought. They made it to the castle and through the locks that were in place to keep the local townsfolk out. There were no other safeguards, which Colind found peculiar and said so.

"Perhaps he doesn't expect to come back," Garret said.

Colind shrugged his shoulders and pushed on to the castle. The castle held the normal furnishings, and it wasn't until they came to Mactar's workshop that things radically changed. They opened the double doors, and Colind sent a tendril of energy out to the orbs that slowly grew brighter. The room was packed, which at first appeared haphazard.

"Is this a storage room?" Garret asked.

Colind glanced around trying to make sense of it all. There were broken swords and shields, along with half-burnt items from twisted crowns to silver bowls. Colind swallowed hard, recognizing some of the items.

"This seems familiar; I think I remember this," Garret said, gesturing to a leather-embroidered chair with its gold paint long since chipped away.

"It's from Shandara. It's one of the council seats from Dragon Hall, where the Safanarion Order used to convene," Colind said, glaring at the items in the room, realizing what this room was. "This is a trophy room. These are pieces he's collected from all his victories."

Garret slowly turned around, taking in the grand room, when he noticed a bare spot on the wall. "I wonder what he had there."

Colind looked over and scanned the wall seeing a dark outline. His lips curved into a smile as he made out what must have hung there for the past twenty-five years. "The standard of Shandara. Particularly the standard for the House Alenzar'seth. I imagine that at some point after learning of Aaron's existence he realized his victory over Shandara wasn't as complete as he had first believed."

Garret scanned the room with a furrowed brow. "Everything in this room is associated with death."

"There is a lot of pride in this room. Let's look through it quickly and see if we can figure out what he is doing and hopefully where he went," Colind said.

Knowing that everything in room had either belonged to someone or was associated with a fallen kingdom weighed heavily on them. They spoke in hushed tones as if they were in a graveyard, and Colind supposed they were. They came to an open area, and along the wall was a metal workbench with tools.

Colind lifted up one of the discarded pieces. "This is Hythariam made."

They found other things that looked out of place, like an old comms device that no longer worked.

"How could he have known about Hythariam technology?" Garret asked.

"Because Mactar is Shandarian. He served the Alenzar'seth when the Hythariam first came to Safanar."

"Shandarian? But he would be over a hundred years old," Garret said in disbelief.

"He hasn't aged in almost sixty years. I knew him. He was my mentor for a time," Colind said.

"I never knew," Garret said.

"Not many do, and that's because the people that did know are all dead and gone. Daverim Alenzar'seth helped establish the Safanarion Order, and Mactar was one of the founding members. He was always experimenting. Pushing things beyond their limits. Reymius had discovered some of the horrible things he had been doing. Many of the practices of the Elitesmen Order had their origins with Mactar's work in Shandara."

"What happened to him?" Garret asked.

"Reymius reported what he found to his father, and Daverim had him banished. Never to return to Shandara," Colind said.

"How is it that he hasn't aged?"

"What I suspect happened is he had help. When the Hythariam first came to Safanar, there were different factions, with some loyal to Halcylon despite his plans for the rest of us. He was injected with the Nanites, but without the constraints that are applied to normal Hythariam, which gives them a lifespan greater than two hundred years."

"How long would he live then?" Garret asked.

"Iranus believes a thousand years or more," Colind answered.

Garrett blew out a heavy breath.

"Exactly, but he won't get the chance. Not if I have anything to say about it," Colind said.

"I can't tell from this stuff what he was doing or where he is going," Garret admitted.

Colind picked up a goblet-sized black piece of metal. "This is from the Drake." He turned it over in his hands and placed it on his wrist. "It's some type of control panel like what the Hythariam wear. The question now is what was the Drake controlling?"

Garret frowned in thought, and then his face lit up. "The Ryakuls. The Drake commanded the Ryakuls, and I would wager that is a power worthy of Mactar's attention."

Colind's eyes widened. "Goddess, if he can control the Ryakuls then..."

"We need to warn the others," Garret said, bringing up his comms device.

Colind continued to scan the room while Garret spoke into the comms device. They never had an accurate count of the Ryakuls, but there were enough of them to cover a mountain. Even with the aid of the Hythariam they would be hard pressed to fight the High King's army if there was a host of Ryakuls aiding them.

"Colind, they want us to return."

"No," Colind answered.

"It's Aaron; he is back."

"He'll understand if we don't come back right away."

Garret stepped up to him. "Mactar won't get away, but they need us back there. We might be able to find him quicker with the help of the Hythariam. All we need to do is track the Ryakuls now."

Colind drew his head up, considering, and nodded. "First we burn this place to the ground," Colind said grimly.

They headed to the main doors, and Colind lingered in the entrance. He reached out with the energy, grasping all the lighted orbs at once, and shattered them. Flames spread eagerly, consuming the old relics in the room, and Colind looked on with grim satisfaction, hoping that the original owners of these relics could rest easier. Mactar had been the foremost pillager laying waste to Shandara, and a warmth spread through his body, knowing that he had been able to take something from Mactar at last.

The flames quickly spread, and soon the entire castle was engulfed. Garret urged them to leave, but Colind wasn't finished yet. He drew in the energy from the earth, pushing deep underground, locating the main supports that kept the castle standing. Tiny cracks spidered their way up, and the ground shook beneath their feet. The flaming castle wavered back and forth before falling in on itself. The hiss of the fire kissed the night air, and the ruins of Mactar's castle vanished from the skyline with nothing but a few remnant walls remaining. The townsfolk gathered outside their homes and watched the flames, but none moved to investigate, and there were more than a few who were relieved that the dark menace that had loomed over their quiet town was gone.

Colind engaged the travel crystal, and he and Garret disappeared. They emerged upon the outskirts of the FNA camp. The sun had risen in this part of Safanar, casting its warmth, and the morning dew slowly retreated.

"Why didn't you take us directly to the castle?" Garret asked.

"Sometimes you can learn a great deal by taking the long way," Colind replied and immediately started walking.

Colind silently looked around, taking in his surroundings. They had been gone a few weeks, but they had kept in contact as best they could. Mostly it was Garret, because Colind wasn't particularly fond of the comms devices. They had their uses and were convenient, but he didn't want to use them. Soldiers who recognized him either bowed their head or saluted. The FNA camp had become a city outside the walls of Rexel, with merchants selling their wares in designated areas. No one in the FNA was foolish enough to allow just anyone to go into the camp proper.

A large group was heading toward the center of the camp, and Colind frowned seeing Aaron leading the group. He was surrounded by the newest members of the De'anjard along with members of the nobility from various kingdoms. Something in the way Aaron carried himself bothered Colind. It shouldn't bother him. He had always known that Aaron would lead these people, and with leadership came the clamoring fools who wanted to carry favor. He just didn't expect it so soon and Aaron to appear so comfortable with it.

Aaron spotted them and walked over.

"Welcome back," Aaron said.

"I should say the same to you," Colind answered, studying him. His skin held remnant scars, and his eyes had a harder cast to them than before.

Aaron recounted how he was imprisoned and came to return to Safanar, and Colind quietly listened.

"Where is Sarah?" Garret asked. "I would hardly expect that she would leave your side since you've been back."

A blank look of uncertainty flashed across Aaron's face, and then his eyes narrowed. "I'm afraid that not everyone was overjoyed with my return."

Now that is a colossal understatement, Colind thought. He had helped nurse Sarah back to health while she recovered from the effects of the Nanites. During that time, the thought of Aaron was hardly a breath away from her thoughts.

He glanced at the others that Aaron had surrounded himself with and noted the absence of his closest friends with the exception of Braden's towering form. Imprisonment had a way of changing those subject to its malicious tendencies. Something Colind was intimately aware of, and the first thing he longed for when he was finally free was to see the faces of his closest friends. The need to be around things familiar and also knowing that most of them were dead had seized his heart. Since his failure to recognize the evil in his son, Tarimus, he had promised himself that if he began making excuses for someone or something that was out of balance in his life, that he would take a step back and refuse the excuses their due. Glancing at Aaron, he knew that things were out of balance here, and he was determined to find out what it was. There wouldn't be another repeat of Shandara, not on his watch.

He told Aaron to carry on and that he would walk with them for a while. It was hard to believe that this was the same person he had first encountered on Earth all those months ago. There had been an unwavering kindness in his eyes, and now they seemed to be constantly measuring everyone and everything. They went to the command tent, which was already filled with people for the morning briefing. Gavril stood in the center and was speaking quietly with Verona and Vaughn.

Gavril called the meeting to order, and after a few moments things settled down to a quiet murmur. Behind Gavril, holographic screens came to life. All of them showed different kingdoms as if someone were watching from above.

"Behind me are feeds from our satellites we have orbiting the planet. Most of them are fixed upon the continent," Gavril said, and after a moment the view on the screens changed. "We're monitoring these feeds for the next attack from the Khamearrians. We have command centers like this set up in Hathenwood, a temporary one in Shandara, in addition to one here in Rexel."

"Why a temporary one in Shandara?" Aaron asked.

"There is a better one in Shandara, but it was buried when the city fell. Our engineers are quite close to getting access to it. Once that happens, we'll have greater access to the bulk of our technology that was lost at Shandara," Gavril said.

There were gasps with some pointing to one of the screens. There was a flash of light, and emerging from the morning mist was the High King's army.

"Where is this? Is this happening right now?" Verona asked.

"This is in Lorric, and yes, the feed is in real time," Gavril answered.

The kingdom of Lorric was one of the bordering kingdoms between Khamearra and the Waylands.

"We need to help them," Verona said, his eyes fixed upon the screen, and then he turned to Aaron. "Some of the Resistance fled Khamearra and are taking refuge there."

Many in the room knew that the Resistance was made up of the former De'anjard.

"We will go," Braden said. "As Warden of the De'anjard it is my duty to stand with my brothers and sisters of the shield."

"I'll go as well," Colind said.

"You can go with the ready team we have on standby. I will inform their king that help is on the way," Gavril said.

"We need to find their focusing crystal to keep them from escaping," Verona said and then he frowned. "I think we should divide our numbers into two groups."

"What do you have in mind?" Gavril asked.

"We need to help the people of Lorric with their defenses, but that doesn't mean we all need to be behind the wall," Verona said, stepping up to the screen and pointing to the outer area of the city beyond the wall. "We should take a smaller force here that can move quickly and take out the focusing crystal."

"First we need to find it, but I agree. We'll use the team you've been putting together as well as some of my own people," Gavril said.

"Having the airships would help, but they can't get there in time," Verona said.

"And they won't fit through the portals. Remember the Keystone Accelerators only have two charges, and one of the charges will be used to get us there. We leave within the hour," Gavril said.

"Won't they need you here coordinating the troop movements?" Colind asked.

"Not today," Gavril answered. "Iranus will take this one."

"I'll go with you," Aaron said to Verona.

"Never doubted it for a second," Verona said.

A short while later, beyond the walls of Rexel, there was an open plain where the troops of the Free Nations Army gathered. Colind advised breaking them up into three groups instead of two. One group to assist in the defense. Another group placed behind the High King's army to strike from behind, and Verona's special squad in the outskirts of the city. They were going to use six of the Keystone Accelerators, leaving four in reserve here in Rexel.

Colind stood near Verona at the head of his group of fifty men. Aaron and Braden joined them. A few moments later, Sarah came. Other than the barest of glances between her and Aaron, they didn't speak. Garret stood by his side, and next to him was Gavril.

A younger Hythariam approached Gavril.

"Sir, Iranus wants me to return to Hathenwood," Tanneth said.

"Did he give a reason?"

Tanneth shook his head. "He didn't say, and the message came through comms."

Gavril pursed his lips in thought and then nodded.

Tanneth saluted Gavril and took off at a run.

The Keystone Accelerator that would open a portal big enough for them to go through was as long as a man's arm and twice as wide. Legs extended from the base. Gavril tapped a few buttons upon his comms device, and the accelerator lit up. In moments, an opaque circle of light appeared before them that was about ten feet tall and twenty feet wide. Colind squinted his eyes, trying to peer through it, but it was just a swirling mass with a small vibration brushing against its skin.

Farther away from them other portals opened, and Gavril gave the command for them to go through. The soldiers of the FNA immediately rushed through, eager to face the Khamearrian army. They were well armed with swords, bows, and spears. A select few carried the plasma pistols of the Hythariam on them, but there weren't enough to arm every FNA soldier with one.

As the last of the soldiers went through, the portals started winking out one by one. With most of the troops having gone through, no one saw the hunched man lumbering onto the field before the remaining open portal. He zigzagged like a crab, as if he couldn't make his legs work right. As the portal diminished in size, he stumbled through just as it closed.

16

THE RETURN

Sarah came through the portal and immediately moved away, scanning for signs of life on the deserted streets. Sounds of fighting could be heard in the distance. Lorric wasn't the biggest city when compared with Shandara, but it was still sizable, covering six square miles. The buildings lining the streets didn't have more than two or three levels, and the streets themselves were wide open. She and Verona took half the men and gathered on one side of the street, while Aaron and Braden took the other half. Orders were given to scout ahead. She looked over at Aaron, and he nodded slowly and smiled. A faint stirring squeezed her chest. More than anything she wanted to believe that by some cruel twist of fate Aaron was still in there somewhere and the stranger before her would just fade away. She longed to fall headlong into the dream that it was him. To feel his powerful arms around her and the press of his lips on hers. She found herself daring to believe, to go against what her heart was telling her, and give in.

The press of the travel crystal nudged against her leg. She had debated on bringing the rune-carved staff, because she knew that it was somehow connected to Aaron. She had taken it for safekeeping and had kept Aaron's medallion, which she still wore nestled on her chest.

"I'm with you, my Lady," Verona said.

Sarah glanced at him and nodded. Gavril had taken the Hythariam and scouted ahead. They caught up and found him frowning at his comms device.

"Is there a problem?" Sarah asked.

"We're getting some strange readings outside the city. I'm not sure what to make of it, but it's being reported by all three groups," Gavril said.

"Have they located the focusing crystals?"

"There is a cluster of troops hanging back from the main force attacking the city. We think it's there, but we'll have to wait for them to commit to their attack before we make our move," Gavril said.

Battle drums of the Khamearrian army thundered through the air. Sarah drew in the energy and leaped to the rooftop to get a better look. The others climbed up while the bulk of their force stayed upon the ground below. William of Lorric ruled this city and divided his troops with half upon the walls, while sending out the other half to harry the Khamearrian army as it came through the sea of buildings beyond the wall. Sudden flashes of light from Elitesmen attack orbs took out the archers on the rooftops. A group of thirty FNA soldiers zoomed away from the walls upon their gliders. Golden bolts of energy returned fire, causing the line of soldiers to pause. Dark streaks of Elitesmen giving chase could be seen from the rooftops, but still the Khamearrian army pushed forward. Flashes of violet appeared on the walls as the Elitesmen used their travel crystals to wreak havoc upon the defenders.

Verona touched her arm and gestured toward the men being held in reserve. That's where the focusing crystal was believed to be held. Colind joined them on the roof and watched the reserve forces of men intently, his eyes scanning. Sarah could sense the energy gathered in him in waves.

"I have it," Colind said. "There is a line of wagons each marked with a designation. The focusing crystal is in one of those."

"How do you know?" Verona asked.

"I could sense the remnants of a large burst of energy. It's the only one in the line, and it would take a lot of energy to move an army of this size," Colind said.

Shouts came from the streets below. A contingent of Khamearrian soldiers had broken off and stumbled upon them. The FNA soldiers charged. Sarah drew her sword and joined them. She caught a glimpse of Aaron sprinting ahead with his swords drawn. There were no Elitesmen with them, but more than a few stopped fighting when they recognized her, bringing both sides to a halt.

"Your Grace," one soldier said. "We're supposed to bring you back with us if we were to find you."

Aaron stepped forward and held his sword to the man's throat.

"No!" Sarah said to him and addressed the soldier. "If you be true Khamearrian sons you will give up this fight."

"I have my orders, your Grace," the soldier replied.

"We can't let them live," Aaron said not taking his eyes from them.

"We can't let them fight or report back to their commanders, but we don't need to kill them," Sarah said and gently lifted Aaron's sword away from the soldier's throat.

"Bind them," Sarah ordered, and an FNA soldier complied.

After the men were bound and locked in a building, they moved on.

"That was a mistake," Aaron said.

"One of many I'm sure to make, but it was the right decision. Something you used to know," Sarah said.

Aaron was about to reply when a screeching cry echoed through the sky above them and was answered by a chorus of others.

"Ryakuls!" Verona hissed.

A great shadow plunged them into momentary darkness as a Ryakul passed overhead and blocked out the sun.

They charged forward and rounded the last corner that would give them a view of the main battle.

"Goddess be merciful," Verona whispered.

The sky was filled with Ryakuls swooping in and killing the Lorric and FNA defenders in droves. The Lorric soldiers were scattering, with groups retreating at an all-out run back to the city walls. The Ryakuls left the Khamearrian line of soldiers untouched.

The FNA ran forward to engage the enemy troops and give the Lorric soldiers a chance to regroup. Sarah darted ahead, dispatching soldiers as she went. Sounds of snarling Ryakuls and men screaming their death cries were all she could hear. The skies were full of them, and they pounced upon any attempt at a regroup.

Aaron stood with a few FNA soldiers around him and watched the Ryakuls, his head cocked to the side as if he had never seen them before.

"Call the Eldarin!" Verona screamed.

Aaron turned to him and looked as if he hadn't heard.

"Call the Eldarin; without them we won't survive," Verona said.

Sarah plunged her hand into her pocket and engaged the travel crystal.

Aaron's eyes narrowed. "She leaves us. She knows we're doomed. Run. Run for your lives!"

The FNA soldiers around them stood with their mouths agape, looking confused. Moments later, Sarah reappeared with the rune-carved staff in her hands and thrust it out to him.

"Call the Eldarin," she said.

Aaron withdrew his hands as if she held a coiled viper.

"If you don't we'll all die," Sarah cried.

"You're already dead," the man pretending to be Aaron sneered, and sprinted toward the walls, yelling for everyone to flee.

Amid the chaotic battle raging outside the walls of Lorric, a lone figure charged forward. He stumbled, regained his footing, and continued forward. His body was a mass of a poorly put together man, but still he lumbered forward amid the retreating soldiers.

"...IGHT!" the crippled man sputtered, his legs carrying him in a half trot. "Fiiiiight!"

The words spewed forth from his malformed mouth, but caught the attention of those around him.

Sarah watched as the crippled man known as Len lumbered forward through a wave of retreating soldiers. Some paused, uncertain of what they were seeing, while others turned to join him.

"Verona..." Sarah gasped, the medallion growing warm against her chest and the crystal's glow showing through her armored shirt.

The Ryakuls screeched in unison and turned sharply in the air. Sarah's breath came in gasps as the Ryakuls closed in on them. She turned back to Len who was still more than a hundred yards from where they stood. He was down on all fours rocking back and forth, his head twisting in anguish. A slight shimmer came from under his tattered shirt.

"Verona..." Sarah called again, and he and Gavril came to her side. FNA soldiers beat back the Khamearrians who attacked.

Sarah turned to them, not believing what she was about to say, but her heart surged with the knowledge. "I think...*that* is Aaron."

Verona's eyes widened as he followed her line of sight to the crippled man. "It can't be—"

Sarah blocked them out and drew in the energy, lunging forward, closing in on Len as he kneeled upon the ground. Soldiers from both armies fought all around him. His eyes met hers, and he cried out, scrambling away.

"No!" Sarah shouted and withdrew the medallion from her shirt. The crystal in the center oozed out a soft glow. Len's eyes widened in fear, his face a mask of struggle.

It has to be you, my love. Sarah quickly reached out and placed the medallion over his head. Len cried out in a deep guttural scream. His misshapen limbs flailed about, jerking wildly, and Sarah stepped back. The rune-carved staff flared to life in her hands as a beam of light surged forth from the medallion. The energy from the staff knocked Sarah and the surrounding soldiers back dozens of feet. A beacon of light shot forth, blazing into the sky. Verona and Braden came to her side and helped her regain her feet.

Elitesmen appeared all around them in a flash, and the High King's soldiers pushed forward. She and Verona drew their swords, and Braden swung his Warden's Hammer. They kept their backs to Aaron as they fought to protect him. *They can't have you,* she thought.

The Ryakuls closed in, swooping down and landing around them, lunging with their saber-tusked maws. Thunder cracked amid a cloudless sky, and a flash of green and white washed over the battlefield. Ryakuls turned away scattering.

The ground rumbled beneath their feet as two massive Dragons landed on either side of the beacon of light. Their growls rolled through the air. The Eldarin attacked, scattering the remaining Ryakuls from the sky, and the Elitesmen pushed forward. Sarah engaged the Elitesmen, fighting with everything she had. Verona guarded her back. Braden smashed his golden war hammer against his shield, and the enemy closing in around them was driven back. Their bodies flung like rag dolls through the air.

One of the Eldarin crouched by Aaron and turned its full attention on him. A sphere of light surrounded Aaron. Sarah focused on guarding Braden, while the power of the Warden's shield blew back the Elitesmen and soldiers alike.

A HUDDLED MASS COILED WITHIN A GLOWING SPHERE, OBLIVIOUS TO THE battle raging around him. He had a purpose once, an identity, but it was gone. A massive shadow loomed over him, and he shrank back.

Yours is a light meant to shine, Shandarian. The Eldarin will always heed the call of those marked by Ferasdiam.

The deep voice that sounded like two granite slabs rubbing together penetrated the fog around him. In the recesses of his mind, an answering call came as a wave of warmth spread through his limbs.

Shandarian... The words twisted and whispered in his mind. *Shandara...* It was important. Synonymous with the name, images flashed in his mind of pristine white walls and a Dragon cradling a single rose.

Len...Alen... a voice whispered inside him. *Alenzar'seth!* Like a beacon stemming from his soul, the floodgates burst open. He was Aaron Jace, the last surviving member of the House Alenzar'seth. He felt the chains that bound his mind shatter, and he opened his eyes, seeing the battle being fought around him. He couldn't move and felt his body being lifted into the air. An Eldarin Dragon focused on him, and thick tendrils of energy locked around him.

The land needs a champion...

The bones in Aaron's body snapped and reformed so fast that the pain of it was gone before it became an impression in his mind. His misshapen legs and arms returned to normal, and a mass of red particles spewed out his mouth, dissipating in the air. Aaron felt his arms lift from his sides and his body rise farther into the air. The Dragon tattoo upon his chest flared, and he felt his heart begin to beat, his mind growing clearer.

Two golden bolts of energy came from the sky and slammed into him, knocking him to the ground. The Eldarin roared, spreading its massive wings, and engulfed him protectively.

"They're firing on him!" Verona shouted.

Gavril's eyes widened as he glanced at the display on his comms device and back up at the sky. "That's not one of ours."

"If it's not ours who the hell could it be?" Verona said.

Plasma bolts continued to rain down upon the Eldarin that held Aaron cradled in its wings.

Gavril's fingers flew across his comms device, and his eyes lit up. "Tanneth, we have a mark sector three from my position."

A golden Hythariam flyer sped into view and returned fire. Sparks flew from two smaller craft as their cloaks lifted and crashed into the ground followed by a small explosion.

"It's the Zekara," Gavril said.

The Ryakuls regrouped and circled around. There were two Eldarin, with one protecting Aaron while the other wheeled around fighting off the Ryakuls in a mass of tooth and claw.

The Eldarin upon the ground drew back, and a man stood. The ground smoked beneath his bare feet. He held the rune-carved staff in his hands, and a white glow surrounded his body.

"Aaron..." whispered Verona. "By the Goddess, Sarah was right."

Aaron drew in the energy around him, feeding off the staff, and took to the sky. He leaped to the nearest Ryakul, swinging the rune-carved staff, sending bolts of energy into each strike, and blowing out parts of the Ryakul's body in a grisly mess.

You are Ferasdiam marked. We heed your call, Safanarion.

The Eldarin's words echoed in his mind as he fought. He danced through the sky, streaking from Ryakul to Ryakul. One of the Eldarin took to the sky and followed him, while the other remained still upon the ground. The energy flowed through Aaron as it hadn't since he had first taken the Nanites into his system. He stood upon the back of a dying Ryakul as it plunged toward the ground. The remaining Ryakuls fled over the backs of the retreating Khamearrian soldiers. Aaron's gaze focused on a single Ryakul with a figure upon its back. His first thought was that of the Drake, but the Drake was gone. Someone else was controlling the Ryakuls.

His mind was as clear as it had not been for so long that it felt as if it was working in overdrive. He turned to the lone Eldarin that flew above him.

We have cleansed your body of the taint.

"Thank you," Aaron said.

He heard a strange growl and saw the other Eldarin struggling to rise. Aaron raced back and winced at the scorched gashes upon its golden hide. The Dragon lord struggled to rise and turned toward him. One of its eyes was missing, and darkness swirled in the other like a storm cloud.

Aaron felt his heart fill his chest at the sight. He reached out, but the Eldarin snarled at him. The other Eldarin landed behind him and growled warily. Aaron leaped back and saw two Ryakul corpses that lay behind the Eldarin. His eyes darted to the wounds and felt the bile rise in his throat.

Please no, Aaron thought and turned to the other Ryakul. "It's the sickness. The same thing that turns the Dragons into Ryakuls."

The snarling Eldarin's hide faded to gray.

"Go!" Aaron shouted to the Eldarin behind him. "Or you'll be infected too. Go!" he screamed.

The Eldarin behind him drew back its head and sent a blast of energy into the Eldarin while releasing a mournful howl at the same time. The sickened Eldarin fell back as the other took to the sky. The infected Eldarin regained its footing and followed. The two streaked away and disappeared in a green flash.

Aaron released the energy and felt his strength leave him. The staff kept him upright. He heard soft footsteps behind him and spun around. Sarah stood before him. Their eyes searched each other's as if they were afraid that the other would fade away.

"I didn't...I didn't know it was you," Sarah said.

His heart filled his chest, and before he knew anything, they held each other. Aaron swung her around in his arms, crying out, losing himself in the blue of her eyes and the feel of her in his arms. They didn't say anything, their eyes speaking the volumes that their mouths couldn't say as they held each other.

The soldiers of the High King's army retreated, no longer having the element of surprise. While the Ryakuls had been an advantage to them, the battle with the Eldarin had shaken their spirit. The Free Nations Army along with the Lorric forces pushed forward until the High King's army disappeared in a blinding flash of light. The soldiers remaining on the field cheered, but those who knew the High King knew that this victory wouldn't go unanswered.

17

WARNING

Rordan was with General Khoiron in the command tent when one of Khamearra's armies returned ahead of schedule. As the reports came in, the more the old general's furrowed brows deepened. He fingered the apprentice amulet he had worn since he had found it. If truth be told, Mactar had left it for him. Since he started wearing it, he had been able to feel more of the energy around him. He hardly noticed the muddled whisperings of souls past that spewed sultry promises of glory and power.

At first he refused to wear it, convincing himself that he didn't need it, but as time went on he found that there were advantages to wearing the amulet in spite of the cost. He could stop the beating hearts of those around him if he focused on it. His experiments on a few random people brought Mactar's attention, as if he had been expecting it all along. He'd been tempted to use his newfound ability on his sister, but decided it would be much more entertaining to watch her struggle against their father.

Rordan looked up and found Khoiron eyeing him. He always felt as if the old general was taking his measure, but his craggy old face gave away nothing in return. The High King had just joined them, having been away on one of the planned assaults. His father had said to him earlier that there were some things best observed with one's own eyes. Rordan knew that despite what his father had said, he had other reasons to go. One thing he had learned about his father was that he had an unquenchable thirst for blood, and it was only a matter of time before he would lead more attacks.

"Bottom line, they were prepared for our attack," Khoiron said.

"How prepared could they have been?" the High King asked.

"They had additional support from the Free Nations Army," Khoiron replied.

"Free Nations Army," the High King sneered.

"Like it or not, your Grace. They are a force to be reckoned with and represent our real enemies in this. Lorric was slated to be an easy victory, and the troops sent in for the attack should have been more than adequate for the job. In fact, with the additional support from Darven and his Ryakuls this attack should have been downright easy," Khoiron said.

The High King eyed the old general for a moment. "As usual, your counsel is as sound as your logic. So tell me how we were defeated and where is Darven."

"Before we delve into the particulars of the battle, there is another thing that warrants your attention," Khoiron said and gestured to the guards.

The guards left the tent, and four Elitesmen returned with a hooded prisoner. The prisoner was broad shouldered and taller than most men in the room. He wore the uniform of the FNA that was almost in tatters, but Rordan could see something painted on his chest. An Elitesman kicked the man behind the knees, driving them to the ground and removed his hood.

The High King's eyes flashed as he studied the prisoner before him. "What's this supposed to be?"

"Do you not recognize the face of your enemy, Father?" Rordan asked. "This is Aaron, the Heir of Shandara."

The High King glanced around the room. "No, it's not."

Rordan glanced at Khoiron. "It is him, Father. I recognize his face."

"As do I, Son, but this is not him. I would know it," the High King said and stepped up to the prisoner, grabbing his face. "The likeness is remarkable. I can see why you would be fooled."

"An impostor," Rordan said.

"He had these on him when we captured him," an Elitesman said and handed the High King two swords.

"Now these I recognize. They are not fake. They are known as the Falcons and have been in the Alenzar'seth family for generations," the High King said and drew one of the blades from its sheath. There was a crystal inlaid into the pommel, and the craftsmanship of the blades with the notches was beyond compare. "There are legends about these swords. In the hands of the right master, the bladesong unleashed could sway the hearts of men." The High King returned the blade to its sheath. "Why don't you tell us who you are?"

The impostor met the High King's gaze. "I am Aaron Jace."

The High King roared, grabbing the impostor by the throat and lifting him off the ground with one arm. "If you really were Aaron Jace, I wouldn't be able to do this to you," the High King said and slammed the impostor back onto the ground.

Rordan watched as his father stepped away. He could sense the energy gathered around his father with such intensity that he had only felt it once before by another man. His father was right, the man before them could never be the true Heir of Shandara.

The High King raised his hand, and the impostor was lifted by forces unseen. The tips of his feet dragged along the floor, but despite the blow that would have killed an ordinary man the impostor appeared to have been untouched. There was a shift in the man's eyes as his narrowed gaze found that of the High King.

"You believe you are powerful. Your people's days are numbered, human. You're already dead, and you don't even know it."

The High King drew his sword, and in the blink of an eye, a deep red slice opened up the impostor from navel to shoulder. The impostor laughed, and Rordan's eyes widened as the skin stitched itself back up again. The High King spun, and the impostor's head left his shoulders, dropping to the ground. The High King thrust out his other hand, sending a blazing orb, and the body of the impostor was reduced to ash in seconds.

"Now we can't question him," Rordan said.

"He wasn't going to tell us anything. He was a spy, judging by the fact that he had these," the High King said gesturing toward the Falcons, "he had some measure of success over our enemies."

Darven entered the tent, and the Elitesmen all but hissed at the man. Darven ignored them and glanced at the blood-stained ground with remnant ashes that swirled around his feet. He saluted the High King, who nodded back and asked him for his report.

"The Ryakuls have been proven effective in the battle, your Grace. We had Lorric on the run. They were scattered, even with the help of the Free Nations Army. Mactar continues to gather more as we speak," Darven said.

General Khoiron frowned. "My reports say you lost control of some of them."

"Yes, that is true," Darven said.

"I hope you can explain why."

"The FNA were able to summon two of the biggest Dragons I've ever seen. It was all I could do to retain control of the ones in my immediate vicinity," Darven said.

"Dragons? Like the ones that came to the arena, the Eldarin?" Rordan asked.

"The very same. As soon as they appeared, the Ryakuls seemed to give in to some primal instinct. We've observed similar behavior while hunting Ryakuls, but it wasn't until today that I learned that the connection between Ryakul and Dragons is much deeper," Darven said and then he described what he saw with the Eldarin before he had been chased off.

"You saw the change actually occur?" the High King asked.

"The beginning stages of it, yes," Darven replied.

"This would explain why we've seen fewer Dragons over the years," the High King said.

"Your Grace," Khoiron said, "we shouldn't overlook the fact that Lorric was prepared for our attack and the Free Nations Army was able to aid them awfully quick. There are only two explanations for this. Either they were already camped in Lorric since we scouted out the kingdom previously, which seems unlikely, or they too have a way to move armies instantaneously. This changes things."

"You are correct, things have changed. We've proven our point by attacking the smaller kingdoms, but now we need to be more aggressive. We need to take the heart of the Free Nations Army at their source. We break that army, and the rest of the kingdoms will fall into line," the High King said.

"A bold plan. We outnumber them, but if we take the fight to them then our greater numbers will be cancelled out because they are well fortified," Khoiron said.

The High King's lips lifted into a wolfish smile. "I find misdirection to be an effective tool in battle. We have the advantage of numbers, Elitesmen, and Ryakuls."

"I know what I'm about to say you've already considered, but I'll say it anyway," Khoiron said. "To commit ourselves to this will require the use of all of our troops and resources."

"Agreed, we have a lot of work to do," the High King said.

They spent the rest of the day coordinating how the attack was going to happen, and at some point it occurred to Rordan that this is what his father had been angling toward for some time. He studied each of the men, from the army generals to the Elite Masters. Each came with their own shroud of darkness and death upon them with the exception of general Khoiron. To him this was a game pure and simple. Though they hadn't discussed it openly, it was implied that the true Heir of Shandara was in Lorric and had turned the tide of the battle there. Rordan knew that his father relished the challenge that Aaron posed. Rordan just thought it would be convenient for him if they both killed each other off and he could be done with it. There were some in the room that didn't favor the High King's plan, but they knew better than to press the issue. One of the conveniences of absolute obedience. Loyalty and fear kept these men in line, and his father was a master at determining which would serve him best.

"I would speak with my son now. We'll reconvene tomorrow afternoon," the High King said.

The men left the tent, but his father didn't say anything.

"How long have you had this planned?" Rordan asked.

"Since the first attack on the city."

"Why not attack them then?"

"People like Mactar are full of great ideas, but without actually having our troops go through the attacks over the last few weeks, they would lack the experience needed to assure victory over our enemies. They have a few victories under their belts and have hardened a bit. Now they're ready for a real battle."

Rordan frowned. "Mactar? I thought it was Gerric who came up with using the focusing crystal to move the army from place to place?"

"Gerric has many talents, but coming up with innovative ways to use the tools we have at our disposal is not one of them."

Rordan shook his head. "I'll never understand the alliance you have with Mactar."

"You need to understand if you're to succeed me as king one day, Son. Mactar lusts for power and freedom. He doesn't wish to rule, and he would fall short if he ever challenged me. I give him the means to carry out things he would probably do anyway, but I get the benefits of his innovation."

"Was it innovation that led Tye to an early grave?" Rordan asked.

"Your brother was ever trying to keep up with you and Primus. Should I blame you for Tye's shortcomings?"

"Of course not, but what Mactar did wasn't right," Rordan said.

His father leveled his gaze at him. "Do you honestly believe that Mactar did anything without my knowing about it first?"

Rordan searched his father's face and almost cursed himself for not seeing it sooner.

"You want to know why?" his father asked. "I had three sons, and only one of you was going to inherit this crown. I had always suspected you would outlast the others. Primus was too impulsive, and Tye was the same though with a bit more jealousy. Mactar had come to me saying that he may have found where Reymius had been hiding all these long years. That Reymius had an heir. Some of the things Mactar says I take with a grain of salt, and that was one of them."

"But you risked Tye on one of Mactar's whims," Rordan said.

"Your brother would have found another way to test himself. I didn't actually believe that Reymius survived the fall of Shandara or got his daughter, Carlowen, out of there. So yes, I allowed Tye his quest. I sent Darven with him. If he had survived, he would have been stronger for it. Good for him and good for me."

"A former Elitesman should have been able to keep him alive," Rordan said.

"Yes, he should have been able to under normal circumstances. But you ought to know by now that dealing with the Alenzar'seth is anything but ordinary. I crushed their kingdom and laid waste to their precious Shandara, but still they survive. This next battle will see their end along with the rest who align themselves with that kingdom."

Rordan was silent for a moment. "What do you think of what the impostor said?"

"I'd like to hear your thoughts on it first."

Rordan frowned, taking a second to collect his thoughts. "The way he called us *humans*, like he utterly detested what we are. Sarah believes there is another race about to invade our world. At first I didn't believe her, but with the impostor, I'm wondering if she was right."

"The Hythariam are a race apart from us. Regardless, until this race shows itself we shouldn't trouble ourselves with it. They will die just as easily as anyone else. After we deal with the Free Nations Army we'll investigate it, but don't let it distract you in the short term."

Rordan said he wouldn't, but the impostor's last words hissed in the back of his mind. *Your people's days are numbered, human.* It didn't even matter to the creature that it was about to die. The creature died believing that they were already dead. There was something in the certainty of it that bothered Rordan, but he wouldn't raise it again to his father. Not until after the attack.

18

A PRICE TO PAY

Aaron breathed in the fresh scents of the forest around him. The smooth call of a lakeside bird skimmed away from them. He and Sarah were the only ones here. Being here with Sarah in his arms, he could almost forget being locked away in a hollowed out mountain, prisoner to the Zekara. The last-ditch effort for a race of beings' attempt at survival. Sarah stole him away shortly after the battle was over, telling Verona, who happened to be closest to them, that she would have him back in Rexel by morning. They had disappeared before anyone could say anything, including Aaron.

"I'll happily be your prisoner as long as you wish," Aaron said.

"They've survived this long without you. A few more hours won't make that much difference," Sarah said, snuggling into his side.

They lay there near the lapping water on a bed of their clothes. They had already been there for hours, and the sun was beginning to rise.

"I still don't know where we are," Aaron said.

"Does it really matter?" Sarah asked, propping up on her elbow. Her long blonde hair caressed her bare shoulder.

Aaron swallowed in the sight of her. "Not really."

Sarah's full lips lifted into a smile halfway between suggestion and invitation. When they had first arrived, hours before, they didn't speak. They didn't need to. They stripped off their clothes and swam in the calm waters of some unnamed lake, washing the battle from them. Hours went by, and it seemed that they had only just embraced as they lay together upon the lakeshore.

Aaron was still piecing together what had happened to him. His memories were a string of disjointed images that he kept trying to put together. Sarah hadn't asked him anything, and he knew it wasn't because she didn't want to know. They had somehow silently agreed to block out all that had happened in order to steal away this precious time to be together as lovers.

After a time he felt more like himself. The Eldarin had somehow rid his body of the Nanites, allowing them to repair the damage to his body that Halcylon had done, but it was his short time here with Sarah that began to heal his soul. He drew in the energy around them, and Sarah did the same. Their golden radiance merged together, and the connection that had gone dormant since his journey to Hytharia blossomed in his chest. Sarah's eyes widened, and Aaron smiled.

The sun had fully risen when they finally dressed themselves. Aaron had only the pants that he had washed in the lake earlier. The medallion lay on his chiseled chest, reflecting the sunlight. He held the rune-carved staff, waiting for Sarah to dress, all the while suppressing his urge to remove her clothing again.

"If you keep looking at me like that, we may never leave," Sarah said playfully.

Aaron glanced away. "That wouldn't be so bad."

"Not at all. The others, I'm sure, are eager to see you."

Aaron turned back to her and pulled her to him. "They can wait."

The comms device chimed, and after a few moments Sarah brought it up.

"You may not know where we are, but it appears that our friends do. It's time for us to return," Sarah said.

Aaron grabbed her hand before she could retrieve the travel crystal. "If it were just me, I would never leave here."

Sarah's hand brushed down past his face, coming to rest on his shoulder. "Neither would I," she said softly.

"Thank you for saving me."

"I had to keep things even," she replied and brought out the travel crystal.

Sarah took them to the Free Nations Army camp outside the walls of Rexel. Aaron sucked in a quick breath, his eyes darting around at the massive camp that was in the midst of transforming into an extension of the city. Dark banners with the Alenzar'seth coat of arms swayed in the breeze. Men and women wearing similar green uniforms traveled in groups.

They found suitable replacements for his clothing and Hythariam-made boots that molded themselves to his feet. When he stood back up, he really appreciated how comfortable they were. The acrid smell of the Hythariam tech nearby snapped him back to the Zekara's base, where he was chained to a column. The tent walls closed in around him, and he took several deep breaths to steady himself. Outside the supply tent, Roselyn and Verona waited with Sarah, both looking relieved to see him. He pulled Roselyn into a quick embrace, and Verona laughed.

"The only reason I am here is because of the Keystone Accelerator you modified for me," Aaron said and told them of the creature that had helped him. "The portal was only opened for seconds, but Thraw pulled me through it."

"I wish I could meet this creature and thank him," Verona said.

"I'm glad it worked," Roselyn said. "I would like to examine you though, just to make sure..."

Aaron nodded. "I feel fine, but I would feel better if you did."

Roselyn's eyes widened and a smile lit up her face. She turned to the others.

"How could we have ever thought that other creature could have possibly been him?"

Aaron clamped his mouth shut. Sarah had told him what had happened. Halcylon had cloned him somehow and sent it here. Some of the soldiers that passed by glanced at him strangely.

Verona leaned in. "Give it some time. After all, the other you told them to retreat and that all hope was lost."

Aaron nodded. "Have they been able to find it?"

He had been anxious to meet this creature since Sarah had first told him about it.

"There has been no sign of him since the battle," Verona said.

"I shouldn't have given them to him," Sarah said.

"Given what?" Roselyn asked.

"Aaron's swords."

"We'll get them back somehow," Aaron said.

Verona frowned in thought and looked at Roselyn. "What puzzles me is how you knew there was, in fact, an impostor?"

"It was in his blood," Roselyn said. "We had samples of Aaron's original blood when he was infected with the Ryakul poison. I compared them. They matched up almost perfectly with one exception. Age. The clone was only a month old, and his cells were deteriorating fast."

"A month old," Verona gasped. "Your people can create a full grown person in a month?"

"Apparently. We'll need to ask Gavril and my father. With the advent of the Nanites, the need for cloning anything was gone," Roselyn said and looked at Aaron, her eyes downcast. "I scanned you while you were getting dressed."

Aaron was more startled than anything else at the admission and glanced at the others.

"The impostor wouldn't let her examine him," Sarah said.

"Oh. It's all right," Aaron said.

"There is no trace of the Nanites having ever been in your system. What is quite strange is that there are no impurities at all in your system now. It's as if your body was completely remade," Roselyn said.

Aaron frowned. "Well, it's a good thing the Nanites aren't there anymore, but you look concerned about the remade part."

"As we grow older our bodies show signs of aging, but we can also tell a lot about an environment that a person has been exposed to. Toxins in the air. You come from a technically advanced society not all that different from Hytharia so you've been exposed to some of that, which shows up. Only now all that is gone. It's still you at your current age, but it's as if the slate has been wiped completely clean," Roselyn said.

Aaron pursed his lips in thought. "The Eldarin healed me, and perhaps they took care of... well, everything. I'm not sure, but I've never felt better."

"We'll keep an eye on you to see that you stay that way," Sarah said.

"You were completely unrecognizable, my friend," Verona said. "It is a strange thing that there are those who have the power to inflict such change. Now that I think back to Len's...your behavior, it was as if there were parts of you that continued to shine through."

Aaron held almost no memory of his time as Len. After coming through the portal, his memory blanked out, but he did recall Thraw telling him that he didn't look right, and it would be a mercy to kill him. He wondered where the creature was now. Sarah had told him of a man named Wes who looked after him, and Aaron made a mental note to find the man and thank him.

Braden joined them, saying that they were waiting for them at the palace. Aaron caught Braden studying him out of the corner of his eye as they made their way through the FNA camp to a smaller airship field. Braden quickly looked away. He had the rod that fanned out into a shield hanging on his belt and a war hammer of blackened steel with gold runes carved on the side.

"If you're going to be the Warden of the De'anjard, you can't be at my side all the time anymore," Aaron said.

"We'll see about that," Braden grunted.

They came to an airfield with smaller ships that were designed to carry groups of people.

"I take it we're not walking to the palace then?" Aaron asked.

"It would take some of us longer to get there. Besides these give us a nice view of the city if we're required to go all the way to the palace anyway," Verona said.

"What are they?" Aaron asked.

"They're prototypes," Roselyn answered. "We don't have the means to build more flyers yet, but we could improve upon the design of the airships already in use. Before Prince Cyrus and the other rulers would agree to put up the resources, they required proof that it would work."

"That's my uncle. He's quite reluctant to raid the treasury unless it's absolutely necessary," Verona grinned.

Roselyn nodded. "So we built working models that could be used to help ferry people around."

The airship in front of them was only twenty-five feet in length and sported two smaller engines on the wings as well as an engine over the cell floating above the ship itself. Jopher opened the gate and invited them on board. Aaron shook hands with him and noticed the quick glance that Jopher had with the others.

They're still checking to see if it's me, Aaron thought.

Joining them onboard were two Hythariam in black uniforms. Each armed with a plasma pistol and a helmet that covered their face.

Aaron nodded to himself, both relieved that they were taking these steps yet at the same time it bothered him that they felt they needed to.

The airship lurched upward, and Jopher engaged the engines. The small airship was quite agile, and Aaron grabbed onto the railing. Sarik leaped up from the ground as the airship ascended, and Aaron helped pull him over the railing.

"Have you decided whether it's really me or not yet?" Aaron asked.

Sarah glanced at the others in surprise, but the rest of them cast their eyes downward with the exception of the two Hythariam soldiers. The soldiers glanced at each other, and their helmets folded away, becoming part of their armor. Tanneth's lips curved into a half smile.

"We couldn't afford to take any chances," Gavril said.

Sarah glared at them for a moment before laughing. "If you could see the look on your faces when he asked you if you thought it was him..."

Aaron smiled, and after a moment the rest of them joined in.

"We, being the ones who knew you best, decided to take it upon ourselves to give a final check to see whether we all agreed that you were who you said you were," Verona said. "Sarah had no knowledge."

"It was actually a good idea," Aaron said. It did feel good to be among his friends again.

The small airship got them to the palace in no time. Jopher secured the ship outside one of the taller towers nearest the main hall.

Verona darted ahead, "Better let me go in first, otherwise the welcome might not be so...welcoming."

The tension that drained out of them all on the airship seemed to creep back in. The main hall was filled with people from different places around Safanar. Jopher went to stand with his father, who narrowed his gaze when he looked at Aaron.

Colind came to his side. "When we're done here, you and I need to speak."

Aaron nodded. As they came to the front of the hall, he noticed that the throne had been removed. Hovering in its place was a large holographic map of Safanar with the major nations marked and color-coded.

Prince Cyrus stepped up to him. "Welcome back. Thanks to you and the soldiers of the FNA, we were able to keep the High King from taking the Kingdom of Lorric. Now that you're all here we can continue."

"We're planning our next move, or trying to," Colind said.

Verona and the others had told Aaron about the High King's attacks and their ability to use the focusing crystals to teleport their armies throughout the continent.

"You're planning to attack the High King?" Aaron asked.

"That is one possibility," Colind said.

Aaron turned to Gavril. "What about the Zekara? They're here."

Gavril nodded. "We know they are here, but we don't know where they are. We were hoping that you knew."

"I only saw the portal they used to get here, but never saw where they actually went," Aaron said.

Gavril frowned. "During the battle we detected strange readings on our equipment. They turned out to be two drones that were cloaked. There were no actual Zekara in the area, but we know they're here because they took a shot at you."

Aaron's throat thickened as he recalled the mournful howl of the Eldarin. "One of the Eldarin became infected with Ryakul venom; are they beyond hope now?"

Colind shook his head. "I would never count against the Eldarin."

"They are a life form the likes of which we have never encountered before,"

Roselyn said. "They are able to shift between physical forms and become almost pure energy."

Aaron nodded. It was something at least. "I don't know what's already been done regarding the High King, but have you reached out to him about the Zekara threat?"

"I went to my father," Sarah said. "He doesn't believe the threat exists, and if he did, he doesn't understand the threat that they pose for all of us. Khamearra is a kingdom divided."

"That may be," Colind began, "but they are firmly under the High King's control. I don't think we have any choice but to bring this war back to the High King. I am sorry, my Lady."

Sarah nodded, and Aaron knew she understood what was at stake.

"We should give shelter and aid to anyone from Khamearra that wants it," Aaron said.

"We have been, but our resources are being stretched thin as it is, and most nations who are allied with us are facing the same issues," Prince Cyrus said.

Aaron glanced around the room and saw the same resignation. He remembered the Resistance—people who lived in fear day after day in the High King's city. "Send them to Shandara, or at least give them the option."

There was a quiet murmuring, but Aaron knew that no one could make any compelling argument. Most of them believe that Shandara was his by right, and he didn't see the harm in giving the people of Khamearra a safe haven.

"One thing at a time," Gavril said. "We have the High King to face."

"Whatever they do, you can be assured that my father will be present at the next battle," Sarah said.

"Are we able to bring the Free Nations Army to Khamearra?" Aaron asked.

After a long moment, Gavril shook his head.

"I have an idea."

Aaron turned to see Jopher standing next to his father, who had spoken. "Firstly, my first son and heir speaks very highly of you."

Aaron looked at Jopher and gave a slow nod of appreciation. "What's your idea...uh...your Grace?"

King Melchoir Nasim drew his head up. "Jopher has informed me that you are not familiar with our customs, so I will grant that we can do away with formalities at this time and speak plainly. If we cannot take our fight to the enemy, then we need to make our enemy take the fight to a place of our choosing. Knowing the High King, he will not take the slight of defeat lightly and will yearn for a crushing victory."

"Until now, he's been hitting smaller kingdoms, but we think he'll direct his efforts at the larger ones from here on out," Gavril said.

King Nasim nodded. "With Zsensibar and Rexel being among them."

"You think he'll attack one of those places?" Aaron asked.

"Or both," the king said. "I proposed that Zsensibar quit the field and break with the alliance. Rexel will become an irresistible target for the High King."

"I can see why you like this idea," Prince Cyrus said. "It's my city being used as bait."

"Uncle, this fight would have come here eventually," Verona said.

"Regardless of what we decide, we do need to move quickly," Colind said. "There might not be an attack today, but it could come from anywhere in the next few days."

Prince Cyrus looked as if he swallowed something bitter. "The reports from Lorric are that they are using Ryakuls to attack the cities."

"Can we clear the city? Get the people who can't fight out?" Aaron asked.

The question caught some of them by surprise, and Prince Cyrus's eyebrows drew up. "Reymius would be proud of you, Aaron. He was ever one for placing the safety of his people among his highest priorities."

Despite himself, Aaron smiled at being compared to his grandfather, and for a moment his thoughts drifted to one of his last conversations with his father. "There are no perfect solutions. We can only do the best we can, but one thing we can all agree on is that the High King will strike. The question is, what are we going to do to face his armies when they do come."

"There is one thing that I don't like about this," Gavril said.

"Only one thing?" asked Verona.

"The High King is on the offensive, and besides the Khamearrian Resistance, he hasn't been attacked at all by the FNA. We can't use the Keystone Accelerators to move an army big enough to challenge the High King, but that doesn't mean we can't hit him. There are other ways to wage war than large-scale battles," Gavril said, drawing several nods of approval among them.

"I like the idea of bringing the battle to them," Aaron said.

"What I propose is hitting their military camps, and I want them to know that the Free Nations Army is responsible. They need to know they are not safe," Gavril said.

The old Hythariam soldier spoke as one who had fought many battles, and many had come to trust his judgment, including Aaron. They continued planning and making preparations. People still stared at him when they thought he wasn't looking, and he could hardly blame them. Almost all of them had been fooled by Halcylon's clone of him, and Aaron never expected it. Not that he could have done anything about it. This whole alliance would spiral out of control if they couldn't trust one another. Prince Cyrus agreed to start moving his people to Shandara. King Nasim would order his armies to withdraw from the borders of the north and send word to the High King, offering his provisional support. Aaron wasn't sure whether the High King would believe it, but it was worth a try.

The council session was about to end when a guard came racing into the main hall. He saluted the prince and spoke softly so that only he could hear. Prince Cyrus looked up in alarm and then turned to Sarah.

"My Lady, it appears that you have visitors," the Prince said.

Sarah glanced at Aaron uncertainly. "Who, may I ask, my Lord?"

The prince hesitated for a moment. "They say they are Elitesmen. They've requested an audience with their queen."

Aaron's hands shifted to the swords that he no longer had and cursed their loss.

"They came through one of the main gates and surrendered themselves to the guards," Prince Cyrus said.

"How many of them are there?" Aaron asked.

"Twenty," the guard answered.

Braden hefted his war hammer, with more than a few of the guards following his lead.

"Stay your hands," the prince ordered. "They are unarmed and have surrendered themselves."

"Elitesmen generally don't use the front door," Aaron said.

"Look among you," Verona said. "Even if the Elitesmen's intentions were less than honorable, it would be a path to a quick end for them."

Aaron glanced at Braden, who lowered his hammer but still kept it in his hands. Gavril's fingers flashed across his comms device, killing the holo image of the continent.

"Please send them in, my Lord," Sarah said.

Prince Cyrus gestured to the guards at the entranceway to the main hall. The guard saluted to his prince, unlatched the great doors, and pulled them open. Several lines of men entered. Soldiers of the FNA flanked each of the Elitesmen, clad in their black uniforms. The Elitesmen's hands were shackled in front of them.

Aaron studied the approaching Elitesmen, and none of them held the energy. Half of their number were quite old with the rest being near his own age or younger. Some had the pristine arrogance that Aaron had come to associate with the Elitesmen, but not all of them. The last Elitesman to come in wore a dark-leather duster and had long gray hair. Isaac's gaze darted to Aaron almost immediately and then focused on Sarah.

Isaac came forward and sank to one knee with the other Elitesmen doing the same. "My Queen, we have come to pledge ourselves to you."

Sarah stepped away from Aaron's side. "You must be mistaken. Khamearra has no queen."

Isaac's eyes never left the floor. "You are Sarah Faergrace of the rightful ruling family of Khamearra. Many of our great kingdom will support your claim, my Queen."

Aaron came to Sarah's side. "Do all Elitesmen change their loyalties on a whim? Maybe not you, Isaac, but these younger men would have gladly killed any of us should we have crossed their paths."

A young dark-haired Elitesman raised his head. "You speak the truth, Heir of Shandara. Until recently we have been loyal to the Order."

"What, pray tell, has had such a calamitous effect that would lead you to change where your loyalties lie?" Verona asked.

The remaining Elitesmen looked up from the ground and their gazes shifted to Aaron, but when the dark-haired Elitesman spoke, he addressed everyone around them. "The Alenzar'seth fought our brethren in the arena, bringing to a halt a practice that we of the Elite should have ended long ago," the Elitesman said.

Aaron saw that some of the people were confused. "The Elitesmen recruit young initiates and as a rite of passage make them compete to save their families. The competition is designed to make killers out of them with none having a hope to succeed," Aaron said.

There was a murmuring of general disgust sweeping through the room, and the Elitesmen paid it no more mind than the air they breathed. They did, however, remain focused on Aaron.

"You didn't have to come here to change things in the Order of the Elite," Aaron said.

"We didn't. We came to pledge our loyalty to the rightful ruler of Khamearra," the Elitesman said. "We will die to protect her."

"Protect her!" Braden scowled. "Weeks ago you took up arms against her."

"Warden," Isaac said with a half smile for Braden, "that was not us or anyone else associated with our group." Isaac looked at Sarah. "Your Grace, those of us who honor the old code of the Elite have watched over you your whole life, and when you came of age one of our order was sent to train you in our ways."

"Please get off your knees," Sarah said. "How many factions of the Elitesmen are there?" Sarah asked.

Despite being shackled, the Elitesmen rose smoothly to their feet. Aaron kept a wary eye on them, not believing for a second that those shackles kept them from doing anything they didn't want to do.

"There is the faction that is loyal to your father," Isaac began. "They compose the majority of Elitesmen. Then there are us, who were able to survive by staying out of the way. We aided the Resistance where we could. Then there are those who either follow the majority or are too scared to do anything different. For obvious reasons we are quite careful in our own recruitment."

"Are there only twenty of you?" Sarah asked.

"No, your Grace," Isaac said. "Our numbers are in the hundreds. Most of which are serving in the High King's army. I thought a larger number to bring would be too risky, given the current tensions between the kingdoms."

Colind, who had been quiet, cleared his throat. "How can you expect us to trust you at all, Elitesman?"

Isaac glanced at the other Elitesmen and nodded. As one, the shackles binding their wrists fell to the floor, but the Elitesmen remained still. The soldiers around them drew swords and pistols alike and trained them on the group.

"As you can see, my Lord Guardian of the Safanarion Order, I think you will find us to be indispensable in the coming battle. By now you realize that the High King is preparing to strike," Isaac said.

Sarah narrowed her gaze. "You tell us nothing we don't already know. If you are truly loyal to Khamearra and would make me your queen, then you need to bring something to the table. I trusted Bek and the Resistance, but I never knew that there were so many Elitesmen who would break with the current regime."

"Understandable," Isaac said. "Most don't leave the order once inducted. We ask that you allow us to prove ourselves."

"Isaac did help us get into the Citadel tower and has been involved with the Resistance in the past," Aaron said. "Him I can extend a certain measure of trust, but the rest of you? I don't think so."

"With all due respect, we came here to pledge our loyalty and service to our queen and not to *you,*" the young dark-haired Elitesmen said.

"Have a care with how you speak, Elitesman," Sarah said coldly. "You know to whom you speak, so I don't need to remind you, but know this. Aaron is my love. His voice is my voice. His will is my will. In this life we are one, now and forever. If Khamearra is to have me as their queen then they will be aligned with Shandara and the Alenzar'seth."

The silence of the hall swallowed them up, and Aaron's mouth hung open. He loved Sarah and knew she loved him. No force on Safanar or any other world would ever keep them apart, but to hear her speak those words sent shockwaves through him.

"My Lady," Colind said softly. "You speak the old oaths."

"Would you expect anything less, my Lord Guardian?" Sarah answered.

Aaron and Sarah spared each other a glance with hints of a smile.

"You would align the kingdoms of the west with those of the east?" Colind asked.

"Be more than a kingdom then," Aaron said, drawing everyone's attention. "Be a nation of men and women united. The promises and oaths sworn between kings die with them. Be a nation of people, and those laws won't die because the ruling families change."

Colind smiled thoughtfully. "It's never far from you, is it?"

"It's the best way forward. You, my grandfather, and others of the Safanarion Order began this work," Aaron said. "Why would anyone trade one tyrant for another? The bonds of this alliance should be strong enough to survive the death of one man even if he is Ferasdiam marked."

"Not all the kingdoms would agree to this," Colind said.

"Then that is their prerogative, but given time they will come around," Sarah said.

"We still offer our services," Isaac said. "Any leader among you knows the value of having well-placed agents in the enemy. We can give you information about the focusing crystals and how they are being used. How many there are and how they are being protected."

Gavril and the other generals of the Free Nations Army perked up at this.

Sarah regarded the Elitesmen. "I'll accept your service on the following conditions, and they are not negotiable," she said, capturing all within her regal gaze. "Your powers are a privilege, and from this day forth will be used in the service of protecting others. You will have dominion over no one but yourself. The Elitesmen are not a law unto themselves and have much to atone for. Part of that atonement will be met by service in the Free Nations Army. You will enter service at the lowest possible rank, and you will only be given privileges through achievement. If you can agree to that, then you can be in my service. If not, then the door is over there, gentlemen. I won't have you in my company or in Khamearra. Is that clear?"

Isaac already nodded before looking at the others, and they spoke in unison. "By the grace of our Queen we serve."

"There is one more thing," Sarah said and then paused. "You will no longer call yourselves Elitesmen. My first act as queen will be to disband the Order of the Elite."

Some of them sucked in a breath with an angry glint in their eyes.

"What may we call ourselves then?" one of them asked.

"You have names, why don't you start with those," Sarah said. "Perhaps in time and if you prove yourselves worthy, you can apply to enter into the Safanarion Order."

Colind sucked in a breath, and Aaron felt his mouth hang open again. After a few moments' thought, he found that he agreed with her. Real change can come from a new identity, and inside he applauded her genius.

"I would honor that," Aaron said.

"But they're Elitesmen," Colind said before he could stop himself.

"Look at them. The younger ones held no part in the fall of Shandara," Aaron said.

"And what of the older ones?" Colind asked, narrowing his thunderous gaze.

"They broke with the Order and were hunted as any of the Safanarion Order were," Aaron said.

Colind drew up his chin stubbornly, considering what Aaron had said. "You took the Safanarion Oath. One day this will fall to you and the others when I am gone. I hope this isn't a mistake, but I will consider any man or woman into the Safanarion Order should they be worthy."

The council session ended. Isaac and the other former Elitesmen left with Gavril and some others, eager to glean whatever intelligence there was to be learned. Sarah stayed by his side along with Verona and Roselyn. Braden kept a wary eye on the former Elitesmen. Aaron nodded for him to go on, and Braden gave him a salute and stalked off to follow them.

Sarah glanced at him.

"Braden won't rest until he's sure about them," Aaron said.

"I thought now that you were back that things would calm down, but there is never a dull moment when you two are together," Verona said, dividing his gaze between Aaron and Sarah. "Did you ever think that Elitesmen would come asking to join us? Or more specifically, pledge their loyalty to their queen?"

"I knew there were factions, but I never thought any of them would give up being an Elitesman," Aaron said.

"Actions will prove their conviction in this case," Sarah said. "It seemed obvious that if they were going to help us then they needed to be reforged. If they follow through, they will be better for it. I just hope I haven't made us more vulnerable if they don't."

"Some things are worth the risk," Aaron said.

Colind approached them and asked to speak with Aaron. Then after a moment's consideration, he asked for Sarah to stay with them.

"What I'm about to tell you will affect you as well," Colind said to her.

They left the main hall, leaving the palace, and headed into gardens that were meticulously maintained. The fresh air felt good after being stuck inside.

"Ferasdiam marked," Colind said. "Do you know what it means?"

Aaron frowned. "I think I have a pretty good idea."

Colind's lips lifted into a small smile. "Enlighten me."

"You believe that I've been touched by the Goddess Ferasdiam. This has granted me powers beyond that of an ordinary person," Aaron said.

"You sound as if you don't believe it," Colind said quietly.

"I'm not sure what to believe. I do believe that anything I can do, can be done by someone else," Aaron answered.

"Do you think Braden can jump as high as you do? Or Verona move as fast as you do? Channel enough energy through that staff to kill a Ryakul? You've surpassed anyone who has been Ferasdiam marked before with the possible exception of the Amorak," Colind said.

"My father? He's Ferasdiam marked?" she asked looking from Colind to Aaron.

"He is," Aaron said. "When I faced him atop the Citadel tower the Dragon tattoo felt strange."

"How so?" Sarah asked.

"It was like it was reacting to being near him," Aaron said, thinking back to his encounter with the High King. "I think he felt it too. He kept rubbing his arm."

Colind nodded. "Having two Ferasdiam marked within the same lifespan hasn't happened before."

"What I don't understand is why the Goddess would bestow her mark on one such as he? It makes me think that this is up to chance. You say my ability to move faster and be stronger than the others is a mark of me being special. What if it's just talent, like a musician's skill with an instrument?" Aaron said.

"But you've heard her message. The Eldarin honor their vows, and that is not something to take lightly," Colind said.

"The land needs a champion," Aaron quoted. "That is what she told me. What vow do the Eldarin honor?"

"Even on your Earth there must have been those among you who had talents in things that went beyond that of ordinary people. Despite you being raised on another world, your bond with Safanar is strong. I can sense your connection to it, and this is a good thing," Colind said.

Aaron glanced at Sarah, and she took his hand in hers. Safanar had become home to him. He did miss Earth sometimes, and his sister, but his place was here.

"There is a danger in being Ferasdiam marked," Colind said.

Aaron met Colind's gaze and mentally braced himself. "What danger?"

"Reymius bid me to let you make your own way, and he was right. But if something happens to me, there would be no one left to tell you. Those who bore the mark before came during times of great change. Some were a force for good, and others became as Amorak—drunk on power," Colind said.

"It wasn't always so with him," Sarah said.

"I believe you, my Lady. Tapping into the energy opens ourselves to the knowledge of past souls. This can cause madness in some. We are defined by our actions. It is our actions that carry the weight and bares the measure of us. Too much death and destruction can wither person's soul. I remember when Amorak was much younger and not as he is today. He was seduced by the power of being Ferasdiam marked and views himself almost as a god."

Sarah withdrew her hand from Aaron's. "Worship of the Goddess is outlawed in Khamearra, but the people still do in secret."

"Exactly," Colind said. "The Ferasdiam marked have a special connection to the higher orders, but Aaron, you are quite different. You spent the measure of your life never knowing about any of this. Your dedication to people governing themselves is quite remarkable."

"Darkness can find its way into anyone's soul," Aaron said. When journeying to Safanar he had been on the path of vengeance, and it nearly sucked the life out of him to a fate worse than death.

"I knew you would understand, but there is more. The more powerful you become, the more tenuous your connection to who you are becomes," Colind said.

Aaron frowned. "Are you saying I will become like the High King?"

"It's not outside the realm of possibilities. The Eldarin are creatures of two worlds with a foothold in this realm and one beyond. They become pure energy and transcend these planes, ascending to the higher orders," Colind said.

Aaron studied Colind's face, trying to glean the meaning behind his words. "Are you saying that I can do the same?"

Colind slowly nodded. "Except that the Eldarin return to heed your call. If you were to transcend you may not return, ever."

Sarah's eyes darted to his. "I would never leave," Aaron said.

"Love keeps you here. What would you do if you lost each other?" Colind asked.

An icy weight shifted in Aaron's stomach. "Anyone who has ever loved fears the loss of a loved one. I've lost those dear to me, and while I mourn that loss each day, it doesn't define me. I won't become like the High King."

"That is good to hear," Colind said.

It wasn't beyond the realm of possibilities that Aaron could become like the High King, so he could understand Colind's concern. He didn't like killing. He killed because there was no other choice, but even those deaths weighed heavily on him at times. Colind left them, and he was once again alone with Sarah.

"Queen?" Aaron asked.

The question caught her off guard. "Of all the things that's been said, you latch onto that."

Aaron grinned. "Well it popped in there, my Queen."

Sarah punched him in the arm. "I have as much desire to be queen as you do being king. I do worry about you. You fight with honor. My father won't, and neither will Halcylon."

"We can't fight if we don't have hope. I won't become like them," Aaron said.

"Do you think that they didn't believe the same thing or something similar at one time or another?" Sarah asked.

"This is a burden shared by anyone, whether they are king or queen or just your everyday average person."

"You're right, this is a burden shared by all. Desperation has a way of sapping the souls of men, and once you make a compromise on one thing the next becomes easier, until one day you find yourself doing despicable things you never would have thought you would be doing. That is what Colind is trying to warn you about, my love."

Aaron nodded. "I understand. That's why it's important for you to keep me in line. No, seriously, we all look out for each other. What Verona and the others did so they could be sure that I was really me and not some impostor was right on."

They came to the tower where a small airship waited to take them back to the FNA camp. Sarah stopped just before the gangplank and glanced back at him, then looked from the ship to the city beyond. She tilted her head to the side and smiled at him. Aaron smiled back and gasped as she jumped away from the tower, streaking away from him in a blur. *It's like the forest all over again,* Aaron thought and launched into the air, racing to catch up with her. They raced along the rooftops of Rexel as only they could.

19

ONE LAST LESSON

Aaron met up with Verona to see the group of FNA soldiers that Colind had sent him. The training area was only half-filled, as many were helping Rexel prepare for attack. Some groups were evacuating those who couldn't fight to Shandara. Many of the local Rexellians chose to stay and defend their homes. Most of those going to Shandara were children with their mothers and older people who offered to look after the families of those staying behind. What was hard to see were the young boys barely more than teenagers, too old to go with the younger children, but not old enough to fight. Finding them jobs that kept them out of harm's way was proving to be difficult.

What had come to be known as the training area was comprised of various fields of previously unused land outside the city of Rexel. The soldiers of the FNA all went through basic field training where they were evaluated on their skills with common weapons, particularly the knife and staff. They were called upon to navigate a five-mile track that ran through the forest that held challenges of its own. After their basic training, they were divided into various groups with some being taught how to use Hythariam weapons and technology. During all of this, they were called upon to work at whatever task was required for keeping the camp operating.

Sarah had left them a few moments before, saying she would be back soon.

"We caught sight of you two from the airship. I was sorry I couldn't join you," Verona said.

"It was spur of the moment. The airship's pilot nearly jumped out of his skin when he saw Sarah leap off the gangplank," Aaron grinned.

Verona looked at him for a moment, then clamped his hand on Aaron's shoulder. "It's good to have you back, my friend. I'm glad you're able to take a look these men."

"It was a close thing for all of us. I keep thinking that the spy had unfettered access to all of you and well...things could have been a lot different," Aaron said.

Verona nodded. "Sarah never believed. Somehow she knew it wasn't you. I'm sorry to say that I thought it was some effect of her being influenced by the Drake."

"I could see why you would think that," Aaron said, suppressing a shiver at the image of Sarah attacking him. Her blue eyes glowing yellow like the Drake's. "All of you came together in the end, and that's what's important."

"She blames herself for giving the Falcons to the clone," Verona said.

Aaron nodded and felt the loss of his swords more than he was willing to show. "What choice did she have?"

They were silent as they walked on, and Aaron glanced at the skies above Rexel. "There are a lot of airships now."

"They've been working almost around the clock on them, but there have been much more in the air lately since Lorric," Verona said.

"What do you mean?"

"Our Hythariam friends have been frantically searching for the Zekara but are unable to find them. They revealed themselves at Lorric, but have since gone quiet."

Aaron nodded.

"Will you be able to face the High King without your swords?" Verona asked.

"I won't lie to you, I would feel a lot better facing him with them than without them, but they're lost. At least for now. I still have this," Aaron said lifting the rune-carved staff.

"Oh, that reminds me," Verona said digging into his pack. "Tanneth asked me to give these to you," Verona said, handing him two small curved axes.

"Thanks," Aaron said.

"Two of them in case you miss with the first one. Isn't that what Tolvar's son said?"

"Yeah," Aaron said. "We could sure use his help."

"We can use all the help we can get," Verona grinned.

"Sarah told me that you've come a long a way in being able to tap into the energy," Aaron said.

"She did, did she? Why do I feel like there is a target painted on my back?" Verona laughed nervously.

"I recall you and Sarik getting a good laugh when I first tried to jump on the deck of the Raven," Aaron said.

Verona shook his head. "I knew that someday you would make me pay for that."

"Yup," Aaron said, coming to a halt.

"Really, right now?" Verona asked, glancing around.

"You can already do it. You just don't believe you can," Aaron replied.

"That's because I tried, and it didn't work out so well," Verona said.

"When Sarah was first trying to show me how, I was too focused on the actual act. What you need to focus on is where you're jumping to. Look at that tree branch right up there," Aaron said.

Verona grimaced. "So high up?"

Aaron leaped up to a thick limb about thirty feet from the ground and turned to face his friend. "Your turn." He watched as Verona focused and could sense the energy being drawn into his friend. Verona squatted, pushed up, rose a few feet into the air, and then landed. After a few more attempts, Aaron could see the frustration setting in and leaped back down.

"Close your eyes," Aaron said. "Trust me. Close them. Picture the limb. Build a perfect picture in your mind. Now draw in the energy and feed it into your muscles, but expand to feel it in the air around you." Aaron waited a moment before continuing. "Now I want you imagine yourself jumping to the tree limb. No need to talk." Aaron continued drawing the energy into himself. He could sense it in Verona. The potential was there. "Now imagine Roselyn is up there waiting for you."

"This is stupid," Verona said, but didn't open his eyes.

"No, it's not. The only thing keeping you from reaching that limb is you. Focus, Verona," Aaron said. "Think back to the tower. Everything is riding on you getting to that limb." Aaron felt Verona's lifebeat darken at the mention of the tower, but the energy flared within him. In a burst, Verona launched into the air, passing the tree limb, and the tree for that matter. He crash-landed beyond, and Aaron was at his side in seconds asking if he was okay.

Verona glared at him for a moment, and then his face split into a wide smile. "I just jumped."

"Yes, you did. Landings are a different skill set and will come in time," Aaron snickered and extended his hand, helping his friend up.

"You are having too much fun with this, my friend," Verona said. "But thanks."

Aaron's face grew solemn. "Better here in practice than in a battle with the Elitesmen."

Verona nodded.

"I can't tell you how many trees I crashed into trying to keep up with Sarah," Aaron said.

"Come on, they're right over there, and it looks like we have some company," Verona said.

Aaron glanced at the group of FNA soldiers and saw Sarah standing with them. Two Elitesmen—*former Elitesmen* Aaron corrected himself—were there. They had changed their clothing into the common garb of a soldier, but Aaron could sense their connections to the energy around them. They walked over, and without word, the soldiers of the FNA lined up. The two former Elitesmen joined them.

Isaac appeared, still wearing his dark-leather duster.

"I'll serve, but I'm not wearing a uniform," Isaac said.

"Have you trained anyone before?" Aaron asked.

"Traditionally the Order of the Elite required that senior members be involved with teaching. I know that the Safanarion Order had similar traditions," Isaac answered.

Aaron nodded. "I would appreciate it if you would help us train these men. Colind believes that they have potential."

Isaac's gruff exterior softened as much as his craggy face would allow. "I will do my very best, but what of the others?" asked Isaac, gesturing to the former Elitesmen.

They were close to Aaron's age, and he could tell they didn't like being demoted to a common soldier. Aaron also knew he didn't much care what they liked. "We all need to start somewhere."

Isaac stepped closer and spoke softly. "They joined your cause at great cost to themselves. They are not novices, but highly efficient killing machines."

Aaron shifted his gaze so the two former Elitesmen could hear. "That's the part we need to change. They need to be highly efficient at protecting." Aaron moved to stand directly in front of the former Elitesmen, but he addressed all the men. "Killing is easy. Anyone can kill. Whether with a weapon or with their hands, the act of taking a life is simple and permanent. With the Hythariam weapons it becomes easier still and with less training. Now don't mistake me, I'm not talking about the inner turmoil that comes from killing, even in self-defense. I mean that killing on its most fundamental level, the act of thrusting a knife into your enemy where he is most vulnerable. It is simple and yet at the same time one of the most horrible acts a person can do. Killing changes you, and the more you do it the worse it is.

"The real challenge is keeping those around you alive. Fighting for those who can't fight for themselves is worth a great deal. Teaching others to defend themselves is better still. And creating a world where we're not living by the sword every day is ideal."

"What about your enemies, do they not deserve death?" one of the former Elitesmen asked.

"What's your name?"

"Rohnek, my Lord."

"Sometimes our enemies deserve death. When it comes to survival and it's either you or them is different than using death as a means to remove obstacles in your path," Aaron said.

"But you've killed Elitesmen and many others," Rohnek said.

"They were trying to kill me—" Aaron began.

"Quite a lot of them actually," Verona quipped.

"My point is that killing should be something that is used as a last resort," Aaron continued.

The other former Elitesman raised his hand, and Aaron nodded to him.

"Zedya, my Lord. There is a war. These are soldiers," Zedya said. "There will be death."

"Yes, there will. Too much death, but eventually the war will be over. I've been to Khamearra, and I know the Elitesmen there kill for the slightest offense or to pull innocents into their experiments. We will fight this war because we have no other choice, but one day the war will be over," Aaron said.

Rohnek and Zedya both lowered their eyes. Aaron knew there were some that relished the power of the Elitesmen Order and then there were those who had to function within its confines to survive.

"My promise to you is not to judge you on what you did to survive. You now wear the uniform of the Free Nations Army and will be judged on the actions and achievements you accomplish from this moment forth. You are part of something, and in time it will become part of you. You all have abilities and talents. You are here because there are some who believe that you have the potential to learn. Some of you already know a great deal. Help your fellow soldiers. There is no one standing here right now who doesn't need help or can't learn something new," Aaron said, walking down the line of men.

"We have a short window of time for training. Some of you will be coming with us on a mission. We'll have more on that later. Right now I'd like to see what you can do. Verona tells me that he and Sarah have already gone over the slow fighting forms. Let's see how well you learned," Aaron said.

The training session must have been rudimentary for the former Elitesmen, but they didn't complain. Their form was perfect, and they carried out whatever he asked them to do with rigid focus. Rohnek and Zedya both wore a mask over their thoughts, and at some points Aaron wondered what they were thinking.

Colind had been right to single out these men. Some had real potential in their own unique way, but what was common among them was a strong sense of self. Something they would need if they were ever successful in tapping the energy around them. More than once he wanted to have the Falcons with him and wield them into the bladesong of awakening.

After an hour, they dismissed all but ten of the men, which included Rohnek and Zedya. They needed their help for what they were about to do. Aaron planned to keep a close eye on them and had to trust whatever vetting process Isaac had used to allow them into the Resistance.

Sarik came at a run across the yard and met them.

"Tanneth is waiting for us on the east field," Sarik said.

They met up with the Hythariam who was working among three long tables inside a tent. The young Hythariam had his fine white hair tied back and tucked into his shirt. He wore dark gloves, and next to him were a pile of octagonal containers several inches across. There were several basins that were filled with dark powders and one that contained a powder that shimmered in the light.

"Is that powder from the yellow crystals used to power the airships?" Aaron asked.

Tanneth nodded. "The black and red powders are used to ignite the charged tiny crystallized dust for a truly powerful explosion. One of these can take out this whole area."

"Is it safe for us to be standing here?" Isaac asked.

"It is if you don't sneeze," Braden said, coming from behind the crates stacked on the other side of the tent.

"Warden," Isaac greeted.

"They are safe enough to handle when I've got them inside these canisters. The outer walls are meant to break apart in a wide arc that will shred anything close by. The metal used is something we have that is highly resistant to heat, which is why they don't simply burn up during the explosion," Tanneth said.

"They are so small. How much damage can they really do?" Sarik asked.

"I planted enough of these on the structural supports of one of the Citadel towers and brought it down," Tanneth said.

"I can attest to that as I was on top of the tower when it collapsed," Aaron said. "How many do we have?"

"This is the final batch. I have three crates we can take with us," Tanneth said and picked up one of the octagonal balls. He rotated it to show a small panel. "This is the timer, which I recommend setting after these have been put in place." Tanneth started closing the canisters, and he and Braden stowed them away.

Isaac's bushy gray eyebrows raised as he looked at Aaron. "What do you plan to do with these?"

"We're going to set these around the High King's camp in Khamearra," Aaron replied.

"My Queen, there are those who would be loyal to you there," Isaac said.

Aaron's eyes darted to Sarah, who seemed to go cold in an instant; he knew this wasn't easy for her.

"There are more loyal to my father, and these same soldiers have already been attacking other kingdoms. We cannot halt our actions on the chance that they may support my claim to Khamearra's throne," Sarah said.

Isaac considered this for a moment and nodded.

Tanneth cleared his throat, getting their attention. "We'll be placing the explosives throughout the camp," Tanneth said and brought up an aerial map of the camps outside of the city of Khamearra.

The FNA soldiers had long gotten used to Hythariam technology, but it was interesting to see the reaction from the former Elitesmen who all looked stunned at the display. Aaron watched the flash of recognition as they identified the landmarks unique to Khamearra, including the High King's palace and Citadel of the Elite.

"How is this possible?" Rohnek asked.

Tanneth took a minute to explain how they had machines in the sky that recorded the images. He then entered a few commands into the holographic interface, moving the massive aerial photograph across the viewing area. "These targets in red are our high-priority targets. The ones deemed to have the most impact are also the riskiest of places for us to plant these bombs. These other locations highlighted in yellow and green have a lower priority, but we feel it will get the message across."

Rohnek frowned at the display. "Those marked in red are the command tents for the Khamearrian army, and those others are where lesser officers gather. You're not hitting the common soldier areas at all."

"That's right," Aaron said. "We're attacking their leadership."

"The plan is for us to enter the camp at these locations over here," Tanneth said gesturing on one side of the map. "We make our way through. Plant the bombs and regroup over here," he finished, pointing to another part of the map.

"They're not going to just let you walk through the camp. What's your plan for that?" Isaac asked.

"In those crates over there are Khamearrian army uniforms. We'll wear them and should be able to make our way through the camp with little difficulty," Tanneth said.

Rohnek and Zedya exchanged glances, and Aaron nodded for them to speak.

"They don't let common soldiers up near the areas you have marked without going through checkpoints," Rohnek said.

Tanneth shared a glance with Aaron and nodded. Tanneth had already known about the checkpoints, but was testing the former Elitesmen's loyalties.

"It's a good thing we have two former Elitesmen who have the authority to get us through," Aaron said.

Rohnek glanced at Aaron, considering with the slow realization that he had just been tested and passed.

"We'll break off into teams," Aaron said. Perhaps they were sincere in wanting to serve Sarah. "Rohnek and Zedya, one of you will be with either Sarah or myself. Isaac, you will go with Sarah." Aaron continued giving the team assignments that they had agreed upon earlier. The part that he didn't like was not having Sarah at his side. It wasn't the former Elitesmen that bothered him...well not too much anyway, it was there was the potential for something to go wrong. Since his last trip into Khamearra had resulted in four of them getting captured, he didn't want to take any chances. They were stronger now and better prepared for the Elitesmen, but still anyone could be overwhelmed.

"When do we leave?" Isaac asked.

"As soon as we can get changed," Aaron answered.

Tanneth approached him while the others were changing into the Khamearrian uniforms. "I had this made for you," he said, handing him a sword. "It's well made and should serve you well until you get the Falcons back."

"Thank you," Aaron said. The sword had a slight curve and single edge. The handle was long enough for both his hands to fit. The style of blade was close to what Sarah carried. He pulled it out of its sheath and tested the balance. Tanneth was right—it was a remarkably well-made sword. Aaron thanked him again, and Sarah looked away from him.

Aaron came to her side. "It's not your fault."

"Yes, it is. I should have kept them. They've been in your family for generations, and now they're gone."

"We'll get them back. I truly believe that."

"But we don't know where he went," Sarah said, letting out a frustrated sigh.

Aaron gently caressed her shoulder. "I've been giving this a lot of thought. Either he went back to Halcylon, or he's been captured by your father's army. There wasn't a trace of him left in Lorric, or we would have found him. If he's with you father, then there is a good chance I will get the Falcons back again. The same goes for Halcylon."

"How do you know that either of them won't just melt them down?" Sarah asked.

"Oh, you can't," Tanneth said, who had been listening. "The Falcons aren't made of ordinary steel. It's some type of foreign metallic alloy that we've never come across. I looked into it when you first fought the Drake. No ordinary sword would be able to cut through our armor. Not that the Falcons with the holes cut into the blades could be ordinary, but still quite interesting."

"I never thought about it before. My grandfather left them to me, but I don't know much about their origins. Would you be able to recreate them?" Aaron asked.

Tanneth's gaze drew downward as he shook his head. "I tried at Hathenwood, and while the blades appear to be like your swords, they weren't quite right. When I tried to add the holes into the each blade, they lost too much of their integrity to do you much good in a real fight."

Aaron nodded, hiding his disappointment, but wasn't completely surprised. "I appreciate you trying."

He still had the rune-carved staff, which was leaning against the side wall of the tent. Aaron went to retrieve it, and as his hands grasped the staff, he felt a deep pull from the pit of his stomach.

"Are you okay?" Sarah asked.

Aaron shook his head to clear it. "Yeah, I just had a strange feeling."

"What about?"

"I'm worried about the Eldarin. One of them became infected with the Ryakul poison. I don't plan on calling on them anytime soon, but then again I didn't plan on calling on them that last two times either," Aaron took a moment, thinking about what he wanted to say. "They healed me, Sarah. Took the Nanites from my system and reversed what Halcylon had done to my body. The Dragons and the Eldarin are going to be pulled into this again, and I'm afraid that we'll see an end to them all because of it."

"They chose to honor you, my love. You are Ferasdiam marked and her champion. If they come to your aid, they do so by their own intent," Sarah said.

"Ferasdiam marked," Aaron said. "I'm the possibility of what anyone can achieve."

Sarah shook her head. "What will it take before you accept that the things you do is what puts you beyond ordinary men? It's your heart that makes you great. Not the power that you're capable of. You affect all those around you. They look to you and give better of themselves. They follow you, not because you're Ferasdiam marked or the last scion of the Alenzar'seth line. They follow you because you light the way for us to have something more than we've ever had before. The Eldarin had it right, my love. *Yours is a light meant to shine.* And if they sacrifice themselves so that we might survive these times of trial then we should honor their sacrifice by remaining true and become something greater than we are today."

Aaron lost himself in her eyes. "You heard them?"

Sarah nodded.

Hearing her speak the Eldarin's words ignited their voice deep within. There must be a way that he could help them.

Verona came quietly to his side. "It's time to go."

Tanneth had them gather on one side of the tent. He brought out two metallic cylinders about a foot in length and handed one to Aaron. Aaron glanced at the Keystone Accelerator and gave it to Sarah, who looked at him questioningly.

"I'm not leaving without you. So you hold onto it," Aaron said.

Tanneth opened a portal, and Sarah led her group through.

"Braden and Sarik will be with her," Verona said.

Aaron nodded, "Let's go hit them for a change."

The soldiers of the FNA grinned hungrily, and Rohnek gave Aaron a firm nod. Tanneth opened another portal and handed the spent Keystone Accelerator to the soldier remaining behind. Aaron stepped through the portal with the others following closely on his heels.

20

TRAP

Khamearra had become a place where its citizens were required to contribute to the High King's war. There were still pockets of those who left messages urging the return of the Faergrace line, and Rordan wondered how his perfect sister felt about that. He hadn't seen or heard from her since she openly defied their father, who had attributed her display as being under the influence of the Alenzar'seth. Rordan knew better; no one told Sarah what to do. He knew his father didn't really believe it either, and was using Sarah's open defiance as a means to get what he wanted. He had been watching his father closely, and for him it was a matter of pride and possession. His father yearned for the heads of his enemies, especially the Heir of Shandara; too many times the man had slipped through their fingers. He suspected that his father welcomed the challenge, as no one since the fall of Shandara had dared oppose Amorak. Not since Reymius Alenzar'seth, and the fact that his grandson had returned to Safanar did appear to have awoken something in his father.

Rordan finished strapping on his light armor, the same that the Elitesmen would be wearing, choosing to rely on their powers rather than be weighed down by heavy armor. He engaged the travel crystal and emerged on the fields outside the city. Khamearra's army was mobilizing, preparing to execute his father's plan and end the insurrection in the Waylands and in Shandara before they could fester any further. Rordan nodded to the guards and stepped into the command tent.

"Have you tied up the loose ends?" the High King asked.

"There weren't that many to begin with," Elite Grand Master Gerric answered. "The ones we could find have been dealt with. The bulk of the Order have been preparing for the attack."

"That's something at least," the High King said and lifted up two sheathed swords and put them on the table.

"Are those the Alenzar'seth's swords?" Gerric asked, unable to tear his eyes from them.

"Yes, they are. One of my favorite trophies," Amorak said.

"Your Grace, these blades are legendary," Elite Grand Master Gerric said.

The High King glanced at him. "I'll make them a gift to you after the campaign."

"You honor me, your Grace."

"Rordan, I see you're ready," the High King said. "You will be with the Elitesmen."

Rordan nodded. "What of Zsensibar?"

"I've sent word that their offer was accepted," the High King said.

Rordan frowned. "That's it? You accept their offer?"

"Absolutely. I don't trust King Nasim in the slightest, and I will deal with our friends to the south after we crush the Waylands and their Free Nations Army. Zsensibar is quite fond of its slave practices so let's see how the entire kingdom copes with being slaves," the High King said.

"Father," Rordan said, "after we conquer the Waylands, won't our troops be too preoccupied with holding Rexel to be able to fight a war in Zsensibar?"

His father turned to face him, his cold gaze could crack the heart of a stone. "I don't plan to occupy the Waylands, Son. I plan to burn it to the ground. When we're finished there, no other kingdom will dare oppose us."

Rordan nodded and was about to say something else when his father knocked him to the ground. In a flash of light, they emerged some distance away from the command tent. Plumes of orange blossomed throughout the camp, and soldiers closest to them collapsed, clutching bleeding wounds that appeared to come out of nowhere.

Rordan sprang to his feet, his sword drawn, and drew the energy into himself. Elite Grand Master Gerric was nowhere to be found.

"Stay with me," his father said.

Soldiers raced around, trying to keep the fires from spreading. There was nothing but scorched earth near the tent they had been in. The blast actually came from several tents over.

"Could it have been one of the crystals?" Rordan asked.

Soldiers recognizing their king and heir gathered around them, grim faced and weapons drawn.

"This was no mishandled crystal," the High King spat.

The armies had already been gathering to prepare their attack, and the forces remaining with the tents were scheduled to follow soon after.

"Sweep the area. I want them found!" the High King bellowed.

Rordan watched as his father closed his eyes for a moment and he felt the waves of energy coming from him in staggering proportions. Elite Grand Master Gerric stumbled over to them. He had a trickle of blood running down his neck from a shallow wound behind his ear. Khoiron came up the hill, leading a company of soldiers with some breaking off to methodically search the area in teams.

The High King opened his eyes and called for a report from the general.

"This was a coward's attack. Explosions have been set off throughout the upper and lower camps. I don't have a confirmed number, but marking where the smoke is rising, they looked to have targeted us pretty well." Khoiron said.

"Which means we have spies among us," the High King said.

Rordan noticed an Elitesmen walking along the next row of tents leading a group of soldiers.

"Elitesman," Rordan called as he came to the other line of tents.

The Elitesman stopped and turned around, but the group of soldiers kept going.

"Your Grace," he said and bowed his head.

"Do you know if the other camps have been attacked?" Rordan asked.

"Apologies, your Grace, but I don't know," the Elitesman said, glancing up at the group of soldiers.

Rordan nodded for him to carry on and returned to his father.

"The attack goes as planned—"

"Shouldn't we assess the damage before moving on with the attack?" Rordan asked, looking to Khoiron for support.

"I would advise patience, your Grace," Khoiron said.

"This cowardly act is an attempt to put us off balance, and it will not work. We leave now," the High King said.

Rordan took one last glance at the city behind him and left to join the Elitesmen.

"We're overdue as it is. Who was that?" Verona asked.

"That was Prince Rordan," Rohnek answered. "He didn't suspect anything, but I thought we had more time on the timer."

Verona shrugged his shoulders. "Let's catch up to the others. Their armies are assembling, which means they are about to attack."

Aaron looked up as Verona and Rohnek caught up to them. Making their way through the camp had been easier than they originally expected, but they could not have made their way to the command tents without the former Elitesmen. Elitesmen authority was unquestioned in Khamearra. He kept glancing at the massing army, knowing there were other camps just like this fed the growing fear that they simply didn't have enough soldiers. Verona relayed their brief meeting with Rordan, and Aaron's gaze fixed upon where they had come from, knowing that the High King wouldn't be far from his only living son.

"This isn't the time," Sarah said. "He's too strong here. When you face him it must be with an army at your back."

Aaron frowned. "If we could take out the focusing crystals we could gain more time. Time enough to prepare--"

"They are too well guarded, my love."

"Not for me they're not," Aaron said, clenching his teeth. Then he whispered, "So many people are going to die, Sarah. If I could prevent that I would."

Sarah reached out, taking his hand in her own. "I know you would, and more importantly everyone else serving in the Free Nations Army knows it too. It's why they will fight."

Aaron nodded, saying nothing, but in his mind he was still judging the distance to where he suspected the High King was, but when he looked up they were gone.

"It's time," Tanneth said quietly. He engaged the Keystone Accelerator and opened a portal back to Rexel.

They filed through the portal. Rohnek paused in front for a moment, tilting his head. He spun around, drawing his sword, and raced past Verona. At first it appeared as if he was swinging his sword at the empty air, but then Aaron heard the kiss of steel on steel.

"Keep going," Aaron shouted and dashed ahead to catch up.

"You betray us, brother," an Elitesman said, releasing his shroud that had kept them from seeing them.

"You betray yourselves," Rohnek said, lashing out with his sword maneuvering around the two Elitesmen.

"The penalty for treason against the Order is death, and you will die alone," the Elitesman said.

Aaron brought his staff down, and the Elitesman crumpled to the ground. Rohnek took advantage of the distraction to sweep the other Elitesman off his feet, but paused with his sword at his throat.

The Elitesman on the ground cursed. "Mercy is for the weak, brother, and you will find none here." The Elitesmen tried to roll away, but Rohnek's blade bit into his neck.

"They won't change," Rohnek said, cleaning the blood off his blade.

"Some of them won't," Aaron agreed. "But some will."

The camp around them plunged into silence, and Aaron felt the faint stirring of energy crawl along his skin. There was a massive bubble of energy growing near the center of the High King's army. The flaring brilliance stretched out, engulfing everything in its path. Tanneth shouted for them to hurry, that the portal wouldn't stay open. The rest of them went through the portal until only Tanneth and Aaron remained.

This is it, Aaron thought to himself. They stepped through the portal and emerged upon the quiet fields of the FNA camps outside of Rexel. Aaron scanned the horizon, expecting the High King's army to appear at any moment. The sky was full of airships hovering along the borders of the city and FNA camps alike. The others glanced around at the sky for a moment, and then Verona tore off his Khamearrian soldier's uniform.

"Don't want to be mistaken for the enemy now, do we?" Verona grinned as he put his regular clothes back on from his pack.

They all quickly changed their clothing, and the comms devices began chiming at once. Tanneth answered.

"The High King's army is attacking," Iranus said.

"We're in Rexel, and the army isn't here," Aaron replied.

"Not there. They are in Shandara."

Aaron felt his gut clench as if he had been kicked. They had sent the women and children along with those who couldn't fight to Shandara, believing that the High King would focus on Rexel.

"Roselyn is in Shandara," Verona gasped.

"We're going," Aaron said.

"We can't use the Accelerator until it charges," Tanneth said.

"We can use the crystals," Sarah said and tossed one to Aaron.

Aaron caught it. "Tanneth, you and Sarik head back. We need you in the flyers." He almost said in case the Zekara chose this moment to show themselves, but they had enough to deal with without worrying about the whether Halcylon would attack or not.

Tanneth withdrew two rods from his pack and handed one to Sarik. Two foot pads opened up at the ends, and they stepped on. Within a moment they rose into the air and were racing to the field where the flyers were kept.

Those who remained closed in around Aaron and Sarah, each putting a hand upon the shoulder of the person in front of them until they were all linked. The FNA would be sending soldiers to Shandara at any moment. With a nod to Sarah, they engaged the travel crystals, and the group disappeared.

They emerged in Shandara in the Dragon Hall. The sun was shining, casting its warm glow upon the city. Aaron hadn't been to Shandara since he had brought down the barrier between Safanar to Hytharia. Then the city had been a place of twilight, where the deathly shadows held the land by the throat. It had been months since he had been here, and without the Drake and the Ryakul around, the land was slowly starting to heal.

They raced through the city amid the soldiers heading toward Shandara's walls. Aaron drew in the energy, launched himself into the air, and landed atop of a taller building. He was followed by Sarah and Verona. The former Elitesmen crested the top with ease. Braden came last, pulling himself over the edge. Aaron was relieved to see the gaping holes in Shandara's pristine walls had been repaired.

"They've been fortifying the city since you've been gone," Sarah said.

"That's good. At least now we know we have a chance," Aaron said.

Battle drums could be heard in the distance. Aaron glanced at the others and launched into the air, speeding toward the walls. The others followed as best they could, and only Sarah was able to keep up with him. Aaron reached back, sensing the energy in the others and urged more speed from them. Verona immediately started to break away from the others, quickly followed by Braden. Rohnek and Zedya remained closed off to him. They crested the walls, seeing groups of FNA soldiers spread out. Some of the FNA carried Hythariam weapons and were spaced out among those armed with bows. Nearest them was a group of Hythariam clustered around a large mounted gun. Aaron scanned along the walls and saw others spaced out along the massive walls of Shandara.

"We found them and other weapons hidden throughout the city," Verona said.

"And they work?" Aaron asked.

"We're about to find out, my friend."

Sarah turned toward them. "Iranus was trying to clear a path to the command center, but it has been buried in an area of the city still under rubble. He said they needed you in particular to open it for them."

Aaron nodded and stepped closer to the edge to get a better look at the Khamearrian Army spread out. They were just out of bow range, but Aaron was certain they weren't out of range of the Hythariam weapons. The Khamearrian line stretched far, and Aaron couldn't begin to guess at how many soldiers were out there. There was little movement, and the soldiers appeared smallish from their vantage point.

Aaron narrowed his gaze, scanning down below. "I don't see any Elitesmen."

Sarah frowned, her eyes darting back and forth, searching. A bright light flickered behind them from the streets below. A portal opened, and more soldiers of the Free Nations Army poured through. Aaron noticed similar portals being opened throughout the city below. Squad captains spread the word to hold their fire until the High King's army advanced.

A seed of doubt took root in Aaron's gut. Everything about this felt wrong. He scanned the sky, searching for any sign of Ryakuls, but there was none.

"This is a trap," Aaron said.

"What do you mean?" Sarah asked.

"How else do you explain the lack of Elitesmen presence and no Ryakuls? Prior to Lorric, all of the High King's attacks included the Elitesmen, which were instrumental in taking the smaller kingdoms. Yet here the Khamearrian Army stands, and they do nothing. It's like they're waiting for something."

Aaron brought his comms device. "Gavril, I think this is a trap. The High King wants us to divide our forces. Stop sending soldiers to Shandara."

"How can you be sure?" Gavril asked.

"The army here is just waiting, and there appears to be no Elitesmen in sight. What would the High King hope to gain by attacking Shandara? Even if he had to guess he would know that the bulk of the FNA is in Rexel..." Aaron's eyes widened. "They're coming for you at Rexel."

The comms device went silent. Aaron called Gavril's name, but no reply came. Aaron let out a frustrated breath, his mind racing. Verona tried using his comms device.

"Captain," Aaron called. The FNA captain came over to them. "I want you to start shooting at the High King's army."

The captain frowned. "We have orders to hold fire unless they start attacking."

"This is a diversionary force sent here to draw us out of Rexel. Right now they are out of bow range, but my guess is that they don't realize that you can still get to them," Aaron said.

The captain's eyes widened. "But with our forces divided... I will give the order," he said and left.

"What do we do?" Verona asked.

Aaron glanced at the city behind them and then back to beyond the walls. The FNA armed with Hythariam weapons fired on the High King's army. Screams echoed from down below, and the soldiers scattered, trying in vain to take cover from the golden bolts.

What could they do? They needed to defend the city, but the High King would bring the bulk of his forces to Rexel. He glanced at Braden, whose cold eyes dared him to ask him to stay behind.

Sarah placed her hand on his arm. "You can't be everywhere, and we are needed elsewhere. Trust that the soldiers here can hold the city. We must go."

Aaron swore and grabbed a clump of his hair on top of his head, despising himself for not being able to stand with the FNA to defend Shandara, but Sarah was right. If the High King committed himself to destroying Rexel and the heart of the Free Nations Army, then that is where he was needed most.

Aaron turned to Braden.

"My place is at your side," Braden said.

"A Warden of the De'anjard defends the helpless."

Braden glared at him, but continued the oath. "Through cunning and strength."

"Stands the watch," Aaron continued.

"Protect that which matters most."

"Honor those of the shield," Aaron said.

"Stand as one...sacrifice for the many," Braden finished.

"The Warden's Oath is meant to guide the De'anjard. Be a shield to these people here. Sarah is right. I can't be everywhere at once. I need you to hold this city. Shandara is more than the Alenzar'seth," Aaron said, holding out his hand.

Braden looked at Aaron's hand before taking it in his own. "I swear to you that I will not let this city fall."

Aaron thanked him, and Rohnek and Zedya stepped up.

"We would like to stay and help," Rohnek said.

"Why?" Aaron asked.

"We renounced the Elitesmen Order to join the Free Nations Army. You said that we should focus on protection. The people behind these city walls, some of which are from Khamearra, need protection," Rohnek said.

Zedya gazed at him intently. "People truly follow you. At first I thought it was through fear, but that is the way of the High King. What you are is different. You make us want to give more. Here in this place, at this time, let us use our skills in a cause worth something more. Let us stand with the Warden of the De'anjard and defend these walls."

Aaron looked at them for a moment and then to Braden, who nodded.

"All right," Aaron said, "good luck."

He brought out the travel crystal, and Sarah did the same. The others closed in, and they left the walls of Shandara behind.

21

WAR

The alarms blared through the city of Rexel, reaching into the palace. The FNA soldiers raced to their pre-battle-plan assignments. Colind glanced at Cyrus, who already wore his armored plate covering his torso. Full-plate armor had become less practical over the years, and with so many changes sweeping across Safanar, Colind knew the days of hardened metal armor were numbered.

"I knew this day would come," Cyrus said. "As soon as Aaron showed up at the palace, I knew that this battle with the High King would happen."

"Aaron may be the catalyst for this, but you and I both know that this battle would have happened eventually. The High King wouldn't have settled for treaties," Colind answered.

Prince Cyrus watched the feeds come in on the Hythariam's holo displays. Amorak's army had arrived outside Rexel's walls on the west. Rexel's walls were nowhere near the size of Shandara's, but with the Elitesmen the size of the walls didn't matter.

Cyrus called for his guards then turned to Colind. "You didn't think I'd wait out the battle in here did you, old friend?"

Colind shook his head and followed Cyrus out to the waiting transport that hovered just outside. Garret met them at the small airship, which heaved upward after they were onboard. The skies over Rexel were littered with airships patrolling. Some were still in hiding and waited for the orders to provide support where they were needed. The soldiers with them were armed with swords and Hythariam pistols, putting to use the number of weapons found in Shandara. The shields of Shandara were in short supply, but at least they had more than just the two that been found by Aaron's companions.

"I know you'd rather be hunting Mactar," Cyrus said.

"My place is here doing what I can to help defend the city, and I have no doubts that he will present himself here today," Colind said.

The prince eyed him for a moment. "You should stop blaming yourself for Tarimus's choices."

Colind pressed his lips together. "I can't absolve myself of my son's failings. Who else can his failings fall to if not his father? I keep thinking that perhaps if I had done things differently..."

"Tarimus was always power hungry; even as a child the potential was there. And he paid the price for it. The past...whatever else it is, my friend, is gone. We still need you."

"I have given everything I have for the Safanarion Order, and I understand what you're saying, but I blame *him*. Goddess how I blame that man," Colind said, balling his hands into fists, feeling the blood rush to his chest. He yearned for Mactar's blood and as much as his wrath focused on him, deep inside he still blamed himself for Tarimus. His son of all people should not have been pulled into Mactar's web. *I should have protected him better. Why couldn't Tarimus have been stronger? Why didn't he come to me?* Colind drew the energy into himself on instinct and glared to the west where the High King's army waited.

Why couldn't I have listened better?

Mactar would pay. He could do that much at least. There would be no rest for him until one of them was dead.

Cyrus ordered the pilot to take them higher into the air to get a better vantage point of the battle below. Bright flashes belched from the muzzles of the Hythariam weapons, pouring their destruction into Khamearra's line. There was fighting on the walls as Elitesmen utilized the travel crystals to their advantage. The tactic worked well against the other kingdoms, but the Free Nations Army had been preparing for this type of assault and had designed the posts on the wall to also function as defensible positions. This slowed the Elitesmen down but didn't stop them completely. They needed Aaron. Full-sized airships roared by with their engines at full blast, dropping a lethal mixture of crystallized dust that exploded on impact. Attack orbs from the Elitesmen upon the ground raced up, tearing into the airships as they went by.

The High King's army swallowed up the land beyond Rexel's western walls in a great shadow. Siege towers made their slow progress toward the walls. Cyrus ordered the pilot to take them to what the Hythariam referred to as the operations base, where they could coordinate the battle.

"Be safe, my friend," Colind said after they touched down.

"Where are you going?" Prince Cyrus asked.

"To where I'm needed. The wall," Colind replied.

Garret stayed at his side as they ran with the soldiers heading toward the front line. Garret pulled him to the side as a portal opened on the street before them and out came Verona leading a group of FNA soldiers. Aaron and Sarah soon followed, and the portal closed behind them. Sounds of the battle rocked the walls in the distance, drawing their attention, and Colind noticed Aaron glance at the skies.

"Not yet. They haven't brought the Ryakuls in yet," Colind said.

Aaron nodded. "It's only a matter of time."

Isaac, the former Elitesman came to join them, wearing his dark-leather duster over his FNA uniform. He led eighteen other Elitesmen that had pledged their loyalty to Sarah.

"My Queen," Isaac said, bringing his fist over his heart.

"The Elitesmen are attacking the walls," Colind said.

Sarah nodded and looked at Isaac. "Have your men go and help hold the walls."

Isaac motioned the men ahead, and all but four left them. "We will stay to help you with whatever it is you are planning."

Aaron glanced at Colind. "Has Zsensibar's army returned yet?"

Colind shook his head as a new barrage of alarms raced through the city.

"Aaron," Iranus said over the comms device. "The High King attacks with another army on the eastern side of the city, beyond the FNA camp. They're unprotected there. The army appeared out of nowhere."

All attacks had been assumed to come from the western side, and the High King had obliged their assumptions.

"We need King Nasim to bring his men up behind them. We'll head over there now," Aaron said and closed the comms device.

"Shandara?" Colind asked.

"A smaller army attacks there, but it seems as if the bulk of Khamearra's forces are here. They mean to overwhelm us. Braden stayed behind to help defend Shandara from attack," Aaron said.

"Good. That's really good. He will do well I think," Colind said.

Aaron nodded and frowned. "The High King learns fast. He brought a portion of his army to Shandara first, knowing that we would send some of our number to defend the city. And now here he has divided his forces again."

"He seeks to put us off balance," Colind said.

"I believe it's working," Verona said.

Aaron glanced at Sarah, knowing that she intended to stay at his side.

"I'm with you," Sarah said.

Aaron drew in the energy, and the runes on his staff glowed. He extended tendrils of energy to the others around him, strengthening their own connections. The others around him gasped, including the former Elitesmen.

"Ferasdiam marked," Isaac whispered and with his thumb and forefinger made a small circle upon his brow, marking the sign of the Goddess.

"Today we fight as one," Aaron said.

He came to Colind, saw the blazing orange of his lifebeat, and sensed a deep hollowness. Aaron's eyes widened, but before he could say anything to Colind, a plume of smoke rose in the distance. A faint shimmer rippled through the ground at his feet. Aaron launched himself into the air, and the others followed, moving at speeds blurring them from vision. They raced onward, and miles slipped by as they closed in on the FNA camp. Shafts of light burned from different points along the Khamearrian line, wreaking havoc in the camp. Anyone caught in the beam was cut down almost instantly.

"Oh Goddess, they're using the energy from the focusing crystals," Sarah gasped.

The focusing crystals were housed in small armored domes mounted on wheels. A team of Khamearrian soldiers maneuvered the domes before firing. The FNA were focusing their own fire in waves of crystal-tipped arrows upon the Khamearrian line. For each group of men that fell, more took their place.

Aaron streaked ahead of the others, pulling a torrent of energy through the rune-carved staff. He moved so quickly that he was atop an armored dome before the soldiers could react. Aaron slammed down the staff, releasing the pent-up energy. The crystal inside cracked, and Aaron leaped off just before an explosion demolished the dome into a malformed husk. The soldiers around him attacked, and his staff whirled through the air, beating them back. Each blow sent men back, and the Elitesmen converged on his location, oozing through the ranks of fleeing soldiers.

Aaron dodged the Elitesmen attack orbs and for a fleeting moment wished he had his swords to block their attacks. He closed in on them and brought the fight in closer. Sarah and the others joined in, and more Elitesmen fell until their attackers stepped back looking uncertain at those who came to Aaron's side.

"You betray the Order," one Elitesman said.

"We serve our Queen, the rightful ruler of Khamearra," Isaac answered.

The Elitesman's cold eyes narrowed. A wave of shadows rose in the sky overhead amid the screeching roars of the Ryakuls.

"Then you've chosen death," hissed the Elitesman.

Isaac's sword flashed, and the Elitesman was dead before he realized that Isaac had moved. The FNA regrouped and pushed forward, throwing themselves at the High King's army.

Aaron's gaze drew to the Ryakuls, and a red cloud blossomed around his vision. The Ryakuls were shadows of their former selves. Dragons fallen from grace with death as their only release. He hadn't seen this many Ryakuls in one place since the Drake commanded them, but the Drake was gone. The sky was full, and the Ryakuls spread out, slicing into the FNA with some breaking off to head toward the city.

"Mactar," Colind hissed.

"He's controlling the Ryakuls? If we take him out then they will scatter," Aaron said.

"Excellent, then maybe they will attack the High King's army as well," Verona said.

Aaron nodded and saw another focusing crystal down the line. "I have an idea."

They closed the distance in seconds, but instead of destroying the contraption, Aaron took out the men around it, and the others followed his lead. Aaron studied the different levers, and after a bit of experimentation, figured out the ones to maneuver the dome. He aimed the focusing crystal into the sky and fired at the approaching line of Ryakuls. The energy blast tore through them easily. The Khamearrians pushed forward, eager to take back their asset, but the others fought around him, giving him time to shoot. FNA soldiers caught up to them and began establishing a perimeter. Aaron motioned for one of the soldiers to take over.

The Free Nations Army clustered together in pockets, trying to avoid the attacking Ryakuls that threw themselves relentlessly at their lines. The crystal-tipped arrows helped, but at the rate they were using them they would exhaust their supply in no time. The burning roar of airship engines at full blast plunged over the battlefield, firing their payloads into the Ryakuls. The dark beasts swarmed a single ship, tearing it apart, and Aaron saw men fall to their deaths in the distance. Gritting his teeth, Aaron launched into the air, heading directly into the swarm of Ryakuls. The breath caught in his throat as a dark-speckled presence kept pace with him.

"I hunt Mactar," Colind's voice said from the swirling mass, which charged off in another direction. The Ryakuls took no notice of it.

Aaron landed upon the deck of an airship, unleashing the energy from the staff into the Ryakuls that attacked it. The sailors regrouped and reloaded the platforms that held the giant crossbows and fired. For all the Ryakuls' power, their weakest point was the head.

Aaron leaped from the airship, and a dark swath cut deeply into the lines of the Free Nations Army. Bodies of men were tossed in every direction, and their cries were pebbled amid the snarling Ryakuls overhead.

The High King, Aaron thought. He saw the dark figure slice through lines of FNA soldiers, becoming a tornado of death. The soldiers pulled back, fighting with the weapons that seemed all but ineffectual against the High King. A spark of energy lanced across the Dragon tattoo upon Aaron's chest. He landed upon the ground and launched back into the air, heading straight for the High King.

A Hythariam lay on his back, firing his plasma pistol using his Nanite-augmented senses, but he kept missing. A dark blade hissed through the air, but for once it missed its mark, and the Hythariam gained his feet.

The runes flared on Aaron's staff, and the High King's sword hacked against it, sending sparks into the air. As the High King moved, a trail of darkened shadows followed in his wake. Aaron sensed the tendrils of energy coming from the High King, but instead of strengthening the connection to the energy of those around them, the High King fed from it.

The High King broke off his attack, and the shadows around him faded into the earth. The wailing moans of men dying littered the battlefield around them.

"I've been waiting for you, Shandarian," the High King sneered. "What, no talk of impending doom to strike across the land? No offer of alliances?"

Elitesmen materialized around them and stood waiting. Strapped to the High King's back were the Falcons.

Aaron glanced at the dead FNA soldiers that were sprawled upon the ground and then back at the High King. "You have something that belongs to me," he said.

The High King brought up his sword, a curved blackened blade. "Well, then by all means, take them back. Let's see how well Reymius taught you."

The High King charged, and Aaron sidestepped out of the way on pure instinct alone. The attacks came from all directions, and Aaron moved the staff, blocking the High King. With each blow a small shower of sparks was sent raining to the ground. Silver streaks blurred around the two combatants. A thunderous blow knocked Aaron back, and his body skidded to a halt. A silver-clad Elitesman reached out hungrily for him. Another Elitesman planted his foot, locking the staff to the ground, while another grabbed Aaron by his hair, dragging him up and away. The medallion became as ice against his chest. He let go of the staff and scrambled to bring his feet under him. Aaron clutched the hand that held him and twisted, kicking out with his foot, infusing the crushing blow with energy. The Elitesman cried out and was knocked back. More Elitesmen closed in on him, but Sarah appeared by his side, quickly followed by the others.

"I thought I'd help even things up," Sarah said and engaged the closing Elitesmen.

Aaron sprang to his feet, his eyes locking on the rune-carved staff less than twenty feet from him. The High King kicked the staff away and smiled at him invitingly. An Elitesman charged in front of him, cutting off his view of the High King.

Aaron snatched the curved axe from his belt and hurled it with an energy-enhanced throw. The axe streaked through the air and burst through the Elitesman's chest. Aaron bolted across the fallen Elitesman, avoiding the High King's sword and locking his grip upon the High King's gauntleted wrist. The High King roared, bearing down upon him with all his strength, but Aaron didn't yield. They locked together, two opposing forces matching strength against strength. The High King spun, and Aaron felt himself lift into the air, but he didn't let go. His feet touched the ground again, and Sarah was there swinging her sword down. The High King shifted at the last moment but caught the tip of her blade on his arm. Aaron kicked the side of his knee, sending the High King off balance. Aaron quickly maneuvered around him, grabbed the hilts to his swords, and tore them from their sheaths on the High King's back.

The Falcons were once again his.

Colind flew through the sky, opting to use darker arts to travel through the battlefield. To the untrained eye, he was a dark mist swirling through the air. He had limited time for which to travel this way, lest he not be able to regain his physical form.

The battle raged beneath him. At least they had been better prepared, unlike the firestorm that engulfed Shandara during the fall. He sped along, and while the Ryakuls were focused upon the FNA, he still couldn't locate who was controlling them. Mactar had to be around here somewhere and within view of the battle. Colind sank to the ground and pulled his essence together. He reached out with his senses, following the flow of energy. The battlefield was a wash of clashing forces, but what he sought was much older, and in spite of Mactar being a master manipulator, there were some things that he couldn't hide. Colind bolted for a small hill upon the rise.

Mactar was so focused on the battle before him that he didn't sense Colind's approach until he was almost upon him.

Mactar spun around, his eyes widening. "You never were adept at the dark arts."

Colind pushed his hand out, sending a bolt of energy searing into Mactar, who raised a shield and deflected the bolt.

"You should have wasted away in that prison I left you in," Mactar spat.

"I almost did, but you underestimated *him.* All of you have."

"The Heir of Shandara has proven to be a formidable opponent. Your last hope to rebuild the Safanarion Order," Mactar said.

The two men circled each other.

"If that is his will. Aaron walks his own path. Do the promises of the Zekara still sustain you? Reymius always suspected, but I wasn't sure until the Ryakuls began fighting for the armies of the High King. Then I knew you had somehow harvested the power of the Drake. After all, how else would you know how to repair their technology? That is why you ran from that mountain. Aaron had already defeated the Drake, but you had gotten what you came for and probably would have been gone if it weren't for Tarimus dogging your every move."

Mactar's eyes narrowed, and his face drew down in a sneer. "Reymius," Mactar hissed, "was a fool to spurn the Zekara, like Daverim before him. They are the true power behind the Hythariam and not the pitiful band that remained holed up in Hathenwood after Shandara burned."

Colind clenched his teeth at the mention of Shandara, and then his lips lifted in a satisfied smile. "Speaking of burning. I returned the favor and found a castle overlooking a small town in northern Khamearra. Sarah was kind enough to share that information with me. Your trophy room was particularly interesting. There isn't much left of it, by the way."

Mactar's face twisted into an evil sneer as he lashed out with an attack orb, and at the same time Colind launched his own attack. Colind was knocked back, and the putrid smell of burnt flesh invaded his nose. Mactar's left arm was a charred wreck where the orb struck.

"What have you done!" Mactar cried out, clutching the remains of his wrist.

Echoes of the Ryakuls' mad shrieks could be heard across the skies of Rexel. Colind turned toward the whispers of the bladesong he heard in the distance. To the east, the sky became washed out in a dazzling display of sunlight reflecting off the majestic hides of Safanar's remaining Dragons.

Mactar's mouth fell open at the sight. Colind pulled a dagger from his belt and plunged it into Mactar's back. The essence of Mactar began to dissolve, and Colind brought his hands up, pulling on the energy around them to keep him from escaping. The dark swarm of Mactar turned and enveloped him in a swirling mass.

"You can't stop me," Mactar's voice hissed.

Colind kept his focus, and the energy flowed freely even as parts of him tore away, but still he held Mactar in check.

"You'll kill us both!" Mactar screamed.

"*I know,*" Colind whispered.

Sarah spun around, sensing the attack coming from behind. Rordan grinned, dodging her sword thrust and grabbing her arm. Using the travel crystal, he took her to another part of the battlefield.

Sarah lashed out with her blade, knocking the crystal from his grasp and continued to hack away at her half-brother. Rordan broke off his attack and dashed away. He made a show of glancing off to the side, and it was then that Sarah realized she was surrounded. Elitesmen melted into view from the smoky battlefield, circling around them. She steadied her breathing and held her sword at the ready.

"Afraid to face me, Rordan?" she asked, allowing the energy from the earth to seep into her.

Rordan raised his head, tilting it to the side, studying her through the eyes of a stranger. It was gone in a blink, and he shook his head.

Sarah chanced a look at the Elitesmen surrounding her. "I know some of you don't hold with the Order. Some of you have already made your loyalties known. Are there are any among you that will stand with me now?"

Sarah slowly circled around, but she was met with the hardened gazes of men who had long ago lost any semblance of a moral code. *So be it,* Sarah thought and clenched her teeth.

"You're alone, Sister," Rordan hissed, his pale face and sunken blackish eyes regarded her coldly.

Sarah saw the tendrils of energy flowing into Rordan. He seemed to be drawing upon the Elitesmen around him. Feeding off of them. Rordan raised his sword, and darkness swirled from the tip of his blade.

Sarah stepped back, her eyes darting to the bulge nestled upon Rordan's chest. "You fool," she said, her eyes widening in understanding. "Take off the apprentice amulet before it's too late."

Rordan's face lifted into evil sneer, and when he spoke his voice sounded inhumanly deep. "But I've become so much more. The amulet allows me to tap into undreamed of powers."

Sarah cried out, wincing as something burned her from beneath her skin. She focused the energy around her, calling on her training with Verona, and formed a shield. The burning stopped immediately.

Rordan leaped forward, swinging his sword. Sarah sidestepped, knocking his blade to the side. She had fought Rordan before, but this time it was different. He was descending into madness in his lust for power. The apprentice amulet that the Elitesmen used to unlock the powers and knowledge from souls past had opened a door to something else. Braden had sensed it when they were in Khamearra, but she hadn't.

Sarah maintained her shield and fought her brother. Why the Elitesmen didn't attack she didn't know. She couldn't spare any thoughts for them as all her focus was on the fight before her. Rordan moved as quickly as she did, and in their deadly dance their blades met in a harsh clang.

Rordan broke off his attack and shook his head as if to clear it. Sarah circled around and stretched out with her senses. Along the fringes she heard the bladesong, and her connection to Aaron blossomed like a flower in the dawn. Releasing the shield, she leaped up into the air and closed the distance to Aaron. Rordan's screams echoed in her wake. Dark shadows pursued her. Sarah went as fast as she could, skimming across the Ryakul-filled sky. She heard the snap of saber-tusked teeth as she went by and occasionally the cry of a pursuing Elitesmen. Getting her bearings, she headed toward where Aaron fought. Determined to be at his side, she pushed all other thoughts from her mind as she sped across the battlefield.

The swirling mass of darkness tried to consume Colind, but he stubbornly held on, allowing years of rage to give him vast reserves of strength. This was a reckoning, and he didn't care if he died, just so long as he took Mactar with him. That was all that mattered. He owed all the ghosts of Shandara that much for his failure. He had fulfilled his vow to his old friend, Reymius. Aaron had grown into the champion that Safanar needed. The bladesong reached out to him, and he felt the touch of Reymius's heir, Ferasdiam marked and the last scion of the House Alenzar'seth, he would go beyond any of his forefathers. A weariness spread within him, consuming his remaining strength. The swirling mass receded once again, forming into the man that had haunted Colind's dreams since the fall of Shandara.

Mactar fell to his knees, covered in his own blood. He raised his weary head, his face twisted in pain and surprise. Colind still held him even as his own lifebeat diminished, his essence leaving his body just as the blood soaked the ground beneath it.

A flash of light lit the area around the two dying men.

"Darven," Mactar whispered.

The former Elitesman that had become Mactar's apprentice regarded him and the battlefield around them.

"It seems you have nothing left to teach, my Lord," Darven said coldly, his gaze wandering to Colind before dismissing them both. "The Ryakuls cannot be controlled anymore. Your plan has failed. You are no longer of any use to me," Darven said.

Mactar struggled to rise, and in a swift motion, Darven caught him, holding a knife to his throat.

"You need me," Mactar said, his voice barely above a whisper.

"No. I don't. And I'm going to do to you what you would have done to me eventually," Darven said. His knife bit into Mactar's throat, quickening an already fast approaching death.

Darven engaged the travel crystal and was gone.

Colind had nothing left to give. His vision faded, and he felt his essence, being pulled farther away, drawing him far to the east into the gardens of a palace known as the White Rose. Armies fought along the pristine white walls of his beloved Shandara. The golden shield of a Warden of the De'anjard flashed, driving the High King's army back. The Hythariam fought at his side, and Colind felt himself drawn farther into a grove of trees. Home to a lone white tree where he had been summoned once before by the ghost of his friend, Reymius. The tree sparkled like a beacon of stars washing him in the warm glow of the Goddess, who at last welcomed home her wayward servant.

The lines of the armies blurred, and Sarah sped across the battlefield that had become a place of madness. Elitesmen fought Elitesmen. Ryakuls swarmed anything that moved. Airships littered the ground in burning wrecks. There were still some in the air that continued to fight however they could, but the FNA fleet of airships had been cut in half. The airship captains were careful to avoid the Dragons, who threw themselves at the Ryakuls with reckless abandon.

Sarah continued on, heading toward the heart of this battle being fought between the man she loved and the man who had been her father. Aaron had been careful to avoid the topic that one of them would die in this battle. He would have found another way if it were possible, but Sarah knew that her father was a monster. None of them would be safe from her father the High King until he was stopped. The Resistance in Khamearra had tried to rebel and resurrected the old call of the Faergraces, her mother's line. Even now she heard the rallying cry, and her heart wept at the death upon the battlefield below. If they didn't stop her father here, they would all die, for her father would offer no quarter, and (truth be told) the alliance that had become the Free Nations Army would never surrender. Aaron would never yield to her father. It wasn't a prideful plea for power that pitted Aaron against him. It was his indomitable will to survive and protect those around him. To step up when fate called upon him. The Goddess had marked her champion well, and the Eldarin honored it. She knew deep in her heart that Aaron wouldn't call on the Eldarin again, believing that they had given enough, but she wondered if they would be drawn to this battle anyway. Too many of the Dragons had died along with a horde of Ryakuls for them not to appear. She needed to be at Aaron's side. To fight beside him for their future. This war would plunge Safanar into a time of darkness that they might never escape from if it didn't end here. She raced onward, drawing steadily toward the source of the bladesong that could be heard by all.

Aaron wielded the Falcons, unleashing the bladesong in a battle medley that adapted his style to thwart the attacks of the High King. This battle had taken him out of time. They blurred in and out of the vision of the men around them, but all could hear the wild cracks like thunder splitting the sky open when their blades met. Aaron gave himself over fully to the dance and opened himself to the wisdom of souls past. Ancestral voices sang in unison, lending their skill to his blades beyond what anyone could achieve in one lifetime, but it wasn't enough. In the back of his mind, Colind's warning of too much death corrupting the heart of the Ferasdiam marked kept coming to his mind. Dead Elitesmen and soldiers littered the ground at his feet, but it wasn't until soldiers from the FNA began to attack him did he suspect that the High King was exerting his influence over them.

"I am a god among men," the High King bellowed and leaped into the air. He landed with such force that a small crater dotted the battlefield. "I hold the lives of men at my fingertips." The High King gestured with his free hand, forcing a handful of soldiers from their hiding places. The tips of their feet dragged across the ground. A Hythariam soldier shot at the High King with his plasma pistol, but the shield he had in place deflected them.

"You're no god," Aaron said through clenched teeth, slamming his swords down.

The High King whirled out of the way, and the soldiers dropped to the ground. Aaron swept out with his leg, but the High King leaped away. Aaron bounded after him. Each attack was deflected. They would land, and the dance would begin again. The High King and Aaron were lost within a cocoon of blessed steel and the energy of a raging storm.

"We have no right to control the lives of men," Aaron said.

"We have every right," the High King answered, lashing out with his sword. He dashed forward and seemingly appeared at Aaron's side.

Aaron scrambled out of the way, but the High King kept coming.

"You've felt it, haven't you? The thirst. That feeling of holding people's lives in your hands. They are so easy to manipulate and control," the High King said and smirked.

Aaron risked a glance to the side. Verona stood with a crystal-tipped arrow drawn, his face was a mask of struggle and apprehension. His body shook, straining against the force of the High King.

"Let him go," Aaron said.

Verona's fingers shook as he struggled to hold the bow string taunt. "I can't hold it!"

The arrow flew from his bow, and Aaron dove out of the way. The arrow exploded as it hit a cluster of soldiers upon the field. Aaron moved toward the High King, but Verona called out to him. He had another crystal-tipped arrow drawn. The shadow of a Dragon flew overhead, and Verona cried out as the crystal-tipped arrow was let loose. The arrow struck the Dragon, and the explosion took out part of its wing. The Dragon let out a mournful wail as it tumbled to the ground and the Ryakuls pounced.

Aaron raced to the High King. The crystals set in the Falcons began to glow. Aaron unleashed a barrage of attacks. The High King deflected the blows, but Aaron kept coming, driving him back inch by inch. The High King feinted to the side and backhanded Aaron, sending him sprawling to the ground.

"No, you don't," Sarah cried, startling the High King.

The High King stepped back, blocking Sarah's attacks until she stopped in mid-swing of her blade.

"You see, Shandarian. There are none beyond my power," the High King said.

Verona cried out, aiming a crystal-tipped arrow at Sarah.

"You're so high and mighty, Heir of Shandara. The only way to save them is to control them. If you don't, they both will die," the High King said.

Aaron reached out with the energy to his friend and the woman he loved. The power was there. He could manipulate the lines of energy and had done so to save Sarah when she was infected with the Nanites, but this was different.

"Do it, Aaron!" Verona cried.

Aaron couldn't. If he did, he would become like the High King. The soldiers around them from both armies stopped fighting and circled around them. They had blank expressions, and the High King grinned. The soldiers came closer and held whatever weapons they carried to the throat of the people nearest to them.

The bladesong churned within Aaron, and he felt the energy around him that connected every living thing. He couldn't move, paralyzed at the scene before him. He couldn't protect them all. The knowledge of souls past couldn't help him here. None of them had been Ferasdiam marked. He silenced them, clearing his mind of their influence.

"This is not your purpose," Aaron said.

"My *purpose,*" the High King spat. "An accident of birth gave me these powers, the same as you."

"Maybe, but it doesn't take any great insight to know that forcing people into subservience is a weak man's ploy. You would burn this whole world if it didn't function as you saw fit."

"Weak, am I? I hold the armies on this field within my grasp. Your own friends turn against you," the High King said.

Aaron smiled. "You haven't turned anyone against me. They are your actions through them. You have no followers, but those who are too afraid to do otherwise."

"Fear *is* power!"

Aaron pulled the energy inward and poured all his focus on the High King, whose eyes widened in shock. "I don't need to control anyone on this field. I just need to keep you from doing it."

The crystals in Aaron's sword flared to life. He shot forward, circling the High King and slicing through the web of energy extending from him. The lines of energy melted away as Aaron pushed forward and prevented new lines from forming. The High King howled in rage, slamming his dark blade down. Aaron came to a stop and crisscrossed his blades, blocking the High King's attack. Aaron pushed up, knocking the High King backward and spun, slashing through his armor with glowing blades.

The High King looked down at the shallow wounds that bled from his torso and then up at Aaron in disbelief. Then his face twisted in rage, and he threw himself at Aaron, roaring as he came. Aaron stood his ground, relying upon the strength that came from a calm, focused mind, and met the High King's attack. Each time Aaron knocked the High King's blade aside, he would swing again wildly and with little skill, but still he charged forward. Aaron stepped back just enough to allow the blade to hiss by, but quickly felt his feet be kicked out from under him. Aaron toppled to the ground and scrambled to his feet, but could already feel the downward swing of the High King's blade bearing down upon him.

The death blow never came. Sarah stood over him, catching the blow with her own sword. The High King regarded his daughter with baleful eyes. In the blink of an eye, he knocked her sword aside and held her up by the throat.

"No, don't!" Aaron shouted.

The High King's gaze switched between Sarah and Aaron. Sarah grabbed the dagger from her belt and plunged it into the High King's shoulder. She dropped to the ground, and Aaron rushed forward, plunging his swords through the High King's chest. The High King's eyes widened in shock and his gaze slipped to Sarah before falling to the ground.

The soldiers around them all seemed to move at once, shaking their heads to clear them.

Aaron reached out to Sarah and pulled her away. She resisted for a moment and then buried her face in his shoulder.

"I couldn't let him take you," she whispered.

Aaron just held her amid the stunned silence of those around them from both armies.

A dark vapor rose from the High King's body and lifted away along the breeze. A large swath of wind blew, carrying a deep resonance of the Dragons around them. The Ryakuls had scattered and quit the battlefield with no one there to control them. The Dragons banded together, with some groups flying off to the east while others pursued the Ryakuls.

News of the High King's death spread among both armies, with the late king's generals raising white flags despite the protest from certain groups within the Elite Order. There was so much infighting among the Khamearrian soldiers and Elitesmen alike that had the FNA chosen to do so, they could have decimated the once-superior force.

22

AFTERMATH

In the days that followed, Sarah was proclaimed the High Queen of Khamearra with fealty being sworn by the surviving generals of the army. Rordan, along with a faction of the Elite Order, were nowhere to be found. Other factions of the Elite Order had fought their brethren during the battle, confirming what the former Elitesman Isaac had suspected. Without the High King and certain Elite Masters, the already crumbling Order would fade away. Sarah's first order as High Queen was to formally disband the Elite Order and revoke all their authority. They were to be absorbed into the Free Nations Army and were to be watched carefully. The former members of the Elitesmen were offered a choice: to serve in the FNA or stand trial for their crimes and abuses of power. A number of them fled and were being hunted, but the bulk of them had chosen to take the High Queen up on her offer.

In Shandara, Braden reported minimal losses and that the Hythariam were instrumental at defeating what had come to be known as the High King's diversionary army. The term was used loosely, because they had learned that while the army was sent there to divide the FNA forces at Rexel, they had orders to take the city if they could.

Prince Cyrus of Rexel was all too happy to see the Khamearrian army return to their homelands using the portals created by the Hythariam. A sizable force did stay to integrate with the Free Nations Army, but there were already plans to move them, as the strain on the natural resources in the area around Rexel was proving too costly. Many eyes drew toward Aaron as the option of moving the bulk of the Free Nations Army to Shandara was discussed.

There were still many people missing, with Colind being most notable among them. Some believed the Lord Guardian of the Safanarion Order would turn up, but Aaron felt a deep-seated fear in the base of his stomach that Colind had not survived. Mactar was also absent, and Aaron firmly believed it wasn't happenstance that the two were missing.

At Iranus's urging, Aaron returned to Shandara with Sarah and Verona. There had been no Zekara activity since Aaron returned to Safanar, and while the threat of High King Amorak was gone, those high up in the FNA knew it was but a temporary lull in a larger storm. Aaron had no doubts that Halcylon was preparing for his attack at this very moment, which was one reason Aaron was in Shandara. The other reason being a pressing need to get away from the battlefield. Amorak had turned the gift of being Ferasdiam marked into something monstrous, and he was left wondering if he was walking the same path. Amorak had referred to it as being an accident of birth, but too much of what Aaron had seen led him to question things of that magnitude being up to chance. Was his being here an accident of birth, or was it destiny that brought him to Safanar?

The combined Shandarian and Hythariam defenses of the city could only be unlocked by a member of the Alenzar'seth line of which Aaron was the last. Aaron's great-grandfather, Daverim, had insisted that if they were to give shelter to the Hythariam, than what they accomplished together would be freely shared with the people of Safanar. When it came to Shandara's safety, its defense and control would fall to a member of the Alenzar'seth. For better or worse, it was agreed and was a primary reason why Iranus was so keen to get Aaron back to Shandara.

"There it is," Verona said.

They had used one of the smaller airships to bring them to the command center. The Hythariam had cleared a road to the place, but there were still remnants of the rubbled remains of buildings in this part of the city. The growing population had set themselves to the task of rebuilding. The progress they made was like night and day since Aaron had first seen Shandara all those months ago. It had been a long time since he had first left Earth, and yet so many things had changed. His life on Earth seemed like a dream.

"What is it?" Sarah asked gently.

Aaron looked at her for a moment, knowing that she was hurting inside and there was nothing he could do but give her time. Taking her father's life had saved them, and he knew she didn't regret it in the least, but still the pain was there along the edges of her eyes.

"I was thinking of my sister, Tara. I left her so she would be safe."

"I'm sure she is fine," Sarah said.

Aaron nodded. "I know, but it would be nice if the two of you could meet someday."

"Perhaps," Sarah said.

Aaron had no wish to return to Earth on any permanent basis. His home was at Sarah's side here on Safanar, but Tara was his only link to a life he had before. In the wake of so much death and destruction, it seemed like such a random thought, but the more he thought about it, the more he wondered if it would ever happen.

The small airship landed, and they followed a path that led them underground. Orbs lit the way, and the pathway opened up to two large metallic doors.

"Gavril, we're here," Roselyn spoke into her comms device.

Next to the door was a silver panel, and Roselyn urged Aaron to place his hand upon it. The smooth surface warmed to his touch, but nothing else happened. He drew in the energy and probed with a tendril behind the plate, and a smaller panel opened above, revealing a circular depression. Aaron withdrew the medallion and pressed it to the surface, and after a moment, both panels withdrew into the wall. There was a great shudder beneath the floor, and bits of rock and dust sifted down from the ceiling. The doors slowly opened, and interior lights flickered on, revealing a large cavernous room that extended well away from them. Holographic screens flickered to life, and Aaron could hear the gasps behind them largely from the Hythariam. A map of Shandara came up on the main display with different sections reporting in sync.

They entered, with people exploring in different directions. Aaron eventually came to a set of doors across the way.

"One of those will take you up to the grounds near the palace," Roselyn said after checking one of the screens.

Aaron came to the doors, and they opened automatically, revealing a small chamber beyond. *An elevator?* He stepped on, and Sarah followed. His comms device chimed, and the panel lit up before them. Aaron selected the button that would take them to the surface. After a few moments, the doors opened to an overgrown path. After climbing through, he and Sarah emerged into a grove.

"I know where we are," Aaron said. "Come on, this way."

He and Sarah ran through the grove, coming to a clearing where a lone white tree stood bathing in the sunlight. Shimmering at the bottom of the tree was a translucent cloaked figure that beckoned them forward.

"Colind!" Aaron gasped.

Sarah threaded her fingers in his as they approached the tree where the shade of the last Lord Guardian of the Safanarion Order waited for them.

EPILOGUE

"Sir, have you seen the latest feeds?" the Zekarian soldier asked.

General Halcylon nodded, watching the summary feeds from the drones they had monitoring the continent. "They may be more powerful than we thought. There are definitely some things we can use."

"There is still the issue with powering our equipment," Ronan said. "The power sources we brought from Hytharia will be depleted in a few months."

"They have sources here we can use," Halcylon said. "Besides, since we haven't been able to find the safe haven where the traitors have taken refuge, we've detected another alternative."

"Where?" Ronan asked.

"Just moments ago a place showed up here on the eastern side of the continent. There is a source there that could power whatever we wanted for the next hundred years."

Ronan glanced at the map, and his eyes widened. "Shandara?"

Halcylon's lips curved into a smirk. "That's what the humans call it. When we take over this place it will all be renamed in a fashion more befitting the Zekara. But I have another task for you."

"What is it?"

"I need you to solve the problem with the longevity of the Akasul," Halcylon said.

"I thought we only needed the one to put the locals off balance while we did more reconnaissance?"

Halcylon nodded. "That was the plan, but now I think we have further uses for them, and we'll need many of them."

Halcylon returned his gaze to the feed showing the battle that had unfolded in the center of the continent. The humans were more powerful than he thought, but were weak in every way he already suspected. The wheels spun in his mind as he proceeded with the next phase of his plan. His enemies already knew of their presence here even if they didn't know their exact location. It was a tactical risk to have the drones fire on the Alenzar'seth, and he shrugged off their failure to destroy him. After all, there was nothing one human could do to prevent what he had been planning.

Safanar would be brought under the dominion of the Zekara.

THANK YOU FOR READING

Thank you for reading Amidst the Rising Shadows.

The Safanarion Order series concludes with the 4th book.

Read it now! - Heir of Shandara

If you loved this book, please consider leaving a review. Comments and reviews allow readers to discover authors, so if you want others to enjoy *Amidst the Rising Shadows* as you have, please leave a short note.

ABOUT THE AUTHOR

I've written multiple science fiction and fantasy series. Books have been my way to escape everyday life since I was a teenager to my current ripe old(?) age. What started out as a love of stories has turned into a full-blown passion for writing them.

Overall, I'm just a fan of really good stories regardless of genre. I love the heroic tales, redemption stories, the last stand, or just a good old fashion adventure. Those are the types of stories I like to write. Stories with rich and interesting characters and then I put them into dangerous and sometimes morally gray situations.

My ultimate intent for writing stories is to provide fun escapism for readers. I write stories that I would like to read, and I hope you enjoy them as well.

If you have questions or comments about any of my works I would love to hear from you, even if it's only to drop by to say hello at KenLozito.com

Thanks again for reading ***Amidst the Rising Shadows***

Don't be shy about emails, I love getting them, and try to respond to everyone.

ALSO BY KEN LOZITO

Safanarion Order Series

Road to Shandara

Echoes of a Gloried Past

Amidst the Rising Shadows

Heir of Shandara

Broken Crown Series

Haven of Shadows

Ascension Series

Star Shroud

Star Divide

Star Alliance

Infinity's Edge

Rising Force

Ascension

First Colony Series

genesis

nemesis

legacy

Sanctuary

Discovery

Emergence

Vigilance

Fracture

Harbinger

Insurgent

Federation Chronicles

Acheron Inheritance

Acheron Rising (Prequel Novella)

Made in the USA
Monee, IL
21 February 2021

61016774R10343